"Unlike most modern fantasy, David Drake's *Lord of the Isles* is an epic with the texture of the legends of yore, with rousing action and characters to cheer for."
Terry Goodkind

"*Lord of the Isles* has it all – treacherous queens, faithful and faithless courtiers, peasants and shepherds who are more than they seem, wizardry fair and most foul, quests, love beyond the grave, and all manner of despicable plotting and unabashed heroics ... A fast-reading and complex fantasy adventure."   L. E. Modesitt, Jr.

"True brilliance is as rare as a perfect diamond or a supernova. *Lord of the Isles* is truly brilliant. Plot, pace, excitement, characterization, but most of all the finely honed and superb use of language mark this as one of those exceptional books you will want to have bound in leather and pass on to your grandchildren."
Morgan Llywelyn

"Some authors are powerful storytellers. Others evoke images that we did not believe existed. When the two are combined you have a powerful writer. *Lord of the Isles* is a magnificent example."   Gordon R. Dickson

"A genre fantasy with more suspense, action, and horror than most ... Drake's magic is more complex than fantasy magic, and the dangers of uncontrollable power form an important theme here. His settings and magical creatures provide surprise and drama as well as plenty of color. This substantial fantasy, in which moral and physical threats are serious and the actions of the characters have real consequences, will appeal to those tired of watered-down myth."   *Publishers Weekly*

LORD
OF THE ISLES

DAVID DRAKE

The right of David Drake to be identified as the author
of this work has been asserted by him in accordance with
the Copyright, Designs and Patents Act 1988.

First published in Great Britain in 1999 by
Millennium
An imprint of Orion Books Ltd
Orion House, 5 Upper St Martin's Lane,
London WC2H 9EA

To receive information on the Millennium list, e-mail us at:
smy@orionbooks.co.uk

A CIP catalogue record for this book is available
from the British Library

ISBN 1 85798 591 5

Printed in Great Britain by
Clays Ltd, St Ives plc

To Dan Breen
My first reader, and a striking example of how different
very similar people can be.

ACKNOWLEDGMENTS

Sandra Miesel helped a great deal with the microstructure. Tom Doherty and Harriet McDougal made equally important suggestions regarding the macrostructure at the beginning and the end of the process respectively.

In a different fashion, the fact that I didn't have to revert to composing in longhand in the middle of the novel is due to the efforts of Mark L. Van Name and Allyn Vogel. People who know computers as intimately as Mark and Allyn do find my needs peculiar, but they expended enormous effort to satisfy me.

A NOTE TO THE READER

I've stolen all the verse quoted within this novel from Greek and Latin poets. Celondre is Horace, whose *Odes* I carried through Basic Training and into Vietnam. Rigal is Homer, and the passage quoted—to me, the most moving passage in literature—is from the *Iliad*. Etter is Hildebert of Lavardin; there's more to Medieval Latin than hymns and drinking songs, though I'll admit I found Hildebert a pleasant surprise.

No translation does justice to its original. These—mine—don't purport to do so.

The general religion of the Isles is based on Sumerian beliefs (and to a lesser degree, Sumerian practice). I have very roughly paraphrased the funeral service described herein from verses to the Goddess Inanna.

I think I should mention one thing more. The magical phrases (*voces mysticae*) quoted throughout the novel are real. I don't mean that they really summon magical powers; personally I don't believe that they do. But very many men and women *did* believe in the power of these words and used them in all seriousness to work for good or ill.

Individuals can make their own decisions on the matter, but I didn't pronounce any of the *voces mysticae* while I was writing *Lord of the Isles*.

—Dave Drake
Chatham County, NC

SANDRAKKAN

BLAISE

o Gonalia

Erdin o

reefs

TEGMA

PANDAH

HAFT

the

Barca's Hamlet

Inner

Carcosa o

North

CORDIN

SHENGY

TISAMUR

the Outer Sea

the ISLES

LAUT

ORNIFAL

ATARA

KEPULAKECIL

BIGHT

CHARAX

Sea

TELUT

PARE

KANBESA

SIRIMAT

SERES

reefs

DALOPO

BUWWISAN

ehli '98

PROLOGUE

Tenoctris the Wizard paused on the spiral stairs to catch her breath and twitch a strand of gray hair back behind her ear. The crowd in the courtyard below cheered wildly: the Duke of Yole and his advisors must have come out of the palace to tell his people of the victory that rumor had already proclaimed.

Six months ago Tenoctris would have been one of the inner circle standing with the duke on the palace steps. The Hooded One had replaced her in Duke Tedry's favor.

Tenoctris sighed and resumed her climb. If she were still Yole's court wizard, the people wouldn't have a victory to cheer. Not a victory like this one, at any rate.

Tenoctris wasn't a great wizard in the practical sense. She had a scholar's mind and a jeweler's soul; large-scale works were for other folk. She saw and understood the forces which had to be shifted; she simply didn't have the psychic strength to manipulate them.

And perhaps she saw and understood too well. Tenoctris couldn't possibly have struck the blow that the Hooded One had delivered; but she realized that actions of that magnitude *must* have consequences beyond those the wizard intended. Consequences that even Tenoctris couldn't predict.

A slit window facing the harbor lighted the next turn of the staircase. Tenoctris paused again, though the top of the tower was only one further spiral above her. She wasn't a young woman, and she'd never been an athlete.

It was a bright, brilliant day. When the sun rose higher the courtyard would be a shimmering inferno, but for now the high walls of the citadel shadowed the ground and cooled the air with the mass of their chill stones.

Duke Tedry had come outside to address his people because the audience hall within the palace wasn't nearly large
enough for the crowd this morning. Everyone in the city below the walls had tried to squeeze into the citadel, and many
of the folk from the countryside had come hotfoot as well
when the story winged its way across the island.

Rumor said Duke Tedry had defeated—had utterly destroyed—King Carus and the royal fleet. That much was true.
King Carus—Carus who had crushed a dozen usurpers; Carus, the greatest King of the Isles since King Lorcan, the
founder of the line—was drowned and all his fleet drowned
with him. The other part, the rumor that in a few months the
Duke of Yole would have consolidated his position as the
new King of the Isles . . . that was another matter.

Tenoctris opened the trapdoor and climbed out onto the
small platform she used for observing the courses of the stars.
She could see the many miles to the horizon in all directions.

Tenoctris was perspiring, more from nervous tension than
as a result of the climb. She could feel the powers building,
focused now on Yole itself. She didn't know what was going
to happen, but the feeling boded a cataclysm as surely as the
hair rising on the back of one's neck gives an instant's warning of a lightning bolt.

Below Tenoctris the hats and caps and bonnets of the cit-
izenry of Yole solidly filled the courtyard. Duke Tedry stood
in silvered armor in the deep doorway to the palace proper.
Behind him were five of his closest advisors; and below the
duke, seated in an ornate black throne that servants had carried from the audience hall to the base of the steps, was the
hooded figure of Yole's court wizard.

"My people!" cried the duke, a big man with a voice to
match. Besides his natural speaking ability, three arches of
expanding size framed the doorway and formed a megaphone
to amplify his words. "This is the greatest day in your lives
and in the history of Yole!"

The cheers of the crowd echoed within the stone walls,
frightening seagulls from the battlements. The birds wheeled,

crying a raucous accompaniment to the human noise.

Tenoctris shook her head. A week ago the people of Yole would have jeered their duke except for fear of the soldiers quartered throughout the city. At least the seagulls held to a consistent opinion.

Duke Tedry wasn't a popular ruler, because his taxes and fines squeezed all classes of society to the edge of poverty— and sometimes beyond. The warships drawn up on stone ramps around the harbor were costly to build and even more costly to crew and maintain. The professional soldiers who would fight aboard the triremes at sea and in armored regiments on land were a greater expense still . . . but those soldiers and the well-paid oarsmen guaranteed the duke would stay in power for as long as there was something left on Yole to tax for their pay.

"My might has overwhelmed Carus, the so-called King of the Isles, with all his ships and men!" the duke said "Carus and his forces came to face me. They perished every one beyond the sight of land! My power destroyed them before they could strike a blow!"

The crowd cheered again. Tenoctris wondered if any of them understood what the duke was saying. Duke Tedry himself didn't—of that Tenoctris was certain. As for the Hooded One . . .

The Hooded One refused to give his name, but he'd claimed that the chair he brought to Yole with him was the Throne of Malkar. One who sat on the Throne of Malkar *became* Malkar, became the essence of the black power that was the equal and opposite of the sun.

Tenoctris knew the Hooded One's throne was a replica, built according to descriptions given by the great magicians of ancient times who claimed to have seen or even sat in it. The original was rumored to be older than mankind, older even than life.

King Lorcan had ended ages of chaos when he and a wizard of a prehuman race had hidden the Throne of Malkar forever. The Hooded One was only a wizard himself; but he was a wizard whose power Tenoctris found amazing, even at this time when the forces available for an adept to manipulate were so much greater than they had been for a thousand years.

"Tomorrow my fleet will sweep westward, bringing every island under my control!" Duke Tedry said. "All the way to Carcosa, the city that for centuries has usurped Yole's rightful place as home to the King of the Isles!"

The people cheered. They were cheering their throats raw.

The Hooded One had used his violet wand to stir the mud of a pool in one of the gardens here in Yole, working sympathetic magic. His spell had collapsed the sea bottom beneath the fleet which bore King Carus across the Inner Sea in response to the Duke of Yole's threats and pretensions. Tenoctris had watched the incantation from her high platform as she now watched the duke's announcement of his success.

The Hooded One focused forces that Tenoctris saw as planes of cleavage within the cosmos; to laymen they were shimmering veils of blue light. The hues were subtly different, proving to Tenoctris that the wizard who supplanted her wasn't as completely in control of his magic as he claimed; but the remarkable strength of the forces he sent cascading toward his chosen target nonetheless took her breath away. If she hadn't seen it herself, she would never have believed that a wizard of such ability could exist.

"The wealth which flowed into Carcosa will come now to Yole!" the duke said. "All my people will dress in silk and eat from golden dishes!"

Tenoctris didn't mind being replaced as court wizard. The duke kept her on, perhaps out of sheer forgetfulness that she existed. Her needs were simple: enough food to keep her spare body alive, and the use of Yole's ancient library, which interested no one else in the palace anyway. She didn't care whether Carus was king or Tedry was king, and she would have done what little she could to prevent royal forces from crushing the rebellious Duke of Yole.

But though a victory for King Carus would have disrupted Yole and caused the deaths of many, Tenoctris knew that the

Hooded One's success was a much greater danger than ever flame and swords could be. A wizard who used powers beyond human comprehension *could* not have the judgment to use those powers safely.

"When I was the Duke of Yole I led thousands," Duke Tedry said. "Now that I'm King of the Isles, I'll have a hundred thousand under my banner and the seas will be black with my triremes!"

The crowd cheered wildly. Did none of them feel the planes of force shifting, bearing now on Yole rather than on some stretch of empty seabed? The Hooded One's fingers twitched slightly on the arm of his throne, but even he showed no real sign of understanding the climax of the events he'd put in motion.

Tenoctris understood only too well. She felt the tower shiver beneath her and turned her head. An earthshock had raised wavelets like a forest of spearpoints from the harbor's surface. Neither the duke nor those listening to him in the courtyard appeared to have noticed.

"I am the future!" Duke Tedry cried, raising his armored fist. "All will follow where I lead!"

The second shock hit Yole like a giant hammer. Red tiles rained from roofs in the town below the citadel. A dozen buildings collapsed in mushrooms of dust, shot through with winking shards of window glass.

The tower on which Tenoctris stood waved like a tree branch. Chunks of stone shook from the walls, pelting the crowd into sudden terror.

Tenoctris knelt on the platform and used her plain wooden athame to sketch symbols on the weathered boards. She could do nothing to save Yole. She didn't expect she'd be able to save herself either, but at such a nexus of force there was a chance for even a wizard of her limited practical abilities.

Duke Tedry drew his sword and waved it in defiance at the empty air. He shouted, but that sound and the shouts of the thousands packing the citadel's courtyard were lost in the rumble of the earth.

"Zoapher ton thallassosemon," Tenoctris said, speaking the words of her incantation calmly, as she did all things. She couldn't hear her own voice, but the effect of the syllables would be the same nonetheless.

The Hooded One jumped up in wild amazement, realizing at last the results of his own magic. His false throne split in half, then crumbled to a pile of black sand rippling with the ground shocks and spreading across the wizard's ankles.

The tower lurched as the earth—the citadel, the town, the whole island of Yole—sank fifty feet straight down. Heavy slates slid from the north roof of the palace, shattering on the pavement to fill the passage between the palace and the citadel's outer wall.

Water from the harbor poured through the streets. The sea rose in white foam all around the horizon, poising for the tidal surge that would carry it across the island. The ground dropped again, as inexorably as a rock sinks through hot tar.

"Eulamoe ulamoe lamoeu," Tenoctris said as the earth and sea roared in raging triumph. As her lips formed each syllable her athame touched the corresponding symbol that she'd drawn on the platform. *"Amoeul moeula oeulam . . ."*

Yole continued to sink with a smooth inevitability. The tower on which Tenoctris knelt wavered but didn't topple. The sea rushed from all sides with a thunder greater than that of the earthshocks that preceded it. Waves broke on the walls of the citadel, then overwhelmed the stone in spray turned to rainbows by the brilliant sunshine.

"Amuekarptir erchonsoi razaabua," Tenoctris said. She no longer felt the tension that had gripped her earlier in the morning. The forces which caused her psychic stress were being released in the material plane. The walls partitioning the cosmos had broken; the pressure faded even as it swept all Yole into ruin.

"Druenphisi noinistherga—"

The sea rolled over what had been dry land, bringing lifeforms with it. Only a few yards beneath her platform's coping, Tenoctris saw long cone-toothed jaws seize the body of a drowning man and twist away through the foaming water.

The long fin on the killer's back rippled from side to side in a motion like that of a snake swimming. The creature was a seawolf, one of a species of predatory lizards which had returned to the water. They were rare everywhere in the Isles and almost unknown here in the eastern reaches. For the most part the seawolves preyed on fish in the open waters, but occasionally they returned to land to snatch unwary victims from the shore.

The seawolves would feast well today.

"Bephurorbeth!" Tenoctris concluded.

Though the incantation's final word was inaudible in the thunderous clamor, the cosmos itself vibrated in tune with the shifting powers. Forces met from a thousand angles in perfect balance around Tenoctris. The tower sank beneath the curling waves, but the platform and Tenoctris upon it separated from the remainder of the crumbling structure.

She couldn't save Yole. Perhaps she could save herself.

Bodies and pieces of wood bobbed amid the foam. Tentacles dragged under a window sash, then released it as inedible and fastened on the gray-headed man who had been in charge of tax collection for the Duke of Yole. A huge ammonite rose, its body concealed within a curled shell with all the shimmering colors of a fire opal. Tenoctris stared into one of the great slit-pupiled eyes behind the forest of twenty or more tentacles.

The ammonite sank again, carrying the tax collector with it. Its tentacles were sliding the body toward the parrot's beak in the center of the ammonite's head.

Searing blue light surrounded Tenoctris. The stars spun above her for a thousand years, wiping her memory the way pumice grinds a manuscript clean for another hand to write upon the surface.

Unimaginably far from her in time and space, ocean roiled above the fresh grave of Yole.

BOOK

I

1

When she looked at the game board in the first light of dawn, she saw that a new piece had been added. She grew very still.

The game board was a vast slab of moss agate, its patterning natural but precisely chosen by the wizard who had cut and polished it in the ages before mankind. She kept the board secret, not behind bars and locks but on a plane of its own from which she alone could summon it for meditation.

To an untrained eye the pieces were assorted pebbles of precious tourmaline, uncarved or barely carved by some barbaric gem-cutter with crude vigor but little skill. To a trained eye, to a careful eye . . . to a wizard's eye like hers, the pieces displayed all the subtle differences of the living creatures on whom her will worked; the human pawns that she moved and her unseen opponent moved, and whose movements in turn shifted the pieces on the board.

She had put infinite time and art into studying the tourmaline pieces so that she could perfect her strategy in dealing with the living beings they mimicked. There were hundreds of them on the board, all of some value; but the skill of the game lay in identifying these few pieces which controlled the path to victory. Last night there had been four.

Two were pieces of great power. The hard, brittle stone of which they were shaped was sea green on one end, red with the fire of ruby on the other. The form of the crystals differed from top to base, and in aspect from one piece to the other.

They were Halflings: the offspring of a human and a creature human only in shape, hybrids who had abilities which neither parent shared. They were not wizards, but they could work with forces no human wizard could shape however great her skill and power.

The Halflings would be dangerous if her opponent directed them, but they had no art of their own. If she was unable to turn them to her own ends, she could at worst set them out of play.

The other two pieces were spirals twined as though the pair had been carved from the same tourmaline prism . . . which they had not been, could not have been. One piece had the brown metallic hue of a crystal with a large admixture of iron in its structure. It was darkly translucent, and shapes swam in its depths. The other helix was water-clear, though like water it had the least tinge of color; in this case the gleam of dawn's first rosy figurings.

She touched her fingertip to the twin spirals. They felt cold or hot, but she could not be sure which; in all the time she had spent studying the pieces, some of their aspects remained an enigma. She must separate and examine them individually, for one was *the* key: the piece that would uncover the Throne of Malkar where Lorcan of Haft had hidden it a thousand years before.

All the power in the cosmos lay with that piece, and the piece could be controlled. It would move as she directed or to the direction of her opponent, the hooded figure she sensed but never saw. There was no third player in the game!

And yet . . .

This night between dusk and dawning a spike of blue tourmaline had appeared on the board in conjunction with the four pieces of power. She must learn what it meant, that slim piece, and still more the fact that the piece was *here*.

She tossed a thin silken coverlet over the board and strode to the outer door. The only apparent bolt was a wisp of spiderweb, but anyone attempting to force the panel from the outside would find himself in a place other than where he intended—and very little to his liking.

She opened the door. The cold-faced servitor nodded obsequiously.

"I'm not to be disturbed for any reason," she said. She nodded toward the tray of covered salvers waiting on the small table beside the door. "I'll be fasting, so get that away."

The servitor nodded again. "As you wish, milady queen," he said.

She closed and sealed the door. Her hooded opponent could not have placed the new piece on the board. . . .

And if not him, who?

2

Garric or-Reise tossed in his bed in the garret of his parents' inn, dreaming of a maelstrom.

The water was icy and so thick it seemed solid. Strings of dirty-white foam marked spirals like the bands of an agate. Garric's head and right arm were lifted from the swirling currents but the rest of his body was caught like that of a fly frozen in amber.

"Help me!" he cried, but roaring currents smothered his voice. The pressure squeezing his chest prevented him from drawing in a further breath.

Other creatures were trapped in the maelstrom's slow gyrations. Most were monsters.

A seawolf struggled almost directly across the funnel of water from Garric's dream viewpoint. Seawolves had raided the pastures around Barca's Hamlet several times during Garric's lifetime, but this beast was twenty feet long—twice the length and many times the mass of any that he'd ever heard of. The beast's skull alone was as long as Garric's arm, and the yellow teeth could shear a man's body in half if they closed on it.

Higher on the spiral was a segmented creature whose flattened, chitinous body was longer than a fishing boat. Its scores of paddle legs trembled in vain effort against the gelid water. It had two pincers like those of a nightmare scorpion, and the facets of its bulbous eyes shimmered in the wan light.

Far below was a tentacled ammonite whose shell was the size of a farmhouse. Its yellow eyes glared up at Garric with unreasoning hatred, but it too was a prisoner in the maelstrom's grip.

On the bottom of the sea, infinitely distant, a human figure stood casting a hooked line of quivering violet fire. The figure wore a long black robe with a cowl that hid its face. The crackling purple fire arched upward, ever closer to Garric as the figure laughed louder than the maelstrom. Closer . . .

Garric woke up with a shout trapped in his throat to choke him. He was twisted into his sweat-soaked bedclothes, not bound by the coils of a whirlpool. The glass of his small-paned window was pale with the half-light of the hour before dawn.

"May the Lady and Shepherd protect me," Garric whispered as he waited for his heart's pounding to slow. "May Duzi who watches our flocks watch over me also."

He pulled the window sash open to let the air cool him. The bull's-eye glass of the panes distorted images too greatly to show anything but changes in the general level of light. When Garric looked through the opening he saw a robed figure sprawled on a raft just short of the shoreline.

Garric pulled himself free of the linen sheet and light blanket he'd been sleeping under; the storm had brought cool nights even this late in the spring. He didn't bother to cinch a belt over the tunic he slept in, and like everyone else in Barca's Hamlet he went barefoot as soon as the ground thawed.

He swung from his window and dropped to the ground a few feet below. He didn't call out to rouse the others, because he was afraid he was still dreaming. Garric's first thought was that the figure in the surf was the hooded fisherman of his nightmare. If there was a real person floating offshore on a raft, Garric wouldn't need help to carry him to solid ground. If his imagination was tricking him, then he didn't want other people to know about it.

He ran easily down the retaining wall to the gravel beach, his tunic flapping around his legs. Garric was big for a seventeen-year-old, though he was rangy and hadn't filled out. His sister Sharina was tall also, but with a willowy suppleness that matched the curls of her long blond hair, while their friend Cashel was built like an oak tree. Cashel was so thick and solid that he looked squat despite being almost as tall as Garric.

Fishermen had dragged their six-oared cutters to the top of the wall, but the surge of yesterday's storm had flung them farther. Three were overturned, and the other two were stacked like a couple cuddling—the upper one smashing the thwarts of the lower.

The Inner Sea rubbed against the beach with its usual hiss. The sound was louder than you realized until you went far enough inland that the first line of hills finally blocked it. Wavelets slapped against the raft as well. It and the woman lying facedown on it were as real as the knee-high water Garric splashed through to reach them.

The raft had grounded on a bar of shells and gravel so slight that at low tide you could miss it on the generally flat strand. To Garric's surprise the raft was part of a building, not a ship's hatch cover as he'd assumed.

The woman moaned softly as he lifted her; at least she was alive. She was older than Garric's mother, though he couldn't be sure quite how old in the dim light. She weighed very little in his arms, although seawater washing over the raft's low edge had soaked her robe's thick brocade.

Garric turned and plodded up the sea-washed slope, careful not to lose his footing and dunk the poor victim again. A wave tugged the hem of his tunic as if in a spiteful attempt to bring him down.

"Here's a castaway!" he bawled at the top of his lungs. He couldn't expect anyone to hear him until he reached the inn, though there might be a fisherman looking over damage from the terrible storm of the night and day before. "Get a bed ready and water!"

Garric couldn't imagine where she'd come from. There wasn't another island with heavy-timbered buildings on it within fifty miles of Haft's east coast. If the storm had driven the makeshift raft—and it must have done so—it was a wonder that the castaway had the strength to cling to a flat wooden platform for so long in the worst weather to flail the Inner Sea in a generation.

"Help, I've got a castaway!" He climbed the sloped wall with long, supple steps. Garric had pulled a full-grown sheep from a bog and carried it up a steep bank on his shoulders. This old woman was nothing by comparison.

Garric had done most of the jobs in Barca's Hamlet at one time or another. He and Sharina would own the inn together someday—their father, Reise, had made that clear. Garric didn't know that he wanted to be an innkeeper, though, and as for Sharina—who knew what Sharina wanted? The way their mother, Lora, treated her, Sharina was too good for anything on this earth!

Reise didn't seem to care whether or not his children kept the inn when he was gone. It was his duty to teach them to run the property he left them; what they did with their lives after he gave them that start was no concern of his.

Reise or-Laver never did less than his duty. He was an educated man who'd come from the royal capital of Valles on Ornifal to become a clerk in the court of Count Niard in Carcosa here on the great island of Haft. When Niard and Countess Tera died during the riots seventeen years before, Reise came to Barca's Hamlet with two infants and his wife, Lora, a local girl who'd gone to Carcosa to serve in the count's palace. The folk of Barca's Hamlet still treated Reise as a foreigner, but he'd bought the run-down inn and made it into a paying proposition.

Reise had provided for his children and personally taught them literature and mathematics, not just the ability to read their names and count on their fingers. He worked without complaint and paid his debts without whining. Everybody in Barca's Hamlet respected him—

But Reise was a pinched, angry man whom no one really liked; not even his own son.

The ordinary houses of Barca's Hamlet were simple ones— two or three rooms below a half-loft, with a shed and perhaps a summer kitchen in the yard outside. Their walls were made of wicker woven around vertical posts and chinked with clay and moss, then plastered over for waterproofing. The roofs were steeply thatched, and the fireplace chimney might be either stone, brick, or—for the poorer folk—sticks and clay with a constant hazard of disastrous fire.

The inn was a centuries' old two-story building, built of tawny yellow brick. Wisteria vines as thick as peach trees climbed the western side; in May they dangled sprays of bell-shaped purple flowers. The enclosed courtyard could hold several coaches at the same time, and there were stalls for twenty horses in the stables on the north side. Garric had never seen more than half of them filled, even at the Sheep Fair, when merchants came to buy wool and drovers purchased the excess of the flock that couldn't winter over for lack of fodder.

The hamlet's other large building was the grain mill next door to the inn. The inn was old; the mill was ancient, a structure built of close-fitting stones during the Old Kingdom. Sluices filled the mill's impoundment pool at high tide; gates then drained the pool into the spillway to drive the wheels whenever the miller chose.

Tidal power was far more certain and controllable than wind or a running stream, because the tide came and went regardless of drought or the whims of the atmosphere; but only the strongest constructions could withstand the rush of spring tides when the sun and moon were in conjunction. No one on Haft in a thousand years had dared to build a similar mill.

"Where am I?" the castaway said. Her voice was so

cracked and thin that Garric only heard the words because he'd rested the woman's head on his shoulder to keep it from dangling as he carried her.

The back door of the inn opened. Reise stood there with a lighted hemlock stem soaked in fat to give a hasty yellow illumination.

"You're in Barca's Hamlet," Garric said. "We'll have you in bed in a moment, mistress. And some milk with a whipped egg."

"But where's Barca's Hamlet?" the woman whispered. "Am I on Yole?"

Reise threw the door fully open and stepped aside. Lora was in the central corridor, and Sharina leaned over the balustrade to see what was happening.

"Yole?" said Garric. "What's Yole?"

"Yole?" his father repeated in a questioning tone. "Yole sank into the sea a thousand years ago!"

3

Sharina tied the sash around the waist of the tunic she'd been wearing as a nightdress.

"Sharina! Go get the hermit!" Garric called as he stepped through the doorway sideways to keep the dangling legs of the person he carried from knocking on the doorposts. "This lady needs help!"

"I'll get him!" Sharina said. Her cape was upstairs, but the air's slight chill wasn't worth the delay. She'd be running most of the way to Nonnus' hut, though the last of the path twisting down to the hut at the creekside had to be walked with care even in full daylight.

"No, you can't go out at this hour, Sharina!" her mother cried. "And not dressed like that!"

"Take a light, Sharina!" Reise said, waggling the hemlock stem for emphasis. He couldn't raise it inside without searing the ceiling.

Sharina ignored both Lora and Reise. She didn't need a light any more than she did a cape . . . though she might have taken both if she hadn't known her parents would want her to do that. Sharina was through the front door and into the courtyard before either of them could stop her.

The double gates of the courtyard hadn't been closed in so long that high grass grew beneath the edges of both and one sagged away from its upper hinge. The part-moon was clear above her, but the sky was already too pale for stars to show.

The only real street in Barca's Hamlet followed the line of houses which backed up to the shallow bay. A flat stone bridge crossed the impoundment pool itself; it had been built at the same time as the mill. For the rest, the street was dirt, dust, or mud depending on the weather. After the huge storm of the previous day, water stood in the ruts that ages of traffic had pounded into the surface. Sharina splashed across the road with the ease of long practice and headed up one of the lesser paths out of the community.

Barca's Hamlet didn't have physical boundaries except for the coastline. Houses straggled in all directions, making it hard for a stranger to say where the hamlet ended and out-lying farms began. There were tracts of pasture and forest attached in common to certain households, however, and those households made up what the folk of the region them-selves thought of as Barca's Hamlet.

The path Sharina followed plunged almost immediately into common woodlands where hogs foraged for acorns and certain families had the right to cut deadwood for their fires. Only one person lived in the forest, and he in a sense was owned in common as well.

Instead of going himself, Garric had told Sharina to fetch the hermit Nonnus. Everyone knew that Sharina was the only person whom the hermit seemed to treat *as* a person rather than an event like springtime or the rain.

Sharina's honey-blond hair and gray eyes set her apart from everyone she knew, her parents included. Perhaps it was her looks that made her feel like an outsider among the locals despite her having lived in Barca's Hamlet for all but the first week of her life. The simple acceptance which Nonnus offered her was as reassuring as the feel of the bedclothes when she woke up from a dream of falling.

The path meandered on to join the drove road near Hafner's Ford, but almost no one came this way through the woods except to see Nonnus—which meant almost no one at all. Brambles waved from both sides, occasionally snagging Sharina's shift. She pulled free without slowing, because she knew a life might depend on her haste.

Nonnus acted as the community's healer. Granny Halla said he'd arrived from no one knew where some few years before Lora returned to Barca's Hamlet with a foreign husband and newborn twins.

"Thought he was a bandit, we did," Granny used to say, "but the bailiff back then was the same sort of puffball as Katchin is today. Nobody had enough backbone to interfere when the fellow grubbed himself a place by the creekside. When Trevin or Cessal's son broke his leg—that's the boy who died of a fever the next year—the feller heard the squeals and set the bone neat as neat. That's how we learned he was a holy hermit. But he still looks like a bandit, if you ask me."

If you didn't ask Granny Halla something, she was likely to tell you anyway. To have told you, that is—Sharina had to remind herself that the old woman was dead five years this winter; found in her bed when the neighbors noticed no smoke rose from her chimney.

Even Sharina found it hard to think of Nonnus as a holy man, though he'd knelt so often at the shrine to the Lady which he'd carved in the bark of a tall pine that the ground was packed to the consistency of stone. Besides praying, Nonnus tended his garden, fished, and hunted. When folk asked for his help he gave it. He took produce or the occasional flitch of bacon in payment if someone offered it, but in truth he was as self-sufficient as the squirrels who provided much of his diet.

Priests of the Lady and her consort, the Shepherd, made a tithe circuit through the borough once a year. Nonnus didn't walk the way they did. He moved like a guard dog, always alert and as direct as the flight of the short, all-wood javelins with which he struck down his prey.

A pair of hardwood batons hung on a cord of plaited willow bark where the path to the hermit's hut branched from the common track. Sharina paused long enough to clatter the rods together. "Nonnus?" she called. "My brother's found a lady thrown up from the sea who needs your help!"

The last of the path was down a gully and up the steep other side. Sharina used her hands to slow her, then to tug herself up by the roots of a mighty beech growing on the opposite rim.

If you didn't ring the clacker when you came to see Nonnus, you found him waiting for you just the same. There was one difference: those who hadn't been polite enough to announce their arrival met the hermit with three javelins in his left hand and a fourth poised to throw in his right. No one in the hamlet even claimed to have sneaked up on Nonnus unseen.

The hermit came out of his low hut with a wicker basket of medicines in one hand and his staff in the other. "Broken bones, child?" he asked. His smile of greeting looked as though it had been carved in a briar root.

Nonnus was below middle height for a man—shorter than Sharina even—and had a waist the same diameter as his chest. There was some gray in his hair and more in his beard. Sharina supposed the hermit must be over forty years old, though there was nothing except the hair to suggest so great an age.

He twisted the strap of his basket around the end of the staff and dangled it over his shoulder. His square-cut tunic was of naturally black wool, woven as thick as a cloak and as harsh as horsehair to the touch.

"I don't know, Nonnus," Sharina said, gasping now that

she had a moment to pause. "Garric just said she's been cast away."

Nonnus wore a belt of weatherproof willow bark like the rope that held the clackers. From it hung a long, heavy knife—the only metal tool he appeared to own—in a flapped and riveted sheath.

"Well, you know where my comfrey grows," he said as he plunged down the path ahead of her at an awkward, shuffling pace that nonetheless covered ground. "You can come back and dig enough roots to boil for a cast if we turn out to need them."

Nonnus planted annuals near his hut. Perennials and vegetables cropped in their second year—parsnips, turnips, and adult onions—grew in a separate plot beyond. Though he had only a sharp stick to cultivate his garden, the early growth showed a pattern as regular as a fish's scales.

"Nonnus?" Sharina called to the hermit's back as she hurried after him. His speed had nothing to do with haste; he simply never made a false move. "Where do suppose she came from? The castaway, I mean."

"Ah, child," the hermit said in a suddenly distant voice. "I don't suppose anything about other people. Not anything at all."

His solid black form strode down the path. *And no one should suppose anything about me,* his back said silently to Sharina, who bit her lip in embarrassment as she followed.

4

Ilna os-Kenset carefully arranged the castaway's robe to catch the afternoon sun on the drying rack outside her entrance to the millhouse. Embroidered symbols stood out against the background; they reminded Ilna of the carvings on old stones reused for the foundation of the inn. The fabric shone green from one angle but blue when she looked at it the other way.

It seemed to Ilna that the symbols changed with the light also, but she found the thought disquieting. The feel of the garment disturbed her even more, though in ways she couldn't explain to another person.

She adjusted the wicker screen slightly so that it would continue to shade the fabric from direct sunlight for another hour. By then it would be time to turn the garment anyway. There was enough breeze to dry even such thick brocade before Ilna took the robe in at sundown to avoid the dew.

Pigeons rose with a clatter of flight feathers from the cote on the side of the mill she shared with her brother Cashel. They circled overhead, then banked to settle again on the roof coping. What went through a bird's mind? But it was hard enough to tell what drove another human being. Especially a man.

Especially Garric or-Reise.

Sharina had brought Ilna the robe in the morning, explaining that Garric had found the woman who owned it tossed up on the shore and that the garment needed to be cleaned. Cleaning wasn't precisely the problem. Ilna quickly determined that she didn't need to work oatmeal into the fabric to absorb dirt and body oils which then could be beaten out with the meal. The fabric's colorfast dyes hadn't been damaged by soaking in the sea, but now the salt residues had to be washed out in fresh water.

If the mill had been powered by a creek, Ilna would have suspended the robe in a wicker basket in the millpond or even the spillway. Her uncle Katchin the Miller might have complained; his slatternly young wife, Fedra, certainly would have. Ilna would have done it anyway as her right and no harm to anyone else—her kin included.

Because the impoundment pool was salt, the question hadn't arisen. Part of Ilna—not the part she was proudest of but part nonetheless—regretted the chance to force Katchin to give way even more than she regretted the work of carrying buckets of well-water to sluice salt away under the gentle working of her fingers.

Kenset or-Keldan had been the elder of the miller's two sons. "The adventurous one," folk who'd known him described Kenset. He'd gone away from the hamlet for a year, no one knew where. When he returned as unexpectedly as he'd left, he had with him two puling infants—Ilna and her brother Cashel—but no wife.

Keldan had died while Kenset was away. Ilna had enough experience of her uncle Katchin to know how furious he must have been to have to divide an inheritance he'd thought was his alone, but he'd done it. The law was clear, and Katchin was a stickler for the letter of the law.

The same folk who'd described the young Kenset as adventurous said that the youth who returned with two children was a different man—and less of one. Kenset had left searching for something; but after he returned the only place he looked was the bottom of a mug of hard cider. He borrowed money from his brother against the mill's earnings; and borrowed more money. He didn't pay much attention to anyone, least of all his children; and nobody paid much attention to him.

Kenset died when Ilna and Cashel were seven, not of drink but from the cold of the winter night as he lay drunk in a ditch a few miles from the hamlet. There was nothing left of Kenset's inheritance save an undivided half-interest in the millhouse itself.

The children's grandmother had raised them while she lived. When she died in her sleep two years after her elder son, Ilna took charge of her twin brother and herself. Cashel did jobs that required his growing strength, and he watched sheep; he'd become chief shepherd for most of the farmers in the borough. Ilna wove with such speed and skill that by now a dozen of the local housewives brought the yarn they spun to her rather than weaving the finished cloth themselves.

And Ilna kept house. She took cold pride in the fact that

when Katchin finally married—bought a wife, more like—everyone in Barca's Hamlet could contrast the spotless cleanliness in which Cashel and Ilna lived with the monied squalor of the other half of the millhouse.

In the early years charity for the orphans had been increased by the fact that nobody cared for their uncle. Ilna had seen to it that every kind act was repaid with interest as soon as she and Cashel could.

Katchin had become bailiff, responsible for Count Lascarg's interests in the borough, because he couldn't get respect from his neighbors any other way. The office hadn't changed anything. Katchin the Miller was by far the wealthiest and most successful man in the community. His ancestors had lived in Barca's Hamlet for ten generations. For all that, drunken Sil the Stutterer got warmer greetings from those who met him on Midwinter's Day than Katchin did.

Cashel or-Kenset had grown into the strongest man most people had ever seen. His sister was so petite she could pass for half her eighteen years if she hid her eyes from the person guessing. But if you asked locals who the *hardest* person in the hamlet was, there wasn't a soul but would have named Ilna. She knew that, and because it was true she told herself that it didn't matter.

Her sister-in-law was screaming at her two-year-old again; Fedra was no better a mother than she was a housewife, and she'd never lose the weight she'd gained during pregnancy, either. Ilna smiled coldly. She understood revenge as well as she understood duty. Sometimes the best way to pay someone back was to let nature do it for you.

Ilna had fabric in the loom on her doorstep and no reason to bother with the robe until it was time to turn it and reposition the shade. The cloth kept drawing her eyes nonetheless. Cautiously, almost as if she were reaching toward a cat in pain, Ilna stroked the fabric again.

She'd seen silk before, though mostly as trim to the garments of wealthy drovers; there weren't to her knowledge three silken garments in Barca's Hamlet, and those were sheer, very different from this heavy brocade. But that wasn't what fascinated her about the robe.

Fabric spoke in images to Ilna, when she handled it and especially if she slept in it. For the most part wool was placid in a way that she found calming; Ilna's own personality had a birdlike jumpiness very different from that of a sheep. Still—she'd only worn once the shift she'd been given by a grieving mother, though she'd never told the giver why her daughter took the poison or who the child's father would have been. There had been other visions as clear and certain, and as impossible to describe to others as the sunrise is to a blind man.

The castaway's robe was different in another way. The scenes that shimmered through Ilna's mind as she touched the patterned weave were too brief to leave tracks in her memory, but they weren't disturbing in a normal sense.

The trouble was that when Ilna touched the fabric, she was absolutely certain that it didn't belong in this world.

5

Garric returned to the inn at early evening with the shovel on his shoulder. The stars were barely visible in the east; an early day for a field laborer, but Getha had insisted he'd done as much as two men already and paid him in full.

Getha was a widow with her eldest son only ten. The family could handle most of the farm's chores, but grubbing the drainage ditches meant levering up rocks that might turn out to be the size of a sheep. Getha and the children had helped as they could, but Garric had indeed done more than a man's work.

Chickens clucked peevishly as Garric walked across the courtyard to the stables. For the most part the hens fended for themselves, but Lora tossed a handful of grain into the yard at evening to train the fowl to come where they could be caught and killed at need. Oats spilled when horses were fed in the stable served the same purpose, but there were no guests at the inn at present and no coach in as long as Garric could remember.

Garric hung the shovel on its pegs against the sidewall. The tool was shaped from close-grained hickory but the biting edge of the blade had a shoe of iron. Garric felt the metal critically. It was worn to the wood at one corner and should be replaced the next time a tinker made his rounds through the hamlet.

He heard water slosh and stepped out of the stables. His father was pouring a bucket into the stone wash trough beside the well in the center of the courtyard.

"I saw you come in," Reise said. "You took care of the widow?"

"Yes, sir," Garric said. "She'd let the ditches go too long, so the storm made the lower field a bog. I think we drained it soon enough that her oats'll come through all right."

He plunged his arms to the elbows in cold water and rubbed his hands together. He had the good tiredness of a task that worked all the muscles and had been accomplished fully. He'd been bragging, really, with the amount of work he could do in front of a woman and her four children. The last boulder Garric moved would likely have broken bones if he'd let it roll back from the top of the ditch—and that had almost happened.

Reise handed Garric a loofah to scrub himself with. The gourd's dried interior was harsh on skin that wasn't armored with callus.

"The woman you found is going to be all right, Sharina says," Reise said. "I suppose the hermit told her. Her robe is silk. I don't recognize the cut, but it's of higher quality than this inn has ever seen before."

He paused, then went on, "Why did you ask about Yole, Garric?"

Garric looked at his father. It would have been hard to describe Reise or-Laver in any fashion that didn't make him sound average, but for all that he stood out in Barca's Hamlet like silver plates in a cowshed. Reise was the same height as most of his neighbors. He wasn't slender, not really, but beside him local men looked somehow rugged. Compared with them his hair had been a paler brown before it went gray, his face was slightly foxlike instead of a rectangle with a strong chin, and the sun turned his cheeks rosy instead of deep tan.

Reise had lived in Barca's Hamlet for seventeen years, and in Haft's capital, Carcosa, for six before that. The locals still referred to him as "the foreigner from Ornifal" when they spoke among themselves.

"Well, she thought that's where she was," Garric said. "At least that's what I heard."

Reise shook his head in irritation. "She's an educated person to have been able to say that," he said, "but she was clearly out of her mind. I only hope she becomes lucid enough to tell us who to send for to collect her and pay for her keep. Her clothing's expensive, all right, but she didn't have a purse or any jewelry that she could sell."

Garric grimaced, though he knew that if his father had been another sort of man he'd never have been able to make a go of an inn in this remote spot. Reise wouldn't refuse charity to a castaway, but he'd grudge it and make no secret of the fact.

"Can I see her?" Garric asked.

"I don't see why not," Reise said. "She's in my house, isn't she?"

Garric walked inside. Behind him his father muttered, "The roof's leaking in a dozen places from the storm, and now I've got a madwoman to care for as well!"

Garric had laid the castaway on a truckle bed in the common room. There were smaller rooms upstairs for drovers and merchants with a bit of money, but he'd been afraid of bumping her on the steep, narrow stairs. She was still there; with no guests at the moment, there was no reason to move her.

Nonnus knelt beside the bed of rye straw plaited into thick rope and coiled higher on the edges to keep the sleeper from rolling out. Lora and Sharina were both in the kitchen from the sound of voices. One wick of the hanging oil lamp was lit to provide light to add to what still leaked through the mullioned windows.

"She said her name's Tenoctris," the hermit offered. He spoke in the slow voice of a man who spent most of his time alone. "I think she'll be all right."

Garric squatted. He didn't remember ever being this close to the hermit before. Nonnus' face and arms were ridged with scar tissue emphasized by shadows the lamplight threw.

Garric heard his sister come out of the kitchen. "She looks terrible," he blurted.

Tenoctris wore a woolen shift; one of Lora's worn castoffs, Garric thought. Her breathing was weak, and her skin had a sickly grayish sheen that Garric hadn't noticed when he brought her from the sea.

Nonnus smiled dryly. "Her main trouble was dehydration and sunburn," he said. "She drank as much buttermilk as I thought she could keep down, and I covered the exposed skin with ointment. Also I added lettuce cake to the milk to knock her cold until tomorrow morning."

Garric grimaced. Now that he'd been told, he recognized the smell of the lanolin that was the basis of the hermit's salve. No wonder Tenoctris' skin looked slick.

"Lettuce does that?" Sharina said.

"Oh, yes," Nonnus said. "The juice boiled down to a solid. The sunburn isn't dangerous, but it can hurt bad enough to make you forget an arrow through your thigh."

Garric stood up. "Do you want to move her upstairs?" he said.

Nonnus shook his head. "Your father says she can lie here overnight," he said. "Your sister will stay with her. When she wakes up she'll be able to walk short distances. With the Lady's help."

Garric looked—really looked—at the muscles of the hermit's limbs. Now he felt doubly a fool for suggesting that this man couldn't have carried the castaway himself if he'd wanted to.

"We gave her clothes to Ilna to clean the salt out of," Sharina said. "They're lovely fabric, Garric. Did you notice them?"

Garric shrugged. He'd never been particularly interested in clothing, but he knew that Cashel's sister, Ilna, was the finest weaver in a day's journey. She was the obvious person to take care of cloth of any sort. "How long has she been in the water?" he asked Nonnus.

"A day, a day and a half," he said. "Not long, I think. Her skin's too fair for the sun not to have raised blisters if it had been much more than that."

"Father says she can't have come from Yole," Garric said. "He says Yole sank a thousand years ago."

The hermit smiled minusculely but didn't speak. Garric's words hadn't been a question, though he'd certainly hoped for an answer.

"Have you heard of Yole, Nonnus?" Sharina asked.

"I've heard that it's far to the east," Nonnus said as he rose to his feet. "And that it sank long ago, yes. But I haven't been there, so all I know is what others say."

He nodded to Garric, then turned to Sharina with an expression that didn't change but somehow became softer. "If she surprises me and wakes up in the night, give her more buttermilk—as much as she wants. I'll be back in the morning."

From the doorway—without turning around—Nonnus added, "And I'll pray, of course."

6

Cashel or-Kenset came out of the woods listening to Garric's pipes playing a dance tune from the top of the knoll. One of the sheep in the lush growth of the swale blatted at him.

Garric turned and put his pipes down. "Were you right?" he called.

"Aye, Bodger'd been nipping dogwood buds and got her neck caught when her hind foot slipped," Cashel said as he climbed to his friend. "I keep telling Beilin that he may as well butcher that ewe himself as have the crows get her one day when I'm not quick enough, but he says she's a good milker and I've never let her strangle yet."

"Nor have you," Garric said. His back was to a holly oak that was good shade in high summer, though for the moment he was on the tree's sunny side. Garric's quiver and unstrung bow leaned against the tree, and a book lay open on the satchel that held his lunch. Cashel could write his name and sound out a few words thanks to his friend's tutoring, but Garric was a real scholar who read ancient poetry for his own pleasure.

"I haven't died yet either," Cashel grumbled. "But I have no doubt that'll happen one day too."

He'd noticed three sheep trot from the woodline together. It wasn't exactly the way they looked—a sheep's expression is always one of wild-eyed idiocy—but just a feeling Cashel had that they'd been frightened by something.

He'd gone to check while Garric watched the rest of the flock pastured here on the meadows sloping down to the shore south of the hamlet. Sure enough, he'd found one of Beilin's ewes choking in the crotch of a tree and unable to lift herself out.

"If sheep were as smart as people, farmers wouldn't need to pay a shepherd," Garric said with a grin. "Say, listen to this, would you?"

He opened the book to a place he'd marked with a strip of cloth. The volume was one of a set that Garric's father had brought with him from Ornifal. Its binding was dark leather with pages of good-quality parchment. While Cashel couldn't pretend to read the words, he could appreciate the craftsmanship of the scribe who'd kept his line and letter spacing so uniform throughout the long task of copying the text.

" 'Now shepherds play their pipes to the sheep fattening on spring grasses, and the tunes delight the gods who watch over the flocks and the wooded hills of Haft,' " Garric read. "There, what does that sound like to you?"

Cashel shrugged. "I like it, sure," he said. "The words are pretty. I just wish it was that simple, though."

"That's what I mean," Garric said, putting the book down again on his pack. "Sure, the sheep are filling out on the new grass—but you're out there making sure they don't hang themselves or drown in a boggy spot or walk over the side of a cliff because they're too dumb to know they can't fly. I'll bet things were pretty much the same back in the Old Kingdom when Celondre wrote this. Father says he was a rich man who wrote about shepherds, not a shepherd himself."

"Well, you play the pipes," Cashel said with a wistful smile. He didn't have much talent for music, and he'd never had the leisure to become even passable enough for his own amusement. The ox horn with a wooden mouthpiece he carried for signaling was the only instrument he was any use with. "I don't doubt it pleases Duzi."

He patted the knee-high stone set up on the knoll and roughly carved with a face. Duzi wasn't one of the great gods, wasn't *the* Shepherd; but shepherds had been leaving offerings of garlands and food before the crude figure for as long as there'd been flocks on Haft.

"It pleases me, I know," Cashel added with a wider grin. He squatted, laying his heavy iron-shod staff on the ground to pick up the pipes. They were lengths of hollow cane, chosen to be the same width and cut to decreasing length. The bottom of each tube was plugged with beeswax. Splints and willow bark bound the set of seven into line.

A piper blew across the tops of the canes with a full, carrying tone. When the musician was good enough—and Garric was that good on the right afternoon—Cashel thought the sound of a pipe was more lovely than the song of any bird ever hatched.

"Well, the sheep seem to like it too," Garric admitted. "They don't mistake me for a shepherd who really knows what he's doing, but they don't seem to wander as badly if I play to them."

Cashel surveyed the flock from the top of the knoll, tallying them with the fingers of his right hand marking the ones place and the fingers of his left marking the tens. He knew the sheep—which individuals were in sight and which were likely still in the woods. The black-brown-white mottling of Haft-bred fleece hid sheep at any distance into the trees, even to eyes as trained as Cashel's.

The sea snarled spitefully on the shore just east of the knoll. The water had remained active ever since the great storm, and frequently Cashel saw an unfamiliar hue on the surface in place of the normal pale green off this coast.

Some of the flock were cropping rushes in the marsh where Pattern Creek spilled into the sea's tidal margin. The brackish water gave their mutton a salty flavor that some folk fancied with a sauce of red seaweed. Even from Barca's Hamlet Cashel had seen that it was a big world, and he'd come to believe that everything in it was to the taste of someone.

Crows hopped and cawed over the wrack the storm had flung high up the shore. The waves had scoured dead fish, seaweed festooned with crustaceans, and less identifiable debris from all across the Inner Sea, dumping it here for a scavengers' feast. Cashel reminded himself to double-check the flock for fly bites, since in normal times the crows winkled maggots from the sheep for part of their dinners. They wouldn't need to while this bounty lasted.

He couldn't see anything wrong; but something was wrong nonetheless.

Frowning slightly, Cashel picked up his staff and walked around the holly oak to where he could look over the swale winding northward. He could account for all his charges—by sight or by likelihood—and those he saw calmly cropped grass and chewed it with a side-to-side motion as regular as a sleeping man's breath.

Garric noticed his friend's mood. He didn't say anything, but he braced the lower tip of his bow with his foot and gripped the other with both hands. Using his knee as a fulcrum, Garric curved the thick bowstaff and hooked the string of waxed horsehair to the upper notch, readying the weapon for use.

Garric's bow was a stiff piece of yew with considerable power despite being only four feet long. The all-wood staff would crack if left under tension for too long, so stringing the bow was the last thing a hunter did before he expected to use it.

There was nothing to *do* with the bow, or with the smooth hickory quarterstaff which Cashel balanced as easily as another man might have held a twig. Nothing in sight . . .

Garric nocked an arrow, scanning the peaceful landscape but watching Cashel out of the corner of one eye. He trusted his friend's instincts, though obviously nothing was disturbing Garric himself.

The tannin-dark marsh exploded into spray glittering like diamonds. A ewe bleated, dancing with both forelegs in the air. The splashes hid the seawolf whose fangs gripped the ewe's hindquarters, but a second seawolf wriggled through the reeds, fastening its long jaws on the victim's throat to choke the breath and cries together.

"There's two more!" Garric cried. He bent his bow Haft-style—by throwing his weight onto his left arm rather than pulling back on the string with the fingers of his right hand.

Cashel had already seen the second pair of squat forms tobogganing in on the waves. The seawolves were mottled gray-green-black on the upper surfaces, with ridged bellies the color of fresh cream. One of those in the surf was huge, easily ten feet long and as heavy as a heifer.

Cashel raised the twisted horn to his lips and blew a raucous warning in the direction of the hamlet proper. As the long note echoed from the rolling hills, he started toward the shore holding his staff at the balance with both hands.

Four seawolves together. Old Hudden claimed he'd seen four seawolves when he was a lad, and that hadn't been for forty years even if the story was true. The storm must have driven them westward to Haft. . . .

Garric's bow whacked, then thrummed as the thick bowcord vibrated to silence. A thirty-inch arrow pinned both shoulders of the seawolf holding the ewe by the throat. The seawolf would surely die, but it might take the rest of the day to do so. The only way to kill the beasts quickly was to sever the spine or pierce the braincase.

To pierce the brain, or to crush it. Cashel jogged toward the killers waddling up from the shoreline.

Seawolves were reptiles, monitor lizards which had gone back to the water. A seawolf's tail was flattened into a broad oar that drove side to side with a snaky, sinuous motion. A swimming seawolf kept its limbs plastered tightly against its body except when its webbed feet banked it into a turn, but the legs could still carry the reptiles for a short distance as fast as a man could run.

Seawolves had teeth like spikes; a big one's were as long as Cashel's middle fingers, good for holding and killing but unable to shear flesh. They dragged the animals they killed on land into the water and twisted violently until they ripped a mouthful loose. In the sea they caught fish; when they came on land, a man or child would do as well as a ewe to fill their bellies.

Sheep clattered along the gravel shore, fleeing in panic from the initial attack. Several were running toward the pair of seawolves which had just come out of the surf. Cashel didn't shout, because that would drive the stupid animals closer to the water and certain destruction.

The bow snapped again; Cashel didn't see where the arrow went. Judging from the sound, Garric had come down from the knoll also. Cashel knew his friend had only a few arrows in his quiver. He needed to get closer than a hundred yards to be sure his shots were effective on creatures so hard to kill.

The nearest ewe saw the six-foot-long seawolf crouching before her and jumped back so violently that she fell down. The reptile lunged, lashing its tail against the ground. Gravel and salt water flew.

Cashel thrust into the seawolf's mouth as if his staff had a point instead of a blunt cap. With his strength behind it, the blow penetrated deeply. Teeth sparked on the iron ferrule. The seawolf continued to worry the hickory in murderous reflex, even though it had been brain-dead from the instant of impact.

Cashel lifted his staff and flailed hard against the beach to clear it of the clinging reptile. Though small compared with some of those in this pack, the seawolf weighed almost two hundred pounds. Cashel, bigger still, twitched the corpse away as though it had been a kitten.

The ten-foot seawolf was almost on him, waddling with its head high and its open mouth stinking like a slaughteryard on a hot summer day. Cashel backed, holding the length of the quarterstaff between him and the monster. Seawolves weren't venomous, but the remnants of flesh rotting between their teeth made a bite from one certain to bring fever and blood poisoning unless it was cleaned almost at once.

There was a whack/*toonk*, Garric's bow releasing and the arrow instantly striking bone. The arrow had penetrated half its length below the seawolf's left eye before the cane shaft shattered on dense bone.

The reptile's forked black tongue shot from its lipless jaws with a roar like water poured into hot grease. The seawolf's lunge lifted both clawed forefeet off the ground. Cashel brought the staff down as an iron-shod club, jolting the creature's head to the side even as another arrow punched to the goose-quill fletching in the soft skin of its throat.

The seawolf twisted onto itself, its jaws clopping together near its own tail. Cashel lifted his staff overhead, judged his moment, and brought the ferrule down across the creature's back to crack the spine just behind the shoulders.

The reptile's forelegs continued to spew gravel in wild sweeps, but the tail and hindquarters only twitched as individual muscles tensed without volition. Cashel stepped back, gasping for breath. The seawolves' blood had a cold, medicinal smell.

Garric shouted in surprise. Cashel spun, using the quarterstaff's weight and inertia as a fulcrum for his body.

The seawolves who'd caught the ewe in the marsh thrashed alongside the body of their victim, crippled by Garric's arrows and dying with slow certainty. The fifth seawolf, unseen by either youth as they concentrated on the pair coming from the surf, must have been some distance up Pattern Creek when its fellows launched their attack. The beast had rushed to the noise of the fighting with the instinct of its kind to mob prey. The first Garric had known of the attack was when teeth closed on his right calf.

Cashel shouted in horror. Garric stabbed the lower tip of his bow into the creature's mouth, levering the jaws apart with a splash of his own blood. Cashel smashed the creature's skull, once, twice, and again. Teeth broke and sparkled at the hysterical blows.

Garric was free. He staggered two steps away from the flailing seawolf and said, "I'm all right! I'm—"

.His torn leg collapsed beneath him, throwing him to the ground. His face was suddenly white with shock.

Cashel dropped the quarterstaff and scooped his friend up in both arms. He began running toward the hamlet with the stumping, powerful motion of an ox headed for the creek after a day of plowing.

"Get the hermit!" Cashel bellowed, knowing no one could hear him yet at this distance. "Get the hermit for Garric!"

7

Garric saw two worlds as if painted one in front of the other on walls of clear glass. Part of him wondered which image was real. The other part knew that both were.

He lay on a straw bed in the inn's common room. He could see and hear. He believed he could walk and talk if he wanted to, but the part of Garric's mind that made decisions within its glass walls didn't see any reason that he *should* do those things, or anything.

Nonnus, Tenoctris, and the members of Garric's family were nearby. Even Lora's face bore a look of concern, though for the most part she showed her worry by complaining peevishly about things that didn't matter.

Cashel sat in a corner with his head in his great hands, mumbling apologies for what had happened. Garric would have said—truthfully—that it was his own fault, if he'd chosen to speak. He'd had eyes only for the monstrously large seawolf in front of him. Nobody would have guessed five seawolves together; but nobody would have guessed four either, and the arrows he'd put through the pair in the marsh might not have anchored them so solidly that they couldn't waddle out to attack.

Ilna bustled to and from the common room, doing the necessary work of the inn that the family was too distracted to handle. When Ilna caught Garric's eyes on her, she nodded calmly. Her face was expressionless, but there was a tight line in the muscles of her jaw.

Other members of the community passed through to commiserate, to drink a mug of ale, and mostly to be entertained by the excitement. Garric was well-liked, but this attack was the biggest event to have occurred in Barca's Hamlet during the lifetime of the oldest resident.

"Five of the monsters! And the storm like never a storm before. I tell you, Rasen, this is a portent. I'm going to inform Count Lascarg."

"Katchin, you said it was a portent when the big sea bass jumped over the spillway before you could net him, when all it was is you're as clumsy as a hog on ice. Did you inform your friend the count about the bass too?"

Garric's right calf muscle was badly chewed; the whole leg felt like a block of ice. Nonnus had cleaned the wounds, but instead of cauterizing the deep penetrations with glowing iron he'd packed them with spiderwebs and smeared ointment on top.

"Shouldn't you stitch the tooth marks closed?" Reise's voice, frightened and diffident.

"Piercing wounds have to drain," Nonnus replied quietly. *"Especially when they're made by teeth, and seawolf bites are even worse than human bites for festering. With the Lady's help, these will close into nothing worse than a dimple."*

Tenoctris wore a different shift from that in which she'd been treated the day before, though this one was patched as well. Her right cheek and the backs of her hands were bright red with the sheen of fresh salve, but she appeared otherwise to have made a full recovery from her ordeal. Her skin was startlingly white where she wasn't sunburned.

While the others stood aside, Tenoctris and the hermit worked on Garric in parallel. The castaway had written on a thin board, then chanted as she burned the wood in one of the charcoal braziers Reise kept to heat the upstairs rooms during the winter. The smoke curled about Garric in a ring which air currents didn't seem to disturb. Sometimes he read words in the haze, though the meanings trembled away like fish glimpsed in the depths.

The flames flickered blue; the smoke had a coppery odor very different from the usual resinous warmth of burning pine. Garric knew Tenoctris' actions were part of the reason he felt so oddly dissociated, but the thought didn't disturb him.

Nothing disturbed him now; not even the realization that the woman he'd pulled from the surf was a wizard.

The flames died. The smoke continued to rotate slowly around Garric, but he thought that might be an illusion like the words he read in it. Nonnus rose from where he'd been kneeling beside the inn's stone fireplace and joined Tenoctris by the bed on which Garric lay.

"Will he be all right?" Ilna asked from the door of the kitchen. Garric smelled stew prepared with a wider range of spices than his mother used. The odor was pleasant, but hunger was as foreign to him as it was to a corpse.

"His humors are coming into balance very nicely," Tenoctris said. *"He's a strong young man. And the wounds themselves have been expertly cared for."*

She nodded to Nonnus; her short gray hair looked like a skullcap. *"He should come through with nothing more than a few scars."*

"With the Lady's help," the hermit agreed/cautioned.

"You were praying," Tenoctris said, her voice catching occasionally as though there were rust between the syllables. Garric couldn't identify her accent, even now when part of him seemed to understand the whole workings of the cosmos. *"When you worked on me as well."*

Nonnus shrugged. *"I hope the great gods exist,"* he said. *"I'm sure that the little spirits of place do. I pray because I hope the gods will help me do good, and because I need to hope."*

"*I'll go now,*" Cashel said, rising with the awkward strength of a team dragging its plow through a boggy swale. "*The gear needs to be brought in from the pasture, Garric's book and bow and all. Beilin gathered the flock, or so he says.*"

He stepped over to the bed, knelt, and wrung Garric's right hand in both of his.

"*We'll eat here tonight, Cashel,*" Ilna called from the kitchen doorway.

"*As if I could eat!*" her brother muttered. Then he was gone.

"*I see planes of force,*" Tenoctris said to the hermit, speaking as a specialist in conversation with a craftsman of a differing specialty. "*The other things folk talk about, gods and fate, good and evil—those things I've never seen.*"

"*Oh, I've seen evil,*" Nonnus said. His voice was soft, and his smile was as bleak as a winter sky. "*I've been evil, mistress.*"

Two worlds drifted about Garric, both of them clear: his friends and family, and the whirlpool beneath a lowering fang of rock. The maelstrom's current was as slow as the stars turning. It gripped Garric and the monsters frozen with him in its toils.

On the sea's dry floor, a hooded figure cast for Garric's soul with a line of violet fire.

8

You watched your brother through the night," Ilna said, scuffling gravel with her toes. A tiny black crab scurried to a new hiding place in the gaps between wave-smoothed stones; a castaway from a distant seaweed forest, tossed here like Tenoctris. "How did he seem to you?"

She and Sharina had gone out saying they were combing the beach for flotsam the storm threw up—a chest of silver tableware from a merchantman, or perhaps a chunk of shimmering amber scoured from a fossil tree once buried somewhere far across the Inner Sea. In truth Ilna had come to talk to her friend about the things that had been happening; and perhaps the same was true of Sharina.

"I've never seen anyone sleep so soundly," Sharina said. Like Ilna, she kept her eyes on the beach. "It scared me, but he was breathing all right. He's got a little fever, but Nonnus says that's nothing to worry about; he'd expected much worse."

Ilna looked at her friend. "You trust the hermit, then?" she said.

Sharina met her eyes. "Yes," she said in a clipped tone. "I do."

Ilna nodded and went back to toeing across the gravel. An upturned shell as delicate as a snowflake gleamed against the dark stone. Ilna turned it over, wondering that the five delicate spines hadn't snapped off.

There was a ragged hole in the shell's upper surface; something had gnawed through to devour the animal inside. Ilna grimaced and flung the shell into the sea.

"It was pretty," Sharina said in mild protest.

"Until you look at the other side," Ilna said. She swallowed a sigh. "Then it's like the rest of life."

They walked on. "The woman Garric rescued is a wizard," Sharina said in the direction of her feet. "She spoke a spell over Garric. Right in the open."

"I saw that," Ilna said. She'd felt a creeping coldness in her heart when she looked from the kitchen and saw Tenoctris chanting as smoke rose from the brazier. She'd wanted to say something, but Garric's family was watching as if it were all as natural as daybreak, and the hermit went about his business undeterred. Some of the visitors spoke in shocked whispers, but none of them tried to interfere.

Nor had Ilna.

"I thought wizards did things in the dark," Sharina said in a miserable voice. "I thought they sacrificed babies and called terrible things out of the Underworld. She just burned a piece of kindling and spoke some words. I didn't know what I should do, so I didn't do anything. It seemed so harmless. . . . But she really is a wizard."

"Yes," Ilna agreed. The same thoughts had gone through her mind. The core of her being had decided that she wouldn't interfere with anyone who was obviously trying to help Garric, even if they *had* been practicing blood magic at midnight. "I knew she was . . . something. As soon as I touched the robe she came in. The cloth was different from anything in this world."

Sharina nodded absently, accepting the comment as meaning there was something odd about the fabric rather than about where the fabric came from. She didn't question the statement any more than she'd have doubted something Cashel said about the behavior of sheep.

"Nonnus doesn't mind her," Sharina said after a moment. "I asked him later. He said that he doesn't decide what's right for other people, but anyway Tenoctris wouldn't go any places he wouldn't go himself. I think I understand what he means."

She didn't amplify the last comment, any more than Ilna would have tried to explain why the robe felt unusual.

"I'm afraid about the things that are happening," Ilna said softly. She hadn't been sure she was going to speak. The noon sun flooded the beach and the dancing waves, but she pressed her arms close to her sides because her body felt frozen. "I feel it squeezing me and I don't know what to do."

Sharina glanced at her in the sort of blank-faced silence with which one greets a friend's embarrassing revelation.

Something wriggled on the eastern horizon. Ilna straightened up. "That's a ship," she said. "It's too big for a fishing boat."

Sharina shaded her eyes from above and below with her hands held parallel, forming a slit that cut the glare from the water as well as direct sunlight. "We have to get back," she said in a tight voice. "Let's run."

The girls broke into a trot, tunics fluttering about their legs. They'd strolled half a mile north of the hamlet; it seemed much farther, now that they wanted to return.

"It must be a big merchantman that was caught in the storm," Ilna said as her toes kicked gravel behind her. "It wouldn't be putting in to Barca's Hamlet unless it had been damaged."

"It's not a merchant ship," Sharina said. She glanced over, coldly measuring her friend's stride and deciding whether to go on ahead.

Ilna lengthened her pace, knowing that Sharina could out-run anyone else in the hamlet over a distance this long. "It's too big for a fishing boat!" she gasped.

"It has hundreds of oars, not just a few sweeps like a merchantman," Sharina said. "A merchant couldn't afford to pay so many rowers and still make a profit on his goods. This is a warship like the ones in the epics!"

9

A metallic screech awakened Garric on what he first thought was bright morning. A moment later he realized that he was in the common room, not his own garret, and the sunlight flooding in the south-facing windows meant it was midday and past.

He tried to rise and found his senses spinning to the edge of gray limbo before his head even left the horsehair pillow. He couldn't even be sure of *which* day this was the middle of.

Garric tried to say, "What day is this?" His voice croaked, "Aagh!"

The hermit reached an arm like an oak root beneath Garric's shoulders and lifted him to a half-sitting position. "Here," he said, holding a herdsman's wooden bottle to Garric's lips with the other hand. "Wet your mouth with this. It's ale."

He turned and called toward the kitchen, "Bring a bowl of the broth and a small spoon. Now!"

Lora popped from the kitchen like a squirrel from its nest. "What?" she said. "Nobody gives orders to me in my own house! Certainly not some filthy outcast who lives in a cave!"

"I'll get it," murmured Reise, who'd just entered by the courtyard door. The squealing hinges were probably what had awakened Garric. Lora moved only enough to let him pass in the doorway; husband and wife didn't exchange glances even when they were in brushing contact.

Because the ale was in a bottle, Garric could drink without spilling as he would have done from a mug. He sluiced the first sip through the phlegm which coated his cheeks and tongue, then spat it onto the floor before swallowing down the rest of the ale.

The rushes covering the room's puncheon floor needed replacement anyway. He'd intended to cut more fresh in the marshes but decided at the last moment to spend the morning reading and chatting with his friend Cashel.

"I was the private maid to the Countess Tera herself," Lora said to an audience which didn't really include anyone in the room. "The men said I was more beautiful than any of the fine ladies!"

Garric didn't doubt that was true. His mother was a small woman with delicate features. Even today her skin was smooth and had the lustrous creamy sheen of old ivory.

"I beg your pardon," the hermit said. He sounded as though he meant the words, though he didn't turn his attention from Garric. "I misspoke."

"There's something coming from the sea," Tenoctris said. She'd stood so quietly by the sea-facing window that Garric hadn't noticed her until she spoke. He looked around, but there was no one further in the common room.

"What's coming?" Lora said, her voice rising slightly and growing harder with each syllable. "Are more of those beasts coming, is that what you mean?"

Tenoctris lifted the latch, a wooden bar made sturdy to withstand eastern gales like the one that had recently punished the hamlet, and opened the door. The salt breeze stirred smoke and hinted memories of the wood she'd burned during her incantations. She walked seaward, out of Garric's line of vision from the bed.

Reise reappeared with a steaming wooden bowl and a horn spoon that ordinarily measured spices into a stew. Nonnus must have doubted whether Garric could handle mouthfuls of normal size.

"I think I'm all right, Mother," Garric said. He *did* feel remarkably healthy now that his system had settled from the first shock of waking. Remarkable, because he'd gotten a good look at his leg as he levered the reptile's slavering jaws away from it with the bowtip. He'd seen *through* the hole made by paired upper and lower fangs. It occurred to Garric that whatever Tenoctris meant about "balancing the humors" was surely part of the reason he could move.

Garric used the hermit's arm as a brace while he levered himself into a kneeling position with his hands. His bandaged right leg felt tight and ached as though it were cooking in a slow oven, but the knee bent normally and pain didn't stab up the thigh muscles.

"Garric, what are you doing?" his mother said. "You shouldn't be getting up yet, your leg's like raw bacon!" She turned to her husband and said, "Reise! Make your son lie down!"

"I'm all *right*," Garric said. He bent forward, putting his weight over his feet so that he could stand up—or try to. His head spun momentarily, but his vision didn't blur and his breathing was normal after it caught the first time.

"You may be tough, boy," Nonnus said quietly, "but the

seawolves were tougher yet and they're dead now. Don't overdo.''

Garric stood, letting his left leg do all the work of raising his body. The hermit's arm kept minuscule contact with his shoulders, not helping him rise but assuring him that he wouldn't be permitted to fall down.

"Should he be doing that?" Reise asked Nonnus. Perhaps by instinct he stepped between his wife and Garric.

Garric let the normal load shift onto his right foot. He still felt no pain, though *pressure* throbbed from the calf through his lower body in quick pulses like a shutter rattling in a gust of wind.

"Of course he shouldn't be doing that!" Lora said. "He's going to lose his leg, that's what he's going to do, and you're going to let it happen!"

"If he can move," Nonnus said, ignoring Lora completely, "then that would be good for him and the wound both. More people have rotted lying in a bed than the spear killed the first time. But I didn't expect to see anyone *here* walk with injuries like that."

"There's men on Haft, hermit," Reise snapped. "And on Ornifal too, if it comes to that."

Nonnus nodded. "Your pardon," he said. The heavy knife hanging in its sheath on his belt wobbled as his stance changed slightly. "Pride is a worse sin than anger, I'm afraid, because it slips in unnoticed so easily."

"If there's something coming," Garric said, "I want to see what it is."

He raised his right foot over the lip of the truckle bed and stepped down. The injured limb held his weight. He took another step; Nonnus followed at his side.

"I'll help him," Reise said curtly. He set the soup and spoon on the edge of the bar and walked to his son's side. Lora turned and stamped upstairs, her back stiff.

Garric continued to move toward the door, putting one foot after the other. He was frightened but he felt he had to learn.

He had to learn whether the thing the wizard sensed coming from the sea was the hooded figure of his nightmare.

10

Sharina stood at the edge of the surf, staring as the huge ship maneuvered in the shallows. It looked more like a building which floated offshore than something intended for the sea. The whole community had turned out to watch, and the lone vessel dwarfed them.

The ship's sides were bright crimson; Katchin had painted his window sashes that color, but no one in the borough had ever seen it applied over so broad a surface. More than fifty oars stroked from either side, bringing the vessel's curved stern shoreward for beaching; the blades quivered like the fins of an injured fish. Empty ports indicated that the ship was intended to have nearly twice as many oars as she did at present.

There were other signs of storm damage, even to eyes as inexpert as Sharina's were. The crew had managed to get the mast and yard down and lash them on the raised deck running the length of the vessel's centerline, but tatters of what had been the sail fluttered from the cordage. In several places bright yellow splinters stood out from the brown paint covering the deck railing; waves had carried pieces away. Seen end-on, the vessel canted noticeably to starboard, suggesting damage to the hull beneath the waterline.

The rowers began to stroke in unison, backing the ship toward the beach. Water trailed like strings of jewels from the rising oarblades. Villagers gasped in wonder at the sight.

Sharina was alone, or as much alone as one could be in a crowd that included everyone she knew. Even Garric stood at the back of the inn, leaning against the wall but upright; Reise was to his right and Tenoctris on the other side. Lora was nearby, her arms crossed to indicate that she was angry about something, and Ilna had stayed close. She'd gone to check Garric's condition as soon as she and Sharina had shouted their news to the hamlet.

Sharina stayed apart from her family. She felt a fluttering of fear and anticipation, something more physical than emotional, as she watched the warship. She didn't know why she felt as she did, but she was sure it had nothing to do with her kin.

She looked around. Nonnus was at the edge of the crowd, far enough forward that the larger waves curled about his knees as they ran in. He nodded when he caught Sharina's glance. She started toward him; to her surprise, he waded inshore to join her.

A drum in the ship's interior thumped time to the stroking oarsmen. Sixty or eighty men stood on deck, many more than could have worked there while the vessel was under way, but Sharina didn't see any sign of confusion. The ordinary seamen wore only breechclouts—and headbands for those men who hadn't shaved to bare scalp or mere stubble. Many of them were poised on the outrigger that carried the topmost of the three oarbanks. Officers in tunics cinched by broad leather belts shouted commands, but there was no anger in their harsh voices.

The vessel grounded with a rasp like that of a huge wave combing in while still offshore by her own length of more than a hundred feet. Seamen leaped into the surf. Officers tossed down coiled hawsers, then jumped over the sides also.

The oars slid in through their ports and vanished. More half-naked figures appeared on deck from the ship's interior, then sprang overboard to help with the lines.

"Those are the rowers," Nonnus said, raising his voice to be heard over the rhythmic cadence called by officers and bellowed back by the straining seamen. "There's only twenty or so deck crew to steer and trim the sails, so the heavy work of beaching the ship for the night is the oarsmen's job."

The tide was just short of full. The ship began to inch ashore, each step timed with the rise of the incoming surf.

Now that the deck was no longer crowded by men waiting to haul the drag ropes, Sharina had a better view of the figures still remaining. A stouter, gray-bearded version of the officers who'd jumped into the sea was shouting commands from the curved sternpost: almost certainly the captain. A few other sailors remained on board.

Twenty-odd soldiers in black armor stood in a close mass near the bow. One of them held a banner. There wasn't enough wind to stream the fabric from its pole, so Sharina could see only that there were red markings of some sort on a black field.

She turned to ask Nonnus about the troops, but the question stuck in her throat when she saw his face. The hermit was looking at the soldiers also. His body was still, and his expression was as starkly terrible as an oncoming thunderstorm. There was no emotion in it; nothing human at all.

"Nonnus?" Sharina said in a small voice. She touched his arm.

For a moment the corded muscle had no more give than a briarwood staff; then the arm relaxed and the face relaxed and Nonnus said in a voice with a playful lilt, "The woman there in the red cloak in the bow, she's a high court official indeed, child. Barca's Hamlet is being honored by her presence, as I'm sure she'll be the first to say."

Then in almost the same lilting tone—and "almost" can be the difference between life and death—he added, "The Lady has a bitter sense of humor, it seems, to send them here."

The ship came the rest of the way up the beach in a grating rush. It was lighter by the hundreds of men now pulling it, and the better traction the crew gained from firm beach beneath their feet more than equaled the decreasing buoyancy as the hull left the water.

When the crewmen ended their forward pull, the sternpost was hard against the seawall near the inn's door. Though the vessel was as high on the beach as possible, waves still washed the bronze beak that made the ship's bow a weapon.

Four of the sailors on deck lifted a boarding ramp and pushed the end of it to a pair of their number ready on top of the seawall. The men on board lashed their end to deck-posts while their fellows braced the other with callused feet.

"Not taking any chances with Her Ladyship having a tumble," Nonnus said in a grimly musing voice. "She wouldn't have liked the voyage even before the storm, not in the least. A trireme's not a palace suite, no matter how rich and powerful you were on land."

Sharina touched his arm again. Some of her earliest memories were of the hermit who'd lifted her when she fell, washed her knee clean, and covered the scrape with a salve that drew away her pain with the sudden ease of grass lifting after a storm has wet the meadow.

Nonnus was always reserved and perfectly controlled, to Sharina as well as to everyone else with whom he came in contact. To hear him joking with catlike humor—underlain by catlike cruelty—bothered Sharina worse than had the look of his bleak visage a moment before.

One of the soldiers raised a trumpet, a long cone of silvery metal rather than a cowhorn, and blew a piercing two-note call. The soldier whose helmet crest was white—the others were red—shouted an order.

The whole troop marched forward in unison two-abreast across the boarding ramp. Their hobnailed boots crashed on the planking and the dangling metal fittings of their armor jingled together. Each time their left feet came down the soldiers banged their spearshafts against their shields and shouted to create a harsh cacophony. It made Sharina's muscles tense.

"The noise is to frighten an enemy when they attack," Nonnus said in the same new voice. "It works with some, I'm told."

The sailors still aboard pressed the rail trying to look inconspicuous as the woman followed the troops down the deck. A fillet of silver lace fastened with pins whose diamond embellishments blazed in the sunlight bound her gray hair.

Her face had fine bones and a look of bored resignation.

At the woman's side, a half-step back so that her flaring cape didn't brush his, was a young man in lustrous black: knee-high boots of polished leather, silk tunic, satin cape. His felt hat had rolled sides, three corners, and a black swan's feather waving from its band. His carefully groomed mustache and goatee were probably intended to give gravity to his delicate features; instead they looked as though they'd been painted on a child.

"Another of Ornifal's finest," the hermit said in that icy tone. "Watch them well, child. You'll want to tell your grandchildren about this some day."

"Nonnus," Sharina said. "Please—please don't use that voice. It . . ."

Nonnus flinched as though she'd stabbed him. He knelt in an attitude of prayer, head bent and hands crossed. "I'm sorry, child," he added before rising again from the seafoam. "I remember what was and I forget what should be. With the Lady's help, I won't let it happen again."

To cover her embarrassment, Sharina watched the young man. He'd paused at the stern to let the woman precede him off the ship. "He's only a boy," she murmured.

"About twenty, I'd guess," the hermit said, this time with dispassionate appraisal. "Nobles don't age as fast as common folk."

As the youth strode across the ramp, his black cape fluttering in the sea breeze, Nonnus added, "It's a bad age for a man, twenty. You have the strength to do almost anything you want, but you don't have the judgment to know what the price of some of those things is going to be in later times."

"Let's get closer," Sharina said, in part because she didn't want to think about what Nonnus meant by what he'd just said.

They walked up the seawall's rough face with the ease of long practice and strong legs. The masons of the Old Kingdom built with such skill that even after weathering for a millennium the courses were as tight as splits within individual stones.

The soldiers had formed a double rank between the mill and the inn. The two nobles frowned in puzzlement as they stood with the trumpeter, bannerman, and white-crested officer.

The hamlet's residents watched in a murmuring circle, but none of them spoke to the newcomers. The strangers were an apparition here, a wonder greater than a stranded whale. Katchin the Miller stood sideways at the back of the crowd as though ready to flee.

"Maybe he thinks they're royal tax collectors," Sharina whispered to her companion. "Maybe they are!"

"Not them, child," Nonnus murmured back. "There was never a tax collector who rated an escort of Blood Eagles."

Aboard the ship, sailors brought packets of personal goods from below and tossed them down to their fellows on the beach. A team was attaching a small sail to a frame of oars for a shelter. The sailors seemed cheerful in contrast to the formal discipline of the armored soldiers. They were probably glad to have made a safe landfall despite the storm which battered their vessel.

After conferring with the woman, the officer shouted, "The procurator Asera bos-Gezaman demands food and lodging during the time she stays in this community. In the name of Valence the Third, King of the Isles!"

He turned his head slightly as he spoke so that his demands swept the onlookers in general. "She also requires food and lodging for twenty-five soldiers of the Royal Guard and food for two hundred sailors. Immediately!"

Sharina's father stepped forward. "I'm Reise or-Laver, the innkeeper here," he said to the officer. "I can offer your mistress food and lodging, though not of the sort she'd find in Carcosa or the house of one of her peers."

"Of course not," Asera said, speaking for herself for the first time. "This is Haft, not civilization!"

Reise dropped to one knee, lowered his head, and made an

odd gesture with his outstretched right hand as though he were brushing something across the ground. Sharina had never seen her father do anything like that before. Then he rose and said to Asera, "As Her Ladyship says, of course."

Asera chuckled in a reaction that smoothed her face and made her look unexpectedly attractive. "Court manners on the east coast of Haft?" she said. "Now you have surprised me, innkeeper. Let's go inside and see if your cooking can surprise me as well."

Reise bowed again and started toward the door of the inn. "Are you the village chief or whatever he's called here as well?" Asera asked as she followed, accompanied by the young noble but not the officer. "That damned ship needs repairs and a new sail before we set off again for Carcosa...."

Katchin hurried after the others now that he was sure of the situation. "I'm the count's bailiff for this borough!" he called as the nobles went inside.

The officer gave an order that released his men from their rigid brace. They began looking around the community. The villagers' conversation grew louder, and one or two of the bolder locals approached the strangers with questions or offers.

"They were just blown here," Sharina said, glad to have an explanation for the ship's presence. "Like Tenoctris and the seawolves, I suppose."

"Yes, but more like which of those?" the hermit said. Sharina looked at him in such surprise that he added mildly, "There are times it's easier to deal with seawolves than it is with nobles. Folk with 'bos' and 'bor' in their names don't think they're the same race as commoners ... and perhaps they're right in that."

A gust blew the troops' banner out from its pole. A few broad crimson strokes drew a stylized eagle's head against the black background. Beneath were words in red script that Sharina couldn't read because of the fluttering.

"The Blood Eagles are the king's personal bodyguard,"

Nonnus said without emotion. "If he sent a detachment of them with this Asera, then she's of higher rank than I'd expect of a procurator sent to handle the king's business affairs on Haft."

The breeze died. Villagers and strangers were mixing freely; some of the newcomers started to wander into the hamlet itself. The hermit watched the scene.

"What does the writing on the flag say, Nonnus?" Sharina asked. " 'Stand,' I think?"

Nonnus looked at her. His eyes were as gray as light glancing off an ice floe. "It says 'We stood,' child," he said tonelessly. "They were with King Valence when he fought the Earl of Sandrakkan at the Stone Wall twenty years ago. When the right flank of the king's forces broke, the Blood Eagles stood and guarded him."

Very deliberately the hermit turned and spat toward the sea. "And the king put 'We stood' on the Blood Eagles banner," he continued, "because of the honor they gained that day."

He walked away without speaking again, his heavy knife wobbling at his side. Sharina watched him until he vanished in the direction of his hut in the woods. She wanted to cry, but she didn't know why.

11

Coming through!" Garric shouted into the bedlam of the kitchen. He stepped crook-legged beneath the transom—the ceiling was high enough to clear the iron cauldron on his shoulder, but the doorway wasn't—and advanced toward the hearth deliberately. "I'm going to hook this on the crane!"

Daya and Tilgar, farmwives used to cooking for large groups at harvest time, were helping prepare meals for the soldiers. Garric couldn't see to his right nor turn his head normally because of his burden, and with extra people it'd be easy to trip over somebody. The cauldron was massive and the present ten gallons of water almost doubled the considerable weight.

"Garric, that's too heavy, I *told* you to fill it with buckets and not bring it full from the well!" Lora cried.

Garric knelt very carefully and brought the cauldron's handle onto the wrought-iron crane that pivoted out from the hearth to hold such vessels. The cooks would immediately start simmering soup stock, for tomorrow and however many later days the ship remained.

The crane groaned as it took the weight. Garric rose and stepped back, suppressing a gasp of relief.

He'd been sure he could carry the full cauldron instead of making many trips with a yoke of buckets into the crowded kitchen. He'd succeeded, but his right calf throbbed and the big muscles of both thighs felt cold and flabby as soon as the stress came off them. This was one of those cases where his mother hadn't been wrong.

Sharina had lighted a lamp because the corner where she was chopping vegetables was shaded from the setting sun. Food preparation would go on long into the night; a stick of light wood in the holder at the top of the firedogs wouldn't be enough for the multiple cooks. Tilgar bumped open the inside door with her hips and turned with her basket of fresh bread into the common room.

"You can walk, I see," Reise said, catching the door before it could swing closed. "Can you row?"

"If you're going to talk, do it someplace else!" Tilgar said as she pushed past Reise on her return. "If you want to stay here, then I could use four more hands kneading dough."

Reise smiled faintly. He led Garric into the common room, now full of soldiers and sailors.

"Row?" Garric said. He hunched his shoulders, loosening the muscles, and rubbed his collarbone where the weight of the cauldron had rested.

Reise opened the seaside door for his son and followed him through. "Yes, the dinghy Tarban uses to net bait. Are you up to it?"

"Yes sir," Garric said. He didn't know what else to say. Reise wasn't an outgoing man at the best of times; even his anger was a cold thing. But Garric had never seen his father in a mood quite like this before.

"Good," Reise said, "because I'd probably overset us, as you know. Another of the skills I lack. We won't go far, just out beyond where the waves break."

Firelight gleamed down the beach in both directions as sailors cooked food they'd bought from villagers. The trireme still looked huge to Garric, but he realized that it couldn't carry more than a day or two's rations for so many men. If they'd been at sea ever since the storm, then they had a right to be hungry.

By an unstated decision, the trireme's crew camped here on the beach instead of above the seawall. Barring another great storm the tide wouldn't come so high at this time in the moon's cycle. Despite their segregated living area the sailors weren't without local visitors—many of them women.

Near one of the larger fires a man with one ear missing and a gold ring in the other was dancing to music another sailor plucked on an instrument carved from whalebone. At intervals all the sailors around the fire would shout and the dancer would turn a backflip.

The man's earring and broad grin winked in the firelight. Village girls—and at least one wife Garric could see—cheered in delighted amazement.

The men of the borough watched from a little distance, some of them wearing deep scowls. There'd been a scuffle or two earlier in the day, but there were too many men in the trireme's crew for the villagers to make real trouble. For as long as the ship remained at Barca's Hamlet, the women would make the choice of where they spent their time and what they did. Afterward, well, there'd be shouts and very likely violence within families; but you couldn't expect girls to behave normally when such an exotic wonder appeared on the beach.

The dinghy was upended on the seawall below Tarban's house, well down the beach. Garric untied the painter from a peg hammered between two courses of stone to hold the little boat against winds and unusually high tides.

The painter was frayed. Tarban had been lucky that the storm hadn't snatched off his dinghy, leaving him with the peg and a tag of rope.

Garric righted the boat and lifted it by the bow thwart. "Should I take the other end?" Reise asked.

"Just bring the oars," Garric said with a shake of his head. He began to drag the dinghy seaward. There were no good ports or even sand beaches on this side of Haft. Boats built here had wear strakes—edge keels—that acted as runners when they slid on the shingle. The strakes could be replaced whenever the harsh gravel beach had worn them down.

Men born in the borough were amazed at Reise's physical ineptitude. He was willing and not weak, at least by town standards, but he could be expected to overset the boat he was rowing—as he'd said—or misharness a carthorse, or even spill a bucket of water he tried to carry. Even when something didn't go wrong, Reise was tense from fear that it would. Garric had come to believe that this fear of looking awkward was the reason for much of the anger that simmered in his father's eyes.

The sea rolled as high as Garric's ankles, then foamed back. The tide had turned an hour ago. Garric met the next wave and shoved the boat out in it. "Jump in the bow quick!" he called to his father.

Reise ran alongside and managed to roll over the gunwale without snagging himself on the oarlock; he even kept hold of the oars, for a wonder. Garric braced the dinghy, now fully afloat, from the next wave, then swung over the stern transom and turned to seat himself. He reached back, took the oars from his father, and stroked powerfully out into the breakers.

It was strange to see dozens of orange bonfires winking

across the beach. Occasionally a dancer or dancers would caper in front of the light. The seawall reflected cheerful cries outward.

"There'll be more coined money in the hamlet than there has been since the days of the north-south coaches when the inn was built," Reise said. "Provisions will be short for the next month till the crops start to come in, though. You can't eat silver."

With cold amusement he went on, "The noble procurator said that because they hadn't made provision with a banker on this side of the island, she'd have to pay me with scrip— royal warrants that I could go to the chancellor on Ornifal to redeem for coin. I told her—very politely, of course—that I hoped she liked stewed cabbage for all her meals and didn't mind sleeping in the stables."

"But if they didn't have money . . . ?" Garric said, glancing over his shoulder as he rowed.

Reise snorted. "Oh, they had gold," he said. "Their own rather than the king's, maybe, her and her companion Meder. Nobles like them don't travel without money. It'll be hard enough to change gold without going to Carcosa. As for Ornifal—it'd still be worth my life to show my face in Valles, even if I were willing to make the voyage."

Garric blinked and felt his face stiffen. He concentrated on his rowing. He'd known his father came from Ornifal and had spent his early life in Valles, the royal capital there; but Reise had never talked about that period, to Garric or to anyone else.

"This is far enough," Reise said. "Turn around and face me, Garric."

Garric shipped the oars and shifted his legs to the other side of the thwart he sat on. The dinghy rose and fell slowly, but the breaking water was inshore of them and the empty sky above muted even the rustle of waves on gravel. The moon was past the first quarter. It reflected from the water without really lighting more than the occasional trail of white foam.

"With things the way they are, I have to come out here to expect privacy when I talk to you," Reise said. He didn't say, "for us to talk"; Garric would have been surprised if he had. "Maybe the things that have happened in the past days are all chance; maybe everything in life is. But . . ."

He rubbed his forehead with both hands. There was a neatness, a delicacy, to Reise that made Garric think of finches: perfectly formed little birds with smooth feathers and angry dispositions.

Reise raised his head again. "I'm a failure, boy," he said. "Well, you know that. Sometimes I wonder what my life would have been like if I hadn't been so weak." He snorted bitterly. "I might better wish that I'd never been born."

"Sir?" Garric said. "I've . . . Nobody thinks of you as weak, sir."

He spread his arms to either side, holding the oars steady against the gunwales as the dinghy rocked in the swells. It gave him something to concentrate on to avoid listening, really *listening*, to what his father was saying.

Reise smiled again, an expression as faint as the moonlight on his smooth cheeks. "Nobody takes me for a fool in a bargain, you mean?" he said. "That's not what *I* mean, though. I've never been able to say no to a woman who begged me. I had to leave Valles because of that, and I had to leave Carcosa as well."

His smile became as thin and cold as a winter breeze. "And I'm married to Lora, of course. That too."

"Sir, you left Carcosa in the Troubles; there's not weakness in that," Garric said. He looked at the purse on his father's belt, not his face. In a desperate attempt to change the subject he went on, "I've never understood what the Troubles were about, and why the count and countess were killed."

Reise chuckled with something close to real amusement. "Well, boy," he said, "I was personal secretary to Countess Tera at the time, and I can't tell you why either. The riots started over whether the statue of the Lady or the statue of the Shepherd would be first in the Midsummer Procession.

Lascarg was Commander of the Guard when it happened. He proclaimed himself count when things settled down; some think he was behind it.''

Reise shrugged. ''The Guard didn't do much until after a mob had gone through the palace, that's true, but I've always found incompetence was a more likely answer than treachery when something goes wrong. Nobody even knows how Niard and Tera came to be killed. She was in the last hours of her pregnancy, so her death might even have been from natural causes.''

''I didn't know you were the countess's secretary, sir,'' Garric said. He concentrated on the minute amount the dinghy rotated as the sea rose and fell.

'' 'Were' is the important word there, boy,'' his father said coldly. ''In Valles I *was* an attendant to the Lady Belkala bos-Surman, 'the special friend' as they put it, of the present king's father. What I am now is the innkeeper in Barca's Hamlet, married to a local girl with a tongue like a stone saw.''

''Sir, don't talk like this!'' Garric said. His voice rose. Anger cleared his mind of the empty despair he felt as he listened to his father discussing his life with the dispassion of a butcher pulling the guts from a slaughtered pig. ''You're a real man who's been places and seen things! There's no one else in this borough who can say that. When I'm an old man here in Barca's Hamlet I'll be telling my grandchildren that *my* father wasn't a hick farmer like everyone they know.''

''No!'' Reise said. For the first time Garric heard in his father's voice the fierce determination that had to have been at the core of the man who'd made a success of this run-down inn. ''No, you won't say that, boy, because whatever else I may have done I didn't raise you to be a fool!''

He gripped Garric's right wrist and turned the hand over, palm up. ''Look at this,'' he said. ''You've read the epics, boy. When the Isles were great a thousand years ago, when the kingship *meant* something, those kings were men of Haft!

Hands like yours held the sceptre—and the sword, needs be. Never deny your heritage!''

Garric wet his lips with his tongue. A snatch of pipe music came from the beach, broken by the breeze that carried it. It could almost have been birdsong.

"I'm sorry, sir," Garric said. "I'm sorry. But don't you call yourself a failure either, because you're not."

Reise squeezed Garric's wrist slightly, then released it and leaned back on his own thwart. "We'll never know what might have been," he said in a gentler, musing tone. "But many would have made a worse job of what I did do, that's true. Including raising a child to be a man."

He laughed, to Garric's complete amazement, and added, "And who knows? Maybe Barca's Hamlet needed an inn-keeper more than Valence the Second needed a chief steward, which it might have been otherwise."

Garric cleared his throat. "Ah?" he said. "We're drifting in a little. Should I take us out again, or . . . ?"

Or go in and end this embarrassment? his mind finished while his tongue was silent.

"In a moment," Reise said in the curt tones of the man who would make the decisions without his son's interference—the man Garric had grown up with.

Reise opened his purse and took from it a small wash-leather pouch, which he handed to Garric. "Here," he said. "This is for you. I don't care what you do with it; wear it or don't, that's your business."

He rubbed his forehead, then met Garric's eyes again. "I've always tried to do my duty," Reise added softly. "I've always tried."

The pouch was heavy for its size. Garric untied the draw-strings and slipped his fingers inside rather than shaking the contents into his palm as he might have done on dry land and in better light. He was conscious of his father's eyes on him as he pulled out a coin strung on a silken cord.

Garric raised the coin to catch the moon better. It was a little smaller than the bronze pieces that were virtually the only coined money seen in Barca's Hamlet: about the diameter of Garric's thumb at the knuckle. One side seemed smooth; a face and a hint of Old Script were barely visible on the obverse. To tease more information from the worn metal would take strong daylight, and even that might not be enough.

The coin's surface was only a sheen in the silvery moonlight, but Garric suddenly realized what its weight implied. He clasped the coin between both hands in horror of dropping it and said, "Sir! This is gold!"

"Yes," Reise said, dipping his head in a crisp nod. He didn't add anything to the curt agreement.

"But why are you giving it to me?" Garric said. The metal was cold between his palms, and the cord had supple slickness that made it seem alive.

"Because it's yours, boy," his father said harshly. "You've the right to wear it. That's all that matters. Now, take us back in before Tarban charges me with stealing his boat and that envious fool Katchin assesses for him."

Garric didn't move for a moment. "Did you wear it, sir?" he asked. A wave slapped the dinghy's seaward side; they really were drifting back into the chop.

"It wasn't mine to wear," Reise said. "Just to keep and give to you when it was time. Do as you please with it."

Garric raised the silken loop and let it fall around his neck. He tucked the coin itself beneath his tunic. "Yes sir," he said as he reversed his seat and took the oars again.

He brought the dinghy's bow around with a pair of quick strokes on the left oar. There was something huge stirring. He didn't know what it was or what it wanted with him.

But with the coin tapping his chest as he rowed, Garric felt not fear but a fierce joy and anticipation.

12

Ilna pulled the latch cord with her little finger, then shouldered the door open and entered the main room of her side of the millhouse. Cashel hadn't returned yet with the load of straw beds he was gathering from neighbors, so she dropped the pile of extra quilts on the stone floor.

"Say, it's the princess back and prettier than ever!" said one of the soldiers sitting around the kitchen table. Two of the men stood up when she entered, but none of them moved to help her.

She kicked the door closed herself and said, "What do you do if you don't have a village to stay in? Or don't you get out of the palace most years?"

Fifteen of the Blood Eagles were billeted in the common room of the inn. The remaining ten were in the millhouse, the hamlet's only other substantial building: five on Ilna's side and five on Fedra's.

The Blood Eagles had been bragging to her about their rank and importance in Valles, how in guarding the palace they rubbed shoulders with the top nobility; but they'd arrived at Barca's Hamlet with nothing but the clothes they stood in. The ship's crewmen carried their own blanket rolls, but these proud soldiers would have had to shiver under piles of leaves if the cove had been uninhabited.

"Aw, all that stuff was on the other ships," the youngest of the soldiers said. He was in his mid-twenties, a tall man with pale hair whose ancestry probably involved one of Ornifal's noble houses—though probably *not* by marriage. "I lost a set of court dress that was worth enough to buy this whole dog kennel."

He waved a dismissive hand to include all of Barca's Hamlet.

"We're not supposed to talk about that, Ningir," said the soldier sitting cross-legged in a corner of the room, cleaning his inlaid dagger sheath with a piece of soft leather and a stylus. He was twice Ningir's age, scarred and balding above heavy brows.

"Belt up, Mesilim," a third soldier said. "Who died and made you king, hey?"

He looked at Ilna and went on in what he clearly hoped was an ingratiating tone, "We started with three ships. All of us were with the procurator, but our gear was on the other two. There's damned little room on a trireme, just deck and the smell of those monkeys right underneath breaking their backs rowing."

"Zabar—" Mesilim said, a frown beetling his already low brows.

"Hey, belt up!" Ningir said, and aimed a kick at the older man's booted foot. Their hobnails clashed. "You think you got something to say, you go out and say it to somebody who cares, right?"

Because of the way the soldiers were divided, the five billeted on this side of the mill were all equals of the lowest rank. Those with authority had chosen the inn or the sumptuous appointments of Katchin's quarters for their billets.

Ilna smiled as she knelt to check the stew simmering on the hearth for tomorrow's dinner. Those in the inn would be well served, but the men across the partition wall from her had probably already learned to regret Fedra's cooking. They'd be lucky if they didn't find lice and bedbugs as well!

Ilna stood. "You were separated in the storm, then?" she asked. She wasn't an idle gossip like most of the villagers—there was little enough else to do in the days of blustery drizzle that were typical of winter on this coast—but the ship's arrival *was* a unique event. There hadn't been this many strangers in Barca's Hamlet in living memory.

"Separated!" a fourth soldier said. He mimed drawing his

sword across his throat. "Yeah, you could say that. Separated by about a mile of water, or however deep the Inner Sea is where the storm hit us!"

"Aw, Eshkol..." muttered Mesilim. He hunched his shoulders in frustrated anger and pretended not to hear anything further. Mesilim was an old soldier who could execute familiar orders with single-minded determination, but he was obviously too stupid to promote. His younger, smarter fellows ignored his opinion even when he was probably right.

"It was the damnedest thing," Ningir said. He shook his head. "I mean that: that storm came straight out of Hell."

A moment before, Ningir had been just chatting, bragging to a pretty girl in hopes that she'd turn out to be more willing than she'd thus far given reason to believe. With the memory of the storm, his mood had changed completely.

"It was like somebody pulled a curtain up from the sea," Zabar said in a tone of frowning recollection. "Solid black. I've never seen anything like it in my life."

"Neither had the sailors," Ningir said. "There'd been no wind and we were cruising on one bank of oars."

"All three ships close enough we could shout," the fifth soldier said. His hands were crossed on the table and he didn't look up from them. "A pretty day, just it was too hot in the sun is all."

"And it came right down on us, black as a woman's heart," Zabar continued. "I wasn't even looking in that direction. There were seawolves swimming along with us, just off the stern, and I was watching them. Only it got *dark* and I looked over my shoulder, that fast. And then the wind hit."

Ilna looked at the soldiers, feeling surprise that she kept off her expressionless face. Some of the men were doubtless braver than others, but they were none of them cowards or they couldn't have been members of this elite unit.

The storm had frightened them. All of them.

"A snowbank dumped on me once when I was just a kid," Mesilim said. His fingers continued to rub at the pattern on the sheath, black niello inlay on silver plating. "It was like that again. The wind pressed my chest just that hard.''

"The sailors, they were shouting," said a soldier. "You could only tell because their mouths opened. You couldn't hear anything. The raindrops hit so hard they felt like gravel flying.''

"The mast bent even though the sail was down," Ningir continued. "The rowers kept us headed into the wind and that's all that saved us. They may be monkeys, but if we'd gotten sideways to that storm we'd have been plowed under in less time than—"

He snapped his fingers.

"—that."

"The wizard Meder says he saved us," Eshkol said. His hand continued to rub a cloth over his swordblade, but he was no longer really polishing.

"Wizard, Meder?" Zabar said. "I don't guess he's really anything more than the procurator's fancy boy!''

Eshkol shook his head. "Don't you believe it," he said. "Meder may be a kid, but his family owns thirty square miles of Northern Gainstup Parish. Whatever he is, he's not selling himself for some old lady's bedwarmer.''

"How does he claim to have saved the ship?" Ilna said. "What was it he did?''

Her mind concentrated unexpectedly when the discussion turned to wizardry. It was like feeling a knife twist in her hand toward a lodestone. Perhaps she was reacting because of how she'd felt when she touched the castaway's robe. The silk had awakened something in her.

"They'd been under an awning, him and the procurator," the soldier explained. "It went with the first gust. Meder bent down so the mast was between him and the worst of the wind and scratched something on the deck with a copper knife. I guess he was chanting, too.''

"I looked on the boards the next day," Ningir said. "There were marks but they weren't real words.''

"They're not for people to read, they're for gods!" the

fifth soldier snapped. "Or demons, more likely. If he really is a wizard."

Ilna thought about Meder. Him a wizard? Yet no one could have looked less like á wizard than Tenoctris in a patched woolen shift. Her incantation had clearly helped save Garric's leg and perhaps his very life.

"All I know," Eshkol said stubbornly, "is that the ship on the right broke up like it was eggshells, and then the one on our left went the same way. Nothing left of them but foam, and I saw an arm try to grab air. But we made it through, and the whole time Meder sat there chanting."

"Did it seem to anybody else that things looked sort of *red* during the storm?" Ningir said. "I mean, not real red but sort of rosy?"

"That's right," the fifth soldier said to his hands. "Like we was stuck in a block of pink quartz. I shut my eyes but I still couldn't keep the light out."

"There wasn't anything like that," Zabar said. He looked at his companions in growing consternation as he realized they *had* seen something happen to the light. "I was on deck the whole time. Lightning was all, and that wasn't red."

"The wizard did it," Mesilim said from the floor. Everyone stared at him. Blinking, the old soldier went on, "There was light. After the first ship sank, and more when the second one went down. He's a wizard. It was magic just like at the Stone Wall, only this time on our side."

Ilna stood in the cold silence, looking from one soldier to the next. At last Zabar shivered and said to her, "Say, beautiful, what's it take to get a drink around here?"

"Right," said Eshkol, thrusting his sword back in its sheath with a clack. "Any chance of wine?"

"There's wine at the inn if you want to pay for it," Ilna said. She too was glad for the break in the mood, though a part of her that she didn't recognize squirmed regretfully to leave the subject of wizardry. "I don't know the prices. And there's more beer at seven coppers a bucket, that's half one of your Ornifal silver pieces. What do you want me to bring?''

The swordsman stood up. "I'd better look over the cellar myself," he said. "Doesn't sound like the pretty lady here would know Blue Hills White from stump water."

"Fetch a couple bottles of something red and strong, Eshkol," Ningir said. "None of your fancy stuff that doesn't have any more kick than water."

"I want beer," Mesilim said. He methodically hooked, then locked, the ornate dagger sheath back onto his equipment belt as he rose. "I'll get the beer."

Ilna opened the door. "What is it that the king sent you all to Haft for?" she asked. "There's never been a royal official in this borough since I've been born."

"Oh, that was the storm," Zabar said, taking the door from her in hopeful gallantry. "We were headed for the Passage to Carcosa on the outer coast, but we got blown southeast and were lucky to make any land."

The group, three soldiers and Ilna, stepped into the night. Lights gleamed through the inn's windows, only twenty feet away. The stars were hard in the clear sky.

"But why Haft at all?" Ilna said. "I know Valence is king of all the Isles"—in name, though little more—"but Ornifal's a long way away even without storms."

"Well, ah . . ." Zabar said, suddenly reserved.

"Oh, that's because of the count's heir," Mesilim said. He'd either forgotten their orders or decided that it no longer mattered because his fellows were talking anyway. "The old count, that is. King Valence learned that there was a child born just before they were killed, the count and countess. Countess Tera was of the old line of Haft, and that means the kid's of the *old* royal line that goes back to King Carus!"

13

S harina brought the rack of lamb into what was now the private dining room where her mother served Asera and Meder. The chamber was the storage room most years except during the Sheep Fair, but the extra blankets and crockery were now in use. Wainer, commander of the detachment of Blood Eagles, ate with his men in the common room.

"*Someone* in the parish must have riding horses!" Asera was saying to Lora in irritated surprise. "I don't insist that my escort be mounted, but surely you don't expect Meder and myself to walk to Carcosa?"

"Please, Your Ladyship," Lora said in a flustered voice. She curtsied, her eyes never meeting those of the nobles to whom she spoke. "It's only drovers and merchants from Carcosa who ride here. We plow with oxen and if we go somewhere it's by our own legs, yes."

Sharina set the platter on the sideboard, shifting the knife, steel, and fork she carried in her right hand along with part of the weight of the dish. Normally Sharina tended bar while Reise carved for guests dining privately, but he'd decided to switch their duties after he'd sized up the sailors thronging the common room for something to drink. Garric helped Reise and brought fresh casks of beer and cider up from the cellar at need.

We didn't expect nobles from Ornifal to appear—sailing, walking, or flying, Sharina thought. She was excited to have noble visitors and knew she'd brag for years to come that she, Sharina os-Reise, had served them with her own hands, but her basic attitude was the same as her father's: treat nobles well because it's your duty to do so; take their money; but never mistake them for gods or yourself for a dog. Lora dithered in a combination of pride in the contact and terror that she'd fail to please the great folk.

"What a barbarous place," Asera said, shaking her head. "I suppose we'll have to sail to Carcosa after all."

The room's dozen candles filled all the inn's holders as well as a pair borrowed from Katchin against the promise that he'd be permitted to greet the nobles formally after dinner. Half the lights were tallow dips, not beeswax, and from the way Meder squinted as he picked the last morsels from his flounder he wasn't as impressed by the illumination as locals would have been.

Sharina struck the knife quickly down one side then the other on the steel, straightening the edge to carve. She traded the steel for the fork, only absently aware that Meder had turned and was staring at her. She began to slice the tender meat away from the ribs.

"Asera, look," the young man said. "*Look* at her!"

Lora took away the fish plates, clattering them onto a corner of the sideboard. She must be flustered; her touch was usually deft and silent.

Sharina deliberately didn't turn from her task. The flush starting to color her cheeks was as much anger as embarrassment. If they were talking about *her*, then what right did they have to sound as though she was a, a *horse* herself?

"Girl?" Asera said. "You there—with the knife, for the Lady's sake! Turn around and face me."

"She's my daughter, Your Ladyship," Lora said with another curtsy. She wore a blue and green overskirt of stiffened linen, a garment Sharina had seen only in a storage chest before. It flared when Lora dipped, making her look like a peacock displaying. "Sharina os-Reise. Sharina, curtsy for the lord and lady."

Sharina put down the carving implements and bowed instead, trying to keep disgust for her mother's behavior from her expression. She'd never learned to curtsy properly, despite Lora's attempts to teach her when she was younger. Trying to do so now would be to make a fool of herself.

"Where do you come from, girl?" Meder asked. He'd changed into a doublet of red velvet for the evening; his tawny hair flowed across his shoulders in a contrast that Sharina would have found attractive were his face not quite so tense and white.

"She's my *daughter*, Your Lordship," Lora repeated as though perhaps the nobles hadn't heard her the first time.

"Do you take us for fools, woman?" Meder snapped. He got to his feet, shoving the chair behind him so roughly that it fell over with a loud crash. The inn's furnishings were all of local craftsmanship, sturdy rather than beautiful. "Just look at her!"

He reached for Sharina, his thumb and forefinger extended with the obvious intention of gripping the girl's chin to adjust her profile for him to inspect. She stepped back, feeling cold all over. Her fingers brushed the handle of the carving knife; she jerked her hand away in horror at the image that flashed into her mind.

"Meder," the procurator warned. She stood up also, lifting one of the pewter candlesticks from the table. "If she is . . ."

The young man froze, backed a step, and then to Sharina's utter amazement bowed to her. "I apologize, mistress," he said. "In my excitement I behaved in an uncivilized fashion. It won't happen again."

"What my companion was pointing out . . . Sharina, is it?" Asera said. "Is that you don't look anything like either the maid here or your father. You're tall, you have—"

She moved the candle closer to Sharina's face.

"—gray eyes. And your hair is lighter than that of anyone else I've seen in this village."

"What you look like, in fact," Meder said with controlled delight, "is an Ornifal noble. An Ornifal noble like the late Count Niard. I ask you again: Where do you come from?"

"I'm from here!" Sharina said. "I was born here!"

Lora put a hand on hers to calm her. In a voice with more dignity than anything else she'd shown since the noble guests arrived, Lora said, "My children were born in Carcosa, Your Lordship, where Reise and I were in service in the palace. But we've lived in this hamlet for all our lives since they were born, lacking the few days we took to travel here."

"Born when?" Asera said. She remained motionless, but the focus of her body made Sharina think of a cat poised to leap. "Born seventeen years, five months, and three *days* ago, woman?"

"Or it might have been four days," Meder said with a minute frown. "If a daughter rather than a son, then perhaps four. The sun was on the cusp."

"It might have been," Lora echoed slowly. "About that time, perhaps. But Sharina is my daughter."

Asera looked sharply at her companion. "You said the storm was unnatural. Could it have been meant to bring us here instead of to harm us?"

"Without my magic—" Meder started hotly. He blinked, fully considering the storm in the light of Sharina's presence *here*. "I thought it was hostile. I fought with all my strength and it still was on the edge of overwhelming us. If I hadn't been aboard, the ship wouldn't have survived."

"But you were aboard," Asera said. She replaced the candlestick on the table and fastidiously flicked a spatter of wax from the back of her hand. She and Meder acted as if they were alone with the furniture. "And without the storm blowing us south of the Passage, we'd be searching in Carcosa for traces of something that wasn't there."

Meder and the procurator turned their appraisal again onto Sharina. Lora stepped in front of her, either out of protective instinct or in a claim of ownership. Asera's mouth tightened in something that could have become either a frown or a sneer; Lora shrank away.

"Can you tell for certain?" Asera asked her companion. Her gaze never left Sharina.

"Of course," Meder said, irritated at a question whose answer was so obvious to him. "I have the tools I'll need in my room. We'll carry out the rite there."

The nobles were lodged in her parents' quarters: the procurator in Reise's room, Meder in Lora's side of the upstairs suite. For now Sharina and her mother were squeezed into the girl's corner garret, while Reise had his son's room and Garric slept in the stables.

Asera nodded. "Come along then, child," she said to Sharina in a not-unfriendly voice, rather as though she were speaking to a favorite dog. She gestured and started for the door.

"Wait!" Sharina said.

They stared at her. Lora touched her hand.

"Wait," Sharina repeated in a calmer tone. Her voice didn't tremble. "What is it you're going to do?"

"Do?" Asera said. "We're going to determine if the Count and Countess of Haft were your real parents, child."

"And if they were," Meder added as his arm shepherded Sharina toward the door, "then you've a life ahead of you never *dreamed* by anyone in this miserable sheep pasture!"

14

Garric had hung the oil lamp on the axletree leaning near the stable door; the cartwheels were beside it. An iron tire had come off last winter, and the smith hadn't made his rounds yet through the hamlet to weld another onto the wooden felly.

"Do you need the light anymore?" he called to Tenoctris, making a bed of loose straw at the other end of the stable.

"No, I . . ." Tenoctris said. In a tone of mild surprise she went on, "That's odd. You—"

Both door leaves lay back against the brick walls; the opening was wide enough to pass a team of horses still hitched. The hermit nevertheless stopped outside the building and slapped the wooden panel with his left hand: a quick rap-rap-

rap like a gigantic woodpecker drumming for a mate.

"May I come through?" he asked. His voice sounded harsh, rusty.

"Sure," Garric said. A dozen sailors came out of the inn, making the courtyard echo with laughter. Several of them began to sing chanteys, but they weren't the same chantey. "Ah, there's plenty of room to sleep here if you don't want to go back in the dark."

Nonnus smiled faintly. "I thank you for your offer," he said, "but I find the dark more of a friend than not. Besides, tonight the stars are clear."

He entered the stable, letting his hands relax. He'd been spreading them to prove that he wasn't carrying a weapon, Garric realized. "I thought I'd check on your injuries, both of you. Do you need more ointment, mistress?"

Tenoctris looked at the backs of her hands, then turned them toward the hermit and the light. "There's only a little tenderness now," she said.

Nonnus stepped close and pressed two fingers gently against Tenoctris' cheek. "Pain?" he asked.

"No, though tenderness as I said," Tenoctris said. "Without your help I'd have been in great pain, I realize."

"You've done more to heal yourself than I did," Nonnus said with the same faint smile as before.

"I wouldn't have been able to do that if I'd been out of my head with pain, would I?" she replied.

The hermit turned to Garric. "And you, boy? Let's see the leg."

Garric pivoted and braced his right foot waist-high on the stable wall to show both that the limb was supple and that the wounds were knitting cleanly. The hermit brought the lamp close. The puffy flesh around the fang marks was pink but not red or streaky. When Nonnus prodded the edge of what had been the hole all the way through the leg, Garric felt a localized burning instead of a barbed lance thrusting to his groin.

To cover his wince, Garric bragged, "I've been doing all

my normal work. I could carry you around the courtyard if you like."

"And why would I like to do something so silly?" the hermit said with mild amusement. "You don't need to prove you're a fine brave man to me. Or to anybody."

"He'll be older before he learns that," Tenoctris said. "If he ever does."

Nonnus chuckled, the first time Garric had heard such a sound from him. He slapped Garric's knee with a hand like the flat of a wooden shovel. "You're healing," he said. "But I warn you that in ten years or twenty you'll feel every strain you put your body through now."

He looked at Tenoctris and added, "He won't believe that, either."

"Sir?" said Garric, lowering his foot flat. He was embarrassed to have the older people discussing him as though he were a funny cloud formation. "Can't we pay you something? The least you've done is saved my leg and I know it."

"The folk of this borough didn't run me out as others might have when I settled in the woods here," Nonnus said. "There's nothing else I need—"

The smile again, there and gone like a rainbow.

"Nothing material, at least. If I can set a few bones or cool a fever, that's small enough recompense for what the community has given me."

He nodded toward Tenoctris and added, "Besides, she's the one responsible for you being able to walk already. Well, I never denied that wizardry was real. Healing's a better use for it than others I've seen."

"You're from Pewle Island, aren't you?" Tenoctris said. "They hunted seals there in my day."

Nonnus nodded. "They hunted seals in my day too," he said without intonation. "And still do, I hope. It's an honest life."

"The young man with the procurator is a wizard," Tenoctris said without a transition. She glanced toward Garric to include him in the conversation, but it was obviously the hermit's viewpoint that she sought. "He's powerful, and he's frighteningly ignorant of the forces he's working with."

"How do you tell?" Nonnus said. He had the interest of a craftsman for another's specialty. "Has he been working magic here?"

"How do you tell when a seal's about to rise?" Tenoctris replied. "How does Garric tell which way the tree he cut will fall? Power trails after Meder like the hair of a comet filling half the night sky."

"Then he knows you're a wizard too?" Garric said. "Have you talked to him about it?"

A sailor wandered through the courtyard with a pair of villagers. In a loud, slurred voice he said, "—and the folk on that island didn't wear anything but necklaces of bones. They made me a king, like enough, they did, and that only because I'd saved a silver mirror from the wreck."

There was a pause as a bottle gurgled. Villagers murmured respectfully. The voices moved out the gate.

Garric stepped back from the stable doorway, drawing the others with him. The hanging lamp would deter folk looking for privacy to do things they weren't quite drunk enough or desperate enough to do under the eyes of the community.

Nonnus dropped into a squat, his haunches against the brick base of one of the posts. They and the beams they supported were ancient oak, so black with the grime of ages that only touch could tell their grain.

"Meder bor-Mederman thinks I'm somebody's maiden sister if he thinks anything about me," Tenoctris said. Her smile reminded Garric of Nonnus' expression when he was talking as much to the past as to his companions. "He doesn't really see the forces he works with, much less notice that I attract them also. And of course by Meder's standards, I'm not really a wizard at all."

"Mistress . . ." Garric said. He didn't know how to treat Tenoctris. On the one hand she was a penniless castaway with manners and tastes as simple as those of a Haft shepherd—perfectly willing to sleep in the stable when the inn was full of paying customers. But she was also educated beyond even Reise's standards, a noble and courtier as surely as these two from Valles, and besides that a wizard. The parts were unfamiliar, and the way they fit together was as puzzling to Garric as a river running uphill.

"If you brought yourself here from so far away," he stumbled on, "you're—you must be really powerful. All that kid did"—Meder was some years older than Garric, but he was a wispy fop—"was keep from sinking in a storm. We've fishermen here who could have done that!"

Nonnus grinned. "Spoken like a shepherd, boy," he said. "That storm would have driven under Pewle sealers if it caught them at sea. Don't let the fact you dislike somebody blind you to what he is and what he can do."

Garric blinked as though he'd been struck. He was used to venting his opinions to people who didn't really listen to or *think* about the statements: Cashel, Sharina, other villagers. It shocked him to have somebody poke holes in his words instead of agreeing and adding some equally empty comment. "Ah, sorry," he said.

"I've only once seen a wizard with such power," Tenoctris said. She twisted a lock of her short gray hair, bringing it around to the side to look at out of the corner of her eye. "*That* was power enough to sink Yole like a stone in a millpond. And I shouldn't wonder if Meder doesn't manage to do something similar. That train he spreads is almost certain to catch something from a place he really shouldn't disturb."

"Court folk live in a different world, mistress," Nonnus said softly. Like Tenoctris, he was thinking of other times as he spoke, though of the present as well. "They don't understand the world that simple people live in, where life is always on the edge. Better that the two sorts never touch."

"All I wanted was my library and leisure to study the way the forces touched," Tenoctris said. "I wasn't interested in using them. I wasn't very good at that part anyway."

She smiled ruefully at Garric and added, "I could never have summoned the forces I rode to come here. And 'here' was simply where the crest chanced to bring me—I couldn't control that, I couldn't even predict it. The choice was random."

"Or fated," Nonnus said. He was smiling also; but while the hermit wasn't hostile to Tenoctris, it was clear that he disagreed with her basic assumptions. "Or by the Lady's will."

The lamp guttered as it burned down to the last of its oil. Garric would have to fetch more from the kitchen if he wanted to keep it lit.

"I'll go back, then," Nonnus said. "I just wanted to be sure that you both were healing well."

"Are you sure you wouldn't like to sleep in the stable?" Garric asked. "Or at least I can fetch you a torch."

"I appreciate your kindness," the hermit repeated, shaking his head. The lamplight shrank to a yellow glow around the wick, then flared again for a moment.

"When I look at you now, Garric," Tenoctris said, pitching her voice so that Nonnus would be sure to hear also, "I see two people. But that wasn't true yesterday."

"I don't know what you mean," Garric said. "There's just me."

Both of them faced him. Tenoctris had a musing expression, but the hermit showed his usual calm detachment.

"Do you feel different?" Nonnus asked.

"I don't . . ." Garric said. "I . . . Everything's changing with the ship and the seawolves. And you, mistress."

He nodded to the wizard. She looked incongruous with her aristocratic delicacy garbed in a worn-out shift, but the silk robe would be out of place in Barca's Hamlet—especially for a castaway sleeping in a stable.

"I don't know how I feel," he concluded, though he was uncomfortably aware of a muscular figure standing *some-where*, looking through his eyes and laughing cheerfully.

"True of all of us, I suppose," Tenoctris said. She didn't sound concerned, just curious.

The lamp went out with final certainty. The hermit walked

away in the starlight, his footsteps soundless. Straw rustled as Tenoctris settled herself on the nest she'd made, leaving Garric with his thoughts.

But not quite alone.

15

We'll need more light, surely?'' Lora dithered as she set her candle in the wall sconce inside the door of what was normally her room. ''I'll go fetch—''

''Be silent, woman,'' Asera snapped. ''Better yet, get out and stay out unless I call you.''

Instead of obeying, Lora backed against the sill of the dormer window with a fixed expression on her face. Sharina put the wooden candleholder on the three-legged table. The room's other furniture comprised a bed, two clothes chests, and a round pine chair made by hollowing out the upper half of a section of tree trunk. She glanced at her mother in unvoiced surprise: she'd have guessed that if the procurator asked Lora to jump out the window, she'd have done so.

''No, no, get that off there,'' Meder said in distracted snappishness as he lifted a flat ironbound box about a foot long onto the chair seat. ''I'll use the top for the written invocation.''

He knelt and inserted a key with four pins of varying length in line with the shaft. They rotated a quarter turn as Meder murmured something under his breath.

Sharina took the candle off the table. She thought the box glowed faintly, as if it were reflecting light from a hearth.

''Bring it near,'' Meder ordered as he lifted the lid. The interior was broken into small compartments, each holding an object in neat isolation. A knife of ruddy copper, its handle marked in the ornate curlicues of the Old Script, was clipped to the inside of the lid.

The young magician took out the knife. When he turned and saw Sharina leaning close with the light he said, "No, not you—I need you for the summoning! Give it to one of the others."

Asera opened her mouth to protest at being grouped dismissively with a maid from the hinterlands, but she closed it again without speaking. It was clear to everyone that when Meder focused on his task, he had no consideration for any of the ordinary social parameters.

Sharina gestured to her mother and stepped away as Lora silently took her place with the light.

Meder took out a lump of what looked like ordinary chalk, placed it on the table, and again closed the box. He straightened and looked at Sharina. He appeared taller than he had in the dining room below.

"I'm going to prick your finger with the athame and touch the chalk with a drop of your blood," he said brusquely, gesturing with the copper knife to make his meaning clear. "It's not really necessary to write the entire phrase in blood; the attraction is quite sufficient for the purpose. And I'll take a lock of your hair."

Sharina looked at her mother. There was nothing in Lora's still face; as well look at the tabletop for help.

"All right," Sharina said, extending her left hand. She wondered what Meder would do if she refused. Judging from the way he spoke, the thought literally hadn't crossed his mind.

Meder's touch was surprisingly warm. He glanced up and locked eyes, seeing Sharina as a person rather than a piece of paraphernalia for the first time since he and the procurator had discussed the rite.

He frowned and said, "Hold still," in a return to his former manner. He stabbed the copper point into the ball of her thumb. There was a burning sensation that Sharina's imagination screamed was subtly different from what she'd felt the times she made a mistake with a needle when sewing.

A dome of blood swelled from the slight wound like a mushroom breaking the ground after a rain. Meder traded the athame for the chalk and rubbed it in the blood. He turned and began to write around the tabletop with quick, firm strokes. The phrase had no punctuation nor any gap between individual words. It was in Old Script, like the symbols on the athame's hilt.

Men in the common room spoke in raised voices, quarreling or simply cheerfully enthusiastic. Sharina felt separated from the activity below by more than just the thick oak flooring. A cold wall was rising between her and everything familiar from her past.

Meder scraped the blood from the chalk's surface with the athame and put away the remainder of the lump. "Here," he said as he stepped close to Sharina again. "I'll take the hair now."

He had to saw several times, pulling the roots painfully, before he was able to separate a few strands. The knife was sharp, but hair is tough and quickly dulled the copper edge.

Meder put the honey-colored lock in the center of the little table, surrounded by the chalk writing. "No one speak," he ordered.

Touching the athame's point against the wood, he muttered, "*Huessemigadon iao ao baubo eeaeie . . .*"

To Sharina the words sounded like frogs on a summer night, or the grunting of penned sheep.

"*Sopesan kanthara ereschitigal sankiste . . .*"

Meder shifted the point of his copper knife at each tortured syllable. He moved to the left around the table so that he never had to reach over the surface to touch the next chalked symbol.

"*Akourbore kodere dropide . . .*"

The partition which isolated Sharina from the rest of the world was growing thicker. A red mist suffused the air above the table, though when she blinked the color faded for a moment before seeping back into her consciousness.

"*Tartarouche anoch anoch!*" Meder shouted. He thrust his athame into the lock of Sharina's hair.

Deep red fire billowed soundlessly from the copper point. The cold flames touched the ceiling, then shrank back and coalesced into a head: a man with shoulder-length hair, aristocratic features, and a precise goatee. The image rotated, not as a man turns but instead like a bust displayed on a turntable.

Lora put her left hand to her mouth and bit her knuckles to keep from screaming. The candle in her other hand trembled like a leaf in a windstorm.

The image vanished as suddenly as a lightning flash. The candles, dimmed by the ruby glow, were again the room's only illumination. Meder sank back onto the chair on top of his ironbound box. The color had drained from his face.

"*That* was your father, girl," Asera said with satisfaction. "Not the innkeeper downstairs."

Sharina turned and opened the clothes chest behind her in the corner of the room. She reached down the side, feeling past the layers of shifts and outer tunics to the oval bronze canister she'd first seen when she was a child playing while her mother was downstairs. Lora whimpered but didn't attempt to stop her.

The small container was packed with a scrap of purple satin. Within that nest was a gold-hinged locket. Sharina opened the ivory panels and held the miniature paintings of a young couple out toward her mother in the palm of her hand.

"It's him, isn't it?" Sharina said. "I'm their child, not yours and Reise's!"

The man's features were those of the image Meder's incantation had raised. Above the head of the painting was the legend NIARD, COUNT BY THE LADY'S GRACE. Over the stronger, darker face of the woman was TERA, COUNTESS BY THE SHEPHERD'S GRACE.

Asera dusted her hands together in a gesture of completion.

"We've found the heir we were looking for," she said. "You'll go with us to Valles, girl!"

Meder looked up from the chair with exhausted eyes. "It's your destiny, Sharina," he said.

16

Garric dreamed.

A man was coming toward him through a foreground that seemed to change with every stride. At first it was a meadow; a moment later the man walked in a grove of hard corals, ducking beneath their branches. The reef's vivid colors were dimmed to pastel as if by light filtered through clear water, but the man strode on unaffected.

"Who are you?" the dream Garric called, though a part of him was sure it already knew the answer. His own voice seemed very distant.

The man was a youthful-looking forty years old, with muscular arms and thighs. He wore boots to midcalf and a rich blue tunic; where his skin was bare it was tanned as dark as Haft shepherd's.

The man waved; his lips moved, but Garric couldn't hear the words. He was in a forest now, stepping in and out of shafts of sunlight that waked dazzling richness from his tunic and the metal ornaments he wore.

He smiled broadly. His face looked as though he laughed often and with roaring abandon, the sort of laughter that Garric had heard in his mind all this evening and night.

The dream Garric closed his hand on the coin hanging around his neck on a silken cord. The warm, smooth metal in his fist wasn't a dream.

In rougher clothing the man would pass for a resident of Barca's Hamlet, though he was taller than most and his shoulders broad enough to rouse notice. He looked like an older version of Garric or-Reise, dressed in shimmering cloth. The dark ringlets of his hair were bound with a simple gold diadem.

"Who *are* you?" Garric repeated. His shout sank into fathomless space. His dream self stood in nothingness, separated by eternity from everything and everyone.

"I'm Carus, King of the Isles, lad!" the man called in a distance-muted voice. He splashed through a swamp in boots of leather dyed the same brilliant blue as his tunic. "*You* know me."

Garric stared at the man. It was like looking into a mirror which distorted not images but time itself. "But you're dead," he shouted.

"Am I, lad?" Carus said. His laughter boomed like far-off thunder. Sand blew off a dune and skirled through the air around him, glinting on his sweaty skin like a dusting of jewels. "*Am I?*"

The figure of the ancient king remained the same size, but his voice grew stronger with every stride he took toward Garric. His face showed the tired determination of a man who had journeyed far and would go farther yet—as far as the road led—before he rested.

"I'll help you become King of the Isles, lad," Carus said. "And you'll bring me to Duke Tedry of Yole, who has unfinished business with me."

Garric watched the figure, now being lashed by rain on a rock-strewn slope. Pine trees bent in the wind; Carus hunched against the blast, and his legs scissored forward with the regularity of a pendulum stroking.

"Yole sank a thousand years ago!" Garric cried. "King Carus is dead!"

Carus threw his head back and laughed with the full-throated enthusiasm of a man who took joy wherever he found it: whether in a sunset or the steel-sparkling air of a battlefield.

Garric spun away, his dream self rejoining with the youth sleeping on the straw of his father's stable, wrapped in a thin blanket and clutching the ancient coin he wore around his neck.

17

The mockingbird perched on the dogwood continued its series of liquid calls even when Sharina rattled the clackers only ten feet away. It was a mild, brilliant morning, and the dogwood buds had opened to surround the bird in white profusion.

The weather had done something to lift Sharina's own mood, though it couldn't help cure her confusion. She skipped down the slope to the hut calling, "It's me, Nonnus. I need your help!"

The hermit stood at the creekside where he'd been smoothing an ash sapling held horizontal in a pair of forked stakes. Bark shavings patterned the ground and hung in the reeds at the margin of the creek. The water was no more than six inches deep except for the pool Nonnus had dug out and covered with a bed of colored stones, to make it easier for him to bathe and dip his copper kettle.

"Not because of your health, I trust, child?" he said as he wiped his knifeblade on the hem of his black tunic. He gave Sharina the craggy smile that she saw more often than anyone else in the hamlet. "No, not the way you're cantering along."

Nonnus viewed the edge of his knife with a critical eye, tilting it up and down to catch the light. Satisfied, he slipped it back in its sheath.

Every peasant on Haft carried a knife for a variety of tasks: cutting rope, prizing a stone out of a sheep's hoof, marking a tally stick—the myriad needs of an agricultural community.

Peasants' knives were mostly forged by a local smith from a strip of wrought iron; their scales of bone, horn, or wood were riveted to a flat tang. The blade was typically six or eight inches long, its point rounded, and the edge sharpened at need on the nearest smooth stone.

The hermit's knife was unique, though it was no less practical a tool. Its blade was polished steel, over a foot long and the thickness of a woman's little finger across the straight back. The edge moved in a graceful curve, forming a deep belly near the point to throw the weight outward.

Nonnus used his knife for everything from skinning game to large projects for which the locals would have chosen an axe, a billhook, or a spokeshave. The blade had a working edge, sturdy enough not to bend on tough jobs but sharp enough to trim his hair and beard. Sharina had sometimes watched as the hermit chopped wood with the knife, using an effortless mechanical stroke that sent chips flying onto the far bank of the creek.

"Not my health, no," Sharina agreed. She jumped up, caught a branch, and chinned herself on a whim, then dropped to the ground again.

"Nonnus," she said bluntly. "They want me to go to Ornifal—Asera and Meder do. I want you to come with me because I trust you. And you've been in cities before."

Nonnus smiled faintly. "One way and another, yes," he said. "But I'm not a city man, Sharina. Your father is. He should go with you, or your mother should."

He reached into the creek and lifted a bucket of bark sewn with sinew and waterproofed with tree gum. It was full of birch beer; the hermit kept it almost submerged so that the running water cooled the drink on even the hottest days of August. Two bark cups dangled from the container's handle. He dipped them full and handed the white one—Sharina's cup—to her.

"If Reise or Lora came with me, it'd be for their own reasons," Sharina said morosely into the cup. "I need someone who worries first about me."

Nonnus turned, surveying his hut and garden. "Haft's been kind to me," he said. "I came here because it was as far as I could go without falling off the edge of the world—"

He fixed Sharina again with his eyes and gave her a grin like sunlight glinting from an iceberg.

"—which I was not quite ready to do. It's a long time since I was on Ornifal."

Sharina raised her eyes to the hermit's, then looked down again with a nervous twitch of her mouth. "Nonnus?" she said. "Reise and Lora aren't my parents. Count Niard and Countess Tera are."

Nonnus snorted with mild amusement. "You're a wise girl to be so certain about your parentage," he said. "I've never found it so clear a matter, nor have I ever seen it a useful question to pursue."

"There isn't any doubt," Sharina said. Part of her was irritated that the hermit took her revelation with so little concern. "Meder held a summoning rite. He's a wizard."

"A very powerful one, from what Tenoctris tells me," Nonnus agreed, "but I wouldn't stake my life on what a wizard said or did."

His voice was lightly musing at the start of the spoken thought but by the end the words cracked. The hermit's face had a wooden stiffness.

"Nonnus?" Sharina said. "I don't know anything about wizards. But I think this was real."

Nonnus hooked the cup back onto the bucket with the deliberation of extreme control, then deliberately faced away from Sharina. "Oh, I don't doubt the boy is real," he said in a thick voice. "His sort think they make the world turn with their spells. But they're wrong!"

Sharina held her cup in both hands, no longer drinking from it. She feared that any motion she made would further disturb the hermit in this unexpected mood, so she stood as still as the image of the Lady carved in the trunk of a living tree.

"The Earl of Sandrakkan had wizards on the high walls of

his camp when he met King Valence at the Stone Wall,'' Nonnus said. His voice was a growl that could have come from a beast or out of a blizzard-driving wind. ''The wizards sacrificed chickens and sheep as the armies advanced, cutting their throats so the blood ran down the walls. And they chanted, and the earth shook.''

He glanced at the Lady's simple image and smiled minutely. Turning again toward Sharina, he resumed, ''Their spell made the ground ripple like cloth in a breeze. What did that matter? Waves rise and fall a hundred feet when they smash Pewle Island every storm! But the Ornifal militia on the right wing panicked, and the Sandrakkan cavalry got through the gap to surround King Valence.''

He was trying to speak normally, but emotion thickened his tongue and slurred the words. He looked at Sharina. Because she knew she had to speak she said, ''But the Blood Eagles stood, Nonnus?''

''Oh, aye,'' he said in a thin, despairing voice like nothing she'd heard from a human throat. ''They *stood.*''

Sharina extended a hand toward the hermit the way she would have reached out to touch fabric of unimaginable fineness. He didn't meet her fingers, but he smiled. His staff leaned against a tree near where he'd been working. He took it in his hands.

''The nobles want to carry you to Valles,'' he said conversationally. ''Do you want to go?''

Iron ferrules capped both ends of the hollywood staff. Nonnus looked at them critically, then laid the staff down with one tip on a flat stone.

''Meder tells me it's my destiny,'' Sharina said with embarrassment. Folk in Barca's Hamlet didn't have destinies, only lives. ''Besides, I don't think they'd let me refuse. They have the soldiers, you know.''

''So they do,'' Nonnus said in a tone she couldn't read. ''But I asked you what you wanted.''

He set the tip of a hardwood peg on the rivet holding the ferrule, then gave it a sharp rap with the butt of his big knife.

The rivet head popped a quarter inch from the other side. Nonnus gripped the head and pulled the rivet out; he had enough strength in his fingers to straighten cod hooks.

"I think I want to go, Nonnus," she said. "I'm afraid because I've never been out of the borough, but I want to go."

Instead of replying immediately, the hermit twisted the ferrule off and walked into his hut with it. He returned with a slender package of oiled linen that Sharina had never seen before.

"They're . . ." she said. "They're readying the ship today. They'll leave tomorrow morning."

Nonnus squatted and unwrapped the packet, holding it so that Sharina could see the contents. Within the linen was a socketed steel spearhead with two deep edges and two narrow ones. The point was needle sharp.

He fitted the head to the end of his staff, then looked up at Sharina. "I don't know anything about destiny, child," he said. "But I know about death, and I'll do what I can to keep death away from you."

He smiled gently. He'd always been gentle, with her and the other villagers. But she'd never confused gentleness with weakness.

"Go on back, child," the hermit said. "I'll be there when the ship's ready to sail."

18

Good morning, Mistress Tenoctris," Ilna said as she joined Garric and the castaway at the shearing corral. "I still have your robe, you know. The dyes are excellent to have stood salt water and direct sunlight that way."

Tenoctris looked up; she'd been tracing carvings with her

index finger and discussing them with or reading them to Garric. He turned also and smiled when he saw Ilna.

The corral north of the hamlet was a waist-high structure built from a mixture of fieldstones and building fragments, some of them very old. The stone Tenoctris was viewing was a slate only an inch thick. The edges had been squared, then carved with the cursive characters Ilna knew to call Old Script.

She couldn't read Old Script. She couldn't even read the blockier modern writing derived from it; her childhood hadn't had time for luxuries like schooling.

"It doesn't look like I'll have much use for silk robes, does it?" Tenoctris said. Her smile swept from Ilna to Garric. "Do you suppose the Count of Haft wants a court magician? A not very powerful court magician, I'm afraid."

Garric looked embarrassed; Tenoctris might as well have asked him what lay on the other side of the world. "I don't know, mistress," he said. "Maybe my father would. He knew Lascarg before he became count, he says."

Ilna didn't care what happened about the robe; it was a unique garment and doubtless quite valuable to the right buyer, but she still found its touch disquieting. The garment was merely her immediate excuse for joining Garric. She'd seen almost nothing of him since the ship arrived and brought her the profitable responsibility of catering for five soldiers.

Tenoctris might have noticed that her question had made Garric uncomfortable, because she said, "Garric's been showing me carved stones reused in present-day structures. This one was a grave marker." Her finger again traced the band of writing on the stone's edge.

"From your own time?" Ilna said. She'd heard rumors that the castaway was from the distant past, but she wanted to hear confirmation from the woman's own mouth.

"Much more recent than that," Tenoctris said. "This isn't much older than the inn. They must have retained the Old Script for formal uses like graves long after it ceased to be the normal style of writing."

"How do you tell?" Ilna said, her eyes narrowing at the flaw in the logic. "If you were really from the past, the dates on that stone wouldn't mean anything to you."

The feel of Tenoctris' robe told Ilna that the castaway was from somewhere unimaginably distant, but she'd prefer to believe that the feeling was false. That sort of knowledge didn't belong in the world which Ilna understood.

"This on the edge is just a plea that the Shepherd protect the soul of the departed," Tenoctris said with a smile of faint approval. "Perhaps there's a date on the face where we can't see it. I was judging the stone's age from the forces that infused it when it was put over a grave."

"Ah," Ilna said. She was blushing fiercely. "Mistress, I'm sorry."

"That was a good question," Tenoctris said with no hint of sarcasm or patronizing. She glanced at Garric, then focused on his right hand clasping something against his chest through the tunic's fabric. "Garric, what is it you're wearing there? That's the reason you're . . . different, I think. Isn't it?"

Garric pulled a loop of silk the pale blue of a winter sky from around his neck. He handed it and the suspended gold disk to Tenoctris. Ilna had never seen the ornament before.

"It's a coin my father gave me yesterday," he said apologetically. Consciously or not, he'd touched the object to call it to the wizard's attention. "He won't say anything about it except that it's mine."

Tenoctris held the object in her palm. Her thumb clamped the cord so that it couldn't slip while she peered at both sides in turn. The worn profile of a man showed on one; the other seemed to have writing, though Ilna couldn't be sure.

"Now this *is* from my time," Tenoctris said, looking up at Garric. "It's not a drilled coin, you know: it's a medallion. See how the boss for stringing it was formed in the die?"

She handed it back to Garric. "It's a medallion of Carus," she said. "It was struck on the day of his coronation as King of the Isles."

Shaking her head in faint amusement, Tenoctris went on,

"I can remember most things from before, you know. It's only there at the end when all the memories are jumbled like a fresco painting when the plaster flakes off the wall. When I see the Old Script and touch things of my own day, some of it comes back; but it's still confused."

"Tenoctris?" Garric said carefully. "Did you ever see King Carus?"

Tenoctris shook her head. All her movements were slight and precise. Ilna thought the old woman would be ignored in almost any company, but that would be a mistake. Tenoctris wasn't flashy, but there was an edge to her that could cut glass.

"I was never on Haft before," she explained. She smiled and added, "I suppose if the royal fleet hadn't been sunk, I might have seen him on Yole."

A pair of chipmunks chased each other across the top of the wall, chittering furiously. When they noticed the three humans they stopped dead, stared in rigid silence, and then went racing back the way they'd come.

"Have you ever seen a man in a black robe with a black hood covering his face, even his eyes?" Garric said. He was looking down at his feet. "I don't know how to describe him better because—"

Tenoctris reached out slowly and touched Garric's chin to bring his eyes to meet hers. "Where did you meet the Hooded One?" she asked in a soft, wondering tone.

"It wasn't real," Garric said. He hung the medallion's loop over his head to have an excuse for breaking eye contact again. The business made him uncomfortable, just as the feel of the wizard's robe had Ilna. "It was only a dream."

"Dream perhaps," Tenoctris said, lowering her hand again. "But don't doubt that it was quite real."

She shook her head again as if to settle her shattered memories. "I don't know who he really was or where he came from, though he was the most powerful wizard I ever thought to see. He claimed to be Malkar, but that was a boastful lie."

"He claimed to be *evil*?" Ilna said in amazement. Malkar

was a bogey to frighten children, not a god like the Lady and her consort the Shepherd, or even the Sister who ruled the Underworld. No one worshipped Malkar. It would have been like worshipping a cesspool.

"Malkar isn't—" Tenoctris began. She looked from Ilna to Garric, assessing how they'd react to the phrasing she'd been about to use. She nodded and said, "Ah. Let me put that another way."

Before Tenoctris resumed, she seated herself on the wall. She had to rise up on tiptoes because the corral was otherwise a little high for her. The whole borough used the corral during the spring shearing and at the fall Sheep Fair, when buyers of mutton on the hoof came from Carcosa and more distant cities.

"To a wizard," Tenoctris said, "the sun is an ultimate source of power and Malkar is an ultimate source of power. But no one can reach an ultimate source directly. The forces that a wizard works with aren't pure, any more than the water you drink is pure."

"You're saying that Malkar isn't evil?" Garric said with a frown that Ilna hadn't seen often. Because he usually wore a boyish smile, it was easy to forget how tall and strong Garric or-Reise really was. "That you serve Malkar?"

"No," Tenoctris said, tapping her finger on the wall beside her with sharp emphasis. She was seated on a squared block of white limestone, an ashlar from an ancient temple. "No one *serves* Malkar. And as for using the forces that stem largely from Malkar, I don't drink seawater either. There are differences of degree."

Ilna turned her head to watch the waves dancing in the sunlight. Near shore the water was dark, almost purple, but beyond that and as far as her eye could reach the Inner Sea had a pale green translucence like that of the finest jade. It was much more beautiful than the colorless fluid brought up from a well; but of course no human could drink seawater. . . .

"The Hooded One was very powerful," Tenoctris went on musingly. "He had the power to sink the seabed beneath Carus' fleet. The power to sink Yole as well, though unintentionally. . . . That's quite amazing, nothing any wizard would have believed possible until it happened. But the forces the Hooded One worked with, the forces that *all* wizards work with, had increased a hundredfold in less than a year. There was something more than human influence involved.''

"Was it Malkar that caused the increase?'' Ilna asked. Talking of magic made her feel warm but oddly queasy. It was like imagining that she was swimming out into the shimmering, lovely sea.

Tenoctris shook her head, frustrated at her inability to explain. "That's like asking if winter wills it to be cold,'' she said. "There are cycles, there are forces. They act whether we understand them or not. Malkar waxes and wanes. But they don't—''

She paused and looked at the two younger people in the bright sunlight. "I don't think the sun and Malkar have wills of their own. But I don't really know, do I?''

She smiled engagingly. Though Tenoctris wouldn't have been beautiful even in her youth, her face was as attractive as a sheet of fine vellum. "What I do know,'' she said, "is that the forces are building in the same way that they did in my day; the forces that sank Yole and flung me here to Haft. Perhaps that's a coincidence.''

Garric grimaced. He touched the medallion with an index finger, realized what he was doing, and shook his head ruefully. "I don't know what to think,'' he said. "I guess I don't need to. Barca's Hamlet isn't going to change much no matter what happens.''

Ilna looked at Garric and saw the lie in the tenseness of his facial muscles. The planes of his cheeks were as hard as oak boards.

"I remember at the end,'' Tenoctris said, "that the Hooded One sat on his black throne. He claimed it was the Throne of Malkar, literally the seat of power. But it shattered in the first shock.''

"But Malkar is real?'' Ilna said, her face calm, her mind

filled with an intensity as cold as the depths of the sea.

Tenoctris looked at her with an expression that became appraising during seconds of silence. "Oh, yes," the wizard said. "Malkar is real, just as the sun is real; and is just as eternal. And I'm afraid that the Hooded One may be part of present reality also if Garric sees him in dreams."

Ilna shivered as though a cloud had drifted over the sun. The sky above was a fine clear blue all the way to the eastern horizon, and the green sea danced beneath it.

19

There were hundreds of people on the shore and seawall, more ever than the hamlet had seen at the busiest Sheep Fair. The trireme's arrival had been a surprise, but its launching was scheduled and had drawn the whole borough to watch it.

Sharina had never felt so completely alone.

"I apologize that there's so little space on the ship," Meder chattered happily, "but really, Sharina, none of the clothing available in this backwater was worthy of you. When we reach Valles the king will outfit you like the great lady you are."

Sailors were carrying the last of the supplies across the gangplank and down into the bowels of the ship. At Asera's order, one of them had taken aboard the wicker hamper holding Sharina's blanket and an extra shift. It was a clear, sunny day, but she huddled within her cape because she felt cold nonetheless.

"You're lucky that we found you in time," Meder said. "The queen's agents are looking for you too, you know. They'd have killed you without hesitation if they'd found you first."

Sharina had avoided Meder ever since the summoning ceremony, but now that they were to be together on the ship she had no choice. He was a good-looking young man; wealthy, noble, and a powerful wizard besides. He just made her feel uncomfortable.

"Why would the queen want to kill me?" Sharina asked with a frown. The warning puzzled rather than frightened her; it simply had no place in her world. "Why would *anyone* want to kill me?"

Asera sat nearby on a folding stool, writing with a stylus on a tablet made by laying wax over thin wooden boards. Noble officials would normally have an entourage of servants, secretaries included. These must have traveled on the other triremes, the pair the sea had swallowed.

None of Sharina's friends from Barca's Hamlet came up to her. Even her family stood a few paces away: Lora was crying, Reise stood stone-faced; even Garric held himself stiff with his hands crossed at the small of his back, and the smiles he offered when Sharina's eyes brushed him were forced. It was as though she'd already died.

"Oh, the queen's evil, utter evil, Sharina," Meder explained in a tone of surprise. "I suppose growing up out here you don't see that as much as we do on Ornifal, but there's no depth to which she and her minions wouldn't stoop to destroy the old royal line of Haft. She's not from Ornifal, you know. And she's a wizard herself who bewitched the king into marrying her."

"We don't see *anything* of the queen *or* the king in Barca's Hamlet," Sharina said with a touch of irritation. Did Meder think his artificial world of politics and treachery was the way everyone lived? Maybe he did think that; probably he did. "We don't see anything of Carcosa except tax collectors. And once a year the priests parade their images and collect portions for the Lady and the Shepherd."

Most of the crew was gathered to either side of the trireme's stern, preparing to shove her off the beach. The waves were already lapping their ankles; the tide was near full. A few oarsmen were aboard to steady the vessel when it began to float.

The Blood Eagles formed a gleaming circle around the nobles and Sharina. Their black presence was at least part of the reason no villagers approached Sharina now, though she supposed people could have gotten through if they'd been willing to try.

"Well, trust me," Meder said. "The queen would stop at nothing to destroy you. She knows that you'll provide legitimacy for King Valence. All but the most depraved people will join his party."

Sharina *didn't* trust Meder. She didn't think the wizard would lie to her—he seemed to like her, to respect her even— but his view of the world was so different from hers that she couldn't assume any of his assessments would be the same as she would make.

"I don't see how my being in Valles legitimizes the king," she said. "What am I supposed to do?"

"What?" Meder said. For an instant he looked surprised; then his face closed in fright or embarrassment. Drawing back a little, he resumed, "Of course, I'm only the king's agent. What he. . . . what his plans—"

The procurator looked up from her notebook with a grim expression. "Meder," she said. "Your business is to carry out the duties I assign you. Yammering like a monkey is not one of those duties. Do you understand?"

The younger noble's face clouded with a furious scowl. "How dare—" he began.

His voice choked off as he saw, really *saw*, the look Asera was giving him. The troops' commander, Wainer, tapped the shoulders of the three men nearest him. The soldiers turned around, watching the folk within their circle. Meder was a noble in his own right, but the detachment of Blood Eagles guarded the king's procurator—from any threat.

Meder grimaced and bowed. "Sorry," he said in a tone of honest apology. "You're right, of course." He was a young man, perhaps too young for the power he wielded, but decent enough underneath the arrogance.

The trireme's captain walked toward them from the base of the gangplank and halted just outside the line of soldiers. "Mistress?" he called. "The tide's full. We need to be under way before it turns or we'll be here till dark."

"Yes, all right, Lichnau," the procurator said. She folded the leather hinges of her notebook closed and stood up. "Come along, girl," she said to Sharina as she strode toward the gangplank.

A soldier caught Captain Lichnau by the arm and muttered something. Lichnau looked startled and angry, but he picked up the stool Asera had left and carried it after her. The troops followed.

Sharina ran to Garric and hugged him. He patted her back awkwardly. They'd gotten on the way siblings do—badly; but now that she was leaving, her heart ached at the thought of not seeing him at supper tonight.

"Remember, you're all anybody in Valles sees of Barca's Hamlet, sis," he muttered. "Make us proud of you."

Garric stepped away. Reise offered her his hand to shake. She took it, then stepped closer and hugged him as well. "Stay well, Father," she said.

Reise's smile was as slight and cold as his smiles always were. "Stay well, Sharina," he said. "I'll aid you as circumstances permit."

"Come along, girl!" Asera repeated from the gangplank. Meder hovered nearby, wringing his hands but unwilling to pull Sharina away from her family.

"Mother?" Sharina said.

Lora glared at her with tear-wet eyes. "Oh, you don't have to pretend I'm your mother!" she said. "I treated you like my own daughter, but now that you're going off to the king's palace you can just leave me behind. I'm only the maid, after all!"

Sharina opened her mouth to plead; then closed it again. The only way she could make Lora happy was to bring her along to Valles. Sharina wasn't willing to do that, even if Asera would have permitted it to happen.

She squeezed Lora's arm and said, "Stay well, Mother."

She turned toward the gangplank. Behind her Lora wept with rising hysteria, an act that was taking on as much reality as emotion ever has.

The crowd nearest the gangplank parted. Nonnus stepped through, carrying his spear reversed on his shoulder. A bindle of personal effects dangled from its butt end. His big knife hung on the rope belt.

Two soldiers stepped to block him, shoulder to shoulder. Nonnus stopped short of them. His posture changed in a way Sharina couldn't have specified, but her instincts screamed a warning to her.

"He's with me!" she cried, running a few steps to the hermit's side. "You have to let him on!"

The procurator was already aboard the vessel. "Don't be absurd!" she called from the stern.

The soldiers stiffened. Nonnus smiled faintly; one of the soldiers touched his sword hilt, then took his hand away.

"Nonnus goes or I stay!" Sharina said in a voice that rang like steel. "I mean it! You've no one with you who can catch me if I run!"

"I've known her longer than you have, mistress," Nonnus said, speaking easily over the crowd noise. "I'd take her word for it."

Asera gripped the rail. It was a replacement piece. Sun and salt spray hadn't yet bleached the wood gray-white. "All right, get aboard!" she ordered. "Now!"

Sharina trotted up the gangplank, her arm stretched behind her gripping a fold of the hermit's sleeve. Meder and the two Blood Eagles, the last of the ship's passengers still on shore, followed.

"What a bizarre outfit!" she heard the wizard say. "Where do you come from, peasant?"

And she heard Nonnus answer, "From many different places, friend. And if you're lucky, you won't have to visit any of them yourself."

BOOK

II

1

Cashel stood at a distance from the other spectators, where the southern end of the hamlet's seawall gave way to grass and the natural crumbling rock of the region. He watched the trireme's crew launch their vessel, and he cried.

All the passengers were aboard. The crew had seated the mast in chocks pinned to the keel, below the deck and even the oarsmen's benches, but they hadn't set the yard as yet. They'd sewn all the canvas in Barca's Hamlet into a sail to replace the one the storm shredded. A trireme could only use the mainsail in fine weather, though, because the rig was awkward to adjust and dangerously capable of capsizing the long, narrow warship if a gust struck from abeam. On blustery days a small triangular sail could be spread from the forepost to aid the rowers.

Garric walked toward Cashel along the top of the seawall. He grinned and waved when he caught Cashel's glance.

Cashel waved back and wiped his eyes with his forearm. He didn't want company; that's why he was standing here! But he couldn't turn Garric away without making even more of a fool of himself than he felt already.

The ship's captain cried "Ready!" in a voice that was almost birdlike by the time the onshore breeze carried it to Cashel. The sailors in the surf, over a hundred of them, braced themselves against the hull and the outrigger that carried the upper two oarbanks.

The drummer seated cross-legged on the trireme's stern began to beat time on a section of hollow log: an ordinary drum's leather heads would soften in the sodden air of the ship's belly. Sailors shouted the cadence as they thrust the vessel outward, into the waves. The sea foamed about them, knee-high to those farthest forward.

"These past three days have really confused me," Garric said as they came close enough to hear each other. "It's like it was all happening to somebody else."

"I wish it was," Cashel said. His eyes were filling with tears again. He couldn't help it.

Ship's officers stood in the surf behind their men, shouting guidance as the waves rose and ebbed. The tide was a little past full, but there didn't seem to be any difficulty launching the vessel. Already the bow was free and the stern rocked with each measured thrust from the men in the water. The planking of the lower hull was black with the tar that sealed it against the sea.

Side by side with Cashel, Garric turned to watch the ship. Cashel quickly swiped his eyes dry again, though he knew it wouldn't help for long.

Thirty oars toward the bow on either side were manned, though the blades were raised and motionless for the moment. An officer leaned out from the curving forepost, watching for the abnormal swell that might lift the vessel and fling it broadside onto the shore again. Cashel was no sailor, but anyone who lived near the sea knew to respect its unpredictable strength.

The morning sun lighted the vermilion upper hull; the ship was a streak of fire on the water. The eye on the far bow seemed to blink as the spray slapped it. Garric must have noticed the same thing, because he said, "The captain told me that the eye isn't so the ship can see its way, like I'd thought. It's to scare away sea monsters."

A dozen more oars came out, spaced along the after part of the hull. The trireme was completely afloat. The bow oars began to stroke, holding the vessel steady as the men in the water gripped the oarshafts nearer the stern and lifted themselves back aboard the ship. The drummer beat a changed rhythm.

The nobles and their soldier escort clustered just forward

of the mast where they were least in the way of the deck crew and the oarsmen swarming over the stern rails on both sides. In their midst stood a tall, blond woman shrouded in a winter cloak.

"Goodbye, Sharina!" Garric called. He waved both arms above his head. "Stay well! Stay well!"

He turned to Cashel and said, "I can't get over the fact that Sharina's leaving. This is all happening in another world."

Cashel began to sob openly. He knelt slowly, the way an ox falls after being stabbed to the heart. His grip on his staff steadied him.

"Cashel?" Garric said. "*Cashel?*"

"Just leave me alone, can't you?" he shouted. Tears choked the words to blubbering. "Oh, Duzi, I love her so much. I love her so much."

"You love Sharina?" Garric said. Even in his present state Cashel could hear the disbelief in his friend's voice. Then in a different tone Garric added, "Does she know it, Cashel?"

"No, nobody knows it," Cashel said. He was already feeling better; blurting the truth seemed to have cleansed the poison of hurt from his soul. "Not even my sister knows."

Though he couldn't really be sure of that. Ilna sometimes read his thoughts before they were even formed in his mind.

He got to his feet, still blind with tears but no longer trembling. He wiped his eyes; this time they stayed clear.

Out of embarrassment Garric didn't look directly toward Cashel. "I'm all right," Cashel muttered to his friend's sidelong concern. He supposed he really was. There was a just cold empty place where the emotions had washed out of his heart with the tears.

The ship was already well offshore. Its oars rippled in sequence like the legs of a millipede. Only two banks were in use; the storm must have smashed many of the oars, and there was nothing in Barca's Hamlet to replace them.

"I didn't know people felt that way . . ." Garric said. His mouth worked silently as he tried to decide how to explain what he meant, then chose to let the thought die.

"Like something out of one of your love poems, isn't it?" Cashel said bitterly. "Maybe that's my trouble—I let you read poems to me. Love doesn't belong here. It doesn't belong with people like me."

Barca's Hamlet was too small a community for any child to grow up ignorant of what went on between men and women. When a couple fought, everybody heard the words they screamed at one another. Wives clawed other women, men bludgeoned rivals senseless in muddy farmyards.

But neighbors fought over fencelines and missing sheep, too. Hot anger was natural. The queasy hollowness Cashel felt at the thought of Sharina being gone was like leprosy, a wasting foulness that he couldn't wash off.

"Well, she'll be back, you know, Cashel," Garric said, the lie patent in his brittle cheeriness. "I've been feeling really strange myself lately. I thought it was the seawolf's poison—"

He patted his right calf gently. The wounds had already closed, though the scabs would be some time clearing.

"—but you know, I wonder if it isn't a fever going around that you caught a touch of too?"

"She'll never be back," Cashel said flatly. He was no longer sad; just empty. "I'm going away too, Garric. I can't stay here. It'd remind me the rest of my life that she was here and now she's gone."

"Leave?" Garric said. "But where would you go? And look, I don't see any reason to think Sharina won't be back. Things these past few days have just confused us, that's all. They'll get back to normal."

"I don't know where I'm going or when," Cashel said heavily. "But I won't be staying here long."

He forced a smile at his friend. "Right now I'm going back to the sheep. I shouldn't have left them, but I had to watch."

Garric opened his mouth. "No," Cashel said sharply. "I don't need company. Not today."

He started for the nearby pasture, where ewes moved

slowly over the new grass. At the top of the first rise he paused to look over his shoulder again.

The ship was halfway to the horizon. It was impossible to make out individual figures on the deck, but Sharina's cloak was a blob of blue.

2

Three points north," protested the tall young officer beside Sharina. The headband around his blond hair and the border of his linen breechclout were the same bright red, making him a dandy of greater refinement than the common sailors with their earrings and tattoos. "That's all we'd have to steer to set the mainsail and let the oarsmen rest."

As soon as the vessel got under way, the crew had erected a deckhouse of light lacquered wood just forward of the steering oars, one on either side of the hull, and the captain's seat beneath the overhang of the curving sternpost. The shelter protected Asera and Meder from the sun and windblown spray, but it would have to come down or be blown down in any kind of weather.

Sharina found the deckhouse cramped. On a day like this she preferred the open air anyway, so she'd refused the wizard's invitation to join them.

For all its size, the trireme had remarkably little space for the people aboard it. The Blood Eagles were mostly near the arms chest forward of the mast. There was more space on the outriggers, but the troops were landsmen and clearly uncomfortable about being so close to the foaming sea. The outriggers were planked over, but they didn't have railings.

"We've a full crew, Kizuta," Captain Lichnau replied. "A slow stroke on one bank isn't going to wear anybody out; in fact it'll keep them in condition. And three points north is three points closer to Tegma than I want to chance. Now, go check the forewell and see if the caulking on those started seams is holding.''

Sharina stood almost between the two officers; they ignored her, treating the passengers as absolutely none of their business. The status of seamen on Ornifal—at least among officials of the king's court—must be very low.

And what was the status of peasants from Haft? *May the Shepherd wait with me. May the Lady take me by the hand. I'm so alone. . . .*

Nonnus half-stood, half-reclined in the curve of the forepost. He gripped the rail with one foot. His other leg was crossed under the right knee, and his laced fingers supported his head as he looked back along the trireme's deck. He gave a minuscule nod and smile in response to Sharina's glance.

Even in this mild weather the trireme's bow slapped hard as it came off the top of each swell, because of the weight of the bronze ram. Spray flew, bathing the hermit. It glittered on his hairy limbs and soaked his tunic, though the heavy black wool didn't seem to change.

The conditions had no effect on Nonnus. He was out of the way, and he had a view of everything that happened on deck.

Sharina started toward him. The gods might or might not be on her side. About Nonnus there could be no doubt.

The officers' argument ended with Lichnau saying, ''All right, set the jib sail but I *don't* trust even that after what we met on the run east.''

Kizuta trotted forward on the starboard outrigger, shouting to members of the deck crew. Nonnus bumped himself upright with a twitch of his hips and walked toward Sharina. Sailors carrying a roll of canvas, the jib sail, danced a graceful pirouette with him as they passed in the opposite direction through the crowd of Blood Eagles.

Along with other baggage, the troops' breastplates and helmets clogged the passageway between the oarbenches below. The rowers' own minimal personal effects were under the benches or folded as padding. For now the Blood Eagles wore the jerkins and caps of soft leather which cushioned their metal armor. Dry leather can turn a swordcut, but it becomes a soggy mass of no more protective value than cheese if drenched by waves or a rainstorm.

The Blood Eagles had stowed their weapons in the arms chest, since there was no threat from anything except possibly the weather. In the cramped confines of the ship there was a good chance of losing a spear overboard or injuring a friend. Swords and daggers would knock against the ship's rail and fittings, damaging the ornamented scabbards, and the blades' high-carbon steel was almost certain to rust in the salt air.

Soldiers sat on the long chest or stood nearby, because it was the only part of the vessel to which they felt a connection. One of the younger men looked at Nonnus and said, "Say, some knife you've got there, old man. It'll drag you straight to the bottom of the sea if you go over. Want to stick it in here?"

His heel thumped the arms chest behind him.

"I'll have to be careful not to fall overboard," Nonnus said mildly. He'd placed his javelin in the chest when he came aboard, but Sharina didn't remember the hermit ever being without the big knife except when he was praying.

She pushed quickly to Nonnus' side, then realized she should have held back for a moment. The soldier's eyes hardened to see a pretty young girl on the old man's arm. The other Blood Eagles watched, clearly disinclined to interfere with whatever their comrade had in mind.

"Yeah, an old codger like you could go over the side real easy if he got uppity with his betters," the soldier said. "I figure that knife's a bit big to shave with, so why don't you put it away right now? Better yet, why don't you toss *it* over the side?"

The hermit's face had no more expression than a stone. "I'm sorry if I offended you, sir," he said. His head barely moved, but his eyes flicked in both directions. There were soldiers behind him as well as in front.

"Ningir, what the *hell* do you think you're doing?" Wainer shouted as he burst through the crowd of his men. His face was flushed with anger. He'd rushed forward from where he'd been kneeling by the deckhouse, speaking to the procurator within.

"Well, I—" the soldier said in surprise.

"Listen, you young fool," Wainer snarled. "I never saw work a sword could do that a Pewle knife couldn't; and once I saw Pewle knives do what swordsmen would not. Now, get below and don't come back up until you've made a written inventory of all the baggage!"

"I don't have anything to write on," Ningir protested.

The officer poked him in the chest with an index finger as thick as a broomstick. "Then take off your jerkin and write on that!" he said. "Or stay below till you rot and grow mushrooms, I don't care which. Just get off this deck!"

The shouting pressed Sharina's body away the way a sheep twists from the blades at shearing time. Nonnus was firm as a rooted oak. He didn't hold her, but his side was a supporting buttress.

White-faced, Ningir turned and walked toward the companionway in the stern. The other Blood Eagles had straightened. Those who'd been sitting on the arms chest now stood up. Nobody spoke for a moment.

"*Damned* young fool," Wainer said, looking almost but not quite at Nonnus as he spoke.

"Thank you, sir," Nonnus said, his voice oddly husky. "The Lady was with me, that you came when you did."

Wainer snorted. "The Lady was with Ningir or I miss my bet," he said. He looked from Nonnus to Sharina, frowning slightly as his eyes shifted back to the hermit. He said, "I was at the Stone Wall."

Nonnus nodded calmly, but Sharina felt his body go as hard as it had been while facing Ningir. "You're of an age to have been there," he said.

"So are you," Wainer said, watching the hermit without blinking.

"I'm of an age to live in a hut in the woods, sir," Nonnus said, "as far from the world as I could go without leaving it."

He gave Wainer a crooked grin. "I'll thank the Lady for your intervention, sir," he said; bowed; and shepherded Sharina ahead of him toward the far bow.

The sailors had rigged the jib sail to the boom; it bellied well out to the port side. The outline of a shark's jaws was stenciled in red on the canvas, some sort of military boast or identification.

"What did he mean about the Stone Wall, Nonnus?" Sharina asked in a tiny voice.

"There are others who will tell you, child," Nonnus replied. "I will not."

He stood looking out over the sea. Sharina stood beside him, ignoring the slapping spray. Neither of them spoke again until the sun neared the western horizon and the hermit turned to cry, "Land on the starboard bow!"

3

On the stone stoop of the mill Ilna's shuttle clattered back and forth across the loom with the regularity of water dripping from a hole. She depressed a pedal or pedals, threw the shuttle, and threw it back. Every six threads she lifted the bar to beat the woof firm again.

The border was of gray and white diamonds, surrounding a black field on which she'd picked out in white the constellations as seen from Barca's Hamlet. The moon, gibbous so that shadow detail emphasized its crater walls, was nearly complete; all that remained was the lower border.

The threads were the natural color of the wool. The available dyes were either muted by contrast to the brilliance of nature—birds, flowers, even the rich tones of sunset and sunrise—or they didn't hold their color through sunlight and cleaning. Ilna scorned artificial hues and worked in vivid permanence with the varied fleece of Haft sheep.

The pattern grew with such precision in the afternoon sun that anyone watching would assume that Ilna's whole attention was directed on it. In reality, weaving was a task for Ilna's limbs and the animal part of her brain. Her conscious mind danced over life and her surroundings, so as a result she was the first person in Barca's Hamlet to see the strangers coming down the Carcosa Road.

Four tough-looking men on foot led the party. They wore swords and breastplates of multilayered linen, stiffened with glue and metal-studded for additional protection. Two of the men led pack mules.

The man following was mounted on a fine bay mare. His doublet was purple velvet over black silk tights, and his light sword was clearly for show in contrast to the serviceable weapons of his guards. He was plump, not fat, and probably in his early forties; Ilna found it hard to judge the age of folk with wealth enough to fend away the strains of time.

Behind him rode a woman—a girl—whose cream gelding looked bigger beneath her than the tall bay did under the man. She wore a brown satin jumper that she probably considered traveling garb; Ilna knew there was nothing of equal quality in the whole borough save the robe in which Tenoctris was found.

From the girl's broad-brimmed hat depended a veil so thin that it accentuated her features rather than concealing them. Her hair was the black of a raven's wing, and she was the most beautiful woman Ilna had ever seen.

Two more guards walked at the rear of the procession. One or the other was always looking back over his shoulder, as alert as stags feeding in a forest glen.

Ilna tapped into place the threads she'd just woven and stood up. The strangers were headed for the inn. Dogs began to bark and the bay whinnied, alerting everyone in hearing to the unusual event. Ilna strode across to the inn's back door and entered calling, "Reise! You have wealthy guests coming."

Lora came out of the kitchen, her eyes still red from crying. Weeping for her own hurt pride, not her daughter; though she'd doted on Sharina and slighted Garric as far back as Ilna could remember. That in itself was reason enough for Ilna to scorn the woman, even without her airs and her shrill carping complaints about everything around her save her daughter.

The count and countess's daughter. That made Lora's attitude more in keeping with the rest of her personality, and made Ilna despise her even more.

"The ship's returned?" Lora asked.

"No," Ilna said curtly as she stepped out the front door. Reise set down the bucket he'd just drawn from the well, and the strangers entered the courtyard.

The male rider was in the lead now that the party had safely reached the hamlet. "May I help you, sir?" Reise said. "I'm Reise or-Laver, and I keep this inn."

"I'm Benlo or-Willet," the man said. His voice was melodious but its touch of hurr proved he wasn't born on Haft. "I'll need private accommodations for myself and my daughter Liane, and quarters for my six attendants."

"Certainly, sir," Reise said. "Do you know how long you'll be staying so that I can arrange supplies of food?"

Benlo dismounted, wincing as his feet touched the ground. There was a scum of dust and sweat around the horses' tack. The guards looked worn, though they were all tough men in top condition. The girl's face was too well bred to give anything away, but the tightness around her lips and eyes hinted at considerable strain. Ilna wondered how many miles they'd come since their last halt.

"That I can't tell you, sir," Benlo said easily. "Several days, I'd judge, but it depends on how quickly I can do my business. I'm a drover with a ship in Carcosa Harbor that I'm loading with Haft sheep."

A guard had taken Benlo's bridle; another guard was handing Liane down from her saddle, though she looked perfectly capable of dismounting herself. Two of the men were detaching the mules' wicker packsaddles. Garric had come in from the street and was leading the horses to the stable.

Most of the hamlet's men were in the fields; some of the women as well, but those who were home spinning or cooking wandered toward the inn to view the strangers. There was less excitement and chatter than there would have been a week past, however. The ship's departure this morning had thrown the arrival of a drover out of season completely in the shade.

"It's not the time we sell sheep here, sir," said Katchin, hurrying into the courtyard. He'd put on a fresh tunic with a satin border, but his feet were flour-stained and he was trying without success to mate his dress belt's complex buckle. "I'm Katchin or-Keldan, the count's bailiff. I'll oversee any dealings you have, to insure the long-term good of the borough."

Benlo turned. With a patronizing gentleness that was more crushing than a snub he said, "Thank you, bailiff. I'm confident there'll be no conflict between your duties and my desires. I've a customer on Sandrakkan who wants to improve his flock by crossing it with Haft bloodlines. He wants the easy part of the year to condition the sheep to their new pastures, so I'm here in spring rather than at the slaughtering time in fall."

He looked around the courtyard, now crowded with spectators. Garric had returned from the stable and was taking the leads of the mules now that they'd been unloaded. The drover's eyes locked momentarily on him in appraisal; Ilna felt her own face tighten in protective hostility, though Benlo's glance was there and gone in an instant. Normal enough; Garric was a youth whose build and carriage attracted attention.

"Also I'll be hiring a local lad to badger the flock to Carcosa for me," Benlo added as if in afterthought. "But for now, Reise, put some chickens on the hearth and heat water for myself and Liane to freshen up with."

He slapped his buttocks, emphasizing the strain of the journey. "And after that, your bailiff and I will arrange business."

Benlo and his daughter entered the inn, following Reise with the bucket he'd just drawn. "Lora, we need a brace of chickens!" he shouted.

"I'll take care of that, Reise," Ilna called. The inn was shorthanded with Sharina gone; there was money to be earned from Reise, a benefit to both parties.

Liane had given the villagers a single long glance, then dismissed them as unworthy of further consideration. She walked inside without looking around or showing anything on her face.

Ilna had seen statues of the Lady with more human empathy; but she'd never seen even a statue as beautiful as this cold woman who had come to Barca's Hamlet.

4

The island didn't have a name. At high tide it could have passed for a stretch of rough water to Sharina's untrained eye, even after Nonnus pointed it out to her. The recent storm had stripped it of most vegetation, though tufts of coarse grass grew on the lee side of hillocks and the trunk of a coconut palm lay uprooted on the shore. The crew had started to chop it up for firewood.

The beach was sand. On the eastern horizon were coral heads worn to mushroom shapes by the currents that deposited their scourings here to form the shore on which the trireme rested.

"I've never been this long off land," Sharina said, digging her toes into the sand in sensuous pleasure at footing that didn't sway beneath her. She pirouetted, holding her arms straight out from her shoulders. "And to have so much room again!"

Nonnus smiled. "A Pewle woodskin holds your hips so tightly that you can rotate over and up again without falling out," he said. "That ship is like sailing in a temple."

"Sharina!" Meder called. A team of sailors had reerected the deckhouse on shore, using piles of sand to brace the sides in place of the turnbuckles that normally clamped it to the deck. Asera and the wizard watched, and a sailor holding a pair of live chickens stood nearby. "Come over with us. I'm going to summon a fair wind for the morrow. You can help me."

Sharina glanced at Nonnus. The hermit gave a minuscule shrug, too slight for anyone at a distance to notice. "I'm coming," Sharina said, and walked toward the nobles.

The Blood Eagles had disembarked with their bedrolls, a motley collection of quilts and blankets purchased in Barca's Landing at prices the villagers would be talking about for years. Wainer was organizing a camp near the deckhouse. Most of the troops looked pleased to be on dry land, though a few of the older men seemed as blasé about nautical life as the sailors.

"We'll carry out the rite inside," Meder said with the crisp enthusiasm that filled him when he talked about his wizardry. "It's better that uninitiated yokels not watch, since there's always the risk that one of them will attempt the incantation and actually get something to happen. Not much risk, of course."

"What do you want me to do?" Sharina asked. She wasn't comfortable with Meder; Asera's eyes, assessing her like a farmer deciding which animals to cull before the hungry times of winter, were bad enough. But Sharina had been raised to help and to do. If the wizard had a task for her, she would dive in just as she scrubbed pots and waited table at the inn.

"We'll cut the throat of one of these birds now and I'll draw the circle with its blood," Meder explained. "Then—"

"Must this be in the shelter?" Asera said tartly. "I planned to sleep in it tonight."

"We'll have the men move the walls when we're done," Meder retorted. "The blood will be on the sand. Do you want some buffoon to call down lightning by accident?"

Asera grimaced but shrugged agreement.

"Now, Sharina," Meder resumed, "when I tell you I want you to cut the throat of the—"

"No," Sharina said.

"—other bir . . ." The wizard paused. "What did you say?" he asked.

"No," she repeated, "I won't do that. Get someone else to help you."

"Surely you've killed a chicken before, girl?" Asera said in amazement. Shadows from the setting sun deepened the furrows of her frown.

"I've killed hundreds," Sharina said flatly. "More than that, I suppose. To eat. I don't like magic and I'm not going to be part of it."

She turned and walked away, her body shaking. "I don't under*stand*," Meder called after her.

Sharina didn't understand either. She'd lived too close to chickens to have any affection for them. They were quarrelsome, stupid, and demanding; the best thing about a chicken was the way it tasted fried. She'd often snapped the necks of a pair like those the sailor held, gutted them with a paring knife, and had them ready to scald the feathers for plucking in less than a minute.

But the thought of cutting the birds' throats just to pour their blood out made her skin crawl and her stomach turn. She didn't even like the idea of reboarding the ship in the morning and knowing where the wind that drove it came from.

Her eyes focused. She'd walked into the midst of the Blood Eagles. Ningir put out a hand toward her, but Wainer waved him back silently.

Nonnus was alert, but he watched Sharina only peripherally. She glanced over her shoulder and saw Asera and the wizard going into the shelter while the sailor with the chickens waited to follow. The hermit relaxed slightly.

Sharina felt sudden hot anger. Was she completely a child who had to be protected from a spindly boy she could have broken over her knee?

She knew the reaction was unjustified, a displacement of her formless disgust at Meder's blood magic, but she felt it nonetheless. She glared at Nonnus, then turned to the Blood Eagles' officer and said in a clear voice, "Your name is Wainer, I believe? I have some questions to ask you in private."

A soldier snickered, then swallowed his reaction in a cough as Wainer glared at him. Wainer's expression cleared to neutrality and he said, "If you like, mistress. I think if we go downwind, we can speak and stay in plain sight so nobody misunderstands."

Sharina nodded and strode briskly beyond the limits of the scattered encampment. She glanced over her shoulder. Nonnus watched without expression, but he didn't follow.

"This should do, mistress," Wainer said. He turned so that they both stood in profile to the camp, then stepped a pace inshore. Unlike Sharina, the soldier wore boots that he didn't want soaked in the murmuring surf. "What is it you want of me?"

"You mentioned the Stone Wall," she said. The anger was gone now and doubt at what she was doing was starting to replace it. "I know that was the battle where King Valence defeated the Earl of Sandrakkan twenty years ago, but that isn't what you meant when you asked Nonnus about it. What *did* you mean?"

"Um," Wainer said. "Have you asked him, mistress?"

"I'm asking you," Sharina snapped. "If you want the procurator to order you to tell me, that can be arranged."

Wainer looked straight at the hermit fifty feet away. Nonnus nodded. He was as emotionless as the coral out in the darkening sea.

"All right, mistress," Wainer said slowly, "because I

guess you've got a right to know. But I want to say that the only reason I'm alive to talk to you—that King Valence is on the throne and not a Sandrakkan usurper—is what the Pewle mercenaries did that day.''

He took off his leather cap and wiped his forehead with a kerchief, though the evening wasn't warm. "The thing is," he went on, squinting at the swells of the Inner Sea, "the earl had cavalry. We couldn't bring many horses two hundred miles across the sea, and besides Ornifal isn't horse country. Too hilly. Sandrakkan infantry isn't much, but they had good horsemen and we had to come to them to put the rebellion down.''

Something jumped and splashed out beyond the shoals; a fish, perhaps, or even a seal. Seals were rare in these warm waters, but they swam and bred in their tens of thousands around the rocky islands in the Outer Sea north of the main archipelago.

"So Valence . . ." Wainer continued. "His generals, I mean; he was a boy then, just crowned. His generals hired a band of Pewle mercenaries to hold the right flank against the Sandrakkan cavalry. They didn't wear armor, so they could hop around like rabbits with their javelins and those big knives. The idea was they'd get inside a cavalry charge and hamstring the horses, throw everything into confusion. Pretty much a suicide job, *we* thought, but the Pewlemen didn't seem to think it was much riskier than paddling after seals in a winter storm.''

Wainer hawked and spat into the sea. Sharina looked at the hermit's squat form with new awareness. It would be frightening to watch an armored horseman charge down on you . . . but if you had the quickness and courage to duck under the rider's awkward blow, then lop through the mount's pastern with a knife that Sharina had seen used to split logs—

If you could do those things, then no horsemen would get through you. A hundred men like Nonnus could turn the finest cavalry regiment into a bloody shambles.

"I see," Sharina said; and she did.

"But that's not how it happened," Wainer continued. "The rebels had a big camp, twice the size of ours though the army wasn't any bigger. They were at home, remember, and the troops had brought their servants along. And wives, a lot of them, and plenty of them had their whole family. All that takes room. They put a palisade around it, just like we did ours; only the earl had brought wizards, too. When both sides had lined up facing each other on the plain between, those wizards stood up on the wall sacrificing just like the young fellow's doing in there right now—"

Wainer's thumb hooked quickly in the direction of the deckhouse, but he didn't look around.

"—and raised an earthquake. The militia on our right wing broke, the Sandrakkan horse charged *us* in the center around the king, and nobody paid any attention to a few hundred seal hunters standing off by themselves."

"The Pewlemen attacked the cavalry from behind?" Sharina guessed. She'd read the epics; she could talk of flanks and ambushes even if she'd never seen a real soldier till the Blood Eagles arrived in Barca's Hamlet.

Wainer shook his head. "Wouldn't have helped," he said. "There weren't enough Pewlemen to cut their way through. It's not the same as breaking up a charge, you see. No, what they did was scamper over the walls of the rebel camp like they were goats on a hillside. The Sandrakkan servants were supposed to defend the walls, but they were no more use than tits on a boar when they saw Pewle knives flashing toward them."

"They killed the wizards," Sharina said.

Wainer shrugged. His face was a grim death mask. "I guess they did," he said, "but that wouldn't have helped either. They'd done their damage already, the wizards had. No, mistress, what the Pewlemen did was drag women and children up on the walls where the wizards had been. And they cut their throats there and tossed the bodies down on top of the sheep and chickens from the sacrificing."

"Oh," said Sharina. "I see." She looked at the water; not

at the soldier and especially not at Nonnus until she'd had time to settle her face.

"Well, the rebels broke, then," Wainer said. "They went running back to the camp to save their families. And we were right with them, cutting them down from behind. It wasn't a battle anymore, it was a slaughterhouse and we killed till our arms ached."

"Thank you," Sharina said, "for telling me."

"They had to do it, mistress," Wainer said, knuckling his eyes as if to rub away the memory of what he'd seen twenty years before. "We'd have all died if it wasn't for those Pewlemen, and King Valence would've died with us. We stood, but they won the battle."

The old soldier shook his head in frustration; his mouth was tight. "There's one thing I can't forget," he said in a husky whisper. "And I've prayed to the Lady but it's still there every time I see blond hair like yours. There was a kid, she can't have been three. Blond as blond could be. A Pewleman lifted her by the hair and he cut her throat clear through with that big knife of his. There was blood in the air, mistress, and he waved that head laughing as the little body fell on the pile below. I just can't forget the laughter."

"I don't think he's laughing now," Sharina said. She turned and walked back toward Nonnus, her protector.

5

The women thronging the common room in their finery weren't drinking, and few men braved the mass of overskirts, patterned aprons, and lace shawls to buy a mug of ale from Garric behind the bar. He didn't recall a night that there'd been a greater crowd or less custom. Even the six guards had gone out when they finished their supper.

Tilusina, Revan's wife, laughed in an affected voice and tapped her fan on the table. Her daughter Khila aped the laugh—even more gratingly, so far as Garric was concerned—and twiddled her index finger in the air: the family had only one fan, probably a wedding gift. It was sheet bronze with a punched design of the Count's Palace in Carcosa.

Liane came downstairs. She'd changed her brown tunic for a blue one of similar cut, though this time the sturdy linen had a satin collar.

The women stopped talking, but those sitting stood up and the ones already standing straightened. The rustle of stiffened, multilayered cloth sounded like roosting time in a henhouse.

Liane started as though someone had jumped at her from behind a curtain. She looked as if she'd bitten something sour. The villagers immediately began to talk again, ostensibly to one another though quite obviously none of them was listening to anyone else. Tiaras, hairpins, and rings all twitched so that the glass jewels and faceted metal would catch the light and the stranger's attention.

Liane was the first fashionable woman to arrive in Barca's Hamlet in living memory. Asera was a noble, but that in itself frightened the villagers out of the kind of display they were making for Liane. Besides, the procurator's garb had really been an offical uniform: a beige silk robe of strictly functional lines, falling from shoulders to ankles with a brown sash tucking it at the waist.

Liane was someone the local women could imagine being—if they were young, beautiful, and had more wealth than there was in the whole borough.

"Tapster?" Liane said to Garric. She raised her voice to speak over the women's meaningless chatter, but they stilled the instant she opened her mouth. The word rang in the silence like the cry of a huntsman calling his hounds.

The girl looked shocked. She flushed, then resumed in a normal tone, "I've been reading in my room and I need more candles. Wax, this time, if you have them."

"I'm sorry, mistress," Garric said in embarrassment.

"Usually we would, but every wax taper in the hamlet was burned the past two days when we had a royal procurator staying here. It'll have to be lamps or tallow dips, I'm afraid."

"Well, whatever you have," Liane said in resignation. She kept her gaze fixedly on Garric so that she wouldn't have to make eye contact with the bevy of women waiting breathlessly for an excuse to speak to her.

Candles were kept in the cupboard beneath the stairs. Garric stepped around Liane to get to them, feeling her eyes on him the whole time. "What are you reading, mistress?" he asked with his head in the cupboard.

"Poetry," she said with brusk boredom. "An ancient poet named Rigal, if that means anything to you."

Garric found the candles. He brought out six of them. The wicks hadn't been cut: they dangled as three pairs, the way they'd been dipped.

He turned to Liane, smiled, and quoted, " 'Lady and your Shepherd! Grant that this boy, my son, may be like me first in glory among the men of Sandrakkan. May he be strong and brave, may he rule the Isles in majesty; and may they say one day, "He's a better man even than his father!" ' "

The girl's face changed with the gathering momentum of ice slipping from a roof in spring. "You know Rigal?" she said. "You're quoting Rigal! Oh, Lady, you've heard my prayers!"

The women surged forward, talking again. Liane jumped a step up the stairs; Garric, amazed and horrified, shifted so that he stood between the guest and the villagers. Those at the back of the room pressed those in front, threatening to push them onto Garric's toes. Apparently when the girl took social notice of any local person, she became fair game for all of them.

"Stop this!" Garric shouted. "Duzi take you all for a pack of fools! Is this what you want a stranger to think of us?"

Reise came out of the kitchen. His arms were wet to the elbows, so he must have just washed at the well after laying bedstraw for the horses and mules. "What's happening here?" he said sharply to his son.

"Innkeeper?" Liane asked in tones of icy rigor. "Might I ask your servant here to carry a lantern for me out on the beach? I'll pay you for his lost labor, of course. And I assure you, we'll be lighted at all times. I have no desire to outrage rural conventions."

"I'll handle the trade, Garric," Reise said. He looked at the abashed gathering of fancy dress. "Such as it is."

To Liane he continued, "If my son Garric chooses to escort you, mistress, I'd be glad for him to do so. But that isn't the sort of matter on which I'd give orders to either of my children."

He bowed.

"I'd be honored," Garric said. He barely avoided stumbling over his tongue. "Ah—Father? Her, ah, father is still over at the millhouse with Katchin. You'll let him know where we are if he comes in?"

Reise nodded curtly. To Garric's amazement, he thought he saw his father almost *smile*.

Liane skipped up the stairs. The women were leaving the common room under Reise's disdainful eye. Some talked loudly to one another; others hung their heads. They were all embarrassed, though they expressed the emotion in different ways.

Garric realized that the notion of dressing up to impress the cultured stranger had been a group thing, not an individual decision. Like other animals, the behavior of humans in a pack is almost invariably worse than the behavior of any single member by himself. Herself, in this case. The village women had made fools of themselves, and they knew it when somebody forced them to look at themselves.

At least nobody was dead, the way there sometimes was when a mob of men got a notion into its collective head.

Garric also noticed that Ilna, the one woman in the hamlet who might be able to compete with the stranger in terms of looks and style, hadn't been present. Ilna os-Kenset wasn't the sort to follow anybody's lead, let alone that of a pack of fools.

Liane returned carrying a lantern with lenses of glass, not horn or mica, and a waist-length cape of red-dyed wool. "Will I need my wrap?" she asked Garric, gesturing with the cape.

He shrugged. "Bring it along," he said. "I'll carry it for you if you think it's too warm."

He had no idea how Liane would react to the breeze down on the shingle. To Garric it would be refreshing after an evening in the common room packed with nervously alert villagers.

Garric opened the lantern's lid of slotted brass, judged the height, and trimmed one of the candles to length with the knife dangling from his belt in a sheath of elder laths wrapped with leather. He set the stub in the three-pronged holder, then lit it with a stick of lightwood from the hearth.

Reise nodded to him as he drew a pail of ale for Gilzani to take home for her husband. Garric couldn't read the expression on his father's face, but for once it didn't seem to be covering anger. Sadness, though . . . Perhaps sadness.

Garric opened the seawall door for Liane, bowed, and followed her through with the lantern. The tide was halfway out, and the surf was a muted rumble. He offered Liane his hand and walked down the wall's forty-five-degree slope ahead of the girl as a brace against her slipping and an anchor if she did.

"Oh, thank goodness!" Liane said. She took the cape off and twirled it above her head when her feet touched the beach. "I felt as though I was being *suffocated* by those women. How ever do you stand it, Garric?"

"Well, they're not always like that," he said in embarrassment. "And it's not a matter of standing it, mistress. I'm one of them, you know."

"You're Garric and I'm Liane," she said. "All right?"

"Yes, Liane," he said. He smiled. Her tone was one he'd

grown used to over the years. Like Reise, Liane didn't expect an argument when she gave directions.

They walked slowly up the beach. Garric held the lantern at waist height between them. Its haze of yellow light fell on the ground ahead, but their faces were dark except for an occasional flicker through the air slots in the lid. Liane had on sturdy sandals that crunched on the shingle. When she'd come downstairs for candles she'd been wearing sequined slippers; he was startled that she'd been able to change them so quickly.

"So," she said. "Have you read any other poets, Garric?"

"Oh, yes," Garric said mildly. He was proud beyond telling that he'd been able to impress a girl as beautiful as Liane. "Vardan, Kostradin . . . Most of the ancients, actually. Celondre, Hithum, Maremi the Baron . . ."

Liane giggled. "We weren't permitted to read Maremi in Mistress Gudea's Academy for Girls," she said. "Of course every room in the dormitory had a copy. If we'd read Rigal as diligently, I'd be able to quote him to you."

"It's just that one passage," Garric said with false diffidence. He was bursting with pride that he had *anything* from Rigal in a memory which he could retrieve. "Celondre's really my favorite, because—well, he writes about the way a shepherd's life ought to be, the way maybe it was in the Golden Age before Malkar."

Though they were walking slowly, they'd passed the end of the seawall. There were only a few houses beyond this point and none of their occupants could afford artificial light. The lantern was the only sign of human existence.

"Where were you educated, Garric?" Liane asked. "Carcosa? I'm amazed that they'd have a teacher so good. When I was there it seemed almost as bucolic as this hamlet."

"My father taught us, my sister and me," Garric said. He'd brought extra candles, but he had to light the replacement before the present stub went out or they'd be in darkness until they got back. "He was born on Ornifal. Are you from Ornifal also, mis—"

She tapped his arm.

"Sorry, Liane," he apologized. "Ah, I think we ought to turn around, if that's all right."

"We're from Sandrakkan," the girl said. "I went to school in Valles on Ornifal. Mistress Gudea's, as I said."

She turned on her heel. When Garric started to walk around her to put the lantern in his left hand between them again, she caught his wrist and held him until he fell into step as they stood now.

"The fashions in Carcosa are what women in Valles were wearing ten years ago, Garric," Liane said. "The people all looked at me as if I were the Lady come to save them. I couldn't go anywhere without somebody asking me about my dress or sketching it to copy and glaring at me if I made eye contact. It was like being in a cage! And then here . . ."

"Why did you come then?" Garric said bluntly. "If clothing fashion's the only thing that's important to you, then I guess Valles is the place to be."

These were his people. Sure they were farmers in the back of beyond, sure they looked like clowns to a girl like Liane when they tried to dress up. But he hadn't gone to Valles to insult citizens there because they didn't know how to shear sheep!

It was a moment before Garric realized that the sound he heard was Liane crying into her cupped hands. "Mistress?" he said. "Liane, I didn't mean . . ."

He had absolutely no idea of how to go on. This was as much a shock as the seawolf hitting him from behind had been.

"I'm all right," Liane said. She stopped and blew her nose on a handkerchief she'd tugged from her sleeve. "Let's stand here a moment," she said. "I don't want to go back in the light with my eyes all red and ugly."

"I don't think you could look ugly if you rubbed your face with soot," Garric said, relieved beyond words that Liane had regained her self-possession. "Not so that anybody in *this* borough would say, anyhow."

He lifted the lantern in a gesture toward the beach ahead of them. "We had a whole three-banked warship there this morning, and it didn't impress the folks around here as much as you do."

"The women, you mean," Liane said. The raised lantern painted the corners of her smile.

"No, Liane, I don't mean just the women," Garric said with a laugh. "I certainly do not."

They began to walk again. "I don't know why I'm here, Garric," Liane said softly. "Soldiers came and took me out of school eight months ago. They wouldn't tell me anything. They brought me to a nunnery of the Lady in Valles. I wasn't . . . hurt. But I couldn't leave my room without a Daughter coming with me, and nobody would talk to me at all. A few weeks later my father got me and said that I'd be traveling with him now."

"I—" Garric said. "I'm sorry I said anything, Liane."

"I'm just so frightened," the girl whispered. "I don't know my father anymore, and I don't understand what's happening. I'm so alone!"

Garric opened his mouth to speak, then closed it again in silence. He'd been about to say that he'd felt alone too since everything started to happen in the past week.

But the medallion was a smooth weight against his chest, and somewhere in the back of his mind King Carus was laughing.

6

I can take the bed linen you wanted washed," Ilna said to Lora from the kitchen doorway. "I'll have it back to you tomorrow evening if the weather holds."

Lora was sitting in the corner beside the stone ledge on

which she'd mixed bread dough and set it to rise. She looked up sharply. "I'd given up on you coming," she said with peevish belligerence. Her cheeks were puffy and her eyes red. "I thought you'd forgotten."

"I don't forget work I've said I'll do," Ilna said in cold distaste. "Do you want me to do the wash for you or not?"

Lora rose from her stool and began beating the unbaked loaves into shape again. She'd allowed the dough to rise too high, then collapse in ugly smears across the ledge. The loaves, though made from wheat as table bread, would have the wooden consistency of rye-flour trenchers by the time they came out of the oven.

"Yes, go on, take it," Lora said. "I don't have much choice but pay you, do I, now that Sharina's gone?"

"I was waiting for that *mob* in the common room to leave before I came over," Ilna said. The clothes hamper was a large wicker basket near the courtyard door, handy both for the well and cauldron in which the linen would be boiled if washed in the inn. "I didn't want to be mistaken for one of them. Trying to impress a woman from Ornifal!"

"They're nobles, you know," Lora muttered as she knuckled the dough angrily. "That Benlo may claim he's 'or-Willet,' but there's a 'bor' in the name he was born with or may the Lady withdraw her favor from me."

"Where is she now?" Ilna asked. She stretched a sheet out on the floor, then started to lay the remaining laundry in the center of it. Her grim mood matched Lora's, though the reasons for it were different. "The fancy woman?"

"Out, I gather," Lora said without particular interest. "On the beach with Garric."

Ilna staggered, though the news was exactly what she'd feared from the moment she laid eyes on the strange woman in her fine clothing. Ilna knew Valles fashions. The merchants she sold to made sure that she did when they placed orders for the fabrics she was to weave for them to pick up on their next trip through Barca's Hamlet.

"On the beach?" she repeated coldly. "Well, that doesn't

surprise me. No better than they should be, these fine ladies, I'm sure."

"I treated Sharina as if she was my own daughter!" Lora said. Her hands clenched in the dough. She stood rigid for a moment, looking as if she was about to resume crying. "*Better* than I would have treated my own blood, because I knew she was real nobility. And what does she do? Cast me away as soon as she comes into her due!"

Ilna folded the corners of the bottom sheet over the rest of the laundry and tied a double knot. "Yes," she said, looking at Lora with eyes as hot as the embers beneath the oven, "you did always treat Sharina better than you did your own offspring."

She shouldered the linen, a bundle bigger than she was. The soldiers had soiled every sheet in the inn during their stay.

At the door she looked back. Lora hadn't moved.

In sudden anger Ilna said, "Not every woman in the borough is as great a fool as Garric's mother, unable to see *his* merits, you know!"

And as she stumped out into the night with the bundle of washing she added under her breath, "And that Ornifal slut *won't* have him!"

7

The day was brilliantly fine, and the trireme ran on mainsail with the breeze dead astern. A V of white foam lifted from the bow and a pair of lesser Vs trailed from the steering oars, weaving behind the vessel in a pattern of remarkable complexity on the sea's slow swells.

Also trailing through the water astern were four seawolves: three of them to port, their side-to-side sinuosities synchronized as though they were parts of a single animal. On the starboard side swam a single monster over ten feet long, a ton of ropy muscle with fangs the length of a man's hand.

"I don't like it!" Captain Lichnau said. "Look at those lizards. Just like the morning the storm struck us, isn't it? I think we ought to change course for Sandrakkan."

Sharina and Nonnus squatted on either side of the far stern, behind the captain's seat and the steersmen standing at the ends of the outriggers. The Blood Eagles had taken over the deck forward of the mast as their own preserve. Mixing with them would have been uncomfortable, though Sharina wasn't really concerned about her physical safety or that of the hermit. The Blood Eagles were disciplined troops, under the eye of their officer and the noble they were guarding.

"We can't put in to Sandrakkan," Asera said flatly. The two nobles and Kizuta, the vessel's mate, had joined Lichnau in a conference made public by the trireme's close quarters. Half a dozen sailors were near to the commanders. "At the very best, the earl's hostile to King Valence and will do us an ill turn if he can. At worst, he's in league with the queen's agents."

Only one set of benches was manned, and even there the oars weren't run out. The oarsmen were available for an emergency, but with the wind so favorable rowing would do nothing to speed the vessel.

The off-duty oarsmen sat on the outriggers to either side, though with the seawolves present they didn't dangle their toes in the water sparkling just below. A few men trailed fishing lines, but for the most part they basked in the sun and talked about their luck in not having to rasp their hands raw for the moment on the salt-roughened oarlooms.

"We'll make Kish by midafternoon if this wind holds," Kizuta protested. "The Needles on Sandrakkan aren't an hour nearer and we'd lose some of the wind besides."

"The wind will hold," Meder bor-Mederman said. He glanced beyond his immediate group and assumed a look of hurt when his eyes fell on Sharina.

She turned as if to study the huge seawolf. The low dorsal fin rippled like a ribbon, barely cleaving the surface. The skin between its spines was translucent and tinged with red and purple from the blood vessels feeding it. Even a monster can be beautiful if viewed in the right way.

She shivered and looked at Nonnus. He smiled wanly, as though he knew what she was thinking. Perhaps he did. . . .

"I don't need a boy to help me tally distances, Kizuta," Lichnau said. "It's not distance that worries me."

The captain wore a kerchief to cover his bald head. He touched it, testing the knotted corners as a ploy to gain a moment in the face of general opposition.

"It's what the course takes us close to," he went on. "That's Tegma, and I don't care what your political problems are with the Earl of Sandrakkan, they're not as bad as getting our bottom ripped out on those reefs in a storm."

He pointed over the side to the trio of seawolves weaving easily around a course parallel to the swift trireme's. "If you think those lizards are bad," he said, "you should see what's waiting for shipwrecks there."

"I don't expect a storm, sailor," Meder said coldly.

"With all respect, sir, you didn't expect the first one!" Lichnau protested. "If we'd been as close to the reefs then as this course puts us now, we'd all be lizard food this past week!"

Meder raised his hand to strike the captain. Asera stopped her colleague with a cold glance and a finger tap, then stared at Lichnau with eyes like those of the reptiles alongside.

"Watch your tongue, commoner," she said, each syllable an icepick. "Or you'll find yourself feeding lizards right now."

Lichnau knelt and touched his forehead to the decking. "Mistress," he whimpered from that position, "it's my duty to bring you safely back to Valles. Forgive me if I misspoke in my zeal."

Sharina grimaced in distaste at what she was hearing. She didn't know who had the right of the argument, but the sight of an honest man being humiliated for stating his opinion to a noble offended her deeply. Haft had always been a more egalitarian society than those of most islands of the archipelago. In Barca's Hamlet the question of birth status didn't arise simply because nobles didn't visit the region.

"The seawolves breed on the Reefs of Tegma," Nonnus said, speaking to give Sharina something to concentrate on rather than the abuse still being directed at the prostrate captain. "Sometimes you'll find them a thousand miles away, but that's rare and the reefs are the only place they lay their eggs."

Sharina nodded as the name came into focus in her mind. "I thought Tegma was an island far in the Outer Sea," she said. "That's where Rigal puts it in *The Wanderings of Duke Lachish*."

"I don't know where Tegma was when your Duke Lachish visited it," Nonnus said. His tone was too precise to be quite sneering. "When I was there, it was fifty miles downcurrent from the south coast of Sandrakkan. It was an island once but it sank the same as Yole. It's just a ring of reefs now, as tight as a virgin's—"

The hermit paused and barked out a bitter laugh. "Child," he said, "now that I'm back among men I find I'm falling back into the ways of the man I once was. You may have to forgive me; and I humbly pray that the Lady will do the same if . . ."

He traced a quick pattern on the deck. His finger left no mark on the smooth planks, but Sharina's eyes followed the gesture into an outline of the Lady.

Nonnus raised his eyes to Sharina's again. "If things happen that I do not wish to happen," he concluded.

"May the Shepherd watch over us," Sharina said uncomfortably. The Great Gods had never been a major part of life in Barca's Hamlet, though most houses had a little shrine to the Lady and her consort, and the shepherds of course made offerings to Duzi on the hillside.

Being so close to Nonnus made her realize that the hermit

didn't worship out of inborn faith. His belief was a matter of need, the desperate hope that there was something, somewhere, greater than the world in which he lived.

"When the water's clear in the lagoon," Nonnus said in a mild voice, "you can see the tops of the old buildings from when Tegma was an island. Square gray outlines with just a touch of pink when the sun catches them right. They're hundreds of feet down, now."

The commanders' discussion had ended. Sharina had successfully distanced herself from its latter portion, but the ship continued under sail on the same course as before. Meder heard what Nonnus was saying and stepped closer to him.

"I've intended for some time to visit Tegma," the wizard said, his eyes slightly narrowed. "The reefs, that is. I'd been told that there was no way through them to the lagoon. How did you get there, old man?"

Nonnus looked at Meder with the same dispassionate intensity with which he viewed the sea. "It was a long time ago, when I was a boy hunting seals," he said. He shrugged. "Tegma may have changed since my time."

"Tegma never changes," Meder said. His expression wavered subtly between anger and interest. "Tegma is a nexus of ancient power."

"It sank the way Yole did?" Sharina said to divert the wizard's focus from Nonnus. The hermit couldn't be pushed into communicating more than he wanted to, and there was a chance his noncommittal responses would send Meder into an arrogant rage.

"The same way, perhaps," Meder said, his tone softening with the pleasure of Sharina having shown interest in his knowledge. "But much earlier, infinitely earlier, Sharina. It sank thousands of years before Yole did, and perhaps thousands of *times* as many years earlier."

He looked at the hermit again and said, "How did you get into the lagoon, old man?"

"A Pewle woodskin can go most places," Nonnus said, meeting the younger man's glare with no particular expression of his own. " 'Skim across a meadow on a dewy morning,' we used to say. That was a joke, but I picked a spring tide and there was enough water between coral heads to get me through the atoll.''

He shook his head with a rueful smile. ''I was younger then,'' he added.

Meder slapped his left palm with two fingers of the opposite hand as he thought. His eyes returned to focus on Nonnus. ''You and I will discuss this—'' he began.

Nonnus leaped to his feet, looking past the wizard and pointing to the southern horizon. ''Down sail!'' he roared in a voice that could break rocks. ''Oarsmen to your benches!''

''What?'' Captain Lichnau cried as he and everyone on deck turned their eyes in the direction Nonnus was pointing. ''Who—''

Almost to the horizon the Inner Sea was a soft green with no more chop than a millpond on a hot August afternoon. The horizon itself was a wall of black cloud glittering with jagged teeth of lightning, sweeping toward the ship at the speed of a racing horse.

''Down sail!'' Lichnau screamed as the favoring breeze died and the first gust rocked the trireme's broadside.

8

Cashel awoke, gasping and spluttering as though he'd been plunged into the depths of the winter sea. His skin was cold and it seemed as if iron bands around his chest released as he straightened on his straw mattress.

The millhouse kitchen was silent—too silent even for the dead of night. No cricket chirped, no dove cooed from the cote, and the still air was without a trace of the breeze that normally sighed across the hamlet. Through the window over the indoor oven, the sky had a faint blue haze that wasn't starlight.

Cashel rose and took his staff from beside the door. Ilna slept in one of the two rooms upstairs, but Cashel liked to be on the ground floor where he didn't risk stumbling if someone called him for a late-night emergency. He went outside. The sky was a net of fine blue that concealed all but the brightest stars.

He'd never known the world to be so quiet. Nothing at all moved.

Guided by instinct, Cashel walked around the front of the millhouse. He didn't think he made a sound but Tenoctris, standing in the shelter of the great cypress-wood millwheel, turned and beckoned him urgently to join her. He moved to her side, careful not to rap his quarterstaff against the projecting paddles.

"Don't alert him," Tenoctris whispered, speaking with exaggerated lip movements to make up for the near lack of sound. "I want to learn who he's interested in."

Cashel peered past the rim of the undershot wheel. The spillway feeding the wheel from the tidal impoundment was dry since the millstones weren't turning. The drover, Benlo or-Willet, knelt in the trough. The murmur of his chanting was the first real sound Cashel had heard since awakening on this ominous night.

The ancient stones around Benlo dripped a blue phosphorescence, like that of the sky but more intense. The drover held a knife with which he tapped a circle around some small object on the floor of the spillway. Every time the knifepoint touched stone, a fat blue spark flashed soundlessly.

"He's invoking an identification spell," Tenoctris mouthed to Cashel's ear. "He has an object—it could be hair, bone, anything—and he's summoning the glamour from it to lead him to its correspondent."

"But that's wizardry," Cashel said, trying to copy the old woman's technique of speaking without vocalizing.

"Yes," Tenoctris said with a dry smile. "It is. Benlo is a very powerful wizard."

Blue mist began to ooze from the thing over which the drover chanted. He continued to tap his dagger on the stone. The flashes grew brighter, flaring through the mist the way heat lightning silhouettes a summer cloud.

"The spell can be used on a single coin to find a missing purse," Tenoctris whispered. "But I don't think that's what's going on here."

The fog thickened above the object, then coalesced into the figure of a man. Cashel couldn't make out any distinguishing details, because the illumination was that of the glamour itself. There was no shadow detail as would normally mold the features.

The glamour lifted from the ground and drifted sideways at the rate of a man walking slowly. Its feet seemed to pass through the wall of the spillway. The drover clambered out to follow. He was awkward until he remembered to tuck the blade of his dagger under his belt. He didn't have a sheath for the weapon.

"It's his athame," Tenoctris explained. Her hand was raised, but Cashel didn't need the warning not to move yet. He hunted small game and knew that motionless patience was the greatest key to success. "Forged it himself, I shouldn't wonder, and from *iron*. I doubt it's coincidence that two wizards of such power would visit a hamlet like this."

The glamour's limbs didn't move: its motion was like that of the statues of the Lady and the Shepherd in the carts the priests from Carcosa pulled through the hamlet during the annual Tithe Procession. Benlo followed a few paces behind. His lips moved as though he was still chanting, but the words were inaudible. They passed the front of the millhouse and out of sight.

Tenoctris' hand was still raised. "Why is it so quiet?" Cashel asked. The sea smell was even stronger: salt and drying seaweed and the faint touch of death with an iodine sharpness that differed from that of a carcass on land.

"He put a spell of silence over the hamlet before he started his main enchantment," Tenoctris said. "Most people within the circuit of the spell will sleep until it's lifted. For a wizard, even a poor wizard like me, the spell has the effect of an alarm instead."

She lowered her hand and led Cashel carefully along the side of the millhouse to the corner where they could again watch Benlo and the thing he had raised. The glow saturating the stones of the spillway had dissipated. A bluish track, fading with time, marked the glamour's course the way slime gleams in the morning sun where a slug has passed.

Cashel's skin prickled as if he'd spent a day on a boat, where light burned both from the sky and in reflection from the water's surface. His quarterstaff felt like a wisp of straw. He imagined it would dance into the night if he let it go.

"I woke up too," he mouthed to Tenoctris, "and *I'm* not a wizard."

"Yes," she said. "You awakened too."

The glamour paused in front of the inn, turned and drifted through the open gates. The drover followed, disappearing into the courtyard.

Tenoctris started forward. Cashel touched her hand and led her to the side of the courtyard instead.

During the past winter Garric had cleared the ivy from the outside of the eight-foot wall and removed the bricks which the prying rootlets had loosened over a generation or more. The bricks were neatly stacked, waiting for Anan to burn lime for fresh mortar in the kiln where he also fired his pottery. Cashel pointed Tenoctris to one of the irregular gaps in the wall's fabric and positioned himself to look through a higher one. They had a perfect view across the courtyard, toward the stables on the opposite side of the inn building.

The glamour was motionless in the center of the courtyard, near the well. It rotated and extended its hand and arm toward the stables. One leaf of the stable door was ajar. Garric stepped out. His expression was blank and he moved like a sleepwalker.

Cashel tensed. Tenoctris touched his lips. "He's not in danger," she whispered.

The front door of the inn banged open like a thunderclap. Garric staggered and cried out. The glamour dissolved into mist that flowed over him, merging with Garric's flesh and vanishing.

From the inn walked a creature with the shape of a man, carrying a cutlass dark with rust or blood. There were sounds again and the night stank of death and the sea.

Cashel shouted. He put his left hand on the wall coping and swung upward, using his quarterstaff to brace him. He balanced a moment in the air with his bare foot clawing to gain a toehold in the gap he'd been watching through.

When the blue glow vanished, Benlo toppled like a drunk walking into bright sunlight. The creature strode toward Garric, raising the cutlass to slash. The stars and the newly risen moon were visible.

Cashel found support for his foot and half-lunged, half-flopped onto the top of the wall. Garric twisted backward into the stable. Two of Benlo's guards ran out of the inn with swords bare in their hands. Liane's white face peered from an upstairs window.

Cashel rolled into the courtyard, landing heavily but on his feet. "Kill that thing!" he screamed to the drover's guards, knowing that he and his quarterstaff couldn't reach the stables in time.

Garric stepped out of the stable with an axletree that Cashel himself would have found a burden. "Haft and the Isles!" he shouted in a voice that waked echoes from all corners of the courtyard. He and the creature strode toward one another, each swinging his weapon.

The massive oaken axletree brushed the cutlass aside and crushed the creature itself with a squelch and a snapping of bones. The cutlass hilt flew toward the inn. The broken blade spun high and thunked point-down in the dirt at Cashel's feet.

Garric turned slightly, seemed to smile, and fell on his face beside the creature he had killed.

9

The trireme's oardeck was wet and dark and stinking. More rain than light came through the narrow ventilators between the main deck and the outriggers.

The ship swung almost on her beam ends in the troughs of the mighty waves that swept down on her with the storm. Sharina had followed the oarsmen below at Nonnus' direction. Many of them were still trying to reach their benches. When a particularly fierce sea caught the ship, oarlooms jerked from the hands of men holding them and flailed like quarterstaves in the darkness. Baggage stored in the lower hull flew about, tangling men wholly intent on not losing their grip on their oars.

The crew was trying to turn the vessel out of the wind: there was no possibility of putting her bow into a gale like this one. Rowers on the port side stroked normally while those to starboard backed their oars. Sharina couldn't imagine how the officers communicated their orders. She could barely hear the drummer beside her giving the stroke through the deeper thrumming of the storm.

She huddled in her cloak, trying not to be stepped on. Asera was somewhere ahead on the narrow aisle. Many of the Blood Eagles were with her, though the soldiers' awkwardness meant there was danger they'd crush the procurator when the ship rolled.

Because of the chaos, it was some minutes before Sharina realized that Nonnus hadn't followed her into the belly of the ship. She looked up. The hatch had been closed but not battened down in the confusion. One of the two hinged panels lay open to spray and the black sky.

Sharina stood, stepping over a soldier who lay curled bawling in a fetal position. She gripped the ladder with one hand and tried to lift the other panel with her shoulder and remaining hand. A wave combed the deck, battering and smothering her with its weight.

Sharina continued to hold the ladder. When the green surge passed, she threw the hatch fully open. Before the next wave came over the stern, she'd gained the deck and grabbed the railing with both arms as her eyes tried to pierce the gloom.

Sailors crawled about the deck, trying desperately to hold on with one hand while the other did the business of the ship. The sail and yard were down in an untidy heap amidships, but the mast itself flexed dangerously.

There hadn't been time to strike the deckhouse, so the wind had taken off the roof and two sides. The remaining panels were jammed into a V shape that protected Meder in its lee.

A rosy glow surrounded the wizard. He held his copper athame and his mouth contorted with the spells he shouted inaudibly into the wind. Half a dozen Blood Eagles crouched nearby, either guarding Meder or unwilling to go down into the bowels of a ship they were sure would soon be overwhelmed.

Nonnus sat in the far bow, his feet clamped against the solid bulkhead to either side. Waves foamed over him waist high. He was at work on something; his knife reflected the cold white glitter of lightning. Sharina crawled toward him, pressing her whole body against the rail as she inched along.

The wind weighed against Sharina like a collapsing sandbank; its howl numbed her ears. A section of rail, replaced in Barca's Hamlet after the previous storm, creaked inward against the pegs fixing it to the original fabric. She waited for a minute lull, then scrambled past the weakened section.

She couldn't tell what the hermit was doing, nor did she really care. All she knew was that at this moment she didn't want to die with strangers.

Nonnus looked up and saw her coming. He started to rise. She screamed and waved him back. He remained tense, but he didn't leave the relative shelter of the prow bulkhead except to bend forward and tug her the last of the way toward him with a grip like iron.

"Nonnus," she shouted. "Is the ship going to sink?"

She wasn't afraid. Despite the question, in her own mind Sharina was quite sure that they *were* going to sink and that she was about to die. She was wet and cold. She flinched at each lightning bolt's *flash/crack*, preceding the longer ripping sound of the thunder itself; but death wasn't a fear, only a fact like the clouds that writhed by overhead as dark and textured as a gravel shore.

"I can't save the ship," Nonnus said. He'd put away the big knife and was using the ship's cordage to tie sections of wooden pole into a triangle. "I think I can save you, though, child; which is what I swore to try."

The hermit had lopped the jib pole into three sections and bound them together. Now he pulled the bundled jib sail from under him—he'd been sitting on it like a pillow to keep it from blowing over the side—and began to unfold it.

"You're making a raft!" Sharina said. She caught a corner of the canvas to keep it from whipping violently before Nonnus was ready to tie it to the frame.

"A float, rather," he said. His spread hands worked with the instinctive precision of spiders binding prey with their silk. Neither the wind nor the salt-stiffened cordage caused the hermit's fingers to fumble or have to redo a task. "I'm making loops of rope that we'll hold to while the float supports us."

"But what about the seawolves?" Sharina blurted, then wished she could take the words back. The fang-jawed reptiles had been the first thought that sprang into her mind. She hadn't meant to complain about the efforts of the man who was doing everything humanly possible for her.

"Raw their meat feels like a jellyfish and doesn't taste much better," the hermit said as he went on with his work. She thought he smiled. "I suppose we'll have to make do with it till we get to a place we can build a fire, though."

Sharina laughed until an eddying gust splattered enough

salt water down her throat to choke her silent. He was serious. Doubting Nonnus would be like doubting the sky: it was simply there, night or day, storm or no storm.

She looked down the length of the vessel. The outriggers were alternately awash. A sailor caught Captain Lichnau by the shoulder and pointed over the starboard rail. Lichnau shouted something. Sharina couldn't hear the words, but Lichnau and the two men near him struggled forward toward the flexing mast.

"I wanted you sheltered below as long as you could," Nonnus said, his eyes on his task. "I'm glad you came up, though. We're drifting faster than I'd expected. The current must have changed as well as the wind."

Sharina held down flaps of cord and canvas, but she didn't try to help with the float's construction. The hermit knew what he was doing; she did not. Her involvement would waste time in circumstances where time was very short.

"Drifting where?" she said, leaning back against the wind so that Nonnus could turn the frame over.

"Look to starboard," he said, nodding without turning his head. "I've been hearing them for some minutes now."

Sharina raised her eyes, squinting. The storm threw her hair about her face like a thousand tiny whips; the braids and coil into which she'd bound them hadn't survived this wind.

A line of white separated the black of the sky and the sea's black beneath it. "The Reefs of Tegma," Nonnus said as he tied and tucked and tied again.

An officer stood to grasp a line. His tunic flared in the wind and lifted him from the deck with his limbs flailing.

His feet didn't even touch the railing as he flew over it. The sea drank him down without a bubble.

Lichnau and the men with him were hacking at the mast with axes; even the bare pole caught the wind and accelerated the trireme's sideways drift. The reefs were a line of gnashing foam so close that Sharina could distinguish their rumble from the wind's howl.

The ball of red light surrounding the deckhouse expanded,

reaching the mast and the sailors around it. Its hue paled from rich magenta to the pink of high clouds when the sun still lingers on the horizon.

The mast cracked vertically, twisting against the wind. A dagger-sharp splinter sprang back. It gutted Captain Lichnau in a spray of blood.

The glow boiled up to envelope the whole ship, as fiercely red as a sunstruck ruby. Every hair on Sharina's body stood out. She tried to scream but her throat was a block of marble.

The trireme lifted with a roar louder than the breaking of the earth. The oars were in the air; the keel itself no longer touched the roiling sea. Wrapped in red flame, the vessel and those aboard her sailed over the slashing reefs and landed thunderously in the calm on the other side. Waves spouted higher than the mast had been, but the hull swam up from the trough of its arrival.

The air was gray with warm mist. Sharina struggled to her feet. The wind had died and the sound of the storm was fading in the distance.

The ship grounded softly on a sloping ramp. Lush jungle wrapped cyclopean stone structures on the shore.

The Isle of Tegma had risen from the sea.

10

Garric swam up toward the lights glimmering on the surface of the black water. He could hear the breakers growling. His limbs were icy, but he forced them to move until—

"He's coming around!" Cashel said. "Back up and give him some room."

Garric's eyes were already open. They suddenly focused on the world in which his body lay on the hard ground of the inn's courtyard, his head in Cashel's lap. Scores of people stood around him, some of them holding lanterns or rushlights. Those had been the glimmers he saw in his dream state. . . .

"What happened?" he said. "Did I faint?"

His body ached and his palms felt as though they'd been stepped on by a shod horse. He curled them up so that he could see them. The tough callus wasn't broken, but his flesh still bore the bloodless impressions of whatever he'd been holding in a death grip moments before.

Tenoctris knelt beside him with two fingers of her left hand on his throat. Garric guessed she'd been murmuring a spell, because now he realized the drone of her voice had stopped.

"A lich attacked you, Garric," she said. "You killed it with a log."

"The axletree from inside the stable," Cashel corrected automatically. "You swung it overhead."

"What lich?" Garric said. Had he really picked the axletree up by himself? That'd explain why his shoulder muscles felt like they'd been minced for sausage, all right. "What *is* a lich?"

His father and the visiting drover squatted between Garric and an object on the ground. Reise stood with a grim face. He tapped Benlo's shoulder, saying, "Let the boy see. Maybe he knows what it is."

Garric sat up cautiously. He wasn't dizzy, but in flashes he saw double: two different worlds through the same pair of eyes.

"I'm all right," he said, more to convince himself than Cashel. Reise held a tallow-soaked hemlock stem close so that its soft yellow light gave Garric a good view of the corpse.

It was human. The skeleton was, at least. The axletree lying nearby had crushed the skull and broken the left collarbone as well as several of the upper ribs. Garric could see the damage plainly because the flesh cloaking the bones was jellylike, translucent where it wasn't water-clear.

"I don't remember it," Garric said. He closed his eyes and

touched his temples lightly with his fingertips. He wasn't sure what he *did* remember. He wasn't even sure who he was.

"I was sleeping in the stables," he said with his eyes still closed. "I was dreaming. I dreamed that King Carus called me to get up. He was pointing toward me. I walked out of the stables—"

He opened his eyes and looked around the circle of friends and strangers. Benlo's six guards stood close about the drover with their swords drawn, looking nervous and uncomfortable.

"That's all I remember!" Garric said. He lurched to his feet and looked down at the creature they told him he'd killed. "I've never seen this thing before. I've never seen anything like this thing before. I don't know what it is."

"It's a lich," Tenoctris repeated. "It's the skeleton and soul of a drowned man, clothed with ooze from the deepest trenches of the sea. It's the work of a powerful wizard."

"What wizard?" Benlo asked. He looked dazed and worried; Garric wondered if the drover also was feeling worlds balance in his mind. "Where?"

"I thought you might know, Master Benlo," Cashel said in a tone that made the drover's guards stiffen. Garric was so aware of his friend's gentle nature that he tended to forget how a huge strong man with a quarterstaff would look to strangers who didn't know him.

And the guards were right, of course. The shepherd is gentle with his flock; but the man who'd crushed the skulls of three seawolves in a matter of seconds wasn't gentle under *all* circumstances.

"No," Benlo said. "No, I have no idea." The statement was convincing because of the puzzled frustration with which the drover spoke. He was too distracted to be frightened by Cashel's obvious anger.

Liane moved to the front of the crowd, looking from Garric to her father in double concern. Very deliberately, Ilna stepped in front of the other girl and nodded when she caught Garric's eye.

Garric looked down at the axletree. He toed it, feeling the

weight of oak shift only slightly. "I picked that up?" he said.

"Swung it like a feather," Cashel agreed. "And a good thing you did, because it was coming for you with a sword."

"I don't remember," Garric said. The flesh was already beginning to slump off the lich's bones. The smell of rot and the sea lay heavily in the air. "I just don't remember."

What part of Garric's mind did remember, though, was the feel of a long iron-hilted sword in his hand as he slashed through a band of liches very like the one he'd killed tonight.

11

A soft rain fell and the air was more thickly humid than Sharina had ever felt it at home, even in the depths of August. The sun was a red blur near the western horizon. Huge tree ferns grew wherever the soil was bare, and runners with leaves sprouting from the joints crawled across the stone structures as well.

The double line of men on the drag ropes stretched into the forest. A detachment of Blood Eagles, fully armed and tense, marched at the head of the column, but the sailors themselves seemed calm, even cheerful. Men joked with their fellows on the other rope. Glad to be alive, Sharina supposed. *She* certainly was.

"*Your mother won't help you today,*" called one of the ship's officers, his thumbs hooked in his wide leather belt.

"*Pull!*" roared the rowers, still over a hundred of them despite deaths and injuries in the storm. They leaned into beaching tackle made fast to the sternpost and dragged the trireme another pace up the ramp.

The sailors could relax, because their task was over for the moment: they'd brought the vessel safe to harbor. The duties of the soldiers guarding the procurator had just begun.

Your father won't help you today/Pull!

"This is made for warships, isn't it?" Sharina said to Nonnus beside her. The smooth stone ramp was a hundred yards across, wide enough for dozens of triremes. It enabled ships to be drawn from the water for storage or repair. There were several similar constructions dimly visible around the harbor. "This is a real port, not just a beach where people pull their boats up at night."

"It's a real port," Nonnus agreed without emotion. Like the soldiers he was alert, though in his case it was more the alertness of a hunter than of someone who thinks he may be prey. "They've nothing better than this in Valles. Nothing this good."

He drew his toe deeply across the sloping surface. Leaf mold humped up to either side of the trough. Beneath was the base layer of pinkish-gray gneiss, polished to a dull sheen. Every structure Sharina could see—the roofed shelters, the bollards for holding ships once they'd been drawn to safety, the ramp itself—was of the same dense, millstone-hard material.

Your sister won't help you today/Pull!

"I'd have thought there'd be mud all over everything if it just came up from the sea," Sharina said, hoping she didn't sound nervous. "This is just forest litter like you'd find in the woods back home."

There was nothing as frightening here as what she'd faced in the storm; but during the storm, she'd given up hope. Hope was dangerous because if you hoped, then you had something to lose.

"I would have expected mud too," the hermit said dryly. "But these trees didn't grow under the sea either. Whatever's going on isn't as simple as the sea bottom flexing."

A salamander barked at the humans from the heart of a plant whose spiked leaves formed a cup. The beast's skin was gray with stripes of indigo and blue; its outstretched tongue was blue as well. It looked like nothing Sharina had ever seen before, but it was scarcely a foot long and certainly no threat in itself.

Your brother won't help you today/Pull!

Kizuta, now the trireme's acting captain, stood on the poop, where he oversaw the proceedings. "That's high enough!" he shouted. "Tie her off with double lashings. I *don't* trust this calm weather to stay!"

Sharina walked slowly away from the ship, knowing that the hermit would follow. "You think we're here because of what Meder did, don't you?" she asked in a low voice. She didn't intend to go far, but she wanted Nonnus to be able to give his honest opinion of the situation out of possible earshot of anyone else.

Asera had disembarked, like most of the crew and passengers. She stood beside one of the open-fronted shelters with her arms wrapped tightly around her body in a sign of nervousness. Wainer was at her side, holding a drawn sword and trying to look in all directions at once. Nine more Blood Eagles, carrying spears and sweating in their full armor, formed a rank between the procurator and the jungle beyond.

The mist softened the outlines even of objects only fifty feet away. Leaf mold covered horizontal surfaces, but the vertical edges of structures on shore were all the same polished pinkish-gray color.

Nonnus looked back toward the looming trireme. Meder was still aboard, hunched in the bow behind a screen to shield his actions from others. He had a fire going in a small jug; occasionally a puff of colored smoke rose into the low clouds.

"I don't know," he said. "I don't think Meder raised the storm. Maybe he didn't have anything to do with Tegma either."

The island climbed from the shore, though it was hard to be sure of the exact slope because of fog and the thick vegetation. Paths paved with gneiss blocks led into the forest from the harbor. They were edged with low curbs rather than railings.

Most of the sailors were free to explore now that they'd

pulled the vessel to a dry berth. Their footprints scarred the dark litter and their voices drifted from among the trees, mingled with those of Tegma's wildlife.

There was no sign of the people who had built these remarkable structures.

"I don't think Meder knows whether he's responsible for this or not," Sharina said. Until she forced herself to speak the words, she'd been keeping the fear only half-formed at the back of her mind. "I don't think he understands all of what he's doing. I don't think he understands *half* of what he's doing."

"Tenoctris said the same thing," Nonnus said mildly. "I wish she was here now. But then, I wish a lot of things."

He squatted at the top of the docking facility, his javelin in his right hand. His left index finger poked into the leaf litter with the care of a surgeon working in a victim's chest. A worm twisted away in blind terror, vanishing again into the mold like rain on sand. The subsoil only a few inches beneath the surface was a dense yellow clay.

Sailors were clearing the long, shallow shelters. They had no front wall, only square-sided pillars to support roofs so low that most of the men had to duck to keep from hitting their heads. They provided cover from the rain because there was no wind to blow droplets onto those inside.

Another party of sailors brought ashore the men injured too badly to walk by themselves. There were several dead as well, rowers who'd been brained or had their chests crushed by oars flailing during the storm. Men with mattocks dragged them into the forest. The yellow clay would be difficult to dig; a layer of leaf litter would probably suffice to cover the corpses. Had the trireme not been in port, seawolves would have formed the burial detail.

"Let's look at these trees," Nonnus said. Glancing aside to make sure Sharina was following, he walked toward a stand of smaller growth. Though the plants were jointed like grasses, the inside was a pulpy solid when the hermit severed a six-inch stem with two quick strokes of his Pewle knife.

The rain had stopped or at least paused. Sailors returned from the forest with a salamander the size of a fox that they'd killed with their sheath knives. Some of the group split a fallen branch to reach the dry wood inside; another sharpened a sapling to use for a spit.

The local wildlife was easy to catch and perfectly edible so far as the crew and Sharina were concerned. She wondered if Asera and the wizard would feel the same way about the writhing amphibians.

Nonnus paced thirty feet along the trunk to where the tree narrowed into a dozen ropy branches, then lopped the top off as well. He eyed the remainder of the stand, looking for an exact match.

"Wainer!" a soldier called, running down from the forest. His feet skidded on the fallen debris when he tried to stop. One of the men guarding Asera caught him to keep him from falling flat.

"We've found a city!" the man said. "A whole city up on top of the hill, and there's no one there!"

Wainer and Asera stepped closer to the messenger. All three talked with animation, but too quietly for Sharina to hear from where she stood.

"Nonnus," she said, lowering her own voice although no one was close by. "What do you think is going to happen?"

He shrugged and gave her a wry smile. "I don't suppose we were brought here for any reason that would please me to learn, child," he said. "But better here than the bottom of the Inner Sea or a lizard's belly. Alive is better than dead."

The hermit notched another tree, then pushed it over with a powerful thrust of his shoulders.

"That should take care of the outriggers," he said. "Now, let's go see if we can borrow a proper axe to fell a tree big enough for our dugout's hull."

12

Cashel duckwalked slowly down the spillway, keeping his eyes on the flat bottom so that he wouldn't miss anything unusual. The stones were slick with residue from the seawater that roared down them when the mill was in use, though that hadn't been for some days. The morning sun wasn't high enough to clear the walls of the trough, but there was plenty of light to see by.

If there'd been anything to see, that is.

"I think it was about there," Tenoctris called from the beside the millwheel, where she and Cashel had sheltered during the night to watch the drover.

He *was* in the right place: he could see the faint nicks Benlo's dagger had made on the stones. Had the drover picked up the object he drew the glamour from? Neither Tenoctris nor Cashel himself had seen him bend down to do that, but the only thing here—

"I found a pebble," Cashel called. "Could he have been using a pebble, mistress?"

"Yes!" she replied. "Very possibly he could."

Cashel climbed out of the spillway and walked toward the wizard. He wondered if Benlo would notice them going over the scene of his invocation of the previous night, though he didn't worry about the possibility. Despite the drover's denial and Tenoctris' doubt, Cashel was convinced that Benlo was behind the attack on Garric. If Benlo wanted to make a problem about what Cashel was doing, then he was welcome to try.

Terns skimmed the sea's surface and rose with small fish in their beaks. Their motion kept drawing Cashel's unwilling eyes to seaward. That was the direction Sharina had gone, and he was sure in his heart that she would never return.

Tenoctris took the pebble from his hand and held it to the sun to see its details. "Marble," she said. "Do you have marble around here, Cashel?"

He shook his head. "I thought it was a chip of quartz from the beach," he said. Now that he looked carefully he could see that what he'd taken for natural weathering on one side of the pebble was really carving. The piece was no larger than the end of his thumb.

"I can't do what Benlo did with it," Tenoctris said, eyeing the stone critically. "But I think I have sufficient power to learn what it came from."

She sat down, crossing her legs beneath her instead of squatting the way a villager would have done. She plucked a stalk of the coarse grass growing in the angle between the millhouse and the spillway.

"My athame," she told Cashel with a smile, holding up the blade of grass. "The tools Meder and Benlo use concentrate power wonderfully, but not power from a single source. Much better to use something neutral. Much safer at least."

Cashel squatted beside her, nodding understanding. He didn't know anything about wizardry, but he understood forces the way anyone who worked with his hands did. If you used a long bar to multiply your strength, you needed to be very careful where you set the tip and what you used for a fulcrum—especially if you were as strong as Cashel or Kenset to begin with.

Tenoctris put the pebble on the ground, then frowned and turned it over so the side with carven braiding was up. She drew a circle in the air around it with the grassblade.

Mitir's little daughter peered at them from the back of her house, then tossed out the remainder of the grain she was feeding to their chickens and went back inside. Cashel was vaguely uneasy that they were in plain sight to anyone on the south side of the mill, but Tenoctris clearly didn't care whether or not people watched her working her magic.

Too bad there aren't more folk—let alone wizards—as

willing to do their business in plain sight, he thought. *The world would be a more honest place.*

"*Miuchthan salaam athiaskirtho,*" Tenoctris murmured as she tapped the grassblade to the ground, one station as she spoke each separate word. "*Dabathaa zaas ouach kol—*"

Movement caught Cashel's eye. He looked up, startled. Benlo's pretty daughter watched them from the corner of the millhouse.

"*Semisilam bachaxichuch!*" Tenoctris said, raising her voice as she struck the pebble with the tip of the grassblade.

"I'm sorry," the girl, Liane, said in embarrassment. "I didn't mean to intrude on—"

The form of a building in faint red light swelled from the pebble the way a puffer fish inflates. The ghostly structure had square sides, a low dome, and no opening except a single arched doorway. The corner moldings were ornamented with stone braid like that from which the pebble had come.

"Oh, that's—" Liane said.

Wizardry, Cashel's mind supplied for the next word.

"—the Countess Tera's tomb in Carcosa," Liane continued. "What a marvelous illusion, mistress!"

"Yes," Tenoctris said dryly. "I'm sometimes mistaken for a wizard. By those who haven't seen the real thing, of course."

The image vanished. Cashel realized he didn't know how large it had been. The size of a real building, he'd thought; but he and Tenoctris were only arm's length apart and it hadn't touched either one of them. Had the red form only existed in his mind?

"How do you come to recognize the tomb, mistress?" Tenoctris asked. She looked at the grassblade as if puzzled to find it in her hand, then dropped it on top of the chip of marble.

Liane's eyes narrowed slightly when she looked closely at Tenoctris. Even seated on the ground and wearing a patched tunic, the old woman's fine features marked her as something out of the ordinary for Barca's Hamlet.

"My father was interested in it," the girl said at last. "I

suppose because it looks something like our family tomb in Erdin. He visited it several times while we were in Carcosa."

Cashel rose to his feet. Liane was a pretty enough girl, though he didn't see what all the fuss the village women were making was about. She had her father's jet black hair and pale complexion, here covered by a broad-brimmed hat of stiffened linen. Her face was triangular, not round, and her fine bone structure must also have come from her mother's side.

"Your father's a wizard," he said bluntly. Nothing in his stance was threatening, but he knew that whether he wanted to or not he loomed over the girl like an ox facing a kitten. "Did he bring that thing out of the sea to attack my friend last night?"

Liane blinked in shock, but she didn't flinch. "My father's a good man," she said in a clear voice. "He said he didn't bring the lich here. He's never lied, not to me, not to anyone."

Tenoctris got to her feet. Liane stooped and helped the older woman in a reflex that was controlling even now when she was angry and perhaps frightened.

Cashel cringed internally. She was a nice girl, whatever her father was. But—

"Tenoctris tells me I'm wrong too, mistress," he said. "I'm sorry. But your father *is* a wizard, because I watched him here last night."

Liane swallowed and closed her eyes. When she reopened them, they were focused on the sea and the far horizon. "When I was a little girl," she said, "the nurse would bring me in and put me on Mother's lap, and my father would sing to us. Beautiful songs, love songs from all the lands he'd visited in his travels."

She looked at Cashel with angry eyes on the verge of tears. "He's a *good* man," she said fiercely. She turned and strode off the way she'd come, around the millhouse, where Katchin's wife screamed at their infant and the infant screamed to the world.

"I shouldn't have said that," Cashel muttered. He felt his face redden with embarrassment as he thought of what he'd done under the goad of his slow smoldering anger.

"You're an honest man," Tenoctris said mildly. "I've always believed that an honest man can say anything he feels ought to be said. Besides that—"

She smiled up at him. If Liane was a kitten, Tenoctris was a bird, a bright-eyed sparrow.

"—I found her answers interesting. Perhaps if I get enough pieces to the puzzle, I'll learn whether it was chance or something else that brought me here, now. The hermit would be amused."

"Mistress?" Cashel asked in a thick voice. "Is Benlo as powerful a wizard as you are?"

Tenoctris laughed and patted him on the arm. "Cashel," she said, "I'm not powerful at all. I've read and I see, those are both important. But the skill I have is that of a diamond cutter who knows where to tap to split a stone on the line of cleavage. If you want raw power—Benlo could *crush* diamonds if he knew how to use the strength he has."

Cashel opened his big, capable hands. "What good's a crushed diamond, mistress?" he asked.

Tenoctris laughed again. "You'd be amazed at how few people understand that, Master Cashel," she said. "The Hooded One certainly didn't."

She looked toward the sea, her face settling into lines of quiet determination. "Which still leaves the question of why the Hooded One did cast me *here*. Well, perhaps we'll learn that too."

13

"Gently, girl, gently," Garric murmured to the drover's tall bay mare at the watering trough by the well curb. She twitched her head anyway. It wasn't a serious attempt to break free, but if Garric's hand had slipped on the bridle she'd have been gone through the gate before he could blink.

The mare was mettlesome and apt to kick if he tried to feed or water her with the other animals. Though she was easily the finest horse Garric had ever seen in his life, he'd have preferred to ride Liane's gelding if it came to a choice. In fact he'd prefer to ride one of the saw-backed baggage mules.

"Good afternoon, Master Garric," Benlo said as he walked out of the common room. His guards remained inside, where Garric could see them being served by his mother. "A bit of a handful, isn't she? Her name's Bright Angel."

"I'm just not used to her," Garric said, stroking the horse behind the ear with his free hand. "Come on and drink, Angel, you know you're thirsty."

For one reason or another—perhaps she was just bored with being troublesome—the bay lowered her head to the stone trough and began slurping water. Garric rubbed her neck, up and down the side of the spine.

"On the contrary, Garric," Benlo said. "She behaves better with you than she does with anyone else I've seen. You have a talent for animals, don't you?"

Garric was glad he had an excuse not to meet Benlo's eyes. Though the drover was trying to be friendly, his words had a *roundness* to them that made Garric uncomfortable. He sounded like the underpriest who usually led the Tithe Procession through the borough. He always talked about his sincere affection for Barca's Hamlet, but Garric had the feeling that an aide whispered "Barca's Hamlet" to the fellow just before he spoke. Otherwise he'd get the name of the village wrong.

"Everybody here on Haft is used to animals, sir," Garric muttered, watching the fly that buzzed around Bright Angel's flank. "Here in this borough anyhow."

"You know I'm buying sheep to carry to Sandrakkan," Benlo said. "I'll need a likely lad to badger the flock to Carcosa where my ship's in harbor. How would you like the job, Garric? I'll pay a Haft silver anchor for every day on the road. That's a full man's wage at Carcosa rates."

"No thank you, sir," Garric said, feeling his throat tighten. The mare raised her head from the trough. Garric put his weight against the big bay skull and turned her to the left so that she was between him and her owner. The mare nickered in surprise at treatment rougher than Garric had shown her in the past. "My friend Cashel's the regular badger. He'll do the job for you better than I could; and besides, the pay would help him and his sister a lot."

Garric walked briskly toward the stables, holding the bridle close to the mare's throat. He gave her a sharp jerk when she seemed to lag. Again she complained, though she didn't try to fight him. Strong as Garric was, a twelve-hundred-pound horse could always win a tugging match with a hundred-and-eighty-pound man if she cared deeply enough.

Two fishermen had wrapped the lich in an old tarpaulin and dumped it in a hundred fathoms of water, but the axletree still lay where Garric had dropped it in the early hours of the morning. He led Angel around it, so Benlo caught up with him again.

"Look, boy," the drover said in a voice of command. "Your friend may be a fine badger but it's you I want to hire, not him. Now, I've offered liberal wages, liberal indeed, but if a little more will—"

"Listen, stranger!" Garric said. Maybe it was sight of the axletree, maybe it was just the roiling confusion of his life, but he felt fury rise in him like that he felt in the dreams where he swung a sword. "I don't know where you come from, Carcosa or Erdin or the depths of the sea for all I care! But here in Barca's Hamlet we don't steal each other's livelihoods! If you want a badger, you can hire Cashel."

Benlo's guards spilled into the courtyard in a trampling rush. Garric was seeing through two sets of eyes. He dropped the bridle and reached down for the axletree. The mare shied back but didn't run.

"Go back inside!" the drover shouted. "Rald, get the men inside at once!"

The chief of Benlo's guards, a stocky man with eyes the gray of cast iron, turned and put his hands on the chests of the men closest behind him. "You heard the boss," he said in a loud, tense voice. "Come on, there's no problem. Let's finish our ale."

Garric shuddered and straightened. He was alone again in his head; the laughing figure who'd measured the six guards for a single stroke of the massive axletree had gone back to wherever it was that he watched and waited.

"Come along, Angel," Garric said in a rusty voice. "We'll find you some oats."

"We'll talk again later, Garric," the drover said in tone of glassy cheerfulness. He reentered the inn and shut the door behind him.

Garric closed the bay mare in her stall. Another time he would have stayed and fed carrots to both horses, but after talking to Benlo he felt quiveringly weak. He walked out of the stable, glad there was no one in the courtyard to see him, and into the street.

Everything was changing. He'd gotten angry as a way to hide his fear.

A silver anchor a day wasn't just a liberal wage, it was a remarkable one. Folk in this borough only saw silver during the Sheep Fair, and even then most payments were made in copper coins.

Benlo wanted more than a boy to chivy his flock to Carcosa. Garric wasn't afraid of Benlo, but the offer was one more sign of the way everything he'd known for certain was shifting about him. *That* frightened him terribly.

"I want things to go back the way they were," Garric whispered. He knew that wouldn't happen, that things never went backward. Chickens don't crawl into eggs, the sun doesn't roll from west to east. But he wasn't willing to give up hope of stability even though he knew the hope was false.

He strode along the path with his head down and his shoulders hunched. Folks glanced at him, but they didn't speak or it they spoke he didn't hear.

He needed to think. He'd almost reached the corral north of the hamlet when he noticed that Tenoctris waited there, watching his progress.

"I was just leaving," Tenoctris called. "I come out here to think sometimes."

Garric closed his eyes and shuddered, hugging himself close. He walked the rest of the way to the pen and said, "Mistress, can I talk to you? I don't know who to talk to. I don't understand *anything*."

"Well, that's the first step to wisdom, they say," the old woman said. She shifted slightly, adjusting her seat on the stone wall. "I only today learned that you were the one who pulled me out of the sea, Garric. I should have thanked you sooner."

Garric threw one long leg over the wall and straddled it, facing her. Shadows were lengthening, and out to sea a bank of high clouds was turning pink.

"One of the fishermen would have brought you in if I hadn't been there," he said. He smiled. "If you like you can thank me for having a father who provides better accommodation for castaways than you'd have found in Tarban's hut, though."

"The inn's roof trusses came from ships' timbers," Tenoctris said with a look of vague marvel. "The wood is full of stories of the far past that's still the future of the person I was. I don't fit in this world. At least I haven't yet found the way in which I fit."

Garric nodded fierce agreement. "*I* don't fit," he said. "Or the world doesn't. Benlo just tried to hire me to take his flock to Carcosa, but that's not what he really means. And Sharina going off like that . . . Mistress, what's happening? I don't want things to change!"

"The trouble is," Tenoctris said slowly, looking toward the sea, "that things are going to change. I liked things the way they were a thousand years ago. Most folk did, I think, though they might have wanted a pig of their own or a less grasping tax gatherer. But the Hooded One wanted more than that, and he brought the Kingdom of the Isles down in centuries of war and famine."

She gave Garric a quirked smile. "Times like that make interesting epics," she said, "but they're not the world in which most people want to live. And now that the Isles have finally settled into something closer to peace, Malkar is rising and the changes are coming again."

"I thought you said the Hooded One had drowned," Garric said, pressing his hands together. "That he was dead."

"Malkar isn't dead," Tenoctris said simply. "And the Hooded One lives also, at least in your dreams."

Garric straightened. "Do you think Fate brought you to Haft to fight Malkar?" he said. His voice was harder than a moment ago; self-pity and self-doubt no longer colored it.

"Fate may be a myth," Tenoctris said, firmer also. "The powers aren't myths, and the powers are building just as they did in my own day. I see them, Garric, just as you see the clouds turn black before the storm hits."

She gave him a quick smile to show that she wasn't angry, at least with Garric. "As for Malkar—you don't fight Malkar any more than you fight the sun. But the sun can be eclipsed for a time, and Malkar's influence can be blocked as well."

Tenoctris shook her head and forced a rueful chuckle. "I doubt Malkar's influence can be blocked by a poor stick like me, but I suppose I'm going to try anyway."

Garric leaned forward and gently took the old woman's hands in his. Like holding a sparrow . . . "Mistress," he said.

"What should I do? Should I go with Benlo? And don't tell me it's my decision; I'm asking for help!"

She bobbed her head once, twice, to indicate she was considering the question rather than ignoring it in silence. She took one of her hands from Garric's grip, patted him, and then folded both in her lap as he sat straight.

"If you were to stand in the spillway while the mill was turning," Tenoctris said finally, "the water would sweep you away no matter how hard you struggled. You'd be better off to swim with the flow so that you at least had a little control over where you were going."

Garric nodded.

"You're connected with King Carus, Garric," she continued. "Through the medal at least, and I think by blood as well. Benlo used the royal line of Haft to identify you. If you stay where you are, you'll draw more things to you. To you and to your family and friends."

"The lich," Garric said.

"The lich," Tenoctris agreed. "And other things better unseen. I wish I could tell you that wasn't true."

Garric said, "Telling a man his barn's not on fire isn't a kindness to him if it *is* burning."

He grinned at her. The situation was funny if you looked at it the right way. He'd laughed when drunken Sil screamed about the invisible spiders that were crawling over his face. If Garric told the other villagers what he was thinking now, Sil could have joined in the laughter and repaid the boy's unmeant cruelty of past years.

"I don't think Benlo's hostile to you, Garric," Tenoctris continued with a frown, "but he certainly isn't your friend. He's seeking you for his own reasons and those reasons may be very like the one that sends a housewife into the yard to fetch a chicken before dinner."

"Will you go with me, mistress?" Garric asked. "To Carcosa or wherever he really has in mind?"

"Yes," she said.

Garric stood. There was light on the bluff, but the hamlet

below was in near darkness. "I guess I'll see if Benlo's job is still open," he said. "May I walk you back to the inn?"

"I'll stay here awhile," Tenoctris said. She smiled also. "I came here to view the alignment of a constellation which won't rise for another two hours. I lied in case you wanted to be alone."

Garric walked down the path whistling. It was more bravado than cheerfulness, but it wasn't because he was afraid. If you were out in the rain, you got wet and there wasn't any point in whimpering about the fact. This business, whatever it was, had to be treated just the same.

Candles glimmered through the windows of some of the wealthier houses. The path was as safe and familiar to Garric at night as it was in bright day. He continued whistling through the courtyard and into the common room, where Reise had spelled his wife at the bar.

Local men in from the fields drank together before going home to their families. They noted Garric with only eye flickers; he was a settled and familiar part of their world.

Benlo rose from a table with his guards and called, "Master Garric? I've talked to your friend Cashel and he's agreed to drive the sheep to Carcosa for me."

"Ah!" Garric said in surprise. He'd been so *sure* that the drover's interest was in Garric or Reise, not in a badger for his flock. "Oh, well, that's very good. Cashel's the best man in the borough for sheep."

"Let me pour you some of your family's good ale," Benlo continued, picking up a pair of mugs and the leather pitcher from the trestle table. He nodded Garric to the small booth in the corner. One of the guards rose to fetch another pitcher of ale.

"I appreciate your concern for your friend, Garric," Benlo said as he filled the wooden mugs, "But you see, I'm still looking for an extra hand. A man who can drive sheep, talk poetry with my daughter—and incidentally, fight like a demon if the need arises. You impressed my man Rald this morning. Didn't he, Rald?"

The chief guard looked at Garric with a perfectly blank expression. "Yes he did, sir," Rald said. "Yes you did."

Garric drank from his wooden masar instead of responding immediately. The tar that moisture-proofed the pitcher added its own smoky fillip to the ale; an attractive flavor, at least if you were used to it.

Benlo's smile was growing brittle. "The same wages as I offered before, of course," he said.

"I've decided I can't always run from new things," Garric said. "I'd be pleased to take the job."

Reise's head turned slightly to fix Garric with a glance, but neither father nor son spoke to the other.

"Wonderful, wonderful!" Benlo said enthusiastically. "The flock's already arranged, so we'll be leaving tomorrow morning if that's all right with you."

Since when do drovers ask permission from their badgers? Aloud Garric said, "I think Cashel will say we leave after noon. The first day needs to be a short one to get the sheep used to the idea."

"Noon then," the drover said with a slight tensing of muscles at the back of his jaw. "We'll have a chance to get to know each other better, since we'll be traveling at the pace of the flock."

"By the way," Garric said. "There's a castaway, Tenoctris, staying here at the inn till she got her strength back. She'll be going to Carcosa too. I'll be responsible for her expenses."

"The old woman?" Benlo said. He shrugged. "If you like. I shouldn't think she was up to the trip, but it's no concern of mine."

Garric downed the remainder of his ale and stood. "I'll take care of my duties in the stable, then."

He caught the eye of his father behind the bar and added, "And I'll have a few things to pack, I suppose."

Whistling again, Garric left the common room.

14

The rain had stopped for the moment, but drops continued to fall *pit! pit! pit!* from the high branches. A salamander grunted in the depths of the forest. It must have been bigger than a man to achieve such throbbing volume.

Sharina had taken a knife from the effects of a seaman killed during the storm. She prodded it gently between layers of the hard stone. The point scarcely penetrated. If she pushed harder, she'd only break the blade.

"Nonnus?" she called. "There's no mortar between the stones here, but they fit closer even than the walls of the mill back in Barca's Hamlet. That's Old Kingdom work. Have you looked at these?"

"Enough to know that you're right," the hermit said. "I was never a mason, though. I can't appreciate the fine points of the work."

Nonnus had a slow fire going in a trough along the upper side of a tree trunk thirty inches in diameter. That would be the diameter, at least, when she and the hermit finished scraping the bark off. Sharina used a hand axe from the trireme; the hermit had his knife.

A falling giant four times as thick had pushed this tree over, saving her and Nonnus the work of chopping it down. The bow and stern would require a great deal of shaping, an axeman's job for which Sharina could be very little help. It didn't seem to concern Nonnus.

The tall vegetation drank the high-pitched voices of men calling to one another, though occasionally a word or a few words penetrated to Sharina's ears. The whole crew had vanished up the hill to see the abandoned city. Nonnus had said only, "When I've finished the dugout, there'll be time for cities."

Sharina could have gone with or perhaps without her protector; but she'd asked Nonnus on the voyage because she trusted his judgment and experience above her own. She wasn't about to second-guess him now. She remained and helped, though she didn't have the endurance to work as Nonnus did without an occasional break to explore the immediate vicinity.

"I meant . . ." she said. "Nonnus, I don't think men could have built things like this. Normal men, I mean. Do you think this was an isle of wizards?"

Nonnus straightened and stretched, laughing with a cheerful humor that would have amazed anyone who'd known the dour hermit in Barca's Hamlet. "Well, I'm not an expert on wizardry either, child. But as for what normal men can do . . . they can do anything a wizard can, in my experience. It may take longer and be done in a different way; but we can do anything at all."

He got up on the fallen log to check the fire, making sure that it wasn't burning too close to the edge as it hollowed the trunk into a vessel. Large timber was too valuable on Haft for Sharina to think of fire as a woodworking tool, but the hermit's experience of less settled lands had led him at once to the option.

A slow fire of damp moss and wood chips hollowed the log as fast as a strong man with an adze. The fire never tired and it worked through the night. A twig framework held a roof of large leaves to keep direct rainfall from the trough; splashes and Tegma's saturated humidity served to prevent the smoldering fuel from breaking into open flame.

Sharina and Nonnus hadn't discussed the reason they were building a dugout. They hadn't needed to.

Breakers groaned beyond the curtain of fog. The reefs were distant—and perhaps distant in more than space alone—but they hadn't vanished. The trireme couldn't cross them without the lift of an unnatural storm as well as magic of a sort that

Sharina knew had depended on the captain's bloody death.

The captain's *sacrifice* by Meder, she suspected. She'd rather drown than become a willing participant in an attempt to repass the reefs by similar means.

"Are we going to have a sail?" Sharina asked. "They probably won't let us take canvas from the ship, but I could sew together the capes of the men who were killed. I wish Ilna was—"

She fell silent. The hermit's stance had changed slightly and he picked up the javelin that had never been beyond arm's length since they landed. He rotated it point down: if he brought his arm back, the missile was ready to throw.

"Nonnus?" Sharina said. Still holding the sailor's knife, she stepped quickly behind him to the fallen log where she'd left the hand axe. A blunt-pointed knife was no weapon if there were better available.

A file of six Blood Eagles and Meder bor-Mederman came out of the forest. The soldiers chatted among themselves. They looked sweaty and bored, though two scarred veterans stiffened noticeably when they noticed the hermit's stance.

"Good morning, Meder," Sharina called in a loud voice. "I trust we won't be in the way of whatever business brings you back to the ship?"

"The procurator has decided you should be with her at all times, mistress," Meder said. "You're to come with us to the city, where we'll stay until we better understand the situation."

He gave Nonnus a glance that was meant to be slighting but instead looked hostile. "Your servant can come or stay as you please."

Meder sounded both peevish and uncomfortable. His black velvet garments were sodden. Even Sharina's thin tunic was heavy with the water it had absorbed. The humid air was both unfamiliar and unpleasant.

The young wizard's problem went beyond the weather, though. She felt flattered—any woman would—that a wealthy noble would find her so attractive; but Meder himself, the way his mind worked and the actions he took without hesitation, was repellent to her. Cold disdain was both Sharina's natural response and the best way she knew to keep him at a distance.

It wasn't a matter she wanted to discuss with Nonnus. It *particularly* wasn't a question she wanted to discuss with Nonnus.

"I don't choose to go," Sharina said loudly.

Meder clenched his right fist. The soldiers who stood talking and scratching themselves fell silent and waited for developments.

"Oh, I don't think there's much we need do here for the next few hours," the hermit said in a calm, carrying voice. He deliberately laid the shaft of his spear on his shoulder as if it were merely a staff. He walked along the log, peering in to check the fire. "No, this is under control."

He turned to Meder and smiled; a gesture of goodwill rather than good humor. "A good time to view new things, sir," he said.

Meder scowled like a ditchdigger unable to crush or shoo away a troublesome fly. "Yes, all right," he said. "Whatever Mistress Sharina wants."

He offered Sharina his arm. She strode haughtily past him and up the stone path.

"I think you can put the knife away now, child," Nonnus said from just behind her.

Sharina blushed and thrust the knife back into its sheath. "I wasn't thinking about it," she said. "I'm used to kitchen knives that you carry till you put them down."

The track was serpentine but steep, rising one foot for every three of horizontal distance. The path was wide enough for six men to walk abreast, though it was a moment before Meder caught up to Sharina and Nonnus. The wizard's slick-soled boots slipped awkwardly on the leaf mold. Bare feet were better even than the soldiers' hobnailed footgear; the spongy matter wasn't strong enough to grip the nails without shearing.

Where traffic had worn the path down to the original surface, gneiss gleamed mirror-smooth. Sharina looked at the curb formed of stones individually twenty feet long. "Some of these blocks weigh tons, Nonnus," she said.

"So they do," the hermit agreed. She heard a faint smile in his voice at the argument she had resumed. "But I haven't seen any block that couldn't have been moved by four men on level ground. Four ordinary men."

"The island is a nexus of power," Meder said, almost to himself. He wiped his face with his sleeve. "A wizard here could do great things. Incredible things."

Sharina realized that the wizard's nervous petulance stemmed from more factors than she'd been considering. Whatever the means by which Tegma's buildings were constructed, the island's reappearance from the sea was proof of great magic. That couldn't help but affect another wizard.

Sailors shouted, nearby but invisible among the vegetation. They were hunting something big enough to require a coordinated attack.

There were worms and insects on Tegma, and the salamanders that preyed on both. She'd seen no mammals, no snakes; not even any birds, though at first she'd thought otherwise. Some of the insects had wings as long as Sharina's forearm. They made a deep bass note as they thrummed through the forest.

Reeds crackled as something large wriggled along just out of sight. The forest was so thick that Sharina couldn't see the path beyond the switchbacks above or below them.

The Blood Eagles panted and cursed softly to one another. Their spears were as much help as hindrance, bracing them when their feet slipped, but their helmets and body armor were heavy and must be unbearably hot in these conditions. It was a tribute to the troops' discipline that they continued to wear the gear; but it was also, Sharina thought, a sign of how silly military discipline could be.

Nonnus carried his javelin butt-upward over his shoulder, still gripping the weapon at the balance for instant use. Perhaps he didn't think the Blood Eagles' concern for material enemies was empty as Sharina did. . . .

The hermit gestured with his left hand, drawing Sharina's eyes upward. Because the path rose so steeply through the scores of switchbacks, she'd been led to the instinctual habit of looking down at where she'd step next and ignoring the wider surroundings.

The buildings on the ridge ahead of her were individually larger than every structure in Barca's Hamlet put together. Walls and high bridges bound the gleaming mass into a whole as complex and intertwined as the tunnels of an ants' nest. The mist-reddened light of the sun deepened the pink stone into bloody scarlet. Sailors walked on the battlements or passed the windows of rooms within, calling to one another in voices bright with childish wonder.

The path led to a gateway twenty feet high: a trapezoid whose transom was half the width of the lintel beneath. Sharina's eyes narrowed slightly. The design was perfectly practical, but she would have expected an arch. Now that she was closer, she saw that the many windows were of the same pattern, slits narrowing toward the top.

"The procurator's in the citadel," Meder said. His eyes had a febrile gleam; his hands twitched as though snatching at something others couldn't see. "The tallest building, I mean. To the right."

Nonnus knelt and ran his free hand along the gatepost. The edge was countersunk as if for a hinge, but no sign of that or the gate itself remained; not even the stain of corrosion on the stone.

Words and the click of the troops' hobnails echoed within the enclosing walls. The building to which the wizard pointed was so high that Sharina wasn't sure whether she saw the topmost tower or just the height at which mist hid the remainder of the structure from her.

"Master Meder!" Wainer's powerful voice called. He stood at the corner of a balcony sixty feet above the courtyard, on the side opposite to the gate. Asera was beside him, letting the soldier do the undignified job of bellowing directions. "The procurator asks that you join her immediately!"

The doorway was small and so low that Sharina ducked, though she would probably have cleared the transom by an inch or two anyway; the passage through the fifteen feet of smooth stone walls felt like a tunnel. The building was certainly capable of being used as a defensive citadel, whether or not that was the purpose for which the ancient builders had intended it.

A pair of sailors jogged across the huge odd-angled room inside. They called to another man somewhere in the echoing gloom. Sharina knew that there were more than two hundred men in this structure or the immediate vicinity, but she felt as though she were swimming in empty ocean.

A soldier murmured something to Meder. He turned with a scowl. "Yes, all right, you're dismissed," he snapped.

"It's only that we need to look after our own rations here, you see, sir," the man said with an air of being ill-used.

The troops turned and vanished back through the doorway, already beginning to strip off their armor. The leather pads they wore beneath the metal were sopping wet.

There were a dozen trapezoidal doorways out of the hall, but the windows on the front and back walls were small and just below the high ceiling. Access to the upper stories was by an open-sided helical ramp supported by pillars. A soldier—not Wainer—waved from the opening where the ramp merged with the coffered ceiling.

"Why didn't they build stairs?" Sharina asked as the three of them started up the ramp. It sloped more steeply than the path outside and her shins already ached from that.

"Aesthetic reasons, mistress," Meder said in a patronizing tone. "The builders of these great structures would have been at pains to blend their work with the forces centered here. This is something that can be fully appreciated only by someone adept in the arts."

By a wizard like him, Sharina translated with a moue of distaste.

"Or of course, they may have been snakes," Nonnus said straight-faced. "Using the arts at which they were so adept in place of the hands they lacked."

Meder blinked, unwilling to believe the gnarled old peasant was mocking him. Sharina giggled despite a hand over her mouth to suppress the sound. The wizard's face went pale except for a blotch of hectic red on either cheekbone.

Doorways opened from each wall of the pentagonal foyer at the top of the ramp. The soldier who'd beckoned to them stepped aside. Asera looked over her shoulder through one opening and called, "Yes, come out here. Tell me what you make of it."

She and Wainer were on a long balcony looking down the other side of the ridge. It was thirty inches deep and there was no railing, only a low curb like those of the paths up the slope from the shore. Sharina felt uncomfortable, though no breath of wind had stirred since the trireme landed on Tegma.

A valley in the mist stretched down the opposite slope. From the base of the citadel bubbled a spring, steaming and sulfurous, which gushed down the rocky slope. No vegetation grew within several feet of the water, though precipitated minerals painted its margins yellow and orange. An updraft from the seething fluid scoured the mist from the air above.

"I can see for miles," Sharina said in wonder. Though there was nothing to see but forest like that on the shore side of the ridgeline.

"These might be the buildings I saw in the lagoon of Tegma," Nonnus said quietly. "But the reefs had grown up around a small island, not . . ."

The point of his javelin gestured toward distances rippling in the heated air.

"Do you know anything about this, Meder?" Asera said bluntly. "Do you know where you've really brought us?"

She was tense in a different fashion from Wainer beside her. The soldier's concerns were for what might be lurking in this vast stone warren—an uncertain question but a limited one. The procurator was still thinking about the mission that had brought her to Haft. She was trying to predict a vast and complex future which their landing on Tegma had thrown into confusion.

If they were even on Tegma.

"I didn't bring—" Meder said, but he caught the glint in Asera's eye and swallowed the remainder of his protest. He was right, of course; the storm was no doing of his. But the procurator was both frightened enough and angry enough to react violently if a colleague misspoke himself at this juncture.

"Mistress," he went on, "Tegma is more ancient than any writings that survive. More ancient than Man himself, some have speculated."

Asera frowned. "That's nonsense," she said, tapping the wall beside her with a fingertip. "These buildings prove that's nonsense."

"Despite the buildings, mistress," the wizard said, though he nodded as if in agreement. "But as I say, everything was conjecture because until now it was impossible to reach even the lagoon above the sunken island."

Nonnus had craned his neck to look up the sheer wall. He smiled faintly. Another balcony jutted from a doorway twenty feet higher and fifty feet to the side, but Sharina knew from her first sight from outside that the citadel had several higher stories inset from this massive base level.

"I'll begin studying the matter through my arts," Meder said.

"You'll find us a way out," Asera snapped.

"Yes, yes of course," Meder agreed, "but first I have to determine where it is that the queen's wizards have brought us. I assure you that my abilities are—"

Boots clashed on the floor of the anteroom. "Wainer!" a soldier called. "Mistress Asera, look what's lying on the floors upstairs. Look!"

Two Blood Eagles paused at the doorway onto the narrow balcony and thrust handfuls of jewelry toward their superiors. Torques too strait for a neck, narrow fluted plates joined into tubes tighter than a human torso but too long for even a tall man's limbs, bangles that Sharina's eyes couldn't fit onto a human form in any way her mind could imagine . . .

Made of gold. Gold so pure that it had survived the ages which devoured all else but the stones of Tegma.

"The sailors have been finding this all over, mistress," a Blood Eagle said. The soldier who'd guarded the doorway onto the balcony hovered behind his two fellows, peering past them for a glimpse of the treasure. "They weren't going to say anything about it, I shouldn't wonder. Well, we taught them about discipline, Ningir and me."

Meder lifted a torque so that it better caught the red light of the sun. He turned it, peering closely at the carvings on all surfaces. If they formed writing rather than decorative symbols, they were in a script like nothing Sharina had ever glimpsed.

"This is exactly what I need!" the wizard said. "We'll take this back to the ship—that'll save time over bringing my tools back here. We'll learn *exactly* what's going on here because the ancient inhabitants will *tell* us!"

Still holding the torque, Meder strode through the doorway so quickly that the soldiers could barely jump clear. Seeming to notice them for the first time, he said, "You three—I'll need animals for this, as many as you can catch. And don't kill them yet!"

As Sharina had noticed before, when Meder was wrapped in what he called his art he completely ignored the procurator except as a potential pair of hands to carry out his bidding. Asera looked startled, but her flash of anger faded quickly to one of hopeful interest.

"Come along, girl," she said to Sharina. "If there's a way out of this place, I want to learn about it as soon as possible. Wainer"—turning her head toward the soldier—"I'll want at least six men. Join us at the ship immediately when you've rounded them up."

The head of the guard detachment nodded. He left the balcony at a quick pace.

"Just as well," Nonnus murmured as they went down the ramp to the main hall. "It's getting time to check on our fires."

Sharina thought he sounded mildly amused. She was confident that she and the hermit would be getting off the Isle of Tegma, whatever happened to the remainder of the trireme's folk.

15

The sheep already in the stone corral made a warm, low sound as Garric approached with the last of the herd, a dozen ewes from Beilin. Bodger, the white-eared milch ewe, angled away from the rest of the herd as soon as she saw that Garric didn't have his full attention on her.

He tightened his lips and reached over the backs of three more docile sheep to rap her sharply with the tip of his unstrung bow. Garric and Cashel didn't carry crooks. Attacks by seawolves were rare, but anybody minding sheep near Barca's Hamlet had to be prepared for them. The bow and Cashel's quarterstaff made adequate prods and levers for the normal duties of a shepherd, and that way the weapons were handy when the unexpected lizard writhed in from the sea.

Cashel waited by the gate into the corral with a pan and a bag in his hands. He clucked meaningfully and called, "Bodger! *Get* back here."

The ewe who'd ignored Garric's touch immediately closed back with the rest of her fellows. They began passing the narrow gate. As each sheep entered, Cashel dropped a bean from the bag into the pan.

"There's twelve of them, like we expected," Garric said.

"Good," Cashel said. "I'd been afraid he'd hold out Bodger after all. Must be a hundred times I've heard him say,

'Never had a milker like her, lad.' Let some poor fool on Sandrakkan worry about her breaking her neck or drowning herself, *I* say."

He continued his tally, a bean for a sheep, just as if his friend hadn't spoken. Cashel was like that: finishing each job the way he'd started it, with no shortcuts and no mistakes. Sometimes he made Garric want to scream with frustration, but you never had to worry about the task being done right— eventually.

Garric gently headed off a young ewe who started to wander away when she wasn't able to enter the corral immediately. "No," he said, "Beilin must have finally listened to you; or maybe it was just the price Benlo was offering."

The last of the sheep passed inside. Cashel set the pan down and emptied the sack of counters into his palm as Garric placed the three wooden bars into slotted stones to close the gate. Beilin's sheep were the last of the fifty which the drover had purchased.

"You know," Garric said, "Beilin's farm is right on the Carcosa Road. We could have picked them up when we passed tomorrow and saved a mile and a half either way."

Cashel shook his head. "I want the whole herd to be used to moving together from the start," he said. "Sheep take time to get used to new ideas."

He popped the half-dozen extra beans into his mouth and chewed with quiet contentment. In the morning and at every halt on the drive, Cashel would count the beans out into the pan again.

Garric laughed. "Well, I'm your assistant," he said. "I just do what you tell me, master."

Cashel looked at him, though it wasn't until he'd finished chewing and swallowed that he said, "Garric, I'll be glad of your company, but I still worry about you coming along. I don't trust this Benlo. He's a wizard."

"So you're safe but I'm not?" Garric said. "I don't see that."

Cashel shook his head. "It's you he's after," he explained.

"Tenoctris and I watched him raise a glamour to find *you*. Did she tell you that? Just before the lich attacked."

"I figured something like that," Garric admitted. He felt uncomfortable thinking of himself as somebody important to a wealthy stranger, much less talking to a friend about it. "I asked her to come along because she'll know better than I would if there's something we ought to, you know, be worrying about."

"Anyway . . ." Cashel said. "I want to get away from here, so I'd take the chance to go with Benlo if he was a seawolf walking on his hind legs. Because of Sharina."

"Well," Garric said, looking out to sea. Neither youth wanted to meet the other's eyes at this moment. "I guess if that's what you want."

Garric's life was being disrupted by outside forces. He fingered his calf where the seawolf had torn him; the twinge in the muscles was little more than he'd have expected from the day's normal labors. *And* the trireme, *and* Benlo, and even Tenoctris; though he felt as good about the castaway's arrival as he did about the fine spring weather.

But Cashel's life was coming to pieces as well, and in his case the blows were being delivered by his own mind. How could anyone care so much about a girl? Sure, Garric missed his sister too, but to *choose* to throw up your whole settled life because of Sharina . . . Well, Cashel's decision was nobody else's business.

"I wonder," Cashel said, "what Benlo would have done if you'd refused to come."

Garric nodded, glad both of the changed subject and the chance to discuss a question he'd puzzled over. "I don't see there was anything he could have done about it," he said carefully. "I mean, he had his guards, but there's too many men in the borough for that to have made any difference. We wouldn't let one of our own be dragged off like a pig to the butcher."

"He's a wizard, though," Cashel said. "That doesn't mean much to you, I guess, because you were asleep through it. It made me tingle all over to watch. I don't think you ought to count on being able to get free of Benlo once you go off with him. We're strong, you and me; but it isn't his guards I worry about."

Garric nodded, pretending to watch the cloud bank paralleling the coast about five miles off shore. "Well," he said, "shall we head back?"

"I'm spending the night here," Cashel said. "I've got my cloak and supper. The sheep need to get used to me as part of the flock too."

Garric punched his friend's shoulder gently, then looked at him with a wry smile. "It isn't just sheep that have trouble with new ideas," he said. "But I guess I'll learn."

He started down the hill toward the hamlet, whistling a jig that he'd learned from one of the trireme's sailors.

16

"Ha-*he*!" Nonnus said as he stood on the edges of the dugout, his weight concentrated on his right leg. He swung the adze at the second syllable, sending back a spray of chips—some charred and some the natural ruddy white of the unburned wood.

"Ha-*ho*!" as he swung again, his weight centered. "Ha-*hi*!" and the adze made a third parallel stroke, completing the breadth of the hollow. Sharina knew that if she checked the work, she'd find it impossible to tell where the blade overlapped; the strokes were that well matched in depth. The hermit moved forward slightly, then bent to resume his cutting.

They'd borrowed the adze from the trireme's carpentry stores. The soldiers might have prevented Nonnus from taking the tool—because they were irritated at their humid misery and because a military man finds it easier to say no than yes in any situation. The troops couldn't stop Sharina from taking the adze without involving Asera in the argument, however, and the procurator's equally short temper would probably have been directed at them. When Sharina chose to push the matter, everyone on the trireme treated her as a noble.

Everyone but Nonnus. Nonnus treated her as a friend.

The rain had stopped again; the sun was low in the western sky. Asera walked out of the shelter where she'd huddled, her face hard with rigidly controlled frustration. Thus far Meder's activities in the adjacent shelter had brought smoke, murmured chanting, and unexpected odors. One moment Sharina thought the air had the dry chill of an ancient tomb; at another she breathed perfumes that had nothing to do with the flowerless forests of Tegma.

But no results beyond those. The wizard hadn't even begun to slaughter the salamanders which the guards had gathered into a sack made from a dead man's tunic.

Sharina had continued to work through the rain, scraping clean the pole that would eventually be the dugout's mast. She didn't find the warm slow drops especially bothersome, at least in comparison with the general saturated humidity.

Nonnus ignored the weather also, smoothing the base and sides of the trough his fires had eaten in the log. Using fire alone would have risked the flames spreading through a crack to eat a hole in the bottom.

It was hard to imagine the weather affecting Nonnus one way or the other. As for Sharina, well, she'd been raised to do the work of a village inn. Her comfort had never been a priority for Reise if there was a job to be done.

Six Blood Eagles stood or sat nearby, talking to one another in a desultory fashion. They were bored and the need for them to be—at least to appear—on guard meant they couldn't get out of the rain or discard their armor. Even Wainer looked disgruntled. Sharina had already come to realize that contrary to the impression she'd gotten from the epics, a soldier's life was mostly a mixture of boredom and discomfort.

Asera glanced toward Meder, but she didn't go over the shelter in which he worked. He hadn't bothered to close the front of the three-walled stone structure this time: he needed the light, and the Blood Eagles kept their eyes rigidly averted from what was going on inside.

The procurator walked up behind Sharina as she removed bumps from the pole, using the hand axe as a plane. "What's this you're doing?" Asera demanded. Frustration soured her tone and she stood, probably deliberately, closer than any workman would like.

"Ha-*he*!" Nonnus said as he swung. He'd raised his voice minutely to underscore the fact that he existed in a world different from that of the nobles. "Ha-*ho*!"

"Something to pass the time," Sharina said. She paused and stretched. If she continued to work while Asera was so close, she'd get angry and make a mistake. That could mean a splinter through the hand or even a gash, though the blade's edge wasn't sharp enough to do real damage when she was short-gripping the axe for the present task. "We're building a boat."

Asera sniffed. "A waste of time is right," she muttered. She was angry at the situation and to a lesser degree at the wizard's failure to correct it. She'd look a fool to sneer at the sky, and sneering at Meder would be counterproductive. Sharina and the hermit were safe targets.

It wasn't a new experience for Sharina: her mother had displaced anger in the same fashion, though most often her shrill rages were directed at Reise rather than the children.

"Quick!" Meder shouted. His voice reverberated from the shelter's open side before he turned his head to look out himself. "Bring me the animals. Now! May the Sister snatch you all down! Do you want me to have to do this again?"

The soldiers stiffened. The lines of Asera's face smoothed into an expression of bright interest. She stepped quickly, almost trotting, toward the wizard. Her hand hooked in a gesture to bring Wainer with her, holding the writhing sack.

"Ha-*ho*!" the hermit said. "Ha-*hi*!"

For all her disgust at what the wizard was doing, Sharina walked to the other side of the pole before resuming her work. From her new location she could watch the activities in the shelter.

Meder was chanting and gesturing with his athame. He'd scribed a circle on the ground around the gold torque. When he nodded, Wainer slit the belly of a salamander so that its blood and internal organs spilled onto the metal. The soldier's face was as impassive as the smooth rock surrounding him.

Asera held another salamander, a small one with orange markings. She scowled with discomfort at the feel of the slimy skin. When Meder nodded again she dropped the little creature into the bowl in which the wizard burned his powders on a bed of charcoal. The hiss and desperate croaking made Sharina's nose wrinkle.

The air about Meder crackled as loudly as a tree limb breaking. Red mist swirled above the torque, expanding and becoming denser. Wainer stepped out of the shelter so quickly that he bumped his head as he straightened. The procurator edged backward slightly, but her attention remained riveted on the twisting red glow.

"Nonnus," Sharina said in a low voice. The hermit had already set the adze down. He hopped to the ground as she moved to his side. He took the javelin in his right hand; his fingers moved without a side glance from his eyes.

The glowing mist congealed into a spindle five feet high, darkening like a piece of iron cooling after it comes from the smith's hearth. The light took on features: limbs and a triangular head. A vaporous image of the torque encircled the figure's neck.

The figure had six limbs, not four. Two were splayed into jointed swordblades or toothed flails; two reached out, capable of manipulation with fingerlike cilia; two were legs, chitinous and insectile.

The creature wasn't even remotely human in anything but its upright posture.

"The Archai!" Meder shouted in delight. He scrambled

from the shelter, clapping his hands. "The inhabitants of Tegma were what Cassarion's *Manuscript* calls the Archai!"

The Blood Eagles had turned to watch. Asera and Meder both moved sideways to change the angle from which they viewed the motionless image. The procurator's expression was a puzzled frown in contrast to the wizard's smile.

"How are you going to—" Asera began.

The image expanded. For a moment the mist retained its shape; then it burst like a soap bubble. The rosy glow continued to spread outward, fading minutely. There was a noticeable boundary layer between it and the surrounding air.

"Step behind me, child," Nonnus said in a guttural voice, brushing Sharina back with his right arm and the shaft of the javelin. He drew the Pewle knife and held its heavy steel blade vertically between them and the oncoming glow.

The mist flowed past the sharp edge and over the two of them unaffected. Sharina felt nothing at the contact. The rosy color was less evident now that they were within it.

"What was that?" Asera asked sharply. She plucked at her cheeks to see if the glow had left anything clinging to them. "You didn't tell me it was going to touch me!"

Wainer had his sword out. His eyes searched in all directions.

"It's nothing," Meder said in dismissive irritation. "In order to get the information we need—"

Something twisted in the shelter where the wizard had worked. At first Sharina thought a salamander had gotten out of the sack.

"—I'll have to repeat the incantation—"

A figure humped upward from the shelter's stone floor as if dust was coalescing back into the original shape from which it had crumbled. This wasn't an image of light: it was the solid form of a living creature.

"—but it'll go faster this time because—"

The ground along the whole foreshore trembled; along the path as well. The glow continued to expand at a walking pace; the dust of ages shifted behind it.

"Look!" Sharina said, pointing to the shelter. Everyone's eyes followed her gesture.

A creature, the tawny, chitinous original of the image Meder had raised, lurched to its hind legs. Asera shouted and jumped back, almost stumbling. The Archa slashed at her. Wainer lunged, driving his sword a hand's breadth deep in the creature's thorax.

The Archa collapsed, its limbs thrashing. An upper limb slashed Wainer's forearm. The tip of his sword dripped purple blood when he withdrew it.

The ground seethed like the liquid in a pot coming to a boil. There must have been hundreds, *thousands*, of Archai thronging the port at the time Tegma ceased catastrophically to exist. Blood Eagles thrust furiously, but they might as well have been trying to stab a fire with their spears.

"Run for the city!" Nonnus called, as always the first to react to unexpected danger. "Get ahead of the spell!"

He was speaking to Sharina but the two of them bolted up the path only a few steps ahead of the others, Meder included. Only Wainer's shouted command kept his men from trampling the nobles in panicked haste. Courage against human enemies was one thing; this uncanny threat attacked the Blood Eagles at an instinctive level and momentarily overcame their pride. Recalled to duty, they formed a rear guard.

There had been Archai on the zigzag path when Tegma died also, though the six-limbed figures Sharina dodged on the trampled leaf mold were slightly less developed than those rising behind her. The difference was the matter of seconds by which the glowing touch of wizardry passed.

Sharina skidded at the first dogleg bend. Nonnus grunted in concern, unable to catch her because he held a weapon in either hand. She didn't need help; she balanced by thrusting the hand out as a counterweight and dabbing down the fingertips of her free hand.

An Archa hunched in front of her, almost fully formed. It started to rise. She leaped over the creature and continued to run.

"Should we cut straight uphill?" she cried.

"We don't know the land!" Nonnus said. "All it'd take is a gully in the wrong place."

Archai continued to coalesce on the path. Sharina heard behind her a clash of metal and a scream. She ran on.

17

When Garric entered the common room he found his father standing at the bar, transferring the guests' accounts from tablets to a sheet of paper made from linen rags. There was still enough light through the west window to throw the waxed boards into shadowed relief, and the evening trade hadn't yet begun.

Only charges amounting to more than a silver anchor rated the formality of a paper tally, but Garric knew the total for Bènlo, his daughter,. his guards, and his animals would be well above that figure. The past week had been a uniquely profitable one for the borough in general and the inn in particular.

Reise turned when the door opened. He looked at Garric with inquiry.

"Ah, Father," the boy said. "I thought that, well, things will be busy in the morning. So I ought to say goodbye today while it's, ah, quiet."

Reise nodded approval. "You've always shown foresight," he said. "In addition to your other virtues, of course."

He looked down at the goose quill in his hand. He wiped the nib between thumb and forefinger so that the ink wouldn't dry and clog it, then met Garric's eyes again and continued, "We none of us know what the future will bring; in that sense tomorrow is no different from any other day. I expect you'll return here with a tidy sum in silver and experience of the sort a young man with coins in his pocket can gain in a city.''

Reise smiled with the left side of his face, scarcely more than a nervous tic. ''I expect you to be prudent,'' he said. ''But I'm not a fool, and you're not a charred old stick like your father. Have fun, but don't get in over your head.''

''Ah, I should be back in ten days,'' Garric said. ''I'll probably turn right around, but unless Tenoctris stays in Carcosa I'll still be traveling at her pace.''

He glanced at the sheet of accounts. Reise's handwriting was the best sort of professional script: each letter as clear as those of a book page, but without the embellishments and flourishes that concealed meaning in the name of beauty. Garric wrote as well as anyone else in the hamlet, but he knew that he'd never equal his father's elegant clarity.

''Yes, as I say, the future will be whatever it chooses to be,'' Reise said.

He set the pen down on the edge of the bar, tented his hands, and resumed, ''While I have no doubt of your ability to take care of yourself, Garric . . . and no illusions about *my* ability to take care of anything, least of all another human being. Still and all, you might at some point find yourself in need of some help that I could give you. I'll give you any help within my ability.''

Reise deliberately turned, picked up the pen in one hand, and with the other tilted a wax tablet better to the light. He dipped the nib again in his pot of oak-gall ink.

''Ah, thank you,'' Garric said to his father's back. ''I figure, you know . . . I'll be back in ten days.''

He started for the stairs, planning to decide which clothing to carry. Lora came to the open door of the kitchen and said, ''Garric? Will you come in here? I have a few things to say to you.''

Garric felt his guts tense. His father didn't look up from his accounts. ''Yes, Mother,'' Garric said.

Lora held the door for Garric and closed it behind him. They were alone in the kitchen: Lora could cook for Benlo and his entourage without additional help.

Garric stopped in the middle of the room and crossed his hands behind his back because he didn't know what else to do with them. Lora faced him. She looked like a bitter, angry doll.

"I've always loved you, Garric," she said. "No mother ever loved a child more!"

Her harsh, defensive voice proved that in her heart Lora knew as well as Garric did that she was lying. To the extent that his mother had ever cared for any person beyond herself, that person was Sharina.

The door onto the courtyard opened. Ilna stepped into the kitchen. "I came to get the—" she began.

"It can wait!" Lora shouted. "I suppose because you didn't have a mother, nobody taught you to knock before coming through a door, is that it? I'm having a discussion with my son!"

Garric had turned his head when the door opened beside him. He saw Ilna's face go stiff in an expression that could have broken stones. Lora was a person who blurted out anything she pleased when she was angry. She seemed to think that other people forgot her words because she herself did. Ilna, and especially Ilna's anger, was of a very different sort.

The girl nodded with cold politeness and backed out of the kitchen, closing the door behind her. The panel didn't bang against the jamb. There was nothing hot or fleeting about Ilna's rage.

"You think your mother's an old fool who has nothing to say that you need to hear," Lora said in a wholly different voice from the one with which she'd started the conversation. "Well, I'm old, all right. I don't need you to tell me that when I've got a mirror. But I know things about women, boy; and men too, even after all these years buried here."

It struck Garric, and not for the first time, that his mother wasn't a fool. She couldn't have done as much harm as she had if she'd been stupid.

"Mother," he muttered, looking at water stains on the plaster behind Lora, "I'll be back in ten days. Two weeks at the outside. I'm just driving some sheep to Carcosa.''

Lora sniffed. ''As if you'll come back here after you've seen a city,'' she said. ''As if anybody with sense would. And that girl Liane has her eye on you besides.''

''Mother!'' Garric said. He was ready to crawl under the table in embarrassment.

''Well, that's what I want to tell you about, boy,'' Lora continued. ''Remember that you're in charge when you're dealing with that girl or any girl. Don't let their airs or their looks or the clothes they wear put you off. Don't whine, don't beg. Let them know that they have to come to you.''

She looked Garric up and down in cold appraisal, the way he might have judged the lines of a sheep. He wanted to sink into the stone floor. She nodded approval.

''They'll come,'' she said. ''Never fear that, boy. They'll come in droves.''

''I don't *want* droves of women!'' Garric said. ''Mother, I'm just driving sheep to Carcosa! And anyway—''

He heard his voice catch and drop into a husky lower register.

''—Liane's a fine lady. She wouldn't be interested in me.''

Lora shook her head in wonder and disgust. ''Oh, I've raised a paragon, I have,'' she said. ''The sort of man a good girl dreams about and maybe one in a thousand might find.''

She stepped closer to Garric and lifted his chin with two fingers, forcing him to meet her eyes. ''Listen, boy,'' she said. ''Always remember this: a lady is a woman first.''

It was odd to hear Lora speaking in a tone of authority, so different from the shrill boastfulness that was as much a part of her person as the careful hairdo.

She put her hand on the latch of the common-room door, but she continued to hold her son with her eyes. ''I'm not telling you what to do with this Liane or any of the other fine ladies you'll meet. But I'm telling you to do it on your own terms or you're a fool.''

She pulled the door open and gestured Garric through it in dismissal.

''As great a fool as your father,'' Lora added.

18

The last bend of the path to the Archan city kinked to avoid an outcrop of sheer, dense rock too hard for the roots of tree ferns and giant horsetails to seat themselves. Because there was no vegetation in the way, Sharina could see the ancient buildings as the spell's faint glow merged with the smooth pink stone.

A man shouted in hoarse fear from the undergrowth to the right of the path. Some of the Archai must have been in the forest, perhaps trying to hide from the disaster they knew was overtaking their island. Sailors looking for food found themselves prey for the sword-sharp limbs of monsters undreamed.

Sharina had thought—she'd hoped, she'd prayed—that the wizard's uncontrolled magic would reach its limits short of the city; that the walls when she and Nonnus gained them would be a barrier to their chitinous builders. Meder was a very powerful wizard, just as he'd claimed. *The fool!*

"I should have brought my chest," Meder said in a breathless wail. "I can save us but I need my tools!"

"You fool!" Asera screamed. "You've killed us, *killed us*!"

Sharina's thigh muscles felt like molten lead. She'd been standing and working all day; climbing the hill twice, this second time at a run, would have been an effort even if she hadn't needed to help Nonnus.

The hermit had more strength in his upper body than most men twice his size, but those muscles had been formed while kneeling to paddle a flimsy boat through the waves of the Outer Sea. His legs were sturdy, but they weren't built for running. Sharina's hand on his upper arm had twice kept him from falling because of the slippery footing and had transfused him with her youthful stamina.

But it was hard for her too. So hard that she didn't dare think of failure.

At the dogleg Sharina glanced over her shoulder. She hadn't meant to look back, but an instinctive need to know the worst drew her eyes. The two nobles were twenty feet behind. Asera had thrown off her beige robe and ran in a shift of white silk that the sun now painted red. Meder held his athame in one hand and flailed his left arm sideways for balance as though he were trying to swim through the humid air.

Four of the Blood Eagles struggled up the slope behind the nobles, turning frequently to fight a desperate rearguard action. Wainer carried a spear that he must have taken from one of his fallen men; both the blade and the conical metal buttcap were smeared with purple blood.

The Archai filled the pathway below in a straggling mass; a few filtered through the forest to head off the fleeing humans. A pair of six-limbed monsters came out of the trees with tiny, mincing strides to get between the soldiers and the nobles while Wainer and his men were focused on the Archai behind them.

Sharina screamed, "Wainer!" She missed her footing and slipped to one knee.

"Come!" Nonnus said in a voice like waves breaking. "Mind your own affairs!"

Men in and around the Archan city gaped at what they saw running toward them up the harbor path. Shouts echoing faintly from within the walls indicated that creatures there were already beginning to quiver back to life. Many of the sailors had wooden spears for hunting salamanders; all of them carried knives. They could clear at least one building for defence before the Archai within reached their full lethal vitality. . . .

Sharina and Nonnus rounded the last corner. The gneiss path straightened for the last hundred feet of its course to the city's tall gateway.

Three Archai stepped out of the trees in front of them. Their saw-edged forelimbs were raised like those of a preying mantis about to pounce.

Sharina was half a step ahead of the hermit because she'd been on the inside when they turned the corner. She didn't need to think: she lengthened her stride and brought the hand axe down in an overhead chop as though she were splitting a billet of firewood.

The iron blade was dull, but the girl's strength and desperation buried it to the socket in the creature's triangular skull. Purple blood spurted. It had an acid odor.

Sharina's momentum slammed her into the creature she'd just killed. The segmented chest plates had some give to them, like boiled leather. The Archa's limbs spasmed; the fingerlike cilia brushed like butterfly wings while the saws raked Sharina's back. The Archa toppled to the side of the path, almost wrenching the deep-sunk axe from her hand.

Nonnus thrust an Archa just below where the narrow neck joined the torso. The chitin broke in a fine star pattern where the steel entered. He used the javelin's barbs to jerk the creature sideways like a gigged frog, blocking with its thrashing body the third Archa's attack.

The Pewle knife was in Nonnus' left hand. He brought it up in a stroke that slashed a hand's breadth deep through the third creature's chest. Tough chitin parted like gauze to either side of the blade.

Nonnus vaulted the tangled, twitching bodies, clearing his spearhead in the same graceful motion. He and Sharina ran on, her left hand touching his shoulder.

The cold trickle down her back was blood, not sweat.

19

Ilna walked out of the millhouse carrying two bundles, neither of them very large, on a short staff which she balanced on her shoulder as she locked the door. The door and latch were more recent by nearly a millennium than the stone fabric of the building, but they were sturdy pieces in their own right.

Katchin the Miller was in the street in front of the inn, talking with Benlo. Liane os-Benlo stood with her back to the men. Her eyes were lifted as though she were scrutinizing the pattern of cirrus clouds to the north, making silently clear to the world that speaking to her would be an undesired intrusion.

Two of Benlo's guards were present; while they weren't precisely relaxed, nothing in their bearing suggested that they expected a sudden danger to appear. Their four fellows were with Reise in the courtyard, adjusting the packs and saddles of the animals.

A number of villagers watched nearby, but for the most part the varied excitement of the past week had jaded Barca's Hamlet to the point that a drover leaving town with a flock was no longer enough to draw folk away from their normal occupations. Mistress Kirruri noticed Ilna locking her door and nudged her neighbor; the two of them whispered, viewing Ilna out of the corner of their eyes.

The men didn't pay any attention to Ilna as she walked toward them. Katchin was describing his plan to turn Barca's Hamlet into a port rivaling Carcosa. It was an utterly ludicrous notion even if he found a backer with unlimited wealth: storms across the Inner Sea almost invariably came from due east, making east-coast ports impossible to enter if they provided real shelter in bad weather.

Benlo "listened" with a fixed expression. His mind was clearly on matters that had nothing to do with Katchin; grim matters, if Ilna was any judge of a man's face.

Cashel and Garric were bringing the flock down from the corral in a slow line. The tail of it, where Garric gently chivied the complaining ewes, was still visible on the slope. Cashel at the head hadn't yet appeared around the bend at the hamlet's north end.

"Good day, Uncle Katchin!" Ilna said, loudly enough to break into even the miller's self-absorbed monologue. "Since you're my nearest relative remaining in the hamlet, I'm giving you this for safekeeping."

She held out the four-pin key. When Katchin goggled at her, she took his hand firmly in hers, turned it palm-up, and pressed the key into it.

"In case of emergency, of course," she went on, holding him with her eyes. "I don't expect to find mine and my brother's goods ransacked in our absence."

"What are you talking about, girl?" Katchin said in growing amazement. "Where would you go? You've never left the borough and you couldn't afford to if you wanted to!"

Ilna untied a corner of one bundle. Within the linen cover was a panel of wool in black, white, and subtly patterned gray shades. "I'm carrying the wall hanging I've just finished to market in Carcosa," she said. "It'll fetch three times as much there as a peddler who comes to Barca's Hamlet would pay me."

She glanced toward the north end of the street. The flock wasn't in sight yet but she could hear Cashel calling to the sheep, conditioning them to obey his voice on the road.

"I've never been able to do this before because I had to stay home and take care of my brother," she said. She'd lowered her voice when she had the undivided attention of everyone nearby, but her each syllable still rang like a hammer blow. She looked at Liane as she continued, "Boys have absolutely no sense. No sense at all."

Liane turned to meet Ilna's gaze with one of cool appraisal. She raised an eyebrow minusculely but said nothing.

"These are unsettled times," Benlo said with a frown. His tone became oily. "I don't think a pretty young girl like you should pick this as her first time to leave home."

"I'm aware that the times are unsettled," Ilna said with a cold disdain that anyone in Barca's Hamlet would have warned would be her reaction to being patronized by a man. "I saw the lich myself, as you may remember. But I rather think that the problems may leave as suddenly as the strangers who brought them here."

Katchin moaned in embarrassment, though he'd heard worse from his niece's tongue, and with less justification in his opinion.

Benlo colored. "I had nothing to do with the lich," he said in a husky voice. He turned as if to look up the street. "Are those boys here with the sheep yet?"

"You're welcome to travel along with us to Carcosa, mistress," Liane said unexpectedly. "You'll be safe in our company. But have you given thought as to how you'll return to your little home here?"

The women looked at one another. "It's very kind of you to be concerned, mistress," Ilna said. "I assure you that someone like me who's been raised without your advantages has to think about all aspects of her own welfare— and the welfare of friends who may not have any sense at all."

She smiled. In her mind she visualized Liane bound with a series of complex knots, screaming as she turned over a slow fire.

20

The only door into the citadel was guarded by the seventeen surviving Blood Eagles: armor and better weaponry meant that a much higher percentage of soldiers than sailors had lived through the chaos of the first few minutes after the Archai appeared. Men had made an attempt to barricade the passage with the only material readily at hand within the building—the bodies of the slain, mostly slain Archai.

Sharina tried not to wince as Nonnus dabbed her cuts with ointment. The base was cool and oily—fat of some kind, she thought, rather than the lanolin that was normally used in sheep country—but it contained something astringent that burned for a moment before it settled into the muscles as gentle warmth.

The barricade hadn't worked. Fresh waves of Archai dragged the corpses of their fellows into the courtyard, then attacked and died in turn. Swords dulled, spearshafts cracked, and sometimes an Archa's slashing arms got home on a Blood Eagle where the armor didn't cover. Even when the soldiers weren't injured, they grew tired with killing.

"I didn't see you pick up your medicine box, Nonnus," Sharina said, speaking in part as an excuse not to hear the sound of fighting at the entrance nearby. Of slaughter, really. Soldiers grunted and cursed; steel crunched as it penetrated chitin and occasionally sang as a man withdrew his blade swiftly; Archai wheezed when they died, a high-pitched sound that made Sharina's skin prickle.

"I'm a seal hunter, child," the hermit said with a smile in his voice. "In a small boat, you tie everything you need to yourself. A trained man can roll a woodskin over and upright again with two strokes of his paddle, but he can't keep whatever's loose in the belly of the boat with him from sinking to the bottom of the sea.''

Still the Archai came. Sailors under Kizuta's direction were trying to shift the stone altar across the floor to block the entrance, but even if they succeeded Sharina didn't expect the respite from attacks to last long.

''Nonnus,'' she said, keeping her voice calm. ''How long do you think we can hold out?''

''Oh, I shouldn't be surprised if it was quite a while, child,'' Nonnus said. He reached through the tear in the back of her tunic to check the skin beneath her right shoulder blade. A single long sawtooth had stabbed her there, a puncture rather than a slash like most of her injuries. ''Especially if we manage to block the door.''

The sailors had given up on sliding the entire altar. Now they were attempting to lever off the top with their flimsy wooden spears. That slab alone was six inches thick and must weigh tons, so it should make an adequate barrier.

''But we don't have anything to eat or drink!'' Sharina said, aware that anger and maybe fear was sharpening her tone.

Sailors shouted in glee as stone began to scrape over stone; the slab was moving. A Blood Eagle shrieked a curse and stumbled back from the entrance, clinging with both hands to a thigh that had been sliced to the bone.

''This will hurt for a moment,'' the hermit said. He pinched the swollen flesh at the base of the puncture between thumb and forefinger to spread the opening, and with his other index finger smeared ointment onto the wound.

He went on judiciously, ''Water won't be a problem with as much rain as falls here. We can collect it on the upper floors of the building. Soak it into cloth and wring it out if we can't just stop the roof drains.''

''Don't just drop it!'' Asera shouted, walking closer to the men working on the altar. Her voice was strong, though her hands washed one another nervously. ''We need it whole to be any good! Get something underneath to cushion the shock.''

''We'll starve, then, won't we,'' Sharina said, her tone too dull for the words to be a question. She'd been fired with adrenaline while she ran and fought her way to the citadel. When the hormones burned out of her bloodstream, they left behind only ashes and hopelessness.

Sharina knew it wasn't the real *her* speaking, only a shadow that would by morning be a whole person again. For now she couldn't help her mood, although it disgusted her.

''I've eaten lobster, child,'' Nonnus said calmly. ''I'll eat these insects if they're the food we have.''

She nodded.

''Child?'' Nonnus said.

She looked up to meet the hermit's eyes.

''Before I'll starve and leave you without a protector, I'll eat men,'' he said. ''The Lady forgive me, but I will; and you will too.''

She forced a smile that became real as the corners of her mouth drew up. ''I don't think we'll run out of lobster so quickly,'' she said.

A sailor screamed in sudden terror. Other men shouted. An Archa climbed from the hollow of the altar, through the gap made by sliding the top slab toward the other end. The crewmen focused on shifting the heavy stone stumbled away, unable to deal with an event so unexpected.

The altar was also a tomb. The wizard's runaway magic had raised the body interred there as well.

Wainer turned, alert to the new threat even when his attention was so concentrated on the main assault. The Archa poised like a bird of prey on the lip of its tomb, then launched itself toward the procurator with its forelimbs spread to slash.

Nonnus' javelin caught the creature in midleap, punching in at the base of the throat and out the back by a hand's breadth of sharp steel. The impact rotated the Archa's upper body so that its abdomen, not the thorax segment and flailing limbs, hit Asera and knocked her down.

Sharina hadn't seen the hermit move. She blinked. Her skin was only just becoming aware that his fingers were no longer medicating her wounds. She gripped the hand axe and stood up.

Kizuta, Wainer, and two other of the Blood Eagles ran to Asera. Nonnus was there already, using his grip on the javelin's butt to jerk the Archa away from the procurator. A second quick tug cleared the blade, now smeared purple. At no time did the hermit himself come within range of the creature's chitinous weapons.

Meder saw Sharina as she rose. "Oh dear mistress, you're wounded!" he cried. He held the copper athame as though he'd forgotten about it. She stepped back from the young wizard rushing to her side, afraid that he'd manage to prod her with the point.

"I'm all right," she muttered. She held the hand axe up to examine the edge. She ought to sharpen it for use as a weapon, but she wasn't sure there was a suitable abrasive surface in the citadel. The fine-grained gneiss had too high a polish for the purpose.

"Look, my art can heal you, mistress," Meder said. "Otherwise you'll have scars!"

He put his hand on her shoulder to turn her so that he could better see her wounds. She jerked away from the contact angrily.

"Meder!" Asera said as she rose without aid of the hand Wainer offered to help her. "What are you doing? This is all your fault and you're just standing here gaping!"

"I have to—" Meder said, turning his head.

"Leave me," Sharina said. "I'm fine."

"I—"

Nonnus stepped between Sharina and Meder. Very deliberately he lifted a fold of the wizard's tunic and used the velvet to wipe purple blood from his javelin point.

His eyes met Meder's eyes the whole time. The wizard

backed away, then turned to face the angry procurator.

"My art saved us from the storm," he said. "From both storms. I apologize for the—situation—but my art is the only thing that can save us now."

"I need to sharpen my hatchet, Nonnus," Sharina said in a small voice. Kizuta's crew was struggling with the lid again and the Blood Eagles had returned to defense of the entrance.

He nodded. "After we've finished your cuts," he said. "The edges that the altar slab covered might do, or we'll find something better."

Sharina knelt again and bowed so that the hermit could see her back. The wounds he hadn't reached yet had a hot, dull ache very different from the ointment's tingle.

"I'm going up to the highest tower to use my art!" Meder called. His voice sounded high against death's clashing cacophony.

Sharina didn't turn her head.

"You will have scars, child," Nonnus said as his gentle fingers touched her wounds.

"As bad as yours, Nonnus?" she asked.

The hermit laughed. "Raise your arm, now," he said. Then he added, "Not from this, child. But we're not off Tegma yet, are we?"

They laughed together. Death clanged and grunted around them.

21

Garric leaned his bow against the ancient holly oak, looking down the sloping pasture to the sea. The tide was out. Crows and shorebirds patrolled the flats while gulls wheeled overhead.

There were no seawolves in the surf today. The water twinkled like jade, cool and green and innocent. It was hard for Garric to believe that he'd almost died on a stretch of gravel that was empty even of birds today.

A sandpiper sprinted a few paces and rose in curving flight, keening a bitter cry. Garric turned and craned his neck in an effort to see the track leading westward to Carcosa. Even the hilltop wasn't high enough for that. Well, he'd be back up with the flock within the hour.

Benlo assumed that the thing Garric needed to do before he left the borough had to do with a person; a parent, a lover from whom the boy was taking his leave. The drover didn't mind so long as Garric rejoined before the first halt four miles west of the hamlet. Cashel could handle the flock alone—even Garric could have. The sheep didn't require two boys to badger them along.

Garric walked around the tree and squatted. The chape of his quiver touched the ground and the embroidered lid caught him in the ribs. He didn't usually wear it on his belt, so he wasn't used to allowing for it when he moved.

He twitched the case to the side. Benlo said he'd provide the boys with swords like those his guards wore. The idea was exciting, but Garric couldn't imagine the blade being more than an awkward weight in practice.

He was good with his bow and arrow. Nobody in Barca's Hamlet ever carried a sword, and Garric wasn't fool enough to believe that merely waving a length of steel made an enemy fall over. Even carving a roast took skill and experience.

Cashel hadn't asked where Garric was going; he'd just said that the flock would be no problem. Cashel rarely asked questions and even less often volunteered information of his own. A stranger might easily conclude that he was dull and harmless.

A ewe blatted in the grass nearby, responding to some stimulus known only to herself. Perhaps she was just happy that spring was here at last. Martan and Sanduri, two boys from the western end of the borough, were watching the remaining sheep while Cashel and Garric both were gone. Sanduri at least had a talent for the work.

Ilna hadn't asked where Garric was going, but her eyes had followed him as he left the flock in front of the inn and headed down the path south to the main pasture. He wondered why she was making the trip to Carcosa. Nothing Ilna did could truly be called a surprise, because her vision of the world was so obviously skewed from that of anyone else Garric knew. Like her brother, she kept her own counsel, but nobody would ever mistake Ilna for dull or stupid.

Garric took his shepherd's pipes out from under his belt and bowed to the little squared stone. At this time of day the carven face was in shadow, invisible against the pattern of gray-green lichen.

"Duzi," Garric said, "you're a small god and perhaps you can't help anyone beyond the borough. But I'm a peasant, an innkeeper's son; a small man. I'm leaving the only place I know, and there are things happening that I don't understand. Duzi, I would be grateful of any help you can give me in the coming days."

He set the pipes against the rock, in the position a shepherd would hold them in the moment before bringing them to his lips to play. Garric stood, feeling tears at the corners of his eyes. He didn't really know why it was he wanted to cry. For himself, he supposed.

He wiped his eyes angrily. "Guard the flock well, Duzi," he whispered. "Martan and Sanduri are young, but they'll learn if you watch over them."

Garric started back toward the road, taking a line that would bring him up with the sheep a quarter mile beyond the hamlet. No point in again striding past the houses and eyes of the folk he'd grown up with.

After a moment, Garric snugged the slack bowcord over his right shoulder to free his hands. He plucked daisies and braided them as he walked along. Liane might be amused by a chaplet. Perhaps he'd better weave *two* chaplets, one for either girl. . . .

Whistling, Garric strode through the spring pasture.

1

Cashel awakened suddenly in the stables of Dashen's Place. The sound that roused him wasn't one that his conscious mind could quickly identify in the night's muted buzz. He got up quietly, taking care not to disturb Garric in the straw beside him or Ilna and Tenoctris in the loft. With the quarterstaff in his hand, he walked through the part-open sliding door into the farmyard.

Dashen's Place was a working farm, but because it was located on the drove road to Carcosa the owner and his family provided inn facilities of a sort to travelers. The stables could hold ten horses, which were fed hay and grain from Dashen's fields; the paddock was large enough for two large flocks together; and there was a common room across the dogtrot from the main house where up to a dozen men could drink home-brewed ale, eat Dashen's produce, and sleep in straw beds.

Tonight Dashen and his family shared the common room with Benlo's guards. The drover had the couple's own chamber, while Liane slept where the four daughters of the house normally did. Garric might have been able to squeeze into the common room, but he'd said he preferred the stable.

As for Cashel, even if space had been available he'd have bedded down in either the stable or with the flock in the paddock. The sheep were his duty, and he wasn't going to be distracted from them by the sounds of close-spaced humans.

There was no breeze. The open air was noticeably cooler than the stable heated by the bodies of horses, mules, and humans, but the frogs were in full throat. Cashel could identify three of the smaller species nearby, and from the bottomland half a mile away came the grunt of a bullfrog signaling his hopes for love.

Insects were out as well. Bats dipped in the moonlight; occasionally Cashel heard their pulsing chitters.

He wondered if the frogs and bats of far lands were the same as those of this borough. He'd made up his mind to leave the folk with whom he'd lived all his life; now for the first time he wondered if he was giving up his whole life as well. Would even the stars be the same? Was he going to drift across the Isles like a branch fallen into the sea, never again at home?

Cashel gripped his staff with both hands and stifled a groan. He didn't know the future, but it didn't matter. He'd made up his mind to leave Barca's Hamlet, and so he would. He walked toward the paddock, making no more sound than fog gathering above a pond.

Ilna had worked off her costs. Dashen didn't need extra help to handle these out-of-season travelers, but the farmer wasn't about to refuse when Ilna offered to wash the pots for a bowl of stew, porridge in the morning, and straw in the stable to sleep on. His daughters would have pilloried him if he'd made them do the work instead.

Besides, this close to Barca's Hamlet, the folk all knew Ilna. Their pots would be as clean as they were the day they came from the kiln.

An owl called. The sound had no source, even to ears as trained as Cashel's. A few clouds hung in the moonlight, too straggling to be properly called cumulus. Clouds and drift-wood, crossing the world without a home or a fellow . . .

The sheep were restive though not exactly frightened. For a moment Cashel thought they were just nervous because of unfamiliar surroundings and the absence of some of their usual fellows. They crowded toward the near side of the en-closure; those at the back of the flock kept glancing toward the other end.

A weasel? Some predator too small to be a direct threat but nonetheless a concern to timid sheep . . .

Cashel saw it: a gray fox outside the paddock, scratching and whining as it tried to climb one of the posts. Cashel searched for a pebble in the moonlight. When he found a suitable one he rose and with it in his right hand paced silently around the enclosure. A shout would have spooked the fox, but it would also rouse folk sleeping in the house. No need for that.

Dashen had an extensive woodlot but less fieldstone than was common a few miles east on the coast. His paddock was built with vertical wooden posts supporting rails split from straight trunks. Hill-country sheep jump, so the rails were five feet in the air and the posts were taller yet.

The fox was trying desperately to reach a bluebird hole near the top of one of the posts. She was a vixen in milk, hunting for her kits back in the burrow, but Cashel was still surprised at her extreme degree of focus on a bird's nest. Gray foxes will climb trees, but her claws slid on the post's barkless surface. She hadn't figured out how to use the rails as a ladder to her goal.

Cashel rounded the paddock's corner twenty feet from the fox. He chose his point of aim and threw the pebble overhand, as straight as a sling bullet. It whacked into the vixen's haunch.

The fox yelped and turned a corkscrew in the air, snapping in terrified reflex. Tail streaming, she bolted into the darkness in a low crouch like a running cat.

Cashel brushed his palm on his tunic with a smile. *If foxes swear, I'm being cursed now.* He walked toward the post to see exactly what she'd been after.

He could easily have killed the fox instead of shooing her off with nothing worse than a sting and embarrassment. The pelt would fetch something, but the sheep wouldn't like the smell of it curing on the road.

Besides—and he wouldn't dare admit this to his sister— she was a vixen in milk. Let her find a meal for her kits; just not where she kept Cashel's flock from getting a good sleep.

He bent close to the hole, wondering if he could hear the

sound of birds within. This was too early in the year for the eggs to have hatched.

A woman four inches tall, as naked as a wax candle, stuck her head out of the hole, looked around, and started to climb down.

Cashel snatched her away from the post by reflex. He couldn't *believe* what he'd seen. He could feel her, warm and wriggling in his grip like a bird coming around again after being stunned against its own reflection.

He lifted his hand and spread his fingers slightly to let the moonlight through. He was holding a naked girl!

"By the Shepherd!" Cashel said. "What *are* you?"

"You can see me!" the girl said in amazed delight.

2

Thunder boomed. It seemed to come not out of the permanent overcast covering Tegma but from the high tower to which Meder had climbed. The wizard's voice drifted down to the battlements where Sharina stood watching the Archai prepare to attack the citadel.

"They're like ants," she said to Nonnus, pleased to note that her voice remained steady throughout the observation.

The hermit looked over the chest-high stone coping. There were no arrow slits as there would have been in a human defensive wall.

"If you really watch ants you'll see that they aren't very well organized, child," Nonnus said. "Certainly not as organized as those folk are."

The stone slab had blocked the mindless assaults up the citadel's entrance passage. A few sailors remained on duty there to make sure the Archai didn't dislodge the massive altar top, but six inches of hard stone prevented actual fighting.

In the courtyards surrounding the citadel, Archai mustered in battalions. Labor crews wound their way into the city from the mist-shrouded forest, bearing with them the trunks of tall trees.

The trees were tall enough to reach the upper levels of the citadel—to reach even the platform on which Meder practiced his art. The Archai waiting in tawny masses were the assault troops who would climb the trunks, using the coarse bark as a nonskid surface for their clawed limbs.

"You see?" Nonnus said. "They'd have built the city itself the same way. There's no need of magic to move heavy things. Just a lot of hands and good coordination."

Thunder rolled. Sharina looked at the tower and said bitterly, "Do you think he's trying to bring down lightning on the insects?"

Nonnus shrugged. "Lightning usually starts at the highest point around," he said.

Sharina smiled despite herself. "Do you think we might be that lucky?" she said.

The hermit laughed, then sobered immediately. "The problem isn't that Meder doesn't know what he's doing," he said. "None of us do, after all. We can only hope and pray. The problem with Meder is that he doesn't *realize* how little he knows. And he's very powerful."

Sharina and Nonnus stood on the citadel's third level with only the tower above them. Most of the surviving humans hadn't bothered to come so high: the Archai had no projectile weapons, so until the pole-mounted assault began the windowless concourse on the ground floor was perfectly safe.

No one would be safe when the assault began.

"Will you watch these for me, child?" Nonnus said. He handed Sharina his javelin, then undid the double knot that attached the sheath of the Pewle knife to his belt. "Things should be quiet for a little while longer."

"I—" Sharina said. "Yes, of course."

The javelin was heavier than she would have guessed. It was perfectly balanced, which meant that the butt end must be invisibly thicker than the other to match the additional weight of the steel head. She held it in one hand and the sheathed knife in the other along with her own axe.

"*Abonicticis eristhemia phalasti . . .*" Meder's voice droned. Words in a language known only by wizards and demons; and perhaps not really known by all the wizards who used it.

Sharina grimaced. Nonnus had gone to an angle of the building. He traced a design on the stone with a bit of charcoal. Sharina deliberately looked over the battlements again so that she wouldn't seem to be spying on her protector; on her friend.

The citadel could hold ten times the number of occupants without crowding, but there was no real privacy because there were no doors or material to make any kind of barricade. Everything but gold and the stone walls themselves had rotted to dust and less than dust during the ages Tegma lay beneath the sea. The trireme's crew and passengers had no means of defense or construction except the altar and the exiguous belongings they'd brought with them while fleeing from the unexpected attack.

On the open spaces of the citadel's battlements, a sailor with a knife and an Archa's slashing forelimbs were roughly equal; but there were thousands of Archai and only a few score crewmen. The double handful of armored soldiers couldn't affect the outcome significantly.

Murmured sound drew the girl's eyes reflexively. Nonnus was praying to a sketched outline of the Lady. Sharina turned her head in embarrassment.

Asera entered the battlements with a Blood Eagle following her; not Wainer. The soldier's right arm was bound against his chest with strips of his own tunic; his face was sallow beneath its tan.

The procurator glanced at the tower, then saw Sharina standing alone nearby and strode over to her. When Asera appeared her hands were clasped in front of her, but she straightened and took on a look of authority as she approached the girl.

"Has he made any headway?" she demanded, nodding in the direction of the tower. As if in answer, angry thunder rocked the sky.

"I don't know," Sharina said curtly. "I'm not interested in that."

"Not interested in saving your life, you mean?" Asera said. "You know we've no other hope—thanks to what the fool did to begin with. Wizards!"

"Not interested in saving my life that way," Sharina said.

The procurator was too nervous to pay attention to anything but her preoccupation of the moment. "He did save us from the storms," she muttered. "He just has to find the right formula."

She noticed Nonnus and said, "What's he doing there?"

She stepped toward the squatting hermit. Sharina's hands were full, so she couldn't just grab the procurator. She moved in front of Asera and checked her solidly with her shoulder. Sharina's flash of anger felt good after the hours of formless dread as she watched the Archai preparing to overwhelm the citadel.

The soldier yelped in surprise and tried to intervene. He collided with Asera as she jerked back angrily. "Idiot!" she snarled at the hapless man.

"My friend's praying," Sharina said in a husky voice, embarrassed at the way she'd reacted. What would her father have said if she'd done that to a guest of the inn? "Just let's leave him alone to pray."

"Well, maybe prayer will save us," Asera said in frustration. "I doubt it, but its getting late to depend on wizardry."

Nonnus suddenly stood at Sharina's side. He took the Pewle knife from her hand. "Actually," he said in a voice as light as his fingers' brushing contact, "I wasn't praying for victory. I like to think that fighting is men's business, not the Lady's."

He held the sheathed knife by the hilt in one hand and began fastening the ties to his belt with the other. The knots would have been an easier task for both hands together, but he wouldn't have been quite as ready to clear the knife in an emergency.

"I was praying to the Lady that the souls of those I've killed find peace in Her," Nonnus added as he finished the knots. He took the javelin from Sharina now that his hands were free.

"Killed?" the procurator repeated. "Who did you kill? Only insects that I've seen!"

Nonnus shrugged. "Insects, then," he said. "Killed by my hand nonetheless."

Wainer and seven more soldiers came through the doorway. The Blood Eagles looked worn; only three of them carried spears as well as their swords. They'd wiped the blood from their armor, but darkening purple stains stiffened their tunics and the soft leather backing.

"But they're not human!" Asera said.

Nonnus smiled faintly. "Perhaps," he said. "And if they're not, then it's better for one like me rather than a holy man to pray for their peace."

"Mistress?" Wainer said in a tone that combined diffidence with impatience. "The bugs are starting their attack. If you'll come with us into one of the inner rooms, we can best protect you there."

Sharina touched the hermit's arm and looked over the battlements. Crews of Archai were lifting the tops of the half-dozen giant tree trunks she could see. There were doubtless several times as many more on all sides of the citadel.

The creatures worked without machinery, using the slopes of buildings across the courtyard as hundreds of jointed limbs levered the boles to each next stage where hundreds more waited. Every surface Sharina could see was covered with tawny, chitinous bodies.

When the Archai had the trunks vertical, they would topple them onto the citadel. There weren't enough human defenders to shove away a single slanting bridge before the waiting warriors swarmed up it to attack; and there would be a score of simultaneous assaults.

"Nonnus, you're human," Sharina muttered in the hermit's ear. "No holy man was ever better than you!"

"Mistress Sharina!" Meder called. By squinting through the mist, Sharina could just make out the wizard's figure leaning over the coping of the high platform. "Mistress Asera! Come up! I've succeeded! I'm going to succeed!"

The procurator's expression turned to one of professional approval. "Come along, girl," she said crisply, tugging the sleeve of Sharina's tunic.

"I don't—" Sharina said.

Nonnus touched her between the shoulder blades, a fingertip pressure little greater than the legs of a butterfly lighting to drink sweat. The hermit's face wore a neutral smile, but his eyes were on the nine armed soldiers.

"Yes, all right, we'll go," Sharina said. She reached back with her free hand, the one that didn't hold an axe. Holding Nonnus firmly, she followed Asera to the winding ramp that climbed the tower.

3

Duzi help me!" Cashel said. He spread his fingers wide. "Forgive me, mistress!"

The tiny girl grabbed his thumb to keep from being accidentally spilled onto the ground. She giggled merrily.

"Oh, I'm so glad to have company again!" she said, swinging on his thumb like an acrobat. "It's been so *very* long."

She tossed herself up in a full somersault that landed her again in Cashel's palm. He had to override the reflex that told him to close his hand when he caught something.

"I'm Mellie," she said. She spoke in a melodious soprano, not loud but certainly not the piping bat-squeak he'd have expected for the voice of someone so small. She grinned up at him. "What's your name?"

"Ah?" said Cashel. "I'm Cashel or-Kenset. Mistress? You're a *sprite*."

She nodded, looking critically down at her shoulder. She flicked away a strand of spiderweb she'd picked up in the bluebird nest. She was really quite pretty; indeed, beautiful if you ignored the fact that she wasn't any bigger than his middle finger.

"That's right," she said nonchalantly. She fluffed her hair with both hands. It was red—not the orange-red of human hair but a true deep red that would have suited a tulip better than a flame.

"But sprites are just stories," Cashel said. "They're not real, I mean. I thought."

Mellie stood and climbed his arm with the effortless speed of a squirrel. She seemed to weigh almost nothing—even less than a being her size ought to weigh. "Well, there aren't very many of us," she said. "I wonder if you have sprite blood yourself?"

Cashel laughed. "Oh, mistress—" he said.

"Mellie!" she corrected tartly. "You're Cashel and I'm Mellie."

"Mellie," he agreed. He couldn't focus on the sprite when she was seated as now on his shoulder. That actually made it easier to carry on a conversation, since he wasn't distracted by the competing realizations that *this girl is only four inches tall!* and *this girl is stark naked!* "The difference in our size means, well, we couldn't very well be related."

Maybe sprites didn't understand human reproduction? Cashel felt a blush rising at the mere thought of trying to explain to someone who at least *looked* like a pretty girl.

Mellie's liquid silver laughter trilled across the moonlight.

"Oh, Cashel!" she said. "Someone with your powers should know better than that!"

He felt her touch his earlobe. She was standing, her body a friendly warmth against the side of his neck.

"We used to come and go from your plane all the time," she said. Her tone was studiously indifferent to the meaning of her words, as though none of it was of any real importance. "This plane is so exciting—very different from our own."

She chuckled, but the infectious humor of moments ago was gone from the sound. "After a thousand years, though, 'excitement' isn't quite the word I'd use to describe it. Especially recently when I've been alone."

Cashel raised his hand. She got into his palm without urging; he brought Mellie in front of him where she could meet his frowning gaze. "You're a thousand years old?" he said in wonder.

"Much older than that, Cashel," Mellie said. She looked as though she might be eighteen; might *possibly* be as old as eighteen. "We don't age, you see. Though on this plane we can die. We can be killed, I mean. And eventually that's happened to all of us that I know of; all of us here on Haft, at least."

The sheep had settled down; Cashel's presence and the sound of his soft voice probably did as much for their mood as his shooing off the fox had. He glanced skyward, uneasily aware that a screech owl which ordinarily ate grasshoppers could make a meal from the tiny woman in his palm.

"Why don't you just go home?" he asked. "You said you could."

"The fox was very insistent," Mellie said, answering Cashel's thought rather than his spoken words. "Thank you—but I hope she's all right?"

"I hurt her vanity," he said with a shrug. "Nothing worse than that. She'd have given up and gone away pretty soon anyway, I expect."

He didn't believe anything of the sort, though the paddock

post was hickory that the vixen couldn't have chewed through easily.

"Still," Mellie said, patting his palm with her own minuscule hand. Without changing expression she went on, "I said we used to be able to come and go. A thousand years ago when islands sank and the kingdom died, the paths got . . ."

She shrugged her tiny, perfect shoulders. "Twisted, I guess you'd say. The paths are still there and maybe they still reach my own plane, but in between they go through places that I wouldn't be able to go *through*."

"Yole sank," Cashel said, remembering Tenoctris' story. Should he talk to Tenoctris about seeing Mellie?

The sprite nodded. "Yole was one of them," she agreed. She went on, "Most people can't see us, but animals can. The fox was *very* insistent. I thought, well, that it might be over. And instead—"

She beamed at Cashel, a pixie in all senses of the word.

"—I met a friend!"

Cashel cleared his throat. He wanted to set Mellie back on the post or perhaps on the ground. Some place there wouldn't be a risk that he'd drop her.

"You know," he said, "you really ought to have a sword. Some kind of weapon at least. You could carry a thorn?"

She patted his palm again. "We don't use weapons," she said simply. "And as for a sword—we can't touch iron."

"Ah," Cashel said, feeling embarrassed. He'd turned down the sword Benlo offered, but only because he didn't think he'd be any use with it. The quarterstaff was a better weapon for him. If the drover had offered a big axe Cashel would've taken it. He'd used an axe many times, and a bandit would be no harder to hew than an oak tree.

"Well," he went on. "I need to be up in the morning—"

It was already getting close to first light.

"—and I guess you've got things to do too." Whatever did a sprite do? Did they even eat or sleep? "Would you like me to put you somewhere in particular?"

Mellie's face clouded. "Cashel?" she said. "I've been very lonely. Alone for the last hundred years, except for animals that . . . well, are animals. If you wouldn't mind terribly, could I ride along with you on your shoulder? I won't be any trouble. Your friends won't see me."

"Oh," Cashel said. His future a moment before had been a series of shutters through which darkness oozed. The shutters were flapping open, and light if not solid images lay beyond.

"I'd be very glad of your company, Mellie," Cashel said. "I understand what it means to be lonely."

4

The platform on top of the tower was oval, not round, and about seven feet through the slightly longer axis. It gave Sharina an even better view of the insects' preparations than she'd had from the battlements fifty feet below.

The preparations were over. She was viewing the Archan assault.

"Quickly, quickly!" Meder cried. "We have very little time! Get inside the circle at once, every part of your body!"

The circle was one he'd scribed on the gneiss; with the athame, Sharina assumed, but the line stood out in pulsing red as though the stone itself were on fire. It enclosed most of the platform; a double row of internally glowing symbols was written around its outside.

Meder knelt within, the squirming sack beside him. Pale blood already spattered the stone, and a salamander's drained corpse lay on the low coping. Its jaws lolled open to display the white membranes within.

Sharina felt her diaphragm tense. She started to turn back. Nonnus touched her again between the shoulders.

"Quickly!" the wizard cried.

The climbing poles had sprung up from the city's courts and the roofs of adjacent buildings like a sudden forest. They wavered in the windless air as hundreds of Archai, with the mindless precision of a school of fish, thrust with limbs and long poles to tilt them toward the citadel.

Warm mist blurred the workers' outlines, changing them from individuals into a force of nature as certain and inexorable as waves pounding the shore. Assault battalions waited in massed ranks to take up the task from the work crews.

Sharina stepped into the circle, careful not to put her foot on the line or the Old Script characters surrounding it. Salamander blood felt tacky on her bare soles but she was a girl from the countryside; blood didn't bother her.

What the blood stood for . . . that bothered her very much.

"You," Meder said. He pointed with the athame. "Nonnus. Come here and cut the lizard open when I tell you to. Squeeze it so that all the blood falls in the center of the circle."

Sharina hadn't been sure Meder knew the hermit's name. The air around the platform had a sullen tinge that wasn't quite a color. She was sweating profusely from the climb, but her heart was cold.

The severed trees tilted toward the citadel with glacial slowness. Workers set wedges beneath the base of each tree as the outer edge lifted. All twenty-odd vertical poles trembled inward together.

How did the Archai communicate? Sharina hadn't heard them make a sound except for the high-pitched wheeze as they died.

There was room for four people within the circle, but if they all knelt the way the wizard was doing their knees would be in contact. The circle's glowing boundary was a warning like the black and yellow bands of a hornet, and Sharina had the feeling that to be *outside* the circle might be more dangerous yet.

"No sir," said Nonnus calmly. "I don't work magic. Especially this kind of magic."

He turned his back on Meder, eyeing the tree which had been lifted to the roof of a two-story building to the north of the citadel. From its height and closeness, the tree could touch the platform on which the four of them stood; and since it still appeared to be vertical, Sharina knew it was slanting directly toward her.

"You ignorant savage!" the wizard screamed. "I need the athame as a pointer! You *must* do this if we're to survive!"

"Let's go back down, Nonnus," Sharina said in a cold voice. "I think we can find an easier place to defend."

"May the Sister drag you both down!" Asera said. "Give me the accursed animal, Meder. If I get out of this, I'll never have any truck with wizards again!"

As the procurator spoke, she fumbled in her writing case of black silk under a cutwork bronze sheath. She brought out a knife with a short steel blade, intended for sharpening quill pens.

The poles were toppling, all of them together like the feathers of a bird's wing—individual units acting in perfect uniformity. Nonnus stepped back very slightly and put a hand on Sharina's wrist to steady her.

Meder reached into the sack and brought out its remaining contents, a salamander with a black body, a tail flattened vertically for swimming, and an eye on either horn of the crescent-shaped wings of its skull. The beast moved feebly; its skin was meant to be immersed in water at all times, so the creature was dehydrated even in Tegma's humid atmosphere.

Meder bent over his symbols; Asera took the sacrifice with a look of disgust, holding it around the body just behind the forelegs. Neither noble could see the falling tree.

A dozen of the poles crashed down simultaneously, whacking the stone like a giant's drumsticks. The sound was lightning sharp; it squeezed blocks of stone hard against one another. Sharina flinched; Asera shouted in surprise and dropped her knife. Meder's lips moved, intoning a spell that the crackling chaos smothered.

So close was the Archan timing that the remaining dozen trees struck within the next half-second. The pole aimed at the tower platform was one of them. Bark and fibers of shattered wood sprayed like sand in a windstorm. The tree, four feet in diameter even here two hundred feet up the trunk, flattened noticeably and bounced high from the coping. The noise shocked Sharina into an unmeant scream, but the touch of Nonnus' hand prevented her from lurching out of the circle and perhaps off the platform itself.

Nonnus poised; for a heartbeat he must have been thinking of throwing his weight against the end of the tree before it came slamming down again to rest solidly on the platform coping. Sharina held him back. Despite the hermit's strength, even if he expended it with the perfect timing of which she knew he was capable, the tree's enormous mass would crush him like a bug.

The hermit relaxed. The tree hit again, flexed, and settled. Only two feet of the length projected onto the platform, but that was enough. The end was chipped square as neatly as a skilled man could have done with a broadaxe and unlimited time, but Sharina had seen the Archai use no tools save their own forelimbs.

"Now, woman, now!" Meder cried. "The blood now or it'll be too late!"

Warriors were already climbing the trunk. They moved like a yellow stain being absorbed up the coarse brown surface of the bark.

"Iakoub-ia ai bolchoseth iorbeth—"

Asera fumblingly picked up the quill knife. She looked shaken. Bark and splinters covered the back of her tunic and hung in her hair. She drew the blade down across the salamander's abdomen.

Meder hadn't moved even when the huge tree struck beside his head and made the very fabric of the tower shiver. His fearlessness proved his utter concentration. Even Nonnus had let the impact shock his mouth open in an unvoiced cry.

"*Neuthi iao iae—*"

The salamander curved its body away from the knife. The procurator, her senses numb from fear and the tree's crashing impact, slashed wildly. She opened the little creature in a spill of internal organs, but she cut into the inside of her thumb as well. Pale amphibian blood mixed with drops of bright scarlet splashed to the stone.

"*Io sphe io io—*"

The chitinous warriors were only halfway to the tower platform, but those directed up other poles toward the lower battlements were already locked in combat with the handfuls of human defenders. Tawny masses spread over the stone, their edged forelimbs held high.

"*Abraoth!*" Meder shouted.

Red light curled like smoke from where the blood had spilled. The stone seemed to bubble, but Sharina could see that the block's smooth surface was really unaffected beneath the seething light.

The Archan warriors walked rather than climbed up the side of the pole. Their feet had sharp edges that bit like climbing spurs into the bark. The nearest of the attackers was only twenty feet below; Nonnus readied his javelin to stab, not throw.

The coil of light from the incantation continued to rise, but it remained a narrow corkscrew rather than the spreading bubble which had enveloped Tegma and returned its inhabitants to life. At its top the helix turned the clouds overlying the mist into a pulsing ruddy blur.

"I need more blood!" the wizard cried. "Squeeze it! Squeeze it!"

He flung the sack inside out, proving what its flat folds had made obvious before: he'd used all the sacrificial animals. When Meder tried to grasp the flaccid corpse on the coping beside him, his haste bumped it over the edge instead. He'd completely drained the body anyway.

The leading Archa stepped onto the coping. Nonnus thrust

it through the upper torso. The creature grasped the javelin shaft with its middle pair of limbs, trying to twist the weapon from Nonnus' hands.

Sharina leaned forward and struck with the hand axe, chopping through what would have been the ankle joint in a human. The Archa toppled sideways from the pole. Gravity dragged the javelin out of its grip and pulled the blade from the gaping wound in the creature's thorax.

"Don't cross the circle!" Meder cried in desperate terror.

The second warrior cut at Sharina's head but struck the interposed javelin instead. She swung the axe backhand because she didn't have time to raise it for a proper blow. The creature's abdomen thumped like a struck log. An upward slash of the Pewle knife opened it in a purple spray. The Archa curled backward in a convulsion which spread the wound even wider.

Asera had fallen to her knees, covering her face with her hands. Meder snatched the dead salamander from her and wrung it like a towel. The ruby spiral continued to rise; it rotated faster than before, but it was still a narrow tendril into the clouds.

Six sailors fought for a moment on the battlements immediately below. The tide of Archai swept over them; the warriors' forelimbs rose and fell alternately, hacking their victims apart. Drops of scarlet blood spattered twenty feet in the air.

"Get back!"

Nonnus reached around Sharina's waist with the hand that held his big knife, drawing her back as she raised the axe to strike the next Archa. The creature poised to jump into the midst of the group of humans.

Meder's spinning red column filled the magic circle. The light was like that of the heart of a furnace, but there was no heat at all. Sound stopped, even the screaming of the men being killed in the Archan assault.

As suddenly as a shutter falling, the circle was clear and lightless. The fiery glow spun from the outer edge, enveloping all beyond at the speed of a wind-driven brush fire.

The nearest Archa shriveled, twisting away like a stick figure of itself drawn with charcoal. The creatures following up the pole in close succession flailed their limbs or tried to jump aside as the flame-red light swept toward them. Contact was death as surely as a candle devours the moth it draws within.

Hideous human screams came from within the citadel. The light destroyed not only the Archai it engulfed.

The pole was untouched, but roaches and other insects prowling crevices in the bark blackened and died just as the Archai did. The wizard's spell affected only living animals; but *all* living animals were affected.

Were killed. Except for the four humans sheltering within the magic circle.

The light poured out like blazing lava, reaching the outer walls of the city and continuing to flow unchecked. Despite the mist, Sharina could follow the spell's progress over stone and through the forest as though she were watching in a ruby mirror.

Every creature she saw was dying. Every single creature.

The fiery doom paled and finally vanished. Memory of it lingered in Sharina's mind, especially when she shut her eyes. The sun was low in the western sky.

Tegma was as silent as a tomb.

Meder lay sprawled on the corpse of the sacrificed amphibian. His face was as pale as carven ivory, but his breath stirred the layer of powdered bark on the stone.

The procurator rubbed her slimy, bloody hands over one another as if washing. She probably wasn't aware of what she was doing. Her lips moved in silent entreaty, perhaps praying to the gods she was too sophisticated to believe in.

Sharina looked down at the wizard. Part of her wanted to leap off the platform and fall to a clean death on the stones below. Another part wanted to bury her axe in Meder's skull before she flung herself into oblivion.

The hermit's face was without expression. He wiped the

blade of his knife on his black wool tunic, then sheathed the weapon again.

"It'll be easier to finish the dugout now," Nonnus said, "since we'll be able to take what we need from the trireme's fittings."

5

The Gravel Ford Inn on the Stroma River was eighteen miles, two days' drive for a flock of sheep, from the outskirts of Carcosa. In the common room Garric's body slept with a score of other men: Benlo's guards, wagoners bringing produce into the city, boys going to seek their fortune.

There was always traffic this close to the capital. The innkeeper had an income that Reise would have envied, though Reise would never have allowed rushes so filthy to lie on the floor of *his* inn.

Garric's dream self watched King Carus climb the escarpment of Ladera Castle on a bright spring day. Fifty men followed him, using the fingers and toes of three limbs to grip while the other limb rose to a new hold as slowly as a snake stalks a field mouse.

"We couldn't wear armor, not even helmets," Carus said. He and dream Garric leaned on a rail, but the structure to which the railing was attached blurred at the edges of vision. The landscape, the castle, and the forlorn hope creeping up its walls were in a different time and place. "If anybody'd looked down from the walls, they could have wiped us out by dropping handfuls of gravel off the battlements."

He laughed with rollicking joy. "I was only a few years older than you then, lad," he said. "Just ascended to the throne and too young to know what the risks were. But I was right: it had to be done or the kingdom would have crumbled right then instead of in twenty years, after we sailed for Yole. . . ."

The king's voice sobered as he continued speaking, not into sadness but with a kind of steely anger. If anything his tone grew lighter, flexing like a bowstaff coming to full nock.

In the sea below Ladera Port and the castle at its western end was a fleet of over a hundred war galleys, bow-on to the shore. Their oars moved sluggishly, just enough to hold station against the ebbing tide. Bronze rams dipped and lifted with the swell. Troops were winding back the arms of the catapults on the vessels' foredecks.

"Because of the weight?" dream Garric asked. He'd climbed the fangs of rock off the shore north of Barca's Hamlet every nesting season since he was twelve, coming down with a basket of green, tangy guillemot eggs in his teeth. It made his fingertips ache to watch the climbing soldiers. At least they didn't have salt spray drenching them as their friends waited below at the oars of a small boat.

"Because of the noise," Carus said, his voice soft and cheerful once more. "One clink of steel on stone and Count Rint of Ladera would have been King of the Isles—at least until one of fifty more usurpers cut him down."

Men stood on the castle's battlements, even here on the south side, but all the guards were looking toward the sea and the threatening fleet. Carus, his dark hair restrained by a golden fillet, wore his long sword in a sheath strapped to his back where it was out of the way until needed.

A catapult fired from the castle wall, the arms slapping loudly against their stops as the head-sized missile sailed toward the ships in a flat arc. The stone splashed into the sea among the oarblades of the quinquireme whose gilded prow marked her as the royal flagship. Iridescent water spouted higher than the mast of a ship under sail.

"Wouldn't it have been safer to attack at night?" Garric asked. The figure of the young king was only a few feet below the lip of a tower on which a pair of Laderan guards craned their necks to see the fleet over the castle's opposite walls.

The older Carus shook his head. "It had to be by daylight so that they'd be watching the ships," he said. "They never dreamed that I'd landed the night before with fifty men and crept to the scrub at the back of the castle in the dark."

The young king came over the battlements in a twisting leap that an acrobat would have envied. The guards turned. The long sword was in Carus' hand, striking right and left like twin strokes of lightning. More men swarmed onto the walls, overwhelming the handful of guards on this less-threatened sector before they could even give the alarm.

"And with your help, lad," Carus said again in a voice like sun quivering on a sword edge, "I'll settle things yet with the Duke of Yole."

"Sir, he's dead," the dream Garric protested. "Dead a thousand years!"

Carus shook his head, his eyes on troops running to complete the capture of Ladera Castle. Defenders were already leaving the walls, throwing away weapons and their armor to surrender as unarmed civilians.

"All times are one time, lad," he said. "Later is as good as sooner."

The troops were shouting as they flooded into the castle. The shouts grew louder.

"Attack! Attack!" a man cried.

Someone stumbled over Garric sleeping in the darkness. He lurched to his feet in the Gravel Ford Inn, fully awake but still blinking with the bright dream daylight of a moment before.

"Attack!" the man outside warned. It was Cashel shouting.

Garric groped for the weapons lying beside his bed of woven straw. The bow would be useless at night. He grasped the hilt of the sword the drover had given him and ran for the door along with Benlo's guards.

As Garric's hands started to draw the sword, he felt the laughing form of King Carus merge with him.

6

Cashel awoke from dreamless sleep, his skin prickling. The warm, sweet smell of the flock filled the night; but the sheep were up and pacing too, and there was a faint odor which didn't belong.

He'd been sleeping beneath a wagon parked next to the sheep pen. The wagoner was glad of his presence, because it saved him the need to stay with the load of pottery on a night that looked like rain. Strangers rightly trusted Cashel or-Kenset the way they trusted the sun to rise in the east and the earth not to open beneath their feet.

"Cashel?" Mellie said in his ear. "Somebody's using powers very close by. I don't think they mean well."

A wagoner's ox lowed a nervous challenge from the adjacent cattle pen. The Gravel Ford Inn had separate enclosures for sheep and cattle, and a horse corral besides for those times when there were more riders and pack animals than the stables could accommodate under cover.

It was dangerous to enclose strange horses and oxen together. An energetic horse might kick and bite its neighbor out of nervous irritation; but an ox has horns as well as a temperament beneath its stolid exterior, and not infrequently the ox will finish the fight a horse started. Better to quarter the species apart.

Cashel rolled out from between the wheels, leaving his long traveling cloak on the ground where he'd been lying. He cinched his belt tight over his tunic and surveyed the night with the quarterstaff in his hand.

It wasn't rain Cashel smelled in the air, nor the Stroma River either. There was a salty tang that was out of place so far from the sea; and there as the smell of corruption, of things long dead.

"It's coming closer," Mellie warned. She didn't sound frightened; just alert, like a squirrel high on a trunk following the prowling dog with its eyes.

The inn was even older than the one in Barca's Hamlet. For centuries the Stroma River had been crossed by a bridge raised on pilings above the surface of the river even at flood stage, but the inn's name hadn't changed.

The abutments of the present bridge were Old Kingdom masonry, relics which survived the fall of the span they'd anchored and the civilization of which they were a part. The inn's outbuildings reused ashlars from the villas of wealthy folk of former times.

Nothing unusual seemed to be stirring. With the quarter-staff balanced in his hands, Cashel walked around the paddock toward the river. Water gurgled against a retaining wall that had been ancient when the Old Kingdom fell; the smell of salt and death was stronger.

"Cashel!" Mellie said. Figures rose from behind the retaining wall with a mechanical suddenness. Starlight glimmered on rusty metal and wetly gleaming flesh.

They were liches like the one which Garric killed in the inn yard, but there were many of them this time: more than Cashel could be sure of in this uncertain light. One had a shield which trailed strands of seaweed.

"Attack!" Cashel shouted. "Attack!"

His first thought was for the sprite on his shoulder, but he didn't dare take the time to put her in a place of safety. He stepped forward, using his staff as a spear. The iron ferrule crunched all the bones from wrist to elbow in a lich's arm.

The creature dropped its rusty sword, then picked it up in the other hand. It came on again unaffected, though jellylike flesh and bits of bone sloughed from the shattered limb.

"Attack!" Cashel cried, backing swiftly. Most of the liches ignored him and strode toward the inn, but he still faced three of the monsters.

He spun the quarterstaff overhead; when a lich thrust a spear at his midriff, the ferrule whacked the point aside; Cashel's overhead stroke with the other end crushed the creature's skull. *That* lich collapsed into a dripping pool and stayed down. The other two came on, inhumanly murderous, slightly flanking him from either side.

The first of Benlo's guards spilled out of the inn's door, hacked twice into the lich confronting him on the flagstone porch, and fell when another monster chopped him with a broad-bladed axe. The guard's sword still flopped from the chest of the lich he'd stabbed but not put down.

Cashel blocked a cut from the one-armed lich. The sword-blade was corroded; there were even barnacles on the steel. Nonetheless the stroke was fierce enough to chip wood from the hard hickory staff.

More guards came out of the inn, shouting in hoarse amazement. Steel clanged and flashed red sparks as men met the liches' attack.

Cashel grunted as his heel hit the wall of the paddock. He'd backed as far as he was going to go.

He supposed Mellie would be all right. She'd lived a thousand years without him, after all.

7

Ilna felt the warmth wrap softly around her. She wriggled in pleasure at its embrace. "I'm coming closer," the darkness whispered. "I'll be with you soon."

She couldn't see its face—she didn't know if it had a face—but she knew that it cared for her as no one else could care. It would make sure she became what she *deserved* to be.

Cashel's shout ripped through the dream like a icicle plung-

ing from a high tower. Ilna shot bolt upright from her bed in
the stable loft. The word hadn't penetrated, only the awareness that the brother she'd cared for all her life was in trouble.

"Attack!" Cashel shouted again. Steel met steel in a ringing crash.

Tenoctris was already halfway down the ladder; she'd
awakened before the shout. The older woman must have
heard something in her sleep just as Ilna did.

Rather than wait for Tenoctris to reach the bottom of the
ladder, Ilna gripped the edge of the loft and swung down. Her
feet dangled in the air for a moment; then she let herself drop
in the assumed confidence that there was nothing but the hard-
packed earthen floor beneath her.

"Attack!"

The shock of a three-foot fall into darkness was nothing.
Cashel was in trouble.

Most of the dozen stalls were occupied by horses or mules.
A mare screamed nervously and kicked her box. The stableboy was trying to quiet her, but all the animals were whick-
eringly restive.

There were more shouts and the clang of weapons from
the inn yard. Ilna had been slow to rise, wrapped in her fantasy of contentment. Thinking back, she couldn't pick a single
dream image from memory; and the whole, the gorgeous par-
adise that had enfolded her, had an aftertaste like that of rotting meat.

A man screamed in a voice that rose in pitch until it
stopped as abruptly as glass breaking. Ilna slid open the stable
door. By the open sky's relative light, her eyes searched for
a weapon. Tenoctris scurried past.

Ilna knew that there were rakes and forks in the stables
somewhere, but she didn't have time to search. Hanging from
a peg on the doorpost was a simple halter, a rye-straw rope
spliced into a bight on one end with the other reeved through
to form a running loop. She snatched it down and stepped
into the yard.

Tenoctris seated herself cross-legged by the corner of the

stable building and plucked a blade of the long grass growing from a seam in the stone foundation. A dozen men and liches fought in a confused mass in front of the inn proper. Cashel wasn't among them: his bulk would have marked him to her eyes.

There wasn't anyone as tall as Garric in the melee either, but bodies lay on the stones for living fighters to trample.

Garric burst from the inn's door, holding a sword in one hand and the doorkeeper's long-legged stool in the other. *"Haft and the Isles!"* he bellowed like a herd bull challenging the world.

A lich cut at him. Garric blocked the sword with the stool's seat, stabbed the lich through the eyesocket with a return stroke as quick as a frog's tongue, and smashed the skull of a second monster with a backhand flick of the stool.

Cashel stood across the inn yard, fighting two liches with his back to a stone wall.

"Haft and the Isles!"

Ilna's blood was as cold as a midwinter storm. She sprinted the fifty feet to where her brother defended himself.

The liches moved as though they were the limbs of a single entity: one drew back as the other thrust, then reversed the process the instant Cashel focused his attention on the immediate threat. The creatures reminded Ilna of a praying mantis shifting its weight from side to side as it prepares for the double stroke that will doom its victim.

Cashel knew better than to fight opponents working in perfect unison; instead he concentrated on defending himself. The quarterstaff spun as a dynamic shield before him, its motion as smooth and assured as the shuttle of Ilna's loom.

Cashel's wrists crossed and recrossed, feeding the heavy staff from one hand to the other. He'd get tired eventually, even Cashel; but for now the blurred rotation was as strong and sure as water flowing down the channel of the Stroma River. The liches poised and feinted, but they could not pierce his guard.

Ilna stepped behind one of the creatures, judged her distance, and flipped the loop of the halter as the lich swayed. The rope settled over the hairless, glistening skull. Ilna pulled hard as though she had a stubborn ram in the halter.

The lich jerked backward. A man would have gagged, but this creature twisted and tried to cut the halter with its rusty sword. Ilna ran three steps to pull the lich off its feet; the halter was too short for her to take another hand-over-hand grab on her end.

Cashel shifted the quarterstaff from vertical to horizontal and tore the ribs out of his remaining opponent in the same spinning motion that had protected him for the several previous minutes. The creature fell like a bird with a shattered wing; its sword arm still slashed, but its body could no longer keep itself upright.

Ilna's lich cut at her ankles. She leaped high without letting go of the halter. Cashel took a stride forward and brought the iron-shod cap of his staff down like a thresher swinging his flail. Gelatinous flesh and fragments of bone splashed in all directions.

"Ilna?" Cashel gasped. "Did he hurt you?"

Across the inn yard Garric laughed like a joyous demon. Ilna turned. All the liches were down. Guards and other travelers stood to either side gaping, but Garric was alone in the midst of the carnage.

The sturdy stool in his left hand had been hacked and beaten to splinters; little remained but one leg and fragments of the seat. Garric's blade was twisted like a ribbon fluttering in the breeze.

"*Haft and the Isles!*" Garric shouted. He spun his battered sword high into the air, then as it fell caught it again by the hilt. As though the spinning blade had cut the strings holding him upright, Garric toppled face-first onto the pile of bodies, lich and human.

Ilna ran toward him, but the drover's beautiful daughter Liane darted from the inn to Garric's side before her.

8

It's moving!'' Meder cried as he leaned into the hawser which the four of them were trying to drag up the slope. Nonnus had reeved the other end through a three-hole block joining the dugout's mast to the ram of the trireme. "Is it moving?"

"Pull!" the hermit said.

The dugout's lower hull groaned as it began to slide down the stone ramp. The vessel's own weight drove moisture from its soggy underside as it pressed against the unyielding gneiss.

"It's moving!" Meder repeated.

Sharina staggered forward, picking up the pace as inertia began to work for instead of against them. She trod on Asera's heels. Nonnus held the head of the rope; Sharina was at the lower end near the water. The nobles were between them. Neither Asera nor the wizard had been any real help on the drag, but Sharina wouldn't have allowed them to stand aside even if Nonnus had been willing. Sometimes the principle of a thing is more important than the thing itself.

Always the principle of a thing is more important than the thing itself.

They'd only crudely shaped the log. Nonnus had been particularly scornful of his own handiwork, but his intention had from the first been for the simplest possible dugout, fitted with twin outriggers for stability and a mast for a sail cut down from the trireme's own canvas. A high degree of finish would improve the vessel's looks, make it sail better, and increase the comfort of its crew; but more work meant more time.

The survivors wanted to leave Tegma's deathly silence as soon as humanly possible.

The dugout was moving briskly. "Sharina, board and cast off!" Nonnus.called.

Sharina dropped the rope and jumped lightly onto the dugout as it slid along past her. They didn't have the manpower to launch the vessel by brute force, so Nonnus had rigged the block and tackle to make up for the deficiency. The most seaward point they could reach to attach the tackle was the trireme's bow. Though the warship was solidly ashore, the several feet of water lapping its seaward extremity were enough to float the dugout, overweight though it was.

"Pull as if you're a man!" Nonnus said. Meder must have let go of the rope when Sharina did. "Pull!"

The dugout hit the water with a splash; the bluff bow porpoised and the vessel skewed sideways. Those on shore needed to continue hauling until the vessel was wholly afloat to save untold additional effort.

Sharina hopped over the sail and stood in front of the mast. The tackle ended in a bight attached to another bight on the mast by means of a thigh-thick wooden pin. Removing the pin was the only thing necessary to release the dugout, but that could be done only when the vessel floated free and took the tension off the tackle.

"Ready!" Sharina called. The dugout wallowed and began to swing starboard, away from the tackle's pull to port. Nonnus had taken the end of the port outrigger in his hand and by a combination of lifting and pulling was straightening the vessel's line. The two nobles were still on the rope, pulling with effort but no apparent understanding of the process.

They'd packed the stores under nets in the dugout's belly before they attempted the launch. There'd been some grain aboard the trireme; scarcely a bite for the full complement of hundreds, but a week's supply for the four of them who'd survived the Archan attack and Meder's wizardry. There was a jug of oil, several bunches of root vegetables, and fresh water in plenty: four tarred casks, as much as Nonnus thought the dugout could safely carry.

They had no meat, but the hermit thought he'd be able to

catch fish with dough balls. The bodies of creatures killed in the fighting spoiled quickly in the humid warmth, and there was no animal life remaining on the island.

"Cast off, child!" Nonnus shouted. "Board, you two!"

Sharina kicked down at the pin with her right heel. The wood gave but not enough: the ropes or the wood itself must have swelled since Nonnus had determined the fit.

The dugout bobbed as Nonnus lifted himself over the stern in a motion as graceful as a fish leaping. Sharina tugged the hand axe from her sash and whacked the wood hard with the back of the blade. The pin dropped and the tackle slid over the side, drawn by its own weight.

Crying for help, the nobles splashed through the calm water and grabbed the stern. The hermit ignored them as he prepared to spread the sail. Sharina took a pole cut from an oar and set her weight against it, fending the dugout away from the ramp. They'd launched just as the tide turned, but the harbor water was so still that the ebbing current was no real help.

Nonnus gestured. Sharina stepped over the spar and walked backward along the starboard rail with her seated pole, thrusting the dugout seaward without changing her own position relative to the shore. When she reached the stern, she laid down the pole and reached over the side to lift aboard first Asera, then Meder, with smooth, strong pulls.

Though Sharina kept her face blank, she was contemptuous of the nobles' inability to carry out simple physical tasks. They were both in good health and Meder at least was fairly muscular. She thought of her mother fawning over the pair in Barca's Hamlet . . . and her own marvel that folk so fine would notice *her*.

The dugout's mast had been the trireme's bowsprit; the spar on which Nonnus was raising the sail had been one of the warship's long upper-bank oars. The trireme's mast, split neatly in half, formed the twin outriggers which two more oarshafts bound to the dugout.

It had been easier to cannibalize the warship for the fittings than to shape Tegma's raw vegetation, and the seasoned wood was preferable anyway. The hull was only part of the new vessel which hadn't came from the trireme.

Meder lay panting in the belly of the vessel. "Look at my hands!" he wheezed. His rope burns were worse than Sharina would have expected for the slight help Meder's efforts had been to the process. "I could have launched us without all this tugging and splashing. By using my art!"

"No," said Nonnus as he tied off the sail's lift to a bitt at the base of the mast. "Because I wouldn't have let you."

He walked to the stern, moving with the delicacy of a gull stepping over a swelling wave. "Give me room," he ordered, "but stay back of the mast."

Nonnus took one of the two paddles; Sharina already held the other. They began stroking the dugout forward. Asera and Meder huddled near the mast and spoke in muted voices.

The sail was limp, the air so still that Sharina couldn't feel its motion on her damp skin. Mist already shrouded Tegma's shore, and she thought the sound of waves breaking on the reefs was louder.

She glanced over her shoulder. Nonnus smiled at her in satisfaction. His strokes with the makeshift paddle looked so smooth that only the wake curling behind the blade indicated how extremely powerful they were.

The fog thinned. There was a breeze and it cut like a knife of frozen glass, though Sharina realized that she'd probably have luxuriated in the warmth if she were back on Haft. The days of muggy heat had thrown her body's temperature control awry.

They'd crossed an invisible barrier between worlds. The world in which the risen Tegma existed was behind them. The chill wind came from the world into which Sharina had been born, the real world.

Breakers growled an angry warning. The fog was thinning. Sharina could see foam now, around coral heads like the molars of walruses that grind the hardest shellfish into sand and less than sand. Low vegetation wavered on the rocks, dark against the surf's white warning. The reefs were just as dangerous to a vessel trying to escape as to one thrown against them from the open sea.

Nonnus tucked his paddle under the mesh of a cargo net. Taking two additional turns in the sheet to the port edge of the sail, he adjusted the angle of the canvas to the wind; the bow swung slightly. The dugout was monstrously unhandy in comparison to a Haft fishing boat, but Nonnus wouldn't have risked this escape without the expectation of success.

The sun was just risen; it had been noon an hour before on Tegma, and the blurred red ball had throbbed down through the mist. Here gulls wheeled and called. A large body slid from the reef into the open sea, unseen save for the splash.

The reefs were a solid curving line, foaming as they prepared to receive the dugout and its passengers. Another seawolf dived into the water to wait.

If I looked into the lagoon now, would I see buildings sunk for thousands of years? But the water was gray with foam, opaque more than a few feet below the surface.

Nonnus canted the steering oar. He slacked the starboard sheet and took several more turns around the port bitt. The vessel continued to swing sluggishly. The surf snarled louder as they neared. Meder and Asera looked around in growing agitation; Meder scrabbled at the net covering some of the provisions and his case of magical paraphernalia.

Sharina glared at them stonily, but her own heart was cold. She'd seen the scraps of wreckage thrown up on the strand of Barca's Hamlet, heavy timbers smashed and clawed before being spat out by the reefs of a distant sea.

By the reefs of Tegma.

"There!" the hermit shouted. Gripping the tiller bar in his teeth, he loosed the port sheet and drew the starboard line taut. The dugout's slow turn reversed, bringing the bow again on a direct heading for the reef. A gap showed between two coral heads, but even that spit water high before drying on the surf's ebb stroke.

The breeze freshened. The dugout gained speed, hastening

toward the rocks with suicidal enthusiasm. Although the wind was behind them, spray from the waves' impact spattered Sharina's face.

"When I call you," Nonnus said, shouting to be heard over the hammering surf, "run all the way back to me. Now, *run!*"

The nobles were already up, terrified by the onrushing rocks. Meder hadn't managed to get his case out of the cargo net. He and Asera scrambled over the provisions.

Nonnus hopped onto the stern transom, clinging to the fall supporting the spar as he balanced over the foaming sea. Sharina threw herself into the far stern, the place the hermit had vacated. The steering oar wobbled unnoticed.

The bow rose as the passengers shifted their weight to the stern. Nonnus loosed the fall, dropping the sail with a bang of the spar on the gunwales. The dugout's thick hull struck the reef, scraping over and through the coral on momentum. If the sail had been set, the shock would have snapped the mast off at its base.

The dugout ground to a halt midway over the reef. "Forward!" the hermit shouted. "Into the bow for your *lives'* sake!"

Sharina leaped over the nobles, another pair of obstructions to her course. Nonnus was already raising the sail again. Sharina hopped over the spar. Asera and Meder, though reacting faster than they might have done, had to wait for the wet canvas to rise out of their way.

Sharina climbed onto the bow and grabbed the forestay. Spray shot high about her. The nobles clambered to her side, hunched over and gripping the gunwale as well as the support rope.

The dugout tilted minusculely downward and began to move again. The mast and the sail's center of force were forward of where the reef gripped the hull.

The dugout slid into open sea. The thick, one-piece vessel was scraped, but it had withstood its battering progress through the reefs as no planked ship could have done.

Sharina heard the waves roar in frustrated anger behind them.

9

Who did it?'' Garric demanded, hearing in his voice a
barely suppressed echo of King Carus speaking in a
tone that *would* be obeyed. ''Who sent the liches
against us, Benlo?''

The drover sat on an upturned feed trough beside the stables, working the tongue of his belt in and out of its loop as
a way to occupy his hands. Garric stood in front of him;
Cashel stood behind, looking more like a bank of storm
clouds than anything human.

The inn yard glittered with torches, lanterns, and an occasional candle that was likely to gutter out in the breeze. Folk
bent close to dead liches to be sure of what they were seeing,
then rose with exclamations of horror and disgust. A wounded
guard was moaning; men talked in high, nervous voices about
what had happened and what might easily have happened.

''I don't know,'' Benlo said. His tone wavered between
anger and genuine concern. He glanced past Garric in momentary appraisal.

''Your guards want to know the truth more than they want
to prevent us from forcing the truth from you,'' Garric said
in a low, dangerous voice. ''The survivors do, I mean.''

Cashel grunted. Garric had never seen his friend so angry
before. As soon as he was sure Ilna and Garric were all right,
Cashel had walked Benlo to this seat out of the immediate
way. When the drover tried to protest, Cashel had lifted his
feet off the ground with the strength of the arm that didn't
hold his quarterstaff.

''Why were you searching for Garric?'' Tenoctris asked.
She sat cross-legged in front of the drover with a blade of
grass in her hand, as though she were a child playing in the

dust. If Garric squinted in just the right way, he saw faint trails of blue hanging in the air after the grassblade flicked through it.

"I can't answer that," Benlo said. His voice hardened, "No, I *can't*. All I know is that I was asked to follow a certain trail and to bring back what lay at the end of it if I could. I've broken no laws. I've done no harm and I *mean* no harm."

He pointed his hand imperiously, index and middle fingers extended together, in the direction of the road to Barca's Hamlet. "Go on back to your sheep pasture, boy," he said, "if that's what you want to do. But I didn't bring the liches on you and nothing you do to me will make them leave you alone. I wouldn't even have known what to call them if your friend here—"

He nodded toward Tenoctris.

"—hadn't told me."

Garric remembered the fight as a spectator, though it had been his body slashing liches down like ripe grain. He'd moved fast and struck with lethal assurance, though part of him was aware that the sword's style and balance made it inferior to any blade he'd have chosen for himself. The stool was both weapon and defense; he'd fought liches before and struck for their skulls with either hand, never making a false motion.

He'd been cut once, across the back of the right calf by a lich that one of Benlo's guards had put down without killing. Garric remembered kicking and being surprised when his bare heel instead of a hobnailed bootsole crunched hard against jelly-coated bone. He'd stabbed down then without bothering to look at the target. His sword rasped through the thin bones of the nasal cavity and into the vault that would have contained the brain of a living being.

With only that fractional delay, Garric had proceeded to dispatch the liches still on their feet. He'd seen it all, he remembered it all; but it hadn't been Garric or Reise fighting.

He'd never held a sword in his hand till Benlo gave him one to carry.

He touched his tunic where the medallion of King Carus hung. He said, "Who sent you to find me?"

Benlo shook his head. He'd relaxed slightly, aware by now that the youths wouldn't harm him without reason and apparently confident that there was no reason why they should.

"I don't know," he said. His eyes moved past Garric again, this time in the direction of his daughter. Liane stood alone but just within earshot, staring at her father with a face as still as marble.

Benlo winced with embarrassment but he continued, "I was given funds by a banker in Erdin with instructions to follow a particular trail. The banker certainly didn't know what I'd find at the end of it, and I doubt his principal—I have no idea who the principal was—knew either. Otherwise I'd have been told more."

While Tenoctris murmured a spell, Liane had dressed the cut on Garric's leg. She said her teachers in Valles had been a renounced order of Daughters of the Lady; they'd taught their charges the practical skills of nursing as well as deportment and literature. The bandaged calf stung but even that was barely noticeable if Garric kept his weight off the leg.

"What kind of trail?" Cashel growled. He picked up a handful of straw and began wiping his staff clean of clinging matter. Garric knew Cashel had given the warning, but he had no recollection of what his friend had been doing during the fight.

Ilna stood beside Garric, her eyes on Benlo's daughter rather than the drover himself. She held a rope halter, running the fall in and out of the loop as she measured Liane's throat.

"It's a . . ." Benlo said. He fluttered his hands as though trying to churn words out of the air. "It has to do with a form of art. I can't explain it to you because you don't have enough knowledge to understand."

"You can't explain it," Tenoctris said with more of an edge than Garric had ever expected to hear in the old woman's voice, "because you're too pig ignorant yourself to understand the forces you're putting in motion."

"What?" said Benlo. Cashel pushed down on his shoulder.

Tenoctris turned to look up at Garric, smiling faintly. Perhaps she'd surprised herself with her tone. "This man certainly isn't responsible for the attack, and he's telling the truth about the other things as well. He's performing a task for someone he doesn't know, and facing opponents he doesn't know either."

Tenoctris looked coldly at Benlo and said, "In simple words, he's a fool."

She put a hand on the ground to rise. Garric reached out to help but froze when pain shot through the muscles of his back and chest. The battle hadn't been harder on his body than the rural labor that had been his whole previous life, but fighting used muscles in different fashions. They'd felt the strain and were letting him know it.

Liane bent over Tenoctris and supported the older woman as she stiffly got to her feet. Liane's face still held no emotion.

Benlo glowered and said, "Just who is this, Master Garric? You told me she was a castaway. Is she really your crazy aunt?"

"Tenoctris is a castaway," Garric said. "More important, she's someone I trust."

He didn't know how he felt about Benlo. In effect the fellow seemed to be exactly what he'd claimed in Barca's Hamlet: a drover carrying out an assignment for a backer on Sandrakkan. Benlo had concealed the fact that Garric, not a flock of sheep, was his real object; but he'd paid fair money for the sheep and fair money for Garric's presence as well.

Liane stepped away from Tenoctris. She looked at Garric, and for the first time her eyes were troubled.

"Liane?" the drover said. He stood, reaching toward his daughter. She edged back as though she hadn't seen the gesture. Cashel grunted but didn't thrust Benlo down on the trough the way Garric thought he might.

"Look . . ." Benlo said. He fumbled in his sleeve for a

handkerchief that wasn't there. The sudden attack had drawn him from bed in a pleated linen nightdress. Unlike his daughter, he hadn't snatched up a cloak as well before he ran outdoors.

"I don't know what's going on, I admit that," Benlo continued. "I don't like these attacks any better than you do. When we get to Carcosa I'll be able to learn. I *will* learn, I promise."

Tenoctris watched Benlo without expression. Garric rubbed his forehead with both hands. His fingers were stiff and tingly, on the verge of cramping from their grip on his weapons in the recent fight. He'd hammered the sword into a twisted bar with less remaining edge than a plowshare, and the oak stool was in splinters.

He didn't know what to think. He didn't know anything at all.

Tenoctris began to question Benlo. Her words lost form and became a buzzing in Garric's exhausted mind.

"I'm going back to bed," he said. "I need sleep if I'm going to be fit to walk in the morning."

Garric shambled toward the inn. He was so exhausted in the letdown after the battle that he knew he'd be able to sleep despite all that had happened.

And he knew that he'd have company in his dreams.

10

You should get some sleep too," Mellie said. She lay on her back on Cashel's knee and looked up at him with a worried expression, her fingers laced behind her neck.

"I'll be all right," Cashel said. "The flock's still nervous. They'll settle down better if they know I'm up and watching."

Cashel sat on the wagon tongue, his face toward the paddock. He ran his right hand up and down the quarterstaff. He'd combed loose a handful of lanolin-rich wool from the flock, mixed in a pinch of sand, and used the wad as a gentle abrasive to smooth out the nicks and splinters from the fight.

When he reached Carcosa—or if he met a tinker at the next halt—he'd replace the staff's ferrules. One had a deep cut across it from when Cashel rammed through the sword and arm of the attacking lich; the other iron cap was battered out of shape on the skull of the creature slashing at Ilna when the first blow landed. One stroke with Cashel's full strength would have been enough. The sixth time he hit the creature, he stirred only dust because the bones had been utterly pulverized.

"Still, you should sleep," the sprite said. "I'll warn you if there's danger, you know."

Cashel smiled. It had only been a few days, but he'd already gotten used to talking to a beautiful naked woman the size of his finger. "I'll be all right," he repeated. "I need to calm down too; and my staff needs work."

One cut in the wood was fairly deep, but Cashel was sure he could buff it into nothing worse than a blemish. He couldn't imagine replacing the quarterstaff. He'd been nine years old the day he took the perfect, straight-grained branch as his price for felling the hickory for Taron, its owner. Cashel had seasoned the wood himself, shaped it, and buffed it to a wax-smooth finish. Only the ferrules had been stranger's work, and they'd been replaced three times already during the time he'd used the staff.

Mellie raised one slim leg and sighted along it toward the north star, then giggled. "Benlo is strong, isn't he?" she said.

Cashel frowned, though he continued to rub the wood with long, even strokes. "Benlo?" he repeated. "I wouldn't have said that, no."

Rald, the drover's chief guard, was built like an oak stump and looked about as tough. Sarhad, another of the guards, might well have been even stronger but a lich's axe had cleft him from shoulder to midchest. Benlo, though—

Mellie giggled again and did a backflip onto her feet. "Not strong compared to *you*, silly!" she said. "But pretty strong."

Mellie glanced toward the inn building. A puff of breeze fluffed her radiant hair; she was so utterly *real* that Cashel couldn't believe other folks didn't see her just as he did.

"It was people like Benlo who twisted the path from this plane to mine," she said. She didn't put any particular emotional weight on the words; but then, she'd sounded much the same when she discussed the possibility of the vixen tearing its way into the fencepost and eating her.

Cashel's mind worked over Mellie's words. When she said "strong" she meant a powerful wizard. He didn't doubt that; he'd seen Benlo raise the glamour to point out Garric.

"Maybe they'll open it this time," he said, speaking to be companionable.

Mellie wrinkled her nose and stuck her tongue out at him. "If you drop an egg on the ground," she said tartly, "it breaks. If you drop it again, do the pieces fly together again?"

"I usually think before I speak," Cashel said. That was half true; the whole truth was that he usually thought instead of speaking. "Sorry, Mellie."

She hopped into a handstand, scissoring her legs, and then lifted one arm to support herself entirely on the other. During the midwinter festivities some men in the borough danced and tumbled with curved ram's horns strapped to their feet; Garric was pretty good at it himself. The sprite's acrobatics were like nothing Cashel had ever seen before, though.

"I'd open the path for you if I could, Mellie," he said awkwardly. He held the quarterstaff out at arm's length and rotated it slowly, letting the gleam of starlight show him where he needed to work more on the polish.

A quarterstaff was a dynamic weapon; it didn't have a point or edge to do the wielder's work for him. The hickory had to slip like glass through Cashel's hands; he couldn't afford to have his palm catch on a rough spot when Garric's life or Ilna's might depend on it.

Their lives and now maybe Mellie's.

"Cashel?" the sprite said, on her back again and watching him. "Where are you going to go after we reach Carcosa? Do you plan to stay with Benlo?"

"No," Cashel said. "No, not with him. And not back to Barca's Hamlet either."

He rubbed the hickory with a second handful of wool, this time without adding sand. He hoped never to replace the quarterstaff. It was more than a tool: it was the only real link Cashel would keep with what had been his whole existence all the years till now.

"Away, that's all I meant to do," he continued. He thought of mentioning Sharina, then decided against it. Mellie was easy to talk to—the first time Cashel had felt that way about another person; the sprite *wasn't* a person, of course—but he really didn't know what to say. "Is there somewhere you want to go?"

"The things I've seen on your plane since the path closed," Mellie said, "have mostly involved cats and foxes. I've never taken a sea voyage because of the rats. If I'm traveling with a friend like you, well, it's all new. New since a thousand years, at least."

"I'll try to keep you safe, Mellie," Cashel said. He resumed polishing his quarterstaff. It had to slip like glass . . .

11

The hedges lining this stretch of road chirped and cheeped with birds complaining at the familiar intrusion or gobbling insects stirred by the travelers' feet. Far back at the rear of the flock Cashel called, "Come along, Ginger, you've eaten all you'll be able to digest. Tsk tsk tsk!"

Liane turned to Ilna and said, "Your brother seems very cheerful this morning, mistress."

She sounded friendly; she always did when speaking to Ilna. In Ilna's heart she felt as if Liane was secretly mocking her for being less beautiful, less wealthy, and less well educated; but Ilna also knew that others didn't read the sneer beneath the smile. She'd look a fool if she reacted openly to it.

"Yes, he is, isn't he?" Ilna said with a smile of her own. "Well, it's a lovely day, and maybe he's just happy to be alive after last night's attack. How about you, Garric?"

Garric walked beside the gelding which Tenoctris rode today in Liane's place. Benlo had started to protest, but his daughter's cold glance had silenced him. Tenoctris had protested also; Liane said simply that she needed the exercise and that the older woman needed the rest. It would be very easy, even for Ilna, to see only the kindly surface of Liane's behavior and miss the fact that underneath the rich girl was a scheming bitch.

"Well, I don't know about happy," he said, grinning over his shoulder at the girls. There'd been no pretense of Garric driving the sheep this morning. The wonder was that he'd been able to walk unaided. "I'm sure I'm alive because dead men don't hurt this much."

He stumbled and had to catch himself on Tenoctris' stirrup; he dabbed down with the bow he carried unstrung in his left hand. "You see?" he added in half-mocking despair. "I'm a cripple. Come on up with us so we can talk."

The road from the Stroma River to Carcosa was paved, though a thousand years of use had worn ankle-deep ruts in the stone. Benlo's entourage shared the route with much other traffic: pedestrians, riders and pack animals, and even some wheeled traffic which would be unthinkable on the narrow tracks farther east. Ilna had seen a carriage for the first time. Its windows were shuttered, and the four black horses pulling it had plumes wobbling from their brow harness.

Benlo was at the head of the line with his four surviving

guards clustered close about him. Liane had with apparent deliberation kept Garric and Tenoctris between her and her father. Ilna had thought at first that this was the girl's clever ploy to walk with Garric, but Liane had remained several paces behind the boy for all the first hour of the journey.

Ilna marched along beside her watchfully nonetheless.

Cashel drove the flock from the rear, whistling and calling the sheep by their individual names. He *did* seem remarkably happy, happier than Ilna could remember him being while at home. Maybe he was just glad to have seen the world beyond Barca's Hamlet—and there was the wage he was earning besides, though she knew her brother didn't share her concern about money. Because Cashel had Ilna to take care of him, he didn't *need* to worry about finances himself.

"Well, come on," Garric repeated. "I may need the pair of you to carry me the rest of the way."

Liane looked a question at Ilna. Ilna suppressed a scowl: "Yes, we're coming," she said. Liane lengthened her pace slightly to come abreast of Tenoctris on the right side, putting the gelding between her and Garric.

"Holding up well on the trip?" Garric said as Ilna reached him. He shifted the bow from his left shoulder to his right so that it wasn't a symbolic barrier between the two of them.

Ilna had known Garric all their lives; she could see that he winced every time his right leg took a step and that the skin was drawn close over the strong, high bones of his cheeks. For all that, Garric was in almost as bright a mood as Cashel. After the night's battle he'd been wrung out so completely that she'd been afraid he'd take days to recover.

"I hope I'll always be able to walk at the speed of a ewe, Garric," Ilna said. "Washing sheets is more effort—and more excitement as well."

Garric laughed merrily. His laughter was louder recently than she remembered it being in the past. He'd gained self-assurance. He seemed to have decided that being cheerful was nothing to be ashamed of and that if other people had a problem with it—so much the worse for them.

"I was just saying to Tenoctris," he said, "that ancient poets didn't write about badgering sheep to market—or shearing them, for that matter. It's all about sitting under a holly oak watching the lambs gambol among the flowers. Isn't that so, Liane?"

He wasn't quite the boy Ilna had grown up with. Garric had always been intelligent, friendly, and as hard a worker as anyone in the hamlet. Now he had spine as well; something he certainly hadn't gotten from his father, and a very different thing to his mother's spiteful bitterness as well.

"I had the impression that shepherding involved more crystal springs and song contests than I've seen on Haft, yes," Liane agreed. Deliberately changing the subject she went on, "Mistress Tenoctris, I apologize for mistaking you for a conjuror the other day. May I ask how you came to be a m-ma—"

She paused, obviously afraid that "magician" would be taken as an insult. Ilna wondered if the other girl was blushing; the horse and rider concealed her from those on Tenoctris' other side.

"To study the art?" Liane finished, apparently doubtful about the word "wizard" as well. Someone must have explained to her who Tenoctris really was.

"Someone" was almost certainly Garric, at the times when Ilna worked her score at the inn because she didn't have a rich father to pay her way.

Liane lowered her voice as she asked the question, though her father and the guards were for the present well ahead. The leaders moved faster than the flock and had to halt every ten or twenty minutes to wait. Garric was used to moving at a sheep's pace and held back those with him.

Tenoctris was an awkward rider; she kept one hand on the reins while clinging to the saddlehorn with the other. "There's little enough art in the way most in this age practice wizardry," she said with a grim smile. "Just as it was in my own day, I suppose."

She turned her head toward Garric and Ilna to clearly include them in the conversation, then looked back at Liane and continued, "I had a talent for visualizing forces, Liane. My family had a title but very little money; I was the third daughter, and I think my father would have supported anything I proposed that didn't involve him finding a dowry for me. I studied in the university on Notisson, and after that I took positions all over the Isles in houses where there was a notable library. At the end I was in Yole; by coincidence, perhaps."

"But were you taught by a wizard?" Garric asked. "Were you apprenticed, I mean?"

"There was a healer named Kaeri in Notisson—in the city, not the university—who had great power," Tenoctris said. "I learned a great deal from her in one fashion, but . . ."

She was frowning, obviously bothered by what she was about to say. "Kaeri turned toward the sun, don't mistake me. She wanted nothing but to help others. But it frightened me to watch because she didn't begin to understand the forces she worked with. She was almost illiterate but that wasn't really the problem. The problem was her own strength."

Tenoctris chuckled wryly. "Not a problem I had, I assure you."

"Was the, the Hooded One," Garric said. He paused to swallow and his eyes were on the ground in front of him. "That way too?"

"If you mean was he illiterate," Tenoctris said in a decisive tone, "no, not at all. It was my assumption that he came from the same sort of family that I did—minor nobility, and very possibly not minor at all. I can't say that for sure because quite frankly I had almost no contact with him. Whatever his background, we had nothing that was important to either of us in common."

She turned her head and looked down—at Liane, to Ilna's surprise, not Garric. "The other difference between the Hooded One and my friend Kaeri is that his whole focus was Malkar."

"Evil," Liane said in a clear, emotionless tone. "His focus was on evil."

"In human terms," Tenoctris said/agreed. "He even claimed to be Malkar, a transparent lie that proved he was a fool as well as a fool dedicated to darkness. But he was an extremely powerful wizard and it's that rather than the direction in which he turned his power that made him so dangerous. He destroyed our world, his world and mine, through a mistake rather than as an act of will."

She smiled wistfully. "I'd thought he'd destroyed himself as well, Garric," she said, "until you told me about your dreams."

"I haven't had that dream for, you know . . ." Garric said. "Since my father gave me the good-luck piece."

"Yes, well," Tenoctris said. "More may have survived of my age than one would assume. Persons of great power . . ."

She shook her head with another faint smile. "And myself as well, through the workings of what I suppose was chance."

The old wizard's face changed—grew even more contemplative than usual. Tenoctris at her most animated projected an aura of detached calm; Ilna marveled at a mind so different from her own, where anger seethed under an icy surface, though an outsider might have mistaken the two of them for emotional sisters.

Tenoctris eyed Benlo and his companions, halted fifty feet ahead to wait. "Forces wax and wane, but knowledge takes the same amount of effort in every age," she said in a slightly quieter voice. "My friend in Notisson was very powerful. The Hooded One was very powerful. And your father, Mistress Liane, I'm afraid that he's very powerful as well—and equally ungoverned."

12

The southeast wind was gusty, fierce and dead against them. Nonnus had lowered the sail, but even so each spiteful puff drove the high-sided dugout farther into the Outer Sea.

Sharina sewed grommets into the leaches of the sail; Nonnus carefully split the pole she'd used to fend off Tegma's shore into brails to stiffen the canvas. The improvements would make only a minuscule difference in the vessel's ability to sail into the wind, but it was something to do besides fret.

Asera was in the bow looking grim. Meder faced forward with his back against the mast and his chest of paraphernalia open before him. Occasionally he looked toward the stern; Sharina studiously avoided meeting his eyes.

Asera stood. "This wind never changes!" she burst out. "It's a magical sending, isn't it? Meder, can't you do something about it?"

"No, because that peasant won't let me!" Meder said in a petulant voice. He didn't raise his eyes from the object he held; it looked to Sharina like a small mirror of polished lodestone.

"There's no magic to meeting a southeast wind in the Outer Sea at this time of the year," Nonnus said calmly. "No need of magic to get back to where we want to be either. There'll be a norther in the next week or few weeks, likely enough. We've provisions enough to wait for it, and we'll be catching fish before long."

The hermit didn't have a carpenter's froe and maul to split the brails. He'd trimmed a pair of wedges from what had been the oarloom, opened the grain with a stroke of his Pewle knife, and was using the back of the blade to tap the wedges down the shaft. He stood while he fed the pole forward with one hand as the other struck with a jeweler's care. Nonnus might have been a part of the vessel's hull for all the difference its pitching in the wind-driven swell made.

"A norther?" the procurator repeated in disgust. "A storm, you mean. Gods! why was I such a fool as to volunteer for this mission? I should have just opened a vein and died in my own bed in Valles!"

"A storm," Nonnus agreed mildly, "which we'll use to ride back to the Inner Sea or make landfall on one of the northern isles. I'm not proud of the workmanship of this pig we're sailing in, but she's sturdy and she wouldn't break up in a worse storm than I've seen yet in these seas."

Sharina stopped sewing the grommet that would anchor a clew adjusting the foot of the sail. Jumping fish had caught her eye. What she'd thought was another great gray wave rising behind them instead flicked its tail as it went under the surface again.

"There's nothing wrong with a dugout," the hermit went on in a musing voice. He was no longer speaking to Asera; perhaps he wasn't speaking to anyone at all. "A properly built twin-hull dugout will sail near as well as a planked ship—and swim in a storm better, too. But I didn't take the time to do the job properly."

"How much time would that have taken, Nonnus?" Sharina asked, watching her friend's face.

He smiled. "Yes, there's that, child," he agreed. "A year I'd say. To build her and work her up properly, aligning the hulls just right."

"I didn't want to spend a year on Tegma, Nonnus," she said, deliberately raising her voice so that the nobles would hear her clearly. "Even if we'd been allowed to by whoever put us there."

Nonnus seated himself on the stern crossbar holding the outriggers to the main hull. His eyes were toward the horizon, but Sharina wasn't sure her friend was really looking at anything in the present world.

"Oh, we'll be all right, Mistress Asera," he said. "The sea's bigger than any man or any ship, that's the first rule you learn on Pewle Island. A boy in a woodskin who gets too far north at this time of year is likely to just keep on going, blown all the way to the Ice Capes. But we've got plenty of provisions and we'll just ride the storm back."

Sharina stuck her needle firmly through the canvas and stood. She'd made herself a leather belt and bandolier. From it hung the hand axe, the sewing case, her dagger—a fine steel one in a sheath of nielloed tin, owned by one of the Blood Eagles until every creature on Tegma died—and a satchel containing bread and a bottle of water. It was an awkward burden but she'd taken the hermit's advice to heart: so long as she was aboard the dugout, everything she'd need to live was attached to her body.

She moved a pace forward, trying not to wobble, and sat on the crossbar beside Nonnus. He smiled wanly at her and said, "When I was a boy, so young that I hadn't even made my first woodskin, I stole my brother's. I can't have been but seven years old then; seven sealing seasons and seven hungry seasons, as we call it on the island. It was weather like this."

A gust made the dugout wallow, thrusting the port outrigger deep in the waves as the starboard one lifted briefly above the surface, to which it streamed back water in jeweled droplets. Spray flew from the wave tops, whacking like hail against the dugout's hull and the passengers. Asera glowered sternward; Meder closed his case of implements and materials.

"It took me north for three days," Nonnus said. "I had no food, just a water bottle. A school of jellyfish was swept along in the same current; sea tigers, the big ones with orange-and-black air sacs. Their tentacles were thirty feet long and their touch burned like the whips of demons. They thumped against my hull day and night; I could feel them pressing the other side when I lay against the thin wood."

He laughed, a bleak sound that might have come from a

gull's throat but should not have come from a man's. Sharina put her hand on his shoulder.

"And the weather changed," Nonnus said to all the world around him. "Blew me in one night back the distance three days had carried me north, and the beating my brother gave me was a pleasure to take because so nearly I hadn't been there to get it. But sometimes I think about another boy in another . . . world I suppose. Who kept drifting north until he froze into the pack ice, seven years old, and nothing on his conscience except that he stole a woodskin from his brother."

"He didn't save a girl from Tegma," Sharina said.

Nonnus laughed again but this time a human sound. "No, he didn't, child," he said. "And the wind will change because the wind always changes."

"I can change the wind," Meder said; looking over his shoulder with his case clutched against his chest.

Nonnus stood up. "And so you can, sir, I don't in the least doubt," he said in a pleasant voice. He resumed tapping the wedges down the length of the pole he was splitting. "But if you do it ever on this boat that my friend and I built, I'll put you off into the sea. The fish have lower standards; they won't mind your presence."

Meder blinked in shock. Sharina glared at the young wizard. She was seated beside the hermit though no longer quite touching him.

Sharina was with Nonnus; there could be no question of that. But in her heart of hearts, she felt the wind and thought of the Ice Capes; and thought of her long blond hair frozen into the ice.

13

The aqueduct's central arches had fallen away long years since; their bricks had been reused for the foundations of the houses and barns Garric had seen along the road ever since they'd halted at midday to allow the sheep to chew their cud. The concrete-cored pillars still remained, marching across the barley fields like giants of a former age.

"Our ancestors piped the water all the way from the head-waters of the Stroma," Garric said. "Seventy miles, the route ran. Can you imagine that, Liane? Can you imagine a town needing so much water that you'd go that far to bring it?"

"Erdin has an aqueduct," Liane said, "but that's because the local water is brackish, not that there's any lack of it. All heavy goods in the south of the island travel by canal barge. Our island—Sandrakkan."

They stood at the end of the dock onto Talpin Lake. The sheep were in the paddock; the fishing boats whose catch would provide dinner for travelers here at the inn, the Lake-side Arms, were still out though the sun was casting long shadows onto the water.

Liane surveyed their surroundings. The flat countryside and the lake's smooth surface gave a broader vantage than Garric was used to. Even the sea was a series of hills and valleys no less real for constantly changing. "This reminds me of Erdin," she said. "Of when I was growing up."

Ilna was in the kitchen; Tenoctris wandered by the lake while Cashel sat with the flock—by choice; the sheep didn't need his presence at the moment. Benlo had gone off alone; his guards drank morosely in the common room. Garric didn't particularly want to know what the drover was about.

At another time Garric would probably have been with

Tenoctris, learning about these ancient structures that she could have seen new; or with Cashel, chatting as friends do about shared experiences and nothing in particular. But Liane had looked at him, and though she hadn't exactly asked Garric to walk with her out onto the dock the signals had been clear enough.

They were in plain sight of over a hundred people; the Lakeside Arms did a major trade, and this close to Carcosa there were numerous travelers deciding to push on to the city before dark or at least not long after. No one would look askance at a young man and a lovely woman standing together, even though they were well out of earshot of everyone else.

"The Grove of Tappa was on this side of the water," Liane said. There was tension in her voice. Her hands were clasped on top of one of the support timbers; the dock didn't have a railing. "There aren't any trees now; I'd think it was too wet for trees to grow, except cypress."

"Really!" Garric said in excitement. "I'd always thought Tappa was a myth! The dreaded goddess whose virgin priestesses sacrificed a male traveler every year on the first full moon until the hero Talamis, ah, ended the practice."

"I don't swear Tappa was real," Liane said with a faint smile. "Or that Talamis was either; even for a demigod his exploits seem . . . impressive. But there was a grove here and a cult, that much is true."

Talamis was said to have impregnated the fifty priestesses all in the same night, changing the cult of Tappa from blood sacrifice to one of motherhood which had survived until the fall of the Old Kingdom. Historians in the reign of Carus had written of the site; there was no reason to doubt that it was real. Garric had never connected Tappa and her lakeside grove with Talpin Lake east of Carcosa, though.

"The countryside must have gotten a lot boggier in the past thousand years," he said. "Well, that's a long time. I wonder if Tenoctris knows about the grove?"

"My father does," Liane said, staring across the lake like a statue. "He's looking for it now."

She turned and faced Garric with a grim expression as though daring him to respond. He cleared his throat. "Oh," he said. "I suppose an old temple would be a place where there'd be a lot of what Tenoctris calls 'forces.' "

"You mean a site of human sacrifices, don't you?" Liane said in a challenging tone.

"No," said Garric calmly. "I still think the part about human sacrifice is just legend."

Two winters before, he'd found Gizir weeping and shouting in the inn's stables. That was the night Laya had announced her betrothal to a wealthy widower named Hakkardi, whose farm was a mile north of the hamlet. Gizir was drunk, and he drew his knife when Garric walked in on him in all innocence.

Liane was as likely to go off explosively as Gizir had been. Garric wasn't worried about his personal safety, now or then; but he didn't want to hurt a person he liked and sympathized with.

Liane covered the top of the post with her palms. She laid her cheek on them and began sobbing her heart out.

Garric had worried that Liane would shout at him or maybe even try to claw his face in displaced anger—the sorts of things that living with his mother had falsely taught him to expect from women in general. Liane's tears took him completely by surprise. He blinked and turned so that he wasn't staring directly at the girl.

Liane reached a hand sideways, caught his wrist, and squeezed it. "May the Shepherd forgive me, Garric," she wheezed through her snuffling. "*I* thought that was what he was doing. I still think it is. Looking for the ground of old deaths to work his magic!"

She straightened and turned her back. She used a handkerchief from her sleeve to mop her eyes, then blow her nose. Garric continued to look at the boats out on the water; the fishermen were beginning to row toward the dock with the slow stroke of strong, weary men.

"I don't really know my father anymore," Liane said in a voice with only the vaguest hint of trembling. "He used to be so wonderful. The happiest time of my childhood was listening to him sing love songs he'd learned all over the Inner Sea on his travels and brought back to Mother and me."

She looked at Garric and forced a smile, actually lifting the corners of her mouth with her thumbs and forefingers. The mimed humor made them both giggle in truth.

In a less strained tone Liane continued, "Our family name is bor-Benliman. I'm sorry to have lied to you."

Garric shrugged. "You didn't lie," he said. "If you didn't want to tell people you're noble, that's your business. Anyway, my mother said that's what you were. She, well, cares about that a lot. She was in service in the palace in Carcosa."

Liane nodded, but her attention was clearly on what she was going to say rather than what she was hearing. She placed her hands on the post again and lowered her eyes toward them as she said, "It all changed when my mother died, five years ago. They were very much in love and when she died he didn't . . ."

Liane looked at Garric. "My father didn't accept that she was dead," she resumed coolly. "I know that sounds silly; how can you *not* accept that somebody's dead? But he put everything into bringing her back. He'd always been a wizard, but his art wasn't important to him the way Mother was. Since her death he's concentrated on it, and on kinds of spells that he'd never have considered before."

Garric nodded toward the fishing boat nearing them, its oarlocks creaking. "Ah," he said. "Maybe we should go in?"

"We'll walk a ways along the margin of the lake," Liane said, briefly again the imperious noble speaking to a commoner. "There's light enough for that."

They left the dock together, her slippers hissing on the weathered boards while Garric's bare feet moved soundlessly.

"I was at Mistress Gudea's in Valles," Liane said emotionlessly. "I don't know what happened. Armed men came to the headmistress. They moved me from the school dormitory to a locked cloister. Nobody would tell me anything, just that I couldn't leave but I wouldn't come to any harm if I kept quiet."

Liane began to snuffle again. She dabbed at her nose with the handkerchief. Garric looked around, but it was too deep in the evening for anyone at a distance to see that the girl was crying. The path along the lakeshore had been paved with blocks from the nearby aqueduct, but that was a very long time ago. Some were tilted, and muddy water lapped broad stretches.

"They held me there for a week," Liane said, ignoring the doubtful footing. "Then my father came. He never told me what had happened, only that we no longer owned any property except for the family tomb in Erdin. That's where my mother was buried. It would all be right again soon, though; he just had to do some business for someone else and we'd be back as before. Only for now he was Benlo or-Willet and I was to travel with him until he found what he'd been sent for. That was eight months ago."

Garric placed her left hand in the crook of his right elbow and turned them around. It was just too dark to continue this way. He was uneasily aware that he'd have to explain not only to Benlo but to Ilna if he and Liane managed to fall into the lake together.

"At first we stayed in Valles," Liane said, apparently oblivious of everything but the story she was telling for the first time to another person. "We stayed at various inns around the city. I hid in my room mostly. I was afraid I'd meet one of the other girls from my school. I felt like I had leprosy. My father poked around palaces and tombs. He was able to go most of the places he wanted to, but it was always in secret, at night or wearing a hooded cloak."

"He seems, well, *rich*," Garric said. He swung them wide to avoid the fisherman leaving the dock with a pair of wicker baskets of fish on a yoke across his shoulders. A woman called to the man from the back door of the inn.

Liane nodded in the dimness. "Father never cared much about money," she said. "Of course, we had plenty of it. Since he came and got me out of school he always carries a belt of gold coins and a chest of gold in our luggage. I thought that was why he hired the guards, but now I'm not sure. Not since what happened to . . . in your inn and last night. With the liches."

"That wasn't his doing," Garric said. "Even Tenoctris says that." He didn't add—he didn't have to add—"and Tenoctris doesn't like your father at all."

"Not that he made the attack," Liane said, "but that someone else is trying to block whatever my father is doing. Someone else who won't stop at anything."

It was really dark. Light came through the kitchen windows and glimmered from the inn yard where men with rushlights completed the business of the day. The ground at Garric's feet was pitch black; he knew the path straight back to the inn was clear, but there was nothing else that he was sure of. He stayed where he was with a hand over Liane's hand on his arm to hold her.

"With no warning he chartered a ship and we sailed to Carcosa," Liane said. "For me it was like falling off the edge of the world. Compared to Erdin and Valles, Carcosa is a menagerie of clowns dressed in cast-off clothing and monkeys with no culture. I was so alone. I wanted to *die*, Garric. I wanted to die."

"And then you came to Barca's Hamlet and it was even worse," Garric murmured. He could sympathize with Liane. His life had been dislocated badly enough that he could appreciate how what she was going through must feel.

Liane laughed. "No," she said, "it wasn't. Because the folk in Barca's Hamlet don't think they're nobles when by civilized standards they're not. And because there's real learning in Barca's Hamlet."

Garric laughed in turn. "There're real scholars in Carcosa, Liane," he said. "I'm sure there are."

The clatter of wooden trenchers on trestle tables indicated that the evening meal was being served in the common room. Well, if he missed the stew, he'd eat bread and cheese; as often enough before.

Liane sniffed. "Do you think so?" she said. Then she added, "Your father is a remarkable man, Garric."

"Do you think so?" Garric said in unintended mimicry. "He certainly wouldn't agree with you."

Garric wasn't sure what he thought. It was hard to visualize Reise as a person rather than a fact of existence like the inn itself or a winter storm.

"I don't know my father anymore, Garric," Liane repeated, her features hidden in shadow but her lips' faint tremble audible in her voice. "It's as though when he changed his name he became another person . . . but I know it's not that. The change came when my mother died. Before then I could hide at school and pretend I didn't know what my father was doing."

"I guess we ought to go inside now," Garric said uneasily.

"He must have done something very terrible to lose everything but his life," Liane said, resisting the faint pressure Garric put on her hand. "I wonder who could have saved his life . . . and what the price of my father's life was."

A whippoorwill began calling, using an ancient concrete pier as a sounding board to amplify its sound. After the tenth call in the series the bird paused.

"Yes, we should get in," Liane said crisply. She walked toward the inn, her grip firm on Garric's arm.

14

A t a distance from Carcosa, Ilna had wondered to see houses perched at the top of a sheer cliff. As she came closer she realized that she was seeing not cliffs but the walls of the ancient city, built upon by folk of the present day since there was no longer need to defend the provincial backwater Carcosa had become.

Ilna felt her self-confidence shrivel. She'd been thinking of Carcosa as a very much larger version of Barca's Hamlet—the same in everything but size. The truth was that a city was no more like a hamlet than a human was like a frog.

Ilna felt like a frog in all truth as she viewed the magnificent walls.

" 'Nothing can equal you, Carcosa!' " Garric declaimed loudly. " 'No one today could build the equal of the fragments of your walls which remain, nor restore that part which is fallen.' "

In a laughing voice he added, "You see, Liane? There *are* learned people in Carcosa."

Liane, beside Tenoctris on the gelding two paces ahead of Liane, turned and called back, "There was one in the last century, you mean—and he was an exile from Sandrakkan, don't forget. Besides, 'What a happy city if it could be rid of its residents, or if the residents could be rid of their cheating ways!' "

They both laughed. Ilna felt her heart freeze.

She didn't understand what they'd said or why anyone should think it was funny. She'd lived beside Garric or-Reise all her life; and here he was, joking with a stranger he'd just met and shutting Ilna out completely.

Because of traffic, the flock was closely bunched at the

right side of the road. Ilna had never seen so many people in one place before. There were pedestrians, riders, occasional carriages—and most noticeable and dangerous to others, the huge goods wagons drawn by teams of up to a dozen oxen or six horses. The wagons moved at their own pace, and their iron-shod wheels would crush anything that came between them and the stone roadway.

Some of the wagons returning from the city were empty and rattled along the road with small care for what was in their way; others carried the debris of tanyards and the cesspools to be spread on fields. A rural hamlet is a hard school and no one had ever mistaken Ilna for a squeamish girl; despite that, she found herself wondering if the risk of being run over by the empty wagons was worse than the stench of those laden with urban refuse.

Benlo's guards provided the flock with a right of way that other drovers must envy. Cashel was in the rear, an equally solid bulwark against riders who might have thought in their haste to drive straight through the sheep. Garric kept the flock together and eased it past tight places where buildings had encroached or the road had collapsed after a thousand years without repair.

Garric glanced at Ilna's face. Sobering slightly, he said, "There was a poet of the last century, Etter bor-Lavarman, a priest of the Shepherd from Erdin. He got into difficulties at home—"

"Difficulties regarding a woman of the court," Liane said primly. "Though Daughter Rothi didn't explain it in quite those words."

She giggled. The grin returned to Garric's lips, the chill to Ilna's heart.

"Anyway," Garric said, "Etter came to Carcosa for a few years. The city impressed him, its past at any rate. The people didn't impress him at all. Liane and I were trading quotes from Etter's poems."

"I see," Ilna said, shifting the staff with her bundles from her right shoulder to her left.

She saw, all right. She could no more compare herself to this clever rich girl than she could compare Barca's Hamlet to Carcosa. But Ilna hadn't given up before and she wasn't going to start now.

At the foot of the looming walls was a way station with stock pens and a large corral for coach horses. A drove of cattle filled one of the stone pens; the other held a few score sheep of a short-legged breed with white fleece—to Ilna's eyes, as alien as if they each had two heads.

Benlo turned in his saddle and pointed. "Head them into the paddock, Garric," he called. "I'll hire a town badger at the inn."

He kneed his bay mare to a hitching rail where already a dozen horses were tethered. Benlo didn't bother to tie the animal; rather, he dismounted and let one of his guards attend to the business while he and the three others entered the straggling one-story building.

Garric turned the bellwether, a grizzled ram with wooden clackers around his neck. Ilna trotted ahead of the ram and lifted the pen's three gate bars with a cool glance back at Liane. *Poetry isn't the only thing of use to a countryman's wife, is it, rich girl?*

Garric gave Ilna a quick smile of appreciation. He began counting the flock into the paddock aloud rather than using a physical tally as Cashel, chivying the flock from the rear, would have had to do.

A countryman's wife . . . but would Garric stay a countryman? He didn't belong in Barca's Hamlet, and Ilna didn't belong anywhere else.

The inn's only lodgers would be folk who'd gotten this far in a blinding storm and weren't up to chancing the city's narrow streets in darkness. The trade in ale and hard cider more than made up for it, however, especially on a hot sunny day like this.

Wines too, Ilna supposed. She remembered the soldiers billeted with her drinking wine. They were from Valles, like the drover's fine daughter. . . .

Benlo came out of the inn almost immediately, accompanied by a weedy-looking youth of no more than twenty who wore a broad yellow cummerbund and a bandanna of paler yellow over his head. He had a ginger mustache and wisps of what he probably flattered himself was a beard.

The youth bowed deeply to the drover, then swaggered over toward the sheep pen. He stopped beside Ilna and gestured toward the sheep with his thumb. "Scraggly lot, aren't they?" he said. "Well, not a wonder seeings they come from the back of beyond."

Ilna thought of turning away from him. Instead she asked, "What's wrong with the sheep? Besides five days of travel, of course."

The youth sniffed. "All leg and no meat, that's the first thing," he said. "And look at that wool! All different colors. How are you to dye *that*, I ask you? Isn't good for anything but stuffing pillows, that trash!"

His tunic was a dull green, but the dye had faded to gray in several patches. That was probably a result of poor preparation of the wool, but Ilna had never trusted artificial colors anyway. With the two shades of yellow and the fact that his leather shoes weren't quite the same shade of red either, the fellow looked to her like a mummer in costume.

"Well, time for me to take over from these hicks," the youth said with an ostentatious yawn. "Really, I think the sheep are usually smarter than the locals who badger them here."

He turned toward Ilna as if becoming aware of her for the first time. "You know," he said, "you're not a bad-looking wench. If you'd care to see the city with a real gentleman—"

He took Ilna's chin between a thumb and forefinger, turning her face to view her profile and then turning it back.

"—I could take time out of my schedule to arrange that."

Ilna smiled pleasantly at him. "I've wrung the necks of chickens I fancied more than I do you, you little weasel," she said. She struck his hand away with a *crack* like a branch breaking.

"What?" the youth said. He drew his arm back for a punch.

Garric laid the tip of his bowstaff across the youth's throat. "A word of advice, fellow," he said in a voice that could be heard all the way to the inn despite the traffic noise. "Mistress Ilna doesn't need her friend and brother to handle a worm like you; but she has us nonetheless, do you see?"

Cashel put the fingers of one hand on Ilna's shoulder. The other held his quarterstaff.

Garric was smiling; Cashel was not. It was hard to judge which expression the local youth found the more deservedly terrifying. "No disrespect meant, masters," he croaked.

"That's good," Garric said. The last ewe was entering the paddock. He patted her flank and counted "Fifty!" aloud.

Offering Ilna his arm, Garric walked over to join Tenoctris and Liane as Cashel dropped the bars in place.

15

"The gates used to be painted red," Mellie said from Cashel's shoulder. "That was when there were gates, I mean. And all those niches above had statues in them, King Itaku and his family."

Cashel looked up. The monumental triple gateway was of a rusty sandstone unlike anything on the east side of Haft. He supposed it must be common locally though; even the ancients couldn't have carried such staggering amounts of stone from other islands. . . .

Or could they? Was the city built by wizardry?

"Is the rock from around here?" he asked. His companions were too gogglingly aware of the city they entered behind Benlo and his guards to be concerned that Cashel was talking to himself—if they even noticed it.

"Most of it," Mellie said equably. From the corner of his eye Cashel could see her sitting cross-legged, combing out her brilliant hair with the prongs of a tiny weed seed. "The best marble for building came from the hills to the south. They barged it down the Stroma River and along the coast, then landed it in the harbor."

The gate panels were gone now; so were most of the fittings that had embellished the high structure. Two pillars of yellow-and-brown stone flanked a niche in the third level, and the statue of a woman in flowing garments graced the pergola at the peak. Perhaps she was meant for the Lady; a thousand years had weathered the face featureless.

The streets were crowded with folk wearing dyed clothing who talked loudly, constantly, and in harsh voices. Cashel felt as though he were in a tree under a flock of blackbirds chattering ill-tempered nonsense, all at the same time.

Every few steps a local plucked the sleeve of Cashel's tunic with an offer of some sort. Cashel ignored them except to shift his quarterstaff from one hand to the other. The hucksters and touts went away and usually didn't fasten on any of the others in Cashel's group either.

Garric walked beside Tenoctris on the gelding, just behind Benlo. Ilna and Liane followed them; Liane regally prim, clearly no mark for the sort of city folk who battened on rubes from the country, while Ilna glanced about with the fierce glare of a mother cat defending her kittens. Cashel knew that anybody grabbing his sister would be lucky to get his hand back, and the hustlers seemed to have picked up on that as well.

Cashel was alone at the end of the line. The streets were narrow and he took up a lot of room. His wages in silver coins were in a wash-leather pouch hung from his neck on a thick strap. Even if a thief managed to cut the strap, the purse would drop into the bosom of Cashel's tunic and be held by his belt. It would take more than light fingers to rob him, and nobody taking a look at *this* rube would think of using force.

When they reached Benlo's inn and the drover paid them

the last day's wages, Cashel would be really alone; and alone forever. He turned and smiled toward the point of his shoulder. "Except for you," he said aloud.

"Except for me," Mellie agreed cheerfully, as if she knew what he was talking about.

She waved toward the hillside to their right. A high brick wall, featureless except for simple brick pilasters at intervals to break the sheer line, fronted the street. Over the top of it Cashel could see manicured trees and pavilions with fanciful roofs climbing the slope.

"That all used to be palaces for the King of the Isles and his chief ministers," she said. "Now the buildings are fallen and some new rich man has turned the grounds into a garden. Humans change as fast as clouds do."

Mellie giggled. "Of course, before the kings," she said, "when Carcosa was a fishing village, the whole hillside was covered with black walnut trees. I used to tease the squirrels when I visited. I'd pull their tails and skip under the branch before they could turn around."

A tile-arched walkway zigzagged down into the gardens proper from the hill's craggy top. Cashel thought about how old his companion really was. "Aye, I can see that," he said. "A big old walnut on the ridge and she'd roll her nuts down till they owned the whole slope. Poison other plants out, a walnut will. There's people like that too."

A farrier's stall stood between a pair of open-fronted taverns. Hot iron and the sulfurous smell of coal smoke filled the air. An apprentice walked a treadmill to drive the wheezing bellows, and the street rang with the smith's measured blows. Horses waiting to be shod half-blocked the street; a carter hauling three huge hogsheads of ale shouted threats to drive on through the obstructing animals if they weren't moved.

Donlo's guards held the horses against the wall long enough for their employer's entourage to pass. Cashel brushed the animals with no great affection. He'd always thought horses were too flighty as well as needing an expensive diet of grain, while oxen got along fine on grass and coarse fodder. Horses were quicker at their business, sure; but speed wasn't a virtue about which Cashel troubled overmuch.

"You know . . ." Cashel said. "Walnut's a pretty wood, I grant you. But give me honest oak any day."

Mellie laughed so hard that Cashel lifted his hand in fear that she'd roll off his shoulder in a spasm of silver trills. "What's the matter?" he asked, trying to keep the puzzled hurt out of his voice. "Don't you like oak?"

The sprite stood to pat his earlobe reassuringly. "I like oak very well, Cashel," she said. "I was laughing because you thought you had to tell me that *you* did."

The street the group was following joined what Cashel supposed was a "square"; though it wasn't square and it was *huge*—probably as big as all the houses and yards in Barca's Hamlet put together. It wasn't smooth; outcrops of rubble and worked stone stuck out of the ground in several places, debris of the Old Kingdom. Even so, the space was large enough that for the first time since they'd entered Carcosa, traffic didn't crush the drover's party into a long line.

Garric turned and spoke to Liane; the girl called something between a request and a demand to her father. The group closed up beside a slab which once had been a transom of fine-grained limestone. Now the corner had been broken off and the stylized vine-leaf carvings were worn to shadows of themselves.

Garric was surveying the square with a look of amazement. "These are all new," he said in wonder.

The surrounding buildings didn't look new to Cashel, but they were of a type he'd never seen before—even on his winding progress through Carcosa's streets. They were mostly three floors high. The bottom story of each was windowless. Foliage showed over high parapets, indicating that they had roof gardens.

The front doors were solid and set back within narrow entryways. There were liveried guards in front of each house;

solid men in half-armor, very much of a type with the folk who guarded Benlo himself.

"Are they new?" Cashel murmured to Mellie. He didn't see anything he wouldn't have guessed was as old as Reise's inn.

The sprite poised on the toes of one foot and raised the other leg vertically. Cashel decided that acrobatics were Mellie's equivalent of a shrug. "They weren't here when I last visited Carcosa," she said. "But that hasn't been for a couple centuries. Even longer, I guess."

Benlo clucked impatiently to his mare. The group started around the square, still close enough together to talk to one another as they walked.

Liane pointed to the nearest building. "These are the houses of the nobility," she said. "There's been trouble in Carcosa, worse even than in Valles. They build this way so that if there's a riot after the midweek sacrifice the mob won't be able to break into their houses and loot them."

Benlo led them out of the square by another of the dozen or so streets feeding it. This one was a broad boulevard with a median divider. The shops of fabric-sellers and dressmakers lined both sides. Cashel saw his sister's interest perk like that of a fox sighting prey.

"After the sacrifice?" Garric repeated. "Why then?"

"Generally in Carcosa the nobles and their retainers support the Lady," Liane said, "and the laborers follow the Shepherd. It's the same in Valles, though in Erdin it was just the opposite. If somebody wants to make trouble, he can usually stir things up when people gather at the temples for the sacrifice."

"Is that true?" Cashel said to Mellie. Garric and Ilna looked as shocked as Cashel felt.

"Oh, yes," the sprite agreed as she pirouetted. "Sometimes they fight each other, but mostly the mobs go smash things in a district where the other side lives. It's very exciting to watch."

"It's evil!" Cashel said so loudly that everyone heard him.

Garric and Ilna nodded agreement; Liane looked sober. "Fighting in the name of the Lady and the Shepherd!"

"It's a symptom of the forces becoming greatly stronger, just as they did in my day," Tenoctris said. "Nothing to do with the gods or religion of course; just dynamic tension too extreme to remain in perfect balance."

"It's evil!" Cashel repeated fiercely.

"Nonnus would certainly agree with you," the old woman said, looking back toward Cashel. "And in human terms you're certainly correct."

She smiled faintly, sadly, and added, "I just don't believe the cosmos thinks in human terms, Cashel."

16

On their way through Carcosa, Garric noticed that they'd passed several inns catering to folk from the eastern boroughs of Haft. The Red Ox was near the northern boundary of the present city where most arriving guests would be from the flat north of the island.

Northerners raised more cattle than sheep and by the standards of Barca's Hamlet they were a coarse lot besides. The inn's standard was a red-painted ox skull on a pole: most of the gilt had flaked from the horns. Garric tried to imagine his father putting a sheep's skull over the gates of his inn; he shook his head in disgust at the image.

Carcosa wasn't what Garric had expected. Unlike what he knew his friends from the borough were experiencing, the city was strikingly less than what Garric had thought he'd find. He remembered in his dreams riding through a metropolis of marble and fountains, triumphal arches and the pillared buildings where the whole government of the Isles transacted its business.

King Carus watched from the back of Garric's mind, more sober now than at any time since the night he entered a boy's dreams and drove away the nightmares. Over the days since Garric put on the medallion, the king had continued to stride closer through the planes that separated the two of them. Sometimes even when he was awake Garric thought he could hear King Carus' voice, and the king's memories lay in a haze over Garric's own.

The buildings of today's Carcosa grew like mushrooms on the stump of a fallen elm, covering the surface but with nothing like the density or magnificence of the original. The city had merely a barbaric sparkle, the sort of thing that was well enough in a provincial backwater with no pretensions to greatness.

But what had been great could become great again.

Benlo dismounted in front of the inn. The servant who took the mare spoke in terms of obsequious acquaintance; the drover must have stayed at the Red Ox while he was in Carcosa before.

The place was big and well kept, but it wouldn't have been Garric's choice for accommodation. The roof was of terracotta tiles; he supposed thatch wasn't a practical roofing material in a city. Neither that nor the ox skull was sufficient to make Garric feel so uncomfortable about the inn, but his discomfort was real.

He glanced up to speak to Tenoctris and saw that the old woman peering intently not at the inn but rather toward the enclosure wall across the road. "What's that?" Garric asked. All he could see from his level were the stone roofs of small buildings above the stone perimeter; Tenoctris at saddle height had a better view.

"It's a graveyard," Tenoctris said. "A very old graveyard. Old even in my day, though the tombs are still being reused."

She dismounted stiffly, using Garric's shoulder as a hand brace and his laced fingers as a step. Riding was easier than walking, but neither had been a skill she'd cultivated.

An inn servant whisked the mare into the stables in the

rear. Benlo walked toward the group from Barca's Hamlet with a broad smile that Garric was sure was forced if not faked. "Well, lads," the drover said. "I've arranged for all of us to stay here for a few days."

He nodded at Tenoctris, then to Ilna as well. The smile slipped slightly. "The women too," he said. "I promised you that I'd . . . gain information when we reached the city, so it's only fair that I put you up at my expense."

Garric opened his mouth to speak. Before he could do so, Tenoctris said, "Thanks for your offer, but I believe I'll have to decline it. I don't care for some of the neighbors here."

She nodded her tight gray bun of hair toward the cemetery.

Benlo's face grew darkly furious. "Are you one of those old fools who's afraid of death?" he said. "Best get used to the thought, mistress. It'll be coming for you soon enough!"

"I'm not afraid of death," Tenoctris said simply. "I only fear for the living." She bowed and stepped back, awaiting the decisions of others.

"Master Benlo," Cashel said, planting one end of his quarterstaff on the ground beside him, "if you'll pay me my last day's wage I'll take my leave also." He lifted the purse from beneath his tunic and cocked his head as if listening to someone. Tenoctris squinted, then frowned, at the big youth.

"Yes, all right," Benlo said. He was clearly irritated at being balked even though he'd never cared what Cashel did except to the extent it affected Garric's actions. "Rald"—the chief guard carried the purse of silver and copper—"pay him an anchor."

"As for me," Ilna said with a curtness that would have been anger in another person; Garric knew her well enough to recognize it as her normal attitude, "we owe each other nothing and I don't require charity. I'll find my own lodgings."

All eyes were on Garric. "Sir," he said to the drover, "I'll go with my friends, thank you. I—"

"You can't run from it, boy," Benlo said. Liane blushed. Her father's tone did Garric the further insult of treating him like a recalcitrant beast instead of a human with the right to an opinion. "I don't care how much of a coward you are, *I'm* your only hope of safety!"

Garric saw the same scene twice, through his own eyes and through others that stained everything a bright, pulsing red. He stood still, afraid of what would happen if he moved.

"I'm very sorry you think me a coward, sir," he said. His voice quavered, but it was Garric or-Reise speaking, not the figure whose rage would splatter blood as far as the inn's high roof.

Liane stepped between Garric and her father. Her eyes caught Garric's and held them.

Garric's shackled anger turned inward, filling him with the sick trembling of hormones unburned. He wanted to throw up and he wasn't sure his legs would hold him much longer. He turned his back, squeezed his temples hard, and faced around again.

Cashel and Tenoctris were looking at him with concern, but Ilna's eyes were on the drover. She'd unbound the rope she wore around her waist and held the ends in her hands as she measured the distance to Benlo's throat.

"Be that as it may," Garric resumed, ignoring the repeated catch in his throat, "I don't choose to stay in the present surroundings. It isn't that I fear the dead, Master Benlo; nor the living"—he heard his voice tremble—"if it comes to that."

Garric gripped his temples again, trying to press a fresh surge of rage out of his skull. He opened his eyes. He hated not being his own man; but he was a man, not a boy, in the eyes of Benlo's guards. He could see they were afraid that nothing could save their employer if this dangerous man Garric chose to strike him down.

The drover himself didn't understand the danger; but his daughter did. "Garric . . ." Liane said.

"Yes," Garric said, speaking to himself as a separate person, then merging again to become a single soul in his own body. The spasm had passed. "Yes."

He raised his eyes to Benlo's. "Sir," he said. "I'll visit you again after I've found quarters to my satisfaction. At any rate I'll return before I leave Carcosa. Good day!"

Garric walked away—nowhere in particular, just away. His friends fell in behind him; Tenoctris quick-stepped to keep up until Garric noticed and in embarrassment slowed his pace.

He thought from the corner of his eye he saw Liane start to follow. Her father caught her by the arm.

"Garric?" rumbled Cashel as they turned the first corner they came to.

Garric looked around, finding to his vague amusement that he knew where they were: the buildings were mostly different or mere tree-grown piles of rubble, but the vast pillars of the Temple of Concord of the Isles still stood, even though the roof and most of the entablature had fallen ages ago. The harbor was half a mile south; the Summer Palace—and what did it look like now?—was half a mile north on the same boulevard.

"I'm sorry for the way I acted back there," Garric muttered.

"Huh!" Ilna sniffed. "Sorry for what?"

"Garric," Cashel repeated. "You too, Ilna. You've been good to me and I'll miss you, but I'm going now."

He turned. Garric caught his arm. "Cashel, wait," he said. "Where are you going?"

Cashel shook his head. "I don't know," he said. "Garric, I'd have gone as soon as he paid me, but I didn't want it to look like I was walking out on you. You didn't need me, I saw you with the liches; but I didn't want it to look wrong to other people."

He lowered his arm—not tugging it away, but removing himself from contact nonetheless. Garric realized that his friend was one of the few people who didn't see any point in talk when talk wouldn't change matters.

And talk clearly wasn't going to change Cashel or-Kenset's determination to go off by himself.

"You'll be all right?" Ilna asked sharply.

Cashel gave her a slow smile. "Yeah, I think so," he said. He frowned in concern. "Oh," he went on. "I have money. How much would you like? All of it?"

Ilna shook her head. "I'll be quite all right, brother," she said. "I . . . will·miss having you to take care of."

She turned her back and put a hand to her face.

Garric swallowed and gripped Cashel's hand; he felt like a grapevine wrapping an oak. "Good luck, friend," he said. "I'll miss you."

Cashel smiled, nodded, and walked away. The tip of his quarterstaff was visible long after the crowd had swallowed the rest of his big form.

"Raphik, the merchant from Valles who buys my weaving," Ilna said quietly, "mentioned that in Carcosa he stays in the Captain's Rest near the harbor. Most of the guests are ships' officers. Raphik said it was quiet, clean, and not expensive."

She smiled with uncharacteristic softness. "He compared it to your father's inn, as a matter of fact."

Garric didn't react. He was trying to absorb all the things that had happened in the past few minutes. Losing Cashel, though his big friend had done no more than he'd said in Barca's Hamlet he planned to do; and almost losing his own mind in murderous rage . . . that was even worse.

Ilna's face hardened when Garric ignored her pleasantry. "Of course," she said with icy nonchalance, "you may already have decided to go back to the Red Ox to stay with your fine new friends."

"No," Garric said, recalling himself to his present company. "I'm sorry, Ilna, I was just feeling . . . A lot's been happening. The harbor's straight down this way." He pointed. "Ah, I think."

He set off at a cautious amble that he thought Tenoctris could match without strain. The traffic here wasn't as bad as it had been near the square, but he walked slightly ahead of the women and to their left so that his shoulder took the shock of the occasional traveler too hasty for care.

"I expect I can find work at the Captain's Rest as I did on the road," Ilna said in a mollified tone. "Tomorrow perhaps I'll see to selling my fabric."

"Mistress Tenoctris?" Garric said. "Is it because of the liches that you want to keep away from the graveyard?"

This section of the street was given over to tinker's ware— pots and kettles of bronze and copper and pale white tin, silver's dull sibling. It shocked Garric to see so many metal utensils in one place. In the borough most kitchenware was of wood or cast iron, with other metals generally to mend splits in the *treen*, wooden, dishes.

"It isn't the presence of skeletons that controls the raising of liches," Tenoctris said. "It's the sea itself. I don't believe a lich could travel to the Red Ox so far from all water, much less be created there."

She cleared her throat, aware that she was giving a lecture rather than an answer to Garric's real question. "Garric," she said, "I was more worried by the spells I'm sure Benlo will use to learn who's working against him. There's a great deal of power centered in those ancient tombs, but it's not a clean single force. Strands are knotted in fashions that I couldn't separate and Benlo can't even recognize. I'm afraid he'll manage to do something very dangerous, but I can't even predict what the thing will be."

Garric thought of Liane. He formed a question in his mind, then suppressed it unspoken; Ilna's behavior already made him uncomfortable, and he couldn't drag a girl away from her father without her even asking for help.

"Should we have warned him?" Garric said aloud.

"He wouldn't listen," Tenoctris said. "And Benlo's very powerful, you know. I'd very much like to have the answer if he learns it. The force that's working against Benlo is almost certainly directed against you too, Garric; and I think against anything you would class as 'good' as well."

"You think that Benlo is going to fall into evil by accident with his magic?" Garric said.

A tout for a corner cookshop stepped in front of him. Garric stopped in polite surprise; no one would be so brazen in Barca's Hamlet. Ilna strode straight at the fellow, the end of her short carry-staff aimed at his face. He yelped and hopped back.

"It's not nearly that simple, Garric," Tenoctris said with a sigh. "Not as simple as good and evil, and not merely two choices. Think of how complex a living person is. Is there one human being whose personality you understand perfectly?"

Garric thought of Ilna and Cashel . . . and himself. "No," he said. "Not even close."

Tenoctris nodded. "When a person dies and is buried, forces fill the space his soul—or whatever word you choose to describe the part of a human that isn't flesh . . . the space his soul used to fill. The way quartz replaces the wood of a fallen tree and leaves it agate; different in every detail, yet still recognizable as a tree trunk."

"It does?" Garric said. "Trees become stone?"

"I could never keep to the subject I was trying to explain," Tenoctris said with a rueful smile. "One of the reasons I never managed to explain very much."

The smile passed. "The other reason is that I don't understand very much . . . which is better, I suppose, than thinking like Benlo that I do understand."

She tapped her lips with a finger. "Benlo sees the ancient tombs as a nexus of great power, which they are. He doesn't see that each of what he thinks is a strand of force is a thousand strands spun together, and that some of them lead to consequences that even he with all his powers can't control."

Ilna nodded, watching Tenoctris with perfect understanding. Garric thought of the care with which Ilna chose her thread before she began weaving; each nuance of color judged before she worked it into her pattern. Oh, yes, she would understand.

"Your friend Cashel knew to avoid the Red Ox without me telling him," Tenoctris said. "I suppose it's just that he recognized the forces and chose to avoid them because he doesn't want to use the talent he unquestionably has. But at first I thought that there might be more to it than that.''

"Talent?" Garric asked.

"Yes," Tenoctris said. "I was surprised that even Benlo wasn't able to recognize it, but Benlo's talent is of a very different sort. And Benlo is ignorant, of course.''

Garric glanced at Ilna from the corner of his eyes. She didn't speak.

"I don't think Cashel would've stayed with us anyway," Garric said aloud. "He was really bothered about Sharina leaving the hamlet. He told me he was going to go off by himself. I didn't believe him till it happened, though.''

He shook his head, trying to make sense of a situation whose elements were complete nonsense. "I just can't understand . . . I mean, Sharina's a great kid, sure. But why would anybody be so broken up about a girl leaving? I don't *understand*.''

"No," said Ilna. "I wouldn't have imagined you would.''

To Garric's complete surprise she pushed past him and continued down the street at a walk that was just short of a run. "Ilna?" he called. He looked at Tenoctris; her face was expressionless.

The inn just ahead of them hung a rocking chair above the street for a sign. The words THE CAPTAIN'S REST were painted in gilt on the broad rockers. Ilna, twenty feet ahead, was going past it.

"Ilna!" Garric called, realizing suddenly that his friend couldn't read. "Ilna, this is our inn!''

She stopped and turned back to enter; he'd been afraid she wouldn't. He should have known how much she'd miss her brother, now that he thought about it. He was pretty sure that when Ilna turned around, he'd seen the glitter of tears on her cheeks.

17

Nonnus slept more soundly than anyone else Sharina had met, and her duties at the inn had given her more experience with sleeping men than most properly raised girls could claim. The hermit had made a joke of it: "I sleep like a seal," he'd said, but that was the truth. Danger might awaken him, but the cold sea splashing over the dugout's bows did not.

The moon hadn't risen yet; it would be in its last quarter when it did. Occasionally stars showed between the columns of thin stratus clouds, but they gave no light.

The sea, thick with phosphorescent plankton, was a bright swelling wasteland beneath the dark sky. Sharina looked north and saw nothing but shifting hills vaster than anything in the landscape of Barca's Hamlet. Nothing but water, all the way to the Ice Capes . . .

Sharina pulled her cloak closer about her and wished she could stop shivering. The fitful, contrary breeze wasn't that cold; she wouldn't have bothered with a wrap if she'd been back home, back on land once more.

A fish jumped. Sharina's eyes caught the motion rather than a form: a twisting silhouette against the glowing water, a splash, and a momentary blotch which filled as tiny multilegged swimmers returned to the point from which they'd been disturbed.

The hook and line had already caught several fish. Nonnus had been right: there wasn't the slightest chance that the four of them would starve, no matter how long they drifted.

Except during brief moments when a fish broke surface, the dugout was alone in a sea more vast than Sharina could have dreamed when she looked down on its pleasant expanse from the bluffs north of Barca's Hamlet. The hermit sighed faintly in his sleep.

The sail, furled beneath its lowered spar, lay crossways over the gunwales. When the passengers were hunched in the belly of the dugout the rolled canvas was a barrier between those in the bow and stern. Meder was on duty at the steering oar; Asera was with him. When Nonnus or Sharina was on watch, the nobles went forward together. The groups acknowledged one another's presence by the briefest nods, existing in parallel but without contact as if they were adjacent buildings.

Nonnus hadn't set the sail since the dugout tore through the reefs of Tegma, gaining freedom and the clean, crisp air of the natural world for the folk aboard her. Nothing in the world was more natural than death, nor cleaner than the Ice Capes.

If Sharina listened carefully she could hear the drone of Meder's voice between gusts of the southeast breeze. Sickly red light flickered above the dugout's stern and stained the nearby swell. The hermit sighed again; he slept in a tight ball with his arms curled around his shins.

Sharina turned her face forward and focused her eyes on the northern horizon. She wished she could sleep; she wished a lot of things.

But the sea was so vast . . .

18

"Couldn't you feel the way those old graves pulled, Cashel?" Mellie said. She hugged herself and shivered melodramatically, though the smile she gave him was as bright as ever. "Ooh! As if they were trying to drag us in!"

"My skin prickled," Cashel said. "I figured I'd gotten

some sun. Is the sun brighter on this side of the island, do you suppose? The air seems drier, that's a fact.''

He sauntered down a narrow street whose merchants specialized in coarse leather goods: harness and tack for draft animals, vests and aprons for laborers; hinges and latch cords even in one small alcove. The proprietors sat in front of their shops, ready to help a customer or twitch the sleeve of a passerby; ready also to bar a light-fingered thief.

Some of the shopkeepers tried to stop Cashel; he ignored them, not by plan but because he was so fascinated by the quantities of similar merchandise all in the same location. He supposed that fine goods—rich folks' sandals and gloves; suede cutwork to net milady's hair—were in a separate street, perhaps a separate district. He walked on by, an ox treading slowly through tall grass and completely unaffected by its brushing contact.

The sprite laughed. "I forgot how strong you are," she said. "Well, it wasn't sunburn, it was that nasty tangle of forces there around the tombs. I haven't seen anything like that in a thousand years. The paths back to my plane closed in tangles like that."

"Well," Cashel said, "I didn't want to stay there anyway. Besides, if I was going to leave everything, I had to leave."

He walked with his quarterstaff held vertical and close to his body; occasionally it rapped a sign or the overhanging second floor of a building, but it was as much out of the way as he could manage. Walking in Carcosa was like pushing his way through a thicket after an ewe who'd let greed for ripening berries tangle her in the brambles.

"I've thought of going through an opening like that," Mellie said quietly, lacing her fingers in front of her and gazing at them as she bent them backward at arm's length. "Of course, it wouldn't really be through, just into. I could never find my way home, and there's too many things waiting at the edge of the path now. Better a cat, I think, when it comes to that."

She did a quick aerial somersault, then hopped forward

onto her hands. "Or a fox!" she added as she grinned at Cashel upside down.

Mellie's nonchalance about her own death made Cashel uncomfortable. She wasn't careless of herself; but she didn't seem to care, either. Well, she had him now.

The street ahead was almost completely blocked by a deep-bellied box wagon. A gang of muscular men unloaded covered baskets from the wagon and passed them hand-to-hand into a building site where blocks of masonry were already stacked.

An architect in a striped robe watched the work with a critical frown, tapping the long wooden dividers that were the symbol of his office. Orange tunics and rattles for summoning help marked a pair of city marshals who shouted warnings to be careful; workmen grunted and ignored them.

Cashel sneezed. "Quicklime," he said. The builders were preparing to mix cement.

He looked up at the narrow gap of sky between upper stories encroaching from either side of the street. There were more clouds than he'd have wanted to trust not to rain and slake the lime in its baskets before it could be mixed. Folk in the city took risks because they were always in a hurry. Most folk were in more of a hurry than Cashel thought was safe, he knew.

"To make that lime they burned the pillars of a temple that was over a thousand years old," Mellie said. She rolled upright again. "Can you see how it shimmers with power?"

She giggled. "I wonder what kind of a building they're going to put up? I'll bet they get some surprises!"

Cashel watched the laborers a little longer. He could probably find work with the crew if he wanted to; they were strong men, but he could lift as much as any two of them. Still, he had money in his purse, more money than he'd ever dreamed of. And besides . . .

"It's not right to use a temple for cement," he muttered. He supposed it'd been in ruins like so much else of Carcosa. That didn't make it right.

Mellie dropped into a back-bend, touching her heels with her fingertips. "Humans build and humans tear down," she said. "You folk live very fast."

Cashel waited for two porters carrying a handbarrow and a woman with a large wicker basket of washing to pass the obstruction going the other way. There was room beneath the builder's wagon to creep under, but quicklime seeped through the bottom planks; Cashel might have taken that route if he'd been alone, but not with the sprite on his shoulder.

Three men in dyed tunics tried to follow the washerwoman. They shouted for Cashel to wait. Cashel ignored them and they gave way.

"We're getting close to the harbor," Mellie said. She stuck her tongue out and waggled her fingers from her ears at a cat curled on a stack of canvas dungarees. The cat didn't get up, but its eyes followed Cashel and his passenger down the street. "There used to be dealers here who sold coral and amber and whale-tooth ivory. But that was a thousand years ago."

Even Cashel would have guessed they were in the harbor district. The shops were for the most part open-fronted, selling rugged clothing of the sort the trireme's crew had worn.

Midway in the block was a more substantial business with an outer grate of heavy bars and an inner one of fine-meshed wire to prohibit sneak thieves. The stock displayed was gold jewelry and bright silk sashes—sailors' goods again, but for show on land. Some of the stock was used; the proprietor probably acted as a pawnbroker as well.

Someone brushed Cashel from behind with a murmur he took for apology. He turned his head, saw a pair of willowy, dark-skinned men in brown robes. He stepped into an alcove selling wool caps and sweaters; the proprietor, an old woman knitting on a stool, barely raised her eyes to acknowledge him.

The two men—Cashel assumed they were men, though their bun of hair and long robes gave no real indication of sex—trotted past at just short of a run. Their faces were impassive but tense. More than a dozen rough-looking young townsmen followed them closely.

"Serians," Mellie said. "They live around the coast of an island far to the southeast. A different sort of folk live in the Highlands."

As Cashel watched with narrowing eyes, one of the toughs shouted "Go worship your devils someplace else, dirt!" and threw a stone. It bounced off a Serian's shoulder. The victim staggered and lengthened his stride. He and his fellow tried to duck into the fancy-goods shop. The potbellied shopkeeper slammed a grille across his doorway and stood behind it grinning.

The mob of toughs poured past Cashel, forming a semicircle around the trapped foreigners. Proprietors up and down the street dropped their shutters. The old woman continued to knit with an impassive expression.

A tough grabbed the hem of one long robe and pulled it up. The cloth shimmered in the light: it was fine silk brocade. Ilna would be interested. . . .

Cashel grimaced. "Mellie, hop off, there's a love," he said. He tapped the nearest tough on the shoulder and asked, "What's happening here, master?"

The man, a youth with a tattooed cheek and wiry muscles, turned and snarled, "Do I look like an oracle, sheep-dip? Get out of here or you'll find something you didn't want!"

He turned. Cashel turned him back with the hand that didn't hold his quarterstaff. "In Barca's Hamlet we answer strangers' questions politely," he said.

"Hey, boys, we got another!" the tough shouted as his hand flicked into the opposite sleeve and came out with a knife as Cashel had expected him to do.

Cashel hit him in the face with the fist wrapped around the quarterstaff, a short punch that would have stunned a draft horse. The lightly built tough flew into the mob of his fellows, giving Cashel the space he needed. The second stories were closer than the ground floors. Cashel turned sideways and spun the staff like a grindstone as he crab-walked through the locals.

A man's forearm snapped with a sharp crack; he screamed and the club fell from his fingers. Another tough dropped when the quarterstaff grazed his skull and broke his shoulder; he wouldn't thank his attacker when he awakened, but the blow would have killed him if Cashel hadn't deliberately altered the line of rotation.

A tough flung his knife blindly and ran, forcing his way past fellows who didn't yet know what was happening. The fine-goods shop had a wooden sign on a horizontal pole crossing the street. Cashel couldn't step under it with the staff still spinning, so he judged his distance and struck the pole near its base. Iron-shod hickory met pine with a *whack* that sent the heavy sign flying onto the remnants of the mob.

The toughs still able to run did so, leaving a trail of weapons behind. One man bled from a severe thigh wound that was none of Cashel's doing.

Rattles sounded from both ends of the street, but Cashel noticed that no city marshals entered until the last of the thugs had disappeared around a corner. He looked around him, panting like a blown horse.

Four locals were down, two of them groaning and one the yellow-white color of raw wool as he tried to get his breath. Cashel vaguely remembered kicking him in the pit of the stomach; a lifetime's calluses from rocky soil had done a job hobnailed boots couldn't have bettered.

"Ooh, you were great!" Mellie cried from his shoulder, clapping her hands in glee. She'd ignored his order to get down. "Of course, I knew you would be."

The orange-clad marshals approached gingerly. Both officers were in their late fifties. One gripped the truncheon that was his only weapon, but the other had better sense. Cashel supposed he could run, but he wasn't going to. He'd done what he'd done; he'd take the consequences of it.

The Serians stepped out of the alcove that had become a trap instead of a refuge. One of them bowed to the marshals and said, "Pardon, sirs, but I don't think there's any business here for you."

"When I want to hear dirt's opinion on—" a marshal said. His eyes focused on the Serian's outstretched hand. "Ah?"

The Serian turned his hand palm-up and opened his fingers. Two silver coins winked on the swarthy skin.

The other marshal said in a worried tone—worry at losing the bribe, Cashel was sure, "Look, there's been damage. . . . Them don't matter—"

He toed a groaning tough.

"—but . . ."

"I seen it all," the old woman knitting said unexpectedly. "The sign blew down in the dumdest whirlwind *I* ever seen." She grinned toothlessly at the marshals. "If I was you fellows, I'd take my money and get out afore you meet another of them winds."

Cashel had his breath back, or near enough. He picked up the sign and carried it to the door alcove. The fat proprietor watched through the grate, no longer smiling.

Cashel leaned the sign against the shopfront. "Do you have a problem with anything that's happened here?" he asked in his usual calm, slow voice.

The proprietor stared at the quarterstaff. Blood from a tough's torn scalp was crawling down the shaft and had almost reached Cashel's hand. Instead of answering, the man slammed the solid door panel closed behind the grating.

The first marshal shrugged. "Accidents happen," he said. He took the coins from the Serian's palm and flipped one to his partner. The marshals walked back in the directions from which they'd come.

The Serians talked in low voices. Their heads were together but their eyes followed Cashel. He returned to the knitwear stall and said, "Mistress? Thank you. Could I do something . . ." He didn't know if he ought to offer her money or what.

The old woman cackled. "Oh," she said, "if I was thirty years younger, laddie, there'd be something you could do for me all right. Nowadays I'll take it as pleasure enough to have seen you move."

She looked past him toward the Serians, who now waited with their fingers tented for Cashel to finish. Her hands continued to knit with the detached constancy of a brook purling.

"Besides," she said in a gentler tone, "I used to live with a Serian more years ago than I care to remember. He was a devil worshipper, right enough, but he never beat me—which is more than I could say about certain Haft gentlemen who never missed a midweek sacrifice. Now, you go on before I decide I'm maybe not too old for you after all!"

Cashel turned and faced the Serians. They nodded to him; one pointed toward the end of the street and said, "Sir? Might we speak to you in other surroundings, please? There's a park of sorts this way."

Shop shutters were beginning to open. One of the toughs looked ready to stand up, though Cashel doubted he'd be much threat to anyone for a while. "All right, masters," he said.

Cashel walked between the Serians to the head of the block, where a pipe-fed fountain in the center of a cobblestone square provided water for the surrounding streets. A marble trumpeter with his horn raised vertically to his lips stood in the center of the basin; water bubbled from the bell. The open sky was a relief after so many narrow streets.

"My name is Frasa," the first Serian said; he bowed. Cashel couldn't have told the two apart with any degree of certainty. They looked like identical masks carved from a block of mahogany.

"And I am Jen," said the other, bowing in turn. "We would like to hire you, sir. We will pay more than your present employer."

"Ah," said Cashel. He wondered if he ought to bow. "I'm Cashel or-Kenset. Ah, I'm a shepherd."

"Shepherd!" Mellie giggled from his shoulder.

"We are merchants, Master Cashel," Frasa said. "We have a cargo here in Carcosa. You have noticed that passions are running high against members of our religion. Perhaps you share those passions?''

"I never met a Serian before just now," Cashel said uncomfortably. "If you want to worship devils, I guess that's your business."

Jen blinked, then broke out with a startled guffaw—the first sign of emotion Cashel had seen from the still-faced pair.

"We don't think of what we do as worshipping devils, Master Cashel," Frasa said, "but as you imply, that's neither here nor there. We need a shepherd of sorts; a strong man to shepherd us through the dangers of a hostile city until we can sell our cargo."

"Our faith prevents us from harming another human being, sir," Jen said. "What another person does on our behalf is between him and his gods, however, and we pay well. Highlanders from the interior of Seres protect our ships from pirates, but it wouldn't be practical to bring them out of the compound with us."

"They're cannibals who file their teeth," Mellie said, caressing the lobe of Cashel's right ear. "Some of them can see my people. They eat us, too."

Cashel found listening to three people at the same time meant he didn't understand what any of them were saying. He heard the words; he just couldn't connect them in his mind with anything real. "Look," he said. "You need guards. I'm just . . ."

He glanced back toward the street of clothiers, feeling embarrassed. "Look," he repeated, "I don't want you to think I do this a lot. I just, well . . ."

He couldn't not have acted, any more than he would've let seawolves ravage somebody else's flock. He didn't know how to explain that. Back home, of course, he wouldn't have had to explain, because everybody felt the same way.

About sheep, at least. Maybe not about wooden-faced strangers.

"We're aware that we could hire professional men of violence," Frasa said. "Though perhaps not easily, given the way Count Lascarg is using''—he smiled coldly—''devil worshippers as a scapegoat for social turmoils. In any case, we would prefer to contract with a person whose first concern was justice rather than money. Though we'll willingly pay your price—say, three Haft silver pieces a day?''

"Four," said Jen decisively. "We couldn't hire any two men to do what we were privileged to watch Master Cashel do just now. And of course, we'll pay you for today, sir, whatever your decision as to further employment."

Cashel tried to imagine that kind of money, counting on his fingers. Ilna would be thrilled—

Ilna wouldn't know. He might never see his sister again.

He cocked his head to look at Mellie. The sprite went up on tiptoe, joining her fingers above her head as if she was preparing to dive from his shoulder.

"Oh, don't worry about me, Cashel," she said with a grin. She was too perfectly beautiful to be real; and of course she *wasn't* real in the human sense. "Highlanders don't bother me. Rats are much worse, and if there's Highlanders there aren't any rats—"

She did a handstand, placing her fingertips exactly where her toes had been a moment before.

"—unless the Highlanders are fed *really* well."

The Serians waited. Cashel shrugged and said, "Well, I guess we can try it for a while."

He stuck out his right hand to seal the bargain. Jen and Frasa bowed instead, and Frasa took a well-filled purse from beneath his robe.

The stone trumpeter blew joyous ripples in the sunlight.

19

Carcosa after dark was a smoky, threatening warren. Garric had rented a lantern at the Captain's Rest, but he hadn't bothered to hire a linkman to guide him and Tenoctris back to the Red Ox because he had a good sense of direction and the recollections of King Carus besides. Murmurs and clinks in some of the narrow alleys they passed made him wonder if a third person in the party wouldn't have been a safety measure.

Aloud he said, "Though I'd worry that anybody we hired here would lead us *into* a band of robbers."

"I think we're safe enough with you, Garric," Tenoctris said. Then she added, "With the help of your medallion, if someone should be foolish enough to attack. He's with you, isn't he?"

"Sort of," Garric muttered. He didn't want to think about what Carus' growing presence might mean.

He'd refused to wear a sword following the night at the Stroma River: he didn't like the way his personality shifted when his hand rested on a sword hilt. The rented lantern hung on the end of a three-foot iron rod so that the user could hold it in front of him. In a pinch, the rod could be an effective weapon.

But Garric preferred not to think about that, either.

A man and woman argued in a door alcove; the man was drunk, the woman sober enough to fall silent till the lantern's yellow light passed on. A third figure, another man, watched from across the street—waiting also, but patting a bludgeon into the palm of his other hand.

It was none of Garric's affair, but it made him feel uncomfortable anyway. And yet—he didn't know the real rights or wrongs. The drunken man would be clubbed; probably robbed, possibly killed. But if the woman didn't have a protector present, what would happen to her at the drunk's hands? Garric was beginning to understand why Tenoctris put "good" and "evil" in quotes; but he was still sure that whatever the merits of the particular situation, a society in which violence was the primary means of settling disputes was an evil society.

"There's pressure on the visible world as forces build on other planes," Tenoctris said quietly. She'd described her talent as an ability to see things. That extended to the personality structures of those around her. "Cities are always worse than villages because anonymous people will do things that they wouldn't in the face of their neighbors, but I suspect it's worse now in Carcosa than it was a decade ago."

They rounded a dogleg in the street. "That's the Red Ox," Garric said thankfully.

A lamp hung over the door of the inn. It had a large oil reservoir and sides of glass clearer than any window in Barca's Hamlet. As Garric started inside, he realized that the stocky man leaning next to the doorway was Rald, the drover's chief guard. He was fully armed and looked worried.

"Sir?" Garric asked. "Mistress Tenoctris and I have come to talk with your master as we promised we would. Is he—"

He nodded toward the inn. The common room was huge and raucously busy. The part of his mind that was Reise's son noted professionally that they covered the floors here with sawdust instead of rushes.

Rald shook his head. "Master Benlo went out at nightfall," he said. "I don't know just where for sure, but I shouldn't wonder if he'd gone the usual place—across to the cemetery."

He gestured by moving only his eyes. Under the slanting lamplight Garric could see a gouge that the guard had almost polished out of his helmet; the damage was a reminder of the fight at Stroma River.

"He went there every night we stayed at this inn," Rald continued. "Only he never took his daughter with him before. He—"

"He took Liane?" Garric said.

"This time, yes he did," Rald said. "And he made it real clear that me and the boys wasn't to come with him. But you know, kid, I sure think somebody ought to go see what's happening."

"Somebody will," said Tenoctris. She started across.

"Kid, wait!" Rald called. "Take this."

Garric turned. The guard held out his sword and belt. Garric took the weapon with a nod of thanks. He buckled it on as he crossed the street with Tenoctris.

There was a gate into the cemetery a hundred yards down the street, but when Garric hesitated the old woman patted the wall immediately across from the Red Ox and said, "Lift me up. They're not far from here."

Garric didn't understand how she knew, but that didn't matter. He leaned the lantern against the wall and used both hands to set Tenoctris on the coping five feet up. His fingers almost met around her petite waist.

Tenoctris swung her legs over to the other side, looking as though she planned to jump down. That didn't look safe to Garric, so he swung himself onto the wall and over, then lowered the old woman to the ground as gently as he'd raised her up.

The lantern was still on the street side of the stonework. Garric hunched to go back for it.

"Leave it," said Tenoctris with a decisiveness that was usually beneath the surface of her personality. "It isn't necessary now. It's this way."

The graveyard was a village of tombs the size of shepherds' huts, mixed with many hundreds of stone troughs a foot wide and a few feet long; some of the latter still had lids carved with a crude tree-of-life pattern. They were all empty. Ornamental cypresses had grown to great heights among the human structures.

From his reading Garric knew the troughs had held the bones of the ancient poor in a custom which hadn't survived the collapse of the Old Kingdom. Families removed the bones to these individual ossuaries after the flesh had decayed during a year in the huge common sepulchre in the center of the grounds. The latter's dome had long collapsed and its walls were overgrown with ivy and honeysuckle.

Many of the tombs were still in use by the wealthy and powerful of today's Carcosa. The walls were cleaned, the roof slabs replaced where necessary, and new coats of arms were chiseled over the entrances to replace those of the original builders.

Tenoctris led the way between the larger tombs and over the troughs lying every which way like deliberate ankle-traps among the resting places of their betters. Garric used the city's sky glow and the light of the recently risen moon to help him pick his way, but the old woman moved faster and with a sureness that kept her from tripping as Garric did time after time. *She must have eyes like a cat.*

He was afraid for Liane and afraid as well for himself. He had no idea what they would be meeting. From what Tenoctris had said earlier, even she wasn't certain.

"Sister take you!" Garric snarled as his foot sank in a shadow-hidden hole that could have wrenched his knee and crippled him for life. He was sorry for the words as soon as he spoke them: this was no place or time to be calling on the Queen of the Underworld.

An iron bell rang from the center of the city; Garric didn't know whether it warned of disaster or if it happened every night in Carcosa when the watches changed. He belonged back in Barca's Hamlet.

But for now he was here, and since he was here he'd follow the guidance of an old woman who said she had the good of the cosmos at heart.

Tenoctris held up a hand in warning. They halted ten feet from two tombs built as a facing pair; the one in black basalt, the other a fine-grained granite so light as to be white in the moonlight. A pavement of dark and light blocks joined the pillared doorways. The wreaths of yew and holly on the pale tomb indicated a recent interment there.

"The folk of today, even the wizards, think because the original bodies have rotted to dust that the tombs are empty," Tenoctris whispered in tones of cold disdain. "If they saw what I see, they'd know better than to place their dead here where those who were so much greater lie. They might as well throw their children to seawolves!"

Garric massaged his bruised shin without speaking. A breeze murmured through the cypresses, some of which were so huge and old that their roots had crumbled the vaults they'd been planted to decorate.

Tenoctris twisted a twig from the boxwood tree beside her. "There," she said, pointing her makeshift wand toward the basalt tomb.

The black stone was barely an outline in the dim light, but perhaps for that very reason Garric began to see a blue flickering—not so much light as the ghost of light—from the stone-grated eye window at the roof peak and around the edge of the rusty iron door. The panel was slightly ajar.

Garric reached the tomb in three strides and shoved against the vertical door handle. The heavy door flexed with a groan but didn't open; it was stuck against the sill. Garric heard Benlo chanting unintelligibly while Liane's higher, clearer voice called, "*Phanoibikux petriade kratarnade*—"

"Stop!" Tenoctris shouted. "That spell will—"

Silent red light glared through the basalt the way the sun penetrates flesh. The whole graveyard shone in momentary vivid clarity. Benlo screamed on a rising note that ended in a gurgle.

"Liane!" Garric said, and hit the door panel with all his weight and strength. The wedge holding it shut scraped back and flew into the sunken vault within.

Niches lined the walls. They'd once held the ashes of cremated nobles; now they were empty except for dust and a single black candle lighting the symbols written on the floor three steps below ground level.

Benlo bor-Benliman lay in the middle of a seven-sided star around which were written words in the Old Script. He'd been disemboweled by a single upward stroke; his blood writhed on the stones beneath him.

Liane stood like a reversed image against a portal of intense red light in the middle of the vault. Her hands were raised as if to thrust back an unseen horror. She and the doorway were a flat painting on the air. Her dark hair and clothing were red and the white skin of her face and hands a black that gleamed like obsidian.

"Garric!" Liane's voice cried.

The light winked out and she was gone. Garric's arms snatched at empty air.

Tenoctris stared down at Benlo. His blood traced a word in the Old Script. "Strasedon!" Tenoctris said. "The utter fool! He summoned Strasedon to him!"

The trail of blood slumped into a normal pool and began to congeal in the light of the black candle. Death filled the vault with its familiar slaughterhouse stench.

20

This North Harbor used to be for the fleet alone," said Mellie. "It's all artificial, you know. I've seen three hundred triremes here, covered with bunting and spreading their striped sails."

She surveyed the buildings on the harbor side of the cobblestone street and added, "*My* how it's changed. You humans are such fun to watch!"

"The factory we've rented is this next one here," Frasa said with a nod. "It's owned by a consortium of our own people, though on previous trips we've sometimes used the Ardukh factory when there was already a cargo in ours."

The Serians normally kept their hands within their full sleeves. Their gestures were mostly facial, and slight by the standards of the people Cashel grew up with. That wasn't a problem to him, since for most of his life he'd been interpreting the even subtler body language of sheep.

Cashel hadn't been sure what the Serians meant by "factory." The indicated building was one of at least twenty similar structures: two-story in front with a lower extension in the rear and a walled compound to the side and back, all the way to the water. They were built of stone with sturdy double doors onto the street and only slit windows (if any) on the front. The Serian factory was one of those which had a perfectly blank façade except for the iron-strapped doors.

A team of tall brown men wearing breechclouts was washing recent filth from the factory's façade. Cashel could see speckles high up the masonry: marks left by flung cobblestones, harmless except in intent.

Jen and Frasa walked briskly to the door of the building with their faces lowered to avoid eye contact with the spectators. Cashel strode along with them, but he kept his head turning in all directions as he would when shepherding a flock through certain danger.

The streets near the North Harbor were slums whose tenement rooms were as small as a rural hut, equally windowless, and not as clean. Idlers in the street watched the Serian workmen, but though the locals were hostile they seemed of a more subdued disposition than Cashel had feared.

"Highlanders," Mellie said, pointing with her right leg while she balanced on the toes of her left foot.

Sitting cross-legged in front of the building were four men of wholly different ancestry from that of the docilely toiling workmen. The seated folk were no more than five feet tall and lightly built besides. Their skin was the pale yellow-white of a well-prepared parchment, and their long straight hair was black with no other hues highlighting it even in direct sun.

They chattered cheerfully to one another and passed around a piece of dried meat from which each in turn tore a mouthful.

The Highlanders' front teeth had been filed into triangular fangs. They held short bows on their laps; the bone points of their arrows had been dipped in black gum that was certainly poisonous. The necklace that each Highlander wore was made, Cashel was pretty certain, of dried human ears.

The door of the factory opened unbidden. One of the Highlanders squinted, then pointed at Cashel's right shoulder and called enthusiastically to his fellows. Cashel glared at the man and rapped his quarterstaff down, striking sparks from the cobblestones.

The Highlanders all laughed and patted each other on the back. The man with the slab of meat lifted it for Cashel to take if he wanted.

Cashel grinned and shook his head as he strode past. Giggling, Mellie hugged his neck.

A pair of Serians pushed the door closed behind Cashel; a third man slid the crossbar through its staples. These servants wore robes similar in cut and color to those of Jen and Frasa, but they were woven from some coarse fabric Cashel didn't recognize. He'd like to send a swatch to his sister, but he knew he had to stop thinking that way or he'd never make a break with his memories of Sharina.

Besides, Ilna was here in Carcosa. She was probably learning about all sorts of new things.

In an alcove beside the door stood a life-sized statue of a goddess in saffron robes as beautiful and delicate as the figure herself. She was flanked by a pair of hideous dog-faced demons: one red and the other blue. Though the demons were bipedal, their forelimbs ended in clawed paws rather than human hands. They were obtrusively male.

Jen and Frasa knelt before the goddess. They lowered their heads and placed their palms flat on the stone before them as they murmured together in an unfamiliar language. As they got to their feet again Cashel said, "Masters? Ah, should I do that too?"

The Serians looked at him in surprise. "Surely you don't worship our Goddess of Mercy, do you?" Frasa asked.

"Well, I just thought maybe you'd want me to," Cashel said in even greater embarrassment. He didn't know how to act in Carcosa . . . unless somebody attacked him, of course. The rules then were pretty much the same everywhere.

"I can't imagine why," Frasa said. "Whatever good would come of forcing anyone to *worship*?"

He led the way to the staircase on the opposite side of the hall. Jen nodded Cashel to follow and added from behind him, "Though of course if you wanted to thank the goddess, that would be fine. The decision simply has nothing to do with us."

A cheaply dressed Serian started down the stairs carrying tablets of laced bamboo; the leaves clattered against one another as he moved. He saw Frasa and bounded upstairs again to get out of the way.

"The statues beside the goddess . . ." Cashel said, glancing back over his shoulder from the landing. He let his voice trail off, hoping that his hosts would answer the question he was afraid to articulate for fear he'd use the wrong words. The Serians were decent folks; he didn't want to shock them—as he obviously had earlier when he called them devil worshippers.

"The guardian demons, yes," Frasa said. He'd reached the top of the stairs. A servant wearing a robe with a black border bowed and opened the door of an office facing the harbor.

"You see, Master Cashel," Jen said, "the goddess is perfectly benevolent; she does only good. But beings of such pure innocence need the protection of others to exist in this fallen world. Therefore the goddess is always guarded by demons . . . while we ourselves crew our vessels in part with Highlanders."

"And desire your company as well," Frasa said as he gestured Cashel to one of the low chairs around an even lower table within the office. A servant hovered at the inner door, holding a tray of cups with tiny rice-paper caps over each one.

Jen and Frasa seated themselves as Cashel lowered himself carefully onto the chair. It was sturdier than it looked, but he was more used to stools than chairs and more used to squatting on the floor than either form of furniture.

Mellie hopped down from his shoulder and scampered off to explore on her own. It frightened him to see the sprite's bright hair suddenly pop from behind a lacquered screen and jump to catch a window louver. He had to tell himself that she knew what she was doing much better than he did.

His hosts took cups from the tray and lifted the caps off. "A mixture of fruit juices," Jen explained. "We can provide alcohol for you if you choose?"

"No, this is fine," Cashel said, wondering what to do with his legs. He finally stretched them out in front of him to straddle the table. The Serians crossed their legs under them on the seat, but his joints weren't used to bending that way.

The opposite wall was of shuttered casements overlooking the one-story extension at the rear of the factory. The shutters were open. Cashel could see more Serians and Highlanders relaxing in the closed yard, as well as the wharf to which was tied a square-bowed sailing vessel like nothing ever imagined in Barca's Hamlet.

Cashel sipped his juice. It was tart and cool, but there was an overtone that suggested to his unfamiliar palate that one of the fruits had been rotten before it was squeezed. He continued to drink.

"Our family has been trading to Carcosa for five generations," Frasa said. "There's always been hostility to folk of our religion—"

"Or our race," Jen said. "Perhaps that's the problem."

Cashel didn't speak aloud, but he'd never noticed that folks needed a real reason to throw stones at other people if they were minded to. Red hair or left-handedness or the fact they came from the next borough—any stick was good enough to beat a dog.

Frasa's eyebrows made the equivalent of a shrug. "In any case," he continued, "we have very little contact while we're in Carcosa. We rent a factory and store our goods in it, then contract with a Carcosan broker to arrange buyers for the merchandise and a return cargo for us. The difficulty this time is that the civil unrest is so unexpectedly severe."

Mellie sped across the flat roof of the building extension and vanished through a drain of glazed brick. There were Highlanders is the yard below. . . .

"Do you know Carcosan politics, Master Cashel?" Jen asked politely.

Cashel had to smile. He shook his head. He wasn't sure he knew what *politics* were, much less the particular version practiced in Carcosa.

"Count Lascarg came to power in riots a generation ago," Jen continued. "He has general support among the common people while most of the wealthy class oppose him, but he's worked to conciliate himself to both parties instead of ruling by brute force."

"In part because he lacks the force," Frasa said. "Lascarg deliberately whittled down the size of the Guard so that his successor wouldn't replace him the same way he replaced the former Count and Countess of Haft. Because he doesn't have a real power base of his own, he's desperate to prevent open class warfare from breaking out."

"Whoever won in the end," Jen said, "Lascarg can be sure that he would lose. Therefore he's has tried to unite the populace by stirring up feeling against strangers. Particularly Serians."

Cashel nodded, "Yeah," he said, glad to see Mellie climb onto the drinks tray again. "Well, you're stranger than most."

She fell on her back, holding her sides with laughter. Frasa and Jen stiffened, then smiled.

Cashel blinked at what he'd heard himself say. Either there was *something* in the fruit juice, maybe not alcohol, or the situation of the whole past week was so unreal that his mind saw no reason not to speak what normally would have remained as unspoken thoughts.

"I suppose we are," Frasa said. "Well, our ill luck at finding ourselves in a situation fomented by cowardly deceit has been mitigated by meeting so unusually honest and stalwart a person as you, Master Cashel."

"If we had known the extent of the unrest we would never have sailed here in the *Golden Dragon*," Jen said. He didn't point to the ship at the wharf behind him; rather, his eyes moved minusculely to the side. The motion if continued would have indicated the window and by extension everything beyond it. "Stones were thrown at the factory last night after we docked, but that had happened before. Today my brother and I went out to contact a broker. Without your help, sir, we would not have returned."

Both Serians rose gracefully to their feet, then genuflected as they'd done before the goddess. Cashel blushed; he wanted to sink through the floor in embarrassment.

"Look," he said as he got his legs under him, "I'm glad I could help you; it wasn't right, what was happening. But you're back safe now, and I'll be on my way."

He tugged out his purse. Mellie bounced toward him turning handsprings, her unnaturally red hair flaring each time her head went down.

"*Please*, Master Cashel," Jen said as both Serians jumped up in obvious concern. "We meant you no insult."

"Wasn't right for me to take money for helping you, either," Cashel said as he fumbled for the silver anchors Frasa had given him beside the fountain. "I wish you fellows well and good business."

Mellie's touch on Cashel's leg and up his tunic had been as feather-light as a bumblebee settling for a drink of salty perspiration. From his shoulder she said, "You've never dealt with Serians before, Cashel. Remember that they haven't met many countrymen. Or honest men either in Carcosa, unless things have changed since my last visit."

Cashel paused, frowning in confusion.

"We sail to Haft by the southern route," Frasa said. "There are many pirates in those waters, so we take Highlanders in our crew. They can't navigate so there's no danger that they'll steal the ship themselves; and they have no compunction about killing pirates."

He smiled very slightly. "Or eating them."

Cashel nodded. He didn't see where the Serian's speech was going, but he could wait. He felt silly holding the purse in his left hand. He drew the neck closed and tucked it back within his tunic.

"In Carcosa," Jen said, taking up from his brother, "we have no protection outside the factory. We hope to be able to do our business quickly through the broker we've engaged and not have to go out again, but we can't be sure of that. Master Cashel, even if we don't need your strength ever again, the presence of an honorable man will lighten our tasks. Please stay with us; and permit us to pay you as we agreed, for the sake of *our* honor."

Cashel looked from Jen to Frasa. The pair of them were as similar as the demon statues downstairs. Here, though, he was the demon. . . .

"I like the feel of this place," Mellie said. "Oh, not to stay long, of course. But they really try to be nice—and they don't keep cats."

She giggled.

Cashel thought about the Highlanders. Well, he supposed he could be Mellie's guardian demon inside the compound as well as Jen and Frasa's outside.

"I don't know what got into me," he muttered to the Serians, lowering his eyes. "I said I'd take the job and there I was, going back on my word. Sorry, sirs. I'll stay around till you shift your goods."

Frasa and Jen bowed, smiling; and Mellie hugged at Cashel's throat again.

21

Sharina woke up abruptly. She felt motion beside her and thought that Nonnus must be rising also.

Nonnus was already gone; the motion was the dugout heeling. The wind had backed and now blew from the north.

The hermit stood on the other side of the mast, freeing the lifting fall. Asera and Meder sat close together in the far stern. They didn't offer to help; Nonnus didn't need or want their help anyway. The nobles' eyes were bright and nervous. Their stance reminded Sharina of a pair of marmots tensely aware of the hawk soaring overhead.

Sharina knew why they were afraid. Her own heart thrilled to the change in the wind, but she was miserably ashamed that she hadn't prevented Meder from working the magic she knew had brought that change.

She climbed across the bundled supplies to Nonnus. He could get along without her help also, but she at least knew how to be useful. The fall was reeved through a single block at the masthead. Sharina gripped the spar with both hands and added her strength to the process of raising it and the wet sail while the hermit tugged on the rope. If nothing else, she took some of the strain off the mast.

The canvas began to fill as soon as it rose, shaking salt droplets over Sharina. The spar lifted above the reach of her hands and she stepped back. The breeze was steady though light.

"Not the weather I would have expected," Nonnus said mildly from behind the curtain of the sail. He bent to snub the fall around the bitt at the foot of the mast. "It should serve our purpose so long as it continues; and if it ends, there's still the norther to expect."

Sharina crawled under the lower edge of the sail. The sky was noticeably brighter but the sun hadn't yet risen. The horizon was a rolling unmarked darkness around them.

Asera held the tiller. Meder was tightly beside her, his hands clasped.

"Good morning, Master Nonnus," Asera said as the hermit came back to take over the tiller and the sheets clewing the sail. Normally the nobles would have passed silently along the opposite side of the dugout's narrow hull; this morning they didn't seem ready to go forward at all.

"Good morning mistress, master," Nonnus replied with careful neutrality. "I need to be in the stern to handle the sail."

Meder swallowed and rose to a crouch. He scuttled forward without meeting the hermit's eyes. Asera released the tiller—it was lashed to move only in a short compass anyway—and said, "Yes, of course," as she got up. Though her progress was as stately as the close confines allowed, Sharina could see tension in the line of the procurator's back.

Meder's chest of paraphernalia was tucked under the edge of a cargo net, but it wasn't under the same net as it had been at midnight when the wizard went sternward to take over the watch. Sharina swallowed as she noticed the change. The hermit's eyes flicked over the case but nothing in his set, bleak expression indicated that he'd noticed anything different.

And perhaps the sun would rise in the west this morning. . . .

Nonnus adjusted the angle of the spar, then unshipped the tiller and added the rudder's help to the dugout's slow change of direction. They heeled hard onto the starboard outrigger. Sharina handled the lines to the lower edge of the sail, flattening its angle gradually as the clumsy vessel came about. Too abrupt a change of tack wouldn't overset them—the outriggers prevented that—but it might crack or unstep the mast.

As Nonnus adjusted the spar, his eyes on the line at which spray flew from the canvas, he said, "There's a smear of blood here on the sternpost, Meder."

"I cut my hand," the wizard called in a high-pitched voice from behind the sail. "I cut the back of my hand on a splinter, that's all!"

Sharina turned her face outboard to hide her expression. She felt sick at her inaction the previous night; sicker yet that she was pretending to conceal what the hermit already knew. "Nonnus—" she began.

There was a line of white off the starboard bow. Sharina hopped onto the crosspole which attached the outrigger to the hull, gripping the starboard mainbrace. It wasn't an illusion, nor was it a line of white gulls waiting for full dawn to rise from the swell where they'd spent the night.

"Land!" Sharina called. "Land to starboard! Look, Nonnus, land!"

Nonnus jumped onto the gunwale and leaned outward. He didn't have a sheet or cable to hold on to, but he stretched his javelin behind him in his left hand to balance the weight of his head and torso. He teetered there, frightening for Sharina to watch.

The hermit dropped back into the stern and adjusted the set of the sail still further. He said nothing.

Asera and Meder ducked beneath the canvas as Sharina came back aboard. The nobles' expressions added a mixture of hope and puzzlement to the previous fear.

"Is it really land?" Meder blurted.

"It appears to be, yes," Nonnus said. He tweaked a clew before Sharina squatted to take the line again. "There shouldn't be an island in this part of the sea."

The procurator scowled. "How can anybody tell where we really are? The sky's been overcast ever since we left Tegma."

"Yes, Tegma," Nonnus said with a humorless grin. He handed the lines to Sharina. "I assure you, procurator, I know where we are. And I know that Tegma wouldn't have risen without wizardry."

"I didn't make this island rise!" Meder said. "I had nothing to do with this!"

"I don't suppose it matters now, does it?" the hermit said without emotion. He adjusted the spar, holding the tiller between his side and left arm.

"I didn't do this," Meder whispered, but the looks he and Asera exchanged were full of doubt.

22

The air of the tomb was hot and dry. The black candle's flame wavered slowly as Tenoctris moved, always keeping her boxwood twig before her. The candlelight was clear and smokeless, though the dull, dark stone drank it in without reflection.

Tenoctris crossed her legs and sat down. She looked with distaste at Benlo's corpse. The drover lay on his back; he'd been opened from pelvis almost to his throat. His face was set in a rictus of fear. The trauma of death had stiffened Benlo's body instantaneously into rigor mortis. Garric had seen that happen once before, when an ox leaping from a horsefly's bite had gored Zaki or-Mesli as terribly as this.

Benlo's arms were spread wide. His right hand still held the athame.

"Can we do anything?" Garric asked. He'd remained motionless on the bottom step while the old woman surveyed the vault.

"Possibly," Tenoctris said as she turned her face toward him. "But anything we attempt will be very dangerous. You'll have to make the decision."

"Then we'll act," Garric said without moving.

"Let me explain," Tenoctris said sharply. "This happened because Benlo opened the wrong door by accident. A demon, invulnerable on this plane, came through the opening Benlo made and killed him; then the demon returned, taking Liane to its own plane."

Garric met the old woman's eyes without speaking. She felt she needed to explain, so he'd listen to the explanation. Perhaps he'd have to understand what was going on before he took the action Tenoctris would set out for him; in any case, interrupting would only delay a resolution further.

But if the decision was Garric's to make, then nothing Tenoctris could say would change his mind.

"Because I know who the demon is," she continued, "I should be able to reach its plane. Benlo used brute force to open the gate; I don't have the strength to do that, but I can *re*open a way if I act promptly."

Her twig waggled toward the pool of blood which was still spreading sluggishly. The word STRASEDON had blurred away within seconds of the time they'd entered the vault, but he knew what she was referring to. Garric didn't repeat the word aloud for fear of summoning the thing named.

"All right," Garric said with a shrug. "You said he was invulnerable?"

He put his hands together because they were beginning to tremble with anticipation. He knew he ought to be afraid but all he felt was an urge to move, to act, to *finish* this—even if it meant his own finish.

"*Here* it was invulnerable. Strasedon can be killed on its own plane," Tenoctris said, showing that it was all right to speak the name. The corner of her lip lifted in almost a smile. "But a tiger can be killed in its own jungle too, Garric. This is a difficult and dangerous business, and there'll be dangers besides Strasedon."

Garric shook his head. "It doesn't matter," he said. "Not because it's Liane, mistress. I'd say the same thing if it was Benlo himself. I'm not going to walk away and leave a human being in the hands of something that does—"

He bobbed his chin toward the corpse.

"—that."

Tenoctris nodded. "Good," she said, "but I had to tell you first."

She took the athame from Benlo's hand. She had to work it back and forth several times to break the fingers' convulsive grip. "Get him out of the way, please," she ordered crisply. "If we survive, then we can see to some proper disposal of the remains."

Garric dragged the corpse to the back of the vault. Tenoctris dabbed the butt of the athame into the congealing blood and began to draw on the floor with it, partially covering the drover's own words of power.

"It's a good thing you can read the Old Script," she said as she wrote. "For this conjuration two voices are necessary. I suppose that's why Benlo brought Liane with him. Of course, if he'd really known what he was doing . . ."

Her voice trailed off without finishing the observation—or needing to.

Garric wondered whether Tenoctris used the blood for some special power or simply because it was the handiest material with which to mark the stone. The old woman had a streak of ruthless pragmatism that a youth raised in a rural hamlet could fully appreciate.

Tenoctris wiped up more blood. "Benlo must have made this athame himself," she muttered. "Amazing, though iron's the ideal element if you have the power to bind it as he did. But what he bound was a skein of varied forces that even I couldn't untangle. No wonder it took him to the wrong plane!"

"You can't use it, then?" Garric said. While he watched the words she drew on the basalt he deliberately kept his jaws clenched to keep from accidentally subvocalizing them with untold result.

"Oh, I'll use my twig," Tenoctris said absently. "A neutral athame is much safer. With the forces surging about this nexus, only a madman or a reckless ignoramus would use a tool designed to multiply their effect."

She leaned back, having drawn two concentric circles of

words in the Old Script on the floor between her and where Garric stood. She gestured toward them with the point of Benlo's athame and said, "You can read these?"

Garric nodded. "Yes, mistress," he said.

"All right," Tenoctris said. She rose to her feet, cautious of her creaking joints. "I'll speak the words in the outer circle myself. When I come to the inner circle you'll speak the words with me. Follow the rhythm I set in the outer circle. Do you understand?"

"Yes, mistress," Garric said. He felt poised and slightly outside himself, as if he were about to dive from a high cliff.

"When the portal opens we'll step through together," the old woman said. "We must be prompt. Do you understand?"

"Yes, mistress," Garric said. She was leaving nothing to chance. That was as it should be.

"Then," said Tenoctris with a wan smile, "I'll proceed."

Dipping the boxwood twig toward the writing at each syllable, she said, "*Anoch ai akrammachamari . . .*"

Her voice was clear and had the relentless quality of a good sawyer stroking through wood.

"*Lampsouer lameer lamhore . . .*"

The last of the outer circle. Taking up the rhythm from the twig and the previous words of power, Garric and the old woman cried together, "*Iao barbathiaoth ablanathanalba!*"

A pane of light as red and dull as iron after the smith's first stroke hung in the air beside them. Tenoctris reached across and took Garric's right hand in her left.

"*Garric . . .*" Liane's voice wailed from a distance greater than worlds.

Hand in hand, Garric and the old woman stepped into the fire.

23

Ilna saw the crowd in the street in front of the Red Ox. Something was wrong and it involved Garric. She stumbled for the first time since she'd left the Captain's Rest at a near run.

She'd finished the duties she'd bargained against her room and board: all the chickens killed, plucked, and cleaned for the next day's dinners. The cook had been delighted with the neat dispatch with which she worked, though Ilna herself was scornful of the number of usable feathers she'd wasted in her hurry.

Nobody else faulted her for sloppy workmanship, but Ilna os-Kenset had never cared what others thought. *She* knew the true facts.

If Ilna had been able to, she'd have returned to the Red Ox with Garric. He and Tenoctris left not long before Ilna finished her duties; they'd had no idea she wanted to come with them or they'd have waited for her. It wasn't Ilna's style to feel beholden to anyone: she'd hastened along after, without guide or lantern. The twisting streets that were to others a maze were a childishly simple pattern for a mind trained to weave complex perfection on a loom.

Ilna had used her own bone-handled knife to clean and joint the chickens, good steel worn thin with years of service. The last thing she'd done before leaving the kitchen of the Captain's Rest was to touch up the blade on the smooth limestone lintel.

She pushed her way into the crowd. Folk were looking toward the graveyard across the street from the inn, talking excitedly among themselves. A few even sat on the wall, though they leaned instinctively back toward the street, tempering bravado with caution. It needn't have anything to do with Garric—

But Ilna knew it did. She could feel the pattern forming.

Benlo's guards stood together beside the wall, looking into the graveyard and talking through scowls of concern. Icy with purpose, Ilna joined them and said, "Master Rald? Where's Garric?"

Rald reached for hilt of the sword he wasn't wearing as his head jerked around to see who had spoken. It was her tone rather than her words, she knew, but she was no mood for mincing delicacy, not now or ever.

"Sorry, mistress," the chief guard muttered in embarrassment. The men had gotten to know and respect, if not exactly like, Ilna during the drive from Barca's Hamlet. He bobbed his helmet toward the moonlit tombs. "He's in there and the old lady with him. And Master Benlo and his daughter, I suppose."

"Then why are you here?" she said. "What else happened?"

She wanted to climb over the wall immediately but there was more to learn before she acted. Ilna determined the pattern even before she strung the warp. Those who wove free-hand were fools and worse: they were bad craftsmen.

"There was a light from there not long after your friend went over the wall," Rald said. "A flash, like; and it wasn't lightning, it was red as . . . it was bright red."

Red as blood.

The guard's voice was neutral but the expression on his grizzled face was uncomfortable. Even without the girl's cold disapproval he must have felt that a better man would ignore orders and go look for his employer. But when you knew your employer was a wizard, some things took a different sort of courage than that of a man who thought he'd been hired to face swords. . . .

"Somebody screamed," another guard said without looking in Ilna's direction. "Could've been any of them. And I guess somebody shouted too."

"Has anybody gone to see what happened?" Ilna said. "Since Garric went in, I mean."

The second guard turned and glared into her cold eyes. "No," he said, "nobody's been that great a fool. Maybe by daylight somebody'll go but it won't be me. And nobody's come out, either!"

"Then it's time for someone to play the man, isn't it?" Ilna said disdainfully. She gripped the wall coping with both hands and set her right toes between the second and third course of masonry from the ground.

A guard, probably Rald, tried to brace her heel. She kicked back in anger, then found the toehold again and lifted herself onto and over the wall unaided. Conversation picked up excitedly behind her; those near where she'd climbed the wall called fanciful explanations to friends farther away. She didn't hear anyone following her, though; and thirty paces from the wall the sound of the spectators was no louder than the buzz of insects and nightbirds.

Ilna had an invisible thread to follow; she couldn't have described or explained her feeling, but she trusted it implicitly nonetheless. That thread didn't light a path for her, however, and the open stone boxes littering the ground among the larger tombs tripped her again and again. Stone had never been a friend; but it wouldn't stop her, either.

She thought she heard something ahead, but she wasn't sure the seeming sound reached her through her ears. It was a rhythmic pulse like that of waves being swallowed in a cavern. Not voices, she thought; or at any rate not human voices.

Ilna stepped beneath a thick-trunked cedar; birds exploded into flight above her head. She ducked in reflex, ashamed of her weakness even before the rattle of wing feathers identified the roosting pigeons that her presence had disturbed.

The kitchen knife was in its case of sheep femur thrust under her belt; she'd tucked it there when she joined the crowd outside the graveyard. Rather than draw the knife, Ilna uncoiled the length of rope she carried around her waist. It was the halter she'd picked up at Stroma River; of no particular use to her now except that holding it between her hands calmed her.

She'd reached a pair of tombs in contrasting stone. The pale one to the right was wreathed in flowers redolent of recent death. The entrance of its black basalt companion was ajar; candlelight shone from within and Ilna heard voices.

Ilna started toward the door. Light that throbbed like a volcano's heart filled the tomb. She stepped inside and saw silhouetted the figures of Garric and old Tenoctris hand in hand.

Benlo lay dead and Liane had vanished.

Garric and Tenoctris stepped together into a portal of hellfire. It began to shrink.

They had to be going after Liane. Garric was going after Liane.

"She *won't* have him," Ilna said; and leaped into the light in which the others had vanished.

24

The wave broke on the shore of the island and ran well up the gentle slope, splashing and spuming as it crossed each deeply weathered channel. "Is the Outer Sea always this calm?" Sharina asked.

The dugout slid a few feet inshore on the lift of the swell. Nonnus gave the hawser another wrap around the pair of long spikes he'd hammered into the rock: the four humans didn't have the strength to drag the heavy dugout above the tide line, so the hermit had taken other measures to prevent it from floating away during the night.

Panting slightly with exertion he said, "Until today, child, I'd have said it's never this calm. This journey has been many kinds of education for me."

Asera and Meder were carrying personal effects up the hill to where they'd camp, out of reach of the spray. The island was about a half mile in diameter, solid rock, and only fifty feet above sea level at the top of the central ridge. There hadn't been time yet to explore, but Sharina didn't expect they'd find fresh water. Barnacles and a dozen species of seaweed clung to the rocks as high as she could see; waves had to wash over the island regularly to permit such marine life to flourish.

There were no trees, bushes, or land animals—even insects. Crabs scuttled in the flat-bottomed ravines, raising their claws defiantly if a human came close.

Sharina didn't care for crabs: they always seemed angry, reminding her of her mother. They'd make a change of diet from fish and grain, she supposed.

"Do you have any idea where we are, Nonnus?" she asked, lowering her voice even though the nobles were too distant to hear anything less than a shout.

He sighed and shook his head. "I've never seen anything like it," he said. "All rock but not volcanic; and in a part of the sea I'd have said you could go a thousand fathoms straight down and not touch bottom."

"Are we in the part of the world we came from?" Sharina asked. She remembered Tegma and the sky of another time that covered what the trireme's crew had found when they crossed those reefs.

"Oh, yes," Nonnus said. He laughed. "The currents are right, the water tastes right; the sun rose where it ought to, and the gulls were the same gulls that've stolen scraps from me a thousand times when I sailed these seas. The only thing that's wrong is there's an island where there never was before."

The rock had the smooth, slippery feel of a pebble washed for generations in a quick-flowing stream. The broad ravines were its only physical feature. They formed a mosaic covering the entire domed surface, at least on this side of the island. Sharina hadn't seen any gravel; for all she could tell, the whole island was a single reddish-brown mass.

"It's ancient," she said quietly. The feeling of age was almost overwhelming. Tegma had been alien; this island was simply *old*.

"Yes," Nonnus said. "But it didn't grow old here."

The surge swept up the shelving beach again, wetting Sharina's ankles and spitting spray as high as her bare knees. Though the dugout shivered, its keel remained solidly fixed.

"Well, we're not going to grow old here either, child," the hermit said. "I don't mind having solid ground underfoot again, but if the breeze holds we'll cast off at dawn."

He looked out to sea, then shaded his eyes with his hand to peer eastward toward the crest of the hill. Asera and the wizard seemed determined to climb all the way to the top. They slipped frequently. The stone and slick weed made the going difficult. The ravines, though generally only a few feet deep, had occasional deeper pits from which seawater crept to wet the surrounding rock.

"I'll look for driftwood," Sharina said. "It'd be nice to have a fire."

Nonnus nodded. "Yes . . ." he said with the slow agreement of someone who didn't expect success but didn't see any harm in trying. "I'll gather seaweed. We can eat some of these kinds."

He looked up the hill again with the grim smile that Sharina by now found familiar. "Our companions will complain about the taste, but it may keep their teeth from falling out."

He looked at her. "And I'll build a little shrine to the Lady," he said, "to thank her for our deliverance thus far."

"Nonnus?" Sharina said. "Where will you and I camp?"

"Just above the spray line," he said, nodding up the rock's hummocky surface. "Fifty feet should do. I set these spikes deep, but our pig of a boat weighs tons and the sea has a sense of humor. Especially this sea, it appears."

He patted his big toe on the stone.

Sharina started clockwise around the shore. She'd seen no sign of driftwood or other debris when they beached the dugout, but there could be a limb or trunk lying in one of the ravines. Besides, it felt good to be able to walk for the first time in days.

"Child?" Nonnus called.

She turned.

"Be careful, please," he said. "I think we'll leave at dawn whatever the wind is doing. This isn't a place where we belong."

He smiled and Sharina smiled back; but the hermit's hand was on the hilt of his Pewle knife as surely as she was touching the hatchet she carried on her belt.

25

The sun was black in a red sky. The heat was the worst Garric had felt since haying last August, but with this difference: there was no moisture in the air. No moisture at all.

Garric touched the hilt of the borrowed sword. The grip was a dowel of hazelwood with shallow finger grooves. That was well enough, but the filbert-shaped pommel and the crossguard were silvered bronze that would soon grow hot enough to burn in this black light. With a reflex not his own, Garric tugged an additional fold of tunic up over his belt and let it flop to cover the metal parts of the hilt. Otherwise he might flinch when he gripped the weapon at a time when there was no room for mistakes.

The figure in the back of Garric's mind knew swords; oh, yes, he knew swords.

"Is it always like this, mistress?" Garric said. He looked around at desolation in shades of red and black alone. There was no wind, and his voice was the only sound in this world. "Is this where demons live?"

"This is where Strasedon lives," Tenoctris said. "As for planes inhabited by other demons—Garric, nobody's ever done this before. Not and come back to leave a record, at least."

"Oh," said Garric. "Well, I don't guess it matters."

Tenoctris settled to the ground with her legs crossed beneath her and began to draw symbols with her boxwood twig. The soil had the texture of sandy loam. When the heat seeped through his calloused soles Garric reflexively moved into a dark patch that past experience told him was shadow.

It was like stepping on live coals. He hopped instantly back to ground that shimmered red.

Reflex could hurt him here. Reflex could kill him.

Tenoctris had drawn the stick figure of a man and placed unfamiliar symbols between the four limbs and head. Now she was encircling the image with words in the Old Script.

Garric resumed surveying the landscape. It looked unappealing but not bizarre if he allowed for the reversal of light and darkness. This was a place of weathered badlands, banks that climbed hundreds of feet in a series of eroded steps. Cones and plateaus stood out against the red sky.

There was no vegetation. Whenever Garric turned his head he sensed tiny, scampering motion just beyond the range of his vision. His fingertips lay on the covered pommel of his sword.

Tenoctris finished writing on the soil and looked up with a kind of smile. "I need to wait a few minutes before I read the spell," she said. "Noon will be the best time and that's almost on us."

Garric fluffed the sweat-soaked tunic away from his chest and tried to echo the old woman's smile. *I wish I'd worn a hat against this sun.* He supposed he was thinking about that to keep his mind off real problems.

"The spell is to take us to Strasedon?" he asked, wondering how much it hurt to die the way Benlo had. The broken landscape would give no warning of the demon's presence. Runnels of earth reached into this valley from a dozen places in either direction; a seawolf or a demon could be waiting behind any one of them. Ravines crosscut the ground, bright red streaks of shadow that were yards across, shelter for monsters to hide.

Benlo had screamed, but not for very long.

Tenoctris shook her head. "Strasedon is the whole plane that we see," she said. She picked up a pinch of gritty soil and let it trickle away again. "I'm going to find Liane because she's the only variation in perfect uniformity."

She looked around her. "This is . . ." She smiled ruefully at her own foolishness. "I find this a wonderful experience, something I never dreamed I'd see. So much power is resident here that it's *solid*."

She waggled her hand at the air as if patting an invisible wall. "It's pure, not the mix of forces one finds on our plane, what you call the real world," she went on. "The very intensity is what may save us: Strasedon's own strength limits its ability to work *through* itself."

The back of Garric's throat was dry from breathing and his lips were already beginning to crack. "Do you mean there isn't a demon here like the one that met Benlo?" he said. Killed Benlo. "We just find Liane and take her back with us?"

"There's a demon," Tenoctris said. "And until it dies, it won't release Liane."

She lifted her free hand to end the conversation. "It's time now," she said. Ignoring Garric, the old woman dipped her twig wand and began murmuring the words of her spell.

Garric nodded, and touched his sword hilt, and wondered. The center of Tenoctris' crude circle popped with a sound like a knot cracking in the fire. A streak of white light extended: at first slowly, then with the gathering momentum of a stone dropping from a sheer cliff toward the sea. The line rippled across the soil and finally raced up the side of a flat-topped knoll to vanish. Remembrance of the light's purity settled Garric's nerves and warned him how keyed up he'd been an instant before.

"That way, then," he said aloud. He offered Tenoctris his left hand to help her rise. The sides of knoll were steep, but cracks and gullies formed paths in the friable soil.

A thought struck Garric. He looked around again and said, "Mistress? The doorway we came by doesn't show from this side. How do we get back?"

"Time enough to worry about that after we've killed Strasedon, Garric," Tenoctris said. "Otherwise it really won't matter."

26

The mob in front of the Serian factory had grown larger with each passing minute after nightfall, the way some of the showiest flowers open in the darkness. A few of the locals had thrown stones, but for the most part they watched with the grinning malice of a cat with its paws spread, waiting for a vole to move.

"Your broker would have done better to come by daylight," Cashel said uneasily. The killers were prowling around his flock and there was nothing he could do about it.

Frasa extended both little fingers in the equivalent of a shrug. "It was Themo's decision," he said. "He's lived here for twenty years, so we can only hope that he has better judgment about this sort of situation than we do."

"He was in Carcosa during the Troubles seventeen years ago," Jen agreed. "We can only hope."

Mellie was prowling about the roof, peeking into drains and sometimes reappearing over the coping several feet from where Cashel had last seen her. The sprite was visible in light or shadow as though she were illuminated by a sky different from the one she walked under. Cashel knew he'd never get used to the blithe nonchalance with which Mellie took risks;

but like most things, his concern would never reach his tongue.

"The man you're dealing with isn't a Carcosan?" Cashel said aloud. It gave him an odd feeling to be standing on a flat roof looking down on the world. Roofs in Barca's Hamlet were peaked and mostly thatch. Even the ancient slates of the millhouse sloped steeply and fed an equally old cistern with rainwater that Ilna saved for washing delicate fabrics.

"We've used two brokers here in the past," Frasa explained. "The other one, Sidras or-Morr, is a local man."

"He seemed honest and satisfactory in the past," Jen said. "Under the present circumstances, though, we thought that Themo or-Casmon was the better choice. His family is on Ornifal, so he'll be less swayed by local passions."

"Folks from Ornifal don't hate devil worshippers?" Cashel said with a frown.

Jen stiffened again, then broke into the broadest smile Cashel had thus far seen on his face. Frasa merely said, "Master Cashel, under the present circumstances I wouldn't trust a Serian out of my own family to deal honestly with me; but we decided to choose a broker whose allegiance isn't to Count Lascarg."

It didn't seem to Cashel that anybody's real allegiance was to Count Lascarg, or that Lascarg felt responsibility for anything except his own skin. Tenoctris had said that outside forces were breaking down society, but pressure on society doesn't make a man evil or weak: it just allows those qualities to show through if they were there in the first place.

The city folk below with bricks in their hands and empty hate in their hearts were making their own decision; wizardry wasn't responsible. Cashel and his quarterstaff had already shown what he thought of picking on strangers. The way things were looking, he'd have more chances to repeat the lesson.

Harbor Street was a broad relic of the Old Kingdom. The tenements on the other side overlooked the factories. Because of the backdrop of the dark sky, the mob in the street couldn't see Cashel and the Serian merchants, but they showed up against the roof's pale brickwork to folk on the tenement roofs.

"Dirt! Dirt! Dirt!" screamed a girl not even Cashel's age. She flung a roofing tile. The missile flew less than halfway to the intended target, dropping to shatter among the mob in the street.

"Arrows!" cried a man as the mob surged away from the sharp-edged fragments. "The dirt's shooting arrows!"

"Maybe we'd better stay back," Cashel suggested, wondering as he spoke where Mellie had gone to. The roof was in easy range of stones thrown from the street. If the mob realized it was being watched from above, there'd be a hail that might hurt somebody before they got under cover.

"There he comes," said Frasa. "That's Themo now."

Half a dozen men in steel caps and quilted leather armor came up the street from the south. Five of them carried spears and wore small round shields on their left forearms; the sixth had a larger shield and no spear.

The crowd saw the broker's men at about the same time Frasa did. A murmur grew, spreading from the edge back to the mob's heart. Themo's guards raised their spears pointforward over their right shoulders, ready to stab or throw.

The rioters nearest the weapons backed or sidled away; those to the rear began throwing stones. The blind shower of missiles scattered the front of the mob faster than the oncoming spears could have done. Themo and his men broke into a run toward the factory door.

Frasa and Jen started for the stairs down into the building proper. Cashel backed behind them, alert to block a missile flung from the street as a farewell but also looking desperately for Mellie.

"They aren't serious about it yet," the sprite said from his shoulder. Cashel whirled his staff in a startled half-circle, responding to nonexistent threats to either side. "You can smell when a mob means business."

"Don't scare me like that!" Cashel hissed. He hadn't felt

the touch of her climbing his leg; had she hopped to his shoulder from the roof coping?

Mellie giggled but cuddled his throat repentantly.

Shouts and curses echoed briefly through the entryway, then muted when Serian servants slammed the door behind Themo and his men. The broker dropped his oversized shield and flung his helmet down on the stone. He was a thin-faced man whose blond hair was going gray. Glaring up the staircase at Jen and Frasa, he said, "You didn't tell me what it was like out there! Were you trying to get me killed?"

"Your pardon, Master Themo," Jen said with a deep bow. Except that he and his brother were standing at the top of stairs, Cashel was pretty sure they'd have fallen on their knees in full obeisance. "We didn't want to have the Highlanders out in the street to await your coming lest we give the civic authorities an excuse to bring their own troops against us."

It was none of Cashel's business but it bothered him to see anyway. The Serians had nothing to apologize for: it wasn't their city, their mob, or their decision to delay so long. Besides, there weren't a hundred people in the street at present. Cashel, Garric, and four more of the right lads from the borough with quarterstaves could have sent a wispy rabble like that packing with less effort than as many minutes on the threshing floor after every harvest.

"He didn't want people to see him by good light," Mellie said, lying on her back and somehow managing to touch her toes with her fingertips from that position. "Consorting with devil worshippers."

She gave a trill of liquid laughter and added, "Who'd want to worship a demon anyway? Most of them are too stupid even to be good company."

Themo stamped up the stairs with two of his guards, a red-haired man and one whose flat nose and scarred cheekbones marked him as a longtime fistfighter. They'd laid their spears aside but they wore their steel caps and carried swords on shoulder belts over their leather jacks.

The guards eyed Cashel with the same generalized contempt they offered everyone else in the factory including the brothers and the four Highlanders laughing just off the entrance hall. Contempt for those little killers seemed to Cashel as stupid as scorning a poisonous snake because it was small.

"I don't like this man," Mellie said, following Themo with her eyes. Cashel said nothing as he walked behind the Serians and their visitors into the office, but he sure didn't disagree.

"Who's that?" Themo demanded, pointing his thumb at Cashel as he addressed his question to the brothers. A servant closed the door behind Cashel.

"This is our aide, Master Cashel or-Kenset," Frasa said calmly. "He is a native of this island."

Themo assessed Cashel and frowned in puzzlement before dismissing him again. Cashel knew he looked like exactly what he was: a big shepherd who had no business in a discussion of this sort.

He kept right hand firmly on the quarterstaff upright at his side; that avoided the possibility that Themo would try to clasp hands with him out of normal politeness. Themo didn't seem the sort who was normally polite anyway.

The broker sat down without waiting for the offer of the chair and pulled several folded sheets of rice paper out of his belt pouch. "All right," he said, "I've looked at your manifest and most of it seems in order. I haven't been able to move the figured pottery at anything like the price the celadon brings—why do you insist on trying to change people's tastes when they know what they like?"

Jen bobbed his head in apology. "The figured ware is very popular in Valles," he said. "We hoped that when news of the court's tastes reached Haft, there would be a surge in demand."

"Well, it's a drug on the market here," Themo grunted. "I've half a mind to tell you to keep it aboard as ballast, but since we've done business so many years I'll do you the favor of taking it off your hands."

The brothers said nothing. Themo fumbled again in his

scrip and came out with another list, this one written on a pair of thin boards.

"Here's what I'm offering in return," he said, tossing the boards on the table instead of handing them across. "Understand, it's going to be a lot of trouble to me to move *any* Serian stuff for the next who-knows-how-long. It might be I'll just have to dump it all at sea to keep from getting charged with devil worship myself. And there's not going to be more cargoes from you lot anytime soon, that I know."

Still without speaking, the brothers each picked up one of the boards, read it through, and then exchanged it for the other. They looked at one another expressionlessly. Frasa handed the board he now held to his brother and said, "This appears satisfactory, Master Themo. Though it's not in my interest to say so, it's quite a generous offer under the circumstances. We'll have a contract prepared."

Jen handed the list to a long-robed servant, who turned with it to a slanted writing desk against the wall near Cashel.

"I already had that made up," the broker said and pulled a third document from his purse; this one a narrow parchment scroll, the ends of the hide left ragged but the roll done up with a red ribbon for show.

He tossed it to Frasa, who untied it expressionlessly. Jen tented his hands and looked calmly accepting.

Cashel would've liked to ask Mellie what she made of what was going on, but she'd left him to climb over the three visitors. Cashel was horrified to see the sprite disappear into the broker's open purse, then pop out again an instant before he buckled it closed again.

"I've got six wagons waiting at Fountain Court," Themo said. "There's a man on top of the Arch of Verucca who can take a signal from your roof and relay it to the wagoners. The only thing is, they're coming empty. I'll have to deliver the return cargo tomorrow."

Frasa put down the parchment scroll. "It's traditional to make the exchange of merchandise at the factory before goods are either loaded on shipboard or carried off the premises," Jen said.

"It's not traditional that there's a mob waiting at the door to knock the heads in of anybody who deals with you Serians!" Themo said. "And the Sister take you if you can't see that. I won't take the chance of unloading the wagons while that lot—"

He gestured toward the street behind him. There was scar tissue on the ball of his thumb and the nail was twisted into a claw.

"—gathers up all their friends and brothers with maybe some of the Count's guard too and waits for us to come back out. I want a quick in and out. Tomorrow when things settle down I'll bring your goods."

He pointed at the parchment. "It's all right there, already signed."

All Cashel knew about contracts was two men spitting on their palms and shaking hands, but he had a notion of how far a Serian would get trying to sue today before Count Lascarg's judges. They'd be as likely to leave court alive as a sickly ewe was to survive the Hungry Time in February before the new grass came in.

Frasa met the broker's eyes for a long moment. "Yes, I can see that," he said at last.

Jen held out his hand. The secretary brought a bronze pen and alabaster inkwell to him, moving with steps so tiny that the long robe appeared to glide over the floor by itself.

"Good, good," Themo said. He'd visibly relaxed; so did his pair of guards. "I figured you'd see reason. The signal's three lanterns from the roof. You've got that here, right."

"Yes," said Frasa. Cashel had seen stones with more overt emotion. The Serians knew the risk they were taking with this man, but they were hoping against hope of a good result for their trust.

"Master Cashel will witness my signature," Jen said, rotating the document on the table and setting the pen across the inkwell where Cashel could reach it.

"Yes you can," Mellie said. She hopped from Cashel's shoulder to the floor in three long jumps that would have frightened the youth if he hadn't already been frozen by Jen's words. Garric had taught him to write his name, but he couldn't imagine doing it under the eyes of so many educated strangers.

"I can't—" he began before the meaning of what the sprite had said sank in. Mellie sat cross-legged on the contract, grinning up at Cashel as her right index finger pointed to a spot above a scribe's trained calligraphy.

Cashel coughed as if clearing his throat. He handed his quarterstaff to the secretary—the Serian accepted it gravely—then squatted in front of the low table and took the pen. He'd seen people writing effortlessly, but people had watched Cashel spin a quarterstaff, too, and that didn't mean they could do it because he had.

"It's easy," Mellie said. "Stick the point in the ink and then start here where my finger is. I'll guide you."

The contract had a short preamble, then an indented list followed by a closing. Below that to the right of the sheet was a signature Cashel took to be the broker's—the ink was dry—written above a scribe's notation; and the signature Jen had just affixed above a similar notation. Jen's writing was if anything more precise than that of the scribe.

Someone had signed below Themo; Mellie was pointing to the similar spot below Jen's name. The scribal notation was the same: Cashel could recognize the shapes of characters even though they didn't project sound or meaning to him. With the laborious care of a man who was used to tasks where the least fraction of his strength would smash the tools he was using, Cashel began to draw his name on the parchment following the line of Mellie's finger.

The parchment grew suddenly warm beneath the heel of his hand. Mellie looked at him, raising her eyebrows in question. Blue fire seemed to tremble from the edges of the document—but that must have been Cashel's imagination, since otherwise the others watching him sign would have said something.

Cashel concentrated silently on his task. Something was happening but he didn't know what; it could wait until he finished what he was doing without humiliating himself in front of friends and enemies alike.

The sprite gave him a wicked grin. Her arm traced a flourish that Cashel followed by the expedient of disconnecting his conscious mind from the motion his hand was making. The pen was out of ink by the time he finished the stroke, leaving only scratches and a tracery of shading on the tough parchment. Mellie crossed her arms in completion, then turned a handspring onto Cashel's wrist.

He straightened and stepped back. Frasa reached for the contract but paused before his fingers touched it. He looked at Cashel in wonder.

Themo stared at the document. "What kind of joke is this?" he roared. He leaped up, kicking the low chair away behind him.

Cashel blinked. The signatures of the broker and his witness weren't the same as they had been when Cashel's hand covered them while drawing his own name. He was sure he hadn't even let his palm brush the parchment, though.

Themo looked at Cashel with a fury the youth had never seen on another man's face. "I'll have your guts for garters!" he said. "Get him, boys!"

The boxer reached for Cashel's arm; the red-haired man tried to draw his sword. A servant dropped a drinks tray and ran out the door shouting; Jen was calling into the courtyard through the louvered windows. The table flipped over, though Cashel didn't see who or what hit it.

Cashel grabbed the guards by their throats. Because he was usually slow and methodical, he always moved faster than people expected when there was a need for haste. The boxer punched him on the side of the head, a glancing blow but enough to send Cashel's vision momentarily black and white.

He swung the two big men together. Their steel caps

clashed like anvils colliding. The helmets flew off as their heads bounced apart. The red-haired man had gone limp; the boxer's eyes crossed but his left arm windmilled blindly.

Cashel slammed their heads together again and flung them both straight-arm against the wall. They smacked hard against the masonry and dropped as though boneless. Themo backed with his hands raised and a distorted look on his face, screaming unintelligibly.

Mellie cheered from Cashel's shoulder. The secretary stood where he'd been, wearing a dazed expression. Cashell snatched the quarterstaff from the man's hand, more to have it than as a useful weapon inside even as large a room as this.

The door flung open again. Highlanders poured in with half-drawn bows and raised stone axes. None of them carried metal weapons; Cashel wondered if it had something to do with their religion. *If the Serians are devil worshippers, what's the Highlanders' god like?* More of the jabbering little men climbed in through the windows.

Jen called a command. From his throat the Highlanders' language sounded like birdsong. One of the little men regretfully lowered the axe that had been an eyeblink from decapitating the broker. He pleaded with Jen, who merely tented his fingers and stared into space with a grim expression.

"Show Master Themo and his companions out of the building," Frasa said to the robed secretary. "You'll need some help with the two gentlemen who fell, I suppose."

Cashel started to say that he'd carry the guards out; then he decided he hadn't better touch them again. He hadn't needed to throw them into the wall that way. He knew he shouldn't get angry and hated it afterward when he did, but the cold rage that the boxer's punch had dropped him into hadn't yet dissipated. Better to let somebody else move the fellows.

Cashel bent and picked up the contract that had flown into a corner when the table overset. The writing still didn't mean anything to him, but he could see that the broker and witness signatures were not only different from what they'd been, they were in squared block letters unlike anything else on the page.

"Themo's name reads LIAR," Mellie said, sitting in the crook of Cashel's right elbow. "And the foreman who signed below him is LIAR'S WITNESS. My, but you're naughty, Cashel!"

She went off into peals of familiar laughter.

"I didn't do this!" Cashel said in amazement. That's what he'd thought of the broker, sure, but . . . "I *couldn't* do anything like that!"

"Of course you did it, silly!" the sprite said. "And you were right, too. He's a *nasty* man."

Servants, sailors from the Serian ship judging from their callused hands, were carrying the guards out. Four held each unconscious man. There was blood on the wall where the fellows had hit. Cashel grimaced and looked away.

Frasa and Jen stood before him. When he looked toward them, they bowed. "Master Cashel," Frasa said, "we had no idea what you were. Thank you from our deepest hearts."

"Were you sent to us, sir?" Jen asked.

Cashel didn't know what to say or do. For want of a better choice he handed the contract to Frasa. "I shouldn't have hit those fellows," he muttered. "On the wall, I mean."

"If you'll consent to act for us further," Frasa said, "our only remaining hope is to contact our other broker, Sidras or-Morr. We can't go out ourselves, and Sidras may reasonably feel that it's unsafe to come here to negotiate with us."

The outside door opened. The crowd roared; the clang of a stone hitting the helmet of a member of Themo's entourage rang through the factory. Nobody in the street was a worse enemy to the Serians now than the disgruntled broker, but with luck the two groups would bloody each other well before the mob realized they were all on the same side.

"He lives in a house on Government Square," Jen said. "We haven't contacted him since we landed, however."

"I know where it is," Cashel said. He'd passed through the square with Benlo. He supposed he could find it again. If he got confused, well, he had Mellie to help him. "But I don't think I ought to be doing that sort of business for you."

"We trust you implicitly, Master Cashel," Jen said. "Of course the risk to you is terrible. Perhaps we'd better reload the cargo and take a loss for the trip."

Cashel shrugged. "It doesn't look that bad a risk," he said. "I mean, if I wait till things settle down for a while out there."

He picked up one of the steel caps lying on the floor. It had been the boxer's; he had a big head.

Jen took the cap from Cashel's hands. "We'll have the dent hammered out of it, Master Cashel," he said. "Is there anything else you'd like?"

I'd like to know what's going on, Cashel thought. Aloud he said, "No, I guess I'll be all right."

"Of course we'll be all right!" Mellie said, stretching like a grinning cat. "It'll be fun!"

27

Ilna was alone.

She'd thought she'd see Garric and Tenoctris ahead of her when she plunged through the portal, but there was nothing: no figures, no ahead; even the portal had vanished.

She stood on a gray plain, though even the notion of standing was a distortion of reality when she couldn't feel ground beneath her feet. She had no sense of falling; no sense of anything really.

"Garric!" Ilna called. She could hear her voice but it had no overtones or echoes. There was no other sound.

The horizon was dead flat in all directions. The sky was minusculely lighter than the ground, but even that difference could have been a self-created illusion, a small madness her mind had worked on itself to keep from shattering completely.

Ilna reached behind her and waggled a hand through empty air. She couldn't have been more than inches from the gate of light by which she'd entered this limbo, but there was no sign of it now. She walked around the imagined doorway, hoping in vain it was visible from the other side.

She began to walk. One direction was the same as all others. She left no footprints behind her, nor were there any landmarks to prevent her from going in circles.

The horizon shifted as she moved toward it: sometimes the line of gray over gray was higher, as though she was looking up a hill, sometimes lower, as though she was on the crest. Each stride took the same amount of effort as the one before it, and the line of the horizon was always horizontal.

They abandoned you here, Ilna.

She held a steady pace, a ground-devouring pace that she could keep up all day and half the night besides. She wouldn't run. There was no place to run to.

They tricked you into coming here. They're laughing now about the way they got rid of you.

Her hands knotted the halter as she strode on. When they finished, the rope was a single mass the size of a man's head. Her fingers began to pick it apart again.

You weren't good enough for Garric and his new friends. They were embarrassed to have you around.

There was a point of light in the sky directly ahead of her. It was too small to be the sun, but it shone brilliantly sharp against the gray. She continued to walk.

The anonymous surface beneath her feet gave way to coarse gravel, though it was minutes of further walking before Ilna could see anything but undifferentiated gray. Her stride hadn't changed since she began walking. Her hands were knotting the rope again in a fashion wholly different from the first time, though the result would seem identical to anyone else.

The ground was like the shingle beach of Barca's Hamlet. *They all laughed at you there too, Ilna.*

When she first saw the tree she felt that she'd always known its presence. It was in black silhouette against the light gray sky, and the sun was behind it. She walked on.

You would have sacrificed everything for them, Ilna. But they cast you away.

The tree's trunk and surface roots seemed normal enough, but Ilna found herself wondering how far away it really was. Her strides didn't appear to bring the tree any closer.

Its branches were leafless and twisted into a loose knot, a stylized tree-of-life pattern. They began to move.

You're lucky to have found me, Ilna. There are terrible things in this place.

"Who are you?" Ilna said. Her voice vanished without an echo. There was nothing in any direction except the tree.

I'm your friend. I'll give you everything you want.

There were tears on her cheeks. "I want to go back!" She wouldn't beg. "Please let me go back!"

Of course I'll take you back, Ilna; I'm your friend. I know that you don't belong in this place, so I'll take you to where you should be. But you're a weaver. Wouldn't you first like to learn how to really weave?

"I don't understand," Ilna said. She didn't know when she'd stopped walking; she now stood motionless on the gravel plain. The rope was a limp coil in her hands.

I can teach you to weave patterns that will make you a queen, Ilna; a goddess, even.

"How can you . . ." Ilna said. Then she said, "Why?"

They won't sneer at you again, Ilna. Garric left you to run after that stuck-up hussy, but he'll never leave you again. They'll all notice you.

"I want to go back . . ." Ilna whispered.

But first shall I teach you to weave, Ilna?

"Yes," she said. She dropped the halter of rye straw and shouted again, *"Yes!"*

Then I'll teach you, because I'm your friend.

The branches were moving faster. The pinpoint sun glared hotter, brighter. Ilna had to turn her head.

Your only friend.

The branches continued to weave patterns in her mind; ever deeper in her mind. For the first time in her life, Ilna was not alone.

28

Nonnus had a fire of dried seaweed going. The pot over it bubbled merrily, though Sharina supposed the crabs being cooked weren't very cheerful about it.

Before Tegma it wouldn't have occurred to her to think about how a crab felt. She wondered if the Archai ate men.

The flames were clear and colored a dozen pastel shades by salts in the dried strands. Occasionally a nodule cracked with a puff of steam. Nonnus had to constantly feed the fire. For a moment Sharina doubted there'd be enough seaweed to finish cooking the meal, but she realized that meant doubting the hermit's judgment.

Nonnus was human; he could make mistakes. But she hadn't seen him make any mistake that mattered since they boarded the trireme together.

Except, perhaps, that he *had* boarded the trireme when he could have remained in prayerful contemplation near the hamlet.

"Shall I—" Sharina said. Nonnus jumped as though she'd stabbed.

"Oh, I'm—" she blurted, then fell silent in embarrassment.

"Child," the hermit said in equal embarrassment, "I've spent so much of my life alone that sometimes I forget that other folk are around now."

He smiled slowly. "Feeding the fire, smelling the salt

smoke and crabs boiling . . . It's like I was your age again, before other things happened.''

The smile vanished like hoarfrost in the sun. "Before I did the other things," he added.

"I was thinking that I could call Asera and Meder down," Sharina said. She spoke in the direction of the island's crest so that she didn't have to meet Nonnus' eyes for the moment. "I don't think they even carried food up the hill with them."

The island was a featureless hump, visible against the sky only as an absence of stars. A twinkle could have meant Meder or the procurator had walked across the skyline, but the heavens weren't light enough to show anything as small as a human a quarter mile away.

"This isn't a hot fire," the hermit said. "Give them another half hour or so."

Sharina had circled the whole island without finding driftwood or any terrain different from the spot where they'd beached their vessel. She'd been doubtful when she returned to find the dugout's mast and spar festooned with seaweed drying for fuel, but it had worked just the way Nonnus said it would.

Occasionally as she'd walked Sharina could see Asera and Meder on the hilltop. The nobles hadn't managed to raise a shelter during daylight; if they wanted to come down to the shore again, there was room for them behind the windbreak. Nonnus had erected a tarpaulin on spikes like the ones that held the dugout.

"Besides," Nonnus said, "I find the night more peaceful the way it is."

He smiled and added, "Charity is one of the things I pray for, but there's a long list."

"There's plenty of food on this island," Sharina said. "Barnacles and crabs. And we can have a fire."

She hadn't realized how glad she'd been to be on dry land until midway on her walk around the island. Of course she wanted to get to one of the major isles. She wanted even more to get home and to curl up in her own bed, letting the notion that she was Count Niard's daughter vanish into fantasy like everything else that had happened since the trireme landed in Barca's Hamlet. But just for now, Sharina would like a few days when she had more space than a dugout's hull and her universe didn't rise and fall with the waves.

"Best we leave, child," Nonnus said as he fed his fire. "This land doesn't hate us the way Tegma did, but it isn't a place we belong either. There'll be roads to walk on Sandrakkan; and houses to live in as well."

Sharina looked up the hill, wondering how close she'd have to get to the nobles' camp for them to hear her offer of dinner. Climbing the channeled rock at night wouldn't be easy. If Asera and Meder wanted a meal they could see the fire burning, couldn't they?

There was light behind the hilltop.

For an instant Sharina thought her eyes were throwing flashes of their own the way they sometimes did when closed in the middle of the night. She opened her mouth to speak but held the words.

The night flickered again, rosy pink.

Sharina got up and ran to the dugout. "Child?" the hermit called behind her.

She knew where the wizard's chest of paraphernalia had been stored near the stern. She clambered over the cargo, pawing at the nets. The boat's belly was in darkness, but nothing else had the shape and feel of that metal-strapped case.

It wasn't where it had been. Meder hadn't brought it out; Sharina had watched to make sure. Asera must have carried the chest for him, concealed in the folds of her robe.

"Child?" Nonnus repeated.

Sharina pointed. "He's doing magic," she said. As she spoke, a flare of red light bathed the darkened hillcrest.

"So he is," the hermit said in a voice like a glacier. He lifted his javelin in his right hand and started up the hill. Sharina jumped to the ground to go with him.

A vast tremor shook the island.

29

Garric had the shepherd's trick of keeping his head raised while walking uphill when the reflex is to look down at your feet. He scanned the crest ahead of them and the stark emptiness of their surroundings.

The ground was grit rather than gravel, apt to crumble out from underfoot when any weight was put on it. The slopes were steep, the sun fiercely hot, and the texture wrong because the reversed light and dark image tricked Garric's eyes into expecting something subtly different from what his feet touched. For all that he slid rarely, dabbed his hand down to hold himself only once, and never fell.

Tenoctris bounced like a pinecone being kicked by a circle of children. "Shall I—" Garric offered for the third or fourth time.

"Your task is to keep us alive when Strasedon appears," the old woman snapped. "Trying to carry me and getting us both killed won't make the situation better."

"Yes, mistress," Garric said submissively.

He'd have traveled much faster if he hadn't had to suit his pace to Tenoctris, but he couldn't very well leave her behind. They knew where Liane had been; not necessarily where she was, and not certainly where the demon itself was. Garric couldn't locate Strasedon again if the demon wasn't waiting over the ridge.

The black sun would kill before long if Strasedon's claws did not.

"I never expected to be doing anything like this," Tenoctris said, panting but surprisingly cheerful. "I don't mean that I didn't want to visit another plane myself: it's just that

I knew I didn't have the power to do anything of the sort. As well wish I could fly."

She chuckled. "When Yole sank, the tower roof and I lifted into the air. I really did fly. And now I'm on a demon plane. Tenoctris the scholar, Tenoctris who read about wondrous explorations and the researches of other folk, who had the power to cleave time and space."

The plateau up which the pointer of light had streaked was three-leveled; the hillsides between sloped at about one foot in four, maybe a little steeper. From below, the top of each next step looked like the top of the plateau itself. This time Garric thought that the edge above them was the real peak.

He walked at a slant, his left side to the higher ground. His left hand rested on the fold of his tunic, ready to snatch it away from the sword hilt for his right hand to grip.

"All those books that were my life," Tenoctris mused. "Sunken for a thousand years. And here I am, doing what—"

Strasedon came over the crest twenty feet above Garric.

The demon walked like a man, but its legs were short and bowed while its arms were so long that the clawed fingers could almost brush the ground. The big toes carried particularly large hooked claws: Strasedon's right leg was still covered with Benlo's black crusted blood.

Strasedon held Liane around the waist in its left hand. The girl was alive. She gripped the demon's upper arm to take some of the weight off her abdomen while her feet dangled in the air.

When Liane saw Garric her face froze. She didn't call out.

Strasedon's skin was the dark translucent red of fine garnets. The creature's face was flat and noseless; the lower jaw rose and fell vertically instead of pivoting at the back. The upper and lower teeth slid past each other as close as scissor blades; the jagged points clicked softly as the demon advanced.

Garric drew his borrowed sword and felt King Carus fill his flesh the way a man shrugs into a tunic. He began to sidle left and away from the demon to gain the advantage of height or at least parity. If Strasedon went for Tenoctris, so much the better: that would open the demon's back to Garric's leaping, slashing attack.

The part of Garric's mind that still *was* Garric felt horrified at the cold calculation that the old woman's danger was his own opportunity. And yet—Garric had culled herds for the winter. A farmer who saved more animals than he could feed until spring lost all of them, not just the ones he should have slaughtered. If Tenoctris could distract the demon long enough for Garric's sword to thrust home, it might save both of them and Liane as well.

Strasedon tossed Liane to the side and shambled toward Garric. The creature called *"Hoo! Hoo! Hoo!"* as it advanced.

Laughing demonically himself, Garric lifted his point for a sweeping blow and charged. Dirt sprayed beneath his thrusting toes.

He cut. The swordblade glittered black in the still, dry air. Strasedon snatched at the weapon. The edge sheared off the thumb of the demon's three-fingered hand, but its touch deflected the stroke to glance off the side of Strasedon's hairless skull instead chopping into it squarely.

Rald's sword was good steel. The blade rang like a giant tuning fork in Garric's hand.

Garric leaped sideways—uphill—to avoid Strasedon's grasp. The soil gave way underfoot. He slashed sidearm at the demon. He was falling away and the blow lacked its full force.

The demon's blood was the color of fire. Droplets showered from the sword edge.

Strasedon gripped Garric's right forearm with its injured hand and reached for his throat with the other. Garric's left hand caught the demon's wrist. It was like trying to hold back an ox one-handed. Garric's muscles bulged. Strasedon's clawed fingers clenched and unclenched, but they didn't quite reach his flesh.

The demon bent toward Garric, its jaws sliding open wide

enough to shear off the youth's face. Garric half-thrust, half-twisted the swordpoint into the open mouth.

The demon's teeth clamped on the steel, holding the last three inches of the tip like a vise. Garric tried to work the blade deeper the inch or less it would take him to slash through the back of Strasedon's throat, but the jaws held as if the blade had been cast in rock.

Both of them put all their strength into their upper bodies and lost their footing, rolling down the slope together in a whirlwind of sand and rock. The demon was heavy even for its great size, but when it was on top Garric could always twist so that they went over again.

Garric arched his back and clamped his legs around Strasedon's waist. Not a moment too soon: the demon's right leg slashed upward, trying to duplicate the stroke that left Benlo and his guts spread across separate portions of the tomb floor. The talons raked Garric's back, shredding his tunic and tearing his skin, but the demon couldn't get the point of its great hook under the youth's rib cage.

They hit the floor of the valley. Garric's frame was so tensed that the shock didn't drive out his breath, but Strasedon was nonetheless on top of him. Garric tried to lever the demon sideways by using the point of his right shoulder for a fulcrum. He might as profitably have tried to move the mill at Barca's Hamlet.

Strasedon shuddered, then lurched upright so suddenly that Garric lost his death grip on the hilt of his sword. He sprawled on the ground; his back and hips felt cool from the coating of his own drying blood.

The demon spat the sword out. Its teeth had left deep gouges in the steel. Garric tried to get up; his muscles were liquid with exhaustion, unable to obey.

Strasedon turned its face to the red sky and screamed like all the winds of winter. The hilt of Benlo's iron athame projected from the base of the demon's skull.

Tenoctris rested on her hands and knees beside Strasedon where she'd fallen when the demon straightened. Liane stood on the creature's other flank, holding a stone that all the strength of both her arms couldn't raise high enough to strike the demon now that it was upright.

Strasedon turned slowly. The black sun was paler and it seemed to Garric that the whole landscape was crumbling. He couldn't move; most likely what he saw was a fantasy as his brain dissociated from the intense pain.

The world was white light and he was falling. King Carus laughed triumphantly, and somewhere Garric saw the Hooded One clenching his fists in fury.

30

The outward-spreading wave was a perfect visual echo of the shore, a vast wall across the sea's face that ignored the water's own swelling rhythms. The dugout had bucked and pitched when the tremor first struck; now it merely whispered urgently in the play of wavelets against its hull.

Sharina stood up beside the vessel where she'd fallen at the initial shock. The wave had combed a hundred feet up the slope, dousing the fire, but Nonnus had snatched the handle of the bronze cookpot before it vanished into the rolling sea. The crabs still steamed with a memory of the flames.

Moving with practiced ease, Nonnus set the pot and his javelin into the dugout's bow cavity, then stepped to the iron shore fasts. He gripped one pin with both hands and kicked the shaft with the heel of his foot.

"Nonnus!" Sharina cried. "The others!"

The island shook itself again even more violently. Sharina leaped onto the port outrigger and wrapped both arms around the mast stay. The dugout lifted, fought the line, and crashed again onto the rock with an impact that would have threatened the frames of a planked hull.

"If we're afloat," Nonnus said, shouting over the sea's bass roar, "we've a chance to pick them out of the water. If we're hard on shore and the next wave flips the boat over, we'll never right her again!"

Foam surged around Sharina's waist and spewed into her face. She blinked in the salt but didn't close her eyes. Nonnus stood like an outcrop of rock, unmoving in the white bubbling chaos.

The sea settled again in nervous anticipation. The surface had an oily sheen; tiny life-forms circled in the frothing water, feeding and fodder alike in the disturbed conditions. Though the water was gurglingly alive, Sharina didn't hear a volcanic rumble from the rocks beneath her. What was shaking it this way?

Nonnus kicked the shore fast again, working it in the crack where he'd set it. The pin came loose in his grip. He tugged it clear and tossed it into the bow as he stepped to the remaining iron.

Sharina could see the nobles struggling downslope with the chest between them. Whenever one slipped, they both fell. It took them longer each time to get up again.

"I'm going up there," Sharina said, springing from her perch.

"No!" Nonnus called. "Child, no!"

Sharina ran with a surefootedness that reason would have told her was impossible, bounding from one wave-wet rock to the next without slipping. Dissipating foam gleamed in the channels, marking them as clearly as they were by daylight. She managed to stay upright even during the third tremor. She was above the reach of the waves, though a halo of foam crowned the hillcrest from the other side.

She'd reached the nobles before they saw her coming. Meder cried, "Help—"

Sharina wrenched the heavy chest from his hands and swung it to her right shoulder. The wizard was probably stronger than she was in absolute terms, but he didn't know how to carry a load. The nobles had made things worse by sharing the burden. If one fell, both did. Asera was holding her knee as she crawled out of the channel she'd fallen into.

"Come on or you'll have to swim!" Sharina shouted as she started back, running as she'd never run before. The chest's inertia gave her leaps a ponderous majesty that would mean disaster if she put a foot wrong.

She didn't. Tonight she couldn't. With the nobles staggering in her wake, freed from each other and the heavy container, Sharina sprinted to the flank of the dugout as the fourth tremor sent the sea rising to meet her.

Sharina wrapped her left arm around the brace of the port outrigger. The wave poured in. Nonnus stood at the remaining shore fast with his legs locked on the hawser to free his hands. He grabbed both Meder and Asera by the wrist. They lost their footing and streamed at full length in the rushing current.

Sounds dissolved in the boiling water, but Asera opened her mouth in a scream of pain. She was trying to loosen the hermit's iron grip with her free hand. She might as well have tried to drag down the crescent moon just rising: Nonnus wasn't going to let her drown to save her wrist from a bruise.

The wave started to subside. Nonnus sent Meder, then the procurator, scrambling along the hawser and over the dugout's bows. He looked toward Sharina.

Sharina released the brace and stood upright with both hands holding the chest. She took two steps along the outrigger and hurled the magical paraphernalia seaward with all her strength.

She heard Meder scream like a balked eagle. The case rolled twice in the receding waves, then vanished forever toward the bottom of the Outer Sea. She turned to face the wizard. He was white: his mouth was open, his eyes staring.

Sharina clambered into the dugout and took the tiller. Nonnus' smile was brighter than the moon's. He kicked the shore fast free and hopped onto the vessel's bow, then ran sternward along the gunwale to join Sharina.

The dugout pitched bow-down as the rock tilted beneath it, then righted as the sea rushed in with a smash of thunder and foam. "We're sinking!" Meder cried. "We're sinking!"

The vessel wasn't sinking, though the violence with which the sea thrashed it threatened to capsize them despite the outriggers. The island was sinking.

The island had sunk; completely and utterly, into a salt waste tossed by its departure.

A vast bulk rose again above the surface to westward, streaming water. For a long moment moonlight gleamed on the eye of a creature whose shell was more than half a mile in diameter; a creature the size of an island floating in the sea.

The front flippers rotated forward again. With the gravity of something unimaginably ancient, the turtle dived out of the world of men.

31

Every time Garric's heart beat, pain pulsed blindingly white, then deep bloody red. The buildings around the square blurred and sprang back into focus in the same throbbing rhythm. He lay on cobblestones. That would have hurt if his brain could make room for such lesser matters.

Tenoctris knelt beside him, droning a spell. The moon was at zenith and the clouds of earlier in the evening had blown away.

Garric's back felt as though it had been minced for sausage. There were spectators, mostly workmen. One nobleman gaped from his sedan chair as his entourage of servants and toadies whispered and pointed. Liane, wobbly but upright, fumbled in the folds of her silken sash. She called to the grandee for help.

Garric's sight steadied and he realized that he was sprawling before the semicircular steps that ornamented the approach to the count's palace. The masonry had been quarried from Old Kingdom buildings, but the construction was regular and ornate in the modern manner.

The windows of the lowest story were small and protected by heavy iron gratings; those of the second story alternated arched and triangular pediments over the openings, while the third-story windows were framed with pilasters supporting flat brows beetling out from the wall. Towering above the real façade was a false front aping a temple of former times, crowned in turn by a gilded statue that gleamed in the moonlight.

Some of the lower windows were lighted; the count's bureaucrats lived and worked in the palace, and in these troubled times they worked late.

"How did we get here?" Garric mumbled. He wasn't sure he even spoke aloud. Tenoctris continued her chant, touching the tip of her boxwood twig to points in the air around Garric. A leaden numbness began to replace the pain of his wounds, and he wondered if he was going into shock.

He and Tenoctris had entered the demon's plane in the graveyard half a mile from here, the Government Square of modern Carcosa. The distance they'd traveled to where Strasedon waited was about right; the moon's greater height now in the sky also matched the time they'd spent searching the other dimension.

Garric couldn't guess at the direction they'd gone in that place of black sun. Perhaps that was right as well.

He was exhausted but he couldn't rest. His back was a mass of live coals, burning him to wakefulness. The demon's claws carried a fiery poison like the touch of certain caterpillars; he would never sleep again, he'd blaze forever until he died. . . .

A pair of porters holding a handbarrow between them stared in horror. Garric and his companions must have dropped into sight directly in front of the men as Strasedon's plane dissolved. Giving up on the noble, Liane called to the porters, "You there! Get this man on your pallet!"

The man at the front of the barrow shied from the girl's attention, but his partner remained motionless in amazement. The barrow twitched but the men didn't go off down the street as the leader intended. They carried a roll of wet hide reeking with the stench of the tannery.

"Look!" Liane said, bringing her hands up from her sash. She let coins cascade from one palm to the other. Even if the porters didn't recognize the chime as that of gold—where would they have seen gold?—the implication of even that much copper was enough to hold them now.

"Carry this man to the Captain's Rest," Liane ordered. "You know where it is, don't you? Get him there alive and there's a gold Sandrakkan rider for each of you!"

"But mistress," the man at the front of the barrow said. The pair had been too shocked even to lower their burden to the cobblestones as they gaped. "We have to deliver this to Chilsen the Cobbler in Boot Lane."

"You idiots!" the grandee shouted in amazement from his chair. "A gold rider would buy Chilsen's whole shop and his daughter besides!"

The porter at the back raised his right handle and lowered the left one, dumping the roll of hide on the ground before his partner fully realized what was happening. The men exchanged glances, then set the barrow down beside Garric. They lifted him with surprising gentleness. They were workingmen, well used to injuries.

Tenoctris continued to chant as the porters raised their barrow with Garric aboard it. Pain faded slowly as waxen darkness diffused through Garric's mind.

BOOK
IV

1

Ilna os-Kenset stepped from gray limbo into the shadows of an alley too narrow for even a donkey to navigate. Wooden balconies were built out from windows in the walls above; from a few hung knotted ropes by which an agile occupant could come or go.

One end of the alley was closed by a blank wall. Hazy light edged the kink in the other direction, where a knuckle of the building to the right pressed toward the wall opposite, squeezing the passage so that Ilna had to turn sideways to round it.

She walked out onto the street beyond. It was late afternoon; too little of the sky was visible from within the alley for her to have been sure. There was a good deal of traffic, both pedestrians and carts. A recent rain had left the pavement slick and pools standing where bricks were missing or sunken; it wasn't raining now.

Ilna had never seen this street before in her life. She didn't think she was in Carcosa—the building styles, the brick street, the dress of the inhabitants all suggested otherwise. She caught the eye of a woman carrying a wicker basket of vegetables and a swatch of salt meat.

"Excuse me, mistress," Ilna said. The woman turned her head aside and strode past grim-faced.

Ilna's own expression hardened. This was a city, not a hamlet where people were polite because everyone knew everyone else and knew that they'd be seeing the same faces for the rest of their lives.

She surveyed the street and began walking. A shop selling earthenware. A tavern; the pavement in front was stained dark by the dregs of beer pails emptied there by children fetching fresh for the family's next-day use. A dairy used a butter churn for a sign. A ewe bleated from the yard in back, touching the part of Ilna that didn't remember it had no home in this world.

The buildings were two and three floors high, some of them even taller. Upper-story windows had cards in the windows; from the uniformity of the characters she assumed they advertised lodgings.

Ilna had always wondered what it would be like to read. She didn't need that skill now. People would read for her. People would do anything she ordered them to do.

Ilna came to a grocer's. A handcart of turnips and parsnips stood to one side of the entrance, blocking the raised sidewalk. On the other side was a tray of oranges covered with coarse sacking to shield them from the direct sun. The proprietor sat just inside where he could keep an eye on the sidewalk display.

Ilna lifted the sacking and began to strip weft fibers from the edge of the cloth. She didn't recognize the material, but her fingers felt an image of dry soil and clumps of leaves like swordblades.

The proprietor was counting eggs into a housewife's basket. He took the woman's copper coins without checking them for weight and followed her out of the shop. "Hey you!" he said to Ilna.

Ilna ignored him. She had a dozen strands loose; her fingers began to plait them together.

The shopkeeper jabbed Ilna's shoulder with the tips of his fingers. Passersby eyed sidelong what they thought was an argument; no one stopped to intervene. "You!" the man shouted. "Are you some kind of booby? Get away from my store or I'll—"

Ilna finished the design. She raised the fibers for the shopkeeper to see. The man froze mute, his mouth open but the threat frozen on his tongue.

A woman moved in the back of the shop. "Arrek?" she called.

"What city is this?" Ilna said in a voice as cold as a serpent's. She held the pattern rigid in the frame of her hands.

"This is Erdin on Sandrakkan," the proprietor said. His words were only sound; there was no life at all in them.

Ilna nodded crisply, a reflexive acknowledgment that the shopkeeper couldn't even see. "Where is the nearest mercer's shop?" she asked. The woman was coming up the aisle of the grocery, wiping her hands on her apron.

"Beltar or-Holman has a shop in the next block," the man said in the tones of the dead. "On the corner of the street and a close."

"Arrek?" the woman from the shop said. She grabbed the man's shoulder. "Arrek!"

"Point the way," Ilna ordered, ignoring the woman just as the man she controlled did. He extended his right arm.

She tossed the plaited fibers to the ground and strode away. She didn't know what a "close" was, but the shop would be obvious. Behind her the woman was chirruping to the shopkeeper in growing agitation. He gasped like a whale blowing and staggered into the cart of root vegetables.

Shops in Erdin weren't grouped like those of Carcosa. She passed a cobbler, a salt seller, and a cookshop selling fish stew. The pavement near the doorway glittered with iridescent scales.

The air was thick with smell of brackish groundwater as well as the recent rain. It was a hot day and the gutters reeked.

The mercer's was across the street; she hadn't asked that. The shopkeeper hadn't had the will to volunteer the information even if he'd had the desire to do so. The close proved to be a dead-end alley like the one she'd entered Erdin by.

Ilna crossed despite the traffic, never touching and never endangered by any of the pedestrians and carts clattering over the bricks. She'd always been good at judging patterns; now she knew how every moving object interacted with every other object.

She entered the shop beneath the swatch of bias-woven fabric that acted as a sign. The brown and blue dyes were colorfast, though city grime had darkened the cloth to the point that you almost had to know the pattern to recognize it.

The shop specialized in fancy weaves, thin stripes and checks. Ilna had noticed similar fabrics on the better-dressed locals, though the patterns were too busy for her taste. No matter.

The shop assistant, a girl with a thin face and straw-colored hair, was showing a matron a roll of cloth from the rack on the other side of the display room. Ilna looked through the part-bolts stacked end-on along the counter, leaving only a yard of the wood bare for transactions. The selvage of loose warp threads hung from each roll.

Ilna found the one she wanted, a bolt of red cloth stacked on the bottom of the pile where its width couldn't easily be compared with that of others. She tugged it out a few inches. The assistant glanced over but continued dealing with her present customer.

A pair of shears lay on the counter; the backspring was inlaid with brass lilies. Ilna ignored them and drew her knife from its case.

"Mistress?" the shop assistant called. "Mistress, I'll help you in—"

Ilna trimmed the selvage off the end of the roll, keeping the threads under firm tension as the steel parted them.

"Master Beltar!" the assistant screamed. The matron stared, backing against a rack of cloth. "Master Beltar!"

A middle-aged man with a broad face and reddish facial hair came from the back room. He held a pen and his fingers were stained with ink. "Yes, mistress?" he said sharply, following his assistant's eyes to Ilna.

She laid the handful of loose threads on the empty portion of the counter and began interweaving them. Windows along the two outside walls provided good illumination even at this time of day, but she could have worked in the dark. The matron took the opportunity to dart past Ilna to the street.

"Mistress!" Beltar said when he saw the bolt that had been

pulled out and trimmed. "What are you doing? Sarhad, get the Patrol!"

"Don't, girl," Ilna said. She looked over at Beltar and continued, "This bolt was short width. You can lose your whole stock if you sell short cloth without marking it by cutting the selvage."

The girl had already reached the street door. "Sarhad, stop," Beltar snapped. "I'll take care of this. Ah, sweep out the back room and the stairs."

Looking wide eyed at her employer and the strange woman, the assistant vanished behind the curtain into the back. Ilna returned to her task. The red dye was a muddy hue; the fabric was shoddy in all respects and didn't belong in a shop with the pretensions of Beltar's.

"Are you from the chancellor's office?" he asked when Ilna remained silent. "I assure you that if any under-width cloth found its way into my shop by accident, I'm more than willing to correct the error in a reasonable manner. . . ."

Ilna smiled coldly. He was offering a bribe. She'd quoted Valles commercial practice, since that was where her market and experience was, but apparently Erdin's regulations were equally stringent.

"I'm not from the chancellor's office," she said. "I'm here to make you rich beyond your dreams. For now you'll set me up in a room above your shop. I'll need a loom and yarn."

"Mistress," Beltar said in frank puzzlement, "I buy cloth—I don't hire weavers. If you've fabric to sell me I might be interested, but you'll have to find your own lodgings and materials."

"No," Ilna said, turning her face toward him again. "I won't. Look at this."

She uncovered the pattern on the countertop. Beltar bent forward to get a better view. His eyes narrowed, then he jerked back as the image came in focus. He brushed his hands in front of his face, trying to grasp what he'd seen or thought he'd seen.

"That's your real future," Ilna said without emotion. "That and a great deal more."

The mercer stared at her in growing wonder. "Who are you?" he whispered.

A pair of women came in the street door. "Go away!" Ilna snapped without looking around.

"Yes, we're closed now!" Beltar said. "You'll have to leave!"

They backed out, gabbling complaints. Ilna waited until she and the owner were alone again and repeated, "I'm the woman who's going to make you rich. That's all that need concern you."

The mercer touched the air again. His face was regaining its normal ruddy coloration but sweat beaded on his sandy eyebrows. "All right," he said. "Mistress Nirari has a room open across the street. I'll rent it for you. I won't have you in my house, but you'll have your space."

Ilna's fingers combed the red threads into two separate clumps, destroying the pattern as if it had never existed. "All right," she said. "We'll go there now. I have much to do."

She smiled. Beltar looked as though he might never smile again; but for all that his expression was warmer than hers.

2

"There's eels here in this harbor as big as a man's leg," Sidras or-Morr said with gloomy assurance. "Oh, they won't fool with a living man. But let a body go into the water and *fst*! it's gone. We'd never be seen again."

"Not as big as *your* leg, Cashel," Mellie said cheerfully. "Anyway, there wouldn't be so many scavengers if people didn't dump garbage into the water the way they do."

Cashel brought the oars forward close to the surface so that water streaming from the blade wouldn't make too much noise. He stroked with gentle grace. There was enough mist over the harbor basin to shroud a small boat, but sound carried.

"You've been a waterman yourself, I shouldn't wonder," the broker said. "That's the only luck there is in this whole business. Listen to them!"

The snarl of the mob in Harbor Street filled the night the way a storm does. Down on the water the deeper notes predominated, but occasionally a scream of bestial rage carried across the mist-wrapped piers and jetties.

"They're serious now," Mellie said. "It won't be long, I think." Then she added, "I like him."

"I'm a shepherd, sir," Cashel said with his easy return and stroke. "I've helped the fishermen, sure; and if you've rowed a loaded fishing boat in from the sea with a storm building, then a harbor skiff is no great shakes."

"That's the *Golden Dragon* or her twin," Sidras murmured. "Nothing on the seas looks like a Serian cargo hauler, but they swim like ducks for all their strangeness."

"Call out from here, Cashel," Mellie directed. "Otherwise the Highlander watching on top of the mast may shoot. They're not really very accurate at any range, but"—She laughed—"you're a big target."

Cashel looked over his shoulder and called, "Jen! Frasa? This is Cashel returned by boat. Don't shoot!"

Voices called in the mist. Either the words were distorted or they were spoken in an unfamiliar language. Somewhere oars hit the water raggedly. Cashel couldn't judge distance by sound over this enclosed water. No one out this night was their friend, and no few were enemies.

Sidras rose to his feet in the stern without rocking the skiff. He was middle-aged and below middle height, from the way he moved Cashel judged that more of the broker's bulk was muscle than fat; but there was fat as well. He shouted in a powerful voice, speaking first in what Cashel assumed was

Serian, then in a mixture of clicking and gutturals that had to be the Highlanders' separate tongue.

The quarterstaff lay lengthways over the skiff's thwarts. Cashel wasn't sure how good a weapon it'd be for a struggle between light watercraft, but he supposed it'd serve. It always had in the past.

A voice jabbered quickly and enthusiastically from the *Golden Dragon*'s dark bulk. Sidras seated himself again. "Take us to the dock, lad," he said. "I make sure there's always a mirror and some glass beads for each of those upland cannibals when I come by the factory. They'd give me a bite of their grandmother's liver, they love me so much."

Cashel brought the skiff the remainder of the way in to the dock ladder near the vessel's stern. The quay was parallel to the shore and extended far enough into the harbor that a good-sized vessel didn't ground. The *Golden Dragon* was moored alongside, its squared bows toward the harbor mouth where signal fires marked the passage between the jetties.

He thought of asking Mellie if Highlanders really ate their own grandmothers. He decided that it wasn't a subject he needed or wanted to pursue.

Servants carrying large lanterns made of yellow paper trotted onto the quay through the gate from the factory yard. One of the brothers—Cashel couldn't tell which as he tied the bow line to the ladder—was among them. He heard Highlanders talking but he couldn't see any of the little men.

"Master Cashel, we were praying that you wouldn't try to return tonight!" said Frasa. Cashel found the Serians' voices more distinct than their features. "We've been concerned that we might be attacked from the water. Is it safe?"

"It is *not* safe, Master Frasa," said Sidras as he swung himself onto the quay behind Cashel. "Don't even think of taking your cargo off by lighters. My colleague Themo appears to have organized the watermen against you. Spent no small sum of money doing it, too."

"My brother's in the office," Frasa said. "Perhaps you'd join us there?"

"I didn't come here to admire the harbor view," Sidras grunted, striding into the factory with the nonchalance of a familiar guest. "And if you're wondering how we managed to hire a boat ourselves, your envoy Master Cashel has a persuasive way about him."

"They shouldn't have spit at me," Cashel muttered in embarrassment. "I'm not a dog to be kicked and spit at."

"There's three boatmen who got a bath in the harbor they didn't expect," Sidras said in satisfaction as he led the way through the goods stacked in the yard. "And they didn't chase us, either, because he knocked a bottom plank out of the other boats with that battering ram he uses for a stick. Impressive lad, that."

The *Dragon*'s cargo was packed in hardwood chests rather than barrels or wicker baskets in the fashion with which Cashel was familiar. There were few enough buildings in Barca's Hamlet as sturdy as these Serian crates.

Aloud Cashel said, "I'll go back by daylight and pay them for the damage. When the one fellow spit, I lost my temper and then there wasn't much choice I could see."

The lantern bearers didn't enter the building. Inside, oil lamps hung from hooks on the walls in a brighter artificial illumination than Cashel had ever seen before.

"Oh, I'll square them, lad," the broker said as he stumped up the stairs. He moved heavily because of the weight of the money belt Cashel had seen him wind around his waist beneath the tunic. "I know all three of them; they do jobs for me more days during the year than they don't. Which wouldn't have kept them from knocking *me* on the head when they're full of Themo's wine and nonsense about devil worshippers."

Jen waited at the stairhead and bowed Sidras into the office. The broker bowed back. He remained standing until Frasa shifted the chair behind him and nodded toward it. Cashel backed against the wall and smiled at the secretary standing stiffly beside him.

The sound of the mob on Harbor Street made the walls of

the factory vibrate. It had been obvious to Cashel that there was no way to return to the factory by land tonight, and even the broker's suggestion of hiring a boat had proved risky.

"You boys got under Themo's skin like a horsefly," Sidras said musingly.

"Master Sidras," Frasa said, "my brother and I attempted to engage Themo to job our present cargo. He became enraged when his dishonesty was demonstrated. I offer you our abject apologies."

Sidras shrugged. "Personally I've always thought Themo crawled up from the bottom of the harbor," he said, "but that's neither here nor there. It's just how the situation is that matters; and that's a problem."

The brothers seated themselves with tented fingers. The rap of stones being thrown against the thick outside wall sounded in the office like hail on the mill's slate roof.

The broker hitched up the skirt of his tunic without the least concern for propriety and began undoing the triple buckles of the multipouched leather belt against his skin. He wore a breechclout like a peasant, though it was linen rather than wool. His thighs were startlingly white beneath a coat of fine blond hair.

"I've gone through your inventory," he said. "It's a good cargo and one I wish I could sell here. But I can't, not the way things are now in Carcosa. They'd burn my warehouse, Themo'd see to that, and *that's* only if I could carry it out of here by wagon—which I could not."

He twitched his short auburn beard toward Harbor Street again.

"So it's got to go to Erdin," Sidras continued. "Sandrakkan's got its own problems but they're not lynching Serians there, not yet."

"We don't have a broker in Erdin," Jen said with the least hint of anger.

"Ah, but I do," Sidras said. "A Serian, as a matter of fact: Master Latias. His compound's hard by the Fellowship Hall just up from the harbor."

"You propose to give us a note on Master Latias, then?" Frasa said in the same distant tone his brother had used. "The gentleman may be of our race but he's not known to us personally, sir."

Sidras laid his belt on the table with a jingle like that of muffled bells. "I propose to give you gold, here and now," he said. "This gold. I'll tell you frankly that it's only sixty percent of what I'd offer for the goods in normal times, but these aren't normal. I can bring gold to you here. I *can't* move goods through the streets, not to you or to take yours away."

"You're accepting the risk of transporting our cargo to Erdin," Jen said, touching the belt with two fingers without trying to open it. He was making a statement, not asking a question.

"Aye, but you're providing the labor," Sidras said. He grimaced and said, "I figured after Themo you'd be shy of trusting Carcosa brokers." He slapped the table with his palm, making the coins ring again. "Gold you can trust."

"You we can trust," Frasa said, rising to his feet. He spoke a quick command to the secretary in his own language. The man went out of the room, repeating the orders at shrill volume.

"We are having the *Golden Dragon* reloaded," Jen explained as he rose also. "The situation outside appears to be becoming more serious."

"That's Themo too," Sidras said, standing and tucking his tunic back down over his thighs. "I don't know if he figures to loot the place or just burn you out for spite. Nasty piece of work I've always thought, but I guess he satisfies some."

He nodded toward the money belt. "The coins are a mixed bag, mostly Haft but I used whatever I had on hand to make up the weight. There's an account in the first pouch you'll want to check them against."

"I don't think we'll need to do that," Frasa said. "If the Goddess permits us to survive, Master Sidras, you'll won't be the loser for your trust."

The secretary reentered the office; every time the door

opened, the mob's voice was harsher. Jen picked up the belt by the buckle end and handed it to the servant with a low-voiced instruction.

"I'll head home then," the broker said. He stepped toward the door.

"Should I . . . ?" Cashel said, his question for Sidras as well as the Serians.

Sidras grinned at him. "I grew up on the water, lad," he said. "I'm willing enough to let a youngster do the work when he's available, but I don't guess I've forgotten what a pair of oars feels like."

He pointed a finger toward the ship. Lines of sailors, chattering with excitement and seeming lack of organization, were grabbing cargo chests and lugging them toward the twin gangplanks. "You're needed here to help get my goods aboard—and like enough for other things if I judge the temper of the folks out in the street. Just remember what I said about the eels."

Sidras left the office. Cashel was a step behind him, delayed fractionally to slant his long staff so that it didn't catch in the doorway. Frasa and Jen stayed to talk with their heads close together.

"Sir?" Cashel asked quietly as he followed the broker down the stairs. The entrance hall was empty except for the quartet of Highlanders, drinking some sort of thick liquid from wooden mugs as they ignored the impacts hammering the outside door.

"Lad?" Sidras said over his shoulder.

"Sir, why are you doing this?" Cashel said. "You and I arranged for earnest money and a note on Latias, not the full amount in gold."

"Aye, so we did," Sidras agreed as he strode through the bustle in the rear of the factory building. Fabrics and spices were stored under cover, though the packing chests seemed to Cashel proof against the worst storm of *his* lifetime. "And Jen and Frasa would've taken the deal: they're over a barrel, right enough, and they'd given me the whip when they didn't let Themo rob them like he'd planned. But you know . . ."

He waved his arm back toward the Goddess of Mercy and her attendant demons. "It's not that I hold with devil worship, but I've been dealing with that pair and their father for twenty years now. In all that time there's never been a short weight or second-quality goods packed under a sample layer of first-rate stuff. I guess if the Sister drags them down to the Underworld when they die, that's her business. *My* business is to treat a man like he's treated me."

The two Haft citizens strode side by side into the lantern-lit chaos of the factory yard. "Besides which," Sidras added, "if I can do that boat-worm Themo one in the eye and make a fat profit on the deal, well, either part would be worth the risk I'm taking."

The broker and the sprite on Cashel's shoulder laughed together in perfect harmony.

3

Nonnus adjusted the sail with the same precise care Sharina had seen him use in cleaning a wound before he sewed it up. The breeze was fretful and varied, a fitting counterpart to the gray skies above.

The hermit let go of the shrouds and sank back to his squat beside the tiller. Sharina smiled at him; not too desperately, she hoped.

"It's possible," Nonnus said with jagged calm, "that this air will take us in a direction that I'd be willing to go if asked. But I wouldn't stake my life on it."

His expression grew bleaker. He added, "I wouldn't stake my soul. I've already staked all our lives, I'm afraid."

"You didn't hold a knife to any of our throats to get us aboard," Sharina said. She wasn't just trying to cheer up a friend: it was the truth. "And we had to get off Tegma."

"That we did," Nonnus agreed as he scanned the overcast. Sharina knew the winds driving the high clouds weren't the same as those here on the surface that would fill the sail, but there might be connections between the two.

Of course, many folks thought there was a connection between the stars and human lives. Likely there was: it was all one cosmos. But it was a very complex cosmos, it seemed to Sharina, and certainly beyond the capacity of a human mind to chart all its interactions.

Asera and Meder huddled in the bow looking as bedraggled and angry as cats caught in a downpour. When things settled down after the turtle dived, Meder had made an attempt to explain to Sharina why she'd been wrong to dispose of his chest of paraphernalia.

Memory of that last conversation made Sharina glare toward the wizard afresh. *She* hadn't needed to pitch her voice low to prevent Nonnus from hearing her words.

Nobody likes to be called a fool and a skulking liar while everybody in the present circumscribed community listens. Meder hadn't spoken to her since.

"There's rocks well north of the Isles where seals breed," Nonnus said, shifting his attention back to the empty horizon. "If we made landfall on one of them, there's a chance we'd meet some Pewle hunters. Of course, it's the wrong season for that now."

"We have fish and even if it doesn't rain our water—" Sharina began.

Nonnus leaped up and sprang to the mast in three strides along the port gunwale. He snatched the lifting tackle free of the bitt to which it was tied; for a moment Sharina thought he was going to cut through the line instead of taking the few extra seconds to unlash it.

Instead of releasing the fall to drop the spar, Nonnus sagged and wrapped it back around the horns of the bitt. "Too late," he said as he straightened. "They'll have seen us by now."

"Land!" the procurator cried. She stood with the creaking awkwardness of an old woman, pointing off the port bow. "Look! Look! There's land on the horizon!"

"It's not land," Nonnus said as Meder wobbled to his feet also. Sharina wondered if either of the pair could swim well enough to be saved if they went overboard. "It's a colony of the Floating Folk."

Sharina saw a brownish blur that looked like land to her; it was certainly too big for a ship. Flecks left the main mass, bobbing in the direction of the dugout.

Nonnus sighed. "Catcher boats," he said. "Well, they had to have seen us."

He returned to the tiller with a cold tension very different from the flaring activity of a moment before. "Maybe it's just as well. We're farther into the Outer Sea than I ever wanted to be on a floating log."

The nobles were coming sternward with a care that their clumsiness fully justified. "Are these your own people, my man?" Asera demanded. "Or friends of yours?"

Nonnus his head slightly. "Pewlemen and the Floating Folk know each other," he said. "We're about the only ones who do know the Folk, since there's nothing in these seas to bring settled people out. But friends, no. The Folk don't have any friends except others of their own sort."

Half of his mouth quirked in a grin. "And not really even of their own sort."

He hauled on the sheets, furling the sail instead of dropping it and the spar in a tangle as he'd started to do. "We don't want them to think we're trying to get away from them," he explained. "Since we can't. Not with the breeze as it is."

The two boats approaching the dugout had no masts or sails; they were being paddled by a dozen men apiece. The vessels rode much higher than any boat Sharina had seen previously, and their hulls writhed over the waves like swimming snakes.

"When they reach us . . ." Nonnus said. His eyes were on the boats; his three companions watched him with an unease

Sharina hoped she hid better than the nobles did theirs. "Let me do the talking, if you please."

"Yes," the procurator said. "Yes, of course."

"If I had my . . ." Meder murmured. He broke off when his eyes turned reflexively toward Sharina and realized that she was almost tense enough and angry enough to throw him into the sea.

"They never come ashore," Nonnus explained quietly. "Oh, they'll set up hunting camps on the Ice Capes and they comb the rocks beyond the Isles for driftwood, but except for that they spend their whole lives in their boats."

"Boats like those?" Meder said, staring at the vessels squirming nearer. The hulls were made of skin: where the sunlight slanted onto the inside, Sharina could see the shadows of the vessels' ribs and the kneeling crew.

"These are catcher boats," Nonnus said, watching the Folk with an appearance of utter calm. "They use them to hunt. The houseboats are much bigger and they lash them together."

He paused and almost smiled. "Though I don't think you'll find them comfortable," he added.

The skin boats had come close enough that Sharina could see some of the paddlers were women: all the Folk were naked to the waist. They had red hair and very white skins gleaming with grease. Straps, bone jewelry, and either tattoos or paint adorned their bodies.

"There'll be fifty or a hundred houseboats in a tribe," Nonnus said. His javelin lay across the gunwales before him; the fingers of his right hand rested on the shaft as if merely to keep the weapon from rolling away. "That's what we're seeing on the horizon. In these latitudes the communities of the Folk ride the currents and the winds in a circle between the Isles and the Ice Capes, never touching land unless a storm strands a catcher boat."

"You said 'hunt,' " Sharina said, trying to copy the hermit's placid voice and manner as she watched the Folk approach. A harpoon with a savagely barbed ivory point lay beside each paddler. "What do they hunt?"

"Whales mostly," Nonnus said. "They build their houseboats from the skin and ribs of whales. Other sea beasts. Driftwood. Shipwrecked sailors when they think the odds are right."

Asera's face went cold; Meder glanced from Nonnus to the catcher boats with wild surmise. The hermit didn't look directly at the nobles, but Sharina saw the hint of a smile play across his lips. "We should be all right," he said. "They know better than to play games with a Pewleman. But let me do the talking."

The boats came alongside the dugout, one to either flank. They were amazingly handy but Sharina noticed that they drifted almost as easily as the spume from their paddle-blades: because of the boats' high sides and shallow draft, they'd be almost impossible to paddle against a serious wind. Paddlers caught the dugout's outriggers to keep the three vessels together.

The Folk wore straps and bangles for adornment. The notion of clothing for modesty's sake clearly wasn't a part of their culture.

The skin boats and their crews gave off a charnel reek. Meder gagged and the procurator covered her nose with a fold of her cape. Even Sharina found the smell dizzying, though her own standards of hygiene had slipped considerably since she'd embarked on the trireme.

The Folk weatherproofed their bodies with blubber that quickly turned rancid. Whalebone had been formed fresh into the frames of the catcher boats: rotting marrow added to the blubber's effluvium, as did the half-cured hides of the hull.

"Hey Sleepsalot!" a crewman of one boat called to the older man in the stern of the other. His accent was thick but intelligible. "This log's got wood-lice in it!"

"That's easy enough to fix," said the wormy-looking youth in the bow of Sleepsalot's boat. He hefted his harpoon; his right hand was missing the last two fingers. The crews were in a joking mood, but it was the cheerfulness of a cat which knows its prey has nowhere to run.

Nonnus rose to his feet. He faced Sleepsalot and deliberately slanted his javelin over his shoulder with the point in the air behind him. "I claim the right to join your community, Sleepsalot!" he said. "For myself, my women, and my son!"

"It's a Pewleman!" a woman snarled. "What's a puking Pewleman doing floating on a chunk of driftwood like this?"

Sharina kept her eyes on the other boat rather than Nonnus and the Folk leader. She knew that the hermit for all his apparent nonchalance could spit anybody who threatened him in the direction he was facing, but even Nonnus didn't have eyes in the back of his head.

A woman whose breasts sagged to her waist despite being within a few years of Sharina's age made a stealthy adjustment of her harpoon. Sharina tweaked her hand axe so that sunlight glanced from the blade into the woman's eyes. The would-be backstabber snarled deep in her throat, but both her hands lifted from the harpoon.

"I claim the right to join your community!" Nonnus repeated. "I bring you wood worth six men's price: we are only four. Take me to your king, Sleepsalot—or fight me, as the Law is, if you refuse my gift!"

Sharina risked a glance behind her. The hermit barely moved: only a slight shift in the way his knees bent, but still a crouch from which he could spring into the skin boat's stern.

Sleepsalot cringed visibly. "Fah!" he said. "Threefingers, Gulleater, tie lines to this log."

"We'll break our backs getting it to Home," Threefingers muttered.

Sleepsalot ignored him. "All right, Pewleman," he added in a venomous tone. "The Law says you can join the tribe, that's true. But you'll never leave!"

4

K ing Carus leaned on the balcony rail, his fingers laced and an unusually somber expression on his face as he watched events below the vantage point he shared with Garric's dream self. Six women in white pleated robes and white headgear of varied height and complexity faced a younger Carus on the throne. In the midst of the court's glitter and plush, the straight-backed women looked like so many daggers of ice.

"The Abbess of the Renounced Daughters of the Lady," Carus said, pointing toward the elderly head of the delegation. Two younger women had supported the abbess when she came forward; they waited now to catch her if she swayed. "Land willed to the temples wasn't taxed. My advisors told me I ought to change that custom—it wasn't law. It seemed a simple enough thing to me."

The abbess began to speak. It was amazing that so frail a body held a voice and spirit of such iron strength. Garric would rather have taken a whipping than had that cold scorn directed at him. He looked at his dream companion.

Carus smiled ruefully and shook his head. "A lot of things seem simple until you think them through, lad," he said. "If the temples were to be taxed, then would the state care for the sick as the Renounced Daughters had been doing?"

He met Garric's eyes. For Garric it was like seeing his reflection among the leaves of a woodland pool, distorted but clearly himself. "Fighting comes naturally to me," Carus said. "I was good at it and men followed where I led. Ruling was another thing."

The figure on the throne was fidgeting. Men in fur-trimmed robes whispered into his ears from either side. One of them held a sheet of parchment as if trying to shield the young king's eyes from the petitioner. The abbess continued to speak, and her words were a saw on stone.

"I decided to deal with the Duke of Yole in the way I *knew* how to deal," said the figure on the balcony softly. "I decided to crush him like a bug."

"Maybe there was no other choice," the dream Garric said.

His companion nodded. "Maybe there wasn't," he agreed. "But I didn't even think about other ways. I took the easy route, and it took me straight to the bottom of the sea."

The man on the throne stood, his face a mass of frustration. The abbess pointed her bony arm; one of the advisors plucked the puffed sleeve of the king's court doublet. The king shouted in fury and stamped out through a doorway behind the throne.

"Maybe this time we can do a better job ruling the Isles, lad," said Garric's companion. "And I *will* crush the Duke of Yole like a bug."

He laughed his familiar ringing peals as the throne room dissolved and the balcony dissolved and the dream Garric merged with the aching form of the youth awakening on the bed of a room lighted through a west-facing window above Carcosa's South Harbor.

Pale smoke with a pungent odor drifted in the sunlit air. Charcoal burned in a brazier on a brass tripod beside the bed; the legs were paired serpents twining. Tenoctris dropped pinches of herbs on the fire with one hand while the other swung the boxwood twig through the smoke in an intricate pattern. She noted Garric's eyes opening with a nod, but she continued to chant and stroke the air.

Garric lay on his belly. He started to lift himself onto his left elbow. "Don't move!" Liane said sharply.

Garric jerked his head around. He'd been stripped bare; Liane was rubbing ointment into the gashes on his back and thighs. The ointment's touch was tinglingly warm, but it quenched the sharper pain of the wounds the way a backfire blocks a dangerous blaze.

Strasedon hadn't left much of the tunic anyway. Cutting the remainder off him didn't make any difference for modesty. Garric still turned his face resolutely toward the window and tried not to blush.

There was a quick knock at the door. "Mistress Liane?" a voice called. "There's a boy from Nuzi the Apothecary with the drugs you ordered."

"Yes, bring them in," Liane said as her strong fingers continued to work on Garric. "I can't get money out right now, so pay him and put the charge on my account. I'll settle it with my bill."

The mistress of the Captain's Rest bustled in with a packet wrapped in oiled paper. A pimply boy of twelve or so stared at Garric through the doorway until the woman shooed him back angrily and closed the door behind her. Garric's proper bed was in the common room; this was one of the private apartments on the inn's second floor. From its size and location it was probably the best in the house.

"Ah . . . ." he said, meeting Liane's eyes again. He supposed his father would send money if he had to. . . . "Do you know how much this is going to cost?"

"It very nearly cost your life!" the girl said in a savage tone. "Now just don't move!"

Garric blinked in surprise before he realized that Liane's anger was directed at herself, not him. He didn't speak, but his muscles had gone hard when she snapped.

"I'm sorry," Liane whispered. Tears began to fall from her eyes. She continued to dab ointment from a stoneware pot and work it in instead of just smearing it lightly onto Garric's skin. "Oh, Lady help me, I'm so sorry. It was my fault it all happened. I should have stopped him. . . ."

She dropped to her knees beside the bed as though her legs could no longer hold her. She clasped her hands, shiny with the ointment. "But he was my father! He said he needed my help because there was nobody else he could trust."

"Anybody would have done the same thing," Garric muttered, lacing his own fingers and looking out the window again. "I would have done it if my father asked me."

Except that Reise wasn't arrogant. Liane's father had been arrogant and worse: he'd been the sort of man who would unhesitatingly put his daughter at risk simply because she was available.

Tenoctris finished her soft chanting. She put the cutwork lid on the brazier with a sigh and settled herself on the window ledge. There was sweat on her forehead. Whatever she was doing involved more than merely waving a twig in circles, though that might be the only visible aspect of it. Garric's mind was alert but he felt a numb detachment from his body: he was aware of physical pain, but he didn't really *feel* it.

He smiled at Tenoctris. "I thought you said Benlo's athame was too dangerous to use?" he said.

She smiled back. "Too dangerous to do magic with, certainly," she said. "As a dagger it proved very useful."

Tenoctris touched her left fingertips to the palm of her right hand, the hand with which she'd stabbed the demon. "I'm having all manner of experiences I'd never dreamed of in my own time."

Liane filled the pewter mug with water from the pitcher on the washtable and added powder from the apothecary's packets. She set the mixture to warm on the lid of the brazier.

Noticing Garric watching her, she said, "It's lettuce cake, a mild dose. It'll help you sleep."

Perhaps because he didn't react she added in a defensive tone, "I'm quite competent to treat you. The Daughters trained us in both medicine and in surgery."

Garric smiled. Liane's face hardened, thinking that he was mocking her for her pretensions. Quickly he said, "The Renounced Daughters of the Lady, yes, you'd said. Do you know if they pay taxes to the Earl of Sandrakkan?"

"What?" Liane said. She was as flustered as if he'd asked her what clothing the inhabitants of the moon wore. "Well, I really don't have any idea."

She fiddled with the rag on which she'd wiped her hands.

It was a strip of Garric's tunic; he wondered if it would be all right to put something on, but he didn't guess he'd say anything to call attention to the fact he was buck naked.

"My father had sufficient funds," Liane said toward the rag. "More than sufficient for my purposes."

She looked at Garric. Her expression was set and her tone clipped as she continued, "I've arranged to have my father embalmed here. I'll take him back to Erdin; the tomb is still ours, he told me repeatedly. I'll place him beside my mother. That's what he'd want."

Garric nodded, avoiding the girl's eyes. She'd watched her father being killed; it'd been shocking enough just to see the drover's gutted corpse afterward. He didn't know if he ought to say anything. He surely didn't know *what* to say.

"I'll carry back the flock as he contracted to do," Liane said. Fiercely, coldly she continued, "I'll find the person who sent my father here. And I'll learn why my father died!"

Tenoctris watched the girl. The old woman's face was never closed, but neither did her minute smile give any suggestion of the thoughts beneath it.

"My father's guards have left me," Liane said. "I don't blame them particularly, and in any case it's their right. I'd like to hire you to accompany me, Master Garric. You can set your own wage."

Tears were running down her cheeks again. She ignored them for a moment, her face as stiff as a marble statue's; then she wiped the back of her bare arm across her eyes with a deliberately exaggerated motion.

"Mistress . . ." Garric said.

"I don't need to tell you how very dangerous it may be to be around me," Liane said harshly. She started to wipe her eyes again. Instead she covered her face with both hands and sobbed openly into them.

"Does Ilna know what's happened?" Garric asked Tenoctris, his voice slightly lowered. Part of him wanted to help Liane; but home was already far away, and the thought of what Ilna would say if he went *off* made him uncomfortable.

The two women exchanged glances that Garric couldn't read. "Ilna followed us to the tomb, Garric," Tenoctris said quietly. "She hasn't been seen since then—last night. I've made a search of sorts for her; not a complete one because I was dealing with your injuries too, but complete enough."

"I'm very sorry, Garric," Liane said. She laced her fingers firmly together. "Your friend may be dead."

Garric's mind tried to get around the thought. It was as if he'd been told that the inn and his family had fallen into the sea. He said nothing.

Tenoctris handed Garric the mug from the brazier. He drank the bitter fluid mechanically, then set the empty vessel on the floor beside him.

Everything was changing.

"I think I'd like to be alone for a while," Garric said without looking around. The women left the room silently. He heard them murmur together as the door closed behind them.

Garric began to cry.

5

Jabbering and hunched over like crabs, the Serian sailors staggered up the gangplank onto the bow of the *Golden Dragon*. Each carried on his back a chest that Cashel had been sure was a load for two of them. The sailors didn't look nearly as sturdy or well fed as Frasa and Jen, and even the Serian nobles were wispy-looking folk by the standards of Barca's Hamlet.

"They're tough little buggers," Cashel said to the sprite as he strode ponderously up the gangplank. It flexed noticeably under his weight and that of the two cargo chests he carried, one on either shoulder. "Hard to believe how strong they are when they look like they'd blow over in a good wind."

Mellie laughed above him. The sprite was a tiny weight in his hair, as though a lock had become twisted by the breeze. "Oh, very strong," she said, but it sounded to Cashel as though she was mocking him.

The *Golden Dragon* had seven transverse cargo holds, each completely separated from the others. The design made it hard to rebalance the cargo at sea, but it also made the vessel extremely sturdy and seaworthy. A hole beneath the waterline could only fill one compartment, leaving a more than adequate reserve of buoyancy.

The ship's captain was stripped to a breechclout like his men but he wore a sash of red silk to indicate his rank. The sailor ahead of Cashel started to lower his case into an open hold. The captain screamed furiously at him, waggling a switch made from the spine of a large stingray. He pushed the man toward the last hold sternward.

The captain turned his attention to the next bearer: Cashel. The Serian's tone changed in midchirp, though Cashel of course couldn't understand a word of it anyway. Bowing, he directed the youth on to the next hold.

A pair of sailors were pegging the hatch cover onto the nearer hold. A third man followed, lashing the pegs with cords made from the bark of some fibrous plant.

Cashel knelt. Sailors in the hold grabbed both chests and swung them down to be cross-laid among others. They flashed him bright smiles, but the clipped rat-tat-tat of their speech made him *feel*, falsely he knew, that they were hostile.

Paper lanterns dangling from the main spar threw twisted shadows as Cashel straightened, breathing hard. Two chests were a heavy load, though he wouldn't have admitted that aloud. He climbed the six narrow steps to the quarterdeck from which a rope gangplank connected the vessel to the arm of the quay reaching out from the shore.

The *Golden Dragon*'s hull was entirely given over to cargo. The three small cabins were arranged in a square-bottomed U around the stern; their combined roof formed the quarterdeck where Jen and Frasa now stood, watching but not directing the loading. A skiff hung from a platform off the stern.

The brothers had brought the Goddess of Mercy and her consorts aboard in three careful trips, placing them in the central cabin. After that the pair took no more part in the proceedings. They nodded to Cashel as he passed them. He guessed the common sailors slept on deck on nights the *Golden Dragon* was at sea, and he wouldn't be surprised if the ship's officers did also.

The Highlanders were fascinated by the work going on around them, but they were no more involved in it than Frasa and Jen were. Pound for pound the little men were probably as strong as anybody in the compound, Cashel included. They prodded one another and laughed as Cashel walked by with Mellie back in her usual spot on his shoulder.

"Couldn't they help?" he murmured to her. He knew several Highlanders were on guard in the foyer, but the rest of the contingent was cheerfully idle while everybody around them worked.

"Why should they?" Mellie asked. "Why are you working so hard?"

"What?" he said. The whole notion surprised him. "Well, people work, Mellie," he said.

"I don't work," the sprite said. "*They* don't."

She stuck her thumbs in her ears and waggled her fingers at a watching Highlander who wore a six-inch hardwood splinter through his upper lip. A swastika was tattooed on the white skin of one cheek and a sunburst on the other. The grotesque little gnome laughed so hard he fell over backward, holding his sides.

Cashel waited for three sailors to hunch out through the courtyard gate beneath their loads. The yard was almost empty. Cashel started on through to the covered storage, but the secretary met him in the door, waving. The Serian spoke only his own language—or at least not that of Haft—but his gestures and a glimpse past him convinced Cashel that the building had already been cleared.

He turned to gather up the last case from the yard. Serians at work scurried about in a fashion that struck Cashel as hopelessly uncoordinated. Maybe that was true, but they still managed to get the job done. It'd drive a normal fellow to madness having a crew of these folk chatter and bustle about the field during harvest, but Cashel guessed they'd get the hay in.

"Cashel," Mellie said in the flat voice she used for things that weren't a joke, "it's time to leave. They're coming in."

"Huh?" said Cashel.

Wood sagged with a crash in the factory building. The secretary ran out onto the quay, jabbering twenty to the dozen. Another impact threw the remnants of the stout front door against the inside walls. The mob must have gotten a proper battering ram, because there'd been no chopping and delay: they'd smashed straight through in two blows.

Cashel had leaned his quarterstaff against the back wall of the yard, near the gateway. He located it with his eyes, then picked up the remaining cargo chest with both hands: his right on the back handle, his left underneath the dense hardwood a little forward of center. He guessed it held pottery, but that didn't much matter.

The remaining sailors scampered out of the yard on the heels of the secretary. There were triumphant shouts from inside the building, then the snap of bows and high-pitched screams.

"Oh, Cashel!" the sprite said. Funny how he could hear her so clearly in this bellowing chaos.

Three Highlanders came out of the building in a bowlegged run. The last of the group lagged several steps behind. He bled from a cut in his thigh and carried a human ear, also bloody, in one hand. Cashel planted his left foot and started his throw.

The doorway filled with locals, street toughs of the sort Cashel dealt with when he met Jen and Frasa. Several of

Themo's guards were close behind in the mob, delayed by their bulky armor. Cashel launched the case with a stiff-armed motion, as though he were casting the stone at the Harvest Festival.

He didn't know how much the missile weighed: two hundred pounds or so, he judged, enough that the thrust turned him neatly around to face the gate.

The hardwood case crashed into the mob at about throat height. Men burst but the missile didn't: it was still in one piece as it vanished behind flailing limbs, well back into the press where folk had thought they were safe. Those who'd been in its path weren't in nearly as good condition as the box.

Cashel grabbed his staff as he ran for the bow gangplank. He wasn't quick but he moved fast enough when he got going. Lanterns dangled from poles along the quay. All the Serian sailors were aboard the *Golden Dragon*, but several Highlanders waited along the quay.

As Cashel cleared the gateway the Highlanders shot arrows toward the yard behind him. He heard one missile *whack!* against a guard's shield, but the screams of unprotected thugs indicated that others had found softer targets.

"Duck!" Mellie cried. Cashel hunched over as he ran. An arrow snapped close enough to ruffle his short hair. The archer was a Highlander with his legs wrapped around the main spar at the head of the vessel's mast. Mellie had said that they weren't very good shots. . . .

Normally a sailing ship worked out of harbor with the help of rowed tugboats, but that was out of the question tonight. Sailors were poling the *Golden Dragon* away from the quay on the port side to get room to back the vessel with its four long sweeps. The gangplank from the shore to the ship's prow was still in place. The Highlanders galloped up it like monkeys running.

Cashel turned at the foot of the gangplank. "Mellie, dear one, you'd best get clear," he said though he didn't expect her to pay him any attention. Lanterns bobbed overhead, throwing a fairy-soft pastel illumination over the scene.

There might have been a thousand rioters in Harbor Street, but relatively few of them had come straight through the building and out the back of the yard. Cashel heard the sound of breakage from inside; furniture and the window sashes, he supposed. All the cargo had been reloaded, with the exception of the case he'd used as a missile.

The first men through the gate arches were a pair of Themo's guards, and even they moved cautiously. Their shields were proof against the Highlanders' light bows, but the pair who'd met the box Cashel threw would be nursing bruised ribs if nothing worse.

"This way!" one of them shouted over his shoulder. "Here's the loot, here's where the devil worshippers are hiding!"

They sidled forward, staying behind their shields. Another guard and a dozen civilians, one of them with blood that couldn't be his own dyeing his whole left side, ran out to join them. Light bloomed through the upper-story windows. The rioters had managed to set fire to the factory office.

A few arrows zinged toward the rioters, but the Highlanders were hunters rather than soldiers. Their quivers were narrow bamboo tubes with only three or four arrows in each.

Cashel waited, saying nothing, aware only of motion. Faces didn't matter anymore. More rioters darted out of the factory yard.

The guards brandished swords. "Let's get him!" one shouted as he feinted toward Cashel. Another guard bulled forward, his shield high to completely protect his head. Cashel swung the full length of his staff in a low arc that smashed the guard's ankles and swept both legs out from under him.

The man hit the path screaming at the pain of crushed joints. His helmet fell off and his shield bonged against the ground. The third guard had lunged an instant later. He tripped over his comrade's legs and pitched onto his face. Cashel hit him on the back of the head with the quarterstaff's butt as he shifted his hands to centergrip the weapon.

Cashel began to rotate the staff, crossing his wrists with each revolution. He watched the mob through the spinning hickory, saying nothing.

Another armored guard had joined the survivor of the trio who'd rushed the gangplank, but this man was limping and showed no sign of wanting to try conclusions with the man who'd thrown the cargo chest. Several score civilians, some of them women, were on the quay; more joined them every moment as the fire took firm hold of the building behind them.

One threw a stone; Cashel's quarterstaff batted it away, but it wouldn't have hit him anyway. Most of the civilians carried clubs or metal bars, though there were a few swords. The rioters hadn't brought missiles into the factory with them, and the yard wasn't paved to supply the lack.

Cashel risked a glance over his shoulder. The vessel was heavily loaded, so the sailors were having trouble pushing it away from the quay. Rioters began to jump the narrow gap, disrupting efforts to move the ship. Somebody hurled a lantern. The paper shell flared up and the oil oozed across the wood in a spreading blaze.

Cashel spun the staff. Everything else stopped in his mind. Blue fire danced from the ferrules, as cold as the hoarfrost that coats twigs in winter.

The staff spun faster. Cashel's arms couldn't keep up with it, yet they did. . . . A wind was blowing, snarling, roaring.

The *Golden Dragon* lurched away from the shore. The gangplank fell out from under Cashel's feet and splashed in the harbor. He was still standing and the staff spun. Its iron tips swept a glowing blue circle beyond which the rioters screamed in horror.

"Jump!" Mellie cried.

Cashel jumped backward, over the bows of the *Golden Dragon*. He collapsed on the deck. The ship quivered under him, still sliding backward from the shore. Cashel lay on his stomach. He was so tired that he felt the muscles of his mighty chest straining just to breathe.

Serian sailors were thrusting the long sweeps through oarlocks on the deckrail as the captain screamed and slashed at them with his ray-spine baton. The mob on the quay crowded through the factory gate again, too frightened to care that the building was fully involved by fire and likely to spill blazing debris in all directions when it collapsed.

"You're so *strong*, Cashel!" Mellie cooed as she cuddled his ear.

There were squeals like those of a pig being butchered. One of the rioters was still aboard the *Golden Dragon*. Several laughing Highlanders pinned the man to the deck as another sawed at his throat with a bone knife.

Cashel clutched his quarterstaff, sucking in deep breaths, and let oblivion sweep over him in shadows lit by the occasional blue flare.

6

As long as Sharina held her breath, the most amazing thing about the village of Floating Folk was the iceberg in the middle of it. The ice winked in sunlight like an immense jewel in a bezel of skin boats; the ice mountain's size dwarfed Folk houseboats which were impressive by any other standard.

When Sharina had to breathe, it was still the smell that made the greatest impression.

"I suppose I'll get used to it," she muttered. That was the most frightening thought of all.

The four islanders rode in the belly of Sleepsalot's boat. Nonnus and Sharina squatted side by side, facing forward. The nobles were just ahead with their backs to the bow, so close that Asera's knees almost touched Sharina's.

As soon as the catcher boats reached the village, Sleepsalot's crew had moored the dugout to their own houseboat—
one of sixty or eighty similar vessels tethered by long lines
in a circle around the iceberg. Then the catcher boats with all
the family's healthy adults set off toward the pair of houseboats tied together catamaran fashion a quarter mile around
the circuit.

"Where are they taking us now?" Meder asked; he no
longer added "my man" when he directed a question to Nonnus, though Sharina wasn't sure whether appreciation of the
hermit's abilities or simple fear had led to the change.

"It's the royal residence," Nonnus said, nodding toward
the double vessel. "The king lives there with his family and
guards. There's a deck between the hulls where the citizens
can gather for a council."

"Citizens?" Sharina asked.

"If you can help crew a catcher boat," the hermit explained, "you're a citizen. Otherwise you're the property of
anybody who chooses to feed you. And if nobody wants to
take that responsibility, well, it's a big sea out there."

The islanders had boarded Sleepsalot's houseboat while
Folk tied the dugout to it. Sharina had gotten a view of the
remainder of the family, a score of prepubescent children and
six old adults—five of them women—who gaped at the islanders in a mixture of awe and loathing. The children hid
from the strangers' direct glance.

One little boy hung on the outside of the hull. He dipped
down every time Sharina looked in his direction and popped
his head back up over the gunwale as her gaze passed. His
toes must be in the water, but the sea didn't seem to concern
the Folk at any age.

Threefingers stood in the bow of Sleepsalot's boat. The
youth was apparently Sleepsalot's son, but Sharina suspected
that kinship among the Floating Folk was a complicated question.

At intervals, every twenty or so paddle-strokes, Threefin-

gers blew on an ammonite's coiled shell; it would have made
a horn eight feet long if straightened. The shell's surface reflected sunlight in a soft iridescence that should have been
lovely; to Sharina it unexpectedly touched her the way the
stench of the village did.

Nonnus was looking at the horn also. "They say the Folk
worship the Great Ones of the deep," he said, pitching his
voice just above a whisper. "But they say a lot of things, and
they say things about Pewlemen too."

He smiled with sad memory. "The truth is usually bad
enough, I've found."

Meder listened to the hermit's words while glancing about
his new surroundings with an expression of lively interest.
The procurator by contrast sat in abject silence, too miserable
for her face to have any expression at all. Sharina was
shocked at how much thinner Asera had become since she'd
arrived in Barca's Hamlet. The change hadn't been obvious
till now when Sharina saw her among other people for the
first long time.

The iceberg was an incongruous mass dominating the floating village. Depending on how light struck the ice, its facets
glittered blue or white or green.

Nonnus followed Sharina's eyes to the iceberg. "Food isn't
a problem at sea," he said. "Fresh water can be. You can't
count on rainwater and besides, it's hard to store."

He gestured to the ice. "Glaciers on the Ice Capes calve
bergs every spring. They follow the same pattern of winds
and currents that the Folk do. A village circles a berg until
in a year or more it's melted enough to break up; then they
find another."

"Are icebergs *fresh* water?" Sharina said. "Oh. I guess
they must be if they come from land."

"It's rare a tribe has to move more than half a mile,"
Nonnus said, "but sometimes you can see a whole village
paddling across the open sea because they waited too long to
shift. That *is* a sight."

Horns wound from the royal catamaran. Members of the

Folk left the other houseboats to head for the residence in catcher boats and strange little one-person pontoons—skin bladders with a whalebone outrigger on one side; the user rode the bladder like a horse and drove himself along with strokes from a double-ended paddle. The sea crawled with vessels built in styles undreamt of on Haft.

"They'll have a palaver," Nonnus said. He spoke softly, but his right hand lightly caressed the shaft of his javelin. That displayed his tension to one who knew him the way Sharina did. "There'll be an argument over us, but not much of one. And there'll be an argument over how the log's divided—*that* may go on all night."

The skin boat moved as if it were alive and ill-tempered. The frame was sawn from sections of whale rib, pegged together and tied with sinews. The hull sheathing was whale-skin, sewn on the inside with standing seams; at no point did a needle pass completely through the hull. Even so the seams were caulked with thick grease, probably the renderings of whale blubber.

Sharina found it odd to be at sea in a boat driven by paddlers looking forward rather than oarsmen facing the stern. The high sides made her feel trapped rather than protected; she didn't like the way the boat flexed, and she *really* didn't like the way it smelled.

But she could see that these craft would ride out storms that overwhelmed a planked boat: they floated like oil on the water. They'd have to if they were to survive winter in northern latitudes.

Sleepsalot's boat drew alongside the residence and halted with a quick swirl of all the paddles together. Sharina hadn't heard any commands during the quarter-mile spurt to the catamaran: Threefingers' horn signals were directed at the village, not to the crew of his own boat. The paddlers stroked to time without any outside control.

Sharina thought of schools of fish or flocks of pigeons, scores or even thousands of individuals acting as one without visible signals. And the Lady knew, from what she'd seen thus far the Floating Folk were like beasts in more ways than their ability to work together.

Folk lined the gunwale of the catamaran. Sleepsalot's family hopped aboard carrying harpoons, jostling and being jostled by the king's household. A woman fell into the water, bobbed up, and pulled herself onto the catamaran in a motion that reminded Sharina of a porpoise leaping.

"Hey!" Sleepsalot shouted. "Tie the boat up, you! Somebody tie her up!"

The crew ignored him. Sleepsalot, heavier than his juniors, clambered over the catamaran's gunwale. Nonnus gave Sharina a wry grin. He strode to the bow and looped the painter in the bow around one of the upjutting ribs of the houseboat's hull.

The rope was cut as a single square section of hide instead of being braided from multiple strands. Only half-cured, the leather was stiff and thick enough that the muscles of the hermit's forearms bulged as he twisted it into a knot.

"What would they do if their boat floated away?" Sharina asked.

"Swim after it," Nonnus said with a shrug. "The Folk can do most anything in the water. On land, well, I suppose they'd make about as good fertilizer as the same weight of seal guts."

He grimaced as he thought about what he'd just said. "Sorry, child," he murmured. "I'm back where I was when I was a younger man, and I'm sounding like I did when I was young and stupid too."

Though Sleepsalot's crew left the islanders—old news to them—behind without a glance, members of the king's household packed the side of the vessel to look at the strangers.

The men were loudly interested in Sharina. Her face stiffened. She'd worked the bar during Sheep Fairs with a lot of outsiders in the hamlet, but Reise kept a respectable house. If a drover drank too much to remember that, well, Garric and the neighbor men were on hand to remind them.

Here she had Nonnus.

The hermit leaped in a single motion to the houseboat's rail. "Make room for my women!" he roared, twirling the javelin above his head between the thumb and first two fingers of his left hand. "Make room for my son!"

There was a briefly angry response from the Folk. Nonnus kicked with his right foot, then his left, then his right again. From behind he looked as if he were executing a complex dance. In a manner of speaking that's what the hermit was doing: every time his foot lashed out, the callused heel smacked one of the Folk in the forehead and flung him back from the railing.

"Come on!" Sharina snapped to Asera and Meder. She let the hatchet slip back into its belt loop and half-helped, half-dragged the procurator onto the catcher boat's rail. "Nonnus, we're coming!"

The breeze was light and the catcher boat was in the lee of the high-sided residence. Sharina boosted Asera onto the houseboat's gunwale squawking; Nonnus bent and snatched the procurator over the side, dropping her into the bigger vessel at his feet. He and Sharina couldn't have done better if they'd practiced the maneuver.

Meder climbed up himself and rolled over the railing. He was awkward, but at least he spared himself the indignity of being tossed like a sack of grain.

Sharina knew she hadn't the hermit's balance, but she was young, proud, and keyed up by the circumstances. She hopped to the railing beside Nonnus, poised there for a moment, and dropped into the belly of the houseboat without stumbling. Chuckling deep in his throat, Nonnus walked down the frames as if they were steep stair-treads instead of jumping as she had done.

Forty-odd Folk clustered around the islanders. Seated or kneeling in their boats, the Floating Folk had the physique of gods. Their chests were deep, and rippling muscles corded their throats and arms.

Standing, their stunted lower quarters gave the Folk a misshapen, nightmare look. They walked with a shamble like monkeys just down from the trees. A houseboat's length was as far as any of them ever moved on his own legs.

"Get them over here!" shouted a man on the platform joining the two hulls. "Don't you be fooling with them! They're mine to judge!"

"You heard the king," Nonnus said to the crowd with a grim smile. He swept the butt of his javelin before him to clear a path. "Keep close," he murmured to the other islanders as he strode toward the platform.

The houseboats were blunt-ended tubs a hundred feet long and forty broad. Bow and stern were decked over with whale-skin on a frame of whalebone, the same construction as the rest of the hull. The covered portions were fetid caves, filthy even by the standards of the Floating Folk.

The open well—the middle half of the vessel—wasn't a great deal better. There was no covering for the bilges nor means of pumping them. Vermin crawled through the muck. The four islanders crossed on the raised frames, but the Folk themselves splashed along oblivious of what might be underfoot.

"This is insane!" Asera muttered.

"This is what magic brought us to!" Sharina snapped in reply. Nonnus said nothing as he swaggered ahead of the others, holding the javelin crossways before him as a bumper, but he smiled faintly.

The houseboat's structure was an intricate mass of triangles with no cross-frames. It flexed even in the present moderate sea, but it wouldn't break in the most violent storm. The whalehide covering was tough, and the sinew-sewn seams could work to a degree no wooden hull could equal without cracking or leaking.

A platform forty feet square, made with a layer of whale-skin both above and below the bone frame, joined the two hulls at the gunwales. The houseboats had only about five feet of freeboard, so even on a quiet day like this waves whacked the bottom of the platform or even washed onto it as the hulls rose and fell on different cycles. The scores of Folk already standing or kneeling on the platform ignored the water.

Nonnus shepherded his charges onto the shifting platform, then followed them in a motion that was half a jump, half a lithe twist of his lower body. Sharina knew the hermit was almost as old as the procurator, but no one would guess that from the way he moved.

The man on the throne of walrus ivory and mother-of-pearl was heavy without being fat and older than most of the others on the platform. Six young men in good condition flanked the throne. They wore caps of seawolf hide and carried long, narrow shields of the same material; one of them had a steel cutlass as well as the ivory-headed harpoon that seemed the universal mark of a citizen of the Folk.

"They call the guards the King's Sons," Nonnus murmured into Sharina's ear. "They *are* his kin, like enough, but they don't have to be."

The old woman kneeling beside the throne peered at the islanders with sharp interest. At first the woman seemed to be wearing a blue garment, but as she hunched to her feet Sharina saw that her body had been tattooed in intricate swirls. She shuffled around the edge of the platform, leaning on a staff carved from a narwhal tusk.

Sleepsalot stood before the king, so close that a guard lowered his harpoon and pricked him back as he bellowed, "King Longtoes, these islanders were floating in the sea beside the driftwood I found. I claim the wood and the strangers also as my slaves."

Sharina put her hand on her hatchet. Nonnus thrust the butt of his javelin between Sleepsalot's ankles from behind and levered the man forward onto his face. A guard rolled Sleepsalot backward with his foot. The watching Folk laughed and pounded their palms against the platform to make it rumble like a drum.

"King Longtoes," the hermit said, "I am Nonnus, son of Bran, son of Pewle Island. I bring you the following wood as payment for my family's joining the tribe. Five poles this diameter—''

He formed the fingers of his left hand into a semicircle the diameter of an oarshaft like the four braces and the mainspar; his javelin point scratched a complete circle on the whalehide.

''—and this long.'' Nonnus strode twenty feet out from the throne. The crowd parted for him because he followed his javelin. ''Three pieces *this* diameter—'' The outriggers and mast made from the trireme's spars. He stepped another four feet outboard. ''—and this long. And a log *this* diameter—''

Nonnus arched both arms into a broad crescent.

''—and this long, but hollowed out by a third of the volume. On my honor as a Pewleman!''

The crowd hooted in wonder. The Folk could make do with bone for most purposes, but scarcity gave wood a certain value. Logs the size of the dugout must rarely enter the great circuit in which the Floating Folk lived.

''And what's a Pewleman's honor worth!'' demanded a voice from Sleepsalot's entourage.

''It's worth your teeth to me to wear and your heart to eat if there's a handspan's less wood than I say!'' Nonnus said. ''Shall we make that bargain, Threefingers?''

Threefingers retreated behind his father's bulkier body. Nonnus stalked forward again to face the king, his javelin resting on his shoulder. ''The price of six citizens!'' he said to Longtoes. ''For me, my two wives, and the son in my care. He's sickly and can't hunt, but I swore an oath to my gods to care for him nonetheless.''

''So-o-o, Pewleman,'' Longtoes said. It was the first time Sharina had heard the king speak since he demanded their presence before him. His voice was harsh and penetrating. ''If you join the tribe, what family will you own? Sleepsalot's?''

The crowd continued to grow as folk from the outlying houseboats reached the residence. There was a general chuckle at the suggestion. It was pretty obvious that it would mean a death shortly—Sleepsalot's, beyond any question in Sharina's mind at least.

"I'm father of a family myself!" Nonnus said. "I'll live here at the residence, King, until I build my own houseboat."

The tattooed woman had vanished into the crowd. She appeared unexpectedly beside Meder and said something low-voiced. Meder jumped; Sharina half lifted the hand axe which her hand had never left since they boarded the royal residence.

"No, Pewleman, I don't think that's what we'll do," Longtoes said in a lazy drawl. His head turned slowly as he scanned the spectators. "Motherhugger, you'll take the Pewleman and his slaves aboard your boat. I don't think the extra weight will sink it, but—"

He smiled; he was missing the front teeth of his upper jaw.

"—if the gods are that angry, then I wouldn't want to lose a better-found boat. Hey?"

Everybody laughed except for a hulking, bald-headed man and the dozen Folk standing near him. "My boat's not so very bad," he muttered angrily.

Meder and the tattooed woman were talking with animation, their heads close together. Even Asera watched with some interest. Sharina relaxed, though it wasn't a development she felt comfortable with.

"All right, my king," Nonnus said, bowing. "I obey you under the Law."

He stepped back. Wrangling resumed with Sleepsalot and Motherhugger among the half-dozen older men who immediately put in claims for a share of the wood.

"This way," Nonnus murmured. "We'll be going off in Motherhugger's catcher boat and I want to be ready when he is. I was never much of a swimmer."

"I'm staying here, my man," Meder said unexpectedly. "Leadsthestars and I want to talk more. She says she'll see that I get to you before dark."

"Does she?" Nonnus said without expression. "As you choose, Master Meder. Any path you choose to take."

He turned away abruptly and said to Sharina and Asera, "Come!" Sharina wasn't sure what the procurator would do, but Asera followed willingly enough. She'd straightened noticeably since Meder and the old woman started talking.

Sharina couldn't imagine how the hermit had managed to place Motherhugger's boat among the scores that had descended on the residence, but it didn't occur to her to doubt his statement. The vessel, moored to the other hull of the catamaran, was in all respects like that of Sleepsalot's family.

"Will the houseboat really be in danger of sinking?" Sharina asked quietly.

Nonnus shrugged. "Things start to fall apart as soon as they're built," he said, "but the Folk's houseboats are better built than most things you'll find on land. If there's pegging and patching needed, well, that'll give us something to do while we figure out how to get out of this place."

A score of young males broke away from the council and surrounded the islanders at a harpoon's distance. They weren't hostile, precisely, but they obviously knew their presence wouldn't be welcomed.

Threefingers was one of them. "Look here, Pewleman," he said. "You're an old man. You can't do a young wife any good. We think you ought to give her up right now since you know she'll be sneaking around to us anyway."

Sharina pulled her hand axe from its loop.

The hermit's laugh was a challenge out of nightmare. He walked up the bone frames of the hull backward, never taking his eyes from the young men.

"Who'll take my women from me?" he demanded in a high, harsh voice, dancing on the gunwale. He leaped up and passed the javelin from hand to hand beneath his feet before he came down again. "Who'll do that? Threefingers, will you try me?"

The youths backed another step. Others of the Folk, mostly children from the royal household, were watching with interest.

"Oh, we can't fight you because you've got a metal spear," muttered a paddler from Sleepsalot's boat.

Nonnus jumped from the gunwale more suddenly than even Sharina, who knew to expect something, could follow. He switched his javelin from right hand to left while in midair and snatched the harpoon out of Threefinger's grip.

"Oh!" Threefingers shouted as he leaped backward, colliding with several of his fellows.

Nonnus hurled the harpoon butt-forward into the chest of the youth who'd spoken. Ribs cracked; the victim's breath whooshed out as he went over on his back.

"Do you fear my steel, little men?" Nonnus crowed as he backed to his perch on the gunwale. "Fear *me*. Fear *me*!"

The youths' startlement turned to uproarious good humor, all but Threefingers and the fellow who lay wheezing as his chest refused to suck in the air his lungs so desperately needed. One of his erstwhile comrades kicked the victim when he thrashed close.

The group broke up and drifted away, still laughing. The injured man managed to roll over and crawl off with his head hanging, making little mewling sounds.

Nonnus stepped back beside Sharina. "We'll be all right for now," he said softly. "But it wouldn't do to have us separated."

Sharina nodded.

Meder and the tattooed woman squatted on a corner of the platform, facing one another. Meder now held what looked like a carved walrus tooth. He gestured as he spoke. A faint helix of red light lifted from the platform before him.

7

Ilna didn't move from the window when she heard the knock at her door: light, apologetic. "Come in," she said a moment before she knew it would have been repeated.

She continued to look past the tilted casement onto the street.

Noise rustling up the stairs from the hardware shop below entered the room, then cut off again as Beltar closed the door behind him. "I've come for more ribbons if you've any done," he said diffidently. "Some of the customers are very excited. They, ah, are used to having their way."

"Erdin's finest," Ilna said without inflection. In the same tone she added, "Threads for my pattern."

Three parked carriages and a sedan chair with curtains of red plush choked the right-of-way. The owners were in Beltar's shop. It was just as well that the draper had insisted on taking rooms for Ilna across and down the street instead of on his own premises. Their racket might have become disturbing otherwise. The pattern wove even when she wasn't conscious of it.

"I've been wondering..." Beltar said. "Should we limit the length of ribbon that we sell to any single customer, do you think, mistress?"

The draper preferred talking to Ilna's back rather than having her face him, she knew. She didn't care one way or another whether he was comfortable. Beltar had a place which he filled acceptably.

"That doesn't concern me," Ilna said. "I told you before: all business questions are for your determination." She turned. "Don't bother me with something like this again."

Beltar shifted his weight and brought his heels together unconsciously. "Yes, mistress," he said, meeting her direct gaze with only a brief twitch at the corner of his mouth to show how nervous he was. "The only thing is, there's a belief..."

He paused to consider the word he'd chosen, accepted it, and went on, "A belief that not only do your ribbons have the effects rumored for them, but that a greater length increases the effect."

Ilna smiled faintly. "Yes, that's quite correct," she said. "The fabric I weave really does attract the attention of men to the women wearing it; and the greater the amount of fabric displayed, the more intense the interest it arouses.''

The room was a single gallery across the front of the building's second story. The three casement windows provided excellent illumination from midmorning to near dusk, though that was no longer a concern for Ilna. She could work in full darkness and never weave a thread out of place.

Beltar had rented the quarters unfurnished. They remained unfurnished with the exception of a straw bed, the six looms of varied sizes, and baskets of the fine yarn with which she worked. Neither prisoners nor ascetic saints lived lives simpler than that of Ilna os-Kenset, but she was well on the way to becoming the most powerful person on Sandrakkan.

Beltar's face had grown pale. Ilna smiled at him.

"You poor fool," she said in amused contempt. "You thought it was all a charlatan's trick, didn't you? I was going to start the rumor that my ribbons were love potions and silly women would *believe* that they worked. Well, silly they may be, but they're buying exactly what they think they're buying, Beltar.''

He closed his eyes. "I can't let anyone else handle the ribbons," he said in a low voice. "I can't trust even my own wife. I've had women, some of the wealthiest women in Erdin, offer me ten times my price if I could find them more of your cloth.''

Ilna touched the ribbon that she'd begun weaving a few minutes before Beltar came upstairs. It was only a finger's breadth wide. The pattern was complete in two inches and she normally tied off the piece after three repetitions, but there was no fixed rule.

For these she worked in only two shades: bleached and unbleached thread, no dyed stock. She preferred flax over an animal product like wool or silk for this purpose, but she could have used any fiber. A fabric isn't a maze with only a single pathway: the thousands of threads knot and twist in a dance as complex as that of life itself. Follow any one of them and it takes you to the end of the pattern.

"Raise your prices, Beltar," Ilna said. "Cut the ribbons

into little scraps or hoard my weaving for a month and sell it for the price of all Sandrakkan—it's your choice."

Her voice changed subtly. "But you'll have to come up with more money somehow, because you need to rent me a house on Palace Square to replace this location."

She gave him a crooked smile. "I'm going up in the world, you see."

"But mistress . . ." Beltar said. "It's only nobles who can afford to live there. The rentals on Palace Square are a hundred times the lease of my whole premises!"

"Then raise your prices," Ilna said coldly. "I told you, the details are your affair. I'm only interested in the results."

She turned back to the window. There was a fourth carriage in the street now. Liveried attendants were arguing loudly and waggling whips; veiled women looked on. There'd be a riot before long.

Ilna smiled again. All the fury was useless. Beltar had no more stock in his shop. Servants could shout and crack each others' heads, but nothing would change that basic reality.

"They'll pay, you know," she said aloud. "Women who spend fortunes for herbal packs that're supposed to smooth wrinkles but do nothing—what *won't* they pay for what I provide? All the fine clothing and jewelry, all the cosmetics, they're just roundabout routes to what my ribbons do directly: draw men to women!"

"I see," said Beltar. From the unhappy tone of the draper's voice, he really was beginning to understand. "I'll inquire about mansions on Palace Square, as you request, mistress."

He gave a laugh of sorts. "I don't even know where to find an agent for such things, but no doubt they're available. And I'll give thought to our price schedule. No doubt you're correct regarding that matter also."

Three of the men who carried the sedan chair climbed onto the box of a carriage while the driver struck at them with the loaded butt of his whip. A woman with a lace mantilla hanging askew over a dress of horizon blue screamed encouragement to one side or the other. She waved a hairpin that looked like a gold dagger.

"Yes," Ilna said with a faint smile. "I'm quite correct."

The first ribbons had gone to prostitutes and servants at modest prices—less than the women would have paid for a love charm of no worth at all. Word traveled upward quickly; very quickly indeed.

"Erdin's finest," Ilna repeated in a whisper. She didn't hate them. There was nothing to hate. Like the linen thread, they were the material with which she wove.

Beltar coughed to clear the hoarseness from his throat. "Given the demand, mistress," he said carefully, "have you considered taking apprentices to, ah, lighten your load?"

She looked at him. He cringed, wringing his fashionable purple-dyed beret between his hands as he waited for the blast of anger he expected.

"I couldn't teach what I know, Beltar," Ilna said with an odd gentleness the draper had never before heard in her voice. "And if I could, it still isn't anything I'd choose to do to some fool girl who's never harmed me."

"Ah," Beltar said, nodding in order to give the false impression that he understood. "It was just that with the demand so high I thought . . ."

He let his voice trail off. Looking at the window—he couldn't see the street from his angle—in order to avoid Ilna's calm eyes, he went on, "Well, if you have a few more lengths woven, I'll take them across to the shop and . . . ?"

"There'll be nothing more for a day or two," Ilna said flatly. "I have a project of my own that I'll be working on instead. You may as well close up your shop and find me the dwelling I require. When you reopen they'll beg you to take their money."

She walked to the double-span loom that filled half the room's floorspace. She was working in silk on it. Thus far there was only a hand's breadth of fabric on the frame. It was so sheer that Beltar saw it as a distortion in the sunlight.

Ilna's hand caressed the shuttle. The draper tried to focus

on the gossamer pattern. There was nothing for his eyes; almost he would have said that Ilna was weaving a panel as clear as spring water, a cloth without visible substance.

Almost. He felt a surge of desire too primal even to be called lust: it was more akin to the forces that cause a seed to germinate in the springtime, sending a shoot bursting upward toward the sunlight. He gasped and jerked his eyes away, hunching over involuntarily as though he'd been kicked in the groin.

"As you will, mistress," Beltar whispered, his face to the door. He reached for the latch. "I'll return after I've looked into dwellings on Palace Square."

The draper closed the door hastily behind him. He stood for a time in the corridor with his forehead against the wall, trying to catch his breath. He was already beginning to deny the full impact of what he'd felt when he looked at the panel Ilna had begun weaving, just as he'd been able to suppress the reality of the vision she'd shown him on the counter of his shop the day they met.

But one question kept droning through his mind: if size determined the strength of the spell the fabrics cast—as rumor and Ilna herself claimed it did—then what would be the effect of this panel the witchwoman had framed two yards wide?

8

Sheep grazed among the burial jars on the hillside. They were of the short-legged flat-country breed with white fleece, but they made Garric feel homesick regardless.

"O Shepherd, kindly to your children," the underpriest said. He was a young man but already balding; the afternoon sun had raised beads of sweat on his high forehead. "Do not let this your son Benlo be put to death in the Underworld."

Benlo's body lay in the outdoor chapel. Over him was a rented pall of crimson silk with gold borders; his face, arranged by the chapel's cosmeticians into an expression of stern grandeur, was bare to the open sky. During the brief time Garric knew him, the drover's visage had generally been hidden behind a mask of false good humor; if Benlo's life had gone other ways, the image on the bier might really have been his.

"Do not let the bright jewels of Benlo's eyes be covered with the dust of the Underworld," the priest intoned. His robe of bleached wool was too hot for this weather. The garment was a relic of ancient times: the formal wear of the Old Kingdom. Memories of King Carus judging legal disputes whispered through Garric's mind; court officials wore colored garments, but the mass of litigants, attorneys, and jurors gleamed in white wool.

The funeral chapel on the hilltop overlooking Carcosa was a low rectangular building with workrooms and storage inside. There was an entrance in one wall and a different deity's statue in a niche outside each of the others. Services were in the open air: each statue was fronted by a stone bier and pavement. Garric supposed the chapel could accommodate three funerals at once, but he doubted that was normal practice.

Liane cried softly. Perhaps this noble-looking corpse was the father she remembered from her childhood, the man who sang to his wife and daughter.

"Do not let the marble of Benlo's teeth be burned in the lime-maker's kiln," the priest said. He seemed a decent sort of man. The condolences he'd offered Liane before the service had sounded sincere, not just the mouthing of a bureaucrat looking ahead to the largest fee he'd collect in this next week or longer. For all that, he'd run through this service too often for the words to be much more than words.

Tenoctris stood with Garric and Liane as the only mourners. The old woman watched things that Garric didn't see, couldn't see. Her hands were clasped and her face would have been grim if it had any expression at all.

Garric wondered which deity presided over most funerals here in Carcosa. In the borough no one doubted that the Lady was queen of heaven, but her consort the Shepherd was closer to people's normal lives. Folks were more likely to spill a drop of milk or crumble a bit of bread to Duzi or before a little carving against the back wall of their hut anyway. The Great Gods ruled heaven from temples elsewhere, but a peasant lived with sheep dung and the pain of childbirth.

"Do not let the lustrous wood of Benlo's flesh be broken for kindling," said the priest, mopping his brow unconsciously with a fold of his robe. Garric wondered what they did when it rained.

Four local laborers waited to transport the body. They were solid, middle-aged men; obviously bored but maintaining the polite silence that was part of their stock-in-trade.

Would Benlo have had more mourners if he'd died on Sandrakkan? Probably not: whatever the man had done involved his utter ruin and disgrace. It took a better person than the one Liane described her father having become to retain his friends after a disaster so complete.

"Loving Shepherd, do not let your son Benlo be put to death in the Underworld!"

Nobody in Barca's Hamlet prayed to the Sister. Her name was simply a curse and a rare one at that: people had the ingrained suspicion that to name a thing was to call it to you. Here, the third face of the funeral chapel held a statue of the Sister in all her majesty as Queen of the Underworld: snake-headed scepter, skirt of thighbones, and necklace of human skulls.

The Sister's bier and pavement looked as well-worn as those serving the Shepherd and the Lady. Garric supposed it made sense to ask the blessing of the mistress of the dead at a funeral, but the notion still made him uncomfortable. Death wasn't evil: you culled your herd for the winter and Nature culled *her* herd, mankind included, for the same reason. But nonetheless there was something perverse about praying to death.

"Benlo bor-Benliman," the priest said, stumbling slightly over the family name. He wouldn't have officiated over many nobles out of all the hundreds of funerals he'd conducted. "Accept the water of life, that you may spring forth from the Underworld."

It was a hot day; the aromatics with which the chapel's staff had embalmed Benlo masked but did not fully conceal the odor of decay. The process normally involved the surgical removal of the dead man's organs so that his body cavity could be packed with spices.

Strasedon had simplified the task of Benlo's embalmers.

The priest dipped a golden aspergillum into the bowl of water on a stand beside the bier and flicked a few droplets on the face of the corpse. Replacing the aspergillum, the priest took a pinch of barley meal from golden salver beside the bowl. "Benlo bor-Benliman, accept the bread of life that you may rise refreshed from the Underworld."

The gold dishes came with the pall of silk brocade for funerals of the highest quality. Middle-class folk were memorialized with silver and a linen covering; the priests used pottery bowls and dealt with the poor in groups; if there was a pall, the deceased's family had provided it themselves.

If the deceased was wealthy, his or her household was expected to wail and follow the coffin. A chorus of six professional mourners came with the price of a first-class funeral; additional mourners could be hired as well. Liane had refused even the six, to the considerable surprise of the chapel's priest.

The priest dusted the barley meal over Benlo's face. The pads of his thumb and forefinger were sweaty: much of the white powder clung to them till he rubbed them surreptitiously on the sleeve of his robe. It was only symbolic anyway.

The priest drew the pall over Benlo's face and bowed three times to the image of the Shepherd: a slender youth standing with his staff slanted over his right shoulder. Turning to Liane, the priest said, "Mistress, the service is complete. Shall I . . . ?"

"Please do," the girl said curtly. She wiped her eyes with a handkerchief, then folded it neatly and returned it to her left sleeve.

The priest nodded to the laborers, who came forward with practiced smoothness; each man went to his allotted corner of the bier without fumbling for position. They lifted the frame supporting the corpse and walked with it into the chapel.

The bier remained. Its sides were decorated with tree-of-life carvings. Garric thought of the similarly decorated coffins in the ancient graveyard near the Red Ox. Families buried their dead simply in the borough, returning to the soil the bodies of those who'd worked it in life.

Garric didn't know which way was right. Maybe what mattered was that people followed their own traditions, whatever those traditions were. Deep in Garric's mind, King Carus chuckled in agreement.

"Ah," said the priest to Liane. "I'll go with them and oversee matters, if I may?"

"Of course," Liane said. She was completely under control now. She wore the blue garment in which she'd arrived at Barca's Hamlet. Her only concession to the occasion was to wear a bonnet of pure white, the color of high mourning.

Nodding again, the priest followed the laborers into the building. Farther down the hillside, an old woman knelt beside a burial jar whose paint had mostly weathered away to the pale red of sun-bleached terra-cotta. As Garric watched, she placed a bunch of flowers on the jar.

Liane turned and touched hands with Garric and Tenoctris both. She smiled sadly. "You two are all I have left now that I've lost my father," she said. "Will you come with me to Erdin to learn what happened to him?"

Tenoctris looked at Garric, then at the younger woman. "The path to the answer may lead much farther than to Sandrakkan, Liane," Tenoctris said. "And it will certainly be dangerous. More dangerous than even you realize. I'm afraid that there are worse things than death."

"I can't live without trying to learn," Liane said simply. "I lost my father years ago but I looked the other way, I pretended what I saw wasn't really happening. I won't do that again."

Tenoctris nodded. "So long as you understand," she said. She turned and went on, "Then it's up to you, Garric. My path lies with you."

She smiled broadly; it made her look like a different woman, far younger and more feminine. "I suppose it does, anyway. If I'm simply a pebble rolling downhill, then I suppose one bounce is as good as another."

The priest preceded the four laborers from the building. They carried poles which were thrust through the ears of the jar into which Benlo's corpse had been folded. The only decoration on the jar's side was a starburst in white paint. The hot tar that sealed the lid over the body had a resinous, piney odor.

The two women were looking at Garric. "Yes," he said. "I'll come with you, Liane."

King Carus bellowed his world-filling laugh.

9

Hali didn't often take her clients so far into the graveyard, but this boy was a butcher's assistant who was engaged to his employer's daughter. Being caught with a prostitute would cost him his job as well as a profitable marriage.

Business among the cattlemen at the Red Ox was slow this evening. Hali didn't want to lose a potential customer just because he was nervous.

"Come along, lad," she coaxed. "Here, this'll be a nice spot, don't you think?"

She patted the white stone wall of the tomb beside her. The graveyard was shaded and cool even during daylight; the flowers hanging on the door and laid on the pavement before the tomb were still fresh enough to perfume the air. "Now, just give me the money and we'll have a *good* time."

The boy hesitated. He was a big youth with eyes too small and close-set to be attractive in his round face, but he had Hali's price, three coppers, in his purse. It was early evening; the sun had just set. Hali hadn't had a drink since noon and she *really* needed one. She planned to earn the three coppers and get straight back to the bar of the Red Ox with them.

She hitched up her tunic slightly, giving the boy a bit of a show. There was a vine-leaf pattern around the hem, worn now but good needlework. Hali had embroidered it herself not so many years ago when she was an honest woman earning an honest living; back when drink was a pleasure, not a need. A few years ago, and a whole lifetime past.

The boy wore his leather butcher's apron. He fumbled loose the strings to get at the purse hanging underneath, then paused again. "Say," he said, looking about him in cowlike wonder. "Isn't this where the trouble was the other day?"

Sister take me for a fool, he's right! Hali thought. *And the Sister take this pie-faced booby too, for insisting we come so far in when leaning against the inside wall is privacy enough!*

The stableman from the Red Ox had gone along with the crew of undertakers and city marshals who collected the body two days past. He'd described the place where it happened: paired tombs facing one another across a stone patio. The white one was in use by the bor-Rusamans, a family in the shipping trade; the killing had taken place in the black tomb whose reputation had kept it vacant despite its good physical condition.

"No, no," Hali lied. "That was clear the other side of the cemetery, honey. I went and saw the place myself and it was nowhere around here."

She patted the tomb wall again. "Now, give me the money, sweetheart, and let's take care of our business, right?"

Now that the boy had brought the matter up, Hali started to worry. She wasn't a flighty woman, but the stableman had been too shaken by what he'd seen in the tomb to embellish the story the way he'd probably intended to do. His description of a disemboweled corpse with an expression of stark terror on its face was the more frightening to hear because it had obviously frightened the man talking.

The boy stared at her. The young fool had no more sense than the sheep he butchered. *How does he manage not to get hit on the head with a hammer himself and have his throat slit?*

She sighed and stepped over to the boy, rotating the unfastened apron around to his back so that it wouldn't be in the way of business—and of the purse hanging from the boy's waist belt. It was getting noticeably darker.

His hands closed over the top of his purse. "Now, don't be a silly boy," Hali wheedled. "You're too handsome to worry about nothing, now aren't you?"

Something crashed inside the tomb behind them. The boy jerked away from Hali. She turned. It was the sort of sound a burial jar would make in breaking apart.

"Now, don't worry about a few tiles falling off an old roof!" Hali said, her voice rising in desperation as she saw the evening's wine vanishing along with the frightened customer. "It's nothing—"

Blue light flared within the tomb, leaking out the iris ventilators in the gable peaks. The door's metal bolt sheared with a sharp crack.

The boy bellowed like a stuck pig and blundered off into the gathering night. Hali heard him fall over a stone coffin. She hoped bitterly for a moment that he'd managed to break his fool neck but he was up a moment later, running on and still screaming.

Hali backed against the side of the tomb. She needed a drink; and suddenly, nothing she might be running away from seemed any worse than the life she'd be running to save.

The iron door squealed open. A man stepped out. He tramped slowly across the cemetery without looking around, vanishing at last behind a stand of centuries-old cypresses on his way toward the gate. There was a faint flicker when the man's legs moved, a dusting of blue light.

Hali recognized the fellow despite the dim light: Arame bor-Rusaman. She'd seen him several times being driven through the streets of Carcosa in a carriage with his coat of arms on the side. He was far too fine to be a customer of hers, of course, but sizing up men was an important part of Hali's business.

Three days ago Hali had seen Arame for the last time as the funeral procession made its way past the Red Ox. His features were painted larger than life on the sides of his burial jar.

10

Sharina steadied the water cask, one of those they'd brought from the trireme, while Nonnus tapped the upper hoop in place with mallet made from a vertebra and a dorsal spine of a large fish. "The seams are holding," the hermit said, "but I'm going to look into the casks the Folk hollow from whale bones. I don't trust these staves not to shrink if they're in sunlight for too long."

"I don't see what possible difference it makes," Asera said bitterly. She held herself as though she were cold, despite the warmth of the bright sun. "We'll never be rescued from here. You said yourself that there's no chance of civilized people coming this far north."

In the week they'd spent with the Floating Folk, the procurator had lost her fear of imminent death. She hadn't become more hopeful, though, and she had the energy to be angry about the situation.

Members of Motherhugger's extended family relaxed in the pleasant weather. More of them were in the water, sporting on pontoons or just swimming, than were aboard the houseboat. Motherhugger himself sat in the waist of the boat with three of his wives. The women were crushing seaweed in bone querns while the chief sipped from a bronze goblet, the loot of some ancient shipwreck.

The prepared weed fermented into the mildly alcoholic beverage that Motherhugger was drinking. It was reserved for chiefs and their special favorites, but Sharina wouldn't have been willing to try the stuff even if she'd been permitted to. The women started the fermentation process by spitting into the crushed leaves. The drink was green, fibrous, and smelled to Sharina like the brownish gunk that seeped from the bottom of wet haystacks.

"I don't expect other people to rescue us, true," Nonnus said equably. He worked around the hoop, tapping on one side and then the other. He never struck quite at the same place; Sharina's thumb braced the point on the circlet of pegged willow opposite to each blow. "But that was never my thought, mistress. We haven't come this far to spend the rest of our days wheeling under the Ice Capes. When the chance to leave comes, we'll have our provisions ready."

Twenty or so members of Motherhugger's household used their leisure to stare at the islanders. Nonnus had appropriated a corner of the houseboat's forward deck for him and his entourage. Their gear was lashed to bone extensions the hermit had raised from the ship's ribs: the houseboats didn't have railings, even on the decked portions.

The islanders slept there also, in part to prevent theft. The wooden casks were valuable and their few bits of metal even more so. Most of the iron tools Sharina had seen Motherhugger's family use were made out of nails pulled from the drifting wreckage of islander vessels that had been nailed rather than pegged.

She didn't know what they'd do if the weather changed—she for one would prefer going over the side to sheltering in the noisome caverns belowdecks—but she trusted the hermit to respond to whatever need arose. He'd said he'd barter for hides to make an actual deckhouse if they were still among the Folk by the time of the fall storms.

Nonnus straightened and tested the cask's lid by pressure from his thumb. It remained firm. They'd filled it, he and Sharina, the previous day with blocks of ice they'd chipped from the berg. She didn't think she'd ever be able to competently handle a pontoon like the one she'd borrowed, but at least she'd managed not to overturn it. The single outrigger didn't support you if you let your weight shift to the wrong side.

"Nonnus," she said in a low voice. "Sleepsalot claimed that we wouldn't be permitted to leave the village. Is that true?"

"That's the Law," Nonnus agreed calmly. He examined the cod-drying rack he'd built from baleen strips and flicked a bit of cod into the water. "Cut the fillet too thick on this end and it was starting to spoil."

The islanders had no surplus they were willing to trade, so Nonnus' bargains were his labor—and once that of Sharina to mend nets—against some bit of material he wanted from the Folk. His skill and the Pewle knife's steel blade accomplished more in an hour than a day of desultory labor by a member of Motherhugger's family.

Besides, the Floating Folk rather liked to watch outsiders work. The islanders were now members of the tribe by Law, but in truth a Folk village was a society more parochial than the most rural hamlet on Haft. The rule was intended for Folk fleeing other tribes because of a feud, though Nonnus said there'd been other cases of outlaws from the islands finding haven of sorts in the floating village.

A small shark turned onto its back to suck the meat down in a swirl of bubbles. Fish swarmed about the houseboat, fattening on offal dumped over the side. Children splashed in the same waters, oblivious of the possible risk. Sharina hadn't seen any seawolves or large sharks, though. The Floating Folk were the top predators in the regions they frequented.

"If you're caught leaving a village," Nonnus said, smiling slightly toward Sharina over the top of the drying rack, "you're a traitor and the whole tribe eats you. I wouldn't choose to be caught, no. Better to wait for a norther . . ."

His gaze drifted toward Meder.

"As I recall saying some while ago," Nonnus concluded, his tone flat, his eyes hard.

The wizard sat a little apart from the other three. He'd spent part of each day since their arrival with Leadsthestars at the royal residence, ferried there and back in one of Longtoes' catcher boats. Asera sometimes talked to him privately, but Sharina noticed that Meder had lost all sign of subordination to the procurator since he began meeting with the tattooed woman.

"I wonder what he trades the old woman for the things she gives him?" Sharina murmured to Nonnus, glancing sidelong toward the wizard. Asera was close enough to hear the words, but she didn't object to the question.

From each visit to the catamaran Meder had returned with some new piece of equipment to replace the gear Sharina threw into the sea. He now had an athame of walrus ivory; its blade was honed to a real edge. The hilt was fretted into the semblance of a pair of demons gnawing at one another's bellies.

Leadsthestars had also given Meder a whale-vertebra brazier and a string of pouches made from the swim bladders of large fish. Inside were powders whose colors were visible through the translucent container. At intervals—as now—Meder lit a fire of whale blubber and burned a pinch of powder in it; but he never chanted aloud.

"He's a powerful wizard, Tenoctris said," Nonnus answered as he checked the bung of the second water cask. "Leadsthestars is pleased to meet him, I shouldn't wonder.

She's probably as much alone here as I was in the borough—"

He paused and grinned at Sharina. "But *that* was my choice."

Blue smoke puffed from the brazier as Meder dropped something on the flame. The dry powder had been red. "We can't choose Meder's path for him," Nonnus said softly, still looking at the wizard.

Most of the Folk kept a cautious distance from the islanders. A boy of three or four, red-haired with freckled shoulders and arms like all the Folk, was the exception. Meder fascinated him. He lay for hours with his chin on his hands, looking up at the young wizard across the brazier.

Meder had shouted at the boy when first he appeared. One of the women crushing seaweed had walked over to the pair and clouted Meder with a pestle carved from whale jawbone. Nonnus sponged and bound up the wizard's bloodied scalp while he was unconscious; after that Meder pretended to ignore the boy.

"He says he'll get us out of this place," Asera muttered. "But he's said that before, and every time we find ourselves in a worse place yet."

"You've noticed that too?" Sharina said sarcastically. "I should take all that stuff away from him and throw it into the sea the way I did the chest!"

Meder added another ingredient to the bubbling flames. White smoke rose oddly, clingingly, as if unwilling to leave the brazier. Wizard and child stared intently as the smoke twisted itself into a shape as vaguely humanoid as a mandrake root, then dissipated with the suddenness of snow melting in water.

"No," Nonnus said. "We should choose our own paths and let others choose theirs."

Without any change of tone he went on, "Sloopoulot's catcher boat is on its way here from the residence."

Asera caught danger in the implications of Nonnus' words, though there was nothing in his tone to cause alarm. "What do you mean?'' she said, leaning forward unsteadily to peer over the bow.

Sharina put out a hand to keep the other woman from over-balancing. She didn't like Asera: days in an open dugout had caused the apparent majesty of a royal procurator to decay faster than a beached fish in the summer sun. She'd still feel obliged to jump in after Asera if she were drowning, so it was easier to prevent the situation from arising.

"We can deal with Sleepsalot," Nonnus said quietly. He held his javelin again. "I didn't say that we had to let others choose paths for *us*."

Motherhugger's family viewed the arrival of their neighbor's boat without overmuch interest one way or the other. One of Sleepsalot's wives waddled to the rail and displayed her buttocks to the catcher boat. Children in the water dived about it; one grabbed a paddle by the blade and tried unsuccessfully to wrest it away. Sharina couldn't tell how much was horseplay and how much might indicate real hostility between the families.

Sleepsalot sat in the stern of the catcher boat with Three-fingers in the bow as before. Threefingers hadn't signaled with the ammonite-shell horn, though it rested on the frames beside him. The shell must be a considerable weight even though the internal walls had been knocked out to create a musical instrument.

Sleepsalot directed his paddlers to the bow of the house-boat, ten feet from the islanders. Threefingers tossed a hawser around the high prow and tied it off to hold the catcher boat. Sharina wondered why the crew was showing greater concern than they had at the royal residence.

"What are you doing here, Sleepsalot?" Motherhugger demanded. He stood at the break of the waist, watching the other chief and the dozen members of the boat's crew clamber onto the deck. Motherhugger didn't bother to climb up to meet Sleepsalot eye to eye. "You still owe me five feathers of baleen. Are you here to pay?"

"My business isn't with you, Motherhugger," Sleepsalot

said airily. "Anyway, Blackteeth was supposed to pay that as part of the bride-price for my sister. Go talk to him."

The visitors advanced in a line abreast. Sleepsalot halted six feet in front of Nonnus and put his hands on his hips. "So, Pewleman," he said. "I'm going out after whale tomorrow. The Law gives me the right to pick a man from another family to make up the crew of my boat. I pick you for my harpooner."

"You can't challenge!" said Threefingers on the other end of the line from his father. "It's the Law!"

Almost everyone on the houseboat was watching the confrontation; people came out from the beneath the decks and many of those in the water squirmed aboard. Asera moved to put the drying rack between her and the rank of Sleepsalot's crew, all of them trying to look threatening to cow Nonnus.

Sharina stepped to the hermit's side and pulled the hand axe from its loop. Nonnus rolled his face upward and started to chuckle. The laughter sounded real to Sharina.

Sleepsalot seemed startled. He was watching the steel point of the javelin glittering on the hermit's shoulder. Sharina knew that was a mistake: the weapon would go where Nonnus sent it. Sleepsalot should have been watching Nonnus' eyes.

"It's a dangerous post, harpooner!" Threefingers said angrily. He shook his own harpoon, but he was extremely careful to keep the point vertical so that Nonnus couldn't claim it was a threat and grounds for a challenge. "Standing up there in the prow where somebody might bump you overboard by accident!"

Sharina heard Meder chanting behind her in a low voice, but she didn't dare turn around now. She understood that Sleepsalot and his son were actually bargaining with Nonnus: frightening the hermit so that he'd agree to hand over an item of value.

Agree to hand over Sharina herself.

They didn't know Nonnus. When they realized their threat wasn't going to work, anything could happen. The rules that prevented a member of the Folk from stabbing another mem-

ber almost certainly wouldn't apply if the hermit were foolish
enough to turn his back now.

"I'm honored that you would choose me to join your fine
crew, Sleepsalot," Nonnus said politely. The remnants of
laughter still lubricated his voice. "I'm afraid that I won't be
able accept, though. You see—"

"You can't refuse!" Threefingers sputtered. "It's the Law
that we can take you!"

"Unfortunately," Nonnus said in the tone of an amused
adult talking to a child, "I'm just on my way over to the
royal residence to challenge Longtoes for the kingship of the
tribe. Tomorrow, well, things will be different, you see. Since
it's the king who decides the crews of boats for the hunt."

The fire in Meder's brazier hissed angrily around whatever
he'd added to the flames. Sharina smelled a bitter odor but
her eyes continued to scan the line of Sleepsalot's crew.

Sleepsalot eased back, probably unconsciously. "You have
to defeat all the King's Sons to challenge the king!" he said;
but his confidence was clearly bluster.

"I don't think the King's Sons look like much, do you?"
Nonnus said nonchalantly. He spun his javelin between his
thumb and two fingers, then transferred it into his left hand
behind his back, still spinning. "Of course . . ."

The woman beside Sleepsalot turned so that the twenty-
armed starburst tattooed on her shoulder was toward the hermit. Sharina remembered what Nonnus had said about the
Folk worshipping the monsters of the deep.

". . . it might be that Longtoes will decide to make you the
harpooner in a boat that *I* captain, tomorrow," Nonnus said,
grinning at the chief and spinning the javelin back into his
right hand. "If Longtoes did that, why, I wouldn't feel a need
to challenge him."

Sleepsalot's jaw dropped. He looked as though the hermit
was dangling him over the open jaws of a seawolf—which
was pretty close to the reality of the situation. The members
of his crew were backing away noticeably; even Threefingers
was looking at his father as if they'd met for the first time.

"Barbathiathiao brimaiao chermari!" Meder shouted, completing his incantation. The fire hissed, then *cracked* as sharply as a blow on the ear.

All of Sleepsalot's crew retreated. Sharina risked a glance behind her.

A cloud of pulsing white smoke rose from the brazier. It was humanoid in shape and already the size of a man as it continued to grow. The child jumped to his feet to stare at the image wide-eyed. Meder grabbed the boy by his long hair.

Nonnus stepped sideways so that he could look at the wizard without turning his back on Sleepsalot, though the chief and his people weren't the threat they might have been a minute earlier. "Meder!" the hermit said. "Put the boy down! I've got this under control."

The child screamed and kicked. Meder punched him with the butt of the athame, then held the point to his throat.

Meder's eyes were wide with fear and anticipation. "You have to give us your boat and let us go!" he called to Sleepsalot. The image of smoke gyrated as though it were dancing on top of the fire. It was about seven feet tall; hulking, faceless, the arms and torso much longer than the legs.

Threefingers and Sleepsalot exchanged glances. The younger man laughed and stepped forward, careful to skirt Nonnus. "Or what, islander?" Threefingers said. "If you think your tricks—"

Meder flushed. He thrust his ivory blade through the child's throat in a spray of blood. The child's screams ended in a gurgle, but Sharina screamed in his place.

A spurt of dark blood from the neck arteries splashed onto the fire. The brazier geysered red flame as though the blood had stoked the fire instead of quenching it. Liquid sparks spewed in all directions, some charring the whaleskin decking while others went over the side to sizzle in the water.

Meder stood unharmed and unmoving in the midst of the blaze, though the dead child's hair was beginning to burn. The image of white smoke dissipated.

The sea roared. A humanoid shape formed from water as

red as flame. It caught the houseboat's gunwale in one hand and pulled itself up on deck. Its limbs rippled bonelessly.

Sleepsalot shouted and stabbed the creature in the chest. The harpoon stuck as though thrust into warm pitch. The creature roared. Seizing Sleepsalot by the scalp and one shoulder, it pulled his head off.

Meder laughed like a demon. He tossed the child's corpse away. The fire had vanished. The brazier was shards of blackened bone, destroyed by the powers it had initiated.

Threefingers flung his harpoon into the creature's back and leaped over the far side of the houseboat in a dive as graceful as a tern's. Sleepsalot's crew ran for the bow, some of them jumping into the water while a few tried to get into the boat. The creature caught two of the hindmost and crushed them together in its arms.

Dropping the corpses, the creature took the hawser in its hands and drew the bow of the catcher boat out of the water. The three crewmen aboard her went over the side. They swam toward the houseboat hundreds of yards distant instead of trying to reboard Motherhugger's vessel. Members of Motherhugger's family were in the water also or poised to dive.

The creature dropped the whaleskin rope and turned toward Nonnus. The hermit cocked the javelin to throw. Sharina stepped in front of him, facing the creature.

Meder shouted a word lost in thunder. The creature's form sagged like wax in a fire. The color washed away. The figure became water, sooty water, splashing across the deck and over the houseboat's side.

Sharina dropped the hand axe. She turned sobbing and threw her arms around Nonnus. All she could see was the face of the boy as his cries drowned in his own blood.

"The past is past, child," the hermit whispered. His ribs beneath his coarse black tunic were as hard and ridged as the bark of an oak tree. "For the child, for you and me. The past is past."

He shifted slightly as he turned his head, though Sharina was still blind with tears and memory. "As for Meder, well, we all have our ghosts. But I'll pray for the soul of his as well as for my own.''

"I had to do it," Meder said in a high-pitched voice. "Procurator, you saw that there was no choice. You saw that!"

"Help me load our provisions onto the boat, child," Nonnus said softly in Sharina's ear. "They won't come chasing us, I think."

He sighed. "Skin boats don't sail much better against the wind than a dugout does, but we'll manage. With the help of the Lady, we'll manage."

11

Ilna heard the voices in the hallway. She stepped away from the loom before the faint, fearful knock at the door.

"Mistress?" the maid called. The door panel was carved with a boar's head, the coat of arms of some former owner. "There's a man who says he has to see you."

The chamber was intended as a winter parlor. Light flooded it through the deep bay window into the garden behind. Ilna used it as a workroom: her looms were set so that the sun was always over her shoulder as she wove.

She'd neglected the garden since Beltar rented the mansion for her, but it remained awash with striking color. Pink and yellow hollyhocks mounted from planters among the brick walks; red and white roses covered the walls against the adjoining properties and Erdin's central canal across the back.

The flowers' beauty didn't matter to Ilna. She never looked around while working, never noticed the play of light on the petals through the day or the tranquil buzzing of the insects they attracted. They weren't a part of her pattern.

The maid who opened the door was small, dark, young,

and terrified. She'd been told that Ilna must never be interrupted while working. The least she expected for violating that order was that she'd lose the well-paid position on which she depended. Rumors about her employer opened much more frightening possibilities.

Ilna nodded. "Show him in," she said.

The girl needn't have worried: she would only have disobeyed Ilna if she'd been forced to do so. Ilna understood compulsion very well. She lacked compassion for those others compelled as she lacked compassion in all things, but neither did she mete out punishment without a reason for doing so.

The maid curtsied. "Voder or-Tettigan, mistress," she said with a sob of relief. "From the chancellor's office."

The man she gestured in before closing the door was compact, reasonably well dressed, and in his late thirties. He had a bit of a paunch on him and enough rank that the hickory baton he carried only served to identify him as a member of the City Patrols.

He hadn't always had the rank. The wood had seen its share of hard knocks, as had the man carrying it.

"Mistress," he said, bowing a hair deeper than bare politeness required. He'd been sizing her up just as she had him.

"I make a regular donation to the district captain," Ilna said coldly. "If you have a problem with his division of the spoils, I suggest you take it up with him. Good day, sir!"

Voder shook his head. "I work out of the central office, mistress," he said. "I'm not here to squeeze you. I'm here to close you down."

His voice was low, slow, and had a slight burr. His build and manner reminded her of Cashel; Voder lacked her brother's size, but they shared a rocklike solidity and a determination as certain as Ilna's own.

"There's a law against a gentlewoman weaving in her own home?" Ilna said. If she'd been speaking to the usual sort of man there'd have been contempt in her tone, but there was nothing contemptible about this man. "I transact no business in this dwelling. I transact no business at all, Master Voder.

If the chancellor has questions about the quality of my work, let him take them up with Beltar or-Holman at his shop on Glass Street.''

Voder shook his head again. "I'm sorry, mistress," he said and sounded like he meant the words. "There's been a dozen killings already over your ribbons. Men killing their wives, wives killing their husbands' girlfriends . . . people drowning themselves because somebody left them, and there was one poor devil last night who hung himself because of the way *he'd* treated his wife. He really loved her, I guess. There's people like that."

His eyes had been surveying the room as he spoke: the looms, the worktable, the ironbound chest bolted to the floor; the lack of any amenities whatever. He met Ilna's eyes again, gave her a lopsided smile, and said, "It's got to stop, mistress. It's got to."

Ilna sniffed as she walked across the room to the strongbox. "All right," she said dismissively, though she knew that it wasn't going to be right; not this time. "How much do you want?"

"Mistress, I really wish it was that simple," Voder said; again she heard the ring of sincerity. "I won't tell you any lies: I've got a family and sure, I've done what I've had to do to make sure they didn't starve. But that's not what I'm here for this time. You're doing evil, mistress. You know it, I know it. If you were just breaking the law I could maybe look the other way, but this has got to stop."

She faced him. "You've said what you came to say," she said icily. "Now leave."

"Mistress," Voder said. "I came up the hard way. I guess you did too so you understand what I'm saying: either you stop this or I do. I'm as sorry as I can be, but that's just what I mean."

Their eyes locked: hers brown, his gray, and as hard as pairs of millstones.

"Mistress," Voder said, "I live here. I've lived in Erdin all my life." He shook his head in self-disgust. "I guess I love the place, fool though I sound to say that. I won't let this go on."

"Good day, Master Voder," Ilna repeated without inflection.

Voder nodded. "I'm sorry," he said. He opened the door and closed it behind him, firmly but quietly.

Ilna walked over to the loom on which she was weaving a portrait. She looked at the image in the shimmering fabric for some moments, then returned to the door and opened it. The maid was waiting in the hall, as stiff as if she expected a sentence of death.

Ilna smiled in disdain. "Send a courier to Beltar or-Holman at his shop," she said. "I need him at once."

"Master Beltar is in the reception room waiting for you to finish your work, mistress," the maid babbled. "Shall I—"

Ilna shooed the girl off with a silent wave of her hand. It angered her to be treated as though she was some sort of capricious monster. She'd never harmed anything without a reason . . . and the cosmos gave her reason for much greater harm than she chose to do.

Beltar came up the hallway, forcing a smile when he saw Ilna. She ushered him into the workroom. The draper now dressed expensively though in conservative colors: his tunic had thin stripes of brown and olive green, and the toes of his black leather slippers curled up to end in horsehair tassels.

He'd lost weight and his face had the gray sheen of an image in a zinc mirror.

"A problem's arisen," Ilna said as she closed the door. She walked between a pair of her looms. The largest, the double-span giant, was covered with muslin to conceal the work upon it. "Come here. You know the woman Leah os-Wenzel? The chancellor's mistress?"

"I know of her," Beltar said cautiously. He'd never been invited to see the looms from the front, where the patterns being created were visible. "Leah bos-Zelliman, she calls herself now. She's been a customer."

There were several ribbon looms. The patterns of the works

in progress were subtly modified from one to the next; nothing that Beltar could see, but he could recognize the variations by the different effects the pieces had on him.

"As if a name mattered," Ilna sniffed. Her lip curled. "As if noble birth meant anything!"

That was as much emotion as the draper had ever seen her display; he blinked. Ilna grimaced at her failure of control and stepped to the loom on which she'd woven a panel—a shawl, it might be—a full yard wide and some eight inches deep. The thread was a mixture of wool and goat hair, both of them black, so that the pattern showed in the texture rather than the color of the fabric.

Beltar looked at the panel, gasped, and averted his eyes. Ilna smiled coldly as she clipped the piece out of the frame.

"I want you to take this to Mistress Leah," she said as she carried the cloth to her worktable. "Tell her that it's a gift from me. A free gift."

Ilna laid the piece flat on the table, smoothed out the wrinkles, and picked up her uncased knife; another weaver would have used shears. She held the upper left corner of the fabric to the table with her free thumb and forefinger.

"Tell Mistress Leah," she continued as she drew the keen steel diagonally down across the fabric, severing it into two perfect triangles, "that she'll get the other half of the panel when a police official from the central office, one Voder or-Tettigan, is arrested."

She looked at Beltar. He winced back from her expression. "A charge of accepting bribes should do," she said. "I can't imagine a policeman in Erdin that the charge couldn't be truthfully brought against."

She smiled. The heart of a glacier had more warmth. "Not that I require the charge be truthful, of course," she said.

Ilna set one of the neat triangles on a strip of the baize she kept for wrappers. She rolled it so that the coarse cloth concealed her own creation.

Beltar cleared his throat. "Ah—is there something I should know, mistress?" he asked.

"You should know better than to get in my way!" Ilna snapped. She grimaced again; in contempt for the draper, and with contempt as well for her own loss of control.

"But you already know better than that, don't you?" she added mildly. "You wouldn't dare cross me."

Beltar's throat worked as he swallowed, but he didn't say anything. Ilna looked at him sharply as another thought struck her. "Why were you waiting to see me?" she demanded. "You came to tell me you weren't going to work for me anymore, weren't you?"

The draper swayed as though she'd stabbed him through the heart; his face was sweat-slicked and blotchy with fear. Ilna laughed with the amusement of an adult for a child's misguided efforts.

"I didn't . . ." Beltar whispered hoarsely. "I never said . . ."

"No, well, it doesn't matter," Ilna said with good-natured scorn. "You're not going to quit, because I still have use for you."

She held out the rolled fabric. "Get this to the lady at once," she ordered. "She'll be quite pleased with the result; the chancellor hasn't been coming by as often as he used to. If he drops Mistress Leah, she goes back to selling oranges to the spectators at stage shows, doesn't she?"

Beltar took the packet. The remaining triangle lay on the worktable. Seeing it was like hearing the sound of a beast breathing in pitch darkness: there was nothing fearsome in what was visible, but something hugely powerful lurked just beyond the realm of vision.

"That may well be the case, mistress," Beltar said in a gray voice. She'd crushed his rebellion before he'd even had the courage to voice it. He knew—as he'd known from the first—that he was Ilna's tool and that she would use him until he broke. "Voder or-Tettigan is to be arrested immediately for taking bribes."

Beltar's eyes fell on the panel being woven on the other

standard loom. It was a full-length image of the Lady, woven in silk and threads of precious metals.

It was the most beautiful thing he'd ever seen in his life.

"Mistress!" Beltar said in awe and wonder. He fell to his knees. The image was about three-quarters complete. A ram and a ewe rose on their hind legs to kiss the Lady's hands; the mists of heaven surrounded Her head in supernal glory. "Mistress! So beautiful!"

Ilna looked at the panel critically. "Yes, isn't it?" she said. She gripped the top of the fabric, stretching the warp threads, and twisted. The cloth was thin but silk and therefore strong; Ilna's face was stark and terrible as she ripped the image nonetheless.

Beltar screamed. He lurched to his feet and put out a hand to stop her, but it was already too late. Ilna tossed the shreds of fabric aside; they hung from the loom like the husks of butterflies drained in a spider's web.

"Go take care of my business, Beltar," she said hoarsely. "And be thankful that you're not man enough to oppose me."

Ilna took the draper by the hand and led him, sobbing and tear-blinded, to the door which she closed behind him. She walked back to the rank of looms.

Mistress Leah would take care of the matter, of that Ilna had no doubt. If the chancellor himself hesitated to do Leah's will, she'd give orders to subordinates in his name. No one would question the matter until it had happened and then—well, it would be too great an embarrassment to undo. Voder had been dealt with before he could damage the pattern Ilna wove.

Ilna resumed work on one of the ribbons she'd begun before Voder's arrival; a simple thing, barely an hour's work for fingers that never made a mistake. After a moment she paused and started to fold the part of the divided shawl still on her worktable.

Ilna put the triangle down, half folded. She stretched out her hands to the panel she'd just torn from the frame, caressing the gleaming tangles with her fingertips. She had been weaving the panel to prove to herself that her talent was just that: a talent, not a manifestation of evil.

Ilna knelt before the loom. She gathered the ruined fabric in her palms and began to cry.

12

With a pair of Serian sailors apiece pulling three of the sweeps and Cashel alone on the fourth, the *Golden Dragon* nosed slowly onto the beach. The westering sun cast the ship's shadow far across the landscape of sand and tamarisk bushes.

"Hooray!" Mellie cried from Cashel's shoulder, bouncing from her toes into a handstand and back again. "Oh! it's so good to be back on land again, isn't it?"

Cashel grinned as he drew in the sweep, careful not to jab the sailors doing the same thing on the other side of the ship's waist. Strictly speaking Mellie stood on his shoulder and *he* stood on the deck of the *Golden Dragon*. Personally, he didn't care that the ship's flat bottom was aground on sand instead of gliding through shallow water.

"Well, I'm not a watersprite!" Mellie said as tartly as if she was reading Cashel's mind. "Ooh, come along, Cashel!"

She dropped from his shoulder to his waist, catching herself by one hand on his leather belt, and trickled like a breeze down his hairy right leg on her way to the ground.

"Hey, wait for me!" Cashel called. Sometimes he forgot that other people couldn't see the sprite the way he did, but it probably didn't matter a lot. The Serians treated him as though he were a member of a different species anyway. The fact that he talked to himself or the empty air didn't make him any stranger in their eyes.

The Highlanders *could* see Mellie, and they acted as though

Cashel were a bigger version of themselves besides. That was even more disturbing when Cashel let himself think about it.

The Highlanders had all scrambled off the ship; many of them while the square prow still slid through the surf. The little men capered and chortled in their joy: Mellie wasn't the only person aboard the *Golden Dragon* who was glad to be on firm ground again. One of the Highlanders gave a fluting call and pointed; the whole dozen vanished up one of the weathered draws into the scrub.

The Highlanders were the reason the *Golden Dragon* had made landfall here, one of the hundreds of uninhabited islets dotting the Inner Sea. Because the Serian vessel had been driven from port without time to load properly, it was short of the fresh vegetables and meat that to the Highlanders were the only imaginable foods. The Serian crewmen were on three-quarter rations of oatcakes and onions supplemented by the occasional fish, adequate until the *Golden Dragon* docked at a real port, but the Highlanders would starve unless something was done promptly.

Food was always a concern on a long voyage even when it wasn't a matter of life or death. Sail-driven merchant vessels could be becalmed for over a month, creeping along by the crews' backbreaking labor with sweeps meant only for maneuvering in harbor. Over the centuries, prudent captains had landed goats on most of the islets with a modicum of vegetation and pools to collect rainwater. The hardy little animals provided occasional meals for seawolves and a source of fresh meat for sailors willing to hunt them.

"Willing" wasn't the word to describe the Highlanders. Cashel doubted they'd even bother to cook the first goat or two they caught.

The sweeps fit into slotted racks on either rail. Cashel set his in place and stepped back, leaving it to the sailors manning the other starboard sweep to tie them both down in the fashion their tradition thought proper. Knots were as culturally individual as hairstyles; Cashel knew the Serians would quietly redo his work as soon as he turned his back.

He bent and scooped Mellie from the bridge of his instep, planting her on his shoulder again despite her squawks of complaint. "Masters?" he called to Jen and Frasa on the quarterdeck. "May I go ashore too?"

One of the brothers—Cashel still couldn't tell them apart at any distance—turned from a discussion with the captain and bowed low. "Of course, Master Cashel," he replied.

"You'd think that you were the one who'd spent the last thousand years learning how to stay alive on this plane," Mellie grumbled as Cashel picked up his quarterstaff and strode for the bow.

"There's likely rats here," he said, unperturbed by the complaints. "And we know there's Highlanders. I'm not going to let something happen to you when you're my responsibility."

Sailors hopped over the side and splashed up on shore. They'd build brush shelters for the night and heat their oatcakes, but unlike Mellie and the Highlanders they felt no great concern as to whether or not they were on land. The Serians—and this was true of Frasa and Jen as surely as it was of the common sailors—lived in self-contained units. It made little difference to them whether they were enclosed by a ship's hull or the walls of a trading compound.

A quartet of sailors staggered up the beach under the iron weight of the main anchor while other sailors payed out the cable behind them. They'd set it forty feet inland to keep the *Golden Dragon* from drifting away in the night. More sailors were lowering the bower anchor from the stern to prevent abnormal wind or waves from driving the vessel too hard aground to float off on the morning tide.

Jen and Frasa were convinced that there was no risk to this landfall, but Cashel kept remembering the storm that had raked Barca's Hamlet and driven the trireme to them. Well, he hadn't been asked his opinion; and the Highlanders needed meat, true enough.

Mellie sniffed and sat cross-legged, facing back over Cashel's shoulder. "There's no rats," she said. "I'd smell them. And the Highlanders won't bother me now because they think I'm your pet."

She turned her head and stuck her tongue out at him. "I guess that's what you think too," she added.

Cashel thrust one end of his staff down into the sand; the surf-washed upper few inches gave, but the packed lime substrate just below was firm. Instead of jumping down as the Highlanders and sailors had done, he lowered himself gently, supported by the quarterstaff and the bow railing. A man of Cashel's weight and strength learned early not to move hastily; and anyhow, he wasn't a hasty man.

Cashel hadn't minded life on shipboard but he found it surprisingly pleasant to be among greenery, even if it was mostly the minute, bitter-tasting leaves of tamarisks. He wondered how goats survived with no better fodder, and what their flesh tasted like if they did. He didn't suppose the Highlanders were finicky eaters.

Mellie hopped to the ground as soon as Cashel strode beyond the upper line of the surf. She scampered up a bush and plucked one of the tiny pink flowers to stick behind her ear: on the sprite, it looked like the bloom of a poinsettia.

"Oh!" she called, leaping to the ground again. "It feels so *good*!"

The gully was less a watercourse than a trough the wind had worn, though it probably channeled the runoff when storms swept across the little island. Shrubs stood on pedestals of coral sand which their roots bound, but between those miniature plateaus the wind scoured twisting passages.

Cashel paused at the gully's head to check the bare ground for the footprints of goats—or, of much greater concern, rats. Mellie might say she'd smell rats if they were present, but he was the one who—

He looked up just in time to see the sprite vanish up the gully, turning cartwheels every few strides. Her laughter trailed back around the bend twenty feet away; then the sound was gone too.

"Mellie!" Cashel shouted. He raised his staff vertically so

that he could move without it catching in the tough branches
and broke into a trot. He hoped that when he turned the angle
he'd find the sprite waiting for him with her tongue sticking
out in mockery.

He rounded the corner. Mellie wasn't there. To Cashel's
amazement, a hut made of huge fossilized bones squatted in
the middle of a wide spot in the gully. An old man wearing
only a breechclout squatted at a fire of tamarisk stems in front
of the hut; he was heating dark liquid in a chipped stoneware
bowl.

"Oh!" Cashel said, skidding to a halt. He hadn't expected
to meet even a goat. A human with a permanent though crude
dwelling was more than a surprise.

"Good day, sir!" the old man said. He stood up spryly.
"*Very* good to see you! Very! Won't you have some tea with
me?"

"I . . ." Cashel said. He lowered his staff, embarrassed that
he must have looked as though he was ready to smash something flat with the weapon. "Ah, no, I'm looking for a—"

He paused, realizing that the old man might have seen the
Highlanders but Mellie would have been invisible to him.

"A friend," he finished lamely. He stepped to where the
hut squeezed close to the gully wall, tight for a human but a
broad thoroughfare for the sprite.

"The little red-haired girl?" the old man said. He held his
right thumb and index finger up in a close approximation of
Mellie's height. "Why yes, she came by. I hoped she'd stay
for a moment and talk, but she ran into the bushes there."

He pointed generally to the side. The gully's wall, textured
by a net of rootlets, was about four feet high; the tamarisks
waved another eight or ten feet in the air. Cashel frowned at
the tangle of scrub.

"I'm sure she'll be back here any time, good sir," the old
man said politely. "Why don't you wait with me and we'll
have tea while we talk?"

Cashel frowned at the thicket, as featureless as the sea itself. He could force his way through the tamarisks if he

wanted to, but he certainly couldn't find the sprite among them if she wanted to hide. Was she that upset at his attempt to keep her close?

"Mellie!" he called. "I'm sorry, Mellie. Come back and don't scare me this way!"

Silence answered.

Cashel turned, feeling as though the clear sky were crushing him down. He didn't know what to do.

"Poor boy," the old man said. "But she'll be back soon, I'm sure. Come sit with me, please."

With a smile that seemed both sad and desperate he added, "I haven't talked with anyone for a very long time. I came here to be alone, but I'm afraid I succeeded better than I'd intended."

"I—" Cashel began. He thought about what it would be like to live for years on this barren islet with no company except the occasional hunting party of sailors. The old fellow looked to be a cultured man.

"Well, I guess I can sit with you a moment," he said. "But I won't have anything, thank you. Till my friend comes back anyway."

"Perhaps later," the old man said, lifting the bowl off the fire by its thickened rim. He seemed tense though as friendly as a little puppy. Gesturing toward the hut with his free hand, he added, "Would you care to see my dwelling?"

The hut was like nothing in Cashel's experience. The walls were made of petrified thighbones, each of them the diameter of a fruit tree's trunk. Ribs of similarly huge size formed the roof. The gaps were chinked with seaweed, but Cashel couldn't imagine the place being either dry or comfortable in bad weather. He'd slept in drystone sheep byres himself, but there he'd had the sheep to keep him warm.

"I'm a hermit, you see, though I know it sounds pretentious to say so," the old man chirruped. When Cashel hesitated, the old man scooted inside himself as if to prove that there was nothing sinister about his dwelling. "I decided to find a barren island like this to study, meditate, and purify myself in absolute privacy.''

He shook his head and tittered, a sound that had as much madness as humor in it. ''Oh, my goodness, how well I succeeded! Absolute privacy! Oh, yes!''

Cashel squatted to look into the hut without blocking the light. He was uncomfortable; maybe it was just worry over Mellie, because he could *feel* the sincerity of the hermit's friendliness. He was a weird old man, sure, but not a lot different from Tenoctris, Cashel suspected.

Besides, the hermit was utterly harmless. Cashel could have broken him in half with one hand, not that he could imagine a circumstance that would make him want to do that.

The hermit had laid a bed of seaweed and tamarisk branches against one wall. An iron cooking pot, somewhat larger than the pottery vessel now on the fire, rested upside down against the other wall. Beside it was a dovetailed wooden box of about a half-bushel's capacity, its lid resting askew. Cashel could see that the interior was a series of vertical pigeonholes, each holding a parchment scroll that had been used so much that the varnish was gone from the roller tips. Though worn, the books were obviously kept with love.

There were no manufactured articles in the hut apart from the two pots and the book safe: not a knife, not a lamp; not even piece of cloth. The hermit's breechclout was inexpertly woven from fibrous tamarisk bark, obviously by the wearer himself.

Cashel leaned his staff against the front of the hut. He eyed the doorway, then knelt and turned his torso sideways in order to fit. The opening was high enough or nearly so, but it was very narrow.

He looked around again, certain that there must be more than what he was seeing. ''Do you live on goats, then?'' he asked. Though there was no sign of bones or butchering; no smell, either, and that you couldn't hide.

''I'm a vegetarian,'' the old man said. ''I—and I don't mean to preach, good sir, please don't take what I'm saying as disapproval of whatever philosophy you may hold. But for me it wouldn't be right to preserve my life by taking the life of another creature.''

He smiled in embarrassment. ''It was part of the purification, you see. I live on the sea's bounty: the currents carry weed of many varieties onto the beach here, as regularly as the sun rises. I like to think that Nature herself aids those who live in harmony with her.''

''Ah,'' Cashel said in soft-voiced amazement. He looked around the hut again, wondering how the old man had managed to move anything as heavy as these petrified bones. ''I couldn't . . . I mean, I don't eat off gold plates myself. But this . . .''

The hermit smiled shyly. ''I don't miss it,'' he said. ''The food; the, well, 'comforts' people would call them. I have my studies.''

He nodded toward the books Cashel squatted beside. ''I've achieved many of the purposes for which I came here,'' he went on. ''I'll admit, though, that I've been lonely at times. Very lonely, I'm afraid.''

Cashel heard the desperation in the poor man's voice. ''How long have you been here, sir?'' he asked.

They hadn't exchanged names. Cashel wasn't sure how he'd respond if the old man asked his name; perhaps understanding that, he *hadn't* asked. There was power in being able to call something, someone, by the right name.

Cashel wished Mellie was with him. He missed her, missed her more even than he'd have expected to; but especially he missed her advice on the situation. Mellie would understand the things that Cashel felt pressing down on him.

''A long time,'' the hermit said. His soft voice trembled; he forced a smile. ''Longer than I can say for sure. At first I wasn't interested in time, and after a while . . . I'm afraid I can't even guess.''

Cashel had heard a widow weeping over the grave of her only child. The old man's words were even sadder, even lonelier.

"You know . . ." Cashel said. Did he sound suspicious? "My friend that I'm looking for, most people don't see her."

The hermit smiled at the implied question. "You're puzzled that I do?" he said. "Really, good sir, it's scarcely more amazing that you do see her than it would be if I didn't. I've given a long life over to the study of such matters, while you . . . ?"

He let his voice trail off delicately.

Cashel managed to chuckle. "I've studied sheep," he admitted. "And woodcutting and a few other things. But no, I can't even read—though I've a friend who does."

He blushed, aware as he spoke the words that bragging to this man that Garric could read was about as silly a statement as had ever come out of his mouth. "I don't know how it is that I see Mellie," he added. "I just did."

He looked directly at the old man. "I know a lady who's a wizard," he said. "I guess you're one too, sir?"

The old man smiled. "More of a philospher, I would say," he replied. "But there's a point where all knowledge joins, I admit."

Cashel felt the pressure growing. The thick stone walls seemed strangely insubstantial but the world beyond the doorway—the sand, the rustling tamarisks—squeezed in on him. The air itself thickened, changing the quality of the light.

"I've got to go find Mellie," he said hoarsely. He felt as if he were buried in wet sand. He could move but it weighed him down.

"Have some tea, please, and I'm sure you'll see your friend again," the hermit said as he leaned toward Cashel with the bowl. The fluid was probably cooked from some form of seaweed; certainly it wasn't tea, but it had a spicy, pleasant odor.

"Please, good sir," the hermit said. "I've been alone for so long. Drink with me."

The old man lifted the bowl to his lips, sipped the dark liquid, and swallowed. His eyes were on Cashel. Cashel started to get up, struggling against a weight as great as the world itself.

"Please . . ." the old man pleaded.

Blue light. A tiny figure of blue light, a bright shadow *thrown on the inside of the upturned iron pot.*

Mellie!

Cashel snatched the pot away and flung it clanging against the stone ribs of the roof. Mellie leaped onto his hand and danced up his bare arm, caroling her joy.

The pottery bowl lay overturned on the ground; the hermit cringed back. Cashel stood, pressing upward against the roof and sidewall.

"Please—"

Cashel roared, lifting his arms. A blue glare enveloped him. The stones were light as thistle down, light as spiderweb. He thrust his hands to either side, ripping apart the walls of the world that held him. Sunlight and wind and the waxy green leaves of tamarisks locked into focus with Cashel's shouting triumph.

Words drifting in limbo as the blue light faded into the black peace of unconsciousness: . . . *so very lonely* . . .

The ground on which he lay was in darkness, but only a few stars shone in the purple sky. Cashel heard the Highlanders' happy chatter as they came down the gully toward him. He raised his head.

"Shall I ask them to help you?" Mellie offered. "You must be very tired, Cashel. Even you."

Three Highlanders came around a twist in the passage, moving jauntily despite the fact that each of the little men carried across his shoulders a goat of at least half his own body weight.

They halted in surprise when they saw Cashel lying on the ground. The rate of their chattering increased like that of chicks in the nest when the mother bird appears.

"No, I can . . ." Cashel said as he rolled to plant his hands flat on the ground. Existence rippled like cloth in the wind. He'd never felt so weak before in his life. What had happened to him?

"Cashel, don't—" the sprite said.

"I *can*," Cashel grunted. Everything closed down to the feel of his palms against the gritty soil. He didn't want to live if he couldn't get up. He wouldn't lie here like a foundered horse.

"I can!" and he pushed his torso up, rising to his knees, lurching back and upright all as part of the same motion. He swayed, towering before the astounded Highlanders.

The world was firm again and Cashel's feet were set firmly on it. He began to laugh in relief. The Highlanders twittered about him like a flock of birds; Mellie trilled merrily, caressing his ear.

"Oh!" she said. "You're so strong, Cashel. The pot was iron!"

There was no sign of the hut. Cashel sobered. He turned, thinking it must be behind him.

The hut wasn't there. Bending over, he could see his own faint footprints despite the twilight, but the gigantic bones and the fire-blackened ground that *couldn't* have vanished—

Had vanished.

"Was I dreaming?" Cashel said, as much to himself as to the sprite on his shoulder. "There was an old man, a philosopher . . ."

The Highlanders closed around him, touching him with friendly hands and tugging him gently toward the ship. The long-haired goats they carried were still warm.

Cashel spread his arms. The muscles ached but they moved normally. He walked along with the little men, glad of their company and Mellie's.

"I dreamed I tore his hut apart," Cashel murmured. Fires gleamed on the beach; the western horizon was a pall of red flame that threw the *Golden Dragon* into ungainly silhouette. "I shouldn't have done that."

"If you'd eaten or drunk anything, Cashel," Mellie said, "we could never have left."

The Highlanders trotted toward a group of their fellows who'd already begun grilling their prey with the hides still on. Hair singed with a stench the cooks didn't seem to notice. Frasa and Jen rose in greeting at a fire placed upwind of the Highlanders.

"He was just a lonely old man," Cashel said.

He glanced at Mellie. The sprite stared back at him in wonder and puzzlement.

13

"We'll pay our port duties in Erdin!" bellowed Aran, the captain of the two-masted trading vessel. His voice was louder than Garric would have thought a man's could be without aid of a megaphone. "Go play navy with somebody who's got the time to waste!"

"There's a wizard aboard her," Tenoctris said to Garric and Liane, who stood with her along the merchantman's lee rail. She grinned minutely and added, "He probably calls himself a wizard, at least."

The officer in the bow of the single-banked warship *did* use a megaphone. "Lay to," he thundered, "or we'll sink you and you can try your wit on the fishes!"

"It's a royal vessel from Ornifal," Liane said quietly. Her hands rested lightly on the railing, the fingers spread. "Do you see the eagle on the pennon? If they were from Sandrakkan they'd have a horse's head there instead."

"Fah!" Aran snarled. "The first time this year the wind's fair to take us up the River Erd without tacking and some nobleman's by-blow decides to hold us up. Till the tide turns, I shouldn't wonder."

He glared at his waiting crewmen and added, "Yes, drop the sails! The fool with the kettle on his head insists!"

Garric eyed the warship paralleling the merchantman's course fifty yards away. Its twenty-five oars per side moved with the rhythm of a millipede's legs. The stroke looked slow to Garric because he was used to the smaller, lighter equipment of a fishing dory, but he didn't doubt that it could drive the ship's bronze beak through the merchantman's hull with no difficulty.

"What's a royal ship doing here?" Garric asked. "Isn't the Earl of Sandrakkan an enemy of the king?"

"It's not open war," Liane said, "but the Earl of Sandrakkan is about the worst enemy the king has. Except perhaps for the queen."

Garric looked sharply at her to see if she was joking. There was nothing but polite interest on the surface of the girl's face, though the muscles below were hard as marble.

The mainspar clattered down. Sailors grabbed handfuls of the sail, furling it and cursing the breeze. It was fair for their destination, Erdin, and strong enough that it had bellied the canvas against the forestay. Sandrakkan sailors believed that a bulging sail held the wind like water in a pail, though the Haft fishermen Garric grew up with swore by board-flat canvas.

"Since there's a wizard aboard," Tenoctris said with her usual detachment, "I think we can assume they're looking for us. For your father at least, Liane."

Two sailors were drawing in the foresail and its spar. They couldn't let gravity do the work because the mast slanted like a bowsprit so that the yard was attached well forward of the hull. That was a necessary but awkward adaptation to the fact the mainsail bellied so far, though Garric admitted that the foresail's leverage meant the tubby merchantman was remarkably quick to change tacks.

"The *king* is looking for us?" Liane said.

"If this is a royal ship as you say," Tenoctris said, "then yes, I think he is."

Liane looked as though she were sucking something sour. "I wonder if my father was working for the queen," she said.

Tenoctris shrugged. "There're more parties than two involved," she said. "Though I'm afraid if you followed most of them back you'd find the same thing at the end of all the chains.''

"The Hooded One?" Garric said, his eyes on the nearing warship. Only a few oarsmen in the bow and stern were rowing.

"No," Tenoctris said, "though he'd like to pretend otherwise. I mean Malkar."

The oarsmen sat on separate benches divided by a central runway so narrow that sailors would have to turn sideways to pass one another along it. There was a mast step at midkeel, but the vessel didn't carry a mast and spar at present; probably they'd been landed on shore so as not to be in the way while the vessel patrolled under oar power. A small sail was furled against the jib boom projecting above the ram.

A single helmsman in the narrow stern handled the paired steering oars. Two belt-wearing officers, one in the bow and the other seated near the helmsman with a drum between his legs, were the only deck crew. Presumably rowers got up from their benches when it was necessary to adjust the sail.

The merchantman lost way, wallowing in the swell. Because the hull was short and the stern higher than the bow, the vessel began to rotate slowly counterclockwise. That complicated the task of coming alongside for the warship's captain.

"Toss us a line," he shouted. When Captain Aran ignored him he added, "Toss me a line or the Sister take me if I don't pull your rails off with a grappling iron!"

"Playing navy!" Aran sneered, but he stepped to the rail beside Garric and lifted the coil of one-inch docking hawser there. He threw it with a sidearm motion that spun the coil open as it flew through the air. The warship's captain caught the last of the coil with equal skill and took a turn around a jibsail bitt, binding the vessels as the oarsmen eased them the last of the way together.

The sheep in the merchantman's hold blatted. They'd been generally docile during the voyage, but the vessel's present nervous pitching would make a veteran sailor queasy. Garric thought of going below, but there wasn't much he could do to help their discomfort. Even with the hatch open the hold was dimly lit and the sheep were packed more tightly together than the warship's oarsmen. There wasn't any good reason to subject himself to that.

The warship carried three men in addition to the rowers. The military officer who'd hailed the merchantman wore a brass helmet and brass cuirass which mimicked a demigod's muscles. The fellow—more likely his servant—must polish the metal every morning to keep it so bright in the salt air.

The second soldier wore an iron helmet and a coat of mail. He looked glum, as he had every right to do. The armor must be terribly uncomfortable in the sunlight. Besides, the man probably realized as Garric did that the weight of the iron would carry him straight to the bottom of the sea if he managed to fall in.

Both men carried swords, and the line soldier had a spear besides. The weapons were merely for show: Aran's eight-man crew could easily have tossed both soldiers over the side and gone about their business if that had been the only constraint. It was the ram that provided the warship with its real authority.

The vessels' prows touched, the merchantman's starboard to the warship's port side. Even at the bow the merchantman was three feet higher than the other. The officer grimaced with distaste, but he and his subordinate clambered up without having to ask help from sailors who weren't going to volunteer it. They must have gotten plenty of experience in the recent past.

Garric's eyes were on the third member of the boarding party, a scrawny old man in deliberately outlandish costume. Instead of a tunic, he wore pinned at the throat a cape made from the skins of dozens of different wild birds and animals. He carried a staff carven intricately from wood so dark that it was almost black.

As soon as the fellow scrambled over the merchantman's rail he began to hop on one foot while snarling and gesturing at the sky. His staff had a knob on one end and a point on the other.

"Playacting," Tenoctris muttered with disdain. "The times being what they are, he has more power than he ever dreamed was possible. Unfortunately he's still a hedge wizard with no more understanding than he had when he was hunting for lost brooches and mixing love charms in some crossroads village."

Garric had brought out his weapons when the warship hailed them, but he hadn't strung the bow and the sword was still within the oilcloth wrapper where he'd packed it for the sea voyage. He was tense. He knew that he could hand the problems over to King Carus simply by grasping the sword hilt, but that was the wrong response here. Besides, Garric or-Reise would never be completely out of his depth in a place where sheep bleated nearby.

"Nasdir," the officer snapped to the wizard. "Quit jumping around and get to work."

The wizard raised his chin in an attempt to look imperious. His drooping mustache was white, though the sparse hair on his scalp was still black. "You don't understand my art," he said.

"I understand that the quicker we find this Benlo, the quicker we can leave a spit of rock that's baking when it's not wet," the officer said. "Get to work!"

"*And* leave off wondering whether what comes over the horizon next'll be a storm or couple hundred Sandrakkan troops to cut our throats," the line soldier said. He glared at Nasdir as if deciding where he'd stick his spear if the wizard gave him the slightest excuse. The warship's base off the shore of the duke's domains might not be quite as bad as the soldiers implied, but it was obviously bad enough that tempers had begun to fray during the time this search operation had gone on.

"You're not the duke's customs inspectors?" Captain Aran said. He shaved his black hair short, but he had a great bush of a beard that bristled as he considered the situation. "Just who are you then, you Sister-loving rats?"

"We're the representatives of your king," the officer said coldly. "We're looking for a man, Benlo bor-Benliman; and I'll tell you right now that if he's aboard your vessel you'll save yourself trouble and maybe worse to hand him over at once."

Liane stood a little straighter; her lips curled in a dismissive sneer. Garric couldn't imagine that anyone looking at the girl wouldn't realize that she was of noble birth. Mostly people didn't look, though. They saw and heard what they expected, and nobody expected a young noblewoman to be traveling from Carcosa to Erdin on a freighter full of sheep.

Aran grunted. "You're seeing everybody aboard," he said. "None of us is named Benlo as best I know, but if you see him you go ahead and take him off. And take yourselves off, so an honest man can get on with his business!"

"Let's see your palms," the officer said, tapping the back of Aran's right hand with his paired index and middle finger.

"And you two as well," he added, gesturing toward the pair of middle-aged sailors who'd taken in the foresail. Neither they nor their captain looked anything like Benlo, but they were close to the right age. The others were too young, except for the helmsman with brown skin, spiky hair, and no tongue.

The officer glanced at the three men's palms. Ropes and oarlooms give a sailor calluses like those of no other profession; a nobleman like Benlo couldn't possibly hope to pass for a seaman if his hands were examined.

"Now," Aran said, "do you want me to show you my bum too, or can I maybe raise sail with a prayer of making the tide?"

"Not yet," the officer snapped. He looked around to find the wizard; Nasdir squatted on the other side of the mainmast with several sailors staring intently at him. He'd drawn a six-pointed star on the deck planks with the tip of his hardwood staff.

The warship's captain slacked the line so that the vessels no longer rubbed in the swell. Four oarsmen kept up a slow stroke to hold the ships' relative positions.

The officer looked at Garric with narrowing eyes. "And what have you got there, boyo?" he demanded, pointing to the oilskin bundle. "Looks like a sword to me."

"It's a sword," Garric said, deliberately thickening his voice into the accent of the most rural of his neighbors in the borough. "And a bow, too, if you're as blind as you're daft and you can't see for yourself. And down below there's fifty sheep, the cargo I'm taking to Sandrakkan for Master Hakar or-Mulin."

He turned and spit over the side. With the wind favoring it, the gobbet splashed not far from the warship's oarblades. Sullen disrespect was the natural reaction of a peasant being troubled by authority, and it also served to hide Garric's fear.

"I don't guess any of the sheep're named Benlo," he continued, "but you'd better ask them."

Captain Aran guffawed and pounded Garric on the back. "Yeah, you do that, soldier boy!" he said. "Maybe you can find some recruits down in the hold, too. Baaaa! Baaaa!"

The officer flushed but he wasn't fool enough to start trouble he was sure to lose personally, even if the merchantman's crew came out of it badly as well. The line soldier grinned, though his face stiffened when his superior glanced around.

The wizard stood; he began a shuffling dance around his hexagram. Garric stepped back so that he had a better view of the proceedings. Everyone else aboard was also watching Nasdir.

"*Salbathbal authgerotabal basuthateo!*" Nasdir shouted. At every word he rapped the staff's black tip against the deck. Garric noticed that the wizard hadn't written the words around the hexagram, only marked a dimple between each pair of points. He wondered if Nasdir could read the Old Script. Was he literate at all?

"*Aleo sambethor amuekarptir!*" cried Nasdir, his motley cape flapping as he pranced. He was naked beneath it.

Tenoctris stared at the peak of the merchantman's foremast with the intensity of a judge passing sentence. Her face was set. Did she disapprove of Nasdir's technique or was there something more to her concentration?

"Benlo bor-Benliman *erchonsoi razaabua*!" Nasdir said, stabbing his staff down into the center of the hexagram. The two sailors nearest him gasped and jumped back, hiding their thumbs in their fists in a gesture to turn away evil.

A wraith resembling light on dustmotes rotated twinkling up from the hexagram. Its color shifted between red and blue, like the shimmering of a cat's-eye gem.

The wraith was a pale image of Benlo. It slowly raised its right arm, pointing toward the deckhouse which held the two passenger cabins.

"We've got him!" the officer cried. He drew his sword. "By the Lady we've got him at last!"

The warship's crew could hear the shouts but they were too low in the water to see what was happening on the merchantman's deck. The drummer put his right foot on the stern rail and bobbed up for a better view. His narrow vessel rocked alarmingly; the captain turned and shouted angrily.

Liane was as still as a winter sunrise. Tenoctris kept her back to the wraith but her lips moved silently. Garric thought he saw the hint of a smile on them.

The two doors of the deckhouse faced the bow. The wraith was pointing at the one on the right where Garric slept. The common soldier moved to it carefully. He held his spear waist-high at the balance, cocked back to thrust if anyone rushed through the doorway.

He jerked the door open. Red and blue sparks swirled in the small cabin, a combination Garric knew meant that Nasdir couldn't discriminate among the forces he put into motion.

"Benlo bor-Benliman!" the wizard repeated. *"Erchonsoi razaabua!"*

There was a loud crack. The lid of the burial jar sharing Garric's cabin rose. Part of the rim split and lifted also, gripped by the pitch seal.

Benlo's nude corpse stood up slowly. The torn body cavity had been sewn with coarse twine. The perfume of aromatic spices mixed with but could not hide the stench of rotting flesh.

The soldier bellowed, turned, and ran straight into the mainmast. He bounced back with a clang. His spear clattered to one side of the mast; his helmet fell off and landed behind him. He got up again and staggered off àt an angle, still blind with fear.

Nasdir shrieked like a hog being gelded and crossed his arms in front of his face, still holding the heavy black staff. The officer backed into him; both men fell in a tangle of limbs and screaming terror.

The soldier started to throw himself over the rail. Liane caught the man's left hand in both of hers and dragged him sideways so that his elbow crooked over the line tethering the vessels together. The warship's captain was shouting questions, and the oarsmen, relaxed a moment before, settled into place on their benches to grip the oarlooms.

Sparks of blue and red light gouted from the open doorway like the last flare of a dying fire, then vanished to normal sunlight. Benlo's corpse sank back into the burial jar; one arm still dangled over the broken rim.

Nasdir and the officer scrambled to the railing on all fours. Drenching in the sea awakened the soldier at least to some degree of function: he'd slid into the belly of the line and was now climbing hand over hand to reach the warship's side.

The officer grabbed the line, shoving the wizard aside, and realized that he was still holding his sword. He dropped the weapon into the sea to get it out of his way. The ivory hilt and the gold inlays on the blade's ricasso gleamed for some while as the weapon sank through the clear water.

Nasdir rose screaming and slashed the air with his staff. Liane ducked from a blow that would have broken bones.

Garric felt the same revulsion he'd known the night he found a rat lapping the blood of the pigeon whose throat it had gnawed out. He stepped forward.

"*Watch*—" Liane called.

Garric raised his open left hand. The staff whistled into it with a smack. The textured heartwood had a greasy feel in Garric's grip. His palm stung, but he'd come by his calluses through hard work; pain was nothing new to him. He tossed the staff over the port rail as his right hand closed on the wizard's throat.

Nasdir bleated for an instant. Garric lifted him, caught one of his thrashing legs—spindly things with less muscle than an honest man's arms—and hurled the wizard so far that he landed among the shafts of the warship's extended oars.

The old man managed to hang on to an oar long enough for a sailor to pull him aboard. Garric was glad of that, but he hadn't worried much when he threw Nasdir over the side. He bent over and supported his body on the railing, breathing deeply.

Most of the merchantman's crew had backed into the bow, but the helmsman stared at his fellows in voiceless wonder. From his position on the roof of the deckhouse he'd only seen Nasdir's wraith. The following general terror puzzled him.

The warship's captain and the dripping military officer shouted into one another's faces. Tenoctris hadn't moved since the boarding party arrived; now she extended her right hand toward the warship. Blue fire as dense and pure as the heart of a sapphire quivered above her index finger.

The military officer flung himself down in the narrow aisle. The captain shouted a hoarse command. The oarsmen began to stroke, raggedly until the drummer took up the beat and brought them into rhythm.

The little vessel drew away at nearly the speed of a man running. Tenoctris lowered her arm, looking worn but still smiling.

"Sister take you all!" Captain Aran said to her in a voice like that of a wounded bear.

He pointed to the cabin. "*That* thing goes over the side now!" he added. "And you can count yourself lucky if I don't decide to do the same with the lot of you."

"No!" Liane said. "He's my father!"

Aran stepped toward the deckhouse. Four of his men followed him.

"No," said Garric. He knew what would happen if he snatched his sword from its oilskin wrapper. Instead he picked up the spear the soldier had lost when he collided with the mast. "No, you're going to land us and our belongings in Erdin as you contracted, so in a couple hours we none of us have to see the others ever again in our lives."

Aran gestured his men to either side. He pulled a hardwood belaying pin from its socket on the port railing.

Garric lifted the spear and spun it on the fingers of his right hand. The spear was sturdy but still slimmer than a quarterstaff. Garric wasn't as skillful as Cashel, but he could make this lighter weapon dance.

"Set your sails, Captain!" Garric shouted. "Or shall I call my friend out of the cabin to help me?"

Tenoctris made a minuscule gesture. Garric didn't know for sure what happened behind him, but Aran dropped the belaying pin as though he'd burned his fingers on it. The sailors stumbled back.

"Set your sails," Garric repeated, this time a plea rather than a challenge. He whirled the spear over his head; needs must he could give a good account of himself with it, though he didn't imagine he could stop the ship's whole crew if they rushed him.

Aran held his ground. He pointed past Garric. "You close that door," he said. "Then we'll go about our business. And by the Shepherd! you'll never set foot on this deck again once you leave it."

"Yes," said Liane as she walked into the cabin with her father's corpse. "That's what we'll do."

She slammed the door behind her. Sailors jumped to the mainspar's lifting tackle before Aran could even give the order. They'd accepted that the only way they'd be free of Benlo was to land him on shore.

Garric planted the spearbutt on the deck and leaned his weight onto it, utterly exhausted. An ewe bleated plaintively from belowdecks.

Garric felt just the same way.

14

Lightning strobed, followed by a monstrous triple crash of thunder as Sharina loosed the mainfall. The boat's sodden leather sail dropped despite the wind's snatching grip. Sharina's right arm ached and she'd been feverish for the past three days of storm, ever since she'd put her hand on the stinging tentacles of a jellyfish that came over the side on the spume of a wave. Despite her dizziness, neither she nor the hermit could imagine trusting Asera or Meder with anything to do with the vessel.

The surf roared around them, displaying fangs of foam in the blue-white glare of lightning. The storm tried to swing the skin boat broadside, but Nonnus dug in his steering oar. Though the vessel shimmied, it drove high up on the northern shore of Sandrakkan safely on its double keel. Without the hermit's skill they'd have overset and very possibly drowned beneath grinding tons of whalebone and hide.

The wave receded. The boat toppled slowly onto its starboard side. Because the Floating Folk never came ashore they didn't build their vessels with wear strakes along the sides as bumpers, but the sandy beach was no direct threat to the boat's hull.

Sharina let the tipping motion spill her out onto the ground. She hunched on all fours, digging her fingers into the sand. She'd have prayed never to leave dry land again except that even after the ordeal of the past weeks she didn't want to spend the rest of her life on Sandrakkan—

And because being around Nonnus had made her unwilling to call on the gods lightly.

The hermit had jumped from the catcher boat while the incoming wave still foamed. He grabbed the bow rope— hemp cordage he'd brought from the trireme, not the stiff leather strap the Folk had used before the islanders appropriated the vessel—and trotted to one of the line of pilings at the head of the beach. A score of plank-built fishing dories were already drawn up on shore, overturned to keep the slashing rain from filling them.

Lightning pulsed for twenty seconds behind the cloudbanks, illuminating both sky and land. Sharina got to her feet. She wanted to help Nonnus, but just now standing upright was as much as she could handle.

"Why, this is Gonalia!" Meder said enthusiastically. "Gonalia Bay! I recognize the castle there on the headland."

He paused as thunder rolled, shaking the dark land beneath. In a much different tone he said, "There's a light in the castle. Who would be there? It's not a place to visit at night."

"What do you mean?" Asera demanded. She was fully the procurator again, commanding in voice and demeanor. She shook out her robe. She might better have wrung it. The fabric was so wet that it dripped during the present lull in the rain.

Nonnus was coming back. Meder watched the hermit and lowered his voice as he said, "A wizard built the castle a thousand years ago. He left no account of his activities but others did, and the stories weren't the sort to draw others here. The whole region was unpopulated for centuries after he died."

"Wizards!" Asera said, the word a curse and a hissing reminder of the lightning of moments before.

The hermit joined them. He laid three fingertips against Sharina's forehead. His touch was cold; she'd known she was running a fever but hadn't realized it was this serious.

"You need to get inside," he said. "Can you walk?"

"We'll all get inside," the procurator said crisply. Even a renewed spatter of rain did nothing to quench her newly recovered sense of authority. "If this is Gonalia—"

"Yes," Nonnus said.

Asera frowned at the interruption. "Then there'll be a coach south to Erdin. We'll buy passage on a ship there."

Her eyes swept the group, then settled on Nonnus. Distant lightning turned her pupils into balls of blue glass.

"And hold your tongues!" she ordered. "I'll travel as a shipwrecked Ornifal noble with you as my servants. I have enough money for immediate needs and I'll be able to arrange credit in Erdin. If word gets out that I'm an emissary for the king, though, it's our lives. Do you understand?"

Sharina wanted to slap her. The thought of the way everybody in Barca's Hamlet had felt honored by the procurator's presence now turned her stomach.

Nonnus smiled faintly. "Yes, mistress," he said. "I understand life and death."

He gestured with the butt of his javelin toward the wooden houses on the corniche above the beach; lights showed through the chinks of shutters but no one was out at night in this weather. "Go on to the inn. I'll follow you shortly."

The procurator frowned, sniffed, and took the small bag of her belongings from the vessel. Sharina thought she'd been about to tell the hermit to carry her luggage, but she wasn't quite such a fool.

Meder already had his satchel. He carried the ivory athame thrust beneath his sash as if a weapon. Sharina looked at him, then said to Nonnus, "I'll stay with you."

"No, child, you won't," he said, touching her cheek with his fingers. "You're too sick. But I'll thank the Lady for you also in my prayers."

Asera trudged toward the wooden staircase to the corniche. Meder looked at Sharina, then closed his mouth without speaking and went off with the procurator.

Sharina squeezed Nonnus' hand and followed them, carrying her own bundle. The rain started again. Its drops chilled her soul without seeming to cool her hot flesh.

Meder muttered to the procurator at the top of the stairs;

they paused for Sharina. Lightning shimmered on wet wood and the nobles' rain-streaked faces.

"The Pewleman served us well, I'll grant that," Asera said to Sharina as she took the last step. "But he'd best recollect his position now that we've returned to civilization. If you're his friend, you'll see that he heeds my warning."

"He did nothing for *you*, mistress," Sharina said. The inn was on the other side of the street. She continued walking as she spoke because she wasn't sure she'd be able to move again if she stopped after climbing the stairs. "And since we're giving warnings—if anything happens to Nonnus, you'll learn how good a friend of his I am."

She didn't suppose she'd have said that if it weren't for the fever. That was all right. It was the truth and they needed to know it.

The road was cobblestone, slick and cold and hard against Sharina's unfamiliar feet. Her calluses didn't cushion the shock. The nobles showed no signs of discomfort; Meder wore boots but the procurator's thin-soled slippers shouldn't have been much help.

Life in the palace would be that way in all things. Sharina might be Count Niard's daughter and of royal blood—she hadn't really let herself think about that—but she didn't know anything about the life she'd be expected to live in Valles. Every aspect of it would pound her, bruise her, just as these civilized cobblestones were doing to her feet. . . .

Asera struggled for a moment with the inn's front door; she raised the latch easily enough, but the weight of braced timber was a surprise. She probably had servants to open doors for her.

Meder bowed Sharina into the common room ahead of him. He'd have taken her bundle of personal effects if she'd let him. Both nobles had changed as a result of their return to civilization. While Asera had become brusquely commanding, the wizard had changed from a sullen youth into a polished gentleman attending a lady.

On balance Sharina thought she preferred the sullen youth.

In that frame of mind Meder had kept as far away from her as possible.

The air of the common room was dank. The innkeeper rose from one side of the chimney alcove; on the opposite seat the sole guest present merely turned his head and gave the newcomers a morose glance. The fire was tiny, dwarfed by the massive limestone hearth.

"You're the host?" Asera said. "Well, start acting like one, then! I'll want food and a hot bath besides. Do you have a wine heater?"

The innkeeper looked astounded. The front door blew open: Meder hadn't latched it properly behind him. Sharina checked to be sure that Nonnus hadn't followed them after all, then slammed it shut herself.

"Well I . . ." the innkeeper said. Three guests coming out of the storm were as surprising as a lightning bolt. "I can mull some, I suppose."

He looked up the staircase. "Enzi! Come down here! Pao! Pao! Where are you, boy?"

The innkeeper thrust a poker into the fire, looked at Asera's face, and hurriedly set three more billets of split wood on.

Sharina dropped onto one of the bench seats built out from the walls of the common room. Her surroundings shimmered in a pastel haze. Her right arm no longer ached but she thought she heard it buzzing. She opened and closed the fingers; they moved normally.

A woman who coiled her hair in twin braids on top of her head looked over the upstairs railing, took in the guests' aristocratic features, and bustled down without snarling the prepared response to her husband's summons. A gangling boy ran into the room from a back corridor.

Asera seated herself on the hearth bench the innkeeper had vacated. She leaned forward and warmed her hands over the growing fire.

Meder glanced at the man on the other seat as if considering ordering him to get up. Sharina suspected the only question was whether the fellow simply refused to move or whether he knocked the wizard down with the sturdy stick he held between his knees. Meder apparently came to the same conclusion; he sat beside Sharina instead.

The innkeeper walked the boy to the door, talking earnestly to him in a voice too low to be overheard. The boy's eyes widened. The innkeeper sent him out the door and slammed it shut again behind him.

"Get wine, woman," he said to his wife. "Our guests want mulled wine to warm them!"

She scurried to the bar and set a copper pail under a small cask on the wall rack. With an oily expression the innkeeper tented his fingers and turned to Asera. "Mistress?" he said. "May I ask how long you'll be staying?"

"No longer than the first coach leaves for Erdin," Asera said. "When will that be?"

"Ah," the innkeeper said. Instead of answering he took the pail of wine from his wife and carried it over to the hearth. "How did mistress come to arrive here, if I may ask?"

"You may get the skin flayed off your back if you don't keep to your own affairs!" Asera said. "Are you worried about your pay? Don't be!"

She took a coin from her purse and rapped it on the mantel; the gold rang musically. "Besides seats in the coach for me and my household, I'll need to replace some of the wardrobe lost when I was shipwrecked. Now, when *is* the next coach?"

"The boy should be back with that information shortly," the innkeeper said. "Let me fix your wine."

He took the poker from the fire, knocked ash from the glowing metal, and thrust it into the pail. The smell of hot wine and spices filled the common room, reminding Sharina of winter evenings at home.

She thought about the past. For the first time she really understood that she'd never be able to go home, at least not back to the home she'd known in the past. She was a pawn in the hands of strangers who'd never leave her alone, who'd hound her if she tried to return.

Sharina closed her eyes. She felt tears on her cheeks but

she didn't care. Voices swirled about her; the innkeeper talked about the weather and making up beds. Someone offered Sharina wine; she took the pottery mug and held it between her palms. She didn't want to drink, but the warm clay felt good in her hands.

Horses clattered up to the front door. Their shod hooves had a nasty, unfamiliar ring on the cobblestones. Horse*men*, not a coach; there was no sound of iron tires accompanying the hooves.

The door banged back. Sharina opened her eyes. Six armored soldiers crashed into the room with swords drawn. Over their mail shirts they wore white linen tabards with a black horsehead on the right breast. Their shouting presence filled the room.

Meder jumped to his feet. A soldier pushed him back onto the bench; another soldier put his sword to the wizard's throat and snarled, ''*Don't* move or we'll see if that's sawdust you're stuffed with!''

Asera cried out in wordless anger. Sharina couldn't see her through the press of armored men.

Sharina raised the mug to her lips and sipped her wine. A soldier looked at her; he frowned but said nothing.

The innkeeper's wife had put too much nutmeg and not enough cinnamon in the wine, but it was a good vintage. Sharina didn't drink wine often, but her father had seen to it that she and Garric had an understanding of the subject.

Sights and sounds were as clear to her as the air of a frozen morning. The fever had burned all the dross out of her mind, leaving her wits sharper than ever before.

An officer entered; he wore a muscled cuirass and a bronze helmet with a trailing horsehair plume instead of the mail shirt and iron pot of the common soldiers. He didn't have a tabard but he wore a separate linen sleeve tied to hooks on his breastplate; there was a black horsehead at the shoulder.

Two soldiers straightened, keeping their grip on Asera between them. Another soldier had his sword half-raised to threaten the fellow in the other chimney seat, but the traveler's lifted cudgel made that a standoff for the moment.

"Callin!" Asera said to the officer. "What are you doing wearing Sandrakkan colors? Did the queen decide you were too slimy for even her to stomach?"

Callin laughed merrily. He swept off his helmet and bowed to the procurator.

"Mistress Asera," he said, "I can't *tell* you how pleased I am that the king chose you for his agent and that I was here to greet you. I haven't forgotten your interference in the matter of the chief steward's wife, you see."

Callin was a tall man with handsome features and shoulder-length hair as blond as Sharina's own. His eyes were blue; they glittered the way a snake's do. He swept them around the room before returning to the man in the chimney alcove.

"Not him, master," the innkeeper said hurriedly. "Master Eskal inspects the earl's properties in this district and to the west. I know him well."

Callin nodded and gestured away the soldier fronting Eskal. He turned his attention to Sharina and Meder. The queen's agent was supple and shone with a lacquered perfection despite having ridden here through the rain.

Sharina sipped her mulled wine. She thought of the hatchet in her belt, thought of Nonnus still outside; and waited.

"Does the earl know that you're meddling in his domains?" Asera said to Callin's back. "What do you suppose he'll do to this inn and everyone in Gonalia when he learns they've been aiding you?"

Callin chuckled. He fingered the horsehead on his sleeve. "Oh, the earl and my mistress are very good friends, Asera," he said. "I'm acting for both of them in this matter, and these men—"

He patted the cheek guard of the soldier beside him; the man looked as though he'd swallowed something unpleasant.

"—are the earl's own troops, right enough. Aren't you, boys?"

The soldiers grunted. Sharina had seen poisonous snakes

she liked better than she did Callin; but as did those snakes, the queen's agent had a glittering beauty.

He looked at Meder and all the humor left his face. "Yes," Callin said, "I know you too, don't I, Meder bor Mederman?"

He took the ivory athame from the wizard's sash, looked at it with distaste, and tossed it accurately into the center of the fire with only a glance to judge distance and angle. He smiled again.

"Master Meder," he said. "My directions from the queen are to take all of you alive if possible. You're believed to have valuable information. If you make a sound that I imagine could be charm or curse, however, I'll have your tongue torn out."

Callin smiled more broadly. "No, I misspoke," he said. "I'll tear your tongue out myself."

The soldier still held Meder against the wall. Callin chucked the wizard under the chin with two fingers.

"Wizards are quite all right in their proper place," he said pleasantly to the room at large. "There was doubtless wizardry behind the decision to send me to this godforsaken place to await the king's agent. But if some little toad of a wizard tries to get in my way, well, he won't like the place I think proper to put him in."

Callin stood in front of Sharina and put his hands on his waist. "And just who have we here, mistress?" he said.

The mug was empty. Sharina set it on the bench beside her. "I'm Sharina os-Reise from Barca's Hamlet on Haft," she said, looking up at the tall, smiling man. "Mistress Asera engaged me as her maid."

"Oh, I think you're rather more than that, my dear," Callin said. "More even than the prettiest little girl I've ever seen on Sandrakkan, I rather think."

He drew the hand axe from the loops of her shoulder belt and looked at it critically. There was rust on the blade because she hadn't wiped it down since coming out of the rain and spray, but the steel was honed to a working edge without nicks or dull spots.

"We were shipwrecked," Sharina said simply.

Callin's smile wavered into one of real appraisal. "Well, we'll see to it that you're not shipwrecked again," he said. He looked around and flipped the hand axe into the molding above the bar. The edge banged a finger's breadth deep in the wood. The innkeeper's wife bleated in fear, then stuffed the hem of her apron in her mouth with both hands.

"Let's go," Callin said to his men in a hard voice. "I'll take care of Mistress Sharina here. Two of you tie the others' hands to the tail of your horses."

He grinned at the procurator. "If I'm feeling kindly, Asera my dear, I'll walk you back to the castle. But I warn you, my mount has a very comfortable trot."

Callin started to offer his arm to Sharina. The outside door opened. Soldiers jerked around. Callin drew his sword so swiftly that the blade sang against the bronze lips of his scabbard. The layered steel shimmered in a pattern like the ripples of a running stream.

Nonnus walked into the common room. He carried his javelin point-forward over his left shoulder with his bindle hanging behind him.

A soldier tried to grab him by the throat. Nonnus kicked the man in the groin and shoved him gasping aside. Nobody else moved for a moment.

"And who are you, my man?" Callin asked. Sharina picked up the mug. It was heavy enough to be useful. . . .

"I'm Nonnus son of Bran, son of Pewle," the hermit said in a voice from deep in his throat. "And who are *you*, buddy, besides the man who's going to be looking at his guts on the floor if he doesn't point that sword someplace else?"

"No!" Callin said to one of his soldiers. Sharina hadn't seen the man tense to move, but Nonnus nodded to the officer with a wolfish grin.

"What are you doing here, Master Nonnus?" Callin asked.

He didn't move his sword, but the situation no longer teetered quite on the edge of a bloody abyss.

"I'm looking for Waley the Merchant," Nonnus said. He looked around the common room with cold, angry eyes whose expression didn't change wherever they lighted. "Any of you lot know where he lives?"

Callin raised an eyebrow to the innkeeper. "Waley's been dead these ten years past," the innkeeper said in a nervous voice. "His stepson Arduk handles what sealskin business comes through here nowadays. He's the ostler, three doors down on this side of the street."

"Right," Nonnus said, nodding. "I'll leave you lot to your fun, then."

He looked at Callin. Callin relaxed minutely and gave Nonnus a curt nod.

The hermit slammed the door shut behind him. Callin sheathed his sword, and Sharina put down the mug.

"Let's go," Callin repeated, his face still showing the strain of the past few moments. Whatever else the young courtier had done, he'd met Pewlemen before.

"Mistress—" He extended his arm to Sharina. "—you'll ride on my saddle ahead of me. I regret I didn't think to bring an extra horse for you."

Sharina ignored the arm as she stood and walked to the door. Every sight and sound was crystalline, and she moved as though crystal knives surrounded her.

15

The captain fanned himself with his cap, the most wind anybody on the open-decked trading yawl had felt all day. He spat over the stern rail, a recognized custom for summoning a breeze. His lips and those of his four crewmen were stiff with puckering to spit, all for nothing.

"If we don't get a breeze come morning," the captain said, "it's out with the sweeps. There's no help for it."

"It's mighty hot," the wizened mate said, looking toward the northern horizon. Erdin was there, a good day's sail distant. An eternity distant if they didn't get a wind.

The yawl was loaded with oranges from the island of Shengy in the southern arc. Citrus fruit brought a good price in Erdin. The captain had decided to risk being becalmed in the center of the Inner Sea rather than take the slow but safe voyage around the western periphery—Shengy, Cordin, Haft, and finally Sandrakkan across the long passage. They'd had a steady south wind for the whole trip—until now, when they should have been making the final run for port.

The captain tried to spit again. His mouth was too dry. The three ordinary sailors watched him glumly. "Tomorrow, the sweeps," he croaked. "Unless there's a wind."

The mate stood, then scrambled like the monkey he resembled to the top of the short, forward-slanting mast. He wrapped his legs around the pole and stared north, shading his eyes with his paired hands. "On the horizon!" he called. "There's something moving."

The captain hopped onto the rail and walked along it until he could see past the limp triangle of the lateen sail. There *was* something moving.

"It's a man on a raft," the mate said. "Sister swallow me down but it looks to be a man on a raft!"

"How's he moving, then?" asked the helmsman, standing also. The yawl rocked gently as her crew's weight shifted.

The thing, whatever it was, disappeared; either over the northern horizon or under the oil-smooth surface of the sea. The yawl was alone again except for the pair of gulls circling near the zenith of the sky.

"No," said the captain. He shivered as he stepped down from the rail. "It was a whale that spouted. That's what looked like a man."

The mate looked at him, then lowered himself to the deck again in three long arm-over-arm snatches at the mainstay. He said nothing.

"I feel a wind," the captain said, as much a prayer as an announcement to his crew. He turned his head slightly; the long hairs growing from the upper curve of his ear tingled.

"I feel a wind!" he repeated, this time with pleased assurance. "On the starboard quarter. Get the mast around and we'll be in Erdin by midday!"

He grabbed one of the lines himself, glad not only for the wind but because it let him forget what he thought he'd seen. The captain's eyes were better than those of any other man he knew, but the distance had been too great for any certainty.

The object had looked very like a plump man in a burial sheet, seated on a simple raft with nothing else aboard it. A blue haze surrounded the thing; and it moved. There could be no question but that it moved.

No question either that the captain hoped he'd never see the thing again.

16

Garric had never seen any place as flat as Erdin. The sea on a calm day had more hills than did this city, where the natural elevation changed less than three feet in a block.

Even the buildings were limited to two or three stories—a contrast from Carcosa, where the tenements rose five or even six rickety levels above the ground. Garric supposed Erdin's soil wasn't firm enough to support the weight of tall buildings.

Tenoctris looked around with interest as she, Garric, and Liane followed the two-man handcart along the broad brick street. Erdin was a growing city, not a backwater. In Carcosa there was more past than present and little hope for a future.

"In my day . . ." Tenoctris said. She smiled at the contrast between the millennium she meant by the words and the decades that most old women would be indicating. "In my day the Earl of Sandrakkan didn't really rule much more than bowshot from his castle on the eastern tip of the island. More of a bandit chief than a major ruler. And I never heard of Erdin."

"Stancon the Fourth founded the city in place of the old port of Zabir ten miles up the coast," Liane said primly. In one sense all nobles in the Isles were of a single class, no matter where they were born, but a girl from Sandrakkan would have heard more than her share of slights directed at her homeland in school on Ornifal. "That was a full three hundred years ago."

Garric—Garric's mind, not Garric's self—remembered a swampy bottom extending to either side of the River Erd, brown with sediment brought halfway across the island. The only similarity between that landscape and the solid, bustling city of Erdin was that both were flat.

"Did, ah, Stancon put the city here because it was easier to defend a marsh?" Garric asked. He looked at Liane, uncertain of how much of the question that popped into his mind would have been there without his dream-guest, Carus.

Liane bridled, then broke into a laugh of embarrassment. "Yes he did," she said. "Pirates from Ornifal were raiding the south coast every spring. He built a new city with no landing places nearby except for on the river, and that he could close with a chain. I shouldn't be defensive, I know."

"All I could really say about the earl of my day," Tenoctris said, "is that he didn't have a library good enough to draw me to his castle. Yole *did* have a fine library and it's been under the sea the past thousand years. On the evidence, the Earl of Sandrakkan's choice was the wiser one."

The two laborers plodded on, one pulling and the other pushing the handcart with Benlo's body. Garric had sealed the lid of the burial jar back in place with hot pitch. The crack was above the jar's ears so they could still be used to handle the weight. Traffic was thick even now that they'd left the commercial district around the harbor. Apartment blocks had given way to single-family dwellings. They were built row-house fashion, but each had its walled pool or garden between the house and the street.

It amazed Garric to see heavy wagons drawn by only a pair of horses or mules. Erdin was flat, and the hard paving meant that wheels didn't sink into the road. Two horses could haul loads that would require six or eight oxen back home.

They'd crossed three canals on their way east from the harbor. Flat-bottomed barges plied the black water, drawn by lines of boatmen singing dismal songs to synchronize their pace. The barges were bigger than any ship to land in Barca's Hamlet before the trireme's arrival.

"My father never cared what people thought of Erdin or Sandrakkan," Liane said in explanation; almost in apology. "I don't know why I do."

"Benlo thought of himself as a citizen of the whole Isles?" Garric asked. It was his question, not that of King Carus, but it wouldn't have occurred to him except for his dream visits with the last ruler of the united Isles. It was all right to come from Barca's Hamlet, from Haft, from anywhere, and to be proud of your home; but if that made you want to knock in the head of anybody from the next borough or next hamlet—

That was wrong. That led to kings who ruled with a sword in their hands, and who turned to that sword first because so often they'd found there was no other answer.

Liane looked at Garric in mild surprise. He realized that some of his questions weren't those of a Haft peasant, even a very well read Haft peasant. Garric or-Reise wasn't simply a Haft peasant anymore, though he was that too. He'd always be a peasant *also*.

"No," she said, "it wasn't that. My father didn't think of himself as a part of anything. He traveled everywhere in the Isles and I suspect beyond, but it didn't matter any more to him than the sea matters to a fish. He was *in* the world, not of it.''

Her eyes focused on the burial jar ahead of her. The terracotta was waxed on the outside so that it wouldn't absorb rainwater and shatter at the first hard freeze, a coarse piece of workmanship even before Garric repaired it with a black smear of tar.

Liane didn't see the jar or even the man who'd died. Her eyes were on the father who sang of far places when she was a child. A tear dribbled from the corner of her eye; she blotted it without embarrassment.

''I don't think anything ever touched him except my mother,'' she said. ''He was always good to me, Garric, but I think that was because he saw Mother through me.''

Garric cleared his throat. He couldn't think of anything to say.

The street widened still further; the right and left lanes were divided by a line of dwarf cypresses interspersed with round ornamental ponds. Garric tried to imagine the cost of building and maintaining facilities like these. For the first time he was gaining an appreciation for the world of wealth and power in which Liane had been raised.

''Even the public streets are luxurious,'' he said aloud.

Tenoctris looked at him. ''It took three centuries for this city to rise from the swamps,'' she said. ''If the darkness comes again, the swamps can return in three years.''

Garric squeezed the medallion beneath his tunic. He nodded.

A sedan chair passed at a quick pace. The trotting bearers wore thick-soled leather sandals and grunted ''Ho!'' when their right feet struck the pavement. The woman sitting upright under a shade of purple velvet was as perfect as an ivory statue of the Lady, but the image would have had more warmth.

The houses here were very fine. Each stood within its own grounds behind a wall or wrought-iron fence. Liane returned to the present with a look of surprise and called, "Cartmen? Turn here—down this alley."

The man pushing from the back of the cart looked over his shoulder. He and his fellow slowed but continued walking onward through the boulevard's intersection with an alley only twelve feet broad—still wider than most of the thoroughfares Garric had seen in modern Carcosa.

"No, miss," the carter said. "The tradesman's entrance is on the other side. We've made deliveries here before."

"We're not making a delivery," Liane said with a flush of anger on her high cheekbones. "Turn down here if you expect to be paid."

With a shrug of put-upon tolerance the men halted, then swapped ends and turned the handcart up the street they'd just passed. Apparently one always led and the other always followed.

"She'll see," the man at the front said without looking around. Liane's expression could have chipped stone.

A high spiked fence surrounded the grounds, but through the bars Garric could see the house, whose brick walls were weathered to a rusty brown. The sash windows were narrow and glazed with small diamond panes, another sign that the house had been built in a previous century before glassmakers had learned to roll larger plates.

He looked at Liane. "Was this . . ." he asked, and nodded toward the house to complete the question.

"Yes," she said without inflection. "This is where I was born and where I lived until my mother died."

She turned and called to the carters, "Stop here."

"This isn't—" one of the men said. "Say, this is a tomb! What is this we've got here?"

Until the man spoke in a tone of rising anger, Garric hadn't realized that the carters were unaware that they were carrying a corpse. The burial jars of the Carcosa district were as unfamiliar to Erdin citizens as they had been to Garric.

"It's the burden you've been hired to bring here," Liane said, taking an intricate bronze key from a fold of her sash.

"And because you've brought it without superstitious mumbling, I'm going to double your pay as soon as you've placed it inside."

The carters looked at one another. The one in the front shrugged. "Just as you say, miss," he said respectfully.

Garric had assumed that all city people followed the same customs. That was as silly as assuming that everybody on Haft raised sheep. At least he hadn't embarrassed himself in public by saying something.

Somewhere out of time King Carus was laughing. There were worse false assumptions a man could make, and worse results than embarrassment.

The tomb was a low brick building at the back corner of the property, separated from the remainder of the tract by its own fence. Garric supposed bodies couldn't be buried in the ground where the water table was as high as here in Erdin. The ivy that grew on the fence and structure hadn't been trimmed in too long. Rootlets had dug out the mortar and loosened some of the bricks. There were no windows in the front half of the building and only one—small and round—in the rear.

Liane unlocked the gate in the outer fence. There was a paved court in front of the tomb and a stone bench beside the door. The rusty hinges fought her; Garric stepped to her side and pushed, forcing the gate open with a squeal.

Tenoctris was looking through a gap in the ivy toward the house. The overgrown fence almost completely hid the tomb from the main building. That was probably deliberate on the part of the new owners. How much did they know about the man who'd lived in the house before them?

Garric was ready to lend his strength in moving the tomb door as Liane inserted the same key into its lock, but these hinges were bronze and sheltered by the overhanging gable besides. The door swung outward easily for the girl. She stepped aside and said to the carters, "Place the jar as close as you can to the bier against the back wall, please."

She touched the tie-strings of her purse as a reminder to

the men. They muscled the burial jar off the cart and carried it inside without complaint.

The coat of arms carved into the marble keystone of the door arch was a bunch of grapes above a slanting line—a *bend*, other memory whispered—and a human skull below. Liane followed Garric's eyes and said, "Our lands in the west of the island were famous for their wines. I don't know why my ancestor chose the skull."

She laughed with a tinge of bitterness. "The lands still are famous for their wines, I suppose. They're just not ours. Nothing is ours but this tomb."

The carters had placed the burial jar as directed. They left the tomb quickly, sneezing from the dust. Liane took a coin from her purse—silver, as she'd promised. With the men no longer blocking the narrow aisle, Garric was able for the first time to see the building's interior.

There were two sets of brick racks on either side of the tomb. Each could hold four oblong wooden caskets. Most of the places were filled; debris on the dimly lit floor indicated that still more caskets had rotted away with their contents in past years. Garric thought of the dust and held his breath.

There was a single, wider shelf against the back wall. Five-branched candelabra stood at the head and foot of the bronze casket resting there. The candles had burned down to stalactites of wax so long ago that even the odor of their flames had vanished; the holders, though tarnished, were almost certainly silver.

"My mother," Liane said simply. The cartwheels rumbled away as the men returned to their station near the harbor. "He'd want to be close to her. I wish . . ."

Her voice trailed off. In a wooden tone she resumed, "I wish that Mother hadn't died. I wish that my father had died with her. And sometimes I wish I'd never been born, Garric."

He put his hand around the girl's shoulder and held her, keeping his face rigidly toward the back of the tomb while she sobbed. After a time she straightened and blew her nose.

Garric released her but continued to look at the building's interior.

"There aren't any windows here," he said. "There's another room behind this one."

"The groundskeeper's shed is built onto the other side of the tomb," Liane said in a more-or-less normal voice. "It's quite separate."

She cleared her throat and added, "Thank you, Garric. I think we can close up this building and leave now. I don't expect ever to return."

Garric looked at her. She gestured toward the coffins. "Those aren't my mother and father," she said. "It's a shame my father was never able to understand that. I might still have him if he'd seen that dust isn't a real person."

Garric stepped back so that Liane could close the tomb door. Tenoctris said, "Your father must have worked here for many years. He imprinted the bricks and even the soil with his power. I've never seen anything like this except at the site of ancient temples."

Liane closed the door firmly and relocked it. She stepped into the street and waited while Garric pulled the iron gate to.

"We'll find Polew the Banker, my father's contact," she said. "From him we'll find the person who actually hired my father. And then . . ."

And then, Garric thought, *what?* There wasn't an answer to that question, even in Liane's mind.

They started back toward the harbor and Polew's offices. The day was wearing toward evening.

"Your father was a very powerful wizard, Liane," Tenoctris said musingly. "I wonder what he might have accomplished if your mother's death hadn't so warped him. And if he hadn't been killed, of course."

17

A rat startled by the torchlight ran over Sharina's foot. She heard the Outer Sea surging and sighing through the drains cut beneath the dungeons, though she'd have guessed that Callin had already brought his prisoners below sea level.

"Not the most luxurious lodgings for our guests, hey boys?" Callin called cheerfully from the back of the line. "But they're clever people so I'm sure they'll adapt."

Perhaps they *were* beneath the sea. Like the mill in Barca's Hamlet, the castle was Old Kingdom masonry: great stones fitted without mortar. But the castle was also wizard's work, and perhaps a wizard could contrive that water drained upward.

"If I'm not able to deal with you myself, Callin," the procurator said, "then I'll at least have the satisfaction of knowing that the queen will do it for me. She's the only person whom I'd describe as even more treacherous than you!"

Asera's voice had its old authority again. The immensity of sea and storm had beaten her spirit down, but no human enemy would cow her.

Meder was shivering so violently that two of the soldiers half-dragged, half-carried him down the circular stairs and along the corridor of black stone. Callin thought Meder was shamming; Sharina was sure that he wasn't. The young wizard had been exhausted when the guards loosed him from the horse to which he'd been tied, but it was only after Meder entered the lowering castle that he'd begun to shake and stumble.

Sharina didn't like Meder, but she'd had too many proofs to doubt that he was really a powerful wizard. The soul of the man who'd built this castle a thousand years before still imbued its stones. To Meder's receptive mind, it must be as overwhelming as being imprisoned in a drum while a giant pounds it.

"I understand!" Meder cried. He began to laugh. "I really understand!"

The soldier holding the wizard's left arm snarled in disgust and anger. He punched Meder on the side of the head, an awkward blow but a hard one.

Meder went limp for a moment. The soldier on the wizard's right said to his fellow, "Why'd you do that? Do you want to carry him yourself?"

Meder resumed walking, though his eyes were closed and his knees would have buckled if the soldiers let him go. He giggled occasionally.

The low ceiling dripped, and condensate beaded on the twisted pillars in the center of the corridor. The pair of soldiers at the head of the procession held their torches out at waist height; even so the air hissed and steamed with moisture which their flames licked off the stone.

Another torchbearer walked beside Callin. There were candles and lanterns in the living quarters upstairs in the castle; from the glimpse Sharina got as the soldiers led her downward, she realized that Callin had come to Gonalia with the furnishings to create what he thought of as civilized surroundings out of barbarous wilderness. His men used torches here because he knew their flickering light would make the dungeons seem even more wild and terrifying.

They were bad enough as it was. Sharina wondered what the rats ate normally; certainly they found something to keep them healthy. The largest of the rodents must weigh several pounds.

"Quite extensive, aren't they, these dungeons?" Callin said. "The original owner must have been a very interesting man."

He laughed. Like the torches, Callin's banter was intended to break his prisoners' spirits. It wouldn't work with Meder,.

because the castle's aura had driven him mad. It wouldn't work with Asera, because the procurator's pride and hatred for Callin were too strong.

Sharina was determined that she wouldn't break either, but being surrounded by the dripping black stone was like being buried alive. When the soldiers left, they would take all the light with them. . . .

The leading torchbearers halted. They'd reached the end of the corridor. There were cells on all three sides of the terminus.

"Put the boy here," Callin said, kicking the bars of the cell on the right. Like everything else Callin did, "boy" was chosen to demoralize his prisoner; there was truth to the word nonetheless. Though Callin was scarcely thirty himself, he had a worldly sophistication that Meder would never equal.

The barred door was closed. A torchbearer unlocked it with an iron key and pulled it screechingly open. He thrust his torch inside so that the three prisoners could get a good look at their surroundings.

The cell's floor and back wall were seamless, part of the bedrock on which the castle rested. The sidewalls were masonry eighteen inches thick, sawn from the same black basalt as the rest of the castle.

The long bones of a man's forearm hung from a manacle riveted to one wall; a few human teeth lay in the slimy detritus beneath, but the remainder of the skeleton had disappeared. Sharina thought of rodents gnawing at bones. She wondered if the rats waited for prisoners to die before starting to devour them.

Meder looked at Asera with a lopsided grin. "I should have come here sooner," he said, then giggled again. "It's all so simple when you—"

One of the soldiers holding the wizard cursed in disgust. They hurled him into the cell and banged the door closed.

"Put Mistress Asera across the corridor," Callin said. His drawling voice was deliberately nonchalant. "That way she and her wizard can look at each other."

He laughed and went on, "But wait! I forgot that there won't be any light for them to see by! What a pity."

Sharina caught one soldier grimace at his partner as a third man unlocked the indicated cell with the same key. The men didn't like the commander who'd been sent to them from Valles, though that didn't prevent then from carrying out their orders efficiently.

Asera walked into the cell with her head high and a look of cold disdain on her face. Water pooled in the rough oval pattern a man's feet would wear in dense stone over decades of pacing his cell. Eyes glinted from the shallow pool, then vanished in a swirl of ripples.

The guards closed and locked the door behind her. The hinges were stiff. While the stonework could date—doubtless did date—from the Old Kingdom, iron would have rusted away long since in this dank environment. Bone decayed in even less time. Somebody had been using the castle more recently than Meder believed, though it might not have been any time in the past century.

The guard unlocked the cell facing down the long corridor. It was only six feet square; the floor and walls were covered with a gelatinous slime that glimmered pale yellow in the torchlight.

Callin put a hand on Sharina's shoulder. "I'm afraid the third one's for you, my dear," he said. "Unless . . ."

He smiled the way a weasel smiles at a pullet trapped in the henhouse. "You know," he went on, "I'm sure there can be a better outcome for a sweet girl like you. Why don't you come upstairs with me and we can discuss matters while we have a bite to eat?"

Callin set off briskly down the corridor, still holding Sharina. The soldiers, obviously told what to expect, fell into step at once, the torchbearer who'd been in the rear with Callin now led the procession.

"Have a pleasant night, Asera," Callin called over his shoulder. "Perhaps I'll send some food down to you tomorrow."

Sharina kept her back straight and her face set, ignoring the feel of the wet stone beneath her feet. The dungeons smelled of salt and corruption, like a sailor's corpse.

The columns supporting the dungeons' roof seemed to have been cut from the living rock. The flaring torchlight made them appear to writhe in pain.

She wouldn't weep. She wouldn't beg. Nonnus would save her.

They climbed three full rotations of the circular staircase to the hall which in turn led to the apartments Callin had marked out for himself on the castle's ground floor. The walls were the omnipresent basalt, but they'd been covered with tapestries and there were fresh reeds on the floor.

The soldiers lighted oil lamps and tossed their torches onto the massive hearth, igniting the wood already laid there. The wind moaned, but the sky visible through slit windows in one wall was bright with moonlight; the storm had blown over.

"Here, my dear," Callin said, pulling a cushioned bench closer to the fire. "The men will bring a meal in to us. Cold meats, I'm afraid, but I'll try to do better in the future. I didn't know exactly when you'd be arriving, you see."

Two soldiers entered carrying a table already laid with cheese, ham, and bread. A third man carried two bottles of wine in one hand and a pair of glasses in the other. They seemed both competent and willing to act as Callin's stewards; surprising after the sudden violence with which they'd burst into the inn.

Sharina seated herself carefully, facing the fire. The couch sloped; it was intended to be used reclining in the style of the royal court and those aristocrats who aped the royal court. Lora had made sure that her daughter was acquainted with court fashions, but Sharina had no intention of attempting to eat lying down now. For one thing, she knew it would please Callin if she did.

The soldiers set the table near the end of the couch. Callin pulled a second couch onto the opposite side and reclined on his left elbow, looking up at Sharina with his usual mocking grin. He prodded the serving fork into ham and held a slice out to her. "Try a little of this, my dear," he said. "I think you'll like it. It's a pepper cure from my own estates."

"Thank you," Sharina said, but she picked up a wedge of cheese with her fingers and nibbled at it. She was ravenously hungry; it took all her control not to stuff the whole chunk in her mouth and reach for more. "How long have you been waiting here, master?"

Callin chuckled and took a bite of the ham himself. "How we came to meet, my dear," he said, "is a matter for the past and therefore of no importance. What you and I need to consider is your future. You're a very valuable person—to others. It's important that you not neglect your value to yourself."

"I'm a lady's maid," Sharina said. She finished the cheese and reached for one of the large round loaves of bread.

Callin extended a hand to help, then paused when the girl's strong fingers ripped the tough crust without difficulty. He raised an eyebrow and said, "I think we can drop that fiction, my dear. The fact that I was here waiting for you should convince you that I know perfectly well what's going on. Rather better than you do yourself, I'm sure. You're descended from the last great King of the Isles, worthy to be queen yourself. And able to make the right man king."

The soldier with the wine filled both glasses, placing one on the table near either diner. "I hope you won't spurn the wine also," Callin said archly. "It's a vintage I'm quite fond of, though I admit that it's none the better for a sea voyage."

"Thank you," Sharina repeated; she raised the glass and drank. The wine was sweet and very strong. She didn't care for the taste, but the bread was dry and her mouth was extremely dry.

"You see," Callin said, "as things stand at present you're merely a pawn. I'm very much afraid that this is as true if you're in the hands of my mistress the queen as it would be if Asera delivered you to the king as she intended. Neither king nor queen would have any compunction about using you or even disposing of you if it suited their convenience."

There was the faintest hint of irritation in Callin's voice. Sharina took a slice of ham. Her coolness had been having the effect she intended, putting the courtier off-balance although he was in total control of the situation.

"What you need to do is to become a player yourself," Callin said as Sharina chewed deliberately. "Since you have no power of your own, you need to marry the power of a well-connected aristocrat whose family is very nearly as old as yours. I offer myself, of course."

He reached for Sharina's hand as she tore off another piece of bread. She turned the loaf slightly to block him.

A flash of anger turned Callin's expression into something real and unpleasant; it then smoothed into cultured neutrality.

"You needn't be concerned that this arrangement will hinder your personal life," he said in a voice whose edge was just below the surface. "You can have any number and type of lovers you please, as I assure you I will myself."

Sharina looked directly at the courtier for the first time since they'd returned from the dungeons. "I'd think making love to a mirror would be at best uncomfortable," she said, "but I can't imagine you caring about anything else. Or anyone else caring about you."

Callin's face went as blank as a shark's. He caught her left hand; his wrist and fingers had a swordsman's strength. He dragged her toward him. She threw the wine in his face and tried to gouge his eyes out with the glass.

The nearest soldier dropped the bottle and grabbed Sharina's arm. Callin let go and jumped up from the couch, wiping his face with his velvet sleeve. Sharina's couch went over as another soldier seized her left arm.

Callin slapped her. Her head bounced into the shoulder of the man on her right. The soldiers had taken off their armor when they reached the castle, but the impact of hand and bone turned her surroundings into a white blur.

"All right, my fine lady!" Callin shouted. "I wish you all the comfort you deserve in your new quarters!"

Snatching a taper from a wall sconce, Callin strode toward the staircase leading to rats and slime and blackness. The soldiers carried Sharina after him, dragging her feet through the rushes on the floor.

18

The moon had set and it was still an hour short of dawn. The usual morning haze lay over Erdin. The vegetable seller halted his pushcart outside the gatekeeper's wicket.

"Reava baked cherry tarts this morning," he said. He unwrapped the broad mullein leaf from around the pastry the cook had given him when he delivered the day's produce to the kitchen at the back of the house.

"I'd hang around her even if there was nothing but her cooking to keep me warm," the gatekeeper said as the two men divided the tart in their usual fashion. The vegetable seller muttered agreement around a mouthful.

The cook and the gatekeeper had an arrangement during the long periods when the cook's husband was at sea. The sailor was home in Erdin now; the gatekeeper discreetly avoided the kitchen and the cook never came to the front gate. She invariably slipped a tidbit from the family's table to the vegetable seller for delivery, though.

"Quiet, I guess?" the vegetable seller said. The men had known each other for a decade; the bor-Mulliman family had kept the same staff and the same method of provisioning when they'd moved from the outskirts of Erdin to this mansion in a wealthy district. Each was probably the other's closest friend, though they had little contact except for the early-morning greeting and chat.

"As the grave," the gatekeeper agreed from the other side of the wrought-iron fence. "Mind you, I'm not complaining.

Better quiet than watching a mob come up the street to rape and pillage the rich folks.''

The vegetable seller laughed. ''Guess you'd sell your life dearly to protect the master and mistress, hey Esil?'' he said.

The gatekeeper snorted. ''They don't pay me enough to convince me I'm rich, Toze,'' he said. He licked the last of the filling off his fingers. ''Mind, I'd go some lengths to get Reava clear. She *can* cook.''

''Shepherd spurn me if it's not the truth,'' the vegetable seller agreed as he chewed. His jaws slowed and he frowned along the foggy street. ''There's a fellow just went down the side alley,'' he said.

''No law against that,'' the gatekeeper said, but his eyes narrowed. ''Probably just a drunk watering the ivy. He'll be back out in a minute.''

''He walked an all-fired long ways to take a whiz,'' the vegetable seller muttered.

He continued to watch for movement where the alley joined the boulevard. Unless the gatekeeper opened the gates and went out, he could only see the wedge of street directly in front of the wicket.

''He wasn't anything special,'' the vegetable seller said, working his tongue over his teeth to clean them. ''A fat guy in a white tunic. He must've had a light with him, though . . .''

He wanted to describe the blue glow he thought he'd seen, but he wasn't sure how to.

Iron rubbed from the back corner of the property. ''Sister take him!'' the gatekeeper muttered. He got up from his stool and lifted the axe-bladed halberd leaning against the wicket. ''Guess I earn my wages.''

He looked at the vegetable seller. ''Want to come along?'' he asked.

The vegetable seller grimaced. ''Yeah, sure,'' he said. He turned and got the three-foot oak cudgel from the pushcart while his friend unlocked the gate.

The grounds within the vine-grown fence were well man-icured. Shrubs that the previous owners had ignored for years were pruned back, or cut down and replaced where they'd been allowed to spread beyond normal maintenance.

The men didn't speak as they walked in the direction of the sound. In order to screen the tomb at the back of the property, the bor-Mullimans had built a brick planter after they moved in. While the men were just the other side of its profusion of scarlet lobelias, a blue flash lit the night. When it vanished, it sucked the darkness deeper than before. Metal snapped with a clang.

The gatekeeper cursed softly and shifted his grip slightly on the shaft of his halberd. He stepped forward. The vegetable seller caught his sleeve and held him.

A door opened, then thumped closed. The haze of blue light glowing through the foliage was as insubstantial as the odor of rotting meat.

The men looked at one another. The vegetable seller tugged his friend away. Together they walked slowly toward the front gate, looking over their shoulders.

"It's not your job, right?" the vegetable seller said. "It's not part of the grounds that come with the house. You told me that."

"Yeah," the gatekeeper muttered. "It's not my job."

He opened the gate for the vegetable seller, then ran his hand up and down the bars. The feel of cold iron settled his mind a little.

"You could tell somebody come morning when you go off duty," the vegetable seller said slowly. "Of course if you did, then they might wonder why you waited."

"Right," the gatekeeper said, staring toward darkness and wishing the sun would rise a little sooner. "There wasn't anything there, you know. I'm not sure there was even a light."

Then he added, "You know, Toze? If that mob came down the street right now, I'd welcome their company."

19

Two soldiers held Sharina's outstretched arms, twisting her torso sideways as they descended the narrow enclosed staircase one ahead of the other. A third soldier, the one with the key to the cells, held a lantern at the front of the line.

Callin was in back. The bare taper in his hand fluttered and frequently sank to a blue spark around the wick, but he managed to prevent it from going out.

Sharina saw the rosy glow pulsing from the corridor while she was still on the staircase. She looked around wildly. Callin and his men appeared not to notice what she thought was obvious. The light quivered like the sea just after the tide turns, when the surf neither gains nor ebbs.

They reached the bottom of the stairs. Meder was chanting in a loud, high voice, but echoes down the long corridor masked the words. The soldier in the lead stopped and raised his lantern. The light from Meder's cell was bright enough to throw the shadows of his bars across the floor of the corridor.

Callin finally saw the glow. "I told him what to expect," he said in a kittenish voice as he drew his sword. "Sister take me if I didn't warn him."

In a completely different tone he added, "Come on."

He strode down the corridor, freeing his left hand by tossing the candle to the floor. The flame guttered but continued to burn. The men holding Sharina trotted along behind the courtier; she lengthened her stride to avoid being dragged.

Asera stood at the front of her cell, touching the bars. Her expression was taut and unreadable, but Sharina thought she was afraid.

Sharina herself was afraid.

Meder sat cross-legged on the floor chanting, *"Sesengen io barpharnices . . ."*

Sharina smelled fresh blood; the corpse of a rat lay at the back of the cell, its throat a ragged wound. Blood smeared the wizard's face: he must have torn the beast open with his teeth.

"Get the door open!" Callin shouted to the man with the key. The soldier fumbled, either nervously clumsy or consciously trying to delay. "Get it *open*!"

The wizard had drawn a six-pointed star in rat's blood on the stone. He'd broken off the end of one of the pair of bones that had been hanging from the manacle to use as his athame. He gestured with it as he chanted, *"Nebouthosaoualeth aktiophi ereschigal . . ."*

The soldier inserted the key into Meder's lock and turned it squealingly. One of the men let go of Sharina to draw his sword. The other tightened his grip unconsciously, his lips drawn back in a snarl.

"Io berbita io thobagra baui!"

Rock pattered to the floor. Sharina and the three soldiers looked around, but Callin ignored the sound and dragged at the cell's sticking door. The man holding the lantern screamed.

The nearest pillar was crumbling. From its heart unfolded the form of a demon as black as the stone itself. Its legs were short but the arms were as grotesquely long as the forelimbs of a crab spider. The creature had small hands with four daggerlike claws splayed from around the edges like flower petals.

Callin glanced behind him and struck, quickly as a cat. The tempered steel of his blade sparked on the demon's head and rebounded, humming like a hawser about to snap. Callin cried out in anger and pain, grasping the sword hilt with his left hand to damp its vibration. The demon gripped his face and pulled it off in a gout of blood.

Bits of rock dribbled from the pillars farther back along the long corridor, clicking and dancing like the start of an avalanche as they bounced on the floor. The man holding the lantern dashed it in the demon's face and tried to dodge past. The demon caught him in both arms and began to pick him apart. Killer and victim were silhouetted against the light of the candle at the other end of the corridor.

The remaining soldiers ran past the creature while it was occupied with their fellow. The man who'd drawn his sword dropped it. The first demon waddled after them, tossing to either side fragments of the man it held. Five more demons twisted free of their rocky prisons farther down the corridor and spread their arms.

Meder's cell was open. Sharina pulled the key out of that lock and turned to release Asera. The procurator's face was as stiff as a skull. Sharina grabbed the older woman by the wrist and shouted, "Come on!"

The only way out of the dungeons was past the demons. They had to try. Cracks ran across the corridor ceiling now that the pillars no longer supported the weight of the building above it. A chunk of rock the size of a man's head crashed to the floor beside Sharina.

The last of the soldiers screamed like a dying rabbit while four demons tore him limb from limb. "Meder!" Sharina said. "Can you control these things?"

Meder walked out of his cell with a look of supernal calm on his face. "Oh, they'll go away," he said. "I don't need them anymore, you see."

He put his hand protectively on Sharina's forearm. She shook him off.

"There were so many things I didn't understand until I came here," Meder said in a satisfied voice. "It's all so clear to me now."

The ceiling crumbled in pieces ranging from gravel to a slab as big as the mantelpiece upstairs. The demons were crumbling also. A long arm fell off the nearest one; then a leg collapsed and the torso shattered like an egg when it hit the floor. Pulling Asera with her and trusting the wizard to follow on his own, Sharina ran toward the distant staircase.

She didn't care if Meder followed. Her bare feet skidded in a pile of human entrails which lay where a demon had dropped them.

Let Meder go where he belongs, to a Hell beneath this Hell.

The wall between a pair of cells collapsed, bringing the ceiling after it in a blast of shattered rock. The roar was louder than the terror in Sharina's mind. The candle had vanished—burned out, buried; smothered in dust too thick to breathe.

Stone turned and fell to sand under Sharina's foot; it was the limb of a demon disintegrating like the castle it had supported. Blind and choking, the girl groped toward where memory told her the stairwell had been.

Light gleamed in a halo of dust so dense that it illuminated only the hand holding the torch.

Nonnus held the torch.

"Upstairs!" the hermit shouted. "I'll cover the back!"

He carried the Pewle knife in his right hand. His javelin would have been awkward on the winding staircase.

"They're all dead!" Sharina said. Another huge slab fell, pumping air full of rockdust into her like the current of a millrace. She gagged. "Only us . . ."

She slid past Nonnus, knowing that he wouldn't precede her. There was no time for argument, maybe no time at all. She continued to hold Asera's wrist but the procurator was moving normally again. The air became cleaner as they climbed the stairs, though each crash in the dungeons blasted more dust up the staircase.

Sharina reached the upstairs corridor. A soldier lay there with a surprised look on his face and a grin from ear to ear carved in his throat. A crack ran along the floor at the base of the sidewall, but the vaulted basements above the dungeons hadn't yet collapsed.

Sharina bent and snatched the man's dagger instead of taking the time to unhook the belt and sheath; the sword would be too heavy and awkward to be any use to her. She missed the familiar heft of the hand axe, and she had to have *some* weapon.

Asera came out of the staircase ahead of Nonnus, who was dragging Meder by the throat of his tunic. The crack in the floor widened; the wall trembled noticeably.

"Outside!" the hermit said. "There's a coach and team in the stables. Out fast because this whole place is going!"

Another soldier was on the floor of the room where Sharina had dined. The fire still burned in the hearth. Soot puffed down the chimney every time the castle shook, covering the corpse with a gray veil.

Sharina put her weight against the outer door and swung it open as the others joined her. She paused on the court of hexagonal basalt pavers, because she didn't know where the stables were. Callin had dismounted at the door, leaving his underlings to care for the horses.

"This way!" Nonnus said, leading the way around the black flank of the castle. He carried his javelin again.

The sky was clear and starlit, though there was no moon. Meder had lost the bone athame. Most of his face and clothing was covered by powdered stone, but he still smiled.

The stable walls stood, but over the years most of the roof had fallen in. Complete, the structure would have held forty horses in individual stone stalls. Part of the original slate roof remained over the near end; Callin's men had cleared additional stalls and covered them with sailcloth.

Horses whickered, made nervous by the trembling of the rock beneath them. A coping fell from a high wall, striking several times before the final crash.

"I saved you, Sharina," the wizard said archly. "You see what I can do for you. You'll always be safe with me."

"Liar!" Sharina screamed. "Nonnus would have saved us! You did nothing! Nothing!"

The hermit touched her hand and turned her toward the stables again. "You'll have to harness the horses, child," he said. "It's not a skill I've ever had to learn."

Then he added in a voice of pale despair, "What's done is done. What he did and what I did. Done."

Sharina tugged Nonnus with her into the stables to find the tack. She didn't want him to be alone just now.

BOOK

V

1

From the outside the building was a brick warehouse exactly like the score of others backing up to the River Erd.

A mule-drawn dray loaded with barrels of turpentine drove out of the double doors as Garric arrived with Liane and Tenoctris. The dray smelled strongly of pines, a welcome change from the harbor's stagnant marshy odor.

Garric looked at Liane, wondering if she'd mistaken the address. She stepped briskly to the pedestrian door and rapped smartly on the cast-iron knocker there, an unexpected piece of furniture for the surroundings.

A small triangular hatch at eye level opened. "Mistress Liane os-Benlo and companions to see Master Polew," Liane said. "My father is indisposed and it's urgent that I talk with the banker."

"One moment," a voice replied. The hatch closed.

Liane turned to her companions and said, "Polew's a Serian. They don't care to advertise their wealth to the world at large."

The door opened. The doorkeeper was a tall, willowy man wearing a jacket and pantaloons of brown silk. "I'll take care of your sword for you, sir," he said to Garric. "Or you can wait outside if you'd prefer."

Garric unbuckled the sword belt and wrapped it around the scabbard before handing the whole ensemble to the doorkeeper. He disliked the weapon. Its weight pulled his hips out of alignment and the chape protecting the bottom of the scabbard regularly knocked against his calf as he walked. Swords were less common in Erdin than they had been in Carcosa, but not so rare that Garric stood out for carrying one. If he was to protect Liane under the present circumstances, he figured he had to go armed whenever possible.

Besides, grasping a sword hilt was a quick way to hand his problems over to King Carus for swift and certain resolution.

Carus chuckled at the back of Garric's mind. There were times when a man had to act without thinking. The problem was to know which times those were.

The doorkeeper stood in an alcove beside stairs leading upward. The brick wall separating the staircase from the rest of the building was so thick that when the door closed behind him Garric could no longer hear the shouting and bustle of the warehouse.

Liane pattered up in the lead, pinching her robe with both hands so that the hem didn't trip her. A glazed skylight illuminated the stairwell, something Garric had never seen before; a five-armed lampholder hung from a chain for use later in the evening.

A young woman with dark skin and black hair pushed aside the door curtain at the head of the stairs and bowed to Liane. Liane bowed in reply, then led her companions into the room beyond.

A tall man, very thin and old, was standing behind a thin-legged writing desk. Garric suspected the man was bald beneath the bonnet made of white silk like his robe. The walls were paneled in bleached oak with gilt ornamentation along the seams, grapevines and passion fruit.

"Master Polew," Liane said, bowing again.

"Mistress Liane," Polew said, returning the bow. "I regret to hear of your father's indisposition. Pray be seated."

There was a chair behind the desk and three chairs in front of it. They were traceries in gilt and white enamel, so spidery that Garric was afraid to trust his weight to one until he'd surreptitiously pressed his hand on the back and found that it didn't flex. He sat down a moment later than the others.

Against one sidewall stood a statue of a slender goddess flanked in separate niches by a pair of demons. Across the room a strongbox was fastened to the floor and the wall by iron bands. The room had no other furnishings.

A Serian of moderate height in a thin cotton robe stood behind Polew's chair. His head was cocked to the side; his arms dangled. He didn't look directly at anything, but Garric had the impression that there was nothing his eyes didn't see.

Garric had expected that a banker would have bodyguards festooned with weapons. This man *was* a weapon.

"Master Polew," Liane said without preamble, "my father was killed on the business his principal set him. It's imperative that I get in touch with that principal at once."

The banker tented his hands. His eyes were cautious. "I am very sorry about your father, mistress," he said. "I will plant a tree in his memory. And I am very sorry also that I cannot help you with your request."

Liane leaned forward to speak. Polew turned one of his hands palm-outward to forestall her.

"Mistress," he said, "my family has handled your family's business for three generations. Unfortunately the account about which you ask was not set up by the bor-Benlimans but rather by another client of the firm. You understand that an honorable man and a prudent businessman cannot discuss the affairs of his clients with third parties."

"Master Benlo was killed by a demon," Garric said. He heard his voice tremble slightly. He laid his palms flat on his thighs and stared at them. "The demon tore him open, then carried Mistress Liane to Hell, sir, *Hell*, from which only a great magician was able to rescue her."

He raised his eyes to meet the banker's. "Master Polew, she has a right to know who was responsible for that."

Polew lowered his hands. His face was without expression. His mouth opened to speak.

"Master Polew," Liane said quickly before the refusal was spoken and therefore final, "I respect your unwillingness to tell me who your client is. But you can tell me who the banker was whose draft opened the account, can't you? That doesn't touch your honor."

The banker smiled slightly. "No, mistress," he said, "but I'm afraid I can't provide that information either. The account wasn't opened by draft, you see. The client provided a quantity of bullion of high quality. Old Kingdom coins, to be precise."

He pursed his lips and added, "Mistress Liane . . . on reflection, I don't think it would hurt to tell you that my client is unknown to me also. The person who set up the account was completely muffled. I wouldn't recognize him again, and I don't assume that he was the principal in any case. Further instructions have come in the hands of boys. They say they were stopped in the street by a veiled figure who told them that I would pay them to deliver a packet to me. That's all I know."

"Do you still have any of the original coins?" Tenoctris asked.

Polew looked at her, appraising for the first time a figure who'd been as silent as the furniture till then. "Yes," he said, "I kept them all, as a matter of fact. They were the most perfect examples of their kind I've ever seen."

He walked to the strongbox, then knelt before it. His robe spread to hide what his hands were doing; certainly he wasn't inserting a key. The bodyguard stepped between Polew and the visitors, giving them a vacant smile. Unless you concentrated on the man's eyes or noticed the flat ropes of muscle directly under his skin, you could imagine he was a dimwitted potboy who'd somehow stumbled into the wrong room.

Polew stood and handed Liane a thin coin the size of Garric's thumbnail. King Carus looked out in rakish majesty, his features as sharp as the die from which they'd been struck.

"No, you needn't pay me, mistress," the banker said as Liane reached into her purse for coins. "Take it as my grave offering for your father. In former times . . ."

Polew looked around the room with a faint smile. The only windows were skylights of hammered glass that distorted images into blurs of color.

"I rarely leave my quarters, you see," he continued. "Your father used to bring me stories of far lands, stories so wonderful that I thought of traveling myself. But the stories wouldn't have been wonderful if it had been me living them, you see; I knew that."

"Before my mother died," Liane said.

Polew nodded. "Before the tragic loss of Mistress Mazzona, yes," he said. "Take the coin, mistress, and take also my regrets for not being able to help you more."

Liane and the banker exchanged bows. She turned and the female attendant held the curtain back for the three visitors.

They didn't speak until they'd reached the street and heard the doorkeeper shoot the bolts behind them. Liane gave the coin to the wizard. "What do you plan to do, Tenoctris?" she asked.

"Tomorrow . . ." Tenoctris said. "Not tonight, because it's already too near sunset, but tomorrow during daylight I'd like to return to your family tomb. There I can have the privacy to do a sourcing ritual that will tell us, I rather think, where the gold came from. At the inn, I'm afraid someone would interfere."

Liane's face tightened.

"She needn't come, need she?" Garric said.

"I'll come," Liane said. "He's my father, Garric. I'm not afraid to do whatever it takes to understand why he had to die that way."

"I *am* afraid," Tenoctris said with a smile that did nothing to rob the statement of its truth. "But the ritual itself shouldn't involve any danger. It's in what comes next that the risk lies. . . ."

2

Sharina led the last of the four coach horses back from the stream where she'd watered them. Meder sat looking at the campfire; Asera was arranging a blanket into a bed for herself under the coach. Privations hadn't changed the procurator, but she bent with the wind when she had to.

"Where's Nonnus?" Sharina asked. They'd come about five miles south of Gonalia. The road was good by any standards a girl from Barca's Hamlet could apply—a firm bed and no ruts deeper than the axles of the coach—but there was no reason to risk driving in darkness once they'd gotten beyond the immediate vicinity of the castle.

Meder turned and looked at her. The fire behind him hid his features; he didn't speak.

"He went into the woods," Asera said. She pointed in a general direction across the road from where the coach stood. "Not long ago. Not too long."

Sharina set the hobbles on the horse. It and its fellows whickered to one another. They were used to stalls at coaching stations. They spent most of their lives either enclosed or harnessed, and they weren't sure they liked this new practice.

The recent rain had brought out the frogs and toads. They weren't the species Sharina knew from Haft. Their cries, particularly the tuneless scream of one of the toads, wore on her temper. She walked into the woods with the coachwhip, using its long butt as a feeler in the dark.

Sharina didn't have a right to be angry at Asera and Meder for being what they were. She was frightened and far from home, but they were as much out of their depth as she was.

She eased her way past a thicket of cedar saplings too

dense to push through. Charity doesn't come easily when you're alone in the dark.

"This way, child," Nonnus said from nearby. He stood at the base of a conifer at least ten feet in diameter.

"I just wanted to see . . ." Sharina said. "I wanted to see that you're all right."

He laughed. "Oh, yes," he said. "I was praying."

Another giant tree had fallen within the past year, smashing a two-hundred-foot hole through the forest. The saplings springing up to fill the gap hadn't yet closed the sky overhead. Starlight showed the hermit's face and the features of the clearing.

Nonnus had shaped the bark at the conifer's base into an image of the Lady. He'd used no more than six quick strokes, but even a stranger would have identified the figure at once. He was an artist with the blade.

His belt and Pewle knife hung from the branch of a larch ten feet back from where he'd been kneeling before the image. The javelin leaned against the same sapling, its fluted blade gleaming in the starlight.

"I had to get away from them," Sharina admitted in a low voice. "I wanted to . . ."

Her features hardened as she allowed them to show what she really felt. "Nonnus," she said, "he shouldn't be alive. His blood magic makes me sick. I'd rather die than be touched by it! You didn't see what happened to Callin and the guards."

The hermit smiled faintly. "No," he said, "I didn't see that."

He looked at her. His face had its usual wooden calm. The only times Sharina had seen any other expression there was when Nonnus held the knife and there was blood on its blade.

"Dead is dead, child," Nonnus said softly. "How one man killed another doesn't matter to the dead man and it doesn't matter to the Lady. I'm not the one to object to the way another fellow does his work."

"Nonnus, he's not human anymore!" she said. She wanted to cry. "I'm not sure he ever was."

"Don't say that!" the hermit ordered. More gently he went on, "Child, don't ever let yourself think that somebody isn't human because you don't like what he does or what he wears or how he prays. Don't ever do that, because if you do you'll find yourself doing things that you'll never be able to forgive. Or forget."

Sharina knelt because her knees were wobbling. She laid her head in her hands and began to cry. Nonnus squatted beside her and put the tips of two fingers on her shoulder.

"Why somebody died and you lived isn't a question for you, child," he said. "It's in the Lady's hands. We have to believe that."

"I hate what he did," Sharina said. Her sobs faded to gulping; she got her voice under control again. "Nonnus, he says he did it for me and I believe him!"

"Yes, I believe him too," Nonnus said. He put his fingers under her chin with a gentle pressure so that she met his eyes.

"I killed the men upstairs," he said. "I didn't take any chances: they had to be dead for you to be safe, so I killed them."

Sharina looked into the hermit's face, wondering what he saw when he looked at her. "If you killed them for me," she said, "then their blood isn't on your hands."

Nonnus said nothing.

Sharina drew the dagger from beneath her sash and walked to the trunk of the fallen tree. She stabbed the point deep enough in the thick bark to hold; she didn't have a belt and sheath to hang the weapon by, out of the way.

She turned, knelt before the image of the Lady, and began to pray for the souls of the enemies who had died that she might live. After a moment, Nonnus knelt beside her.

3

"isely, God hides future outcomes in a mist of night,' "
Liane read from Celondre's *Odes*.

There was a metallic hiss from the tomb behind
them where Tenoctris worked alone. The sound was very
faint. Liane paused a half-beat, then resumed, " 'God laughs
at mortal hopes and fears. Remember to accept whatever
comes with a calm mind!' "

The slim volume was the one unnecessary item Garric had
brought with him from Barca's Hamlet. He'd had to leave
most of his past behind. Celondre remained to anchor him in
simpler times, when all Garric or Reise needed to worry about
was what the sheep were doing and whether his father would
shout at him for being slow starting his chores in the stables.

Celondre's *Odes* had remained the same for a thousand
years, and they would be the same for thousands of years
more: outlasting bronze, as Celondre himself had rightly said.
That vantage point put all present problems into perspective,
even those problems of life and death.

If Tenoctris was right, the danger threatening the cosmos
would sweep away even the *Odes* this time. Garric believed
the old woman, but at an emotional level Celondre's civilized
truths seemed eternal.

A chime climbed a full octave by half-steps within the
tomb. Liane listened, tension evident in her controlled face.
She and Garric had waited all day on the bench in front of
the tomb. The ivy-grown fence surrounding them formed a
sort of arbor that would have been pleasant under other conditions.

The last note faded. Liane set the book down and gave
Garric a trembling smile.

"I'm afraid," she said simply. "I don't want anybody else to be hurt because of me. You and Tenoctris are my only friends now."

Her smile failed. "And I keep thinking about what happened to my father," she said.

"Tenoctris isn't like your father," Garric said. "She does everything one step at a time. And she said this wasn't going to be dangerous."

He couldn't imagine Liane as someone who was afraid. She'd always gone straight ahead with whatever was required: calm, quick, and decisive, despite the fact that she'd watched a demon appear out of thin air to disembowel her father.

"I used to play here when I was a little girl," she said with a smile. "It was always fenced off from the rest of the grounds, though the inner gate wasn't locked then. I didn't think about it being a tomb, of course, but it wouldn't have mattered. I didn't think about death at all until my mother died."

Being afraid didn't change anything about her. If another demon stepped through the doorway in place of Tenoctris, Liane would be stabbing for its eyes with her writing stylus for want of a better weapon.

He nodded. Traffic on the boulevard a few hundred feet away was a constant sound though not an obtrusive one. Only very rarely had anybody come down the alley past them: a group of female servants from another mansion; a coachman driving his empty vehicle to the stables; a delivery boy whistling and running a stick along the rods of the fence. The boy had screamed when he saw Garric and Liane looking at him through the ivy.

"I hadn't thought it would take this long," Garric said. They'd eaten at the inn near the harbor before they left in the morning, but he had a young man's appetite and the midday meal was usually the main one of the day. It was verging toward evening and Tenoctris hadn't come out of the tomb with a report.

The door squeaked. Garric leaped to his feet. He reached

first for the door handle, then for his sword hilt, and in fact
touched neither of them for fear of making the wrong decision.

Tenoctris stepped into the sunlight, looking more tired than
Garric had ever seen her before. Smoke oozed from the doorway with an oily odor: she must have burned a score of the
wax candles she'd taken into the windowless tomb with her.

She smiled at her younger companions. Neither of them
was willing to ask what had happened inside.

"I found where the gold came from," she said. Both of
them helped her as she settled herself onto the pavement, first
kneeling and then crossing her legs beneath her. "It wasn't
difficult, exactly, but there were more steps than I'd expected."

Tenoctris had used a tendril of ivy as an athame. She still
held it, though the curled tip had begun to droop in the hours
since she plucked it.

"I should have known better," she said. She looked at
Liane and then Garric as they hovered to either side of her.
"It took a long time because it's on a plane separate from
this plane. I should have known that it would be. The Hooded
One couldn't have survived in our time, *my* time, if he'd
stayed as the sea rushed in."

"What do we do next?" Liane asked calmly. A candle still
burned on the floor of the tomb, its light a yellowish contrast
to the waning sun.

"I think," Tenoctris said, "that someone should go to the
plane and see what is there. I wish I could go myself, but I'll
have to hold the gate open here."

"I'll go," Liane said.

"No," said Garric. He stood up, feeling more comfortable
than he had since facing down Captain Aran and his crew.
He had something to *do*. "I will. Will it be like the other
place, Strasedon's place?"

"I don't know," Tenoctris said. "I need you to describe
the location to me. Then I can plan the next step."

She grinned with half her face. "For that you have to return, Garric," she said. "There's nothing you can do that's as important as coming back. If there's any danger, turn and run. The gateway will be waiting for you."

"No!" Liane said, standing also. "It's not right that he goes! Benlo was *my* father, so the risk should be mine!"

"If it were only your father I wouldn't be doing any of this," Tenoctris said from her seated position. "I'm sorry, Liane, but this is a matter for the whole cosmos. Garric is the better choice. I'll need your help with the responses."

She looked at Garric with affection and something more, a kind of sad respect. "Garric is perhaps the best choice of anyone alive, which is another of those things that shakes my faith in the random nature of the cosmos. It's a terrible thing to have my beliefs dashed at my advanced age."

Garric laughed with the exultant shadow of King Carus. They'd be together, he and Carus, wherever it was they were going.

He bent down and lifted Tenoctris to her feet. "Now?" he asked. "Or do you need to rest, mistress?"

"Now would be best," she said. "Half the work has been done, you see."

She put her hand on Liane's forearm. The girl was trembling with anger and frustration.

"There's plenty of risk to go around, Liane," Tenoctris said. "For you and the cosmos as well."

4

Jular bor-Raydiman!" announced the maid, bowing as she passed the titular head of Erdin's City Patrols into the drawing room where Ilna waited on a couch beneath the south windows.

Jular bowed as Ilna rose to greet him. "Mistress Ilna," he said. "Such a pleasure to meet you at last."

The nobleman wasn't often up this early—didn't often *get* up this early, though sometimes his nights ran this late. A summons from the mysterious Mistress Ilna wasn't something he cared to turn down, however.

The windows were ceiling-high. Jular had expected tapestries; after all, the woman was supposed to be a weaver. There was nothing of the sort, just a shawl of gray-shaded wool over the couch. The furnishings were limited to a pier glass; a wardrobe chest of burl walnut, well made but of simple design; and the couch. Jular's eyes turned to the couch instinctively.

"No," Ilna said as she walked toward the wardrobe, "that's not why you're here, Master Jular."

She was an attractive little thing. Stiff-backed, but he rather liked that sort. When they finally broke there was no reserve, no spirit left.

Ilna turned to him and smiled. Jular hated spiders, feared them worse than he feared death itself. For an instant—

The world was normal again. Jular lowered the hand he'd instinctively clutched to his heart.

"I told you," the woman said, "that's not why you're here." She opened the lid of the chest.

Jular was a fleshy man but still young enough to appear handsome in a bad light. The light in this east drawing room was very good indeed. He was breathing hard after the shock, the *illusion*, and he'd have sat down without asking if there'd been a chair available.

There was only the couch. He'd rather have died than sit there.

"Come over here," Ilna directed as she closed the wardrobe and laid the three packets she'd taken out on its lid.

Part of Jular's mind told him that he ought to be angry at being ordered around by a commoner—and a woman besides. That wasn't why he hesitated, though.

Ilna gave him a grin that was just short of a sneer.

"Come," she repeated. "I won't bite you. I need you, the position you fill at least."

Jular obeyed because he was afraid of what would happen if he didn't. He hadn't spoken since his initial greeting, a time that seemed from a former life.

"I want two people arrested and brought to me," Ilna said, unrolling one of the packets of cloth. "I don't want them harmed—"

She fixed Jular with a look of anger that he'd done nothing to justify. *He'd done nothing!*

"Under no circumstances are they to be harmed," she said. "Do you understand that? Answer me."

"I understand," Jular said after swallowing. "Ah . . . mistress? I think you may misunderstand the extent of my involvement with, ah, the duties of arresting people and this sort of thing. In fact—"

"Yes, I know," Ilna interrupted. "You're a fat fool who probably doesn't know where the city's prison is. You have the title simply because other nobles think that one of their own *sort* should be in charge of important ministries on paper. But they'll take orders from you if you give them, won't they?"

Jular had been called many vile things during his life. The inflection this woman put on "sort" made it far the worst insult he'd ever heard.

He cleared his throat. "Well," he said. "Yes, I suppose they will. I've done favors in the past, of course. . . ."

For others of my own sort.

Ilna nodded as she spread two of the rolls of cloth on the wardrobe. "That's what I assumed," she said. "A ship chartered by Benlo bor-Benliman arrived in port the day before yesterday. These two persons were probably aboard it. They're the ones I want brought to me. If they've left Erdin, I want to know where they went."

Jular looked at two portraits in fabric; they were astonishingly realistic. They were of a young man with an unfashionably dark complexion, and of a strikingly beautiful black-haired woman.

"They may be going by the names Garric or-Reise and Liane os-Benlo," Ilna said. "You can have these sketched by artists so that every member of the Patrols has a copy of both pictures."

"Yes . . ." Jular said. He'd have agreed that he was the son of a donkey driver under the present circumstances. "I suppose they have people who can do that."

Ilna rolled the portraits again, each within its separate covering of baize. "I suppose you're wondering what's in this for you?" she said as she worked.

All Jular was thinking about was how he was going to get out of this house, away from this *woman*. He didn't know what would happen if he ran. There were a number of husky male servants in the mansion, but it wasn't them whom he feared.

She handed him the portraits and weighed the third roll of fabric in her hand. "This is for you when you've accomplished your task," she said. "It's exactly what you need for your off-duty pursuits."

Her brief smile was insulting, but Jular was beyond insult by now. "You've heard about my work, no doubt?" she added.

"Yes," Jular said, interested despite all the negative emotions boiling through his mind. "Yes I have, mistress. This cloth—"

He gestured but didn't try to touch the roll.

"—has the effect on women that your other cloth is said to have on men?"

"No," Ilna said curtly. "For that you'd have to go to another weaver, a man I suppose—if anything of the sort exists. But this can be used to the same effect."

She unrolled a length of the fabric and held it over the back of her left forearm as though she were a shop assistant and he a customer. Objectively it was black lace of gossamer delicacy, valuable no doubt to a person who cared about such things.

Subjectively it lit in Jular a desire such as he had never imagined could exist. He *wanted* this woman, wanted to abase himself before her, to surrender himself utterly . . .

And all the time he knew that her poison fangs would drain him dry and leave him an empty husk beneath her web. It didn't matter. Nothing mattered except that he had to have her.

Ilna covered the fabric again. Jular caught himself on the wardrobe with his palms flat. He looked out the window until he'd gotten his breath.

"This is of a much higher quality than the ribbons others have purchased," Ilna said to his averted head. There was a cat's smile in her voice. "As a bribe, I think you'll find it more than satisfactory. Virtuous women who couldn't possibly be brought to your bed by gold will nonetheless meet whatever price you set for the chance to be irresistible to the man of *their* desires."

Jular had control of himself. He straightened.

"I suppose they'll hold their noses while they're with you," Ilna continued, "but that isn't a matter of concern, is it, Jular? You're just interested in adding them to your little list."

Jular looked at her. He was no longer afraid: he'd achieved the safety of abject surrender. He would do absolutely anything for this woman in order to be free of her. She knew that, and she was still offering a payment for which he would have exchanged half his considerable personal fortune.

Jular weighed the two rolled portraits, unconsciously mimicking Ilna's gesture of a moment before. "Yes, I'll take care of this at once," he said. "Why are you interested—"

He caught himself. "No, that's none of my business, of course," he said.

He looked again at the rolls and shrugged. "The girl's a pretty thing, isn't she?" he said. "But that's none of my business either, I know. That lace will suffice me for some time to come, I'm sure."

"We understand each other," Ilna said. She rang a small bell. "Good day, Master Jular."

Jular saw himself in the pier glass. His smile was as foul as the expression on the face of a long-dead corpse. He didn't care; he knew what he was, and he didn't care.

"Good day, mistress," he said. The maid opened the door for him. Jular was only peripherally aware that the maid was female. All that mattered was that he was leaving.

And that if he succeeded in arresting two nobodies, he would never have to face Ilna's smile again.

5

The portal was a perfect cerulean blue, the color of the eastern horizon from Barca's Hamlet on a spring evening. It hung in the air before Garric, a thing of light itself which didn't illuminate the floor or the ancient coffins around it.

Liane and Tenoctris sat on opposite sides of the circle Tenoctris had drawn around Garric in wax. The fresh vine shoot the wizard used for an athame bobbed with the words the women spoke alternately.

"—*sterxerx!*" Tenoctris cried, concluding the spell. Sword in hand, Garric stepped through the light and onto a forest path. He gasped with surprise and relief: he'd expected . . .

He didn't know what he'd expected. Something terrible, a lich waiting to seize him or a pit of lava that would swallow him if he moved a finger's breadth.

This wasn't home, exactly, because there were no pines; but the birch, hickory, dogwoods, and oaks were all familiar. Even the wrist-thick hairy stem of poison ivy climbing to open sky along the trunk of a oak was a friend because it was a commonplace of Garric's past.

Poison ivy lived its life and let you live yours unhindered, so long as you left it alone. It didn't come looking for you with fangs or a rusty cutlass. Garric sheathed his sword and felt King Carus recede deeper into his mind.

It was early fall in this place. The trees hadn't started to shed their leaves, but flushes of color marked the early-changing dogwoods and maples. The air had the pleasant coolness of a well-watered woodland on even the hottest summer day.

Garric knelt to examine the ground more closely. There were no tracks on the leaf litter nor other sign of what had worn the path through the undergrowth. It was wide enough for a man walking or for a horseman who didn't mind saplings brushing his knees with their branch tips.

He looked behind him. The portal hung in the air; through its shimmering surface Garric saw more forest, but he knew that if he stepped into the light he'd be in the bor-Benliman tomb again. Tenoctris had told him so. He trusted her.

He trusted her with his life.

Garric started down the path, resisting an urge to whistle. The sound would make him feel better, but he knew he shouldn't call attention to himself. Birds sang to one another, and tree frogs shrilled in the upper branches.

"Help!" a woman called on a rising note. "Oh help me *please*!"

Garric drew his sword, still *his* sword in *his* hand, though the laughing presence of King Carus was as close about him as fog is to a windowpane. Experience was teaching Garric how to retain control even when the ancient monarch's will surged over him with the emotions of danger.

But they both still knew that Garric was no swordsman. If it came to need, well, Carus would respond as no other man who'd ever lived.

The forest was relatively open; the ferns and saplings that grew among the larger trees were no barrier to a man in a hurry. Garric pushed them aside like a curtain.

The woman's voice rose in a scream. She was off to the left of where he'd expected and still some twenty yards away. You couldn't see far in a place like this. Young trees sprouted larger leaves than those of their adult kin, and they wobbled at eye height like so many pennons. They concealed everything more than a dozen feet away.

Garric stopped and held still except for his head and silently darting eyes. Nothing made a sound, not even a tree frog.

A woman laughed far away; she continued laughing musically until even that sound faded.

Garric turned, taking deep breaths through his open mouth as he returned the way he'd come. The forest's pale green light was no less friendly. He looked in every direction, glancing over his shoulders abruptly and scanning the canopy of branches for lurking dangers.

There was nothing wrong until Garric reached what should have been the path and found in its place a cobblestone road.

Birds fluttered among the tree branches; the flash of blue was an indigo bunting that had been picking for seeds between the pavers. The sky was a little darker now, but that was only natural since evening was wearing on.

Everything was natural except that the road shouldn't have been here. Garric's sense of direction was as sure as sunset and sunrise: he hadn't mistaken his way, but the ruts worn in the stones meant this road had been here for centuries.

Garric sheathed the sword. He thought of returning to see if the portal still waited for him, but he was afraid of what he'd find.

If not back, then onward. Garric resumed walking, whistling a pipe tune that he'd often played to the sheep he was watching. After a few steps on the hard, rounded cobblestones he moved aside and continued in the sod ditch to the left of the pavement.

The road curved back and forth as it proceeded, just as the path he'd been following had done. The ground sloped one direction or the other, or perhaps an outcrop of layered rock was easier to avoid than to excavate. All perfectly innocent, a natural landscape shaped minimally by the hand of man.

A quarter mile through the forest, Garric saw the stone wall. It was Old Kingdom work, or at any rate masonry like that of the Old Kingdom: layers of large, squared stones fitted tight without mortar. It was a good twenty feet high but if he'd had to he could have climbed it easily, even with the unfamiliar sword dangling behind him.

He wouldn't need to climb, because the road passed under a pointed arch in the wall. There wasn't a gate. Garric thought at first that the panels and their metal fittings had rotted away from the dense stone, but the sides of the archway showed no signs of ever being cut to accept hinges or other mountings.

The road on the other side of the wall looked the same as the cobblestone surface on which Garric stood. The forest beyond was so similar to what he'd just walked through that it might have been a mirror image, except there wasn't a tall youth on that side wondering what on earth he ought to do.

Garric laughed and stepped forward. There was a feeling of coolness; smooth black stones were above him and to either side. He took another step—

And the world was like nothing he'd seen through the arch.

He was in a water garden. Little streams purled as they ran along mossy channels or fell through rocks arranged in a studiously "natural" fashion. The sound of running water and bees working among the flowers was relaxing and much louder than it seemed at first: a man speaking in a normal voice couldn't be heard more than arm's length away.

Statues of women with smiling, kindly faces stood in wall niches. There were flowers in rich profusion: springing from still pools, growing in borders along the channels, climbing the walls in sprays of pink and blue and violet. Garric didn't recognize any of the varieties of plants.

From this side he couldn't see the top of the walls. He patted the stone. It was cool to the touch, darkened from long exposure to the air, and as solid as the flank of the mountain from which it had been hewn in ages past.

There was no archway or other opening. There never had been, on this side of the wall.

"Oh Garric, we've been waiting for you so long!" girls—two voices, maybe three—called.

Garric spun around. No one was there, but the ropes of white flowers cascading from a trellis wobbled as though somebody had just ducked behind them. Garric walked to the floral curtain and moved it gently aside with his outstretched left hand. The petals felt damp where they touched his bare skin; bees hummed with excitement, and the air was thick with an odor suggesting summer nights.

His right hand hovered over the hilt of his sword, but he didn't touch it. No one was on the other side of the trellis.

"Here we are, Garric!" a girl called.

He spun again and they *were* there, surrounding him as if they'd condensed out of the air. Six nude girls with pastel hair, laughing and plucking at his tunic with long, slender fingers.

"We're so glad to see you, Garric!" said the girl with blue hair that danced like a mountain stream. She took his right wrist between her hands. Her fingertips were delicate and cool.

Two other girls caught his left arm, their pink and green hair flowing over his skin like spray. "Come with us, Garric," they said in unison. "We're so glad you've finally arrived!"

"Please, I—" Garric said. He felt not a touch but an absence of weight—his sword was gone, the belt unbuckled by a girl with hair the color of bleached straw.

Garric turned and snatched unsuccessfully. The girl hopped away giggling and held the weapon in back of her.

Garric encircled her with his arms and groped for the sword. The girl unexpectedly kissed him and ducked out of his arms. Her hands were empty and the sword wasn't in the bed of gorgeous magenta flowers behind where she'd been standing.

All the girls laughed merrily.

At the corners of his eyes, Garric thought he saw the glint of fins and scales. "Give me my sword back!" he said, feeling a complete fool. What was he going to do with a weapon even if they did return it?

The girl with hair of dusty rose touched his hands with her own. "Come with us, then," she said. "We'll give you a much better sword than that."

"Come with us, Garric!" all the girls called. Their hair swirled like pools of colored oils as they moved.

Garric looked behind him at the vine-grown wall that had been the arch through which he entered this garden. The girls' touch was as light as summer raindrops. There really wasn't any choice.

"All right," said Garric. "I'll go with you."

6

Liane leaned back against the wall, coughing to clear her throat. She was already hoarse, and the cloying odor of candle smoke turned her stomach. Across the circle, Tenoctris took up the litany in a low voice: *"Phanoibikux petriade kratarnade . . ."*

The blue plane of the portal hung in the air between them. They'd run through the spell three times, each speaking it individually to give the other a chance to get her voice back and chew her tongue to encourage the flow of saliva. Tenoctris was starting her fourth reading; then it would be Liane's turn again.

"Arthu lailam semisilam . . ."

They should have brought food or at least something to

drink into the tomb with them before they opened the portal
... but Tenoctris said haste was important, Garric was ready
to go, and Liane had been in the most hurry of all in order
finish the task and have Garric back safe.

If anything happened to Garric, it was Liane's fault for
bringing him into this danger.

"Bachuch bachaxichuch menebaichuch . . ."

It had grown dark outside. They'd left the door of the tomb
slightly ajar, but light no longer seeped past the edges to
supplement the candle burning beside the coffin of Liane's
mother. The portal *was* light but gave no light.

Liane and Tenoctris would remain here repeating the spell
until Garric returned or they fainted from effort. If the sequence of words lapsed for more than a minute or two, the
portal would close and trap Garric forever in the plane to
which he'd gone because of Liane and Liane's father. . . .

"Raracharara anaxarnaxa achara . . ."

The door of the tomb swung open.

Liane looked up, thinking it was a groundskeeper or one
of the owners of the house. She was on her own property and
there was gold in her girdle to ease matters if the City Patrols
were called in. The spell *had* to be chanted!

"Belias belioas—"

The man who stepped into the tomb had empty eyes. Liane
screamed and snatched up the bronze stylus she kept within
the hinges of her writing tablet. The intruder caught her by
the wrist.

Time stopped. There was no longer sequence, only a plane
on which all things existed at once.

Liane sprawled over the intruder's shoulder. He was a
heavy man, not so much wearing a sheet as merely wrapped
in it. He struck Tenoctris, knocking her against a rack of
coffins. The bottommost, the oldest, crumbled with the force
of the impact.

The portal faded. The intruder walked around the blue
glow, placing his feet with the weight and caution of a draft
horse on ice. Tenoctris lay where she had fallen.

Mazzona's bronze casket weighed at least five hundred pounds, perhaps a thousand. The intruder lifted it with one arm and turned. The ends of the metal container crushed the wooden caskets it touched.

The intruder walked out into the night, carrying both Liane and the casket of her mother. A blue glare popped and rippled about him even as the portal vanished forever.

7

Who are you?" Garric asked as the girls led him around a pool that jutted out from the wall. The coping was a soft volcanic stone, smoothed and darkened by age. Lotus flowers bloomed above pads floating on the still water.

"We're your friends, Garric!" said the girl with violet hair.

"We live here!" another girl chorused. He wasn't sure who spoke; maybe Pink-Hair. Only rarely were all six of the girls in sight at the same time, though he never saw one vanish or reappear.

Bright-colored fishes swam in reflection on the surface of the pool beside him.

"You're water nymphs, aren't you?" Garric said.

The girls giggled. "Come along, Garric, it's only a little farther!" Green-Hair said as she skipped along with him.

They'd left the water garden for a rocky olive grove. Garric couldn't tell exactly where or how the change had occurred. The trees were ancient; their gnarled trunks were as thick as Garric's own torso. Black fruit hung from their branches. The roots must drive deep in this forbidding soil to find water and nourishment.

He was hungry. He thought of snatching a few of the ripe olives as he ducked under a branch, but after a moment's consideration he decided he wasn't *that* hungry.

"Where are we going?" Garric asked. He didn't think the nymphs meant him harm, but he knew they weren't his friends either. They didn't care what he wanted.

"We're already there!" Blue-Hair trilled. With two nymphs playfully holding either of his wrists and Blue-Hair leading, Garric stepped through a columned doorway. The pillars were of stuccoed stone, oddly wider at the top than at the base. They were painted harsh primary colors with red and blue predominating, though for the most part the walls were creamy white.

"Where *are* we?" Garric said. He was more frustrated than frightened at the moment, but fear was growing too.

The nymphs skipped with him down a corridor. There were pillars on one side and a frescoed wall on the other. The painted images were of men battling monsters whose legs twisted like snakes. The background was a dark landscape picked out by lightning that leaped from cloud to cloud and erupting volcanoes.

"Don't you know?" Rose-Hair said. Garric wasn't sure if she was playing with him or if she really did expect him to recognize his surroundings. "This is the palace, silly. Malkar's palace!"

Garric stopped dead in his tracks. The courtyard on the other side of the colonnade was open to the sky, but that sky was dark with night or storm clouds. He couldn't tell where the corridor's soft gray light came from.

"Why are you taking me to Malkar?" Garric asked quietly. He knew by now that if he turned and ran back the way he'd come that it *wouldn't* be anything like the way he'd come. All flight would do was cost him his dignity. He had little enough of that left, allowing six giggling girls to lead him to death or worse.

"Oh, we aren't taking you to Malkar!" Saffron Hair said in horror. For an instant all her sisters had vanished, though they were staring aghast at Garric before he could have blinked. "Oh, Garric, we wouldn't do that!"

"We're taking you to the sword," Green-Hair said. "You wanted the sword, Garric."

"We don't have anything to do with Malkar," Pink-Hair said. "That would be awful!"

"Come, let's get the sword," Blue-Hair said.

In a reproving tone Violet-Hair added, "You've frightened us by being so silly, Garric!"

Garric jogged along the corridor with the nymphs. He was sure they'd regret it if anything happened to him, the way a child would regret her kitten's death for a day or two. He wondered if this place he'd been lured into even had time.

He'd been wrong about the frescoes: they really showed monsters battling men, not the reverse. Snake-legged creatures exulted in the ruins of human cities, brandishing their torches and weapons triumphantly. Garric tried to avoid seeing the images as he passed them.

The nymphs led him into a room with a high ceiling and bands of geometric designs across the walls. From wall pegs hung huge shields of an unfamiliar type: they were shaped like figure eights and covered with the hides of piebald oxen, hair-side out. A long bronze-pointed spear was racked beside each shield.

"This is the guardroom," Pink-Hair said in what seemed to Garric a loud voice.

Blue-Hair pointed to the coffered wooden door at the other end of the room. It was the first doorway Garric had seen in this palace that wasn't open. "That's the throne room through there," she said. "But we won't go there."

"Oh, no!" several of the nymphs said together.

"But here's the sword, Garric," Green-Hair said, pointing to the weapon hanging from a peg on the right doorpost. "Just as we promised you."

"Don't you recognize it?" asked Rose-Hair, reaching back with both hands and combing her fingers through her marvelous mane. "It's King Carus' sword."

It was King Carus' sword!

"Well, take it, silly!" said Saffron-Hair.

Garric stepped forward and lifted the sword and belt. He gripped the leather-wrapped hilt and drew the blade a few inches from its sheath. A lifetime of images cascaded through his mind—images of Carus' life, not his own. It was like walking from a darkened room into sunlight: everything Garric or-Reise had done paled by contrast.

"Touch the metal, Garric," Violet-Hair said. "You can't be enchanted if you're touching this iron."

The straight blade was longer than that of the sword Benlo provided, though perfectly balanced and not uncomfortably heavy. The hilt and cross guards, quillons, were forged from the same billet of steel; Garric looked at the hilt closely to be sure, but there was no line indicating that the pieces had been made separately and welded together.

A ring for the index finger was part of one of the quillons, so that the user would always be in contact with the metal. Garric slid his finger through the ring. The hilt fitted his hand perfectly.

Fish with pastel fins floated in the air about him. He jerked his finger out of the ring.

"Let's go out now, Garric," Green-Hair said. "We don't want to stay here too long."

They went through the door by which they'd entered; the nymphs surrounded him like ripples about an oarblade. Outside was a cobblestone courtyard with a fountain in the center. A bronze girl held a pair of geese from whose open beaks streamed water into the basin below.

The six-sided courtyard had at least twenty arched doorways on every face. The architecture was nothing like that of the palace Garric had entered minutes before.

The belt wrapped around the sheathed sword was heavy leather and wide enough that the buckle had two tongues. Garric wondered if he ought to put it on.

"Mistresses?" he said, feeling awkward. "Thank you for the sword, but I need to get back now. I have people waiting for me, ah, where I came from. Can you show me the way out?"

The nymphs laughed merrily. Blue-Hair put her hands on his as she had when she first appeared to him.

"Oh, silly!" she said. "We've given you what you wanted, Garric, so you have to give us what we want!"

"And we want you!" the other nymphs trilled in chorus.

8

Cashel leaned over the *Golden Dragon*'s bow railing, looking down into the phosphorescent spume that rolled past. A sailor near the mast played a lute whose neck was kinked back in a right angle; several of his fellows sat at his feet, their torsos swaying in time with the music.

"I love your stars," Mellie said, lying on the rail beside Cashel with her fingers laced into a cushion behind her head. "They're just like you humans—they move and then they come back just the way they were."

She raised her right leg and extended her foot in line with it as though she was sighting at the waxing moon. "You're always doing the same things, you know," she said to Cashel with a grin. "Building cities and then tearing them down and killing everybody. Do you suppose it's because you use iron?"

Cashel looked at the sprite and tried not to frown. He was never sure when she was joking. He wasn't sure that she ever joked the way people did.

The breeze was light and visibility good, but the ship proceeded with only two brails of the mainsail clewed down from the yard because the captain believed Erdin was just over the horizon. Navigation out of sight of land was more of an art than a science. An error of a hundred miles was possible, especially on this passage that the crew had never made before. A far smaller mistake could run the *Golden Dragon* onto the shore of Sandrakkan if the captain clapped on sail in darkness.

"Iron's good for a lot of things," Cashel said, looking into the water again. "I like the feel of hand-rubbed wood, sure, but for a wagon tire or a plow blade there's nothing like iron."

A Highlander played a bamboo flute from the stern gallery where the skiff swung in davits. He wasn't playing the same tune as the lutist—or any tune at all, it seemed to Cashel—but despite that, the instruments managed to create between them a melody that suited the sea very well.

The sigh of waves passing the hull stilled as Cashel peered into them. It was as though the water had vanished and the vessel floated on air. A fish glowing with its own rosy light swam beneath them. It was thirty feet long and had a simple tailfin, not the flaring tail of the fish Cashel was familiar with.

"What's that?" he said in surprise.

"Umm?" Mellie said, rolling onto her stomach and sticking her head over the railing to look down.

The fish vanished into the immensity of the vanished sea. People danced around an altar on a hillside, executing complicated steps and countersteps. The figures were tiny, but Cashel saw every detail of their features and dress. Their faces were pinched-looking, as though they danced with fear rather than joy.

"Oh, they're worried about their harvest," Mellie said. She cocked her face up toward Cashel with the first frown he'd seen from her. She added, "You should keep away from them, Cashel. They're nobody's friends though they like to pretend they are."

Cashel stared downward. Was he seeing the bottom? The lookout on the mast head didn't seem to notice anything wrong with the sea.

"Who are they?" Cashel said. The hillside had passed under the keel, dancers and all. He couldn't understand what he was seeing.

"Oh look!" Mellie said, pointing. She drummed her legs

up and down in excitement. "It's your friend Garric, Cashel! Oh, the nymphs have got him!"

She giggled at Cashel. "He should have known better," she said. "He's nice enough as humans go, but he isn't strong the way you are."

"Garric?" said Cashel, craning his torso over the railing. "What's he—"

It *was* Garric, looking just as he had when Cashel last saw his friend in Carcosa. Garric stood in a great courtyard surrounded by merry girls, turning his head from side to side with an anguished expression.

"What's he doing under the sea?" Cashel said, finishing his question after the moment's pause.

"The nymphs caught him," Mellie repeated in a patient voice. "Why ever did he go to them, do you suppose? They'll never let him go."

The *Golden Dragon*'s square teak bow slid onward. Cashel had to lean still farther outward to see the courtyard. "Can't we help him?" he asked desperately.

"Well, of course you can," Mellie said. She hopped from the railing and danced monkeylike up Cashel's mighty arm. "Just jump over the side."

She pointed.

With no more hesitation than he would have showed if a seawolf came out of the surf to attack his flock, Cashel raised his right foot to the ship's rail and went over the side in a clean dive. He didn't feel the water as the *Golden Dragon* vanished into the sky above him.

9

Blue-Hair said "Oh!" in surprise. The nymphs looked at something behind Garric. He turned and saw Cashel walk through one of the many doorways onto the courtyard.

There was a tiny girl on his shoulder, perfectly formed and quite normal except for her size and hair of an inhumanly red color.

"Cashel!" he said. "What are you doing here? And what's that on your shoulder?"

'The nymphs drifted closer to Garric. Blue-Hair placed herself between Garric and the newcomers. She and her sisters seemed apprehensive but determined.

Cashel glanced at his shoulder. "Oh, this is Mellie," he said. "I didn't think you could see her. I guess I'm dreaming."

"You've got to let him go, Cyane," said Mellie to the blue-haired nymph.

"Garric's ours!" Blue-Hair insisted. "You have one of your own, Mellie! Why are you coming here?"

Cashel seemed to ignore the women's argument. "Mellie says we can help you leave," he said to Garric. "Though if this is a dream, I don't know. Have you been keeping well?"

"Well enough," Garric said. "It's all pretty confused."

He laughed and added, "It was confused before now. I think I must be dreaming too, but I'd like to wake up."

It was good to see Cashel again. He projected a sense of solidity that nothing in this place and perhaps nothing else in the waking world could match. You could always trust Cashel not to do the wrong thing even if there might be many right things that he didn't bother himself about.

"Cashel wants you to turn his friend loose," said the tiny girl on Cashel's shoulder. "He's even stronger than you think. You have to do what he says, Cyane, or . . ."

She fluttered her little hands in a gesture that was somehow as threatening as the way a storm surge humps as it approaches the shore.

"I dreamed I dived over the side of the ship," Cashel said. He frowned, trying to organize the details of his memory. "But there wasn't any water. I just walked through the door."

"I was following a path but I went off it and got lost," Garric said. "I found this—"

He looked at the sword and wondered again if he ought to belt it around his waist.

"—but I wasn't looking for it. At least I don't think I was."

He frowned too.

"It's not fair!" the nymphs chorused. Green-Hair looked ready to cry with the frustration of having her wishes balked.

"Show Cashel's friend the way out," Mellie said with cruel nonchalance, "or Cashel will make a way for him. You know he will."

"I met Mellie on the way to Carcosa," Cashel said vaguely. "I didn't say anything then because I didn't think you could see her. I guess you only see her in dreams?"

Garric shrugged. He buckled the sword belt. There were five sets of tongue holes; the set tighter than those the previous owner had normally used felt most comfortable on Garric.

"Not fair," Green-Hair whimpered as she took Garric by the hand and tugged gently. He hesitated, looking from the nymph to Cashel.

"Go along with Prasina," Mellie said. Garric heard her voice as clearly as if she'd been the size of a normal woman. "And you should be more careful about what you get yourself into. My Cashel may not be around to help you the next time!"

She put her hands on her hips, leaned forward, and stuck her tongue out at Garric.

"Mellie!" Cashel said in embarrassment. The girl burst into laughter and patted his earlobe with one hand while waving to Garric with the other.

Prasina tugged again. Her sisters had gone somewhere while Garric wasn't looking. He followed the green-haired nymph toward one of the archways.

"Goodbye, Cashel!" he called over his shoulder. "Good to see you again, even this way."

Whatever way that was ...

Prasina stopped at the archway. "This will take you back,

Garric," she said. "The way you came is blocked, but this is shorter anyway."

He smiled awkwardly at the nymph. Cashel and his tiny friend were no longer in the courtyard. Garric was afraid to say anything in case it meant he wouldn't get free after all, so he ducked into the corridor beyond.

"Goodbye, Garric!" a nymph's voice called behind him. "Don't get off the path!"

The corridor was paneled in yellow pine with many knots. The way grew darker with each step Garric took, but patches of fungus on the wood gave off a pale light to which his eyes adapted after a time. Until then he kept his right fingertips against the wall.

He jogged, holding his scabbard with his left hand to keep it from flopping as he moved. It felt natural to do that, instinctive even, though he supposed it was a habit Carus had had to learn a thousand years before.

A hundred yards from the entrance, another corridor crossed the one Garric was following. There were lights burning in the branch to the right; he heard cheerful music coming from that direction.

There was no chance at all that Garric would leave the path he was on this time. If he saw his sister being murdered down another corridor, he'd treat it as an illusion and keep on going.

Keep on going and pray to the Shepherd that he was right.

He came to a place where part of the ceiling had fallen in; he clambered over the debris. A bronze helmet and the gold hilt of a sword lay among the masonry, but the blade and the bones of the man who'd carried it had rotted away in long ages past.

A slime of glowing fungus now covered walls of bare stone. Garric jumped a crack in the floor several feet wide; the air that puffed up from it was hot and sulfurous. The corridor was by now a tunnel through living rock. At one point a metal pipe crossed from one wall to the other. It was cold and hummed when he touched it.

Garric saw light ahead of him. He sucked in his lips and

continued at his previous deliberate pace instead of breaking into a dead run. Something small squealed and crunched beneath his callused foot; it felt like bare bones without a sheath of muscles and fur.

The tunnel ended in a circular room hundreds of feet across. The ceiling was a harsh white blaze. Garric couldn't guess how high it was, but the light itself was a pressure on his shoulders.

He stopped and released the scabbard. His palm ached; he hadn't realized how hard he'd been holding the weapon.

Machinery whose purpose Garric couldn't imagine was bolted to the floor. Most of it had slumped into piles of rust from which poked tubes of a crystalline substance, some of them broken.

The exit was a quarter of the way around the circle. Garric let out a deep breath. Until he saw the rectangular opening in the wall he'd feared that there was no way out of his nightmare after all. He strode to the exit, letting the sword swing and feeling almost jaunty.

The passage grew larger beyond the opening, but it was nearly blocked by the skeleton of the giant who'd crawled as far as he could before he stuck. His right hand was extended: the finger bones lay in the tunnel just short of the circular room.

Garric squeezed past the skull, four feet across through the temples. There was a single eyesocket where the bridge of a man's nose would be. Garric didn't know whether that was a deformity or the way all the creature's kin were born. The giant's bones were relatively heavier than those of a human.

The rib cage was still articulated. Spiders the size of Garric's palm hung from webs marked with a Z-pattern of silk. The creatures scurried to hiding places among the spiky processes of the spine.

The spiders' hairy bodies were dirty yellow; their eight eyes glittered in the light seeping past Garric and the skull behind him. He pushed through the webs, pretending they 'were thin cloth, pretending that he wasn't afraid of fat yellow bodies dropping on his neck in the darkness.

This was the way out of his nightmare. He was going back to his friends. He was going home, and fear wasn't going to stop him.

The passage kinked. It was pitch dark. Garric felt his way over a pelvis more massive than an elephant's. He stepped down, his right hand on a great thighbone, and there was no floor beneath his feet.

Garric shouted. He clutched at the bone but his fingers slipped from the smooth surface. He dropped through darkness, flexing his legs by reflex. Hitting the stone surface was as great a shock as the fact of it being ten feet below where he'd expected it, but he landed on his feet.

He stood in the center of the circle Tenoctris had drawn on the tomb floor. The candle on the empty shelf had fallen over but still burned in a pool of wax. The door was open, and the night was dark outside.

Tenoctris lay on the floor unconscious, and of Liane there was no sign.

10

Cashel awakened. It was past dawn and the Serian crew was taking in sail with a great deal of enthusiastic chattering. Cashel raised his head and saw that the *Golden Dragon* was well up the channel of a broad river; they floated in brown water, and marshes spread to the horizon on either side.

He jumped to his feet. "Mellie?" he called, suddenly afraid that the sprite was all part of a dream.

Mellie swung down on a lock of Cashel's hair, deliberately swishing past his eyes before releasing. She did an aerial somersault, then landed on his shoulder and stood on her hands.

"Did you sleep well, Cashel?" she asked him, upside down.

Cashel let out his breath at shuddering length. His tunic was dry on the underside and only slightly damp over his shoulders where spray had settled while he slept. He hadn't been swimming, that was certain.

"I don't know how I slept through all this," he said, looking around at the crew bustling over the ship's crowded deck. Men must have been almost stepping on him to spread the sail when light allowed and now to take it in as traffic on the river required a more cautious pace. Two grinning sailors began turning the horizontal capstan they'd been unable to use to adjust the yard while Cashel slept against it.

"They should have got me up," he said. The Serians were either too polite or too frightened of him to give him the kick in the ribs he'd deserved. He was ashamed of himself.

Jen and Frasa stood together on one wing of the quarterdeck. When they saw Cashel looking toward the stern they tented their hands and bowed to him. He blushed and nodded back.

It'd be time to get out the sweeps shortly. He'd be useful then.

"I've never seen Erdin," Mellie said, "though I suppose it's just a city. I haven't been on Sandrakkan in a thousand years. It rains a lot, and there's a kind of spotted cat that's way quicker than a fox."

She giggled and dropped into a normal seated posture, looking up at Cashel. "Of course maybe you humans caught all of them to make clothes out of. You're always doing something."

"I had a dream last night, Mellie," Cashel said slowly.

"No, no, Cashel," the sprite said in a laughing tone. "You didn't dream. Don't you remember? You were too busy helping your friend Garric."

11

The procurator swayed in the sedan chair she'd hired as the four bearers lifted the poles to their shoulders and began trotting toward the bor-Dahliman mansion in the heart of Erdin. City regulations forbade wheeled vehicles during daylight hours, and it was still three hours to sunset. Asera hadn't been willing to wait, so she'd hired the chair waiting in front of the inn on the northern outskirts of the city.

Sharina clasped her hands and wondered whether she should feel relief that they'd reached the city. Bor-Dahliman was a Sandrakkan noble who supported the king—more likely, a noble who opposed the Earl of Sandrakkan; all the procurator and her contact had in common might be enmity for the earl, but that was good enough for the purpose.

Asera would arrange for all four of them to be fed, clothed, and given lodging until she could arrange passage to Valles. Political rivalry between Sandrakkan and Ornifal didn't prevent normal trade by the islands' own vessels and by merchants from other isles carrying cargoes between the two.

Sharina didn't remember whether she'd even known that Sandrakkan was ruled by an earl during that past lifetime when she was a girl in Barca's Hamlet. Sandrakkan was a barbarous place during the Old Kingdom, mentioned by the epic poets only as a rocky shore or a home to savages who threatened the heroes.

She turned to Nonnus. "I've been thinking about the old epics, Nonnus," she said. "We've seen the rocky shore of Sandrakkan, I wonder when we'll meet the savages they always talked about?"

The hermit smiled, though it would be a hard question whether his expression could better be described as "wan" or "grim." "Trust a civilized man to think of Sandrakkan as either a bad shore or a land of savages," he said. "Your poets should have come to Pewle Island to find the real things."

This was a government coaching inn, like those they'd stayed in each of the past four nights they'd been driving south. They'd had no choice even if they'd wanted to do otherwise: Callin's coach bore the seal of the Earl of Sandrakkan and to stay elsewhere would have aroused even more suspicion than their motley appearance already did.

The coach was here in the inn yard with two others, one a rich landowner's private conveyance. The postilion, a young lout who looked like a robin in his russet tunic, was washing down the vehicle's lacquered paneling while the driver—an altogether higher form of servant—drank in the common room.

The postilion rode at the back of the coach, taking the worst of the pounding and all the dust the wheels turned up. He was there to add to the grandeur of his master's passage, like the plumes on the horses' brows. Apart from that the postilion opened doors for the coach's passengers and cleaned the coach at halts.

Those weren't the sort of duties that ought to give a man airs, but the postilion thought better of himself than Sharina did. In fact, he seemed to think better of himself than Sharina thought of the king in Valles. She would have been washing their coach now, except that she knew she'd meet the postilion at the water trough.

Nonnus looked over the situation. "Why don't you go inside, child?" he said. "I'll thank the Lady and join you shortly."

Sharina hesitated. She would have offered to go with the hermit, but she knew he preferred privacy for his prayers. He'd suggested she go inside because she wouldn't be bothered there. The stable staff, two ostlers and a boy, were cut from the same cloth as the postilion; it would be certain trouble for a lone woman to stand in their vicinity.

But Meder had entered the inn with the procurator and

stayed after she rode off. Besides, Sharina liked the open air after a day of jouncing in the coach. The vehicle's body was slung from leather straps rather than being mounted directly on the axletrees. That turned fore-and-aft shocks into swaying motions, but it didn't cushion the up and down impacts when the wheels hit a high stone or dropped into a rut.

"I'll go over by the kitchen," Sharina said, nodding to the rear of the main building. As she spoke, a girl backed out the kitchen door and swung, carrying a wooden platter on her head and another in her arms. Beneath muslin drapes to keep the flies off were risen loaves; the girl was taking them to bake in the outdoor oven.

Nonnus nodded that he understood. There'd be enough traffic from the kitchen to the oven and well that the men from the stables on the other side of the compound wouldn't try to trap Sharina alone.

"I won't be far," he said. "Or long."

The hermit still looked doubtful. Sharina patted his hand and strode briskly toward the kitchen door before he could change his mind about leaving her.

Nonnus paused a further moment before walking to the gate into the alley. The stableboy had left it open when he returned from wheeling a barrowload of manure to the pile there. Stable refuse collected at a busy inn like this would be a valuable commodity for sale to neighboring farmers.

Meder came out of the side door of the inn just in time to see Sharina going toward the back. He immediately turned to join her.

The wizard had ably driven the coach from Gonalia, something none of the others could have managed. A nobleman learned as a matter of course to control four horses in a hitch, as complicated a task as baking bread or skinning a seal. Sharina could count on her fingers the number of times she'd seen four horses in Barca's Hamlet at the same time, and she didn't imagine that there'd ever been a horse on Pewle Island.

If it hadn't been for Meder's skill, the nobles would have used the soldiers' riding horses while Sharina and Nonnus walked. There was no way the two commoners could have ridden cavalry mounts on a thoroughfare without breaking their collarbones or worse.

That didn't make Sharina like the wizard or want to be around him, however. He'd changed in the dungeons of Gonalia, but he hadn't changed in a way she found attractive. She met Meder's eyes with a cold look, then deliberately turned her back.

He came up to her anyway. "Mistress Sharina," he said, projecting a false brightness. "You must be thankful that we'll be in civilized surroundings again soon. The bor-Dahlimans are an ancient family. I'm sure their town house will be comfortable."

Sharina turned to him again. Meder probably wouldn't describe as "civilized" any place he'd been since he left Valles. The inns the four of them stayed in south of Gonalia were comfortable by Sharina's standards, though none were as clean as Reise saw to it his house was kept.

The only thing *really* wrong with the inns here on Sandrakkan was that they weren't home. The thought that she'd never see home again made Sharina wish that the sea had drunk her down when the great turtle dived.

Meder blinked at Sharina's silence. His expression looked as though it had been fitted together in mosaic; it moved in a jerky fashion, and the pieces didn't join one another perfectly.

"There's still the voyage to Valles," Meder said. He was trying desperately to force her to accept him as a human being. "But I'm sure that a proper merchant vessel will be far more comfortable than the warships Asera insisted on traveling on."

If nobody attacks us at sea, Sharina thought, though material enemies hadn't been the major threats they'd faced thus far. She wasn't angry at Meder, just disgusted and a little sick every time she thought of him standing in a pool of blood.

"Master Meder—" she began.

She'd intended to tell the wizard bluntly that she didn't

want his company; not now, not ever. Over his shoulder she saw the boy coming out of the stables with a gleeful expression. *Has he been peering at Nonnus through a gap in the gate panels?*

The two ostlers were behind the boy; one of them carried a manure fork. They were going to the alley gate.

Sharina walked toward the gate, brushing past Meder as if he'd been a stake sunk in the inn yard. She knew that she couldn't reach the alley ahead of the men even if she ran.

The hermit's javelin was in the coach; Erdin was a city where ordinary folk didn't carry spears in public. He'd have his Pewle knife, of course.

He'd have taken off the knife while he prayed.

"Nonnus!" Sharina shouted, ten feet short of the gate as the ostlers flung it open together. Both were big men. One had black hair, a beard, and a limp, while the man with the pitchfork was tall and gangly; his joints seemed oversized for his limbs.

The stableboy turned to face Sharina, then lurched back with a gawp of fear when he saw the dagger she brought out from beneath her cloak. He was missing his upper front teeth, and patches of eczema blotched the scalp beneath his dirty blond hair.

The postilion caught Sharina by both elbows from behind. She kicked but she couldn't raise her heel high enough to do any good with bare feet. The postilion rushed her forward and hammered her right hand against the brick wall till she dropped the dagger.

He carried her into the alley; the stableboy entered behind them and closed the gate. He flourished the dagger as he gave Sharina a spiteful glance.

The Pewle knife hung from the gatepost. Nonnus stood against the board fence on the opposite side of the alley, smiling vaguely until he saw Sharina in the postilion's grip. Then his face went perfectly blank.

She understood her mistake at once. The alley was open in both directions, though the large pile of straw and horse manure to the right would be an odorous escape route; the fence itself was no barrier to a man as athletic as the hermit. If Sharina hadn't gotten involved, the only risk would have been loss of the Pewle knife.

Nonnus didn't care about property, not even for a knife he'd probably carried for as long as he'd been a man. All he really cared about were the Lady and the girl who'd just turned an unpleasant incident into catastrophe.

Nonnus had been kneeling before the Lady's image that he'd scratched on the fence. The tall ostler poked his pitchfork toward the hermit's face; Nonnus backed without flinching.

"Guess you'd be enemies of the earl since you're praying to the Lady, huh?" the man with the pitchfork said. "We're loyal folk around here."

"Think we didn't hear how your mistress talks?" the other ostler said. He reached back and took the Pewle knife; drawing it, he tossed the belt and sheath onto the manure pile. "She's from Ornifal. It's all well for rich folks to say it don't matter, but I lost my daddy at the Stone Wall!"

The stableboy picked up manure with his free hand and rubbed it deliberately over the simple image of the Lady. He made a whistling sound through the gap in his teeth.

"I'm no enemy to your earl," Nonnus said. "I didn't mean to offend anyone. I'll willingly pray with you to the Shepherd, friends."

The postilion laughed. "One of you hold this filly's legs apart for me. You can fight over seconds."

Sharina kicked the postilion's knee. He grunted and swore. The ostlers and stableboy glanced toward the motion.

Nonnus gripped the manure fork just back of the tines and rammed the end of the handle into the diaphragm of the man holding it. The ostler fell over, unable to cry out or cling to the fork.

Nonnus rotated the shaft and thrust the fork into the stableboy's face. One of the wooden tines broke in an eyesocket; the boy dropped without a sound.

The remaining ostler jumped back and crashed into the wall around the inn yard. He spread his hands in front of his face, apparently forgetting that he still had the Pewle knife in one of them.

"Say hello to your father!" Nonnus said as he stabbed the ostler in the throat. A tine struck the wall to either side of his neck; the tine in the middle was through the windpipe as well as major blood vessels, because the man made only a croaking sound as he fell to his knees. Nonnus jerked the fork clear. Pulmonary blood frothed down the front of the victim's tunic.

Nonnus looked at the postilion and laughed. The postilion screamed, lifting Sharina as a shield for his face and torso. Sharina kicked him in the crotch.

The postilion doubled up with a horrified gasp. She broke his grip and rolled free, hearing the *thunk!* of the fork thrusting home for the last time.

Sharina got to her knees. The gate swung back. Meder stood in the opening with a blank expression.

Nonnus lifted the first ostler by the hair and cut his throat with the Pewle knife. The victim's legs thrashed violently.

Just like a chicken, but with much more blood . . .

Sharina worked the fork sideways to pull it from the postilion's back. "Get out of here!" she said to Meder. She was crying. "You'll only be in the way while we bury them!"

She began to turn over manure. The pile wouldn't be collected for a week, especially with the disruption to the inn's routine caused when its stable staff absconded with Asera's jewelry from the luggage in the coach. The story would pass without question till the bodies showed up.

The gate closed behind her. She couldn't see much through her tears, but all she needed was a trench in soft manure. The fork's two remaining tines and the stumps of the others were adequate for the job.

"We wear black wool on Pewle Island . . ." Nonnus said between rasping intakes of breath. "Because it doesn't show blood. There's always blood when we slaughter animals. But you'll have to bring me a bucket of water before anybody sees me, child, because my arms are red to the elbows. Just like old times . . .''

He laughed through his sobs.

12

Tenoctris drank greedily from the pitcher, giving no sign that the brackish taste of Erdin's water bothered her. She had a bruise on her right temple. By daylight in six hours, it would look terrible.

"Oh!" she said, setting the container down and taking a breath. Garric had brought her out to the pavement in front of the tomb when he went for the water.

Mosquitoes whined and settled in the darkness; occasionally Garric brushed a hand along his bare arms or over his forehead, but for the most part he ignored the bites. Insects were well down his present list of concerns.

Tenoctris looked at him. She smiled, an expression as dim as the moonlight illuminating her face. "Benlo came back for his daughter," she said. "He was in another body, but his aura is unmistakable."

Her smile grew lopsided. She added, "I thought I'd lost you too, Garric."

"I got lost," he said. "It wasn't your fault. Cashel brought me back."

Tenoctris nodded as though there was nothing surprising in what Garric had said. "Cashel is a fine young man," she said. "His instincts are so good that his lack of—"

She made a moue with her lips to devalue the word she was about to use.

"—education isn't the danger it would be in another wizard of his power. He has quite remarkably good instincts."

"Cashel's a wizard?" Garric said. "*Cashel's* a wizard?"

"Yes," Tenoctris said. She raised the pitcher and took a series of small swallows. When she lowered the pitcher she went on, "Indeed he's a wizard, though I suppose he'd be as surprised to hear it as you are."

She shook her head and added, "I'm less puzzled by the things people don't see than I am about the things they do see, must see, but ignore. Where did you get the water?"

Garric's mind was still struggling with the ludicrous vision of his friend chanting in a dead language as he gestured over a pattern of mystic symbols. It took a moment before he realized that Tenoctris had asked him a question which was grounded in the world he understood.

"Oh!" he said. "Well, I went to the back entrance of the house and tried to buy water at the kitchen. They gave me the pitcher and some bread too, but they wouldn't take my money. I guess I looked . . ."

He laughed, thinking about his mother's reaction if a man with a long sword, wild eyes, and dusty cobwebs in his hair had appeared at her kitchen door.

"Well, I was pretty upset."

If Liane was gone, so was her sash filled with gold coins. Garric still had the silver from his pay, more money than he'd ever seen in one place before he set out from Barca's Hamlet. Money wouldn't be a problem in the near future.

"How do we get Liane back?" he said bluntly.

Tenoctris nodded. "First we have to locate her," she said. "We can't be certain that she's still on this plane, though I think that's the greater likelihood."

She looked at Garric and added, "Benlo took his wife's mummy as well as Liane. This is . . . a matter that gives me concern for Liane. Benlo ceased to be her father at his death. The soul that remains is a very powerful entity, but it isn't fully human."

Garric got to his feet, working out the stiffness and the bruises he'd gotten during his return from—wherever he'd gone. He retightened the belt when he stood. The sword's weight was better distributed when the belt was firm.

"Should we get started now, then?" he said. "I mean, the longer we wait the more likely . . ."

He wasn't sure that was true. He didn't know what Tenoctris was afraid would happen to Liane, and he didn't think he wanted to learn.

"Yes, we should do it now," the old woman said, rising with Garric's help and support from the fence beside her. "The *situs*, here, the tomb, is already prepared."

She went into the darkness; the candle had burned out long before. Old smoke and the stench of corruption mingled in an odor that turned Garric's stomach.

Tenoctris found the satchel containing additional tapers. Garric brought out his flint and iron striker. The wood of one of the coffins had crumbled to punk which would make good tinder.

"Don't bother," Tenoctris said. She murmured something under her breath. A blue spark jumped between her cupped hands, igniting the taper's wick.

Tenoctris set the light on the ledge where Mazzona's coffin had lain, then grinned. "This tomb would make anyone a wizard, Garric," she said. "There's more power focused here than it took to sink Yole into the sea. It's all in balance, fortunately."

She moved to the side of the previous circle and began sketching her symbols on a bare piece of floor. There was very little room. "Garric," she added without looking up from her task. "Please remove Benlo's corpse from the burial jar and stretch it out on the slab. I'm afraid it's necessary."

"Yes, all right," Garric said. He drew his knife and began working its straight iron blade into the pitch the funerary workers in Carcosa had used to seal it. He hated the thought of what he was doing, just as he'd hated crawling among the huge spiders in the passage back to the waking world; but he hadn't been raised to back out of a job because it was unpleasant.

"Tenoctris?" he said as he worked. "Is this dangerous,

what we're about to do? I'm not worried for myself . . ."

Tenoctris chuckled. She continued to write for a moment, using the clear wax of an unburned candle for a crayon, but she began laughing so hard that she had to pause. She looked up at Garric.

"My dear friend," she said. "My dear young friend. Have you ever started running down a hill so steep that you couldn't stop? And you had to run faster and faster or you'd fall?"

Garric nodded.

"That's what the three of us have been doing from the very beginning," Tenoctris explained. "But no, I don't foresee any exceptional risk in the next step."

Garric laughed also. It felt good; he'd been tense for too long, tense and lost and alone.

"I guess that was a pretty silly question," he admitted. Being with a friend was the same as being home; and soon they'd have Liane back with them as well—or die trying.

He laid the corpse full length on the stone bench, ignoring the stickiness of his palms. Farm labor meant you found yourself up to your knees in most kinds of nastiness at one time or another. Garric hadn't moved a half-preserved human body before, but he'd dealt with worse things.

Tenoctris finished drawing her symbols and leaned back with a sigh. The wax characters were only a texture on the stone floor, a rippling reflection. Garric guessed that the words had to be written but that they didn't need to be visible to human eyes.

"Normally this would be a very long incantation," she said, as much to herself as to Garric. "With the forces that are gathered here tonight, I doubt I'll need to repeat the spell more than once; probably not even that."

She looked at Garric. "This is necromancy," she said as if daring him to react in horror. "I'm calling the corpse to life so that it can answer questions."

Garric nodded to show that he didn't object. Disturbing a

dead man's rest was a small price to pay for saving a girl's life. But—

"If Benlo's in another body," he said aloud, "then how will you . . ." He turned up his palms in question.

"I'm summoning the spirit of the man whose body Benlo occupies," Tenoctris said. "He'll still have a link with his former flesh, and I hope that will help us."

She shook her head in wonder. "I find it hard to believe that I'm doing these things," she said. "For *me* to control so much power."

She smiled. "The important thing is 'control,' of course. Not 'power.' "

Her focus sharpened back to Garric and the job at hand. "I'll call on you to continue the incantation if it requires more repetitions than my throat can stand," she said. "But I'd be very surprised if that were the case."

Garric nodded. "I've been surprised often enough recently," he said. "I'll do my best if you need me."

He couldn't read the wax-written words. That shouldn't matter, because he'd be able to memorize the sounds if Tenoctris repeated them so often that she had to take a break.

Tenoctris bobbed the ivy sprig twice in her hand as though to loosen it, then said, *"Catama zauaththeie cerpho . . ."*

Garric laid a finger on his sword's iron pommel and felt Carus rise within him like a man stretching himself out of sleep. The sword, for all its weight and awkward length, felt *right* on his hip.

"Ialada kale cbesi . . ."

The hair on Garric's arms and the back of his neck prickled as though lightning were about to strike. He turned his head to look at the corpse. A blue nimbus surrounded it, slightly veiling features which decay had already begun to soften.

"Iaththa maradtha achilothethee chooo!" Tenoctris concluded.

The corpse sat up slowly. Its arms remained folded over its breast. The white burial tunic was stained with fluids leaking through the terrible wound to the chest and abdomen.

"By the power of Phaboeai, tell me your name!" Tenoctris ordered in a steely voice.

"I am Arame bor-Rusaman," Benlo's corpse said. Its voice had the timbre of wood blocks being rubbed together, a dry whisper. "I am dead."

"Arame, are you aware of your own body?" Tenoctris said. Garric's hand was tightly gripping the sword hilt. He forced himself to release the weapon.

"Yes," the corpse said. Its chest moved the way a bellows does, emptying and filling in long strokes that had nothing to do with the rhythms of human breath. "I am aware of my body. It is not moving."

"Arame," Tenoctris said, "why is your body not moving?"

"My body waits for the full moon," the corpse said. Its lips moved with the slow deliberation of a snake swallowing an egg. "My body waits for tomorrow night."

Garric expected Tenoctris to ask what the body—Benlo— would do at the full moon. Instead she said, "Arame, describe what your body sees."

"My body sees a door," the corpse said. A swatch of scalp slumped from the left side of the skull, baring the bone beneath. Movement was making the revivified body fall apart more quickly than decay alone would have caused. "The door is iron. The door is cold iron."

The corpse's chest pumped up and down more quickly now, but air whistled from the chest cavity and the voice was weaker. The stitches were pulling out of the wound the embalmers in Carcosa had sewed up.

"There is a coat of arms on the door," the corpse continued, wheezing like a runner on the verge of collapse. "A bunch of grapes over a skull. Over a skull. Over a—"

The whisper faded into a dry cackling laughter, Garric would have said if it had been from a healthy man; a death rattle in a sick one. The corpse's lower jaw disarticulated from the socket. It continued to wobble for a moment until the tendons gave way completely and it dropped into the creature's lap.

The corpse sank like a sand figure dissolving in a wave. The finger bones appeared as the flesh liquefied around them. The stench was overpowering.

"Benlo's in the mansion," Garric said, trying to keep his stomach from throwing up the bread he'd eaten while Tenoctris was unconscious. "He had a secret room that the new owners don't know about."

"We can leave," Tenoctris said. She struggled to her feet, breathing hard. "Poor Arame can't tell us any more. And I think I can learn the rest from that hint."

They stumbled into the clean night air.

"Hold it right there!" a voice shouted. A lantern threw their shadows unexpectedly onto the stone front of the tomb.

13

The *Golden Dragon* rubbed gently against the bumpers of old rope hanging between her hull and the stone dock. Mule-drawn wagons loaded with crates and bales and barrels clashed slowly down the street which fronted the river harbor. Erdin was a busy port, and the goods passing through it were packed in more fashions than Cashel could have imagined.

"They're talking about you," Mellie said. She clung to Cashel's earlobe and leaned out, pointing toward Frasa and the Serian who'd come to the dock to meet the *Golden Dragon*. "They'll want you to do something for them."

Cashel stood at the end of the line of Serian crewmen, whom Jen paid as they stepped from the vessel to the dock one by one. The Highlanders clustered on the foredeck around the Erdin customs inspector, apparently fascinated by the official's tunic with its border of gold lace and purple. Cashel was sure the little killers didn't mean any harm, but the resplendent inspector had drawn himself up as though he were in the middle of a pit of poison snakes.

The vipers would have been a safer alternative than Highlanders in a hostile mood, of course.

"I guess that'd be Master Latias, the factor," he said. The Serian was of the same physical type as the brothers. His robe was dark blue rather than brown, but it had the same silken luster.

"That's right," Mellie agreed. "What are you going to tell them?"

Cashel wondered what Ilna was doing now. She'd like all this silk. There were bales of it in the holds, beautiful stuff, but Cashel knew he couldn't appreciate fabric the way Ilna did.

He sniffed the air. "You couldn't graze sheep around here," he said, deliberately avoiding Mellie's question. "Their feet would rot."

The sprite giggled and hugged his neck.

The sailor in front of Cashel received his pay and went to join the group of his fellows chattering with the entourage which accompanied Master Latias. The factor's servants weren't Serians, but they apparently spoke the language well enough to communicate the sort of information a sailor with pay in his purse wanted to know.

Frasa and Latias joined Jen and Cashel. "I told you," Mellie laughed in Cashel's ear.

The brothers whispered together for a moment. Latias acknowledged Cashel with a polite bow; Cashel responded with an awkward smile and a nod.

Latias was probably in his late twenties, though the cool propriety common to all Serian nobles made him seem more mature at first glance. He stood with his hands clasped, waiting for the brothers to finish their discussion.

Frasa turned to Cashel again and said, "First your pay, Master Cashel." He counted out silver coins into the youth's palm—Haft anchors, not the bronze and Erdin silver in which the Serian crewmen had been paid. Without a tally stick, Cashel was lost after the tenth coin.

"They're giving you a bonus," Mellie said. "Serians are nice people, for human beings."

With laughter in her voice she added, "But they'll want you to do something that'll be really hard."

"That's too much," Cashel blurted as Frasa continued to add coins.

Jen and Latias exchanged glances. Within the limited range in which Serians displayed emotions publicly, the factor looked surprised and Jen wore a satisfied smirk.

"Latias has proposed a return cargo at very acceptable terms," Jen said. "Since you negotiated the original transaction with him, we're adding a finder's fee to your wages."

"Cashel," Jen explained, "I've told Latias of the abilities you've demonstrated on our behalf. I believe you might be able to help him with a problem that has previously proven intractable."

The factor made a full formal bow to Cashel. "Master Cashel," he said. "If you would come with us to my compound and listen to my proposition, I'll double the amount you were just paid. If you accept the proposition, I'll pay you very much more."

"Well, that's only if you survive, of course," Mellie noted in the detached tone she used for things she deemed serious. "Whatever they want you to do will be a really hard thing, Cashel. Can you see it in his face?"

Cashel looked at the money in his palm. He didn't think he'd ever seen so many coins in one pile before, let alone *silver* coins.

"Well, I guess . . ." Cashel said. "It can't hurt to listen."

Cashel accompanied the three Serians down one of the streets joining the frontage road. Part of the factor's entourage boarded the *Golden Dragon* to secure the cargo until it could be unloaded; coincidentally they freed the customs inspector from his jabbering audience. The rest of the entourage preceded or followed the nobles, clearing a path through the traffic.

Cashel ran a hand slowly up and down his polished quarterstaff, trying not to think about the number of people crowded around him. It'd be different if they were sheep. . . .

They passed a two-story building with an arcade on the lower floor. "The Fellowship Hall," Latias said, noticing Cashel's interest. "Many shippers and merchants in the overseas trade have offices there. The courtyard serves as a hiring hall for sailors. My family's office is combined with our living quarters so we have a separate compound nearby."

His eyebrows indicated the blank brick wall just across the next street. An arched gateway formed the compound's near corner. Serian servants threw open the gate. Its panels were lacquered a blue indistinguishable from Latias' robe, and the servants' tunics bore a blue stripe also.

Cashel saw three and perhaps the roof of a fourth separate building within the compound, and there were probably more. Pillared archways ran between them, though it didn't seem to him that they'd be much protection from a blowing rain.

Near the Serian doorkeepers were two husky local men carrying knobbed cudgels. They watched Cashel with looks of professional reserve. Cashel figured he and his quarterstaff could handle both of them together—and they figured the same thing. Clearly Serians in Erdin didn't face the sort of hostility Cashel had seen in Carcosa.

The attendants led the party to a tile-roofed building whose windows were made of colored glass. The individual panes were almost as small as the chips used in a mosaic, and the leading between the bits was much finer than anything Cashel had seen in Carcosa.

The interior was a single large room. Folding panels concealed doors in the sidewalls; servants entered on silent feet with trays of varicolored juices and fruit sliced into tidbits.

There was a low table in the center of the room with a chair on one side and three chairs on the other. Strongboxes of metal and metal-strapped hardwood rested against the walls; some of them were ornamented with fanciful moldings and painted designs.

Latias gestured his guests to the trio of chairs and took the one opposite. Cashel leaned his staff carefully against the wall and sat on the right end.

"Ooh . . ." Mellie said. She pointed toward a particularly garish chest on the back wall. A dog-faced demon in red enamel glared out from each of the iron panels. "Look at that one, Cashel. They'll want you to open it. Ooh, this *will* be hard!"

Servants, all of them women with long oval faces, knelt to offer refreshments. Cashel took a glass of pale green juice; it was tart and had a taste that he couldn't describe.

Latias tented his fingers. "Perhaps you already know why I would like to hire you, Master Cashel?" he said.

That was a test, a game. Cashel sensed Frasa stiffening in disapproval on the chair beside him. The factor's test reflected on the brothers' honesty as well as on the youth's.

Angered mainly by the insult to Jen and Frasa, who'd treated him well and paid him well beyond belief, Cashel put the juice glass on the floor. He stood. "If you wanted me to open that box there," he growled, nodding his head toward the enameled chest, "then you could be man enough to say so. I guess I'll leave now."

Latias gaped as if he'd been stabbed through the heart. He threw himself prostrate on the low table and laced his hands over the back of his neck in abject surrender.

Frasa and Jen rose to their feet. "Master Cashel," Frasa said, "my countryman's youth is no excuse for his behavior, but the fate of an entire clan depends on the accomplishment of the task he faces."

"Please," Jen added, "accept the apologies of my brother and me for Latias' boorish behavior, but hear him out."

Mellie laughed and clapped her little hands. "He'll know better than to play with my Cashel again!" she caroled. "Oh! That was just the thing!"

"Sir," Latias said, pressing the table. "I offer you any amends you choose. I have lived so long among folk without honor that I have dishonored myself!"

"Oh . . ." Cashel said, blushing fiercely. "Look, just tell me what you want me to do, all right? I don't know why I got my back up like that anyway."

Though he supposed he did know. People in Barca's Hamlet were as likely to lie and boast as people anywhere else, but nobody back home would think of doubting Cashel's word—or Ilna's either, if they knew what was good for them.

He wasn't home now. He'd likely never see Barca's Hamlet again. He had to get used to people calling him a liar, just as he'd gotten used to the fact that he didn't think very fast.

Latias stood but he kept his eyes cast down on the floor. "Master Cashel," he said, "my father was head of our family in Seres. When he traveled, as he did recently to visit the holdings which I administer on Sandrakkan, he brought with him the clan images so that he could carry out the necessary sacrifices on the anniversary of our descent from the gods. That will be tomorrow."

Frasa and Jen looked very solemn. Cashel nodded, because he was expected to do something. All he felt was a mild puzzlement, like when Garric read a passage from a book that really excited him and all Cashel could hear was words.

"I've never seen a god," Mellie said, combing her hair with the teeth of a tiny burr as she sat cross-legged on his shoulder. She grinned. "Do you think they're something you humans see instead of seeing my people, Cashel?"

"My father died unexpectedly at sea," Latias said. "He—"

"Oh!" Cashel blurted, more embarrassed than ever about the way he'd come down on the poor fellow. He didn't remember losing his own father, but he'd often seen how it hit sons and daughters in the borough. "I'm sorry about the way I acted. I didn't know you were upset."

The three Serians looked at him in guarded puzzlement. After a moment Latias said, "All the obsequies were carried out properly when the ship docked last week. There was no difficulty with that.''

"Oh," Cashel said. He blushed again. He was missing something that the others thought was obvious. It wasn't a new experience, but Mellie rolling with laughter on his shoulder didn't help matters.

"My elder brother accompanied Father from Seres," the factor continued. "He became head of the clan with Father's death, so three days ago he opened the chest to prepare the images for tomorrow's sacrifice. The demon which Father had set to guard the images tore my brother to pieces and closed the chest again.''

Mellie dropped down Cashel's side at her usual dizzying speed and trotted across the mats of woven grasses on the floor. Cashel hadn't seen cats around the Serians either here or back in Carcosa, but he still worried to see the sprite wandering that way.

"A demon *killed* your brother?" he said, trying to make sense of what the factor was telling him. He wished they were still sitting down; squatting, better yet. He thought best when his head was closer to the ground, it sometimes seemed.

"Yes, but we carried out his obsequies also," Latias said. "There was some difficulty finding all the pieces for the funeral pyre, but fortunately it happened in a closed room. I am therefore head of the clan, but I can't remove the images from the chest."

He smiled minusculely.

"Not and remain in condition to carry out the sacrifice, that is."

"Your father and brother were killed and all you're worried about is a, a sacrifice?" Cashel said in amazement. He wondered if this was the room where Latias' brother was torn apart. Those could be recent stains on the ceiling, scrubbed but not quite removed. . . .

Mellie returned from her exploration of the iron chest. She did a backflip on the table, but her heart wasn't in the acrobatics. "The demon's name is Derg," she said nonchalantly. "Cashel, he's very strong."

"My father and brother and all our ancestors can be assured of a peaceful afterlife," Latias said, speaking with the care of a man answering a question that he hadn't fully heard, "so long as the annual rites take place as scheduled. There's no time to make and consecrate a set of replacement images, you see."

"Didn't your brother know that a demon guarded the images, Latias?" Jen asked.

The factor shook his head. "No," he said, "though I can't say it came as a surprise. My father was a private man and, I'm sorry to say, a very suspicious one. He worked with foreign traders all his life until becoming head of the clan five years ago."

Latias stepped to the side of the table so that he could kneel to Cashel in full obeisance. He rose and added, "Obviously I've inherited some of the same attitudes, Master Cashel. Otherwise I wouldn't have doubted the abilities which Frasa and Jen assured me you have."

"Look," Cashel said. Without really thinking about it, he took his staff in his hands again. "I know you folks don't kill or anything, but couldn't you hire somebody local to, you know, be waiting when you open the box?"

"I tried that, yes," Latias agreed. "Points of steel, stone and bronze don't bite on the demon's flesh. A wooden club shattered, and the creature snapped a silken strangling cord. While it was killing all the hirelings, of course."

"Him, not it," said Mellie. She was back on his shoulder again, looking pensive. "Derg is male."

"Did you give them proper obsequies?" Cashel asked, pronouncing the word carefully and wondering what it meant. He'd thought they wanted him to use the quarterstaff.

The Serians looked at one another. Frasa said, "Well, the guards didn't have families—"

"*Serian* families," his brother interjected hastily.

"Serian families," Frasa repeated with a nod. "But I'm

sure their dependents were compensated for their loss.''

"Ah?" the factor said. "Yes, I, ah, compensated the victims' dependents. But the demon remains on guard within the chest.''

"What do you want me to do about Derg?" Cashel said. "I don't understand.''

"We didn't even know the demon's name," Latias said. "You just *named* him?''

"He's Derg," Cashel said, more embarrassed by the Serians' look of awe. "He's male." He swallowed. "I think.''

"Oh, he's male, Cashel," the sprite said coolly. "Just like you.''

"Our father died too suddenly to pass his authority over the demon on to my brother," Latias said. "Let alone to myself.''

He took a deep breath. His face showed more emotion than Cashel had previously seen on a Serian noble, even when the brothers were in immediate danger of being beaten to death in Carcosa.

"Sir," he said. "A wizard of sufficient power can overcome the demon. The only alternative is to have the chest exorcised by whichever priesthood protected it in the first place. There isn't time to return it to Seres for that.''

He knelt in submission. "Sir," he went on, "if you can free the images from their guardian, I'll willingly sign over half my personal fortune to you. The peaceful repose of my ancestors rests on you.''

Cashel swallowed. "I still don't see how I can help," he said. "I knew a wizard, but she was back on Haft. And she said she wasn't very powerful anyway.''

"You aren't a wizard the way they think," Mellie said. She sat with her arms crossed on her raised knees, glowering at the garish chest. "Not the way you think of the word either, Cashel. But you could fight Derg if you wanted to.''

Cashel twisted his head to look directly at the sprite. "Mellie?" he said. He didn't care what the Serians thought about him talking to empty air. "Should I do this? *Can* I do this?''

The factor started to speak. Jen hushed him with a hand gesture. The brothers watched Cashel intently.

Mellie turned her face up to his. "I don't know what you should do, Cashel," she said. "I think you're very strong . . . stronger than Derg. But Derg is very strong."

Cashel didn't understand any of this. Somebody ought to give him a flock of sheep to mind; but then, if he'd wanted to herd sheep he should have stayed home in the borough. He'd wanted something different; and this is what he had.

He chuckled. Even if he didn't understand it.

"Sir," Latias said. He'd gotten up again, so at least Cashel was spared the embarrassment of having somebody kneeling before him like he was a statue of the Shepherd. "Apart from the material rewards I can provide, the man who defeats the demon can demand a wish from it. From him."

"No, no, he's wrong," Mellie said. "What Derg will grant you . . ."

She raised one leg almost straight in the air while she balanced on the toes of the other. Cashel couldn't imagine anybody being as limber as the sprite obviously was.

The Serians stared at him. He ignored them.

". . . is what you'd wish for if you knew everything Derg does," Mellie said, switching legs in a scissors motion as sudden as the movements of a hummingbird's wings. She grinned at him. "And Derg knows a lot more than you do."

"Everybody knows more than I do," Cashel said. He grinned also. "Except about sheep."

"Of course," the sprite added, "first you have to defeat Derg."

"Master Latias," Cashel said, "I don't need your money. I've got more money now than I thought there was in the world."

That was only a small exaggeration. His pay crammed the purse around his neck tighter than a sausage fills its skin. He'd either have to get a bigger purse or change some of the silver into gold. Cashel or-Kenset with gold of his own!

"I guess this is pretty important to you, your ancestors and all," he went on. "And I guess Jen and Frasa want me to do this and—"

"Please, Cashel!" Frasa said. "This can't be anyone's decision but your own. If you would prefer to stay with us, my brother and I will gladly continue to employ you at your previous wage."

"Sure, I know," said Cashel. "But you wouldn't have brought me here if you didn't want me to help. I understand. You two've been good to me and I don't mind doing you a favor."

"The death of a clan by neglect of its rites is a terrible thing, Cashel," Jen said, his hands hidden in the opposite sleeves.

"Anyway," Cashel said, "you've been straight with me and you say Master Latias here has been straight with you."

He met the factor's gaze, wondering as he did so what Mellie was really thinking. He didn't understand the sprite any better than he did people; any better than he did a girl like Sharina, he supposed.

"I don't need your money, Master Latias," Cashel repeated. "But where I come from, people get by themselves by helping each other. I guess I'll help you now, since it seems like you need it."

"Well, I thought you would, Cashel," Mellie said with a tone to her voice that he couldn't identify. "After all, a flock has only one ram. . . ."

14

Part of Garric's mind wanted to draw his sword and cut through the men facing him behind the lantern. That feeling didn't come *only* from the part of him where King

Carus strode in bloody majesty across remembered battle-fields.

But the men were a squad of the City Patrols investigating lights and noises from a tomb in a good section of Erdin. They had every right to be here; but then, so did Garric and Tenoctris.

"Good evening, officers!" Garric said. "We're servants of Mistress Liane bos-Benliman. She sent us to inspect the family tomb for her."

"I want you to arrest them!" said a pudgy man behind the row of patrolmen. "They're plotting to break into my house!"

There were six City Patrolmen. They wore brass helmets and tabards bearing the Sandrakkan horsehead quartered with the wavy symbol of Erdin. Two patrolmen had catchpoles, forked shafts with a spring closure that could be thrust over a suspect's neck or limbs from a safe distance. The others carried cudgels, and all of them wore short swords.

"This property is owned by the Benlimans," Tenoctris said imperiously, speaking as a noble to commoners. That's just what she was, of course, though her family estate had probably vanished a thousand years before. "My master retained it when he sold the remainder of his Sandrakkan properties. Who is this person who disputes his title?"

The officer leading the patrol wore a plume of white feathers in the tube on the right side of his helmet brim. He looked at the pudgy man standing behind him and said, "Is that true, sir?"

"Here's the key to the enclosure," Garric said, reaching into the wallet hanging from his belt to find it. The key had been lying on the floor of the tomb; Liane must have lost it when the corpse carried her away.

"Well, I . . ." the man said. He was obviously the owner of the house and grounds. His wealth was sufficient to get vagrants jailed, even if they weren't trespassing on his own property; but demanding the arrest of agents of another nobleman while on their master's proper business—*that* was another matter.

"If you'd care to look inside, officers," Tenoctris said in a tone of tolerant superiority, "I believe you'll find matters in order. No stash of housebreaking implements or loot, I assure you."

"We're staying at the Ram and Ewe near the river," Garric said. "We can be found there—though Mistress Liane may send us back to her property with further instructions, of course."

"Well . . ." the officer said.

"Corporal?" said a patrolman with one of the catchpoles. "I think he's the one in the picture."

The officer reached into his scrip and brought out a tablet made of two thin wooden plates. "Bring a light!" he ordered peevishly.

Two patrolman held lanterns with glass lenses that could be shuttered to hide the light. They aimed their beams to illuminate the faces painted on the tablet's inner leaves.

Even from Garric's angle, the faces were recognizable as him and Liane.

"By the Shepherd!" the corporal said. "You're right, Challis, it *is* him."

"Watch him!" a patrolman shouted.

Garric spread his empty hands. He might be able to break and run, but Tenoctris couldn't escape that way. He wasn't afraid to fight, but these were human beings, not liches to be killed without compunction.

There were six patrolmen and the homeowner, and he'd have to kill them all. He wasn't willing to do that.

A catchpole thrust for Garric's neck. He batted it away. "I'm going to unbuckle my sword," he said in a loud voice. "Treat it well or it'll be the worse for you!"

He didn't know whether that was Garric speaking or the king shining through Garric's flesh at this crisis. Why were the City Patrols looking for him and Liane?

"Your name's Garric?" the corporal asked.

"Yes," he said. "What's all this about?"

"Well, Garric," the corporal said, "we're to behave with courtesy with you when we take you in, and we'll do just that. But we *are* going to take you in. Got that clear?"

Garric wrapped the sword belt around the scabbard and handed it toward the corporal. Challis, a young, sharp-looking man, took the weapon instead.

"I understand," Garric said.

"How about her, corporal?" a patrolman asked. "She's not the right one, not by forty years."

"Right," said the corporal, putting the tablet away in his scrip again. "But we'll take her in too. It's a lot easier to explain why you arrested somebody than to explain why you didn't."

He looked Garric up and down. "You'll come back to the Patrol hut with us and I'll send a runner to the people who want you. Then it's out of my hands."

"Did the Earl of Sandrakkan order Master Garric's arrest?" Tenoctris demanded.

The corporal shrugged. "I don't know who ordered it," he said. "All I know is that I did my job. But the runner . . ."

He looked at Tenoctris.

"The runner goes to a private house on Palace Square."

15

Everyone but Cashel and Mellie had left the room. The doors were closed and men waited outside with weapons Latias said were useless against the demon. Cashel set his staff against the wall regretfully. He believed Mellie when she said it was his bare hands or nothing, but the smooth, familiar hickory would feel good right now.

The sprite sat on the wooden chest next to the enameled

iron one which held the images. Her legs dangled over the edge.

The iron chest was two feet long and a foot wide and deep. Cashel didn't see how a demon hiding in a space so small could be dangerous. Was Derg poisonous like some snakes?

"What do I do?" he asked.

"You just raise the lid," Mellie said. "And after that, well, it depends, doesn't it?"

She lifted her body off the wood with her hands and rotated her torso upward into an absolutely amazing handstand on the edge of the chest. "Or we could go out and see the rest of Erdin instead," she added from an inverted position. "Though it seems what I thought it would be. Just another city."

The hasp wasn't padlocked. Cashel flipped up the latch.

There was no point in waiting; like Mellie said, this was entirely his own decision. He threw back the heavy lid and straightened, expecting a demon to billow up at him like smoke from a chimney.

A cover of green silk brocade lay over the images within the chest; threads of gold, scarlet, and blue shot through the heavy fabric. A bright red, dog-headed demon no taller than Mellie stood in the center of the cloth looking up at Cashel.

Mellie swung her body in a graceful arc, clearing the iron edge of the chest and landing feet-first on the brocade. "Here or there, Derg?" she demanded.

The demon opened his jaws. The roar wasn't from Derg's throat, though, but from the whole cosmos. The room blurred white, gray, and finally bright flaming red.

Cashel fell. The only point that held firm in the flux was Derg's bestial face, swelling out of the fiery background.

Cashel's feet hit the ground. The soil was thin over a base of dense clay. Ferns and the leaves of pale saplings decorated the bases of giant trees. The air was hot and still.

Mellie was a full-sized woman. She stood with her hands on her hips, her pelvis thrust forward. Derg, as tall as Cashel and so bright that he seemed to vibrate in this waste of green/black/brown, leaped for Cashel's throat.

Cashel was big but not slow. He caught Derg by one outstretched wrist and forearm, then slammed the demon to the ground like a giant flail.

Derg bounced hard, spraying water from the saturated soil. Cashel stepped back. He'd expected Derg to close with him in a wrestling contest. Depending on how strong the demon really was, the fight might have lasted some time, but Cashel hadn't really considered that he might lose. He knew that Garric was smarter than most people; and he knew that Cashel or-Kenset was stronger than anybody he was likely to meet.

Derg rolled over and got to his feet. The demon's legs were relatively shorter than a man's; his torso and arms were longer. The dent in the ground where he'd hit was filling with water.

Derg laughed. In a low, gravelly voice he said, "That was very good, human. Shall I throw you, now?"

"You can try," said Cashel. He and the demon stepped together with their arms outstretched. They struck chest to chest and their hands locked. It was like walking into an oak tree but Cashel didn't give way.

Derg growled a laugh and twisted to set his long jaws in Cashel's throat. Cashel head-butted the doglike muzzle. Fangs gashed his forehead, but the demon yelped and jerked his head away. Cashel turned, using his body as a fulcrum, and hurled Derg over his back.

The demon hit the ground just as hard as before, losing his grip on Cashel's hands. Cashel straightened, sucking huge breaths in through his open mouth.

This time he wasn't surprised when Derg rolled over and got slowly to his feet. The impact would have broken every bone in a human's body.

"You're very strong, human," Derg said with obvious respect. "I'll be sorry to tear your head from your body and devour your entrails."

Cashel was too involved with breathing to speak, and there

wasn't much to say anyhow. He didn't have a lot of use for men who talked about the things they were going to do instead of going out to do them.

A flock of robin-sized green-and-yellow parrots flew into the clearing, noticed Cashel and the demon, and swirled away squawking. Cashel started for his opponent again.

"Cashel," Mellie said from the side of the clearing. "He takes his strength from the earth. Don't let him touch the ground."

Derg snarled and charged him. They slammed together. Like hitting an oak tree, like hitting a boulder the size of an ox . . .

Cashel might have been wrestling one of the marble statues guarding the entrance to Latias' compound. There was no give in the demon's muscles. But Cashel *had* lifted boulders, and he'd once pulled a hickory sapling from the ground to brandish overhead roaring. No other man in the borough could have done that, but Cashel had; and he would do this thing.

He leaned backward, twisting at the waist, and dragged Derg with him despite the demon's attempt to pull in the opposite direction. Derg's legs were shorter than Cashel's. When both of them bent at the axis of the youth's hipbone, the demon's feet came off the ground.

Mellie laughed from the sidelines and turned a somersault in the air. Derg's teeth gnashed a whisker's width from Cashel's throat, but he couldn't force his jaws that slight degree closer.

Cashel started to laugh, a hacking, gasping sound of triumph. Holding Derg in the air was the hardest thing he'd ever done, but he could feel the demon weaken in his grip.

Cashel bent the demon's left arm inexorably back. He didn't have any margin to relax, but he knew now that he was stronger than Derg by a measurable degree.

When the leverage was right, Cashel caught the demon's right ankle. He turned Derg and brought him down across his left knee, ignoring the way the demon's freed right arm clawed him. The claws were short like a dog's, not a cat's rending talons; and not even that would have saved Derg now.

Mellie pranced closer and looked down into the demon's inverted face. "He'll kill you, Derg," she said. "Cashel isn't one of us, you know. He kills things when they get in his way."

The demon sprayed spittle in wordless desperation. He tried to roll sideways, but Cashel's strength prevented him.

Sweat plastered Cashel's hair to his scalp and ran down his chest. The top half of his tunic hung in rags; shredded by Derg's claws or burst from within by the flexing of his own massive torso—he didn't know the cause and it didn't matter. He continued to force the demon's shoulders and legs down on opposite sides of the blade of his knee.

"It's not going to be long now, Derg," Mellie said cheerfully. She gave the demon's nose a little tweak. "Cashel doesn't stop when he gets started, you know. I wonder how loud it'll be when your spine—"

"I yield!" the demon croaked.

Cashel barely heard the sound over the thunder of blood in his ears. He flung Derg away and started to rise.

All color left the cosmos in a white roar. The clearing dissolved. Cashel felt the ground receive him; then he felt nothing.

16

Challis had gone as the runner. Now he sat with the driver on the box of the closed carriage approaching the lockup. Behind him were a pair of postilions with dark faces and eyes whose pupils looked almost yellow in the light from the lamps on the front of the box. The wheels roared even though the vehicle was slowing to a halt.

Challis hopped down and said, "Garric goes with these guys, the old woman goes free. She isn't part of the deal."

The lockup was an open cage in front of the Patrol hut. The corporal's courtesy had extended to ejecting the half-dozen drunks who'd expected to spend the night in the cage, instead of throwing Garric and Tenoctris in with them. The smell and pool of vomit remained, but it hadn't been very long.

And besides, conditions in the lockup weren't the real problem.

The corporal unlatched the door. Tenoctris gave Garric a tiny smile of encouragement as they left the cage under the patrolmen's watchful eyes, but she didn't know what was happening either.

The carriage opened. Two dark, husky men of the same race as the postilions got out and stood to either side of the door while a pale-looking fellow followed. He looked at Garric and nodded. "Yes, he's the one. Get in, sir."

"Here's what he was carrying," the corporal said. The pale man accepted Garric's sword, purse, and wallet and handed them up to the nearer postilion.

Garric had expected the patrolmen to help themselves to his silver; that hadn't happened. Something about the situation worried them enough that they remained scrupulously honest in dealings with their prisoners. .

"Get in, I said," the pale man repeated. His voice was like the popping of a spark, sharp but lifeless.

Tenoctris had vanished into the shadows, getting clear before the Patrol or this civilian changed their mind. She'd murmured she had a plan, but there hadn't been any real discussion with the patrolmen always nearby.

"Yes, all right," Garric said, and climbed into the coach. Two more guards were inside. Garric sat on the bench facing them. The other pair reentered and seated themselves to either side, wedging Garric tightly so that he couldn't jump out a door while the vehicle was moving.

The coach started off as soon as the pale man sat down

across from Garric. The only light inside was the glow of the front lamps through panels of thin horn in the coachwork. The pale man's face and the yellow eyes of the guards beside him seemed to hang in the air.

"Where is Liane bos-Benliman?" the pale man asked over the thunder of the wheels. "You told the Patrol that you were in her service."

"Sure, I'm in her service," Garric said. "I left her at the Ram and Ewe. She's still there, I guess."

That was mostly a lie, but it'd stand up. The truth— "Liane's dead father carried her off"—wouldn't be believed and would probably make the situation worse.

Whatever the situation was.

"Why did you arrest me?" he demanded. The shade of King Carus paced across the back of his mind like a caged cat; restive but not nervous, waiting only for the moment Garric would release him. "Who are you working for?"

The pale man smiled. "You'll not be harmed," he said. "No doubt you'll have the answers to all your questions very shortly."

The coach pulled up with a creak of harness and leather springs. They hadn't driven very long, but the busy sound the tires made on the bricks gave the impression they were traveling faster than Garric guessed was actually the case.

A postilion opened the door. They were in front of a large mansion; lights were on behind the curtained windows. Two of the guards got down and waited watchfully.

"Go on in," the pale man said. "I'm told you'll be treated well."

His face moved in what was either a smile or a nervous tic. "She doesn't lie. That may be the most frightening thing about her. She does exactly what she says she'll do."

"*Who?*" Garric said as he climbed out of the vehicle. "Who are you working for?"

"Go in, Master Garric," the pale man said. "It doesn't do any good to fight her. You can't, you see."

Garric turned and walked up the three steps to the front

door. Two guards preceded him; the other pair and the postilions were directly behind. One of them carried his sword and other effects.

The coffered hardwood door opened before Garric reached it. He looked over his shoulder as he heard the coach driving away. Four men with yellow eyes stared at him; the pale man was gone.

The doorman was another of the yellow-eyed breed, as large and as silent as the others. Garric wondered if they spoke his language or could speak at all.

A woman waited in the foyer with the doorman. "There's a washbasin and fresh clothing waiting for you, Master Garric," she said. Like that of the pale man, her voice was as soulless as a plate of glass.

Candles in mirrored holders hung on the walls, more candles than Garric had ever before seen in one place. The panels were limewood with gilt edging.

Garric blinked. *Bright as day*, he thought, but he knew it wasn't. For all the glitter and whiteness, this building was as surely a tomb as the one in which Liane's ancestors lay.

"Come," said the woman. Garric followed her, because he knew she'd lead him to her mistress; and only the mistress of this place could answer his questions.

A room off the foyer was covered in marble veneer. In it were an alabaster washstand and basin, and in one corner a great copper bath. The room was larger than half the huts in Barca's Hamlet, though it seemed small compared with the mansion of which it was a part.

The woman had withdrawn; a male attendant waited at the open door. The staff, though discreet, would surely appear in time to prevent Garric from running away now.

The bath was half full of steaming water. Garric ignored it and filled the basin from the waiting copper pitcher instead. He scrubbed at his face and arms with a sponge.

A mirror of silvered bronze hung over the washstand. Garric cleared the cobwebs from his hair with the comb provided among the other bath implements. He thought of the spiders in the tunnel through which he'd finally escaped his dream.

Dreams don't leave cobwebs on waking; nor swords.

He had no intention of running. The owner of this house was one of the people trying to control Garric's life. He was going to learn why that was happening.

A fresh tunic and a pair of sandals hung from wall pegs. Garric's own tunic had been clean this morning, but that was a long day past. He didn't change, though: the garment was his, and the only thing of his that remained to him with the exception of his soul.

"You can take me to your mistress now," he said to the attendant.

The yellow-eyed man stepped aside. The thin female waited in the foyer. She said, "Follow me, please," and led Garric down a corridor into the mansion's west wing. The hall was brightly lighted, but all the polished wooden doors opening off it were shut.

The woman tapped on the door at the end. A voice within said, "Yes." She opened the door and closed it softly behind Garric.

The room was darker than the remainder of the mansion, though the pair of three-branched candleholders provided a great deal of light by the standards of the borough. There was a couch opposite the door and a wardrobe chest between the tall, curtained windows on the right-hand wall.

A woman stood with her back to Garric, examining the sword lying on top of the chest with the rest of Garric's effects. The candles on the wall above her threw her figure into shadow.

"The interesting thing about this sword isn't that it's sharp or strong," she said in a conversational, familiar voice. "Though it's obviously that too in the natural sense. Its real virtue is that to touch the metal is to be free of all enchantment. The smith who forged it must have been as skillful as I am."

That was what the nymphs said when they offered him the sword. "Who are you?" he asked.

The woman turned, smiling. "Have you forgotten me, Garric?" she said. "I haven't forgotten you."

She was Ilna.

"Ilna!" he said. He stepped toward her to hug her in greeting, then paused. "Were you arrested too? We didn't even know you were on Sandrakkan!"

She continued to smile. It was that expression which had stopped him. "Not at all, Garric. The house is mine. Sandrakkan nobles pay well for love."

She gave a short laugh. "For lust, at any rate. It's much the same thing, I believe."

Ilna's voice made Garric afraid for her. He felt as if he were watching her climb out onto a high cliff. He remembered his dream of a spike of rock a thousand feet above a foaming maelstrom. . . .

"Ilna?" he said. "What's wrong with you? Is it something I can help?"

She took a packet of fabric from the top of the chest. It was no larger than a folded handkerchief, but Ilna shook it out into a cape of cloth finer than spiderweb. Garric saw the candlelight through the fabric undimmed, but it distorted solid objects in ways he couldn't describe.

Ilna swung the cape over her shoulders and closed the throat with a ribbon tie. Garric felt his chest constrict.

She reached out to him. "Nothing's wrong, Garric," she said. "You aren't ignoring me now, are you? Come."

A fire hotter than a smith's forge swept over Garric's soul, burning away all personality and volition. He couldn't speak. He took a step forward, conscious of himself only as he might be conscious of a statue in a distant room.

Ilna laughed like ice crackling in the dead of winter. She lifted her cape's hood; the peak flopped down over her face in a transparent veil. "Come," the cosmos repeated in a voice as cold as moonlight.

Garric came to her arms. He could no more have refused than water could refuse to run downhill.

Shouts and the clang of weapons sounded in the hallway.

The thunder of Garric's pulse was louder in his ears. He touched Ilna's cheeks through the gossamer fabric.

The windows shattered inward. Curtains fluttered as figures climbed through the transoms. The door burst open.

"Garric!" Ilna shouted. She stepped back. Garric followed her, aware of his surroundings but not affected by them.

A pair of liches stood in the doorway. One held a spear, the other a cutlass red with rust and blood. More of the skeletal creatures were entering through the windows. The air stank like rotting marshes.

The liches stepped forward with their weapons raised. They were already dead. Ilna's magic had no effect whatever on them.

17

Garric!" Ilna cried, afraid for him as she would never fear for herself. The liches came on, smiling skeletally through their translucent flesh.

In the crisis Ilna didn't think of the knife she'd brought from Barca's Hamlet, sharp as a sunbeam within its bone case under her sash. The noose was her weapon, the one she'd die with.

She snatched off her cape, twisting the thin fabric into a rope. It was light as spidersilk, but it was that strong also.

Garric, freed from the enchantment, moved as Ilna had never seen a man move before.

He drew the sword, gripping the hilt in one hand and the chape of the simple, sturdy scabbard in the other. The same motion sheared the skull of the lich coming through the right-hand window.

He spun, blocking an axe with the scabbard while the long sword decapitated a lich with a cutlass. The slash became a thrust so quick that it was through the eyesocket of the creature with the axe while sparks the axeblade had struck from the scabbard's iron mountings still glowed in the air.

Ilna crossed her arms, then snapped them back, catching a lich's sword in the temporary loop. The blade was too corroded to sever the silk that held it. The creature struggled briefly to pull the blade out of Ilna's grip before Garric topped its skull like a soft-boiled egg.

Garric stepped chest to chest with a lich, too close for the creature to spear him. He struck with the sword pommel, turned, and cut a pair of liches across at midchest with a single sweeping motion.

The strength and speed of Garric's sword arm splashed jellylike flesh across the walls and ceiling. The bones of some of the creatures powdered like rotten sticks when struck; others sheared cleanly with a fresh, yellow color and traces of marrow at the core.

There had been at least a dozen liches; all were down but two. That pair came on as fearlessly as logs rolling. Garric struck low, under the kite-shaped shield one carried, and split the other lich to midchest with an overhand stroke.

Ilna picked up the axe. She smashed the head of the lich whose legs were severed at the knees, then did the same to one whose rusty sword flailed wildly even though its pelvis lay to one side of the upper body.

Garric turned. His body sagged with exhaustion; his complexion was gray. Bits of stinking gray gelatine darkened and liquesced, dripping from his limbs and torso.

"Garric!" Ilna said, herself suddenly exhausted. Her cape lay wrapped about the blade of a lich's sword, torn and soaked in the filth of the creatures' dissolution.

Garric's eyes focused at the sound of her familiar voice. The smile that started to form on his wide, strong mouth froze in horror and disgust. In a flash of sudden rapport, Ilna saw herself in the mirror of Garric's eyes:

Foulness stained her thin tunic. A point had thrust through it waist-high, front to back, ripping the fabric without touching her flesh; she hadn't even been aware of the danger.

Behind her, wrapping her in branches whose tips thrust into her ears and eyesockets, was a tree with leprous white bark. The leafless limbs caressed her like maggots crawling over flesh. The trunk and branches wove and swayed in a pattern more disgusting than the flesh dripping from the liches' rotting bones.

Ilna screamed. She grasped the branches filling her eyes, but she might as well have tried to tear down the doorposts.

Garric stepped forward, bringing his sword around with both hands on the hilt. His face was cold, his strength and grace that of a youth who had felled many trees without a missed stroke. The sword's heavy blade sheared through the trunk just below the knot of writhing branches.

The cosmos tore apart with a scream of dying fury. A void spread between Ilna and Garric, between her and everything but a chasm of ashen gray. She slid into the abyss.

But she was free. Ilna os-Kenset was free for the first time since she stepped through the portal in Carcosa, and her soul smiled.

18

The bed was of spun glass, soft and springy in a way that feathers never could be under Cashel's weight. He luxuriated for a moment in its caress, even though he knew he ought to be getting up.

At last he opened his eyes. The sun was a vast ruby dome on the western horizon. The clouds piling at intervals across the summer sky were streaked purple, maroon, and in flecks at the highest levels—gold. Where the city's crystal towers rose through the forest, they reflected all the colors of the rainbow.

Cashel sat up and stretched. He ached about every place a man could: a good feeling, a badge of honest work. Mellie walked onto the broad covered balcony where the bed lay, carrying a cup so clear that it looked as though the green liquor foamed in a blanket of air.

"How long did I sleep?" Cashel asked. He stood, careful but not shaky. His muscles weren't damaged but they needed to be coaxed into their duty.

"A long time," the sprite said cheerfully. It didn't surprise Cashel that she was a full-sized woman—not as tall as Sharina but more fully curved than Sharina would ever be. "Here, drink this and you'll feel better."

"I feel fine," Cashel grumbled, though he wasn't sure if that was true. He didn't feel bad, exactly, but he wasn't ready to do anything harder than walking across the room either.

He drank the liquor in small sips, keeping the glass to his lips all the time, never gulping, never hastening. The bubbles tickled the back of his nose. The liquor itself was cool in his mouth and throat but spread through his body as pleasurable warmth.

Cashel looked down at his chest. The tears Derg had clawed in his skin were already half-healed. Only a few patches of scab remained.

"How long?" he repeated in amazement. "Mellie, you should have waked me up!"

Birds wheeled through the high heavens in a complex dance. The sun was almost wholly below the horizon by now, but occasionally a wing sparkled as it cut a beam of light.

Mellie giggled and put her arm around Cashel's waist. Her muscles were as hard and flat as his own.

"You needed to sleep, Cashel," she said. "I told you, Derg is very strong."

He remembered the fight the way you always remember a fight: bits and pieces, a collection of shattered moments rather than a seamless whole. Fangs snapping a hairsbreadth from his throat, the sight of the stocky red body dripping with *ground water as it rose after an impact that should have been crushingly final . . .*

"He was that," Cashel said. "I hope I never meet anybody stronger."

He touched his forehead. The cuts Derg's canines had made when he butted the demon were still tender, though they too had healed.

"Let's watch the moons rise," Mellie said. She took the empty glass from Cashel's hand and set it on a table with legs like sapphire wires. They walked together, his arm over hers, to the bridge of glass arching off their balcony.

The air was charged and vibrant, though the only scents were those of the forest below: here a flower's perfume, there a whiff of fruit ripening; over all, the green power of life. Quick motions vibrated the canopy. Some of them must be birds roosting, but others were nocturnal animals coming out with the returning shadows, hopping along runways hundreds of feet in the air.

The bridge was six feet wide and had railings so delicate that they were only visible as the sheen of light bending through their structure. The slope was barely noticeable underfoot, but at zenith its rise completely hid the tower a quarter mile away at the other end. The surface had a pleasant, springy solidity, like a thickly sodded meadow.

Cashel had control of his muscles again if not his full strength. He lifted his arms overhead and flexed them, laughing in joy to be alive.

Mellie hugged him. "Yes," she said, again responding to words he hadn't spoken. "Now you're only as strong as any two other people, Cashel!"

She giggled. Cashel put his right hand under her thighs and lifted her into a chair of his arm and shoulder. He walked on, carrying the sprite like a tuft of thistledown. Creatures hooted and whistled musically in the wood below.

They reached the center of the span. Fairy lights gleamed in towers across the darkened forest.

The moons were rising, the lesser one above, and separated

by only a degree of angle the greater moon as well. They
were full, beaming silver light through a pastel haze of gold.

Cashel hugged Mellie to him with both arms; and hugging
her, he awoke.

"Oh!" Cashel cried. He lay in the jungle clearing where
he'd fought Derg. His head was pillowed on a bundle of
springy branches. Mellie sat beside him with a concerned expression; the demon squatted on the other side. They were
both full-sized. Cashel twisted upright, knowing that Derg had
him at a hopeless disadvantage now.

Instead of attacking, the demon knelt and touched his forehead to the ground. "Master," he growled.

"Here, Cashel," Mellie said. She tossed a nut the size of
a fist to Derg. "Drink this and you'll feel better."

The demon set the stem of the nut between his long jaws
and topped it neatly. He spat out the end as he handed the
open nut to Cashel.

"I'm all right," Cashel muttered. He didn't know when
he'd ever ached in so many places at the same time. He sipped
from the nut, expecting coconut milk and finding instead an
effervescent green liquid. The drink warmed and loosened his
muscles like a steambath as it spread through his body.

Cashel looked at the dog-faced demon. "You and me are
all right, then?" he said. In the borough a fight was mostly
over when one of the pair yielded, but there were times the
loser didn't want to leave it at that.

Derg bowed again. "You are my master until I grant your
wish, human," he said. He grinned, a ferocious expression
on a visage with jaws so long. "After that I will look for an
enemy who is not so strong."

Cashel laughed and clasped hands with the demon. "I
guess I'll do that too," he said.

He stood up, letting his muscles unknot slowly. He looked
down at his chest. Mellie—Mellie or Derg—had smeared
brown sap with an astringent odor over the claw marks. He

wrinkled his forehead, feeling the constriction of another daub of sap on the fang cuts.

"I had the strangest dream, Mellie," he said. "I was somebody else."

Derg plucked a purple flower dangling from an air plant on a branch high above. When the demon stood, his long torso made him about Cashel's height.

"The breath of these flowers gives dreams," he said. His growling voice, like the expressions of his inhuman face, took a little getting used to.

The flower didn't seem to Cashel to have any particular smell, but he didn't hesitate to believe Derg. He could identify a ewe by her bleat at a distance so great that nobody else in the borough could tell the sound from the breeze sighing. A nose as long as the demon's should be able to smell things Cashel couldn't.

"What did you think about the dream, Cashel?" the sprite asked. If anybody but Mellie had spoken, Cashel would have thought there was tension in her voice.

He shrugged. "It was fine," he said. "It was just funny, though—dreaming that I was somebody I wasn't."

"The person in the dream," Mellie said. "He couldn't have been you?"

"Oh, no," said Cashel. He laughed, feeling embarrassed and wishing he hadn't brought it up. "No, that was somebody else entirely."

The sprite gave a quick backflip onto her hands, then bounced upright again. Those were the first acrobatics Cashel had seen her perform since they entered this green jungle.

"We'll have to go some ways for Derg to grant your wish," she said. "Shall we start now?"

"Huh?" Cashel said. "Sure, I guess. I'll need to take it slow till I loosen up a little, is all."

"This way, then!" Mellie said brightly, striding off between a pair of man-high fern fronds.

Cashel thought he saw a tear wink on Mellie's cheek. It must have been a trick of the light.

19

"No," Nonnus said to the leader of the four horsemen escorting the carriage Asera had sent back for her companions, "I'll ride on the step, not inside."

The guard scowled. Lantern light winked on his steel cap and breastplate. He wore a long curved sword that hung down by his left thigh and clanked when he moved.

"You'd best not slip, then," he said. "If you fall, you'd better hope it's your head and not your belly that goes under the wheels, that's all I can say."

The carriage was turning around in the inn yard. The box was a wooden framework covered with linen waterproofed with size which required only two horses to draw it. Inn servants waited to transfer the party's meager possessions from the cross-country coach to this lighter, handier city vehicle.

"Yes," said the hermit, "I'll have to remember that."

"Sarko!" the innkeeper cried, calling one of the stablehands who should have been helping him. He himself carried the rug Sharina used for a bedroll. "Brann! Where are you?"

The carriage completed its turn. The innkeeper and two maids handed the baggage to the coachman, who laid it within the low fence on top of the vehicle.

"Sarko!" the innkeeper called again. Sharina tried to remember the faces of the dead men, but all that remained was a moving blur. Even bad men deserved something better than gray oblivion.

"Come on, get aboard then!" the guard said. He twisted his horse in a tight circle and clopped out of the inn yard, shouting orders to his men.

Nonnus looked at Sharina, smiled faintly, and handed her into the vehicle. Meder followed, sitting on the bench opposite. The carriage started to move immediately.

The hermit's left arm reached in through the window to grip the frame. His hard face was in silhouette. The step was small, meant only for the toes of a passenger entering or leaving the box, but Sharina didn't worry that Nonnus might fall.

Her dread was formless. Perhaps the ghosts of the dead stablehands rode her shoulders.

The seats were dark plush. She supposed the carriage was bor-Dahliman's property, but there was no crest or other mark of ownership. The guards weren't in livery either.

Meder was staring at her, though only occasionally did enough light sweep the interior for the wizard's face to appear as more than a vague outline.

"You don't realize how much you need me, mistress," he said. The rumbling tires turned his voice into an iron whisper. "You will, though. Someday I'll save you when nobody else could, and then you'll appreciate me."

Sharina turned her head away. She touched her fingertips to Nonnus' forearm. His lips smiled but he didn't look into the coach. His muscles were like carved bone.

Sharina didn't know how far they drove. The carriage never slowed, but sometimes she heard the escort bellowing threats ahead of them. Once iron clashed.

The noise and vibration of the wheels on brick pavers made her sleepy, but every time her eyes started to close she thought of the killings in the alley. Not the victims' faces, only the horror in their eyes as they died. She jerked upright again, her head buzzing. *Even bad men . . .*

The carriage pulled up so abruptly that Sharina swayed forward in her seat; the driver must have set his brake while shouting to the horses. Nonnus dropped from the carriage step and opened the door with his free hand, his left hand. He held his javelin at the balance in his right.

Sharina got out. They were under a porte cochere, a roof supported on one side by freestanding pillars to protect guests arriving in the rain, in front of a mansion. The air was salt, and humid; they were near the harbor or more likely a canal leading to it, since all the houses on this square were palatial rather than warehouses and tenements serving sailors.

There were no lanterns, but the rising moon was full. A tall woman in gray stood at the doorway; candlelight from the room behind her brushed long shadows across her cheek. "Get in quickly," she said. "Before someone sees you."

Sharina followed Meder into the entryway; Nonnus was a silent presence behind. The floor was laid in a geometric pattern of marble terrazzo; the ceiling was coffered with mythological paintings in the four sections. The single candle's light wasn't good enough for Sharina to see the details, but men rode dragons in one scene.

The woman closed the door and led them into the main hall. High windows let in wedges of chill, bright moonlight. Asera waited there with another servant, male this time but otherwise identical to the first.

The servants' faces were pale. Their hair lacked body or highlights; it lay on their scalps like carded flax.

Sharina heard the carriage and escort clatter away—down the street, not around to stables in the back. She looked about her. The hall was veneered in colored marbles; statuary looked out from wall niches, and the banisters supporting the rail around the mezzanine floor above were miniature statues as well.

Most of the corridors from the hall to other rooms were closed by tall doors of black wood, richly carved and mounted on hinges of gilded bronze. A double staircase faced the formal front door—not the side anteroom by which the trio had entered. Between the wings of the staircase a peaked passageway led straight back to a bronze grating like the portcullis of a castle. Sharina saw a marble dock gleaming in the moonlight beyond. The house had direct access to one of the city's canals.

The bor-Dahliman town house was a mansion of great luxury. There probably wasn't a building in Carcosa to match it. It was empty or nearly so.

Even by moonlight, Sharina could see the film that settles

inexorably over an unused room. The stickiness of salt air attracts dust, and there was no army of servants here to wipe it away. She wondered if the pale couple were the only people in residence.

"Where's the owner?" she demanded sharply. "Who is it we're meeting here?"

Asera's nose wrinkled with irritation at having her judgment questioned. "Regin bor-Dahliman is away. His servants will see to our needs until the morning, when I'll arrange our passage."

Sharina heard faint movement from the upstairs. Nonnus heard the sounds also. There was no obvious change in his behavior—he'd been as tense as a mongoose in a snake pit ever since they arrived at the house—but she could follow his eyes assessing their surroundings.

The front door was barred, pinned, and locked. It would withstand a mob with a battering ram and would take several minutes to open even from the inside. The windows at mezzanine level were grated; any openings in the walls of rooms behind the black doors would be equally well protected. The portcullis onto the canal would have to be cranked up, a lengthy process even if they found the windlass that worked it.

The only way out in a hurry was through the door by which they'd entered. If this was the trap it seemed, the party responsible would have been aware of that also.

The female servant bowed to Sharina. "Mistress," she said, "please come with me to the West Wing. There is a room prepared for you."

"West Wing?" Asera said in puzzlement. "You said all the open rooms were in . . ."

"Let's go," Nonnus said softly. His Pewle knife was in his left hand.

He and Sharina started for the anteroom. She drew her dagger and reached for the door latch with her free hand. The portcullis closing the canal entrance began to creak upward.

"Where are you going?" the procurator demanded. "Are you out of your minds!"

"Mistress," said one of the servants. Their voices were indistinguishable, pale and empty like their gray eyes. Sharina jerked the door back.

The outside door was already open. Liches trailing seaweed filled the anteroom. They shambled forward, raising their dripping weapons.

Nonnus kicked the door shut before Sharina could move. "That way!" he shouted, giving her a nudge toward the closed door directly across the main hall.

Asera shouted in fear and anger. Liches lined the mezzanine railing and were starting down the stairs; more of the creatures came up the corridor from the canal.

The female servant wrapped her arms around Sharina. She had the strength of an octopus. Sharina stabbed upward, a clumsy blow because she'd been thinking of the liches as her only enemies.

The dagger had a needle point and a good edge. It grated through the woman's ribs—if she was even a woman. She continued to grip Sharina. Sharina twisted her broad blade desperately. They fell together and Sharina's head smacked the terrazzo.

The woman suddenly went limp. Her head rolled to the side; a thick, brownish fluid, not blood, oozed from the stump of her severed neck.

Nonnus dragged Sharina to her feet by the back of her tunic. Her eyes focused, but not both on the same point: all objects were haloed by their double. The male servant lay on his side with the hermit's javelin so far through his breastbone that half the blade stuck out from the middle of his back.

Meder already had the door open. Moonlight streamed through the clerestory windows of the room within, illuminating a black throne. Meder ran to it with a cry and caressed the carven arms. Nonnus carried Sharina inside, shoving the procurator ahead of them.

Sharina tried to get her bearings. Brown ichor was already beginning to corrode her dagger's blade.

The large room held only the ornate throne and an ebony table against the opposite wall with a pair of silver candlesticks, oxidized black like the furniture. The windows were too narrow to pass a human and were barred besides.

The only door was the one onto the main hall, filling with liches.

Nonnus glanced at the latch, a complex apparatus that shot two bronze bars into slots in the doorjamb. The bars and the door itself were sturdy, but scores of undead monsters could hack through them in a matter of minutes.

"Lock the door," Nonnus said and stepped back into the hall, pulling the door shut behind him.

"Nonnus!" Sharina said as she staggered to her feet. Asera threw the double bolt. "Nonnus, no!"

Steel clashed. Something hit the other side of the door and bounced away.

"Pray for those I kill this day, child," Nonnus called through the panel.

Because he wouldn't be alive to pray for them himself.

"No!" Sharina repeated as she grasped the locking wheel to open it. The procurator hit her from behind with a silver candlestick.

Sharina lost control over her limbs. She slumped bonelessly onto the floor, still able to see and hear. The dagger slipped from her fingers and clanked on the terrazzo.

Meder knelt on the floor before the great black throne. He was beginning an incantation, while outside the door the fight continued. Metal rang savagely but none of the combatants said a word.

Nonnus could buy only time, not safety, for the girl he'd promised to protect; but he was buying that time, with his Pewle knife and his life.

20

A full-sized stone makes sharpening easier," King Carus said as he drew the small whetstone across the across the edge of the sword near the point. He was working on the reverse of the blade, the edge opposite the ring quillon: his spirit in Garric's body had backhanded the sword through an iron helmet. The metal had parted like wheat before the scythe, but it had left a nick in the blade as well. "This one will do, though."

He grinned at Garric. "Just don't cut your finger off—and that's not a joke, lad, I've seen it happen."

Dream Garric nodded. "When you're tired, you make mistakes," he agreed. "I do, at least."

"Everybody does," Carus said, turning the blade over to work from the other side. With a bigger whetstone you'd move the blade across the stone to sharpen it, but this one, from the pouch attached to the frogs holding the scabbard, was too small for that to be practical. "And you'll never be so tired again as after a battle, but it's then you *must* care for your sword."

He laughed with the joy of a man who finds humor in most of life, not least his own mistakes. "There's nothing worse than waking up to learn your enemy's counterattacking at night *and* your sword doesn't have the edge you'd like because you didn't bother to polish the dings out before you fell asleep."

Carus held the sword to the light and sighted along its edge. "Only the dings, mind. And only a working edge, lad. You don't take a sword into battle with an edge so sharp it turns or cracks when it meets something hard—as it surely will."

"I've sharpened knives," Garric said. "And axes too.

Bone may be harder than the root of an old hickory, but not so very much harder.''

Carus laughed again. "And was your tree wearing armor, lad?" he said. "But I take your meaning."

He sighed. "There's so much to know when you're king. Some of it I never learned, maybe never could learn. You'll do better."

They sat at opposite ends of a curved marble bench in a garden. Roses climbed a long trellis on the other side of a circular pavement. The sky above was blandly neutral; nondescript clouds showed against a faint blue background.

Carus used a rag to wipe the grit of sharpening from the blade, smiled at the weapon, and shot it home again in its sheath. "A good sword," he said. "It never let me down."

"Did a wizard make it for you?" Garric asked. He knew that if he got up and looked through the rose hedge, there'd be nothing to see—swirling grayness perhaps, the raw material from which his mind wove dreams. He didn't need to prove that to himself.

The king laughed. "One gave it to me, at any rate," he said. "I don't think he forged it, though. Wizards know things, but that doesn't make them any good with their hands. The smith who created this sword—"

He tucked the whetstone back into its pouch.

"—must have been like your friend Ilna. I never had much use for wizards, but I can respect a man who makes things."

Carus returned the sword to Garric, who stood and buckled it on again. The king remained seated, a pensive expression on his face.

"I hated wizards," Carus said. "Because I didn't understand what they did, I suppose. That's wrong."

He looked up, his features as sharp as a stamping die. "Don't make that mistake, lad; about wizards or anything else."

Carus' face broadened into its familiar grin. "But also don't make the mistake the Duke of Yole made and trust somebody simply because he knows things you don't."

King Carus got to his feet, his eyes exactly on a level with those of dream Garric. There was a sound in the background, a voice chanting words of power. The hues of the dreamworld brightened and faded with the pulse of every syllable.

"You need to go now," Carus said. He patted the hilt of the sword. "Take care of her, lad. It won't be long now before I need this blade again."

The garden dissolved into pearly light. Garric threw out his arms as he fell, but he was already lying on cool alabaster slabs in a room flooded by moonlight. Tenoctris smiled when she saw Garric's eyes open, but she continued chanting until he managed to sit up.

They were in the ruins of Ilna's drawing room. The bodies of liches lay where Garric's strokes had strewn them; some of the bones were already bare because the flesh had deliquesced in dark pools on the flooring.

A wild mace blow had smashed the walnut wardrobe chest. The destruction of that piece of fine cabinetry disturbed Garric at a deeper level than did the man slashed to death on the threshold, one of Ilna's yellow-eyed servants. He scowled, offended by his own priorities.

Ilna was gone.

"Ilna was here," Garric said. "Have you seen her?"

He remembered the thing clutching the girl; the stroke that cut through the serpentine trunk was Garric's, not that of King Carus in his body. But that might have been a dream, a nightmare like so much else.

Tenoctris shook her head. "You're the only person alive in the house, Garric," she said. "Can you stand up?"

She held out her hand. Garric braced his hands on the floor, avoiding the pools of spreading filth. He raised himself in a series of careful motions. He smiled at the notion that he needed the old woman's help—physical help, at least. He didn't doubt that the reason he *could* stand owed as much to the forces she'd called to his aid as to his own sturdy constitution.

"From the residue Ilna left behind," Tenoctris said, answering the question she'd avoided a moment before, "I'm afraid that she's in a place I'd rather she were not. A very bad place. But the same is true of Liane, and unless we rescue Liane before midnight—"

Her eyes gestured toward the moon, already high in the heavens.

"—it will probably be too late."

Garric glanced around the room instinctively, wondering what Tenoctris meant by "the residue Ilna had left." He saw nothing—recognized nothing at least—and it didn't matter anyway. *We can only do one thing at a time.*

"Let's find Liane, then," he said. "She's in the old family mansion?"

"She's in the groundskeeper's shed that's part of the family tomb," Tenoctris said. "I didn't go there by myself. Not against Benlo."

"You're not by yourself now," Garric said. He stepped across, not onto, the dead servant as he led the way out.

A thought struck him. He paused and drew the long sword, then squinted at the edge in the light of candles still burning in the hallway.

Tenoctris might possibly have belted the sword around Garric's waist while he was unconscious, but she hadn't done this expert job of polishing the nick out of the tip of the blade.

21

Though her body slipped to the throne-room floor, Sharina's mind watched from a place in limbo as the entrance hall filled with liches. Nonnus backed against the door, seemingly at bay, then launched himself low into the figures of gray flesh before they could react to the change.

The Pewle knife winked in moonlight:

A lich fell, its spine split by the blade slicing in through its belly.

A lich fell, its skull crushed by the pommel hammering against the left temple.

A lich fell, its neck cracked when the hermit's blunt fingers jabbed into its eyesockets for a grip and jerked as if to finish a leg-snared rabbit.

Nonnus backed away. The surviving liches had no fear, no hesitation. Those in the center stepped laboriously over the bodies of their own kind; those to either side moved forward unhindered, their weapons raised and their cold gray faces set.

Nonnus breathed in great gasps. As well as the Pewle knife he now held the end of a boarding pike whose shaft was broken off thirty inches beneath the hooked point. He grinned to his right and jumped left, into the gray mass.

Steel sparkled on steel. From the melee spun a skull dead for centuries and now dead forever, losing bits of gelatinous flesh while still in the air.

Nonnus stepped back, but the door was there and no longer space for maneuver. The liches rolled over him from two sides and then the third. The pile of impassive faces and rusty weapons stabbing continued to move much longer than any human being could have lived to fight—

But when the movement ceased, Sharina's mind returned in a wave of black emptiness to her body on the floor of the throne room.

"Phasousouel eistochama nouchael!" Meder called. He and the procurator stood within the circle he'd scribed on the stone floor with Sharina's dagger. The embedded marble chips steamed and bubbled at the touch of the brown ichor remaining on the blade.

Asera looked cold-faced in the direction of the door, taking no part in the ceremony. She was probably afraid, but she was too much an aristocrat to let her fear show now.

"Apraphes! Einath! Adones!"

The door shook with another series of blows. The point of

a rusty boarding axe split the panel near the top and withdrew. A halberd head stabbed halfway through the wood lower down; the liches were using the long shaft as a lever to tear the door apart.

Sharina thought she could move again, though she wasn't sure that she wanted to. When the undead monsters in the hall killed her, they would end her responsibility—and her guilt.

"Dechochtha iathennaouian zaarabem!" Meder called. His voice lilted and his moonlit face held a fierce joy.

Sharina didn't know what the wizard was planning. Based on recent experience it would be something foul, something that a human being would rather die than be associated with.

A mace and the axe together smashed the center of the top panel to splinters. Hands of translucent jelly reached in to pull the broken wood out of the way. Splinters clung to the flesh.

Nonnus wouldn't want her to think of Meder as inhuman. Nonnus wouldn't expect the girl he'd died for to lie on the floor while evil triumphed.

The candlestick that had struck her down lay beside her. Sharina picked it up and stood, backing slightly away from the door and the gray, skeletal creatures who were completing its destruction.

"Namadon! Zamadon! Thestis!"

The door split top to bottom. The latch side sagged and fell into the throne room. Two liches pushed the rest of the door in on its hinges. There was a pile of their kind dismembered just outside the door, as Sharina had known there would be.

She braced herself, raising the heavy candlestick. The liches were already dead, but perhaps her own blood would give Meder the power he needed for his incantation.

"Sharina!" the wizard called. She glanced around by reflex at the sound of her name.

Meder seized Asera by the hair with his left hand. He cut her throat with the dagger.

The procurator's mouth opened wide, but she was too startled even to scream. Blood gouted over her beige robe, then vanished in the jet of red fire filling the protective circle and mushrooming off the ceiling above the black throne.

Even the liches paused. The wizard and his sacrifice both dissolved in the roaring flame. The dagger fell to the floor and bounced away, twisted and glowing. None of the inferno's heat touched Sharina, though she was only arm's length from the protective circle.

The flame vanished, flicked out as if a shutter had fallen. A red-skinned creature with leprous eyes stood in the center of the circle. It was seven feet tall, with shoulders so hunched that the claws on its long fingers brushed the floor.

"I'll save you, Sharina," the demon said in a croaking parody of Meder's voice. He shambled forward, his claws scoring the stone.

Sharina stepped aside, still holding the candlestick. She was too shocked to be frightened.

Half the plastered ceiling dropped with a crash, covering the throne and the burned stone floor. A cloud of white dust spilled outward. Fire twinkled on the bared roofbeams.

Whatever animated the minds of the liches left no room for fear. The pair in the doorway lunged toward the greater monster, swinging their weapons. One's mace clanged from the red skull. The other's swordstroke didn't land because the demon caught the blade in one hand and crumpled the steel like a boy playing with a dandelion stem.

"I'll save you, Sharina," repeated the monster that had been Meder. He squeezed the liches together. When he released them, the bones of their shoulders and upper chests were ground to powder suspended in the jelly of their flesh.

The demon waddled into the main hall on its short legs. There were scores of liches. They attacked with the single-minded fury of bees swarming over a nest-robbing bear, and to as little purpose. The demon pulled his opponents apart or crushed them. Neither the armor some liches wore nor the blows they rained with a variety of weapons on Meder had any effect on his actions.

Sharina dropped to her knees in the pile of liches dismembered outside the door of the throne room. She clawed through putrescent flesh and bones, some of them so ancient that they snapped when she tugged at them.

Nonnus was on the bottom, the Pewle knife in his right hand. His face looked calm; but then, it always had.

"May the Lady cover you with Her cloak, my friend. May the Shepherd guide you to His fold."

Sharina wrapped her fingers around the dead man's. She began to cry.

The demon flung aside fragments of the last remaining lich. He turned with a smile on his flat, lipless face.

"I've saved you, Sharina," Meder said. "Now you're mine."

He started toward her.

22

Derg pointed one long blue arm toward the ruined castle. "There," he said. "We've reached the place where I'll grant your wish."

Cashel rubbed the cuts healing on his chest. At first he'd thought they were approaching a natural hill. He could see squared stones now beneath the foliage but trees grew even on portions of the wall that roots hadn't pried to rubble.

"All right," he said. "What do I do?"

Cashel didn't see much in this ruin worth looking for, but he trusted Derg. And of course Mellie would tell him if anything was wrong. . . .

He smiled at the sprite. It was vaguely disconcerting that Mellie was normal size now. She smiled back, but there was none of the usual joy in her expression; she reached out and squeezed his hand in reassurance.

"It's inside," the demon said, leading the way around the circuit of the wall. "One of the towers still has its roof, and what you want is there."

From on top of a block of masonry, a spotted deer no larger than a goat stared at the three companions. Tree roots wrapped the stone the way water flows about a boulder. For a moment the deer's jaws continued to work, drawing in the remainder of a large leaf with the russet tinge of young vegetation; then it snorted, tossed its tiny spike horns, and leaped deeper into the forest.

Cashel wondered what he *did* want. Not money, certainly. The weight of his purse was already enough to make the thong cut his neck. He'd tied it instead around his waist, outside the breechclout to which he'd reduced his shredded tunic. No one was going to steal his silver in this jungle; and if they did, Cashel wouldn't much care.

If Derg was leading him to a chest of gold or jewels ... he'd take them, he supposed, but for sake of courtesy. It wouldn't be polite to refuse a gift, even one he didn't need.

The gate had collapsed, though the posts and lintel were three of the largest worked stones Cashel had ever seen. The wall was built of fine-grained sandstone with a faint bluish cast, a dense stone that had weathered very little despite the untold ages it had lain exposed. There'd been nothing wrong with the castle's workmanship. Time had simply defeated it, as time defeated all things.

They climbed the ruin of the gateway. Mellie hopped lightly from one bit of bare stone to another. Some of her footholds were upturned corners, still square despite their age. It was like watching a bluebird perch on the spike of the mill's lightning rod.

What do I want? Derg knew better than Cashel himself did, Mellie had said. That wouldn't be hard. Cashel couldn't think of anything, any object at least. People talked about happiness but he didn't know what that could be, not really.

Nor did other people, most of them, from what he'd seen.

Mellie moved with all her usual grace, but she hadn't been skipping and playing with the world about her since, well, since they'd come to this place, really. It was as if when she'd grown to full size—or Cashel had shrunk, he wasn't sure which—she'd gotten staid like ordinary people.

If anybody'd asked him before they came to this place, he'd have said the sprite was happy. Now he didn't know.

The castle's courtyard had been paved with blocks of the same hard stone as formed the walls, but they lay in a jumble among the trees. Roots had found cracks between the pavers, then expanded to lift them.

People thought that rocks were eternal. Life, with all its changing cycles, that's what was really eternal. Rock was all well and good, but Cashel'd take a seasoned hickory pole any day. . . .

He thought about the sword Garric was wearing when they met in their dream. It looked like it belonged with him, belted around his waist.

"Derg?" Cashel said. "Are you taking me to a sword? Because really, I wouldn't want—"

Derg and even Mellie dissolved in laughter, the first real joy Cashel had heard in the sprite's voice in far too long. "Oh, silly!" she said. "What would you do with a sword? You!"

"It's right over here," Derg said. "Inside."

The stables within the courtyard had fallen in or been buried by the collapse of the outer wall. The building across from the gateway still stood, or at least the walls did. Judging from the vacant window openings there had originally been three stories. Roofing tiles were a ruddy litter on the ground inside and out of the structure, and the floors hadn't long survived the roof.

At the left end of the house—the palace? stood a tower two levels higher than the rest of the structure. Its sharply peaked roof remained, though many of the tiles had dropped away. Birds, not the swallows Cashel would've expected back home, flew in and out of the windows on quick, twittering courses.

Derg led the way, going as often on all fours as he did on his hind legs alone. When the demon put his hands down he walked on his knuckles with the claws tucked up into his palms. Mellie skipped like a bird; and Cashel walked as he always did in bad terrain, choosing his footing carefully because a rock that seemed solid might well turn under his weight. He wished he had his staff, but he wasn't too proud to dab a hand down.

He didn't guess there was much of anything he was too proud to do if that's what it took.

Derg led them up a pile of rubble to the door that must originally have been entered from the second floor of the main building: the tower's whole base was a foundation course.

Cashel laughed. Derg and Mellie looked at him. "I was thinking it was a good thing the rubble made a pile for us to reach the door," he explained. "But then I thought, if the roof hadn't fallen in like that we'd have gotten in the regular way. Things have a way of working out, don't they?"

Derg looked puzzled. The sprite smiled at Cashel. "Yes they do, Cashel," she said. "For some people."

The staircase leading to the top of the tower was made of stones sticking out from the inside of the wall. A passion-flower vine ran up the long circuit, sending spiky purple blooms out each slit window and the hole in the roof besides.

Against the tower's curved inner wall, protected by the staircase as well as what remained of the roof, hung a tapestry. It seemed as out of place here as it would have been on the wall of the mill where Cashel and his sister grew up.

"Oh . . ." he said, touching the edge of the fabric with one careful finger. "Ilna would love to see this."

The light in this nook wasn't good, but the woven scene was nevertheless alive. A city of fairy towers rose from the forest in the middle distance. Walkways of crystalline delicacy leaped from tower to tower or sometimes spiraled down into the treetops. The sky was a dome of pastel beauty in which great birds sparkled.

"I dreamed about this!" Cashel said. "I saw this hanging, only I was living in it!"

Derg raised an eyebrow in question, but he was looking at Mellie. The sprite hugged Cashel and said, "Yes you did. But it was only a dream, remember."

The foreground at the bottom of the tapestry was meadow separated from the forest by a broad river. A bridge spanned the swirling water. At the near end the piers were stone with timber decks like the bridges Cashel had seen on his way to Carcosa, but at midstream the span became shimmering glass and swept into the city with no further support.

He couldn't tell what fabric the tapestry was made of. He didn't think it was silk, and even the threads that shimmered gold and silver had a translucence that meant they couldn't be metal.

"Am I to take this to my sister?" Cashel asked. A gift for Ilna, that *was* something he'd like to have.

"No," said Derg. "Step through the doorway behind it. That will take you where you want to be."

Cashel kept his face expressionless. He lifted the hanging a little ways out and found behind it more smooth, slightly curved sandstone blocks like the rest of the the tower's wall.

He looked at his companions.

The demon's long jaws smiled. "The doorway is there," Derg said. "When you step behind the hanging, you'll find it there."

"He's right, Cashel," Mellie said. Her smile was nothing like the cheerful grin he'd grown used to. "That will take you to the place you want most to be."

Cashel shrugged and clasped arms with the demon. "I don't suppose you're coming with us," the youth said. "I'm glad to have met you, Derg. I like you better for a friend than I do an enemy."

The demon's grip was firm on Cashel's biceps; his muscles moved like heavy ropes.

"Friend?" Derg said. "Well, you're human, you understand those things better than I do. May you have success in all your other fights, Cashel."

He stepped back.

"I'm not going either, Cashel," Mellie said.

Cashel frowned. He didn't understand what she'd just said. That happened to him a lot, being told things he didn't understand by people who assumed he would. . . .

"You've brought me to a place where I can go home safely," Mellie said. "I could never have gotten here myself, Cashel. You're very strong."

"I didn't think you'd leave, Mellie," he said. "I've . . ."

He didn't know how to put it. He hadn't *gotten used to the sprite*, that made her sound like the ache in his left knee every time the weather changed, a relic of a tree that fell the wrong way when he was twelve.

"I'll miss you," he said.

Mellie stepped close and kissed him. She felt like a rabbit, all softness and hard muscle in the same form. "May you have success with others as you've had with me," she said.

"Mellie," Cashel said as she backed away.

"Go!" the sprite said. "Go now! It's what you really want!"

Cashel turned quickly because her tears embarrassed him. He lifted the hanging aside and stepped forward as if there wasn't a stone wall before him.

There *wasn't* a stone wall, only darkness. He took another stride. He'd started this course, so there was nothing for him to do but finish it.

BOOK

VI

1

The gate to the bor-Benliman tomb was chained and padlocked: the new owners had decided to bar intruders, even though they didn't own this corner of the property.

Garric felt fierce indignation fill him. "They had no *right*," he whispered as he reached for his sword hilt. With this sword on his waist, his anger was no longer a frustrated, inward-turning thing. If someone wronged him, they'd learn—

Tenoctris touched his sword hand.

Garric looked at the old woman in embarrassment. He let the sword's weight slide it back into the scabbard. "I was just going to cut the chain," he muttered in embarrassment. "It's soft iron. This sword can . . ."

"I think we can do with less noise," Tenoctris said. That was all that reached her lips, but there were questions in her eyes. She lifted the padlock in her cupped palms.

Garric blushed, wondering how much of that outburst was him and how much was the king who laughed in his mind. He'd never thought of himself as someone who threw his weight around; but then, he'd never *had* any weight. He wasn't sure what had changed, but the sword he now wore wasn't the only factor.

Tenoctris murmured a spell while still holding the lock. Cold blue light gleamed from the padlock's interior. Metal pinged musically; the hasp fell open.

"I said I wasn't a very powerful wizard," Tenoctris said as she removed the lock. "I didn't say I wasn't a wizard at all."

Garric unwrapped the chain from around the iron gate and post, being particularly careful not to clank the metal together. Now that he was using his senses rather than reacting to provocation by a fat landowner who didn't believe the law affected a rich man's prerogatives, he could hear low chanting. The air rumbled as though stirred by a distant surf.

Garric thought he saw blue light flicker at the corners of his eyes. He glanced at Tenoctris. She nodded, grim-faced, and walked into the fenced enclosure ahead of him.

Garric thought of drawing the sword; he kept his hands at his sides instead. The only use for the sword at this moment was to be a crutch for his spirit. If Garric couldn't be a man except when he held a sword, he wasn't a man he'd have wanted to know.

The window on this side of the groundskeeper's lodge was round and eight inches in diameter. Crossbars divided the unglazed opening into four, and ivy grew across it as well.

Garric brushed back leaves so that he and Tenoctris had a clear view of the interior. Some moonlight entered by the similar window on the other side, but the real illumination was the haze of blue fire in which stood a plump, balding man who chanted in Benlo's voice.

The bronze casket lay empty against the crosswall separating the lodge from the tomb in the other half of the building. The lid hung open, showing the white satin liner.

The chanting wizard wore a burial shift. On the floor beside him was the mummy of a woman, her cheeks sunken and the tendons of the interlaced fingers standing out like ropes. There was no sign of overt decay.

The other bodies in the family tomb weren't preserved any better than Benlo's own; Garric had spent enough time among the crumbling caskets to know that. It must have been while on his travels that Benlo learned the embalming technique he applied to his late wife—among the Isles, or perhaps on the other planes to which his wizardry took him.

Liane lay on the wizard's other side. She was as still as her dead mother.

Benlo raised the pudgy arms of the body he wore. He spoke, but Garric no longer heard the words of the incantation. The cosmos pulsed, growing alternately tighter and looser with the movements of Benlo's lips.

A thread of blue light as dense as a sword edge bound Mazzona's forehead to that of her silent daughter. The thread grew thicker and even brighter as the wizard chanted.

"Can you distract him?" Tenoctris whispered. "Otherwise I don't have enough power to . . ."

Garric nodded. The door of the groundskeeper's lodge was wood rather than metal, but he could see through the window that it was closed by a bar as thick as his arm. He couldn't kick his way in, and hacking the door down with the sword would take longer than he wanted to delay. Besides, there was another locked gate between him and the doorway.

He stepped away from the window. This was the sort of problem Garric understood. Wizardry and monsters had been no part of his life until he met Tenoctris, but he had plenty of experience with making holes in solid objects.

Garric judged the balance of the stone bench planted in front of the tomb. He knelt and used the strength of his legs to lift the seat off its two supports. He didn't know what the slab weighed. Enough, he expected; and if the wall took more than one blow, well, it'd get whatever was required.

Tenoctris stepped out of the way as Garric waddled forward with his battering ram. The old woman looked impressed as she watched him.

Garric took a last step, swinging the bench with the strength of his shoulders in addition to his forward momentum. The blunt stone hammer hit squarely over the window opening. The frame and wall disintegrated in an avalanche of smashed bricks and old mortar.

The crashing destruction was muted by the soundless weight of Benlo's invocation. The wizard's lips continued to move without missing a beat.

The bench stuck halfway through the crumbling wall. Gar ric shoved the end sideways, levering bricks away. He jerked the slab clear, then crawled into the room shimmering with azure magic.

The wizard's silent thunder paused, though the pressure of unseen forces continued to squeeze Garric. He couldn't imagine how they felt to Tenoctris, who understood them the way Garric understood a towering storm-tossed wave.

Benlo turned his head. All the strength left Garric's limbs. He sprawled on the pile of shattered rubble, choking on mortar dust but unable even to override reflex and hold his breath. His outflung hand touched Liane's arm. Her flesh was as hard as the bricks beneath him.

Benlo extended his hand toward Garric's head. His thumb and fingers were spread like a crab's pincer. Blue flame crackled between the fingertips.

Mazzona sat up behind the wizard. Her chest swelled and she screamed, "Help! Help!"

Benlo turned. "Mazzona!" he said.

Still seated, the mummy backed awkwardly to the far wall. There was a look of horror on Mazzona's pinched face. "Help!" she screamed again. "This monster's killing my daughter! Help!"

"Mazzona my love," Benlo said. He reached out toward his wife. Garric still couldn't move, but he felt the hidden pressure draining from the tomb.

"Monster!" Mazzona cried. She was trying to stand, but there wasn't quite enough strength in her mummified arms to lift her up the wall. "Loathsome monster!"

"My love . . ." Benlo said in a liquid voice that blurred out on the final syllable. The blue radiance faded quickly, like water draining through a hole in a bucket.

The mummified woman stiffened, then slumped sideways. Her right hand broke off as her body fell.

The corpse Benlo wore remained standing for a few moments more. Patches of blue mold spread across the cheeks like fire in dry grass; a stench of corruption filled the narrow room. Weeks of deferred dissolution were taking place in a matter of seconds.

His eyeballs began to drip. The corpse fell onto its face,

no longer animated by Benlo's soul. The flesh squelched wetly as it hit the floor.

"May the Shepherd guide him safe," Garric whispered. He knew he was physically able to get up now, but he wasn't mentally ready.

He hadn't much cared for Benlo when he was a living man. As a dead soul inhabiting another man's corpse, the wizard was terrifying. Garric had been able to function only because he *had* to function, had to act to save Liane and probably Tenoctris despite his fear. To save his friends.

But no human being really deserved the fate that Benlo had brought on himself.

Liane's arm quivered. Her chest rose and fell again.

She was alive.

Garric scrambled to his feet. His muscles prickled as though he'd been sitting in a way that cut off circulation, but full feeling was coming back.

"He was going to transfer his wife's spirit to Liane's body," Tenoctris said softly. She was still outside the tomb. "That's why he had to have Liane. The link between mother and daughter was necessary, even for a wizard as powerful as Benlo. Even for the part of Benlo that remained."

Liane murmured as if she were having a bad dream. Her hands opened and closed.

Garric looked at the old woman. "Don't tell her that," he said. The steel in his voice surprised him. "She doesn't need to know."

"No," Tenoctris said. "She doesn't need to know."

Garric unbarred the door and opened it, then picked up Liane. He needed to get out of this room. He needed to get away from the stench, both physical and spiritual, of what had happened here.

"He was so powerful," Tenoctris said. "It was all I could do just to redirect the forces he'd raised. To nudge them aside by the slightest degree. It was like standing in a millrace. . . ."

She touched the lock on the wicket gate; it clanked open. The door of the groundskeeper's shed gave onto the grounds of the main property, not the alcove of which it was a part. Garric carried Liane into the ivy-bordered alley, leaving both gates ajar behind him. A watchman holding a halberd crosswise at waist height eyed them from near the house. Tenoctris bowed to the man and followed Garric out.

Liane stirred. The old woman put her hand on the girl's forehead. Garric couldn't tell whether the gesture was wizardry or normal human kindness.

Liane opened her eyes and said, "Garric? Am I alive?"

Garric set Liane on her feet, keeping his hold around the girl's shoulders until they were both sure her legs would support her. "I guess you are," he said. "There was a while I wouldn't have bet on it."

"Who was the man who attacked us?" Liane asked. Her voice had a distant quality. Either the girl was still feeling the effects of her captivity or the cool demeanor was her conscious attempt to keep from screaming.

Garric looked toward Tenoctris for an answer. The old woman was staring intently at the sky to the south of them.

"Oh!" she said in embarrassment. "The creature that attacked you, Liane . . . that was a ghoul of sorts, haunting tombs. He's dead now, gone forever."

She shook herself, then sighed. "Something is happening near the palace," she said. "Something very serious."

She gave Liane a smile of tired affection. Garric realized that his lifting the stone bench was nothing compared to the effort this frail old woman must have expended to defeat the greater wizard.

"Liane," Tenoctris said, "the creature who attacked you was acting on his own, at least there at the end. The activities of the Hooded One and those of a rival of his are separate; and one or both are going on nearby."

Liane forced a smile. "Those are what we came to deal with," she said. She noticed Garric's frown and added with a touch of anger, "I'm all right! It's there we'll learn who sent my father to Haft and his death, won't we?"

"We may indeed," Tenoctris said. She put her arm around

Liane's and began walking toward the climax of forces which her wizard's mind saw reflected in the sky.

Garric walked on Liane's other side; glad of the presence of his sword, gladder still to have his companions.

2

Cashel pushed the tapestry out of the way and stepped into a throne room stinking of fire and old death. Sharina stood with her back against the opposite wall, holding the hermit's heavy knife. She faced a long-armed demon with a mottled red body.

Cashel stepped forward, circled his left arm around the demon's throat, and threw the creature backward over his braced left knee. It crashed to the floor so hard the impact cracked the terrazzo.

Sharina stepped forward, raising the big knife. "Get away with that, girl!" Cashel said. "You'll hurt no one but me or yourself with a knife!"

His words surprised him, maybe more than they surprised Sharina. Still, when Cashel saw a straight path to completing a task he'd always taken it, and he didn't have time for folks who got in his way. He didn't know as much about fighting demons as he did about sheep, but it was a thing he'd done.

If he'd had any doubt that the same rules applied to this creature as had to Derg, the wreckage of this room and the hall beyond would have convinced him. Score of liches and their varied weaponry lay strewn and shattered across the polished floors. The demon's ruddy skin was unmarked.

Sharina backed into the angle of the wall and the black throne dominating the room. It was an ugly thing that looked like it was formed by the twined bodies of living snakes instead of being carved out of stone.

But it wasn't Cashel's concern just now.

The demon got to its feet. It was taller than Derg but not nearly as heavily built. The exceptional length of its arms reminded Cashel of a crab, or a crab spider.

"I will kill you now, peasant," the creature said in the voice of Meder, the procurator's wizard.

Cashel tossed his head like a bull clearing his horns. "Better men have tried," he said. "Better demons, too."

They stepped together. Cashel gripped Meder's forearms because his own arms didn't have the span to catch the demon's wrists.

There were no lights in the throne room and only a candle or two burning in the great hall beyond, but the light of a full moon streamed through windows just below the vaulted ceiling. Wall hangings, one of them the tapestry Cashel had emerged behind, fluttered in the violence of the combat. Each woven scene was a distant world depicted with the realism of a death mask.

Cashel butted Meder in the chest. The demon wasn't any heavier than Cashel or at any rate not by much, but he was ungodly strong. Meder's toes scratched for traction, digging furrows in the marble chips and black mortar.

Meder bent his arms, bringing his hands toward the youth's temples like clawed pincers. Cashel didn't have the leverage to prevent him. An instant before his elbows folded and the claws met in his brain, Cashel twisted his torso and flung the demon over his right knee again, this time sideways.

Meder crashed down, skidding on the slick surface. Cashel bent forward, resting his fingertips on the floor as he breathed in great gasps.

The only thing that had saved him thus far was that Meder didn't know how to use his advantages—didn't know how to *fight*. He wasn't greatly stronger than Cashel, but he didn't tire and he wasn't harmed by being slammed down hard enough to crush stone.

The demon had a scarecrow build and a supple spine.

Cashel couldn't bend Meder's back far enough over his knee to break the spine.

Meder stood up. He gave a screeching, angry laugh and started for Cashel.

The only option Cashel saw was going to be fatal to him even if it succeeded, because the demon would have time to claw him apart. Survival—even Sharina's survival—wasn't the most important thing right now. Winning this fight was the most important thing.

Winning was the only thing.

Cashel gave a roar from deep in his throat and lunged toward Meder, catching the demon off-guard. Cashel had his left forearm under Meder's chin and his right forearm around the demon's back for a fulcrum before the red hands closed on his bare back.

Cashel levered his left arm upward with all his strength, ignoring the claws that raked him. Meder resisted, trying to force his chin down. He twisted his head in an attempt to escape the pressure.

Blood streamed down Cashel's back. He'd do all that human strength could do; he'd press his arm into Meder's throat for as long as he could. And then he would die.

A flicker of fierce, red light, a figure only inches high, sprang from one of the tapestries. It bounded toward the combatants like a wolf running and set its jaws above Meder's heel where the Achilles tendon would be in a man.

Meder screamed so loud in startled pain that weapons lying on the stone quivered in sympathy. The scream ended in a *crack!* as sharp as lighting when Cashel broke the demon's neck.

Cashel hurled the body away from him with a cry less of triumph than relief. Meder's gangling form sprawled half on, half beside the black throne. His foreclaws dripped blood on the terrazzo.

"I owed you nothing, human!" Derg cried, his dog-faced form as small as when Cashel first glimpsed him in the strongbox. "This was my gift to a friend!"

He leaped back onto, *into* the tapestry from which he'd come.

Sharina knelt beside Cashel. She began slicing her cloak into bandages with the Pewle knife. "There's a fountain in the main hall, Cashel," she said. "Can you walk that far or shall I bring a helmetful to you here?"

He hadn't thought he'd ever hear Sharina's voice again. Her face had firmer lines than that of the girl he'd known in Barca's Hamlet, and she was even more beautiful.

"I can walk," Cashel said. He took another deep breath, gathering his strength to rise. He'd said the words, so now all that remained was to make them so.

The tapestry he'd come from behind was an almost perfect duplicate of the one in the ruined tower where he'd left Derg and Mellie. In it a bridge crossed a broad river toward a forest and a city of fairy glass.

Two tiny figures stood at the center span of the bridge. They waved toward Cashel. One was a dog-faced demon, and the other was a sprite with rich red hair.

3

That's Cashel!" Garric said in amazement. As unlikely as it seemed, there was no mistaking his friend's big form coming through the crowd filling Palace Square. He wore a breechclout and a crisscross of bandages over his chest.

One of the mansions was afire. Not Ilna's—as Garric first thought with a tensing of his heart—but a place a few doors down which also backed up to the main canal.

Flames leaped from one end of the second story. Members of the Fire Watch worked on the blaze while hundreds of City Patrolmen and soldiers from the palace barracks tried vainly to keep order. The crowd brought out by the excitement wasn't yet a dangerous mob, but the fire was an excuse for ordinary citizens to ransack a rich man's house—and they were doing so.

Garric understood that, but he was surprised to see Cashel carrying a roll of fabric. Cashel was the last person Garric could imagine looting. The last person besides Ilna, at any rate.

"Cashel!" he called, striding ahead of Liane and Tenoctris. There was a woman with Cashel, a tall—

"Sharina!" Garric shouted. "Shepherd guide me! Tenoctris, it's Sharina!"

Cashel grinned broadly. He changed direction but didn't break into a run as Garric and Sharina did, shoving people out of the way in their haste.

Garric hugged his sister, lifting her off the pavement. Until the day she left he'd never thought he'd miss Sharina, and even the emptiness he'd felt as the trireme sailed off gave him no inkling of how good it would feel to see her again.

"What are you doing here?" he said. They both started to laugh half-hysterically, because Sharina had said the same thing simultaneously.

"Garric," Tenoctris said. "I don't believe Liane has met your sister."

Garric put Sharina down. Cashel had joined them. Garric clasped arms with his friend—flesh this time, not a dream—and looked over his shoulder toward the two women. Liane's expression was withdrawn and as cold as the moonlight that illuminated it.

"Ah," Garric said. "Liane, this is my sister Sharina. Liane came to Barca's Hamlet, ah, after you left."

He tried to think how to explain to Sharina what had happened to him since she'd sailed away. The complexity of the whole business—things that he didn't understand, things that weren't over yet; things which might not have happened at all, like the dream in which he got the sword—stunned him silent.

Sharina wore a heavy knife under her sash. Garric blinked

at it. Much else besides about his sister looked different from the last time he'd seen her, but that was a specific, identifiable change.

Sharina followed the line of his eyes. She touched the hilt and said, "Nonnus is dead, Garric. He died because, because ..."

"Ah," Garric said. "I'm sorry. I didn't know him very well."

"Come," Cashel said with a rumbling confidence he used to have only when herding sheep. "There's a, well, the man who employed me; a Serian named Latias. His compound's close, and I think I need to lie down."

The five of them were a strange enough mix that under other circumstances the Patrol would certainly have been asking questions. Garric realized that there hadn't been time to cancel the pickup order for him and Liane, though the fire and the surging mob provided a degree of protection from the authorities at the moment.

Cashel strode through the fringes of the crowd, leading them in the direction he and Sharina had been headed when Garric saw them. On Cashel's back the bandages were soaked through with blood, some of it still seeping from the wounds below. The injuries must have been extremely painful, though apart from a certain stiffness Cashel seemed the same as usual.

The stiffness was usual enough too. Cashel was the sort who plodded along, never hurrying and never stopping till he'd gotten where he was going.

"Want me to take that?" Garric offered, patting the roll of fabric under his friend's left arm. It didn't look heavy, but somebody hurt as badly as Cashel was didn't need extra burdens.

Cashel looked down at the bolt with a smile that Garric couldn't read. The cloth had gleamed with highlights from the fire. Now that they'd left the square and were walking up one of the boulevards feeding it, the moon's softer light lay across it like a shimmering stream.

"It's all right," he said. "The house we were in caught fire, I guess from the fighting before I got there. I thought I'd bring this along in case . . ."

Cashel cleared his throat, uncertain for the first time since Garric had met him here. "In case it was important to some friends of mine that it not burn."

"Meder caused the fire," Sharina said with a tremble that wasn't fear. "With his wizardry. His last wizardry."

"If Master Latias will give us privacy," Tenoctris said, "that will be very helpful. The things I'm afraid we have to do next will be difficult enough without outsiders becoming involved."

Cashel looked at the old woman over his shoulder. "He'll give us whatever I ask, I think," he said.

"There's more to take care of?" Garric said. He wasn't frightened. He was just getting information together so that he'd know what he was to do.

"Yes," said Tenoctris. "The dark power which now holds Ilna."

4

Sharina watched three Serian healers—an old woman, a middle-aged man, and a ten-year-old girl—work on Cashel's back with jabbering enthusiasm while Cashel sat stolidly in a circle on the floor with his four companions. The Serian male cleaned and spread unguent in the long gouges while the child sewed them up under the old woman's direction. The healers might have been digging ditches on another island for all the indication Cashel gave that he was aware of them.

"I need to go after Ilna," Garric said. He'd turned the belt buckle to his right side so that the long sword lay across his lap instead of projecting awkwardly behind him. "It's my fault what happened to her."

Latias had given them the use of an entire building; its ceilings were high and the louvered walls provided ventilation while maintaining privacy. Trays of juices and sliced fruits sat on little serving tripods beside each guest.

Cashel had described Latias as his employer. The Serian's conduct toward Cashel reminded Sharina more of the deference the Blood Eagles had shown to Asera.

"She's my sister," Cashel said. "Besides, I've gone . . ."

He grimaced, either looking for a word or disliking the one he'd found. "I've gone other places. I'll bring her back."

Sharina had always known Cashel was strong. She hadn't appreciated *how* strong he was till she left Barca's Hamlet and saw enough of other men to learn that the boy she'd grown up with wasn't merely the strongest man in the borough.

She'd watched him kill the thing that Meder had become. She'd grown up with a man who tended sheep, and who killed demons with his bare hands.

"It's not a matter of responsibility," Tenoctris said, dividing her glance between the two youths. "Garric, you freed Ilna from a very bad master. That left her vulnerable to another power who needed a servant, but you didn't cause that to happen."

The Serians chirped like a flock of birds as they closed Cashel's wounds. They seemed to speak only their own language; certainly they had no interest in what their master's guests were saying.

"A worse master," Garric said flatly.

Tenoctris shrugged. "I don't think so," she said, "though bad enough. This one is human, or at least he used to be: the Hooded One."

Tenoctris had insisted on pronouncing a healing spell over Cashel despite his objection that she shouldn't strain herself on his behalf, that he'd be all right. Sharina remembered Garric lying torn in their father's inn, with Tenoctris and Nonnus discussing the gods and healing.

Sharina wished she could cry. She didn't know why she couldn't. She would have rather any result than Nonnus lying dead before the throne-room door; but he was dead.

Garric touched his sword hilt. "If the Hooded One has her, then I *do* need to go."

He didn't seem to be her brother anymore; and yet... Cashel was still Cashel, there was just more of him than Sharina had realized before. Maybe the same was true of Garric, that the things he'd encountered had brought out parts of him that nobody in the borough would have had a chance to see. Nobody, Garric himself included.

"I can take you with me to where Ilna is, Garric," the old woman explained, "but I can't take anyone else. I don't have the power to take anyone else."

She looked at Cashel. "Garric has a link to the place, the *time* I believe, where the Hooded One hides. He comes out to do his business, but only through agents."

"People like my father," Liane said. She was beautiful woman, obviously a lady despite looking for the moment as though she'd just dried out after a shipwreck.

Perhaps she had. Sharina, Cashel, and Garric had all blurted the rough headings of how they'd gotten here from Barca's Hamlet, but Liane had remained silent during the discussion.

"I don't think so," Tenoctris said, meeting Liane's eyes. "I believe your father was in the service of another power, a competing power. At the end he served only himself, though. And Malkar, since all evil serves Malkar."

Liane nodded crisply. "I see," she said. "Well, I wanted to know."

"Is the sword what you mean by a link?" Cashel said. He'd listened to what was being said and sifted it for the only question that mattered to him. "Because I can carry it, if that's all it is."

Tenoctris smiled wanly. "No, it's not the sword, it's his ancestry," she said. "Garric by blood and soul is bound to one on the plane in which the Hooded One hides. That's why I can bring Garric to-him.''

She looked around her companions and went on, ''I suppose you all realize this but I'll say it anyway: Garric and I can confront the Hooded One, but the most likely result is that he'll defeat us both.''

The smile quirked her face again. ''If we're more lucky than I expect, he'll kill us.''

Garric shrugged. ''He can try,'' he said.

More than the brother she'd grown up with; but still her brother.

''Garric,'' she said. He looked at her, a little surprised though he smiled. ''Don't get yourself killed for Ilna. She wouldn't—''

Her voice caught. She went on, ''Ilna wouldn't want to know that a friend had died to save her. She'd rather die!''

Nobody said anything for a moment. Sharina wiped her eyes fiercely, then wiped them again.

''It's not a matter of rescuing Ilna,'' Tenoctris said, looking at Garric as she spoke to the group. ''Though that too, of course.''

She held up a tatter of cloth that Ilna had woven and had worn when she and Garric fought the liches. ''Ilna's presence allows me to locate the Hooded One's hiding place. If we only counter when *he* acts, then he'll withdraw whenever he's personally at risk. We have to go *to* him to defeat him completely.''

''There was a throne where Sharina was,'' Cashel said. The male healer wound fresh linen bandages around his chest while the child held the ends in place. ''Black. And ugly.''

Tenoctris nodded. ''I'm not surprised,'' she said. ''I think it's sympathetic magic. Wizards like the Hooded One believe that if they claim to sit on the Throne of Malkar, it will bring the reality closer.''

She shrugged. ''Perhaps he's right,'' she added. ''He's a greater wizard than I am, certainly.''

"When do we go?" Garric asked. The careful nonchalance of the question showed he was tense.

"I'll need to make preparations," Tenoctris said. "Powders of various sorts. Cashel, do you think Master Latias will help us?"

"Sure, I figure he can find whatever you need," Cashel said. "He's a pretty big man in Erdin."

Cashel gave a big, slow smile of contentment. The Serians had started to leave. They paused in the exit—there wasn't a door, just offset panels—and chirped in horror when their patient stretched with his fingers interlaced.

Their bandages held. "His ceremony went real well, he says," Cashel added with quiet pride. "The one I kind of helped him with."

"Garric," Tenoctris said. "You don't have to go with me, though I hope you will, since I'm not fool enough to think I can succeed alone against the Hooded One; but I don't think the pair of us will succeed either."

She shook her head in self-deprecation. "Sharina," she went on, "I told your friend Nonnus that good and evil only mattered in human terms. I find that I'm human also. I hope Nonnus is amused."

Sharina touched the old woman's hand.

Garric stood up. "I have to go with you," he said. He fingered his sword hilt, grinned like another man entirely, and added, "Carus and I have to go with you."

Sharina looked at her brother and thought of Nonnus. And at last she was able to cry.

5

I wish you'd gotten some sleep," Cashel said, clasping arms with Garric at the edge of the room. They'd taken up the grass mats so that Tenoctris could draw a circle ten feet in diameter on the floor of terra-cotta tiles. The circle and the Old Script characters around it, also drawn with powder, took up much of the floor space.

"I wish I'd been able to," Garric said. "Well, I don't guess being tired when I get there is going to be the worst trouble we'll have."

He wondered if Cashel would've been able to sleep in the six hours it took Tenoctris to prepare the incantation. Maybe he would. Garric knew Cashel too well to doubt that Cashel had an imagination, but he didn't let it bother him the way most people did.

Cashel stepped back. "Garric?" he added. "Don't trust that sword. Trust yourself, all right?"

Garric nodded, though he wasn't sure exactly what his friend meant. He'd killed a demon with his hands, Sharina said; Cashel hadn't talked about that himself. But Garric doubted that he meant anything simple.

Tenoctris was within the circle, checking for one last time the symbols she'd drawn. The powders differed from one character to the next and sometimes within individual characters. They included minerals; the hair, horn, and bone of various animals; and vegetable products like wood and dried leaves. All were finely divided and laid with the same care the old woman used when drawing with a brush or a scriber.

Sharina hugged Garric. Her height was a subconscious surprise to him after being around Liane and Tenoctris the past while. Not that Liane was short, he didn't mean that. . . .

"Take care of yourself, brother," she said. "Nonnus told me that he wasn't as good at charity as he thought he should be. I don't have any charity at all. If you find the person responsible for Nonnus dying—kill him, Garric. Kill him like a roach in the pantry."

Garric wasn't surprised by his sister's tone. He'd never doubted that Sharina had the same inner hardness as their mother, though without Lora's peevish bitterness.

Tenoctris had completed her check of the circle of power.

She picked up the wrapper from one of the packets and rolled it into a spill.

Liane offered Garric her hand rather than clasping him forearm to forearm in masculine fashion. Her smile was false, but the goodwill behind it was certainly real.

"Ah," he said. "Goodbye, Liane. I mean—"

Liane kissed him firmly on the mouth. It wasn't what he'd expected. Of course, that just added it to a long list of recent occurrences that he hadn't been expecting.

She stepped back. Her smile was real now. "Go do what you think is right, Garric," she said. "That's what you've been doing ever since I met you. And come back to me."

Tenoctris cleared her throat. Garric nodded. He wasn't sure whether he was responding to Liane or Tenoctris. Maybe to both of them. He turned and stepped over the circle of gleaming gray powder, careful not to disturb it.

A blue spark popped in the air, igniting the tip of the paper spill in the old woman's hand. Garric expected Tenoctris to begin chanting a spell. Instead she touched the flame to the point in the circle where she'd piled powder into a cone.

The powder spluttered for a moment. The flames from the spill sank to a blue rim at the paper's edge, punctuated by an occasional crackling white spark.

The powder caught with a snarl and a gush of gray smoke.

Tenoctris straightened, checked to make sure that the process was fully under way, and tossed the burning spill out onto the tile floor beyond the edge of the circle. She smiled grimly at Garric.

Flames tracked quickly in both directions around the circle, burning with a white glare that leaped and capered through veils of smoke. The Old Script characters burned also, starting at the bottom where they touched the circle. Their flames were lower and lacked the sparkling violence of the protective circuit. Several-colored light flickered like the aurora borealis, reflecting in pastel blurs from the room's white walls

Garric saw his friends watching still-faced within the smoke. Over the continuing angry hiss of the fire he heard what first was a pulse like that of distant thunder. It resolved into words being chanted in an enormous room. The sound reverberated with the power of those syllables.

Tenoctris stood like a post, smiling with the same sort of quiet pride Cashel had worn when he referred to what he'd accomplished for Latias. This wasn't the end of all tasks, but it was a task well done.

Garric's friends had vanished and the walls of the room were growing dim. He could still see beyond the gray veil of smoke, but his surroundings had changed.

For a moment he was in a forest. The trees were evergreens, pines or spruce; snow was piled high up their trunks and blew in swirling eddies around the roughness of their bark.

Smoke and flurries blended, blurred. When the curtain thinned again Garric saw beasts grazing in a meadow. Deer, he thought, but one raised its head to look toward him and he saw horns not only on its brow but also in the middle of its long snout.

Smoke from the spluttering fires rolled across the scene and drew back. A violent storm slashed through a bamboo grove without touching the fires or the protective circle. Lightning struck nearby. In the flash Garric saw a dozen creatures with cat faces and the bodies of human dwarfs, dancing around a pole to which a terrified girl was tied.

One of the dwarfs gestured to Garric. Smoke mercifully blotted the scene.

The fire consumed itself, cooling into a circle of gray ash with craters where an element had burst violently. The characters beyond burned to the top and went out also. When the colored flames ended, so did the echoing power of the ancient words Tenoctris had written.

The smoke dissipated, leaving a bitter aftertaste. Garric and Tenoctris stood on a sandy beach. The air was warm with a light breeze to riffle the palm fronds.

It was night. The moon was full and more than twice as

large as it should have been. Its angry reddish light flooded the sand and rumbling surf.

Behind Garric was a wall on which was carved a scene in high relief. Life-sized figures formed a tableau of the sinking of the royal fleet a thousand years before Garric was born. In the center King Carus raised his fist to heaven as the deck of his flagship plunged beneath the sculptured sea.

In front of Garric and Tenoctris was a figure seated on a black throne at the edge of the shore. It laughed; louder than the ocean, louder than anything living.

"Come closer, humans," the Hooded One said. "I've been waiting for you."

6

Garric stepped out of the circle. Ash from one of the words of power felt soft and warm under his bare heel. He knew he had to move immediately, before his growing fear froze him where he was.

The ash couldn't protect him any longer. He knew that, but he knew also that if fear mastered him he'd cower in the circle like a fool anyway.

"Come," the Hooded One repeated. He gestured with the long rod in his hands; violet light gleamed from the tip. "Come to Malkar, humans."

Tenoctris laughed. "I watched your false throne shatter on Yole, wizard," she said. "The same will happen to this one, as you know."

She stepped out of the circle of ash also. In her hands was another paper wrapper, which she deliberately rolled into a tube, a wand of power. Its crude simplicity implied scorn for the wizard she faced.

The surf rumbled in anger. This was an evil place, for all the quiet beauty of its setting.

"I'm surprised a hedge wizard like you even had the ability to bring the boy to me, old woman," the Hooded One said. He didn't shout, but his voice echoed from the sea and sky regardless. "I appreciate your efforts though. Perhaps I'll kill you quickly as a favor for your help."

Garric stepped forward, putting himself between Tenoctris and the throned figure. He drew the Sword of Carus. Ruddy moonlight washed its blade like a river of blood.

"We've come for Ilna," Garric said. The sword felt as natural in his hand as the sand did beneath his toes, but *he* was speaking; the youth who'd grown up in Barca's Hamlet, not the king poised within him, grinning with a joy that wolves would recognize.

When Garric's fingers touched the steel, the throne and figure lost solidity to become as insubstantial as the moonlight itself. This was an illusion then; the Hooded One wasn't really in this place.

The ghost figure reached into his sleeve and came out with a mannikin he held in his palm. "This is your Ilna," the Hooded One said. "What will you give me to have her back, human? Will you give me the Throne of Malkar?"

When Garric faced the choice, it was his personal reality that mattered. Not great questions of good and evil, empire and chaos, but the safety of the friends whose lives twined with his.

"I'll give you your life, human," Garric said. "I'll take Ilna back to my own proper world and not trouble you so long as you don't trouble us."

It was the truth—Garric's truth. Tenoctris wouldn't agree, nor probably would King Carus; but it was Garric's honest answer.

Not that it mattered. The Hooded One would never accept any terms but his own. This wasn't a fight Garric was provoking; but the fight would come nonetheless, and Garric wouldn't walk away from it now even if he could.

"You show no more intelligence than I expected from a Haft barbarian," the Hooded One said. Neither of his opponents were cowering at his feet, and he was noticeably angry. "Old woman, tell him that he can't touch me here."

Garric wasn't afraid anymore. It helped that he was pretending to be unafraid, because the image of courage tended to become reality. As for Tenoctris—she didn't seem to care enough about the material world for it to matter to her whether or not she remained in it herself.

"I know that you can't be harmed in this place save by a person from your own time, wizard," Tenoctris said. "We haven't reached your real self yet."

"I haven't permitted you to reach the plane on which I exist in a material sense!" the Hooded One thundered. He stood up and banged his staff on the base of the throne beside him. "I'm responsible for you being here, not your own efforts! Do *you* plan to attack me, old woman? Do you?"

"I don't have the physical strength, wizard," Tenoctris said. Her voice was calm and almost playful, it seemed to Garric. She knew something he didn't, and the Hooded One didn't know it either.

Or she was bluffing, of course.

The Hooded One pointed his wand toward the sea. Water spouted as if on a rock at the edge of the breakers.

"You've met liches, I believe," the Hooded One said. "Lesser wizards create them from the souls and bones of drowned sailors, but I have something special for the two of you."

The sea foamed about an object rising a hundred feet from shore. A whale broaching. . . .

It stood up slowly; it was thirty feet tall and shaped like a man. Its legs were pillars, inhumanly thick to support the torso's enormous weight. The bloody moonlight gleamed from the great single eye in the middle of the creature's forehead.

It began walking in from the sea. Surf sprayed and spat as if the legs were stone breakwaters.

Garric had crawled through the rib cage of a giant like this when he'd escaped from the dreamworld. Now he faced another, clothed in gelatinous gray flesh. The creature carried a club, its shaft a young tree to which was lashed a head of gleaming jade as large as a horse's skull.

"A prehuman race," the Hooded One said. He cackled with laughter. "But I've picked the soul of a great warrior to animate the form to my will. Do you remember him, hedge wizard?"

Tenoctris had knelt and was chanting over the symbols she'd drawn in the sand. Garric knew that the old woman didn't have the power to oppose the Hooded One directly, but he was glad to know that she hadn't given up. He took a firm grip on the sword hilt and started forward.

"This is the Duke of Yole!" the Hooded One said in triumph.

Lightning struck Garric. Colors and sound blazed about him, but he had no consciousness except of roaring conflagration. His flesh tingled with a shock as great as that of diving into the winter sea.

He was lying on the sand. King Carus, bearded and wearing the gleaming diadem of Garric's dreams, stepped out of the stone relief. His strong hands helped Garric rise. Carus unbuckled the sword belt and cinched it about his sightly fuller waist, then took the sword itself from Garric's willing fingers.

The Hooded One was a black figure on a black throne again, though Garric was too aware of the illusion to be frightened by its seeming solidity.

Carus smiled broadly at Garric and said, "You've brought me where I wanted to be, lad. Better late than never, hey? You take care of your end and leave Duke Tedry to me."

Carus whirled the sword above his head. "Haft and the Isles!" he cried. With a peal of bloodthirsty laughter he charged the giant just striding heavily from the surf.

For a man to attack a creature so large should have been ridiculous, but there was nothing ridiculous about Carus. His left hand held the scabbard to prevent it from flapping against his thigh, and his boots sprayed sand behind him.

Carus had waited a thousand years for this moment. The size of the body his enemy wore wouldn't change the outcome.

Garric threw back his head and laughed. Good might not triumph, but one evil man would receive the end he deserved even though it was delayed by a thousand years.

The figure on the black throne screamed and slashed his staff down. The cosmos tilted on more than three planes.

Everything was gray. Garric heard Tenoctris continuing to chant. His feet were down, but the direction of *down* shifted again and a third time without any material change. Garric extended his arms for balance and touched the old woman's tunic, though he couldn't see her in the shimmering gray blur.

The world changed a fourth time. Garric stood in a room of flaring torches and stone walls dripping with condensate. Water pooled on the floor, and there was a strong smell of the sea.

Ilna lay beside the black throne, on which sat a hooded figure no more than the size of a tall man. The wand he held was pulsing with angry amethyst light.

"He had the choice of facing your ancestor there, or bringing us here to his lair with him," Tenoctris said at Garric's shoulder. "This is the Hooded One. This is the real man."

Garric strode forward.

The Hooded One rose and struck his staff down again. The cosmos shifted around Garric.

7

Garric stood on a fang of rock-above the sea, facing the monstrously tall figure of the Hooded One. The wizard's head brushed the lightning-shot clouds, but it wasn't quite clear where his feet rested.

Garric looked over his shoulder. A thousand feet below foamed the maelstrom of his nightmare, covering the sea almost to the horizon. Among the flotsam caught in its coils were creatures so huge they were clearly visible even at Garric's distance above them. The spirals of water were as slow and inexorable as the tide itself, and there was no escape from them.

"Tenoctris?" Garric called.

Nothing answered but the howling wind and the roar of the whirlpool below. He and the Hooded One were alone. Though Garric knew the figure's giant size was an illusion, when he raised his head to look at his opponent he felt an emotional effect that his intellect couldn't fully override.

"Would you like to be King of the Isles, Garric or-Reise?" the Hooded One said. His voice was a roar, part of the thunder but louder than that thunder. "Hail, King Garric! Do you like the sound of that? I'll make you a greater king than any of your ancestors, boy. Greater than Carus, for *I* will support you!"

Armored soldiers paraded through the center of a city that dwarfed ancient Carcosa. Huge crowds lined the route of vast temples and colonnades, cheering at the top of their lungs: "Great is Garric, King of the Isles! Great is Garric!"

All the structures were built of black stone, and the sky was the color of soot.

Garric took a deep breath and stepped forward. "I'll take

my friends with me back to where we belong," he said. A gust of wind buffeted him spitefully but he walked on. "You'll leave us alone. That's all I want, and I'll have it or I'll kill you."

"Do you want the woman Ilna?" the Hooded One shouted angrily. "You can have her! You can have any woman, *all* women, boy! Lead me to the Throne of Malkar and I'll give you all the world else!"

Ilna stood before him, wearing a long scarf that wrapped her from shoulders to ankles. She held one end of the diaphanous fabric high and pirouetted beneath it, stripping herself layer by layer.

Behind Ilna were a score of other women: all of them young, all beautiful; all of them offering themselves in varied forms of coquettishness. Liane was among them.

Garric grimaced and stepped forward. The air resisted him. It had a gelid thickness, as if he were walking through cold broth. He was nearer to the Hooded One, though he knew distances were deceiving in this place.

"I'm your queen, you fool!" the wizard said. "Bow down to your queen, Garric or-Reise!"

Garric hadn't seen the change, but a coldly beautiful woman dressed in lace and ribbons of precious metal stood in the place of the hooded wizard. In her right hand she held a sceptre, its head a gleaming purple sapphire.

Garric paused. He'd never seen the queen or even her image, but this woman looked as the queen should look.

"You're a loyal subject, Garric," the woman said. "Because of your courage and loyalty, I'll make you my consort. Prince Garric, King of the Isles in all but name—and you'll have me!"

"No," Garric said as he took another step. "You're not the queen, and it wouldn't matter anyway."

She scowled and dipped her sceptre. There was a violet flash.

Soft golden light flooded over Garric. The ground was a meadow of ankle-high grass thick with pastel flowers. A dome of warm air formed a vault across the sky, though Garric could see lightning continuing to rip between the clouds in the high heavens. The breeze was gentle and breathed sweet spices.

The Lady in Her robe of bleached wool stood before Garric. "Garric, my child," She said in a voice as kindly as a mother nightingale's. "I've tested you to see that you were worthy. Bow to me, Garric. When you rise, I will make you my Shepherd—a god to rule the cosmos beside me. Bow to me, Garric!"

She was beautiful and pure. She was all Good in a single form.

Garric didn't know what the truth was. He and most of his neighbors in the borough had been perfunctory in their worship of the great gods. They gave grudging support of the Tithe Procession, and the better off sacrificed a lamb on their birthday. He couldn't doubt the reality of this shining figure before him, though.

He didn't know the truth. If he was wrong, he'd bear his punishment knowing that it was just.

"Duzi, forgive me if I stray," Garric whispered. He stepped forward. He would take the Lady's throat in his—

Lightning pulsed down in a triple shock, filling the world with its blue-white glare. All was rock and storm and the roaring sea again.

The Hooded One stood before Garric, the size of a normal man. The figure threw back its cowl. The face beneath was hard, smooth, and sexless. His cold eyes were the color of the jewel on his wand. Ten feet separated him from Garric.

"Stop!" he ordered, pointing the wand. The rock between them bubbled in a gush of violet light.

Spatters fell on Garric's shins, blistering the skin. He halted.

"I've kept you alive," the wizard said, "because I want you to find the Throne of Malkar. If you force me, though, I'll blast you utterly to oblivion."

If Garric stepped forward, the Hooded One would dissolve

him in a bath of violet fire. Garric knew he couldn't reach
the wizard before the wand stuck him down.

People in the borough said Garric was a smart lad, just as
they said Cashel was slow. Cashel wasn't as simple as most
of his neighbors thought him, and maybe Garric wasn't quite
so bright either, but he'd always felt he was as likely to find
the answer to a problem as anybody else he knew.

There wasn't an answer this time. He could submit to evil,
or he could die.

Garric laughed, because he understood now what Cashel
had meant when he said, "Don't trust that sword. Trust yourself." There really wasn't a choice after all.

"I won't serve evil," Garric said as he stepped forward.

"Die then for a fool!" the wizard said, and tried to point
his wand.

A net of light as fine as cobwebs bound the wizard's hand
and arm. Red threads crossed blue, gossamer but unyielding.
The Hooded One's wand spewed violet force, gouging the
rock without diminishing the web's strength.

"I am Malkar!" the wizard screamed.

"You're a puppet!" said Garric. "And I see your strings!"

He leaped the glowing rock and gripped the wand in both
hands. It was metal and so cold it burned. He took it from
the wizard's hand and twisted it with the strength of youth
and desperate need.

The wand shattered in a spray of powder and rainbow light.
The fang of rock dissolved like sand as the tide rolls in. Garric
heard the Hooded One scream again.

Garric wasn't falling. He stood—he still stood—before the
empty throne in the room whose walls dripped seawater.

The throne was shivering to powder the way a pile of grain
settles. Ilna lay beside it, gasping with effort. A web of
threads she'd teased from the fringe of her shawl bound her
fingers together.

Tenoctris touched Ilna's shoulder supportively. "She has
such exceptional power," Tenoctris murmured to Garric.
"Even for a woman whose mother was a sprite. But now that

we've succeeded, we need to get out of here very quickly before we drown.''

Garric stepped to Ilna and gathered her up in his arms. Green water bubbled through the porous walls, and the stone was beginning to crack. A single corridor led out of the chamber, slanting upward.

Garric could see and hear normally, but part of his mind remained in another place. The Hooded One's limbs flailed as he fell toward the maelstrom.

His scream went on and on.

8

Ilna was fully conscious, but it took all her remaining strength just to smile. Her weakness in that gray limbo had permitted others to use her.

But she hadn't been as weak as they thought. At the end, the Hooded One must have wished he'd left Ilna os-Kenset alone. Ilna would have laughed if she'd had the strength, but she could smile.

Garric cradled her with his left arm under her thighs and his right supporting her torso. Her head rested against his shoulder. He was breathing hard, but that was from his previous exertions—not her weight.

Water lapped the corridor ahead of them, faintly phosphorescent and the only light since they left the torchlit chamber. Bubbles swirled on the surface, and occasionally a shadow swam past.

Tenoctris was in the lead. The water had risen to the middle of her spindly calves already. Soon the old woman would have to hike up the hem of her tunic.

''A little farther,'' Tenoctris said. ''Though after that—''

Ilna heard a roaring crash behind them. Shock waves

danced across the surface of the water, forming arcs from wall to wall of the corridor.

"Here!" Tenoctris said, stepping to the right into what had looked like solid rock an instant before she reached it.

A surge of water boiled up the corridor. It rose to Garric's waist and dampened Ilna's dangling toes. He ignored the current's pull and followed the old woman up a flight of three steps: two cut into living rock like the corridor from which they branched, the third and topmost made from blocks of yellowish limestone.

"Tenoctris?" Garric said. "Are the Hooded One and the queen really the same person?"

They were in a high vaulted cellar. Air and enough light for eyes adapted to the dim corridor came down an open staircase on the other side of the room.

"I don't think so, Garric," the old woman said as she plodded toward the stairs. A tremor shook the ground. "I think the queen is a wizard in her own right, a rival of the Hooded One, and he merely took on her semblance for a moment. They're both searching for the Throne of Malkar. But I can't be sure."

Drifted sand lay against the pillars and in a thinner sheet across most of the floor. The dry air was harsh with grit that danced wildly at a second ground shock. There was no sign of the water that had flooded the corridor below, if "below" was even the right word.

Tenoctris reached the staircase. She staggered as the cellar trembled violently. The pillars wavered like trees in a high wind, and clouds of fine sand humped up from the floor.

A block fell from one of the arches. It crashed down in a loud cracking clamor as the whole vault began to disintegrate.

Garric spread his left hand to brace Tenoctris while still supporting Ilna's legs with his forearm. The old woman stepped briskly up the stairs, pushing off from the wall with one hand to speed her. There was a fourth shock, a small one, but the air was pregnant with expectation of what was about to come.

Ilna twitched her foot to see if she could move. She doubted she could stand; certainly she couldn't walk unaided.

Tenoctris disappeared out the doorway at the top of the stairs. The cellars shook so violently that fallen blocks bounced waist-high.

Garric leaped forward. The lintel, twisting from the doorposts, grazed his shoulder on its way down. The dust of shattered masonry puffed around them but they were clear—standing at the base of a bluff with the sheer ice wall of a glacier pressing close behind them.

Tenoctris was already climbing the pathway that slanted up the face of the bluff. The ice groaned. It was nighttime with no light but that of the stars; Ilna didn't recognize the constellations.

"They wanted Sharina because she's the daughter of the count and countess," Garric said. "But why do they care about me?"

"Sharina is the daughter of Count Niard," Tenoctris said, "but her mother was the countess's maid—Lora. You're the son of Countess Tera, Garric, and through her descended from King Carus. Only that can explain your link to Carus—and his to you."

Garric stumbled in surprise as he followed the old woman. A slab of rock plunged past them and hammered hard on the ground: ice pressure was causing the cliff to flex and fracture.

"Put me down," Ilna said as loudly as she could. "Go on and I'll follow."

"No," Garric said. "And don't wiggle or you'll kill us both."

They continued upward. "Tenoctris?" Garric said. "My mother said Sharina was the countess's child. She was sure!"

"Lora was numb with the pain of childbirth," Tenoctris said. "A state I've been glad to avoid as a participant. She would have believed whatever your father told her."

After a moment she added, "Reise is a very intelligent man, Garric. And as faithful to his duty as he raised his son to be."

The path was too narrow for Garric to carry Ilna crosswise. He turned his back to the cliff face and sidled upward. Ilna hung off the side of the bluff, over ground that was increasingly far below. The wind eddying between the bluff and glacier was cold and bit with teeth of ice crystals.

"Oh!" Tenoctris cried. Rock broke away under her heel and spun into the shadows below, narrowly missing Ilna's legs.

Garric's left hand flashed out and snatched the old woman as she started to fall; Ilna's weight was in his right arm alone. Ilna snorted in a half-conscious attempt to make herself as small as possible.

Tenoctris caught a root dangling beneath the bluff's overhang and drew herself up. Her feet vanished over the edge. Garric gripped the same root and heaved Ilna up ahead of him. Instead of solid ground she found herself hanging on to a root of a tree that tossed in warm salt water while a hurricane raged.

Tenoctris lay on the trunk, gripping the rough bark with her fingers and toes like a tree frog as a wave burst over her. As soon as the water receded she began crawling again toward the leafless branches nearly two hundred feet distant.

She looked over her shoulder and shouted to Ilna. Wind carried her words away, but Ilna had no doubt of her meaning. Ilna wasn't sure she could walk yet, but she could crawl. She looked behind her to be sure that Garric was following and started on.

The sky was a solid mass of cloud, lit occasionally by magenta lightning. In one flash Ilna thought she saw a giant eye in the side of a wave fifty feet away. *A trick of the foam, not a creature hunting in this heaving waste. . . .*

The tree trunk lifted in the wave's hand. Ilna was gaining strength; already she'd caught up to Tenoctris. She had to be careful not to put her hand on the old woman's foot. They were beyond halfway.

A six-inch lizard peered at them from a crevice in the bark, its tongue flicking the air nervously. How long had it been since the tree fell and stranded its little denizens in a merciless sea?

Lightning flashed. This time Ilna saw not only the slit-pupiled eye but also the pearly shell and a dozen of the ammonite's waving tentacles. The predator was within twenty feet of the trunk now.

Ilna rose to her knees, resting her torso against the thrust of the wind. She spread her hands to either side of her body.

"What are you doing?" Garric said, screaming to be heard.

She ignored him, waiting for the lightning. In the next rippling flash, Ilna moved her fingers in a pattern that she understood as surely as she knew which warp threads to raise as she thrust her shuttle across the loom.

The monster waved a tentacle in a curt, disappointed gesture and sank back into the sea. Its shell was at least thirty feet in diameter, and the beak nested in its tentacles could snap a big man in half.

Tenoctris had reached the lowest branch. Ilna followed, smiling with grim satisfaction. She supposed she could talk to spiders now also. Well, she'd always respected their craftsmanship.

The branch overhung the sea's tossing surface, a foot above or ten depending on the state of the waves. The old woman crawled out to where one branch of a fork had broken so long ago that the stump was covered with a bark callus. She dropped feet-first toward the sea, vanishing before she touched the water.

Ilna checked to be sure that Garric could see what was happening, then jumped after Tenoctris. Her feet hit a slab of coarse limestone with jarring suddenness.

She was on a jungle-covered pyramid which rose in tall steps toward a covered altar. Tenoctris was clambering up the next waist-high platform.

Trees, some of them several feet in diameter, had set their roots into cracks from which they levered the blocks apart. Ilna's quick glance took in scores of different kinds of vegetation. Plants included the great trees, vines, mosses with feathery fronds, and spiky bromeliads.

Garric dropped, apparently from a branch reaching over the platform. The tree had compound leaves and flowers like a mimosa.

"This way!" he said. He draped Ilna over his right shoulder like a sack of grain.

Ilna shouted a protest that didn't make any more difference than she thought it would. Without pausing, Garric snatched Tenoctris with his other hand and threw her over his left shoulder. He jogged along the platform to the flight of ordinary-sized steps running up the center of the pyramid's face. Ilna hadn't noticed them, perhaps because she was close to the point of exhaustion.

The vegetation at the base of the pyramid turned yellow as though a stain were spreading through cloth. Insects were crawling out of the deeper forest. Ilna supposed they were ants, but each individual was the size of her little finger.

There were more of them than any number Ilna could imagine knowing. *Stalks of grain in a field, pebbles on the shore of Barca's Hamlet* . . . They advanced with the inexorable certainty of water boiling on a hot fire.

"I can walk," Ilna said, but she whispered the words. The *tick* of the creatures' mandibles rustled louder than the wind in an aspen grove. They frightened her as she had not thought she could be frightened. *Tiny scissors slicing her flesh a thousand times, a thousand thousand times* . . .

Garric mounted the steps on the toes of his feet, jogging despite the weight he carried. He gasped for breath but he didn't slow. Ilna wasn't sure whether he saw the pursuing ants or if he simply knew there would be something to drive them.

"Tenoctris!" Ilna said. Both women jounced violently on Garric's shoulders with each upward stride. "How much longer?"

The old woman tried to smile. The shocks must be even

more brutal for her, but there was no choice. "Longer," she wheezed.

Garric reached the top of the pyramid. He was weaving from exertion. His foot turned on a wrist-thick root festooned with hairy suckers and he almost fell.

"Inside," Tenoctris said, trying to look past the head of the man holding her.

The ants were a yellow-brown mass only one level below the humans. They covered all four faces of the pyramid.

Garric threw himself and his burdens under the stone canopy. The altar block had a basin for blood and a groove to carry away any excess. The stone sides were carven with scenes from the rites practiced there. The style was chunky but clear enough that Ilna could see that the victims were human and the priests were not.

The ants had reached the highest platform. Tenoctris wriggled onto the top of the altar and faded from sight. Hand in hand, Garric and Ilna followed her. They sprawled in a bowl-shaped crater from whose floor rose jagged, glassy spikes.

Ilna got to her hands and knees. They were all gasping. The air was cold and their breath wreathed them. The sun directly overhead had a greenish tinge.

"This way," Tenoctris said. She pointed to a fracture in the side of the bowl, a path upward in a surface otherwise too smooth and steep to be climbed. "Garric, Ilna, can you . . . ?"

Ilna nodded. She didn't have breath to waste speaking. Garric got to one knee and they rose together.

A creature came over the basin's far rim about a quarter mile away. It had many legs like a centipede, but its gleaming body segments were polished steel. It started down the wall toward the humans.

The creature's sinuous body was over a hundred feet long, and its mandibles were the length and sheen of swordblades.

"Hold the pace, don't hurry," Garric said, gesturing the women ahead of him into the fracture. "We're tired, and if we try to push we'll fall. Steady will see us clear."

He was right about falling if they hurried. Ilna wasn't sure that any pace she could maintain up this jagged pathway would be enough to escape the centipede, but she no longer really cared.

Tenoctris climbed ahead of her, leaving bloody handprints on the surface. The crater wasn't volcanic. Its wall was a web of fracture lines of which this crack was merely one of the largest. Something had smashed the ground so hard that rock fused and spewed skyward.

The centipede came on, its feet clicking like hail on the mill's slate roof. Ilna didn't look over her shoulder. What would be, would be. She remembered every detail of what she'd done in Erdin. Her only regret was that Garric would die also. The fault was hers alone, but this wasn't a pattern of *her* weaving.

The old woman's heels no longer climbed at the level of Ilna's eyes. A moment later Ilna fell forward because the handhold she'd reached for by habit wasn't there to take her weight. She sprawled on a plain as flat as a millstone, featureless except for a black throne looming like an island in a calm sea.

Garric collapsed beside her. They'd escaped the centipede. There was no sound but their breath and their hearts pounding.

"The Throne of Malkar," Garric whispered.

"Yes," said Tenoctris. There was no other sound in this world.

Ilna got her limbs under her and rested her forehead against the ground. The surface had no temperature or texture; its gray hue was a perfect neutral, neither color nor absence of color. It was the palpable form of the limbo in which she had lost her soul.

The three of them were in a vast circle of sourceless light whose center was the black throne. The walls of darkness were moving in.

"Come," Garric said. He stood up.

"Garric, no," Ilna wheezed. She was crying with anger

and frustration; and fear, she recognized the fear. "It's better to die. Garric, I know what lives here."

Tenoctris was rising. "Come," Garric repeated, and touched Ilna's cheek with his hand. She got up, blind with tears but unwilling to deny his command.

They walked toward the throne. Garric was between the two women, a hand on either of them. The wall of darkness squeezed closer behind them, though the distance to the throne didn't seem to change.

Ilna bent forward to look at the other woman. "Tenoctris?" she said.

"This is the only path," Tenoctris said. "I don't know whether it's a path out."

"We started this," Garric said. "We're going to finish it."

Darkness brushed close at their heels; driving them, threatening to engulf them if they hesitated. Ilna felt the damned moaning in stark despair, utter and eternal. *Their* eternity if they let the darkness swallow them, hers and Garric's and the old woman's.

That bleak eternity would be preferable to joining the thing that was the throne.

"Malkar isn't a person," Tenoctris said. Her voice was audible but oddly flat: there were no echoes in this place, not even from the ground. "Malkar simply *is*. The throne exists only as a symbol."

Tenoctris might have been talking to either of them or to herself, marshaling her thoughts here at the end. Tenoctris had lived for her learning, Ilna knew.

What had Ilna os-Kenset lived for? Well, she'd helped defeat the Hooded One. That was at least a result of her existence if not a purpose.

She chuckled. Garric squeezed her hand in comradeship. Did *he* understand, even now? Well, that didn't matter either.

"To sit on the Throne of Malkar is to be the focus of half the power in the cosmos," Tenoctris said. "To *have* half the power in the cosmos. A man with that power could do anything."

"But he wouldn't be a man," Ilna said.

"No," Tenoctris said. "He wouldn't be a man."

Ilna could see details of the throne now, though when she focused on any particular point it blurred away. It was like trying to watch serpents mate in the twilight. The patterns were too complex for even Ilna to grasp fully, but she understood them well enough.

She had been part of the pattern not long ago. The tree she'd surrendered to somewhere in gray limbo was a tiny part of the throne's vast fabric.

"To sit on the Throne of Malkar," Ilna said with a detached smile, "is to become all evil."

"In human terms," said Tenoctris. "In human terms, yes."

They were very close. The throne stood on a three-step platform. It had broad arms and a high back formed of the same material. It was sized for a man—a tall man, a man like Garric—but at the same time Ilna felt its vastness spread through all the darkness of this plain and of the greater universe beyond.

Garric gathered the two women into the cradle of his arms, one in the crook of either elbow. He lifted them and walked forward.

No, but Ilna's mouth didn't speak the denial her mind had formed. If this was what it was to be—

Garric mounted the platform's three steps, moving with the steady grace that had marked him from childhood. He disregarded the weight of the women he carried. He was smiling faintly.

"All the power . . ." Tenoctris whispered.

So be it!

Instead of sitting, Garric stepped onto the throne's seat. He lurched up with his burdens and put his left foot on the carven arm as the next step. Then he leaped as though he wasn't exhausted, as though he wasn't carrying two women who for their different reasons would have been unable to come this far without his strength.

Garric's right foot gained the top of the throne's back. He

rose once more on the power of that leg alone and hurled all three of them up into the darkness.

Arms caught them. The light of paper lanterns was dazzling, and the twilight glow around the door baffles was like the sun at noon.

They were in a room Ilna didn't recognize, though she saw that the furnishings were Serian. Garric was in the arms of Cashel, whose blank expression showed fear for his friend's utter collapse. Sharina held Tenoctris; the girl was reaching for a cup of juice to offer the old woman.

"Here, let me lay you down," Liane said. "It's all right, Ilna. You're safe now."

9

Garric lay with his eyes closed, savoring the fact that he had no responsibilities whatever for the moment. Tiny hands smeared ointment on his scrapes and shallow cuts; as before, the Serian healers chattered birdlike. The only injury that really hurt was the bruise over his ribs, and he wasn't even sure how he'd gotten that one.

But he was tired. He was so very tired.

"Thanks for bringing Ilna back," Cashel said. "I wish I could've helped, but I guess you didn't need me."

Garric tried to laugh. He shouldn't have: it felt like a handful of knives stabbing into his lower rib cage. When he managed to stop gasping he wheezed, "A lot of it was Ilna bringing us. We wouldn't have done it without her."

"He had to carry me most of the way," Ilna said in a thin voice from nearby to Garric's left. She wasn't a person Garric imagined would ever break, but she must have been worn very close to vanishing, like a knife sharpened too often. "But the Hooded One is dead."

Garric opened his eyes and sat up. The Serian child chided him in words he couldn't understand and would have ignored in any case. "That's true isn't it, Tenoctris? The Hooded One *is* dead."

A dozen lanterns hung around the walls of the room, the light of each throwing its lamp's shadow onto the paper shade. A brazier heated medicines in porcelain bowls under observation by the old Serian woman, while the male healer painted styptic on Tenoctris' scratched thigh.

Liane was massaging Ilna, whose muscles looked as flaccid as warm wax. *Worn very close to vanishing . . .*

Tenoctris sat up. She managed a smile, though the lines around her eyes tightened every time the healer's brush touched her.

"I thought the same thing a thousand years ago, you'll recall," she said. "Perhaps it's true this time, but I'm afraid that doesn't really matter."

"It matters to me," Sharina said. She spoke quietly, but her voice had no more mercy in it than an axeblade does. She sat near Cashel, her hands crossed in her lap over the hilt of the Pewle knife.

"Yes," said Tenoctris, nodding with her former quiet authority. "To all of us. And to the Hooded One himself for the considerable length of time it took him to fall. But he was only part of the problem."

Ilna looked up at Garric. She smiled, a disconcertingly cold expression.

"The tree wasn't the Throne of Malkar," she said, a reference that only Tenoctris among the other people in the room might understand. "But it was too much for me. I was weak."

"No," said Tenoctris. "It was your strength, not your weakness, that made you vulnerable. But your point is correct: the Hooded One was the human agent of an impersonal force. The force will work through others as it worked through him, and through what you call the tree. Malkar waxes and wanes. Malkar is rising now, just as it did a thousand years ago. If it continues, it will smash the Isles back into barbarism.''

''Not this time,'' Garric said. He hugged himself, trembling with emotions and memories that were only partly his own. ''Not this time!''

Garric thought he felt at the core of his soul the king laughing. ''Not this time, lad!'' he heard as if in a dream. ''Not this time, King Garric!''

10

She stared at the tourmaline pieces scattered across the game board in a pattern she could not yet understand.

Her hooded opponent was dead, but she had not defeated him and she did not know who had. There were other players, other wizards to whom the cosmos was only a game, playing against her. She was as certain of that as she had been when she denied the possibility only a few months before.

She would identify and defeat her new opponents. She would sit on the Throne of Malkar and crush the cosmos in her hand like a ripe peach if it suited her mood to do so. She alone!

She strode to the door and opened it. The servitor bowed to her, as always impassive.

''I'm not to be disturbed for any reason,'' she said curtly.

''An agent from Erdin has arrived,'' the servitor said. ''He waits in the private interview room.''

''For any reason!'' she said. She raised a hand as if to launch lightning from the bare palm.

''Yes, milady queen,'' said the servitor. He bowed. His face was calm but there were minute droplets of sweat on his forehead.

The door panel was too heavy to slam. She closed it with a measured thump, then returned to the game board.

Sometimes . . . sometimes when she rose from a sleep where nightmare had been her closest companion, the thought lingered in her mind that the pieces might sometimes play themselves—and woe betide the wizard who tried to interfere with them.

The Queen of the Isles scowled and seated herself before the agate board. The chips of tourmaline were pawns, no more. Any other thought was madness.

She *would* set them to her will.